THE CLAY SANSKRIT LIBRARY

FOUNDED BY JOHN & JENNIFER CLAY



www.claysanskritlibrary.com

www.nyupress.org

*Artwork by Robert Beer.*
*Typeset in Adobe Garamond at 10.25 : 12.3+pt.*
*XML-development by Stuart Brown.*
*Editorial input from Dániel Balogh,*
*Tomoyuki Kono & Eszter Somogyi.*
*Printed in Great Britain by St Edmundsbury Press Ltd,*
*Bury St Edmunds, Suffolk, on acid-free paper.*
*Bound by Hunter & Foulis Ltd, Edinburgh, Scotland.*

# MAHĀBHĀRATA

## BOOK FIVE

# PREPARATIONS FOR WAR

## VOLUME ONE

TRANSLATED BY

Kathleen Garbutt

WITH A FOREWORD BY GURCHARAN DAS

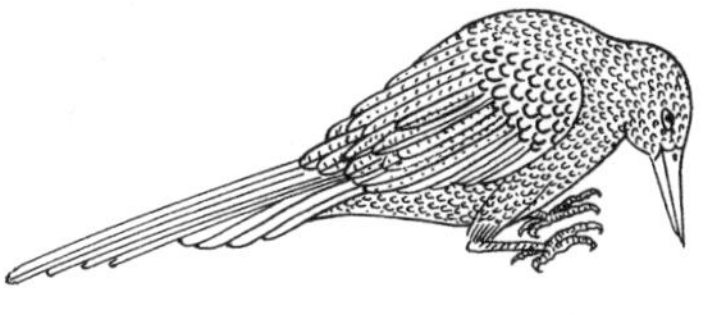


NEW YORK UNIVERSITY PRESS

JJC FOUNDATION

2008

First Edition 2008

The Clay Sanskrit Library is co-published by
New York University Press
and the JJC Foundation.

Further information about this volume
and the rest of the Clay Sanskrit Library
is available at the end of this book
and on the following websites:
**www.claysanskritlibrary.com**
**www.nyupress.org**

ISBN 978-0-8147-3191-8 (cloth : alk. paper)

**Library of Congress Cataloging-in-Publication Data**
Mahābhārata. Udyogaparva. English & Sanskrit.
Mahābhārata. Book five, Preparations for war /
translated by Kathleen Garbutt. -- 1st ed.
p. cm. -- (The Clay Sanskrit library)
Epic poetry.
In English and Sanskrit (romanized) on facing pages;
includes translation from Sanskrit.
Includes bibliographical references and index.
ISBN: 978-0-8147-3191-8 (cloth : alk. paper)
I. Garbutt, Kathleen. II. Title. III. Title: Preparations for war.
BL1138.242.U39E5 2007
294.5'92304521--dc22
2007017336

# CONTENTS

# CSL CONVENTIONS

## Sanskrit Alphabetical Order

| | |
|---|---|
| Vowels: | *a ā i ī u ū ṛ ṝ ḷ ḹ e ai o au ṃ ḥ* |
| Gutturals: | *k kh g gh ṅ* |
| Palatals: | *c ch j jh ñ* |
| Retroflex: | *ṭ ṭh ḍ ḍh ṇ* |
| Dentals: | *t th d dh n* |
| Labials: | *p ph b bh m* |
| Semivowels: | *y r l v* |
| Spirants: | *ś ṣ s h* |

## Guide to Sanskrit Pronunciation

| | |
|---|---|
| *a* | b*u*t |
| *ā, â* | f*a*ther |
| *i* | s*i*t |
| *ī, î* | f*ee* |
| *u* | p*u*t |
| *ū, û* | b*oo* |
| *ṛ* | vocalic *r*, American p*ur*dy or English p*re*tty |
| *ṝ* | lengthened *ṛ* |
| *ḷ* | vocalic *l*, ab*le* |
| *e, ê, ē* | m*a*de, esp. in Welsh pronunciation |
| *ai* | b*i*te |
| *o, ô, ō* | r*o*pe, esp. Welsh pronunciation; Italian s*o*lo |
| *au* | s*ou*nd |
| *ṃ* | *anusvāra* nasalizes the preceding vowel |
| *ḥ* | *visarga*, a voiceless aspiration (resembling the English *h*), or like Scottish lo*ch*, or an aspiration with a faint echoing of the last element of the preceding vowel so that *taiḥ* is pronounced *taih*[i] |
| *k* | lu*ck* |
| *kh* | blo*ckh*ead |
| *g* | *g*o |
| *gh* | bi*gh*ead |
| *ṅ* | a*n*ger |
| *c* | *ch*ill |
| *ch* | mat*chh*ead |
| *j* | *j*og |
| *jh* | aspirated *j*, he*dgeh*og |
| *ñ* | ca*ny*on |
| *ṭ* | retroflex *t*, *t*ry (with the tip of tongue turned up to touch the hard palate) |
| *ṭh* | same as the preceding but aspirated |
| *ḍ* | retroflex *d* (with the tip |

| | |
|---|---|
| | of tongue turned up to touch the hard palate) |
| *ḍh* | same as the preceding but aspirated |
| *ṇ* | retroflex *n* (with the tip of tongue turned up to touch the hard palate) |
| *t* | French *t*out |
| *th* | ten*t h*ook |
| *d* | *d*inner |
| *dh* | guil*dh*all |
| *n* | *n*ow |
| *p* | *p*ill |
| *ph* | u*ph*eaval |
| *b* | *b*efore |
| *bh* | a*bh*orrent |
| *m* | *m*ind |
| *y* | *y*es |
| *r* | trilled, resembling the Italian pronunciation of *r* |
| *l* | *l*inger |
| *v* | *w*ord |
| *ś* | *sh*ore |
| *ṣ* | retroflex *sh* (with the tip of the tongue turned up to touch the hard palate) |
| *s* | hi*ss* |
| *h* | *h*ood |

## CSL Punctuation of English

The acute accent on Sanskrit words when they occur outside of the Sanskrit text itself, marks stress, e.g., Ramáyana. It is not part of traditional Sanskrit orthography, transliteration, or transcription, but we supply it here to guide readers in the pronunciation of these unfamiliar words. Since no Sanskrit word is accented on the last syllable it is not necessary to accent disyllables, e.g., Rama.

The second CSL innovation designed to assist the reader in the pronunciation of lengthy unfamiliar words is to insert an unobtrusive middle dot between semantic word breaks in compound names (provided the word break does not fall on a vowel resulting from the fusion of two vowels), e.g., Maha·bhárata, but Ramáyana (not Rama·áyana). Our dot echoes the punctuating middle dot (·) found in the oldest surviving samples of written Indic, the Ashokan inscriptions of the third century BCE.

The deep layering of Sanskrit narrative has also dictated that we use quotation marks only to announce the beginning and end of every direct speech, and not at the beginning of every paragraph.

## CSL Punctuation of Sanskrit

The Sanskrit text is also punctuated, in accordance with the punctuation of the English translation. In mid-verse, the punctuation will not alter the sandhi or the scansion. Proper names are capitalized. Most Sanskrit meters have four "feet" (*pāda*); where possible we print the common *śloka* meter on two lines. The capitalization of verse beginnings makes it easy for the reader to recognize longer meters where it is necessary to print the four metrical feet over four or eight lines. In the Sanskrit text, we use French *Guillemets* (e.g., *«kva saṃcicīrṣuḥ?»*) instead of English quotation marks (e.g., "Where are you off to?") to avoid confusion with the apostrophes used for vowel elision in sandhi.

### SANDHI

Sanskrit presents the learner with a challenge: *sandhi* (euphonic combination). Sandhi means that when two words are joined in connected speech or writing (which in Sanskrit reflects speech), the last letter (or even letters) of the first word often changes; compare the way we pronounce "the" in "the beginning" and "the end."

In Sanskrit the first letter of the second word may also change; and if both the last letter of the first word and the first letter of the second are vowels, they may fuse. This has a parallel in English: a nasal consonant is inserted between two vowels that would otherwise coalesce: "a pear" and "an apple." Sanskrit vowel fusion may produce ambiguity.

The charts on the following pages give the full sandhi system.

Fortunately it is not necessary to know these changes in order to start reading Sanskrit. All that is important to know is the form of the second word without sandhi (pre-sandhi), so that it can be recognized or looked up in a dictionary. Therefore we are printing Sanskrit with a system of punctuation that will indicate, unambiguously, the original form of the second word, i.e., the form without sandhi. Such sandhi mostly concerns the fusion of two vowels.

In Sanskrit, vowels may be short or long and are written differently accordingly. We follow the general convention that a vowel with no mark above it is short. Other books mark a long vowel either with a bar called a macron (*ā*) or with a circumflex (*â*). Our system uses the

## VOWEL SANDHI

| *Final vowels:* a | ā | i | ī | u | ū | ṛ | e | ai | o | au | *Initial vowels:* |
|---|---|---|---|---|---|---|---|---|---|---|---|
| ' â | " â | y a | y a | v a | v a | r a | e ' | ā a | o ' | āv a | a |
| ' ā | " ā | y ā | y ā | v ā | v ā | r ā | a ā | ā ā | a ā | āv ā | ā |
| ' ê | " ê | ' î | " î | v i | v i | r i | a i | ā i | a i | āv i | i |
| ' ē | " ē | ' ī | " ī | v ī | v ī | r ī | a ī | ā ī | a ī | āv ī | ī |
| ' ô | " ô | y u | y u | ' û | " û | r u | a u | ā u | a u | āv u | u |
| ' ō | " ō | y ū | y ū | ' ū | " ū | r ū | a ū | ā ū | a ū | āv ū | ū |
| a' r | a" r | y ṛ | y ṛ | v ṛ | v ṛ | ' ṝ | a ṛ | ā ṛ | a ṛ | āv ṛ | ṛ |
| ' âi | " âi | y e | y e | v e | v e | r e | a e | ā e | a e | āv e | e |
| ' āi | " āi | y ai | y ai | v ai | v ai | r ai | a ai | ā ai | a ai | āv ai | ai |
| ' âu | " âu | y o | y o | v o | v o | r o | a o | ā o | a o | āv o | o |
| ' āu | " āu | y au | y au | v au | v au | r au | a au | ā au | a au | āv au | au |

## CONSONANT SANDHI

| Permitted finals: k | ṭ | t | p | ṅ | n | m | (Except āḥ/aḥ) ḥ/r | āḥ | aḥ | Initial letters: |
|---|---|---|---|---|---|---|---|---|---|---|
| k | ṭ | t | p | ṅ | n | ṃ | ḥ | āḥ | aḥ | k/kh |
| g | ḍ | d | b | ṅ | n | ṃ | r | ā | o | g/gh |
| k | ṭ | c | p | ṅ | ṃś | ṃ | ś | āś | aś | c/ch |
| g | ḍ | j | b | ṅ | ñ | ṃ | r | ā | o | j/jh |
| k | ṭ | ṭ | p | ṅ | ṃṣ | ṃ | ṣ | āṣ | aṣ | ṭ/ṭh |
| g | ḍ | ḍ | b | ṅ | ṇ | ṃ | r | ā | o | ḍ/ḍh |
| k | ṭ | t | p | ṅ | ṃs | ṃ | s | ās | as | t/th |
| g | ḍ | d | b | ṅ | n | ṃ | r | ā | o | d/dh |
| k | ṭ | t | p | ṅ | n | ṃ | ḥ | āḥ | aḥ | p/ph |
| g | ḍ | d | b | ṅ | n | ṃ | r | ā | o | b/bh |
| ṅ | ṇ | n | m | ṅ | n | ṃ | r | ā | o | *nasals* (n/m) |
| g | ḍ | d | b | ṅ | n | ṃ | r | ā | o | y/v |
| g | ḍ | d | b | ṅ | n | ṃ | *zero*[1] | ā | o | r |
| g | ḍ | l | b | ṅ | l̃[2] | ṃ | r | ā | o | l |
| k | ṭ | c ch | p | ṅ | ñ ś/ch | ṃ | ḥ | āḥ | aḥ | ś |
| k | ṭ | t | p | ṅ | n | ṃ | ḥ | āḥ | aḥ | ṣ/s |
| gg h | ḍḍ h | dd h | bb h | ṅ | n | ṃ | r | ā | o | h |
| g | ḍ | d | b | ṅ/ṅṅ[3] | n/nn[3] | m | r | ā | a[4] | *vowels* |
| k | ṭ | t | p | ṅ | n | m | ḥ | āḥ | aḥ | *zero* |

[1]ḥ or r disappears, and if a/i/u precedes, this lengthens to ā/ī/ū. [2]e.g. tān+lokān=tāl̃ lokān. [3]The doubling occurs if the preceding vowel is short. [4]Except: aḥ+a=o '.

macron, except that for initial vowels in sandhi we use a circumflex to indicate that originally the vowel was short, or the shorter of two possibilities (*e* rather than *ai*, *o* rather than *au*).

| When we print initial | before sandhi that vowel was |
|---|---|
| *â*, | *a* |
| *î* or *ê*, | *i* |
| *û* or *ô*, | *u* |
| *âi*, | *e* |
| *âu*, | *o* |
| *ā*, | *ā* |
| *ī*, | *ī* |
| *ū*, | *ū* |
| *ē*, | *ī* |
| *ō*, | *ū* |
| *ai*, | *ai* |
| *āu*, | *au* |
| ’, before sandhi there was a vowel *a* | |

When a final short vowel (*a*, *i*, or *u*) has merged into a following vowel, we print ’ at the end of the word, and when a final long vowel (*ā*, *ī*, or *ū*) has merged into a following vowel we print ” at the end of the word. The vast majority of these cases will concern a final *a* or *ā*. See, for instance, the following examples:

| What before sandhi was | is represented as |
|---|---|
| *atra asti* | *atr' âsti* |
| *atra āste* | *atr' āste* |
| *kanyā asti* | *kany" âsti* |
| *kanyā āste* | *kany" āste* |
| *atra iti* | *atr' êti* |
| *kanyā iti* | *kany" êti* |
| *kanyā īpsitā* | *kany" ēpsitā* |

Finally, three other points concerning the initial letter of the second word:

(1) A word that before sandhi begins with *ṛ* (vowel), after sandhi begins with *r* followed by a consonant: *yatha" rtu* represents pre-sandhi *yathā ṛtu*.

(2) When before sandhi the previous word ends in *t* and the following word begins with *ś*, after sandhi the last letter of the previous word is *c*

and the following word begins with *ch*: *syāc chāstravit* represents pre-sandhi *syāt śāstravit*.

(3) Where a word begins with *h* and the previous word ends with a double consonant, this is our simplified spelling to show the pre-sandhi form: *tad hasati* is commonly written as *tad dhasati*, but we write *tadd hasati* so that the original initial letter is obvious.

### COMPOUNDS

We also punctuate the division of compounds (*samāsa*), simply by inserting a thin vertical line between words. There are words where the decision whether to regard them as compounds is arbitrary. Our principle has been to try to guide readers to the correct dictionary entries.

## Exemplar of CSL Style

Where the Devanagari script reads:

कुम्भस्थली रक्षतु वो विकीर्णसिन्धूररेणुर्द्विरदाननस्य ।
प्रशान्तये विघ्नतमश्छटानां निष्ठ्यूतबालातपपल्लवेव ॥

Others would print:

kumbhasthalī rakṣatu vo vikīrṇasindūrareṇur dviradānanasya /
praśāntaye vighnatamaśchaṭānāṃ niṣṭhyūtabālātapapallaveva //

We print:

kumbha|sthalī rakṣatu vo vikīrṇa|sindūra|reṇur dvirad'|ānanasya
praśāntaye vighna|tamaś|chaṭānāṃ niṣṭhyūta|bāl'|ātapa|pallav" êva.

And in English:

May Ganésha's domed forehead protect you! Streaked with vermilion dust, it seems to be emitting the spreading rays of the rising sun to pacify the teeming darkness of obstructions.

("Nava·sáhasanka and the Serpent Princess" 1.3)

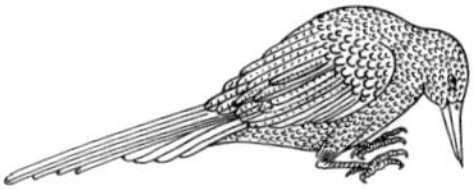

# FOREWORD

Like Tolstoy's "War and Peace," the "Maha·bhárata" can see both sides of war. It glories in immortal feats of courage, daring, and self-sacrifice, like those of Abhimányu, and showers petals over brave heroes like Karna and Duryódhana when they die on the battlefield, honoring acts of courage that are also feats of lunacy. The epic would have had much to say about today's crazed fanatics, who undertake suicide missions certain that they will go to heaven—much like the kshatriyas who fought at Kuru·kshetra.

Yet in 'Preparations for War,' the same "Maha·bhárata" condemns the approaching war in the most savage terms. While lamenting the failure of the peace negotiations, Yudhi·shthira leaves no doubt about what he thinks will be the consequences of the coming war. He expresses his feelings so forcefully that one wonders if Krishna might have given his message to the wrong Pándava in the "Bhagavad Gita."

> *War is entirely disastrous, for which killer is not killed? Victory and defeat are the same to a dead man, Hrishi·kesha. I do not believe there is any distinction between defeat and death. The man who gains victory will certainly also meet his downfall, Krishna. In the end, some other men will kill someone he cares for, and when he has really lost his strength and no longer sees his sons and brothers, disgust for living will completely overwhelm him, Krishna. In fact, the firm, modest, noble, and compassionate are the ones who die in war, but the lesser men escape.* (Clay Sanskrit Library edition (csl) v.72.53–57)[1]

In between these two positions lies the Indian epic hero's fundamental question: How to live one's life? Does the good life consist of dying young in battle and going to heaven? Or should one live a long, peaceful, and probably unremarkable dharmic life of nonviolence and compassion? Where does true honor lie? These questions drive the Pándava heroes' search for the real meaning of dharma and are behind the problem which hangs over the entire 'Preparations for War.' The Pándavas undertake many efforts to negotiate a peace, but the negotiations fail. Krishna concludes, "War is the only course left." With violence inevitable, Yudhi·shthira voices Árjuna's dilemma at the beginning of the "Gita:"

> *The ultimate disaster for which I dwelled in the forest and suffered is upon us in spite of all our striving.... For how can war be waged with men we must not kill? How can we win if we must kill our gurus and elders?* (Critical Edition, v.151.20–22)

It is Árjuna, ironically, who must reassure his elder brother, and remind him of his duty. "It is not right to retreat now without fighting," he says. And to end this unbecoming wavering on the part of mighty warriors, Krishna exclaims impatiently and bluntly, "That is the way it is!" (CE v.151.25–26).

And so the Pándavas resolve to go to war. It is an unhappy ending after the great effort that has gone into negotiating a peace, and also a morally awkward outcome for an epic that is dedicated to preserving dharma. But at the same time, the conclusion—that war is inevitable—is not a surprising one. In fact, 'Preparations for War' marks a turning point in the epic's treatment of dharma. We become aware of this when Sáñjaya suggests to Yudhi·shthira during the second embassy, "Do not destroy yourself! If the Kurus will not grant you your share, Ajáta·shatru, without resorting to war, then in my opinion, a life of begging in the kingdom of the Ándhaka Vrishnis would be better than winning your kingdom through war" (CSL V.27.1–2). The earlier, idealistic Yudhi·shthira might have accepted this recommendation that he turn the other cheek; now, he finds it preposterous.

In a poignant earlier scene in the forest, recounted in 'The Forest,' Yudhi·shthira had tried to persuade Dráupadi that "forgiveness is the strength of the virtuous"[2] when she had wanted him to raise an army to recover their kingdom. Dráupadi had been in tears seeing her royal husband sleeping on the hard earth when he was accustomed to sheets of silk and pillows of down, eating roots from the forest when he should have been feasting like a king served by a thousand retainers.

> *I remember your old bed and I pity you, great king, so unworthy of hardship.... Sorrow stifles me.... I saw you bright as a sun, well-oiled with sandal paste, now I see you dirty and muddy.... I have seen you dressed in bright and expensive silks ... and now I see you wearing bark!* (CE III.28.10–14)

Yudhi·shthira responds to Dráupadi's call for action by reminding her that he has given his word: when he lost the game of dice he had promised to live thus in exile. To fight is easy, to forgive more difficult, he says. To be patient is not to be weak; to seek peace is always the wiser course. He reminds her that forbearance (*kṣamā*) is superior to anger (*krodha*), leaving her wondering why her husband has adopted a stubborn pacifism while their enemies exploit his goodness. She wails, "When I see noble, moral, and modest persons harassed in this way, and the evil and ignoble flourishing and happy, I stagger with wonder.... I can only condemn the Placer, who allows such outrage" (CE III.31.37–39). To which Yudhi·shthira can only reply, "I do not act for the sake of the fruits of dharma.... I act because I must. Whether it bears fruits or not, buxom Dráupadi, I do my duty" (CE III.32.2–4).

This was Yudhi·shthira's high deontological position: he would not fight because he had given his word. His duty is to *satya*, truth, and he must stick to it no matter how inconvenient. It is the same high-souled Yudhi·shthira who, at the end of his exile, parched with thirst and still in shock at discovering the corpses of his brothers, shows amazing determination to play and win the moral game against the interrogating one-eyed *yakṣa* and bring his brothers to life. In that surreal moment, his admirable, winning answer is "Compassion (*ānṛśaṃsya*) I consider the highest Law, superior even to the highest goal" (CSL III.313.129).

When Sáñjaya makes his suggestion about turning the other cheek, it is this earlier Yudhi·shthira whom he has in mind. He reminds him that "non-violence surpasses moral duty" (CSL V.32.12), and chides him:

> *If you must commit an evil act of such hostility, Parthas, after all this time, why then, Pándavas, did you have to live in the forest for those successive years, in miserable exile, just because it was right? … And why have you spent these successive years in the forests if you want to fight now, Pándava, when you have lost so much time? It is a foolish man who fights.* (CSL V.27.16, 20–21)

Yudhi·shthira's answer comes as a surprise:

> *In times of trouble one's duty alters. When one's livelihood is disrupted and one is totally poverty-stricken, one should wish for other means to carry out one's prescribed duties.… which means that in dire situations one may perform normally improper acts.* (CSL V.28.3–5)

'Preparations for War' is a crossroads because it points to a new, pragmatic view of the world. As Yudhi·shthira, chastened by thirteen harsh years in exile, begins to take charge of the war effort and the peace negotiations, he has changed from a passive to an active individual who is "in complete control of his brothers and allies."[3] The first sign of this change comes on the day after Abhimányu's wedding, when Sátyaki proclaims in Viráta's court, "No law can be found against killing enemies who are plotting to kill us" (CSL V.3.20)—a down-to-earth view of dharma, one that recognizes the limits of goodness and is grounded in human self-interest without being amoral. This view avoids both ideological extremes—the Hobbesian amorality of Duryódhana as well as the idealistic super-morality of the earlier Yudhi·shthira in exile.

Yudhi·shthira's moral journey from 'The Forest' to 'Preparations for War' takes him to a position akin to the evolutionary principle of reciprocal altruism: adopt a friendly face to the world but do not allow yourself to be exploited. Recent insights of evolutionary scientists[4] affirm that Yudhi·shthira has attained a fundamental insight not only about the way we live, but about how we ought to.[5] To be sure, human beings have evolved through a long struggle in which only the fittest pass on their genes. But to conclude that life is a tooth and-claw struggle—or that morality is merely in the interest of the strong, as Duryódhana claims[6]—is a mistake. Nature is replete with examples of dharma-like goodness. Wolves and wild dogs bring food back for their young. Dolphins will help lift an injured companion for hours to help him survive. Blackbirds and thrushes give warning calls when they spot a hawk even at risk to their own lives.[7]

Vídura's advice to the insomniac Dhrita·rashtra in 'Preparations for War' is based on the principle of reciprocal altruism:

> *The law dictates that a man must be treated in the manner he behaves. So, an illusionist should be treated with deception, and well-behaved people should be treated well.* (CSL V.37.7)

Dráupadi, too, has reciprocity on her mind when she urges Yudhi·shthira to get up and raise an army:

> *I think, king of men, it is time to use your authority on the greedy Dhartaráshtras, who are always offensive. There is no more time to ply the Kurus with forgiveness; and when the time for authority has come, authority must be*

> *employed. The meek are despised, but people shrink from the severe: he is a king who knows both, when their time has come.* (CE III.29.34–35)

In effect, she is telling her husband, "Don't be a sucker; counter meanness with meanness."

It has taken Yudhi·shthira thirteen years to learn that there will always be crooks in the world, and if necessary, one must be prepared to go to war. But "tit for tat" should not be confused with an aggressive worldview; its default position is to be friendly and collaborative. Yudhi·shthira presents such an affable face to the world when he sends greetings via Sáñjaya not only to the princes and the mighty at the Hástina·pura court but also to elephant riders, charioteers, door-keepers, accountants, courtesans, slaves, and deformed persons (CSL V.30.23–41). Eventually, he makes an exceptionally generous offer to forgo his share of the kingdom and to accept only five villages—a deal that must have appalled the hawks in the Pándava camp. He quickly reminds Sáñjaya of his reciprocal altruism: "I am just as capable of peace as I am of war ... I am as capable of duty and profit as I am of gentleness and severity" (CSL V.31.23).

It is not implausible that, like reciprocal altruism in individuals, societies evolved the principles of dharma in order to get people to cooperate. In 'Preparations for War,' the "Maha·bhárata" has found a middle path between the amoral realism of Duryódhana and the idealism of the earlier Yudhi·shthira. It is a pragmatic path grounded in human self-interest, that upright statesmen—like Bhishma and Krishna, who have the responsibility of running a state

—must try to follow. In a world of power politics, the dharma of the leader cannot be moral perfection; it must be more like EDMUND BURKE's "prudence," which he called a "god of this lower world." Prudence does not mean that one weighs amorally the pros and cons of victory and defeat as King Dhrita·rashtra does:

> *By subtle and clear-sighted calculation of the pros and cons with proper judgment, the sagacious and intelligent man, who desired victory for his sons, precisely weighed up the strengths and weaknesses, and then the lord of men began to work out the capabilities of each side.* (CSL V.60. 2–3)

The considerations of dharma are a part of the deliberations of the prudent ruler of the middle path. As Yudhi·shthira is getting resigned to the war's inevitability, his mind is weighed down with moral issues. He asks Sáñjaya:

> *Why would a man ever go to war? Who, but a man whose fate is cursed, would choose war? The Parthas wish for happiness but they act to fulfill the law and for the welfare of the world.* (CSL V.26.3)

One wishes for more statesmen like Yudhi·shthira who also weigh the dictates of their conscience when they measure the pros and cons of going to war. Politics need not be a dark world of realpolitik in which force and cunning have to be the only currencies.

Societies are held together by laws, customs, and moral habits, as BURKE said, and it is these that make up dharma. When Bhishma and others call dharma "subtle" (*sūkṣma*), they are in effect saying that it is sometimes difficult to know right from wrong. The epic's world of moral haziness and uncertainty is closer to our experience as ordinary human beings—its dizzyingly plural perspectives a nice antidote to the narrow and rigid positions that surround us in the hypertrophied post-9/11 world. The subtle art of dharma teaches that it is in our nature also to be good, and ordinary human lives should not have to be so cruel and humiliating. One must be willing to compromise in a plural world, and reciprocity is a modest, guiding principle of civilized existence. The peace negotiations failed in 'Preparations for War' because Duryódhana was unwilling. The Pándavas merely want to be allowed to live, in five villages, the kinds of lives that they want to lead. No one has the right to control the lives of others, and the only thing one can do is to try to prevent intolerable choices.

The "Maha·bhárata" is a splendid, moving, and wise story "almost in the Marmion class," as Hardy described the "Iliad." But unlike "deep-browed" Homer, it has not invited many acts of homage from translators. Kathleen Garbutt's translation of the first volume of 'Preparations for War' is elegant. The weft and warp of the story leaves one with a combined sense of shock and uplift. It reflects the high standards set by the remarkable Clay Sanskrit Library that is producing true Sanskrit translations for our age.

Gurcharan Das

## Notes

1 I have quoted from KATHLEEN GARBUTT's translation of the first part of the *Udyogaparvan*, 'Preparations for War;' P. WILMOT's translation of the *Sabhāparvan*, 'The Great Hall;' and from W.J. JOHNSON's CSL translation of the fourth part of the *Vanaparvan*, 'The Forest;' and I have adapted quotations from J.A.B. VAN BUITENEN's translations of the remainder of these *parvans* (*Mahābhārata*, vols. 2 & 3, Chicago: University of Chicago Press, 1975, 1978).

2 The good Vídura repeats these words of Yudhi·shthira's in his interminable moral teaching to the insomniac Dhrita·rashtra (CSL V.34.75).

3 J.A.B. VAN BUITENEN, *Mahābhārata*, vol. 3, Chicago: University of Chicago Press, 1975, p. 133.

4 See, for example: W.D. HAMILTON, "The Genetic Evolution of Social Behavior I and II," *Journal of Theoretical Biology* 7, 1964, pp. 1–16, 17–32; E.O. WILSON, *Sociobiology: The New Synthesis*, Cambridge MA: Harvard University Press, 1975; RICHARD D. ALEXANDER, *The Biology of Moral Systems*, New York: Aldine de Gruyter, 1987; RICHARD DAWKINS, *The Selfish Gene*, Oxford: Oxford University Press, 1976; ROBERT WRIGHT, *The Moral Animal: Evolutionary Psychology and Everyday Life*, New York: Vintage Books, 1995; E. SOBER AND D.S. WILSON, *Unto Others: The Evolution and Psychology of Unselfish Behavior*, Cambridge MA: Harvard University Press, 1998.

5 Although you cannot derive moral values from nature's workings—if you do, you're committing what philosophers call the "naturalistic fallacy" or the unwarranted inference of "ought" from "is"—recent insights of evolutionary scientists do help in explaining the moral position that Yudhi·shthira attains.

6 See for example 'The Great Hall' (*Sabhāparvan*) CSL II.55.

7 Similarly, human parents make huge sacrifices for their children with little expectation of return. Although we behave altruistically, "there is no such passion in human minds as the love of mankind, independent of personal qualities, of services, or of relation to ourself" (David Hume, *A Treatise on Human Nature*, Book iii, part 2, section i, Harmondsworth: Penguin Books, 1984).

# INTRODUCTION

'Preparations for War' (*Udyogaparvan*) is a new beginning for both the Kurus and the Pándavas. At the end of 'Viráta' (*Virāṭaparvan*) the Pándavas have fulfilled the terms of their exile and now rightly expect their share of the kingdom. However, that book also ended with a battle between the two parties, serving as a harbinger of the hostilities to follow.

Duryódhana refuses to part even with the five villages the Pándavas request. Both sides realize that war is surely inevitable and make their preparations, thereby overshadowing the series of embassies which constitute the main structure of the book. Both sides, to varying degrees, struggle with the morality of the coming war, and so 'Preparations for War' offers us variously detailed discussions of dharma, culminating in the teachings Sanat·sujáta offers Dhrita·rashtra. Despite their respective consciences, however, this volume ends bleakly, there being little chance left of peace with the intractable Duryódhana. Nevertheless, Krishna sets out for Dhrita·rashtra's court, hoping his neutrality, somewhat compromised though it is, may help in negotiations.

Though I have translated *Udyogaparvan* as "Preparations for War" for convenience, the term *udyoga* is more neutral and can also refer to the peaceful overtures of the book: the embassies.

The two volumes are divided into four embassies of varying importance, the first two of which feature in this volume. The embassies abide by the rules of diplomacy, and all the messengers are official, rather than being classed as spies like the men Dhrita·rashtra employed in the previous book. The choice of ambassador is all-important, for it shows the level of respect, and reveals the attitude of each side to the negotiations. The Pándavas begin by sending Drúpada's family priest. As a brahmin, he is a symbol of high regard. In return the Kurus snub the Pándavas by sending Sáñjaya, a bard (*sūta*). Though Sáñjaya is a friend to the sons of Pandu, the more natural choice would have been Vídura, who is a much closer friend and has acted as an ambassador in the past ('The Beginning,' CE 1.192).

The first envoy is a mere messenger without any power to negotiate. He is given strict instructions on how to behave and what to say. Sáñjaya, on the other hand, is given some flexibility by Dhrita·rashtra, and told that he should say whatever he thinks appropriate (22.40). It is important to note that it is Dhrita·rashtra who sends him and that he is not sanctioned at all by Duryódhana, who has no interest in negotiation.

Finally, at the end of this volume, Krishna sets out for the Kurus. He, however, cannot really be regarded as an envoy, for he is not sent by Yudhi·shthira. He goes on his own authority to negotiate, and Yudhi·shthira eventually tells him to do anything he sees fit.

Despite the ostensibly peaceful structure, 'Preparations for War' is something of a contradiction. Even before the first embassy has been heard, both sides are racing to win the allegiance of powerful neighboring kings in case of war. The Kurus gain the numerical advantage, having more to offer than the impoverished Pándavas. Shalya is a striking example when he succumbs to the luxury and flattery of the Kurus. Nevertheless he does not entirely forsake his allegiance to the sons of Pandu, instead promising Yudhi·shthira that he will do his best to destroy Karna's confidence in battle.

This episode demonstrates the depiction in 'Preparations for War' of war as corrupter and inverter. The normally upright Yudhi·shthira is here shown in a new light. He is sly and willing to play dirty. Normal moral duties are tested and the boundaries are unclear. In this book we see some characters transgressing their usual levels of restraint under new pressures, and we also find corresponding levels of didactic passages. The Pándavas have the moral high ground in this debate, and Duryódhana and his father are clearly shown to be in the wrong when they refuse to honor the agreement made so many years before. Nevertheless, waging war against one's family is not without its problems. This is a question which will return throughout the coming books, but it is here that it is first seriously grappled with.

After the humor of 'Viráta' and its light-hearted attitude to war, the sense of horror in 'Preparations for War' is a stark contrast. This book is permeated with a real dread of battle and its implications, but despite the foreboding, this volume also offers us hope through parables and philosophical insight. The tale Shalya tells of Indra's misery and eventual triumph mirrors the fate of Yudhi·shthira. In the midst of all the uncertainty and doubt that plagues the characters at the beginning of this volume, comes a prophecy of war but eventual victory. Indra, like Yudhi·shthira, is a king without realm or sovereignty, but in the end he is returned to his position, as Yudhi·shthira too will be.

The tale of Indra's misery is a beautifully depicted story of the struggle for power, and the moral dilemmas facing a righteous ruler. It is a complete microcosm of the conflicting pulls to negotiation and retaliation which dominate this volume, and to an extent the entire epic. The imagery of this tale is vivid and entrancing. Indra, in an absolute reversal of fortune, is so far reduced that even his size is diminished. When Agni searches for him, he finds him hiding within the fibre of a lotus stalk, an unsure and minute opponent for Náhusha. And when we look at Náhusha, who do we see but Duryódhana: a human king who robs others of their rightful powers, and whose arrogance ensures his eventual downfall. The pride and obstinacy of Duryódhana are themes heavily explored throughout both volumes of 'Preparations for War,' but here, and again later, we are assured that Duryódhana will pay for his ambition.

There are other similarities to note in this beautiful tale, such as the hero's reaction to his situation. Indra is tormented by the burden of his sins. Unable to ignore the moral consequences of his battles he hides in penance, and Yudhi·shthira too is wary of war. Dhrita·rashtra is also depicted as plagued by worry and insomnia on the brink of war, and even Bhima, normally so keen on conflict, advises Krishna to avoid hostilities if at all possible, saying that they would all rather accept Duryódhana's superiority (74.20). But war is the overriding subject of the book despite attempts at conciliation, and the inevitability of having to fight one's family scares almost everyone but Duryódhana.

Indra's situation mirrors the reality of the Pándavas yet more, for whom does he rely upon to help kill Vritra but Vishnu. All gods and men turn to the preserving deity in times of disaster, and the Pándavas too now turn to this god in the form of Krishna. The Kurus, notably Dhrita·rashtra and Duryódhana, fail to understand his true significance, and therein lies their mistake.

The insight, or lack of it, of both sides is perhaps perfectly depicted in this volume when Árjuna and Duryódhana both stand before Krishna to beg for his allegiance. Faced with the choice of allies—countless mighty warriors—or Krishna as a non-combatant, Árjuna chooses Krishna, but Duryódhana is misguidedly delighted with his army, believing quantity outweighs quality. Arrogance is shown to blind one of intelligence. So Náhusha and Duryódhana seal their fates.

Like father like son, for Dhrita·rashtra too fails to see the significance of Krishna. Sáñjaya tells him, "Where there is truth, where there is morality, where there is modesty and sincerity, there is Go·vinda. Where Krishna is, there is victory" (68.9).

Krishna's role in 'Preparations for War,' and indeed in the epic, is gradually revealed in this volume. Though he reinforces his neutrality at the wedding celebrations, he is quickly and inevitably allied specifically to the Parthas. His decision not to fight is in some ways irrelevant, for as Sáñjaya points out: "Using the Pándavas as his cover, seemingly deceiving the world, he wishes to burn up your foolish sons who take pleasure in lawlessness" (68.11). As this first volume develops, so the true nature of Krishna is exposed. His importance to the proceedings eventually leads to his setting out, at the end of this volume, on his own personal embassy to the Kurus; an embassy which takes place in the second volume and will prove to be the dramatic climax of 'Preparations for War.'

As mentioned above, the tale of Indra's misery is not the only instance where 'Preparations for War' offers us relief and hope in the midst of dread. We are also given moral insights which serve to put human action into perspective.

Much of the dharmic teaching in this book is non-specific to the situation, repeating well-known instructions for the duties of the castes and so on. Vídura's teachings are fairly standard fare and do not really answer any of the important or philosophical questions which the current situation poses, merely reiterating that the Pándavas are in the right. This last-ditch attempt to change Dhrita·rashtra's mind is not particularly strong, but though it is rather repetitive and lengthy, VAN BUITENEN is not entirely fair in calling it a "well-nigh interminable sermon" (1978: 180). Vídura eventually reveals that he cannot tell his brother any real secrets because he himself is low-born, and so he calls Sanat·sujáta, one of the mind-born sons of Brahma.

Sanat·sujáta's teachings are philosophically far more interesting than Vídura's, and as such this passage has attracted a great deal of interest in its own right. Its date is certainly early, though there is disagreement as to whether it is contemporary with the "Bhagavad Gita" or earlier, so that it could be regarded as a late Upanishad.

There is evidence from two standpoints to support the theory that the *Sanatsujātīya* was originally a separate work in its own right, merely inserted into the "Maha·bhárata" after its composition. Firstly there is the apparent age of the passage, as mentioned above, which would put its composition far before the epic itself. Evidence for this comes from the style of the language, such as the sparsity and simplicity of similes, and from the metrical and syntactical anomalies, suggesting that the text is far older than much of the "Maha·bhárata."

The second argument is derived from the position and context of the *Sanatsujātīya* in the text. Dhrita·rashtra is not always portrayed as being terribly concerned with doing the correct thing. Indeed, even after the *Sanatsujātīya* he questions Sáñjaya in the hope that his forces could defeat the Pándavas, and he is still unaware of the true magnificence of Krishna. Perhaps this discrepancy may be due to the fact that the *Sanatsujātīya* was not originally directly before this passage. He is normally characterized by his weakness and his overwhelming favoritism towards Duryódhana, rather than his concern for higher truths. The *Sanatsujātīya* is often compared to the "Bhagavad Gita," as discussed more fully below, but given the context of anxiety before battle, the *Sanatsujātīya* could well be the Kurus' equivalent to the "Bhagavad Gita:" a philosophy which illuminates the true nature of human action when properly undertaken, thereby granting license to the inevitable violence. It seems entirely plausible that the *Sanatsujātīya* could be a late addition to the "Maha·bhárata," but it must be reiterated that this by no means implies that the text itself is late.

The *Sanatsujātīya* is an extremely obscure passage. Readers who follow the Sanskrit will notice the frequent instances of metrical anomalies and highly unusual use of vocabulary. It is probable that the text is intentionally unfathomable due to the esoteric nature of its substance. However, this has made it almost impossible to translate literally, since one would be left in some cases with a text too arcane to make sense of. Therefore, the commentaries of Shánkara and Nila·kantha have been used to elucidate the stranger passages.

The message the *Sanatsujātīya* teaches is that death is mere illusion, and it reveals the secret of how to avoid death. This non-death is not immortality as we may consider it today, but rather release from the world of rebirth and union with the ultimate creative power. Sanat·sujáta stresses knowledge and true understanding as the only valid path, and rejects mere ritualism. The *Sanatsujātīya* is rigidly opposed to what it sees as the hypocrisy of those who perform Vedic rites only to win merit, and who believe themselves to fully understand the Veda when in fact they have no inkling of its true meaning. These men go to the heaven of the gods, but are doomed to fall again. Sanat·sujáta explains that acts tie one to the cycle of rebirth if one undertakes them with any vested interest. Only indifference to the fruits of one's actions leaves the soul untainted by the act itself. Real knowledge is the key to success.

Immortality is gained by uniting with Brahman. Brahman is the ultimate. It cannot be described and is beyond the scope of human language. In Vedánta philosophy Brahman is explained by means of what it is not. Trying to give Brahman attributes and identifying it as something alien to our true selves are traps into which Dhrita·rashtra falls.

Sanat·sujáta tells us that immortality is achieved through realizing that our souls and Brahman are one. The world we live in is created through *māyā*—illusion. Attachment to worldly matters and seeing oneself as separate from Brahman are symptoms of ignorance, which ultimately is what chains us to the cycle of rebirth. Furthermore, merely knowing that one's true self is nothing other than Brahman is not enough to win union with it and win release from reincarnation. The truth must be recognized on every level of one's self, and this takes time and proper *mauna*—strict, silent meditation, which involves absolute focus on the self and absolute renunciation of wordly matters and objects of the senses.

So the heart of the message is essentially that of the "Bhagavad Gita," and it is easy to see why these two philosophical passages are placed where they are, for in both instances the characters are troubled by the enormity of the sin of war. Just as Árjuna feels he cannot kill his family and teachers without incurring sin, so too Dhrita·rashtra, weak though he is, is depicted as being deeply troubled about the morality of the inevitable war. The "Bhagavad Gita" comes directly before battle, and this passage before the decision to go to battle. Both Sanat·sujáta and Krishna respond to these worries by essentially letting their audience off the hook. Acts cannot always be avoided, but by undertaking them with the right attitude one can avoid the repercussions to one's soul.

Now, with this secret teaching, we know that this war is not in itself the huge sin many characters worry it will be. It can, in fact, conform to what is morally right, and so the

Pándavas do not have to be trapped into servitude by their own ethics.

## Note on the Sanskrit Text

I have used KINJAWADEKAR's edition of the "vulgate" established by Nila·kantha as the main text for my translation. On occasion it was felt necessary to emend the text, usually due to a transparent case of typographical error, but also in cases where it seemed faulty or incomprehensible. In such cases, emendations have been made with reference to the text of the Critical Edition and its extensive critical notes.

## Concordance of Canto Numbers with the Critical Edition

| CSL | CE |
|---|---|
| 1–44 | 1–44 |
| 45 | (not in CE) |
| 46–62 | 45–61 |
| 63 | 62.1–62.5* |
| 64–83 | 62.6†–81 |

* CSL 63.7cdef to the end of Canto 63 is not found in CE.
† CSL Canto 64 forms the remainder of Canto 62 in CE.

## Abbreviations

CE = *Mahābhārata* Pune Critical Edition (see Bibliography)
conj. = conjecture
CSL = *Mahābhārata* CLAY SANSKRIT LIBRARY edition
K = KINJAWADEKAR (see Bibliography)

## Bibliography


### THE MAHA·BHÁRATA IN SANSKRIT

*The Mahābhāratam with the Bharata Bhawadeepa Commentary of Nīlakaṇṭha.* Edited by RAMACHANDRASHASTRI KINJAWADEKAR. Poona: Chitrashala Press, 1929–36; reprint, New Delhi: Oriental Books Reprint Corporation, 1978 (2nd ed. 1979). Vol. 5 Udyoga Parva. [K]

*The Mahābhārata.* Critically edited by V.K. SUKTHANKAR, S.K. BELVALKAR, P.L. VAIDYA et al. 1933–66. 19 vols. Poona: Bhandarkar Oriental Research Institute. [CE]

### THE MAHA·BHÁRATA IN TRANSLATION

BOWLES, A. *Maha·bhárata, Book Eight: Karna.* Vol. 1. New York: New York University Press & JJC Foundation, 2006. [CSL]

VAN BUITENEN, J.A.B. *The Mahābhārata, vol. 3. The Book of Virata. The Book of the Effort.* Chicago: University of Chicago Press, 1978.

TELANG, K.T. *The Bhagavadgîtâ with the Sanatsugâtîya and the Anugîtâ* (Sacred Books of the East), 2nd edn. Oxford: Clarendon Press, 1898.

WILMOT, P. *Maha·bhárata, Book Two: The Great Hall.* New York: New York University Press & JJC Foundation, 2006. [CSL]

### SECONDARY SOURCES

AGRAWALA, V.S. "The Mahābhārata: a cultural commentary." *Annals of the Bhandarkar Oriental Research Institute* 37, 1956, pp. 1–26.

BEDEKAR, V.M. 'The Sanatsujātīyam: a fresh study.' *Annals of the Bhandarkar Oriental Research Institute* 58–59, 1977–78, pp. 469–77.

BROCKINGTON, J.L. *The Sanskrit Epics.* Leiden: Brill, 1998.

SHULMAN, D.D. *The King and the Clown in South Indian Myth and Poetry.* Princeton: Princeton University Press, 1985.

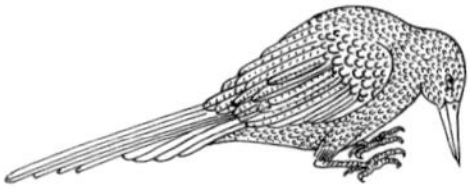

# MAHA·BHÁRATA

## BOOK FIVE

# PREPARATIONS FOR WAR

## VOLUME ONE

NĀRĀYAṆAṂ namas|kṛtya,
Naraṃ c' âiva nar'|ôttamam,
devīṃ Sarasvatīṃ c' âiva,
tato «Jayam» udīrayet.

Having paid obeisance to Naráyana and Nara,
the greatest of men,
as well as to the goddess Sarásvati,
let the word "Victory" be uttered.

1–8

# THE FIRST EMBASSY

VAIŚAMPĀYANA uvāca:

1.1 KṚTVĀ VIVĀHAṂ tu Kuru|pravīrās
tad" Âbhimanyor muditāḥ sva|pakṣāḥ,
viśramya rātrāv uṣasi pratītāḥ
sabhāṃ Virāṭasya tato 'bhijagmuḥ.
sabhā tu sā Matsya|pateḥ samṛddhā
maṇi|pravek'|ôttama|ratna|citrā
nyast'|āsanā mālyavatī su|gandhā.
tām abhyayus te nara|rāja|vṛddhāḥ.
ath' āsanāny āviśatāṃ purastād
ubhau Virāṭa|Drupadau nar'|êndrau,
vṛddhau ca mānyau pṛthivī|patīnāṃ
pitrā samaṃ Rāma|Janārdanau ca.
Pāñcāla|rājasya samīpatas tu
Śini|pravīraḥ saha|Rauhiṇeyaḥ,
Matsyasya rājñas tu su|sannikṛṣṭo
Janārdanaś c' âiva Yudhiṣṭhiraś ca.
1.5 sutāś ca sarve Drupadasya rājño
Bhīm'|Ârjunau Mādravatī|sutau ca,
Pradyumna|Sāmbau ca yudhi pravīrau,
Virāṭa|putraiś ca sah' Âbhimanyuḥ.
sarve ca śūrāḥ pitṛbhiḥ samānā
vīryeṇa rūpeṇa balena c' âiva
upāviśan Draupadeyāḥ kumārāḥ
suvarṇa|citreṣu var'|āsaneṣu.

VAISHAMPÁYANA said:

WHEN THE JOYFUL Kuru heroes had celebrated Abhimányu's marriage with their own parties, they rested for the night, and at dawn they cheerfully set out for Viráta's court. 1.1

The venerable lords of men headed for the Matsyan king's prosperous court, which gleamed brightly with the most exquisite and choicest jewels and gems. Thrones were set out in order, decked with garlands and daubed with bewitching fragrance.

Kings Viráta and Drúpada sat down on the frontmost thrones, and the venerable and respected of the earth-lords, along with Rama, Janárdana, and their father, also took their seats. The hero of the Shini race and Rauhinéya sat near to the king of Pañchála, and Janárdana and Yudhi·
shthira sat close to the Matsyan king. All King Drúpada's 1.5
sons were there, as were Bhima and Árjuna and Madri's twins. So too were Pradyúmna and Samba, both heroes in battle, and Abhimányu, who sat with Viráta's sons. All Dráupadi's brave, princely sons, the images of their fathers in heroism, beauty, and strength, sat on superb gilt-embellished thrones.

tath" ôpaviṣṭeṣu mahā|ratheṣu
virājamān'|ābharaṇ'|âmbareṣu,
rarāja sā rājavatī samṛddhā
grahair iva dyaur vimalair upetā.
tataḥ kathās te samavāya|yuktāḥ
kṛtvā vicitrāḥ puruṣa|pravīrāḥ,
tasthur muhūrtaṃ paricintayantaḥ
Kṛṣṇaṃ nṛpās te samudīkṣamāṇāḥ.
kath"|ântam āsādya ca Mādhavena
saṅghaṭṭitāh Pāṇḍava|kārya|hetoḥ,
te rāja|siṃhāḥ sahitā hy aśṛṇvan
vākyaṃ mah"|ârthaṃ su|mah"|ôdayaṃ ca.

ŚRĪ KṚṢṆA uvāca:

1.10 «sarvair bhavadbhir viditaṃ yath" âyaṃ
Yudhiṣṭhiraḥ Saubalen' âkṣavatyām
jito, nikṛty" âpahṛtaṃ ca rājyaṃ,
vana|pravāse samayaḥ kṛtaś ca.
śaktair vijetuṃ tarasā mahīṃ ca
satye sthitaiḥ satya|rathair yathāvat
Pāṇḍoḥ sutais tad vratam ugra|rūpaṃ
varṣāṇi ṣaṭ sapta ca cīrṇam agryaiḥ.
trayo|daśaś c' âiva su|dustaro 'yam
a|jñāyamānair bhavatāṃ samīpe
kleśān a|sahyān vividhān sahadbhir
mah"|ātmabhiś c' âpi vane niviṣṭam.
etaiḥ para|preṣya|niyoga|yuktair
icchadbhir āptaṃ sva|kulena rājyam.
evaṃ gate Dharma|sutasya rājño
Duryodhanasy' âpi ca yadd hitaṃ syāt
tac cintayadhvaṃ Kuru|puṅgavānāṃ.

Once those mighty chariot warriors were seated in their gleaming robes and ornaments, the flourishing court, full of kings, shone like the heavens teeming with dazzling planets. The heroic men discussed various topics of conversation, making suitable use of the meeting, but then the kings remained lost in thought for a moment, looking attentively towards Krishna. The lion-like sovereigns, whom Mádhava had assembled for the Pándavas' mission, brought their conversations to an end, and together they listened to his advice of great note and significance.

LORD KRISHNA said:

"You all know how Yudhi·shthira was dishonestly beaten 1.10
in a game of dice by Súbala's son, how his kingdom was stolen and how an agreement was made stipulating he would live in exile in the forest. The preeminent, truthful, warrior sons of Pandu observed that terrible vow for thirteen years, duly standing by their true promise, despite the fact that they are capable of forcibly conquering the world. And once their exile in the forest was done, these powerful, high-souled men passed their thirteenth year, highly problematic as it was, in your presence, unrecognized and enduring insufferable hardships.

These men, forced to make a living by entering the service of others, want to take back their kingdom in partnership with their family. So, this being the case, think of a satisfactory solution for the son of Dharma, for King Duryódhana, and for those bull-like Kurus. It must not deviate from moral law, it must be appropriate, and it must bring

dharmyaṃ ca yuktaṃ ca yaśas|karaṃ ca.
a|dharma|yuktaṃ na ca kāmayeta
rājyaṃ surāṇām api dharma|rājaḥ!
1.15 dharm'|ârtha|yuktaṃ tu mahī|patitvaṃ
grāme 'pi kasmiṃś cid ayaṃ bubhūṣet.
pitryaṃ hi rājyaṃ viditaṃ nṛpāṇāṃ
yath" âpakṛṣṭaṃ Dhṛtarāṣṭra|putraiḥ
mithy"|ôpacāreṇa yathā hy anena.
kṛcchraṃ mahat prāptam a|sahya|rūpam.
na c' âpi Pārtho vijito raṇe taiḥ
sva|tejasā Dhṛtarāṣṭrasya putraiḥ.
tath" âpi rājā sahitaḥ suhṛdbhir
abhīpsyate 'n|āmayam eva teṣām!
yat tu svayaṃ Pāṇḍu|sutair vijitya
samāhṛtaṃ bhūmi|patīn prapīḍya,
tat prārthayante puruṣa|pravīrāḥ
Kuntī|sutā Mādravatī|sutau ca.
bālās tv ime tair vividhair upāyaiḥ
samprārthitā hantum a|mitra|saṅghaiḥ
rājyaṃ jihīrṣadbhir a|sadbhir ugraiḥ;
sarvaṃ ca tad vo viditaṃ yathāvat.
teṣāṃ ca lobhaṃ prasamīkṣya vṛddhaṃ,
dharmajñatāṃ c' âpi Yudhiṣṭhirasya,
1.20 saṃbandhitāṃ c' âpi samīkṣya teṣāṃ,
matiḥ kurudhvaṃ sahitāḥ pṛthak ca.
ime ca satye 'bhiratāḥ sad" âiva
taṃ pālayitvā samayaṃ yathāvat.
ato 'nyathā tair upacaryamāṇā
hanyuḥ sametān Dhṛtarāṣṭra|putrān.
tair viprakāraṃ ca niśamya kārye

glory. The king of righteousness would not wish even for the kingdom of the gods if it were inconsistent with moral law! He would wish for lordship even in some village if it 1.15
were righteous and profitable.

All the kings here know how his ancestral kingdom was seized by Dhrita·rashtra's sons through deceitful means. Great and insufferable pain followed. But Dhrita·rashtra's sons failed to even defeat Árjuna Partha in battle by merit of their own splendor.

Despite this, the king and his friends wished only for their health! It is only what the Pándavas themselves accumulated, by harrassing the kings of earth, that the sons of Kunti and Madri's heroic twins wish to take back. Their multitude of enemies sought to kill them by various means while they were still children, for those evil and savage Káuravas wanted to take their kingdom. But you know all this. So, examining the Kurus' increased avarice, Yudhi·shthira's
understanding of moral law, and the Pándavas' family piety, 1.20
make up your minds, first individually and then as a group.

These men always engage in the truth and have observed their agreement accordingly. And so, if they were to be mistreated now, they would kill all Dhrita·rashtra's sons together. And the Pándavas' allies will stand by their side in the crisis, when they hear how those men maltreated the king, and they will drive off the Káuravas in battle. They

suhṛj|janās tān parivārayeyuḥ
yuddhena bādheyur imāṃs tath" âivaṃ
tair bādhyamānā yudhi tāṃś ca hanyuḥ.
tath" âpi ‹n' ême 'lpatayā samarthās
teṣāṃ jayāy', êti› bhaven mataṃ vaḥ
sametya sarve sahitāḥ suhṛdbhis
teṣāṃ vināśāya yateyur iva.
Duryodhanasy' âpi mataṃ yathāvan
na jñāyate, ‹kiṃ nu kariṣyat' îti.›
a|jñāyamāne ca mate parasya
kiṃ syāt samārabhyatamaṃ mataṃ vaḥ?
tasmād ito gacchatu dharma|śīlaḥ
śuciḥ kulīnaḥ puruṣo '|pramattaḥ
1.25 dūtaḥ samarthaḥ praśamāya teṣāṃ,
rājy'|ârdha|dānāya Yudhiṣṭhirasya.
niśamya vākyaṃ tu Janārdanasya
dharm'|ârtha|yuktaṃ madhuraṃ samaṃ ca
samādade vākyam ath' âgra|jo 'sya
saṃpūjya vākyaṃ tad atīva, rājan.»

BALADEVA uvāca:

2.1 «ŚRUTAṂ BHAVADBHIR Gada|pūrvajasya
vākyaṃ yathā dharmavad arthavac ca,
Ajātaśatroś ca hitaṃ, hitaṃ ca
Duryodhanasy' âpi tath" âiva rājñaḥ.
ardhaṃ hi rājyasya visṛjya vīrāḥ
Kuntī|sutās tasya kṛte yatante,
pradāya c' ârdhaṃ Dhṛtarāṣṭra|putraḥ
sukhī sah' âsmāśbhir atīva modet!
labdhvā hi rājyaṃ puruṣa|pravīraḥ,

would kill them in battle even if being oppressed themselves! And if it is your opinion that the Pándavas here are not yet powerful enough in number to defeat them, then be aware that all together, and united with their friends, they will strive for their enemies' destruction.

As yet it is not known what Duryódhana is planning or what he will do, but when you don't know the enemy's strategy, how can you form an opinion? Therefore, let a pure, high-born, and careful man of lawful conduct go as 1.25
our messenger; someone who is able to pacify them and persuade them to give back half of Yudhi·shthira's kingdom."

Having heard Janárdana's charming and balanced advice, which complied with moral law and profit, his elder brother took it upon himself to speak, and he praised the speech in no uncertain terms, my king.

BALA·DEVA said:

"YOU HAVE HEARD Gada's elder brother's righteous and 2.1
profitable words. They are advantageous to both Ajáta·shatru and indeed to King Duryódhana. By letting half of their kingdom go, the hero sons of Kunti strive to put an end to this business, and in giving away only half, Dhrita·rashtra's son should be very pleased and delighted with us! Providing the others act compliantly, those heroic men will surely be pacified when they take their share of the kingdom, and they will find happiness. And peace between the two parties can only be an advantage for their subjects. It would please me if someone would go for the sake of peace

samyak pravṛtteṣu pareṣu c' âiva,
dhruvaṃ praśāntāḥ sukham āviśeyus.
teṣāṃ praśāntiś ca hitaṃ prajānām.
Duryodhanasy' âpi mataṃ ca vettuṃ,
vaktuṃ ca vākyāni Yudhiṣṭhirasya,
priyaṃ ca me syād yadi tatra kaś cid
vrajec cham'|ârthaṃ Kuru|Pāṇḍavānām.
2.5 sa Bhīṣmam āmantrya Kuru|pravīraṃ,
Vaicitravīryaṃ ca mah"|ânubhāvam,
Droṇaṃ sa|putraṃ, Viduraṃ, Kṛpaṃ ca,
Gāndhāra|rājaṃ ca sa|sūta|putram.
sarve ca ye 'nye Dhṛtarāṣṭra|putrāḥ
bala|pradhānā, nigama|pradhānāḥ,
sthitāś ca dharmeṣu tathā svakeṣu,
loka|pravīrāḥ śruta|kāla|vṛddhāḥ.
eteṣu sarveṣu samāgateṣu,
paureṣu vṛddheṣu ca saṃgateṣu,
bravītu vākyaṃ praṇipāta|yuktaṃ
Kuntī|sutasy' ârtha|karaṃ yathā syāt.
sarvāsv avasthāsu ca te na kopyā,
grasto hi so 'rtho balam āśritais taiḥ.
priy'|âbhyupetasya Yudhiṣṭhirasya
dyūte prasaktasya hṛtaṃ ca rājyam.
nivāryamāṇaś ca Kuru|pravīraḥ
sarvaiḥ suhṛdbhir hy ayam apy a|taj|jñaḥ
sa dīvyamānaḥ pratidīvya c' âinaṃ
Gāndhāra|rājasya sutaṃ mat'|âkṣam.
2.10 hitvā hi Karṇaṃ ca Suyodhanaṃ ca,
samāhvayad devitum Ājamīḍhaḥ!
duro|darās tatra sahasraśo 'nye

between the Kurus and Pándavas, to find out Duryódhana's opinion and give him Yudhi·shthira's message.

He should greet Bhishma, the Káuravan hero, the mighty 2.5
son of Vichítra·virya, as well as Drona and his son, Vídura, Kripa, the king of Gandhára and the *suta*'s son.* He should also greet all Dhrita·rashtra's other sons, predominant in strength and doctrine, earthly heroes who abide by their own duties, and are advanced in learning and age. When all those men are assembled, and the elderly citizens have gathered, he should give his speech in an appropriately humble manner in order to fulfill the son of Kunti's aim.

Under no circumstances should they be made angry, for they seized their wealth by relying on force. Yudhi·shthira's kingdom was stolen when he had been approached like a friend and his attention was focused on a game of dice. Even though all the Káuravan hero's friends had discouraged him, and even though he had absolutely no skill, he played and gambled with the king of Gandhára's dice-obsessed son.

Disregarding Karna and Suyódhana, Ajamídha chal- 2.10
lenged him to a game! There were thousands of other gamblers whom Yudhi·shthira could have beaten. But he passed them over for Súbala, whom he challenged and by whom

Yudhiṣṭhiro yān viṣaheta jetum.
utsṛjya tān Saubalam eva c' âyaṃ,
samāhvayat; tena jito 'kṣavatyām.
sa dīvyamānaḥ pratidevanena
akṣeṣu nityaṃ tu parāṅ|mukheṣu
saṃrambhamāṇo vijitaḥ prasahya.
tatr' âparādhaḥ Śakuner na kaś cit!
tasmāt praṇamy' âiva vaco bravītu
Vaicitravīryaṃ bahu|sāma|yuktam.
tathā hi śakyo Dhṛtarāṣṭra|putraḥ
sv'|ârthe niyoktum puruṣeṇa tena.
a|yuddham ākāṅkṣata Kauravāṇāṃ
sāmn" âiva Duryodhanam āhvayadhvam.
sāmnā jito 'rtho 'rtha|karo bhaveta.
yuddhe 'n|ayo bhavitā; n' êha so 'rthaḥ.»

VAIŚAMPĀYANA uvāca:

2.15 evaṃ bruvaty eva Madhu|pravīre,
Śini|pravīraḥ sahas" ôtpapāta.
tac c' âpi vākyaṃ parinindya tasya,
samādade vākyam idaṃ samanyuḥ:

SĀTYAKIR uvāca:

3.1 «YĀDṚŚAḤ PURUṢASY' ātmā, tādṛśaṃ saṃprabhāṣate.
yathā|rūpo 'ntar' ātmā te, tathā|rūpaṃ prabhāṣase!
santi vai puruṣāḥ śūrāḥ, santi kā|puruṣās tathā.
ubhāv etau dṛḍhau pakṣau dṛśyete puruṣān prati.
ekasminn eva jāyete kule klība|mahābalau
phal'|â|phalavatī śākhe yath" âikasmin vanas|patau.

he was beaten in the game of dice. He was played by his opponent and the dice were invariably unkind to him. He got over-excited and was beaten outright. That was not Shákuni's fault! So let the messenger bow and address the son of Vichítra·virya in extremely conciliatory terms. In this manner, the man may be able to bring Dhrita·rashtra's son round to his own purpose. Our hope is to avoid war between the Kurus, so address Duryódhana politely. Profit is won by conciliatory negotiation, so we may achieve our aim. Bad luck is to be found in battle, and is therefore not our aim here."

VAISHAMPÁYANA said:

When the Mádhava hero was speaking, the hero of the 2.15
Shini race quickly flew up and strongly censured what Bala·deva had said. Furious, he began this speech:

SÁTYAKI said:

"THE WAY A MAN speaks betrays his soul. So, the way 3.1
you speak reveals what sort of soul you possess! There are brave men and there are cowards. Both these clearly distinct groups can be discerned among men. A eunuch and a mighty hero are born in one and the same family, just as the same tree can produce a pair of branches—one fruitful, the other not.

n' âbhyasūyāmi te vākyaṃ bruvato, lāṅgala|dhvaja,
ye tu śṛṇvanti te vākyaṃ, tān asūyāmi, Mādhava!
3.5 kathaṃ hi dharma|rājasya doṣam alpam api bruvan
labhate pariṣan|madhye vyāhartum a|kuto|bhayaḥ?
samāhūya mah"|ātmānaṃ jitavanto 'kṣa|kovidāḥ
an|akṣa|jñaṃ yathā|śraddhaṃ, teṣu dharma|jayaḥ kutaḥ?
yadi Kuntī|sutaṃ gehe krīḍantaṃ bhrātṛbhiḥ saha
abhigamya jayeyus te tat teṣāṃ dharmato bhavet.
samāhūya tu rājānaṃ kṣatra|dharma|rataṃ sadā
nikṛtyā jitavantas te—kiṃ nu teṣāṃ paraṃ śubhaṃ?
kathaṃ praṇipatec c' âyam iha kṛtvā paṇaṃ param,
vana|vāsād vimuktas tu, prāptaḥ paitāmahaṃ padam?
yady ayaṃ pāpa|vittāni kāmayeta Yudhiṣṭhiraḥ,
3.10 evam apy ayam atyantaṃ parān n' ârhati yācitum!
kathaṃ ca dharma|yuktās te? na ca rājyaṃ jihīrṣavaḥ
nivṛtta|vāsān Kaunteyān ya āhur ‹viditā› iti?
anunītā hi Bhīṣmeṇa, Droṇena Vidureṇa ca,
na vyavasyanti Pāṇḍūnāṃ pradātuṃ paitṛkaṃ vasu.
ahaṃ tu tāñ śitair bāṇair anunīya raṇe balāt,
pādayoḥ pātayiṣyāmi Kaunteyasya mah"|ātmanaḥ!
atha te na vyavasyanti praṇipātāya dhīmataḥ,
gamiṣyanti sah'|âmātyā Yamasya sadanaṃ prati!
na hi te yuyudhānasya saṃrabdhasya yuyutsataḥ

I am not indignant at the words you speak, plow-bannered hero, but I am displeased with those who listen to your speech, Mádhava! How can one take it upon oneself 3.5
to criticize the king of righteousness, even if only a little, in the midst of this council without fear from any quarter?

Skilled gamblers made the wager with that high-souled man, and he played in good faith despite being an unskilled dice player, and they beat him. Where is the justice in that victory? If the son of Kunti had been gambling in his house with his brothers and they had come and beaten him it may have been morally acceptable. But challenging a king who always concentrated on his kingly duty and beating him through dishonesty—is this really an example of their best behavior?

Why should this man, who played for the highest stakes, grovel to regain his ancestral position now that he has been released from his exile in the forest? Even if Yudhi·shthira
here were to covet the wealth of wicked men, he ought not 3.10
to beg his enemies too excessively! How do those men respect moral law? Aren't they greedy for power, claiming that the sons of Kunti were discovered when in fact their exile was finished? They were entreated by Bhishma, Drona, and Vídura, but they made their decision not to hand back the Pándavas' ancestral property.

I'll entreat them by force in battle with sharp arrows, and topple them at the feet of high-souled Kauntéya! But if they decide not to prostrate themselves before this wise man, then they will go to Yama's realm along with their ministers! For they can no more sustain the powerful force of

3.15 vegam samarthāḥ saṃsoḍhuṃ, vajrasy' êva mahī|dharāḥ!
ko hi Gāṇḍīva|dhanvānaṃ, kaś ca cakr'|āyudhaṃ yudhi,
māṃ c' âpi viṣahet kruddhaṃ, kaś ca Bhīmaṃ dur|āsadam?
yamau ca dṛḍha|dhanvānau Yama|kāl'|ôpama|dyutī,
Virāṭa|Drupadau vīrau Yama|kāl'|ôpama|dyutī?
ko jijīviṣur āsāded Dhṛṣṭadyumnaṃ ca Pārṣatam?
pañc' êmān Pāṇḍaveyāṃs tu Draupadyāḥ kīrti|vardhanān,
sama|pramāṇān Pāṇḍūnāṃ, sama|vīryān, mad'|ôtkaṭān?
Saubhadraṃ ca mah"|êṣvāsam amarair api duḥ|saham,
Gada|Pradyumna|Sāmbāṃś ca kāla|sūry'|ânal'|ôpamān?
te vayaṃ Dhṛtarāṣṭrasya putraṃ Śakuninā saha
3.20 Karṇaṃ c' âiva nihaty' ājāv, abhiṣekṣyāma Pāṇḍavam.
n' â|dharmo vidyate kaś cic chatrūn hatv" ātatāyinaḥ.
a|dharmyam a|yaśasyaṃ ca śātravāṇāṃ prayācanam!
hṛd|gatas tasya yaḥ kāmas, taṃ Kurudhvam a|tandritāḥ.
nisṛṣṭaṃ Dhṛtarāṣṭreṇa rājyaṃ prāpnotu Pāṇḍavaḥ.
adya Pāṇḍu|suto rājyaṃ labhatāṃ vā Yudhiṣṭhiraḥ,
nihatā vā raṇe sarve svapsyanti vasudhā|tale.»

an enraged warrior lusting for battle than mountains can sustain the force of a lightning strike! 3.15

Who can endure the Gandíva bowman or the discus-bearer in battle? Who can withstand me when I am furious, or, for that matter, unparalleled Bhima? Which man would attack the sure-bowed twins, splendid as deathly Yama, or the heroes Viráta and Drúpada, also splendid as deathly Yama, or Dhrishta·dyumna or Párshata, unless he had a death-wish? Which man would attack the five sons of the Pándavas, who increase Dráupadi's renown, those passionate men who emulate the Pándavas in their heroism, unless he had a death-wish? Or who would attack Saubhádra the great archer, a man whom even the gods would struggle to defeat, or Gada, Pradyúmna, and Samba, men to match
time, the sun, and fire respectively? We shall kill Dhrita· 3.20
rashtra's son along with Shákuni and Karna on the battlefield, and then we will consecrate the son of Pandu as king!

No law can be found against killing enemies who are plotting to kill us. But begging one's enemies is both immoral and disgraceful! Do not be slow to bring about the wish of the Kuru king's heart.

Let the Pándava take back the kingdom which Dhrita·rashtra transferred to him. Let Yudhi·shthira, the son of Pandu, either take his kingdom now, or let them all be killed in battle and sleep on the surface of the earth."

DRUPADA uvāca:

4.1 «EVAM ETAN, mahā|bāho, bhaviṣyati, na saṃśayaḥ.
na hi Duryodhano rājyaṃ madhureṇa pradāsyati.
anuvartsyati taṃ c' âpi
Dhṛtarāṣṭraḥ suta|priyaḥ.
Bhīṣma|Droṇau ca kārpaṇyān
maurkhyād Rādheya|Saubalau.

Baladevasya vākyaṃ tu mama jñāne na yujyate,
etadd hi puruṣeṇ' âgre kāryaṃ su|nayam icchatā.
na tu vācyo mṛdu vaco Dhārtarāṣṭraḥ kathañ cana.
na hi mārdava|sādhyo 'sau pāpa|buddhir mato mama.
4.5 gardabhe mārdavaṃ kuryād, goṣu tīkṣṇaṃ samācaret,
mṛdu Duryodhane vākyaṃ yo brūyāt pāpa|cetasi!
mṛdu vai manyate pāpo bhāṣamāṇam a|śaktikam.
jitam arthaṃ vijānīyād a|budho mārdave sati!

etac c' âiva kariṣyāmo, yatnaś ca kriyatām iha:
prasthāpayāma mitrebhyo, balāny udyojayantu naḥ.
Śalyasya, Dhṛṣṭaketoś ca, Jayatsenasya vā, vibho,
Kekayānāṃ ca sarveṣāṃ dūtā gacchantu śighra|gāḥ.
sa tu Duryodhano nūnaṃ preṣayiṣyati sarvaśaḥ;
pūrv'|âbhipannāḥ santaś ca bhajante pūrva|codanam.
4.10 tat tvaradhvaṃ nar'|êndrāṇāṃ pūrvam eva pracodane.
mahadd hi kāryaṃ voḍhavyam, iti me vartate matiḥ.

DRÚPADA said:

"WELL, LONG-ARMED man, no doubt that is how it will be. For Duryódhana will certainly not hand over his kingdom with good grace. And Dhrita·rashtra will obey him because he loves his son. Bhishma and Drona will obey because of their poverty and Radhéya and Súbala's son will obey out of foolishness. 4.1

But in my opinion Bala·deva's speech was not appropriate, for right from the outset it implies dealing with a man who wishes to make use of sensible policy. The son of Dhrita·rashtra should never be addressed with gentle words. I certainly do not believe that evil-minded man will be won over by soft speech.

The man who talks sweetly to wicked-minded Duryó- 4.5
dhana may as well be treating an ass kindly but behaving cruelly to cattle! A wicked man considers a softly spoken person to be powerless. Being conciliatory will only make that idiot believe he has already won!

Let us begin our preparations and do our best: let us go to our allies so they can raise our forces. Let fast-paced messengers go out to Shalya, Dhrishta·ketu, or Jayat·sena, my lord, and all the Kékayas. Duryódhana will presumably send people to all of them too, but good men choose the invitation
of those who ask them first. So hurry and be the first to 4.10
beg help from those kings, for as I see it, it is certainly a considerable task that we must undertake.

Śalyasya preṣyatāṃ śīghraṃ, ye ca tasy' ânugā nṛpāḥ,
Bhagadattāya rājñe ca pūrva|sāgara|vāsine,
a|mit'|âujase tath" Ôgrāya, Hārdikyāy', Ândhakāya ca,
dīrgha|prajñāya Śūrāya, Rocamānāya vā, vibho.
ānīyatāṃ Bṛhantaś ca, Senābinduś ca pārthivaḥ,
Senajit, Prativindhyaś ca, Citravarmā, Suvāstukaḥ,
Bāhlīko, Muñjakeśaś ca, Caidy'|âdhipatir eva ca,
Supārśvaś ca, Subāhuś ca, Pauravaś ca mahā|rathaḥ,
4.15 Śakānāṃ Pahlavānāṃ ca, Daradānāṃ ca ye nṛpāḥ,
Surāriś ca, Nadījaś ca, Karṇaveṣṭaś ca pārthivaḥ,
Nīlaś ca, Vīradharmā ca, Bhūmipālaś ca vīryavān,
Durjayo, Dantavaktraś ca, Rukmī ca, Janamejayaḥ.
Āṣāḍho, Vāyuvegaś ca, Pūrvapālī ca pārthivaḥ,
Bhūritejā, Devakaś ca, Ekalavyaḥ sah' ātma|jaiḥ,
Kārūṣakāś ca rājānaḥ, Kṣemadhūrtiś ca vīryavān,
Kāmbojā, Ṛṣikā* ye ca, paścim'|Ânūpakāś ca ye,
Jayatsenaś ca Kāśyaś ca, tathā pañca|nadā nṛpāḥ.
Krātha|putraś ca dur|dharṣaḥ, pārvatīyāś ca ye nṛpāḥ,
4.20 Jānakiś ca, Suśarmā ca, Maṇimān Pautimatsakaḥ,
Pāṃśu|rāṣṭr'|âdhipaś c' âiva, Dhṛṣṭaketuś ca vīryavān,
Tuṇḍaś ca, Daṇḍadhāraś ca, Bṛhatsenaś ca vīryavān,
Aparājito, Niṣādaś ca, Śreṇimān, Vasumān api,
Bṛhadbalo mah"|âujāś ca, Bāhuḥ para|purañ|jayaḥ,
Samudraseno rājā ca saha putreṇa vīryavān.
Udbhavaḥ, Kṣemakaś c' âiva, Vāṭadhānaś ca pārthivaḥ,
Śrutāyuś ca, Dṛḍhāyuś ca, Śālva|putraś ca vīryavān,
Kumāraś ca Kaliṅgānām īśvaro yuddha|durmadaḥ.
eteṣāṃ preṣyatāṃ śīghram. etadd hi mama rocate.

Let word be sent quickly to Shalya and his subject kings,
and also to King Bhaga·datta of immeasurable energy who
lives by the eastern sea, to Ugra, Hardíkya, Ándhaka, far-
sighted Shura, and Rochamána, my lord. Fetch Brihánta
and King Sena·bindu, Sénajit, Prativíndhya, Chitra·var-
man, and Suvástuka, as well as Bahlíka, Muñja·kesha, and
the lord of the Chedis, and Supárshva, Subáhu, and the
mighty warrior Páurava. Fetch the kings of the Shakas, 4.15
Páhlavas, Dáradas, and the kings Surári, Nadíja, Karna·
veshta, Nila, Vira·dharman, and the mighty Bhumi·pala, as
well as Dúrjaya, Danta·vaktra, Rukmin, and Janam·éjaya.

Fetch Ashádha, Vayu·vega, and King Purva·palin, as well
as Bhuri·tejas, Dévaka, and Eka·lavya along with his sons.
Bring back the Karúshaka kings and heroic Kshema·dhurti,
and the Kambója, Ríshika, and western coastal kings, as
well as Jayat·sena, the king of Kashi, and the kings of the
five rivers. Fetch the unconquerable son of Kratha and the
mountain kings, Jánaki, Susharman, Mánimat, Pauti·mát- 4.20
saka, the king of the Panshu realm, and mighty Dhrishta·
ketu. Bring Tunda, Danda·dhara, and mighty Brihat·sena,
Aparájita, Nisháda, Shrénimat, Vásumat, hugely energetic
Brihad·bala, Bahu the conqueror of enemy cities, heroic
King Samúdra·sena, and his son.

Fetch Údbhava, Kshémaka, King Vata·dhana, Shrutáyus, Dridháyus, the powerful son of Shalva, and Kumára the battle crazed lord of the Kalíngas. Let these men be sent for quickly. This strikes me as a good plan.

4.25 ayaṃ ca brāhmaṇo vidvān mama, rājan, puro|hitaḥ
preṣyatāṃ Dhṛtarāṣṭrāya. vākyam asmai pradīyatām;
yathā Duryodhano vācyo, yathā Śāntanavo nṛpaḥ,
Dhṛtarāṣṭro yathā vācyo, Droṇaś ca rathināṃ varaḥ.»

VĀSUDEVA uvāca:

5.1 «UPAPANNAM IDAṂ vākyaṃ Somakānāṃ dhuraṃ|dhare,
artha|siddhi|karaṃ rājñah Pāṇḍavasy' â|mit'|âujasaḥ.
etac ca pūrvaṃ kāryaṃ naḥ su|nītam abhikāṅkṣatām.
anyathā hy ācaran karma puruṣaḥ syāt su|bāliṣaḥ
kiṃ nu saṃbandhakaṃ tulyam asmākaṃ Kuru|Pāṇḍuṣu,
yath" êṣṭaṃ vartamāneṣu Pāṇḍaveṣu ca teṣu ca.
te vivāh'|ârtham ānītā vayaṃ sarve, tathā bhavān.
kṛte vivāhe muditā gamiṣyāmo gṛhān prati.
5.5 bhavān vṛddhatamo rājñāṃ vayasā ca śrutena ca,
śiṣyavat te vayaṃ sarve bhavāmahe na saṃśayaḥ.
bhavantaṃ Dhṛtarāṣṭraś ca satataṃ bahu manyate,
ācāryayoḥ sakhā c' âsi Droṇasya ca Kṛpasya ca.
sa bhavān preṣayatv adya Pāṇḍav'|ârtha|karaṃ vacaḥ,
sarveṣāṃ niścitaṃ tan naḥ preṣayiṣyati yad bhavān.
yadi tāvac chamaṃ kuryān nyāyena Kuru|puṃgavaḥ,
na bhavet Kuru|Pāṇḍūnāṃ saubhrātreṇa mahān kṣayaḥ.
atha darp'|ânvito mohān na kuryād Dhṛtarāṣṭra|jaḥ,
anyeṣāṃ preṣayitvā ca paścād asmān samāhvayeḥ.
5.10 tato Duryodhano mandaḥ sah'|âmātyaḥ sa|bāndhavaḥ,

My king, send this brahmin, my wise family priest, to 4.25
Dhrita·rashtra. Instruct him on what he must say; how Duryódhana and Lord Bhishma, son of Shántanu, should be addressed, as well as how Dhrita·rashtra, and Drona the greatest of warriors, should be addressed."

VASUDÉVA said:

"THE SÓMAKAS' YOKE bearer's words are fitting and will 5.1
bring success to the immeasurably energetic Pándava king's cause. This is the first thing we must do if we are to strive for wise policy. A man would certainly be extremely foolish to pursue any other course.

But irrespective of how the Pándavas and the others choose to behave, our ties of kinship towards both the Kurus and Pándavas are equal. We have all been brought here, just like you, for a marriage. Now that the marriage ceremony is over, let us go back to our homes in good spirits.

You are the most venerable of the kings in age and in 5.5
learning, and we are all your pupils. There is no doubt about it. Dhrita·rashtra holds you in constant high regard, and you are a friend to both teachers, Drona and Kripa. Now, may you be the one to send a message to accomplish the Pándavas' aim, and whatever message you send will have the sanction of us all.

If the bull-like Kuru should make peace in due course then there will be no great breakdown in brotherly relations between the Kurus and the Pándavas, but if the son of Dhrita·rashtra is full of arrogance and in his idiocy fails to make peace, then invite us back once you have sent for
the others. Then slow-minded, stupid Duryódhana, along 5.10

niṣṭhām āpatsyate mūḍhaḥ kruddhe Gāṇḍīva|dhanvani!»

VAIŚAMPĀYANA uvāca:

tataḥ sat|kṛtya Vārṣṇeyam Virāṭaḥ pṛthivī|patiḥ
gṛhāt prasthāpayām āsa sa|gaṇaṃ saha|bāndhavam.
Dvārakāṃ tu gate Kṛṣṇe Yudhiṣṭhira|purogamāḥ
cakruḥ sāṃgrāmikaṃ sarvaṃ, Virāṭaś ca mahī|patiḥ.
tataḥ saṃpreṣayām āsa Virāṭaḥ saha bāndhavaiḥ
sarveṣām bhūmi|pālānāṃ, Drupadaś ca mahī|patiḥ.
vacanāt Kuru|siṃhānāṃ Matsya|Pāñcālayoś ca te
samājagmur mahī|pālāḥ saṃprahṛṣṭā mahā|balāḥ.
5.15 tac chrutvā Pāṇḍu|putrāṇāṃ samāgacchan mahad balam,
Dhṛtarāṣṭra|sutāś c' âpi samāninyur mahī|patīn.
samākulā mahī, rājan, Kuru|Pāṇḍava|kāraṇāt
tadā samabhavat kṛtsnā saṃprayāṇe mahī|kṣitāṃ.
saṃkulā ca tadā bhūmiś catur|aṅga|bal'|ânvitā.
balāni teṣāṃ vīrāṇām āgacchanti tatas tataḥ,
cālayant' îva gāṃ devīṃ sa|parvata|vanām imām.
tataḥ prajñā|vayo|vṛddhaṃ Pāñcālyaḥ sva|puro|hitam
Kurubhyaḥ preṣayām āsa Yudhiṣṭhira|mate sthitaḥ.

DRUPADA uvāca:

6.1 «BHŪTĀNĀṂ PRĀṆINAḤ śreṣṭhāḥ,
prāṇināṃ buddhi|jīvinaḥ.
buddhimatsu narāḥ śreṣṭhā,
nareṣv api dvi|jātayaḥ.
dvi|jeṣu vaidyāḥ śreyāṃso, vaidyeṣu kṛta|buddhayaḥ.

with his ministers and relatives, will meet his end in the form of the furious wielder of the Gandíva!"

VAISHAMPÁYANA said:

Once King Viráta had properly accommodated Varshnéya, he sent him on his way home from his palace with his attendants and relatives. And when Krishna had gone to Dváraka, King Viráta and the Pándavas, led by Yudhi·shthira, made all their war plans. Viráta and his relatives and King Drúpada sent word to all the lords of the earth. Upon receiving word from those lion-like Kurus and from the kings of Matsya and Pañchála, those mighty sovereigns of the earth set out in high spirits.

And when Dhrita·rashtra's sons heard that the sons of 5.15
Pandu were gathering a great force, they too fetched kings. So it was, my king, that the whole earth was brimming with monarchs setting out for either the Káurava or the Pándava cause. The earth was teeming, full as it was with four flanked armies. Battalions of heroes came from here and there and seemed to rock goddess earth herself with her forests and mountains. Then the king of Pañchála, abiding by Yudhi·shthira's decision, sent his family priest, venerable in both years and learning, to the Kurus.

DRÚPADA said:

"CREATURES THAT breathe are the best of all creatures, 6.1
and intelligent creatures are the best of those that breathe. Men are the best of intelligent creatures, and the twiceborn are the best of men. Men learned in the Veda are the best of the twiceborn, and among Vedic scholars the best are those who have achieved understanding. Among those with

kṛta|buddhiṣu kartāraḥ, kartṛṣu brahma|vādinaḥ.
sa bhavān kṛta|buddhīnāṃ pradhāna, iti me matiḥ.
kulena ca viśiṣṭo 'si, vayasā ca śrutena ca.
prajñayā sadṛśaś c' âsi Śukreṇ' Āṅgirasena ca.
viditaṃ c' âpi te sarvaṃ, yathā|vṛttaḥ sa Kauravaḥ,
6.5 Pāṇḍavaś ca yathā|vṛttaḥ Kuntī|putro Yudhiṣṭhiraḥ.
Dhṛtarāṣṭrasya vidite vañcitāḥ Pāṇḍavāḥ paraiḥ.
Vidureṇ' ânunīto 'pi putram ev' ânuvartate.
Śakunir buddhi|pūrvaṃ hi Kuntī|putraṃ samāhvayat
an|akṣa|jñaṃ mat'|âkṣaḥ san, kṣatra|vṛtte sthitaṃ śucim.
te tathā vañcayitvā tu dharma|rājaṃ Yudhiṣṭhiram
na kasyāñ cid avasthāyāṃ rājyaṃ dāsyanti vai svayam.
bhavāṃs tu dharma|saṃyuktaṃ
Dhṛtarāṣṭraṃ bruvan vacaḥ
manāṃsi tasya yodhānāṃ
dhruvam āvartayiṣyati.
Viduraś c' âpi tad vākyaṃ sādhayiṣyati tāvakam
6.10 Bhīṣma|Droṇa|Kṛp'|ādīnāṃ bhedaṃ saṃjanayiṣyati.
amātyeṣu ca bhinneṣu, yodheṣu vimukheṣu ca,
punar ekatra|karaṇaṃ teṣāṃ karma bhaviṣyati.
etasminn antare Pārthāḥ sukham ek'|âgra|buddhayaḥ
senā|karma kariṣyanti, dravyāṇāṃ c' âiva sañcayam.
vidyamāneṣu ca sveṣu lambamāne tathā tvayi
na tathā te kariṣyanti senā|karma, na saṃśayaḥ.
etat prayojanaṃ c' âtra prādhānyen' ôpalabhyate.
saṃgatyā Dhṛtarāṣṭraś ca kuryād dharmyaṃ vacas tava!

understanding the best are those who apply it, and among these men who apply their understanding the best are those who expound the Veda. In my opinion, you are the first of those who have achieved understanding. You are distinguished by your family, your age, and your learning. You are equal to Shukra and Ángirasa in your wisdom.

You know all about how the Káurava behaves and how 6.5
Yudhi·shthira, the son of Kunti and Pandu, behaves. The
Pándavas were deceived by their enemies with Dhrita·
rashtra's knowledge. Despite being advised by Vídura he
obeys only his son. Shákuni laid his plan in advance and
challenged Kunti's son, although he was a novice at dice, being pure and devoted to his kshatriyan duties, and Shákuni
was gambling-crazed. And now that they have cheated
Yudhi·shthira, the king of righteousness, they will never return his kingdom of their own accord.

But by speaking to Dhrita·rashtra in words which conform to moral law, you will certainly bring round the minds
of his warriors. Vídura will promote what you say as well,
and breed dissent, starting with Bhishma, Drona, and 6.10
Kripa. Then, when his ministers are divided and the warriors are unwilling, he will have a job uniting them again in
a single cause.

In the meantime, the Parthas will happily focus all their attention on the task of the army and gathering supplies, but with you hanging around and with dissension among their own ranks, the others will doubtless not be organizing their army's affairs in the same way. You must consider this your top priority. And Dhrita·rashtra may even take your righteous advice once he has met you!

sa bhavān dharma|yuktaś ca dharmyaṃ teṣu samācaran
6.15 kṛpāluṣu parikleśān Pāṇḍavīyān prakīrtayan.
vṛddheṣu kula|dharmaṃ ca bruvan pūrvair anuṣṭhitam,
vibhetsyati manāṃsy eṣāṃ, iti me n' âtra saṃśayaḥ.
na ca tebhyo bhayaṃ te 'sti, brāhmaṇo hy asi veda|vit,
dūta|karmaṇi yuktaś ca, sthaviraś ca viśeṣataḥ.
sa bhavān Puṣya|yogena, muhūrtena Jayena ca
Kauraveyān prayātv āśu Kaunteyasy' ârtha|siddhaye.»

VAIŚAMPĀYANA uvāca:

tath" ânuśiṣṭaḥ prayayau Drupadena mah"|ātmanā
puro|dhā vṛtta|sampanno nagaraṃ nāga|sāhvayam.
śiṣyaiḥ parivṛto vidvān nīti|śāstr'|ârtha|kovidaḥ
Pāṇḍavānāṃ hit'|ârthāya Kauravān prati jagmivān.

VAIŚAMPĀYANA uvāca:

7.1 PURO|HITAṂ TE prasthāpya nagaraṃ nāga|sāhvayam,
dūtān prasthāpayām āsuḥ pārthivebhyas tatas tataḥ.
prasthāpya dūtān anyatra Dvārakāṃ puruṣa'|rṣabhaḥ
svayaṃ jagāma Kauravyaḥ Kuntī|putro Dhanañjayaḥ.
gate Dvāravatīṃ Kṛṣṇe Baladeve ca Mādhave,
saha Vṛṣṇy|Andhakaiḥ sarvair Bhojaiś ca śataśas tadā,
sarvam āgamayām āsa Pāṇḍavānāṃ viceṣṭitam
Dhṛtarāṣṭr'|ātmajo rājā gūḍhaiḥ praṇihitaiś caraiḥ.

As you yourself, endowed with virtue and acting virtuously among them, mention the Pándavas' troubles to com- 6.15
passionate men and talk to the elderly of the family of the morality which was upheld by their ancestors, I have no doubt that you will cause division in their minds. You have nothing to fear from them, for you are a brahmin who knows the Veda, you are employed as a messenger, and especially since you are an elderly man. When the Pushya constellation is in conjunction with the hour of Jaya then you should go to the Káuravas with all speed, for the successful completion of the son of Kunti's aim."

VAISHAMPÁYANA said:

Once he had been given his orders by high-souled Drúpada, the virtuous family priest set out for Hástina·pura, the city named after elephants. So, that knowledgable man skilled in the aims of political treatise, surrounded by his pupils, set out towards the Káuravas in order to achieve an advantageous deal for the Pándavas.

VAISHAMPÁYANA said:

AFTER THEY HAD sent the family priest to Hástina·pura, 7.1
the city named after elephants, they dispatched messengers to kings scattered here and there. Once Dhanañ·jaya, Kunti's bull-like Káurava son, had sent messengers to other places, he then set out for Dváraka himself. But when Krishna Mádhava and Bala·deva had gone to Dváravati with their hundreds of Vrishnis, Ándhakas, and Bhojas, Dhrita·rashtra's sovereign son ascertained all the Pándavas' arrangements by means of the spies he had sent out in secret. When 7.5
he heard that Mádhava had gone, he set out himself, with

7.5 sa śrutvā Mādhavaṃ yāntaṃ, sad|aśvair anil'|ôpamaiḥ
balena n' âti|mahatā Dvārakām abhyayāt purīm.
tam eva divasaṃ c' âpi Kaunteyaḥ Pāṇḍu|nandanaḥ
Ānarta|nagarīṃ ramyāṃ jagām' āśu Dhanañjayaḥ.
tau yātvā puruṣa|vyāghrau Dvārakāṃ Kuru|nandanau
suptaṃ dadṛśatuḥ Kṛṣṇaṃ, śayānaṃ c' âbhijagmatuḥ.
tataḥ śayāne Govinde praviveśa Suyodhanaḥ
ucchīrṣataś ca Kṛṣṇasya niṣasāda var'|āsane.
tataḥ Kirīṭī tasy' ânu praviveśa mahā|manāḥ
paścāc c' âiva sa Kṛṣṇasya prahvo 'tiṣṭhat kṛt'|âñjaliḥ.
7.10 pratibuddhaḥ sa Vārṣṇeyo dadarś' âgre Kirīṭinam.
sa tayoḥ svāgataṃ kṛtvā, yathāvat pratipūjya tau,
tad|āgamana|jaṃ hetuṃ papraccha Madhusūdanaḥ.
tato Duryodhanaḥ Kṛṣṇam uvāca prahasann iva:
«vigrahe 'smin bhavān sāhyaṃ mama dātum ih' ârhati.
samaṃ hi bhavataḥ sakhyaṃ mama c' âiv' Ârjune 'pi ca,
tathā saṃbandhakaṃ tulyam asmākaṃ tvayi, Mādhava.
ahaṃ c' âbhigataḥ pūrvaṃ tvām adya, Madhusūdana,
pūrvaṃ c' âbhigataṃ santo bhajante pūrva|sāriṇaḥ.
tvaṃ ca śreṣṭhatamo loke satām adya, Janārdana,
7.15 satataṃ saṃmataś c' âiva, sad|vṛttam anupālaya.»

KṚṢṆA uvāca:

«bhavān abhigataḥ pūrvam, atra me n' âsti saṃśayaḥ.
dṛṣṭas tu prathamaṃ, rājan, mayā Pārtho Dhanañjayaḥ.
tava pūrv'|âbhigamanāt pūrvaṃ c' âpy asya darśanāt
sāhāyyam ubhayor eva kariṣyāmi, Suyodhana.
pravāraṇaṃ tu bālānāṃ pūrvaṃ kāryam, iti śrutiḥ.
tasmāt pravāraṇaṃ pūrvam arhaḥ Pārtho Dhanañjayaḥ.

excellent horses swift like the wind and a moderate force, towards the city of Dváraka. And it was on that very same day that Dhanañ·jaya, the son of Kunti and Pandu, set out at speed for the lovely city of Anárta.

When those two tiger-like men, both descendants of the Kuru race, reached Dváraka, they saw Krishna was asleep and they approached him as he slept. While Go·vinda slept, Suyódhana entered and sat down on a very fine seat by Krishna's head. Then high-minded Kirítin entered and stood, hands together, bowing at Krishna's feet.

When Varshnéya awoke, he saw Kirítin first, but wel- 7.10
comed both men, duly paying his respects to both. Then Madhu·súdana asked them the reason for their visit. Duryódhana almost laughed as he replied to Krishna, saying:

"You ought to give me your allegiance in this war. For your ties of friendship to me and Árjuna are equal, and our alliance to you is correspondingly matched, Mádhava. I was the first to arrive here today, Madhu·súdana, and good men who respect precedence choose the man who comes to them first. At this moment in time, you are the greatest of the
good in this world, Janárdana, and constantly honored as 7.15
such. Keep up your excellent conduct."

KRISHNA said:

"I have no doubt that you arrived first. But I saw Dhanañ·jaya Partha first, king. So, since you came first, and I saw him first, I will give my help to you both, Suyódhana. It is traditional that first choice goes to the youngest. And so Dhanañ·jaya Partha ought to have first choice.

mat|saṃhanana|tulyānāṃ gopānām arbudaṃ mahat,
Nārāyaṇā iti khyātāḥ, sarve saṅgrāma|yodhinaḥ.
te vā yudhi dur|ādharṣā bhavantv ekasya sainikāḥ,
a|yudhyamānaḥ saṅgrāme nyasta|śastro 'ham ekataḥ.
7.20 ābhyām anyataraṃ, Pārtha, yat te hṛdyataraṃ matam,
tad vṛṇītāṃ bhavān agre; pravāryas tvaṃ hi dharmataḥ.»

VAIŚAMPĀYANA uvāca:

evam uktas tu Kṛṣṇena Kuntī|putro Dhanañjayaḥ
a|yudhyamānaṃ saṅgrāme varayām āsa Keśavam;
Nārāyaṇam a|mitra|ghnaṃ kāmāj jātam a|jaṃ nṛṣu,
sarva|kṣatrasya purato deva|dānavayor api.
Duryodhanas tu tat sainyaṃ sarvam āvarayat tadā.
sahasrāṇāṃ sahasraṃ tu yodhānāṃ prāpya, Bhārata,
Kṛṣṇaṃ c' âpahṛtaṃ jñātvā saṃprāpa paramāṃ mudam.
Duryodhanas tu tat sainyaṃ sarvam ādāya pārthivaḥ,
7.25 tato 'bhyayād bhīma|balo Rauhiṇeyaṃ mahā|balam,
sarvaṃ c' āgamane hetuṃ sa tasmai saṃnyavedayat.
pratyuvāca tataḥ ŚaurirDhārtarāṣṭram idaṃ vacaḥ:

BALADEVA uvāca:

«viditaṃ te, nara|vyāghra, sarvaṃ bhavitum arhati,
yan may" ôktaṃ Virāṭasya purā vaivāhike tadā.
nigṛhy' ôkto Hṛṣīkeśas tvad|arthaṃ, Kuru|nandana,
‹mayā saṃbandhakaṃ tulyam iti› , rājan, punaḥ punaḥ.
na ca tad vākyam uktaṃ vai Keśavaḥ pratyapadyata
na c' âham utsahe Kṛṣṇaṃ vinā sthātum api kṣaṇam.

The great multitude of cow-herds, renowned as the Nárayanas, are my equals in strength and are all veteran soldiers of war. Let one of you have these near invincible men in war as your soldiers, and I will go to the other, but I will lay down my weapons and I will not fight in the conflict. So, 7.20
Partha, according to the law it's your turn first to choose whichever of these two is dearer to your heart."

VAISHAMPÁYANA said:

So, being addressed in this way by Krishna, Dhanañ·jaya, the son of Kunti, even though he would not fight in the war, chose Késhava, the increate Naráyana, the slayer of his enemies, born among men through his own will; the foremost of all kshatriyas and even gods and Dánavas. Duryódhana then chose his whole army. Taking the thousands upon thousands of warriors, descendant of Bharata, and knowing that Krishna had removed himself from battle, Duryódhana felt exceedingly happy. So it was that King
Duryódhana took his entire army, and then the terrifyingly 7.25
powerful man headed for mighty Rauhinéya. He explained to him fully why he had come, and then Shauri replied to Dhrita·rashtra's son in these words:

BALA·DEVA said:

"You ought to know everything I said before at Viráta's wedding celebration, tiger-like man. I spoke to curb Hrishi·kesha on your behalf, descendant of Kuru, repeating again and again, my king, that my allegiance was equal. Krishna did not confirm what I said, and I do not for one moment dare to continue without Krishna. So looking to Vasudéva

‹n' âhaṃ sahāyaḥ Pārthasya, n' âpi Duryodhanasya vai,›
iti me niścitā buddhir Vāsudevam avekṣya ha!
7.30 jāto 'si Bhārate vaṃśe, sarva|pārthiva|pūjite,
gaccha yudhyasva dharmeṇa kṣātreṇa, puruṣa'|rṣabha.»

VAIŚAMPĀYANA uvāca:

ity evam uktas tu tadā, pariṣvajya Halāyudham,
Kṛṣṇaṃ c' âpahṛtaṃ jñātvā yuddhān mene jitaṃ jayam.
so 'bhyayāt Kṛtavarmāṇaṃ Dhṛtarāṣṭra|suto nṛpaḥ.
Kṛtavarmā dadau tasya senām akṣauhiṇīṃ tadā.
sa tena sarva|sainyena bhīmena Kuru|nandanaḥ
vṛtaḥ pariyayau hṛṣṭaḥ suhṛdaḥ saṃpraharṣayan.
tataḥ pīt'|âmbara|dharo jagat|sraṣṭā Janārdanaḥ
gate Duryodhane Kṛṣṇaḥ Kirīṭinam ath' âbravīt:
7.35 «a|yudhyamānaḥ kāṃ buddhim āsthāy' âhaṃ vṛtas tvayā?»

ARJUNA uvāca:

«bhavān samarthas tān sarvān
nihantuṃ, n' âtra saṃśayaḥ;
nihantum aham apy ekaḥ
samarthaḥ, puruṣa'|rṣabha.
bhavāṃs tu kīrtimāl loke, tad yaśas tvāṃ gamiṣyati.
yaśasāṃ c' âham apy arthī, tasmād asi mayā vṛtaḥ.
sārathyaṃ tu tvayā kāryam, iti me mānasaṃ sadā
cira|rātr'|ēpsitaṃ kāmaṃ. tad bhavān kartum arhati!»

VĀSUDEVA uvāca:

«upapannam idaṃ, Pārtha, yat spardhasi mayā saha.
sārathyaṃ te kariṣyāmi. kāmaḥ sampadyatāṃ tava!»

I have made up my mind that I will not be Partha's or Duryódhana's ally! You have been born into the family of Bha- 7.30
rata, a line esteemed by all kings, so go and fight according
to kshatriyan law, bull-like man!"

VAISHAMPÁYANA said:

When he had said these things, Duryódhana embraced plow-weaponed Bala·rama. And knowing that Krishna had removed himself from the war, he assumed that his victory was already won. Next Dhrita·rashtra's sovereign son visited Krita·varman, and Krita·varman gave him a battalion. So the descendant of Kuru returned delighted, surrounded by the full breadth of his formidable army, and by so doing he brought joy to his friends.

Once Duryódhana had left, Krishna Janárdana, the
yellow-robed creator of the world, said to Kirítin: "What 7.35
were you thinking by choosing me when I will not fight?"

ÁRJUNA said:

"There is no doubt that you can kill them all, but I can also kill them single-handedly, bull-like man. You are renowned throughout this world and the glory will go to you. But I too aim for glory and so I chose you. In my heart I have always wished for you to be my charioteer. It is a wish I have longed for over many long nights, and so you should oblige me!"

VASUDÉVA said:

"It is appropriate for you to emulate me, Partha, so I will indeed be your charioteer! May your wish be granted!"

VAIŚAMPĀYANA uvāca:

evaṃ pramuditaḥ Pārthaḥ Kṛṣṇena sahitas tadā
vṛto Dāśārha|pravaraiḥ punar āyād Yudhiṣṭhiram.

VAIŚAMPĀYANA uvāca:

8.1 ŚALYAḤ ŚRUTVĀ TU dūtānāṃ, sainyena mahatā vṛtaḥ
abhyayāt Pāṇḍavān, rājan, saha putrair maha|rathaiḥ.
tasya senā|niveśo 'bhūd adhyardham iva yojanam,
tathā hi vipulāṃ senāṃ bibharti sa nara'|rṣabhaḥ,
akṣauhiṇī|patī, rājan, mahā|vīrya|parākramaḥ.
vicitra|kavacāḥ śūrā, vicitra|dhvaja|kārmukāḥ,
vicitr'|ābharaṇāḥ sarve, vicitra|ratha|vāhanāḥ.
vicitra|srag|dharāḥ sarve, vicitr'|âmbara|bhūṣaṇāḥ.
8.5 sva|deśa|veṣ'|ābharaṇā vīrāḥ śata|sahasraśaḥ
tasya senā|praṇetāro babhūvuḥ kṣatriya'|rṣabhāḥ.
vyathayann iva bhūtāni, kampayann iva medinīm,
śanair viśrāmayan senāṃ sa yayau yena Pāṇḍavaḥ.
tato Duryodhanaḥ śrutvā mah"|ātmānaṃ mahā|ratham
upāyāntam abhidrutya svayam ānarca, Bhārata.
kārayām āsa pūj"|ârthaṃ tasya Duryodhanaḥ sabhāḥ
ramaṇīyeṣu deśeṣu ratna|citrāḥ sv|alaṅkṛtāḥ.
śilpibhir vividhaiś c' âiva krīḍās tatra prayojitāḥ,
tatra mālyāni, māṃsāni, bhakṣyaṃ peyaṃ ca sat|kṛtam.
8.10 kūpāś ca vividh'|ākārā mano|harṣa|vivardhanāḥ,
vāpyaś ca vividh'|ākārā, audakāni gṛhāṇi ca.

VAISHAMPÁYANA said:

So it was that Partha went back to Yudhi·shthira delighted, together with Krishna, and surrounded by the leading Dashárhas.

VAISHAMPÁYANA said:

WHEN SHALYA HEARD from the messengers, he set out 8.1
to the Pándavas, my king, accompanied by a massive army and his great warrior sons. That bull-like man, the mightily heroic general of his battalion, my king, supported so large a force that his army encampment was about thirteen and a half miles wide. The heroes all wore colorful armor and variegated ornaments, carried multicolored banners and bows, and rode on colorfully decorated chariots and horses. They all wore garlands of multiple hues and were dressed in colorful clothes.
8.5
Kshatriya-bull heroes, dressed in their own regional costumes and ornaments, numbering hundreds of thousands, became his officers. Terrifying all creatures and making the earth tremble, he went to the place where the Pándava was, traveling at a slow pace and letting his army rest.

But when Duryódhana heard that the high-souled mighty warrior was approaching, he hurried towards him and paid homage to him himself, descendant of Bharata. Duryódhana ensured that beautifully decorated traveling palaces, full of brightly gleaming jewels, were set up in pleasant spots in his honor. Amusements were arranged in those places by various artisans, and an excellent spread was laid on of garlands, meat, and food and drink.
8.10
There were diversely designed wells which augmented the thrill in one's

sa tāḥ sabhāḥ samāsādya, pūjyamāno yath" âmaraḥ,
Duryodhanasya sacivair deśe deśe samantataḥ,
ājagāma sabhām anyāṃ dev'|âvasatha|varcasam.
sa tatra viṣaye yuktaḥ kalyāṇair atimānuṣaiḥ
mene 'bhyadhikam ātmānam, avamene Puraṃ|daram.
papraccha sa tataḥ preṣyān prahṛṣṭaḥ kṣatriya'|rṣabhaḥ:
«Yudhiṣṭhirasya puruṣāḥ ke 'tra cakruḥ sabhā imāḥ?
ānīyantāṃ sabhā|kārāḥ, pradey'|ârhā hi me matāḥ.
8.15 prasādam eṣāṃ dāsyāmi. Kuntī|putro 'numanyatām.»
Duryodhanāya tat sarvaṃ kathayanti sma vismitāḥ;
saṃprahṛṣṭo yadā Śalyo diditsur api jīvitam.
gūḍho Duryodhanas tatra darśayām āsa mātulam.
taṃ dṛṣṭvā Madra|rājaś ca, jñātvā yatnaṃ ca tasya tam,
pariṣvyajy' âbravīt, «prīta iṣṭo 'rtho gṛhyatām! iti.»

DURYODHANA uvāca:

«satya|vāg bhava, kalyāṇa, varo vai mama dīyatām.
sarva|senā|praṇetā vai bhavān bhavitum arhati.»

VAIŚAMPĀYANA uvāca:

«kṛtam, ity» abravīc Chalyaḥ, «kim anyat kriyatām? iti»
«kṛtam, ity» eva Gāndhāriḥ pratyuvāca punaḥ punaḥ.

mind, and variously designed ponds and pavillions on the water. Duryódhana's court and ministers approached him and worshipped him on all sides in every place as though he were a god.

Then he came to another wayside palace as brilliant as the dwelling of a god, and was furnished with sensual delights and heavenly pleasures. He began to consider himself superior and treated the Sacker of Cities contemptuously. Then the bull-like kshatriya happily asked the servants: "Which of Yudhi·shthira's men have built such wayside palaces here? Bring in the men who built the palaces, for to my mind they
deserve to be rewarded. I will grant them a favor. May the 8.15
son of Kunti give his permission."

The people were amazed and told the whole matter to Duryódhana; how Shalya was so happy that he was now prepared to sacrifice even his life. Then Duryódhana, who was hidden, showed himself to his maternal uncle. When the king of the Madras saw him and understood the effort he had made, he embraced him and said, "Take whatever you most want!"

DURYÓDHANA said:

"Be true to your word, my good man, and grant me a favor. You ought to become the general of my whole army."

VAISHAMPÁYANA said:

"Done!" said Shalya, "What else can I do?" But the son of Gandhári replied again and again, "That's it! You've done enough."

ŚALYA uvāca:

8.20 «gaccha, Duryodhana, puraṃ svakam eva, nara'|rṣabha.
ahaṃ gamiṣye draṣṭuṃ vai Yudhiṣtshiram arin|damam.
dṛṣṭvā Yudhiṣṭhiraṃ, rājan, kṣipram eṣye, nar'|âdhipa,
a|vaśyaṃ c' âpi draṣṭavyaḥ Pāṇḍavaḥ puruṣa'|rṣabhaḥ.»

DURYODHANA uvāca:

«kṣipram āgamyatāṃ, rājan, Pāṇḍavaṃ vīkṣya, pārthiva,
tvayy adhīnaḥ sma, rāj'|êndra. vara|dānaṃ smarasva naḥ!»

ŚALYA uvāca:

«kṣipram eṣyāmi, bhadram te.
gacchasva sva|puraṃ, nṛpa.»
pariṣvajya tath" ânyonyaṃ
Śalya|Duryodhanāv ubhau.
sa tathā Śalyam āmantrya punar āyāt svakaṃ puram.
Śalyo jagāma Kaunteyān ākhyātuṃ karma tasya tat,
8.25 Upaplavyaṃ sa gatvā tu, skandh'|āvāraṃ praviśya ca.
Pāṇḍavān atha tān sarvān Śalyas tatra dadarśa ha.
sametya ca mahā|bāhuḥ Śalyaḥ Pāṇḍu|sutais tadā
pādyam arghyaṃ ca gāṃ c' âiva pratyagṛhṇād yathā|vidhi.
tataḥ kuśala|pūrvaṃ hi Madra|rājo 'ri|sūdanaḥ
prītyā paramayā yuktaḥ samāśliṣyad Yudhiṣṭhiram.
tathā Bhīm'|Ârjunau, Kṛṣṇau, svasrīyau ca yamāv ubhau.
āsane c' ôpaviṣṭas tu Śalyaḥ Pārtham uvāca ha:
«kuśalaṃ, rāja|śārdūla, kac cit te, Kuru|nandana?
araṇya|vāsād diṣṭy" âsi vimukto, jayatāṃ vara!
8.30 su|duṣkaraṃ kṛtaṃ, rājan, nirjane vasatā tvayā
bhrātṛbhiḥ saha, rāj'|êndra, Kṛṣṇayā c' ânayā saha.

SHALYA said:

"Go back to your city, bull-like Duryódhana. I will go 8.20
to see Yudhi·shthira, the tamer of his enemies. Once I have seen Yudhi·shthira, my king, I will leave quickly, lord of men, but I must inevitably see the bull-like Pándava."

DURYÓDHANA said:

"Go quickly, king, to see the Pándava, my lord, for we are depending on you, lord of kings. Remember the favor you promised us!"

SHALYA replied:

"I will go quickly, my good man. You go back to your own city, my king." And Shalya and Duryódhana both embraced one another. So, having bid Shalya farewell, Duryódhana went back to his own city once again. But Shalya
went to the Kauntéyas to tell them what he had done, and 8.25
once he had reached Upaplávya, he entered the royal residence. There Shalya saw all the Pándavas.

In accordance with custom, long-armed Shalya came up to the sons of Pandu and accepted water for his feet and a cow as a gift. The king of the Madras, the destroyer of his enemies, first asked after their health and then embraced Yudhi·shthira, filled with the greatest happiness, as well as Bhima and Árjuna, the two Krishnas, and his twin nephews by his sister. Then Shalya sat on his seat and said to Partha:

"Are you in good health, tiger-like sovereign descendant of Kuru? Thank heaven you are free of your exile in the forest, best of victors! You have achieved an enormously diffi- 8.30
cult task, my king—living in the desolate forest with your brothers, lord of kings, and of course with the lady Krishná

a|jñāta|vāsaṃ ghoraṃ ca vasatā duṣ|karaṃ kṛtam.
duḥkham eva kutaḥ saukhyaṃ bhraṣṭa|rājyasya, Bhārata.
duḥkhasy' âitasya mahato Dhārtarāṣṭra|kṛtasya vai,
avāpsyasi sukhaṃ, rājan, hatvā śatrūn, paraṃ|tapa.
viditaṃ te, mahā|rāja, loka|tantraṃ, nar'|âdhipa,
tasmāl lobha|kṛtaṃ kiñ cit tava, tāta, na vidyate.
rāja'|rṣīṇāṃ purāṇānāṃ mārgam anviccha, Bhārata.
dāne tapasi satye ca bhava, tāta, Yudhiṣṭhira.
8.35 kṣamā, damaś ca, satyaṃ ca, a|hiṃsā ca, Yudhiṣṭhira,
adbhutaś ca punar lokas tvayi, rājan, pratiṣṭhitaḥ,
mṛdur, vadānyo, brahmaṇyo, dātā, dharma|parāyaṇaḥ.
dharmās te viditā, rājan, bahavo loka|sākṣikāḥ
sarvaṃ jagad idaṃ, tāta, viditaṃ te, paran|tapa.
diṣṭyā kṛcchram idaṃ, rājan, pāritaṃ, Bharata'|rṣabha!
diṣṭyā paśyāmi, rāj'|êndra,
dharm'|ātmānaṃ sah'|ânugam,
nistīrṇaṃ duṣ|karaṃ, rājaṃs,
tvāṃ dharma|nicayaṃ, prabho!»

VAIŚAMPĀYANA uvāca:

tato 'sy' âkathayad rājā Duryodhana|samāgamam,
tac ca śuśrūṣitaṃ sarvaṃ, vara|dānaṃ ca, Bhārata.

here. You have also accomplished a terribly onerous task in living unknown. Where can the man who has been banished from his own kingdom find comfort, Bhárata? There is only pain.

But you will find happiness, my king, after the great distress which Dhrita·rashtra's son has caused you, by killing your enemies, scorcher of the foe. Great king, you know the way of the world, and therefore, lord of men, nothing you do is done out of avarice, my friend. Bhárata, seek the path of the ancient royal sages. Yudhi·shthira, my friend, live your life in liberality, religious austerity, and truth.

Patience, self-restraint, truth, and non-violence, Yudhi· 8.35
shthira, and a marvelous world, reside in you, my king. You are gentle, eloquent, liberal to brahmins, and intent on virtue. Your numerous virtues, my king, are known and attested by the world. This whole world, my friend, is known to you, scorcher of your enemies. Thank heavens, my king, that this troublesome task of yours has now been completed, bull of the Bharata race! Lord of kings, thank heavens that I see you, righteous-souled as you are, a man who has amassed virtue, along with your followers, my king, now that you have accomplished your wretched task, lord!"

VAISHAMPÁYANA said:

Then the king told him about his meeting with Duryódhana and all about his pledge of allegiance and the favor he had granted him, descendant of Bharata.

YUDHIṢṬHIRA uvāca:

8.40 «su|kṛtaṃ te kṛtaṃ, rājan, prahṛṣṭen' ântar'|ātmanā,
Duryodhanasya yad, vīra, tvayā vācā pratiśrutam.
ekaṃ tv icchāmi, bhadraṃ te, kriyamāṇaṃ, mahī|pa, te.
rājann, a|kartavyam api kartum arhasi, sattama.
mama tv avekṣayā, vīra, śṛṇu, vijñāpayāmi te;
bhavān iha, mahā|rāja, Vāsudeva|samo yudhi.
Karṇ'|Ârjunābhyāṃ saṃprāpte dvairathe, rāja|sattama,
Karṇasya bhavatā kāryaṃ sārathyaṃ n' âtra saṃśayaḥ.
tatra pālyo 'rjuno, rājan, yadi mat|priyam icchasi.
tejo|vadhaś ca te kāryaḥ Sauter asmaj|jay'|āvahaḥ.
8.45 a|kartavyam api hy etat kartum arhasi, mātula.»

ŚALYA uvāca:

«śṛṇu, Pāṇḍava, te bhadraṃ. yad bravīṣi mah"|ātmanaḥ
tejo|vadha|nimittaṃ māṃ sūta|putrasya saṅgame.
ahaṃ tasya bhaviṣyāmi saṅgrāme sārathir dhruvam,
Vāsudevena hi samaṃ nityaṃ māṃ sa hi manyate.
tasy' âhaṃ, Kuru|śārdūla, pratīpam a|hitaṃ vacaḥ
dhruvaṃ saṃkathayiṣyāmi yoddhu|kāmasya saṃyuge,
yathā sa hṛta|darpaś ca hṛta|tejāś ca, Pāṇḍava,
bhaviṣyati sukhaṃ hantuṃ. satyam etad bravīmi te.

YUDHI·SHTHIRA said:

"My lord, you have done well to act with a joyful soul 8.40
upon what you promised Duryódhana with your words, hero. But, bless you, I want you to do one thing for me, earth-lord. Most excellent king, you ought to do me this favor, even though it is improper. In my experience, hero, you are Vasudéva's equal in battle, great king, so listen as I ask this of you. Greatest of kings, when the single combat on chariots between Karna and Árjuna gets under way, you will doubtless have to be Karna's charioteer. If you wish to do me a favor, king, then guard Árjuna. Make sure the *suta*'s son's splendor is extinguished in order to bring us victory.
It is certainly improper, but you ought to do it, uncle." 8.45

SHALYA replied:

"Listen, Pándava, bless you. High-souled man that you are, you are telling me to sabotage the *suta*'s son's splendor in battle. I will surely be his charioteer in battle since he has always considered me Vasudéva's equal. Very well, tiger of the Kurus, I will certainly speak discouragingly and dispiritingly to him in battle when he is fired up for the fight, to rob him of his pride and his magnificence, Pándava, so that he will become easy to kill. I swear this to you truthfully.

evam etat kariṣyāmi yathā, tāta, tvam āttha mām,
yac c' ânyad api śakṣyāmi, tat kariṣyāmi te priyam.
8.50 yac ca duḥkhaṃ tvayā prāptaṃ dyūte vai Kṛṣṇayā saha,
paruṣāṇi ca vākyāni sūta|putra|kṛtāni vai,
Jaṭāsurāt parikleśaḥ, Kīcakāc ca, mahā|dyute,
Draupady" âdhigataṃ sarvaṃ
Damayantyā yath" â|śubham,
sarvaṃ duḥkham idaṃ, vīra,
sukh'|ôdarkaṃ bhaviṣyati.
n' âtra manyus tvayā kāryo, vidhir hi balavattaraḥ.
duḥkhāni hi mah"|ātmānaḥ prāpnuvanti, Yudhiṣṭhira,
devair api hi duḥkhāni prāptāni, jagatī|pate.
Indreṇa śrūyate, rājan, sa|bhāryeṇa mah"|ātmanā
anubhūtaṃ mahad duḥkhaṃ deva|rājena, Bhārata.»

I will do what you ask of me, my son, and whatever else you wish that is within my power. This torment that came 8.50
down on you and Krishná when playing dice, the abusive words which the *suta*'s son directed at you, the difficulty you experienced from Jatásura and Kíchaka, great glorious man, and all the sinful propositions made to Dráupadi, like those made to Damayánti—all this misery, hero, will transform into future happiness.

You should not be angry about this, for the law of the universe is stronger. High-souled men, Yudhi·shthira, come across troubles, and even the gods suffer misery, lord of the universe. Tradition has it, my king, that mighty-souled Indra and his wife experienced great sorrow, Bhárata."

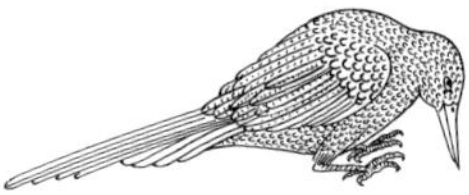

# 9–19

# INDRA'S MISERY

YUDHIṢṬHIRA uvāca:

9.1 «KATHAM INDREṆA, rāj'|êndra,
sa|bhāryeṇa mah"|ātmanā
duḥkhaṃ prāptaṃ paraṃ ghoram,
etad icchāmi veditum.»

ŚALYA uvāca:

«śṛṇu, rājan, purā vṛttam itihāsaṃ purātanam,
sa|bhāryeṇa yathā prāptaṃ duḥkham Indreṇa, Bhārata.
Tvaṣṭā Prajāpatir hy āsīd deva|śreṣṭho mahā|tapāḥ,
sa putraṃ vai tri|śirasam Indra|drohāt kil' âsṛjat.
Aindraṃ sa prārthayat sthānaṃ viśva|rūpo mahā|dyutiḥ,
tais tribhir vadanair ghoraiḥ sūry'|êndu|jvalan'|ôpamaiḥ.
9.5 vedān ekena so 'dhīte, surām ekena c' âpibat,
ekena ca diśaḥ sarvāḥ pibann iva nirīkṣate.
sa tapasvī mṛdur dānto dharme tapasi c' ôdyataḥ,
tapas tasya mahat tīvraṃ su|duścaram, arin|dama.
tasya dṛṣṭvā tapo|vīryaṃ, satyaṃ c' â|mita|tejasaḥ
viṣādam agamac Chakra, ‹Indro 'yaṃ mā bhaved iti.›
‹kathaṃ sajjec ca bhogeṣu, na ca tapyen mahat tapaḥ?
vivardhamānas tri|śirāḥ sarvaṃ hi bhuvanaṃ graset!›
iti sañcintya bahudhā buddhimān, Bharata'|rṣabha,
ājñāpayat so 'psarasas Tvaṣṭṛ|putra|pralobhane:
9.10 ‹yathā sa sajjet tri|śirāḥ kāma|bhogeṣu vai bhṛśam,
kṣipraṃ kuruta, gacchadhvaṃ, pralobhayata mā|ciram.

YUDHI·SHTHIRA said:

"LORD OF KINGS, I would like to know how high-souled Indra and his wife met with terrible and utter misery." 9.1

SHALYA said:

"Very well, my king, listen to this ancient legend of events from days gone by, of how misery befell Indra and his wife, Bhárata. Once upon a time Tvashtri Praja·pati, the best of gods and the great ascetic, produced a three-headed son out of maliciousness towards Indra, or so they say. And this great glorious creature of various forms, with three terrible faces resembling the sun, moon, and fire, coveted Indra's position.

With one face he learned the Veda, with another he drank 9.5
wine, and with the third he watched all directions, as though he were drinking them down. As a moderate and restrained ascetic fixed on the law and religious austerity, his asceticism was of a great but violent form, and one extremely difficult to master, enemy-tamer. But upon seeing the valiant austerity and purity of this boundlessly energetic creature, Shakra fell into despondency at the thought that he might assume the position of Indra.

'How might he become hooked on hedonistic pleasures rather than practicing this great feat of asceticism? As that three-headed creature increases in strength he will swallow the entire world!' So the wise god thought long and hard, bull of the Bharata race, and then he commanded the
*ápsaras*es to seduce Tvashtri's son, saying to them: 'Go 9.10
quickly and make the three-headed creature heavily

śṛṅgāra|veṣāḥ, su|śroṇyo, hārair yuktā mano|haraiḥ,
hāva|bhāva|samāyuktāḥ, sarvāḥ saundarya|śobhitāḥ,
pralobhayata, bhadraṃ vaḥ, śamayadhvaṃ bhayaṃ mama.
a|svasthaṃ hy ātman" ātmānaṃ lakṣayāmi, var'|âṅganāḥ.
bhayaṃ tan me mahā|ghoraṃ kṣipraṃ nāśayat', â|balāḥ.›

APSARASA ūcuḥ:

‹tathā yatnaṃ kariṣyāmaḥ, Śakra, tasya pralobhane,
yathā n' âvāpsyasi bhayaṃ tasmād, Bala|niṣūdana!
nirdahann iva cakṣurbhyāṃ yo 'sāv āste tapo|nidhiḥ,
taṃ pralobhayituṃ, deva, gacchāmaḥ sahitā vayam.
9.15 yatiṣyāmo vaśe kartuṃ, vyapanetuṃ ca te bhayam.›

ŚALYA uvāca:

Indreṇa tās tv anujñātā jagmus tri|śiraso 'ntikam.
tatra tā vividhair bhāvair lobhayantyo var'|âṅganāḥ
nityaṃ saṃdarśayām āsus tath" âiv' âṅgeṣu sauṣṭhavam.
n' âbhyagacchat praharṣaṃ tāḥ sa paśyan su|mahā|tapāḥ,
indriyāṇi vaśe kṛtvā pūrva|sāgara|sannibhaḥ.
tās tu yatnaṃ paraṃ kṛtvā punaḥ Śakram upasthitāḥ.
kṛt'|âñjali|puṭāḥ sarvā deva|rājam ath' âbruvan:
‹na sa śakyaḥ su|durdharṣo dhairyāc cālayituṃ, prabho.
yat te kāryaṃ, mahā|bhāga, kriyatāṃ tad an|antaram.›
saṃpūjy' âpsarasaḥ Śakro, visṛjya ca mahā|matiḥ,
9.20 cintayām āsa tasy' âiva vadh'|ôpāyaṃ, Yudhiṣṭhira.
sa tūṣṇīṃ cintayan, vīro, deva|rājaḥ pratāpavān

addicted to the pleasures of love: seduce him without delay. Dressed in alluring clothes, shapely hipped ladies, all furnished with breathtaking charms and a ravishing appearance, sparkling with beauty, seduce him, bless you, and alleviate my fear. For I feel uneasy in my heart, beautiful ladies. Quickly destroy my great and terrible terror, ladies.'

THE ÁPSARASES said:

'We will do our best to seduce him, Shakra, so that you have nothing to fear from him, slayer of Bala! We will go together, god, to seduce that eminently austere man who sits there as though he were burning the horizon with his eyes. We will endeavor to bring him under our control and 9.15
to rid you of your fear.'

SHALYA said:

So, commanded by Indra, they entered the three-headed creature's presence, and there the shapely women began to seduce him with their various charms. They continually exhibited the beauty of their bodies without ceasing, but the fantastically strong-willed ascetic did not become aroused while watching them. Instead he kept his senses under control and remained as calm as the eastern ocean. So, having tried their utmost, they stood before Shakra once again.

Folding their hands in obeisance they all said to the king of the gods: 'That most inviolable creature could not be distracted from his composure, my lord. So arrange whatever diversion is required next.' Wise Shakra paid his respects to the *ápsaras*es, sent them away, and pondered over a means 9.20
to destroy his enemy, Yudhi·shthira. The wise and majestic king of the gods remained in silent contemplation, hero,

viniścita|matir dhīmān vadhe tri|śiraso 'bhavat.
‹vajram asya kṣipāmy adya; sa kṣipraṃ na bhaviṣyati!
śatruḥ pravṛddho n' ôpekṣyo dur|balo 'pi balīyasā.›
śāstra|buddhyā viniścitya, kṛtvā buddhiṃ vadhe dṛḍhām,
atha vaiśvānara|nibhaṃ, ghora|rūpaṃ, bhay'|âvaham
mumoca vajraṃ saṅkruddhaḥ Śakras tri|śirasaṃ prati.
sa papāta hatas tena vajreṇa dṛḍham āhataḥ,
parvatasy' êva śikharaṃ praṇunnaṃ medinī|tale.
9.25 taṃ tu vajra|hataṃ dṛṣṭvā śayānam acal'|ôpamam,
na śarma lebhe dev'|êndro dīpitas tasya tejasā.
hato 'pi dīpta|tejāḥ sa jīvann iva hi dṛśyate.
ghātitasya śirāṃsy ājau jīvant' îv' âdbhutāni vai.
tato 'ti|bhīta|gātras tu Śakra āste vicārayan,
ath' âjagāma paraśuṃ skandhen' ādāya vardhakiḥ.
tad araṇyaṃ, mahā|rāja, yatr' āste 'sau nipātitaḥ,
sa bhītas tatra takṣāṇaṃ ghaṭamānaṃ Śacī|patiḥ
apaśyad, abravīc c' âinaṃ sa|tvaraṃ Pāka|śāsanaḥ:
‹kṣipraṃ chindhi śirāṃsy asya. kuruṣva vacanaṃ mama!›

TAKṢ' ôvāca:

9.30 ‹mahā|skandho bhṛśaṃ hy eṣa. paraśur na tariṣyati.*
kartuṃ c' âhaṃ na śakṣyāmi karma sadbhir vigarhitam.›

determinedly focused upon the destruction of the three-headed creature.

'I will hurl my thunderbolt at him today, and he will soon be torn apart! When he's growing, even a weak enemy should not be overlooked by the stronger party.' Once he had made his decision, based on this learning derived from the shastras, and set his mind resolutely on murder, furious Shakra then threw his terror-inspiring, horrifying-looking, and fire-like thunderbolt at the three-headed creature. Struck hard by the thunderbolt, he collapsed dead just as a mountain peak crashes to the surface of the earth when struck.

But when he saw him lying like a mountain hit by the 9.25
thunderbolt, the chief of the gods could find no comfort and was scorched by his opponent's splendor. Though dead, he seemed to blaze with magnificence as if he were still living. The heads of the creature slaughtered on the field of conflict seemed miraculously alive. And as Shakra sat in reflection, his body filled with extraordinary terror, along came a carpenter carrying an axe on his shoulder. Then, in the forest where the creature happened to be lying, great king, Shachi's terrified husband saw him as he was busy cutting wood, and so the punisher of Paka hastily said to him: 'Quickly cut off that creature's heads. Do what I say!'

THE WOODCUTTER said:

'He is certainly very broad-shouldered! This axe won't cut 9.30
through, and I cannot commit an act which is censured by good men.'

INDRA uvāca:
‹mā bhais tvaṃ. śīghram etad vai kuruṣva vacanaṃ mama,
mat|prasādādd hi te śastraṃ vajra|kalpaṃ bhaviṣyati.›

TAKṢ' ôvāca:
‹kaṃ bhavantam ahaṃ vidyāṃ
ghora|karmāṇam adya vai?
etad icchāmy ahaṃ śrotuṃ,
tattvena kathayasva me.›

INDRA uvāca:
‹aham Indro deva|rājas, takṣan, viditam astu te.
kuruṣv' âitad yath" ôktaṃ me, takṣan, m" âtra vicāraya.›

TAKṢ' ôvāca:
‹krūreṇa n âpatrapase kathaṃ, Śakr', êha karmaṇā?
ṛṣi|putram imaṃ hatvā brahma|hatyā|bhayaṃ na te?›

ŚAKRA uvāca:
9.35 ‹paścād dharmaṃ cariṣyāmi pāvan'|ârthaṃ su|duścaram.
śatrur eṣa mahā|vīryo vajreṇa nihato mayā.
ady' âpi c' âhaṃ udvignas, takṣann, asmād bibhemi vai.
kṣipraṃ chindhi śirāṃsi tvaṃ, kariṣye 'nugrahaṃ tava.
śiraḥ paśos te dāsyanti bhāgaṃ yajñeṣu mānavāḥ.
eṣa te 'nugrahas, takṣan, kṣipraṃ kuru mama priyam.›

ŚALYA uvāca:
etac chrutvā tu takṣā sa mah"|Êndra|vacanāt tadā
śirāṃsy atha tri|śirasaḥ kuṭhāreṇ' âcchinat tadā.
nikṛtteṣu tatas teṣu niṣkrāmann aṇḍa|jās tv atha:

INDRA said:

'Don't be afraid. Just do what I tell you, and quickly, for by my favor your axe will become as competent as my thunderbolt.'

THE WOODCUTTER replied:

'Who should I know you as, you who have committed this awful deed today? I wish to hear it, so tell me truthfully.'

INDRA said:

'Let it be known that I am Indra, king of the gods, woodcutter. Now do what I commanded, woodcutter, and don't dwell on it.'

THE WOODCUTTER said:

'How are you not ashamed of this vicious deed, Shakra? Having killed this seer's son, are you not afraid of brahmanicide?'

SHAKRA said:

'I will perform a very difficult act of virtue later in order 9.35
to purify myself. This enemy was very heroic, and I killed him with my thunderbolt. I am grieving now, woodcutter, and I am still afraid of him. Quickly cut off his heads and I will grant you a favor. Men will give you the beast's head as your share during sacrifices. This is the favor I grant you, woodcutter, so quickly do what I want.'

SHALYA continued:

When the woodcutter had heard great Indra's words he cut off the three-headed beast's heads with his axe. But when they had been cut off, birds emerged: heathcocks, partridges, and sparrows, on all sides. Heathcocks flew swiftly 9.40

kapiñjalās, tittirāś ca, kalaviṅkāś ca sarvaśaḥ.
9.40 yena vedān adhīte sma, pibate somam eva ca,
tasmād vaktrād viniśceruḥ kṣipraṃ tasya kapiñjalāḥ.
yena sarvā diśo, rājan, pibann iva nirīkṣate,
tasmād vaktrād viniścerus tittirās tasya, Pāṇḍava.
yat surā|paṃ tu tasy' āsīd vaktraṃ tri|śirasas tadā,
kalaviṅkāḥ samutpetuḥ, śyenāś ca, Bharata'|rṣabha.
tatas teṣu nikṛtteṣu vijvaro Maghavān atha
jagāma tri|divaṃ hṛṣṭas, takṣ" âpi sva|gṛhān yayau.
mene kṛt'|ârtham atmānaṃ hatvā śatruṃ Surāri|hā.
Tvaṣṭā Prajāpatiḥ śrutvā Śakreṇ' âtha hataṃ sutam
9.45 krodha|saṃrakta|nayana idaṃ vacanam abravīt:

TVAṢṬ' ôvāca:

‹tapyamānaṃ tapo nityaṃ,
kṣāntaṃ, dāntaṃ, jit'|êndriyam,
vin" âparādhena yataḥ putraṃ
hiṃsitavān mama,
tasmāc Chakra|vināśāya Vṛtram utpādayāṃy aham.
lokāḥ paśyantu me vīryaṃ tapasaś ca balaṃ mahat,
sa ca paśyatu dev'|êndro dur|ātmā pāpa|cetanaḥ!›
upaspṛśya tataḥ kruddhas tapasvī su|mahā|yaśāḥ
agnau hutvā samutpādya ghoraṃ Vṛtram uvāca ha:
‹Indra|śatro, vivardhasva prabhāvāt tapaso mama!›
so 'vardhata divaṃ stabdhvā sūrya|vaiśvānar'|ôpamaḥ.
‹kiṃ karom'? îti› c' ôvāca kāla|sūrya iv' ôditaḥ.
9.50 ‹Śakraṃ jah' îti› c' âpy ukto jagāma tri|divaṃ tataḥ.
tato yuddhaṃ samabhavad Vṛtra|Vāsavayor mahat
saṅkruddhayor mahā|ghoraṃ prasaktaṃ, Kuru|sattama.

from the mouth with which he had studied the Veda and drunk *soma*. Partridges flew from the mouth with which he had seemed to be drinking down all directions, Pándava king, and sparrows and birds of prey flew up out of the three-headed creature's wine-drinking head, bull of the Bharata race.

Once the heads were severed Mághavat was free from his anxiety and went happily to heaven, and the woodcutter went to his own home. Now that he had killed his enemy, the slayer of Surári considered himself to have achieved his aim. But when Tvashtri Praja·pati heard that his son had
been murdered by Shakra, his eyes became red with fury 9.45
and he said these words:

TVASHTRI said:

'Since he has killed my religiously austere, controlled, ascetic, ever-forgiving, and sinless son of disciplined senses, I will therefore produce Vritra for Shakra's destruction. Let the worlds witness my prowess, austerity, and great strength, and let the wicked-minded and evil-hearted king of the gods behold it too!'

So the extremely glorious but furious ascetic cleansed himself, poured an oblation into the fire, produced the terrifying Vritra, and said to him: 'Enemy of Indra, grow by the power of my asceticism!' So he grew and supported the sky, resembling the sun and fire. Once he had risen like the sun dawning at the end of the world, he said, 'What
do I do?' When told in reply 'Kill Shakra,' he went up to 9.50
heaven. Then a great battle broke out between Vritra and

tato jagrāha dev'|êndraṃ Vṛtro vīraḥ śata|kratum,
apāvṛty' ākṣipad vaktre Śakraṃ kopa|samanvitaḥ.
graste Vṛtreṇa Śakre tu saṃbhrāntās tri|div'|ēśvarāḥ
asṛjaṃs te mahā|sattvā jṛmbhikāṃ Vṛtra|nāśinīm.
vijṛmbhamāṇasya tato Vṛtrasy' âsyād apāvṛtāt
svāny aṅgāny abhisaṅkṣipya niṣkrānto Bala|nāśanaḥ.
tataḥ prabhṛti lokasya jṛmbhikā prāṇa|saṃśritā.

9.55 jahṛṣuś ca surāḥ sarve Śakraṃ dṛṣṭvā viniḥsṛtam,
tataḥ pravavṛte yuddhaṃ Vṛtra|Vāsavayoḥ punaḥ,
saṃrabdhayos tadā ghoraṃ su|ciraṃ, Bharata'|rṣabha.
tadā vyavardhata raṇe Vṛtro bala|samanvitaḥ,
Tvaṣṭus tejo|bal'|āviddhas, tadā Śakro nyavartata.
nivṛtte ca tadā devā viṣādam agaman param.

sametya saha Śakreṇa Tvaṣṭus tejo|vimohitāḥ
amantrayanta te sarve munibhiḥ saha, Bhārata.
‹kiṃ kāryam? iti› vai, rājan, vicintya bhaya|mohitāḥ,
jagmuḥ sarve mah"|ātmānaṃ manobhir Viṣṇum a|vyayam,
upaviṣṭā Mandar'|âgre sarve Vṛtra|vadh'|ēpsavaḥ.

Vásava, enraged as they were, and the battle was constant and horrifically terrifying, best of the Kurus.

Heroic Vritra grabbed the king of the gods, who had performed a hundred sacrifices, and full of rage, opening his mouth, he threw Shakra inside. But when Vritra had swallowed Shakra, the noble heavenly lords became agitated and created the yawn, which was to be Vritra's downfall. For when Vritra yawned, the slayer of Bala compressed his limbs and emerged from the open mouth. And beginning from that time onwards, the yawn has been a feature of breathing creatures.

When the gods all saw Shakra emerge they were de- 9.55
lighted, and then the grisly battle between the enraged Vritra and Vásava began again immediately, bull of the Bharata race. But when Vritra, filled with strength, grew in the battle, stirred up by the power of Tvashtri's austerity, Shakra then retreated. Once he had withdrawn, the gods fell into the greatest despondency.

Anxious about Tvashtri's ascetic power, they came together with Shakra and all consulted with the sages, Bhárata. They all sat together on the peak of the Mándara mountain, confused by their fear and eager for Vritra's destruction; and as they contemplated what should be done, my king, they all struck upon high-souled imperishable Vishnu in their minds.

INDRA uvāca:

10.1 ‹SARVAṂ VYĀPTAM idaṃ, devā, Vṛtreṇa jagad a|vyayam,
na hy asya sadṛśaṃ kiñ cit pratighātāya yad bhavet.
samartho hy abhavaṃ pūrvam,
a|samartho 'smi sāṃpratam.
kathaṃ nu kāryaṃ, bhadraṃ vo?
dur|dharṣaḥ sa hi me mataḥ.
tejasvī ca, mah"|ātmā ca, yuddhe c' â|mita|vikramaḥ,
graset tri|bhuvanaṃ sarvaṃ sa|dev'|âsura|mānuṣam.
tasmād viniścayam imaṃ śṛṇudhvaṃ, tri|div'|âukasaḥ,
Viṣṇoḥ kṣayam upāgamya sametya ca mah"|ātmanā
10.5 tena sammantrya vetsyāmo vadh'|ôpāyaṃ dur|ātmanaḥ.›

ŚALYA uvāca:

evam ukto Maghavatā devāḥ sa'|ṛṣi|gaṇās tadā
śaraṇyaṃ śaraṇaṃ devaṃ jagmur Viṣṇuṃ mahā|balam.
ūcuś ca sarve dev'|ēśaṃ Viṣṇuṃ Vṛtra|bhay'|ârditāḥ:
‹trayo lokās tvayā krāntās tribhir vikramaṇaiḥ purā,
amṛtaṃ c' āhṛtaṃ, Viṣṇo, daityāś ca nihatā raṇe.
Baliṃ baddhvā mahā|daityaṃ Śakro dev'|âdhipaḥ kṛtaḥ.
tvaṃ prabhuḥ sarva|devānāṃ, tvayā sarvam idaṃ tatam.
tvaṃ hi devo, mahā|deva, sarva|loka|namaskṛtaḥ.
gatir bhava tvaṃ devānāṃ s'|Êndrāṇām, amar'|ôttama!
jagad vyāptam idaṃ sarvaṃ Vṛtreṇ', âsura|sūdana!›

INDRA said:

'THIS WHOLE IMPERISHABLE world is pervaded by Vritra, 10.1
gods, for he has no equal to resist him. There was a time
long ago when I was a match for him, but I am no longer
able to challenge him. How can we do it, bless you? To
my mind he is near invincible. This high-souled and magnificent creature possesses immeasurable prowess in battle,
and he will devour all three worlds along with gods, *ásura*s,
and men. Therefore, heaven dwellers, listen to my decision. 10.5
Let's go to Vishnu's abode and consult together with that
high-souled god, and let's find a way to kill that evil-souled
creature.'

SHALYA said:

So the gods and flocks of sages, addressed in these words by Mághavat, went to the mighty protecting god Vishnu for refuge. Tormented by fear of Vritra they all said to Vishnu, lord of the gods: 'Long ago you crossed the three worlds with three forceful strides, you brought us ambrosia, Vishnu, and killed the Daityas in battle. Once you had bound the mighty Daitya Bali, you made Shakra lord of the gods. You are the lord of all gods and this whole universe is dependent on you. You are the god, great god, who is worshipped by all worlds. Become the refuge of the gods and Indra, greatest of immortals! This whole universe is pervaded by Vritra, O slayer of the *ásura*s!'

VIṢṆUR uvāca:

10.10 ‹avaśyaṃ karaṇīyaṃ me bhavatāṃ hitam uttamam.
tasmād upāyaṃ vakṣyāmi, yath" âsau na bhaviṣyati.
gacchadhvaṃ sa'|rṣi|gandharvā yatr' âsau viśva|rūpa|dhṛk;
sāma tasya prayuñjadhvaṃ. tata enaṃ vijeṣyatha.
bhaviṣyati jayo, devāḥ, Śakrasya mama tejasā.
a|dṛśyaś ca pravekṣyāmi vajre hy asy' āyudh'|ôttame.
gacchadhvam ṛṣibhiḥ sārdhaṃ,
gandharvaiś ca, sur'|ôttamāḥ,
Vṛtrasya saha Śakreṇa
sandhiṃ kuruta mā|ciram.›

ŚALYA uvāca:

evam ukte tu devena ṛṣayas tri|daśās tathā
yayuḥ sametya sahitāḥ Śakraṃ kṛtvā puraḥ|saram.
10.15 samīpam etya ca yadā sarva eva mah"|âujasaḥ,
taṃ tejasā prajvalitaṃ pratapantaṃ diśo daśa,
grasantam iva lokāṃs trīn, sūryā|candramasau yathā,
dadṛśus te tato Vṛtraṃ Śakreṇa saha devatāḥ.
ṛṣayo 'tha tato 'bhyetya Vṛtram ūcuḥ priyaṃ vacaḥ:
‹vyāptaṃ jagad idaṃ sarvaṃ tejasā tava, dur|jaya!
na ca śaknoṣi nirjetuṃ Vāsavaṃ, balināṃ vara.
yudhyatoś c' âpi vāṃ kālo vyatītaḥ su|mahān iha,
pīḍyante ca prajāḥ sarvāḥ sa|dev'|âsura|mānuṣāḥ.
sakhyaṃ bhavatu te, Vṛtra, Śakreṇa saha nityadā,
10.20 avāpsyasi sukhaṃ tvaṃ ca, Śakra|lokāṃś ca śāśvatān.›

VISHNU replied:

'Inevitably I must accomplish this task which is most ad- 10.10
vantageous to you. Therefore, I will tell you the means by which that creature will be annihilated. Go with sages and *gandhárvas* to the place where that creature who adopts all guises resides, and employ conciliatory techniques towards him. This is the way you will defeat him. Gods, by my magnificence Shakra will have his victory. I will invisibly enter his greatest weapon, the thunderbolt. So go together with the sages and *gandhárvas*, most excellent celestials, and bring about a reconciliation between Vritra and Shakra without delay.'

SHALYA continued:

Addressed by the god in these words, the sages and the
thirty celestials, with Shakra at their head, left together. All 10.15
those powerful beings reached Vritra's vicinity as he blazed with magnificence and scorched the ten directions. Shakra and the gods gazed at Vritra as he seemed to gobble down the three worlds and the sun and moon. Then the sages went up to Vritra and spoke to him in mollifying words:

'This whole universe is pervaded by your magnificence, unconquerable being! You are not able to defeat Vásava, strongest of beings. A very long time has passed while you two have been fighting, and all creatures and gods, *ásuras*, and men are afflicted by it. So, Vritra, form an eternal alliance with Shakra, and you will attain happiness and the 10.20
perpetual worlds belonging to Shakra.'

ṛṣi|vākyaṃ niśamy' âtha Vṛtraḥ sa tu mahā|balaḥ
uvāca tān ṛṣīn sarvān praṇamya śiras" âsuraḥ:
‹sarve yūyaṃ, mahā|bhāgā, gandharvāś c' âiva sarvaśaḥ,
yad brūtha, tac chrutaṃ sarvaṃ. mam' âpi śṛṇut,' ân|aghāḥ.
sandhiḥ kathaṃ vai bhavitā mama Śakrasya c' ôbhayoḥ?
tejasor hi dvayor, devāḥ, sakhyaṃ vai bhavitā katham?›

ṚṢAYA ūcuḥ:

‹sakṛt satāṃ saṅgataṃ lipsitavyaṃ.
tataḥ paraṃ bhavitā bhavyam eva.
n' âtikrāmet sat|puruṣeṇa saṅgataṃ
tasmāt satām saṅgataṃ lipsitavyam.
dṛḍhaṃ satāṃ saṅgataṃ c' âpi nityaṃ.
brūyāc c' ârthaṃ hy artha|kṛcchreṣu dhīraḥ.
mah"|ârthavat sat|puruṣeṇa saṅgataṃ,
tasmāt santaṃ na jighāṃseta dhīraḥ.
10.25 Indraḥ satāṃ saṃmataś ca, nivāsaś ca mah"|ātmanām,
satya|vādī hy, a|nindyaś ca, dharma|vit, sūkṣma|niścayaḥ.
tena te saha Śakreṇa sandhir bhavatu nityadā.
evaṃ viśvāsam āgaccha, mā te bhūd buddhir anyathā.›

ŚALYA uvāca:

maha"|ṛṣi|vacanaṃ śrutvā tān uvāca mahā|dyutiḥ,
‹avaśyaṃ bhagavanto me mānanīyās tapasvinaḥ.
bravīmi yad ahaṃ, devās, tat sarvaṃ kriyate yadi,
tataḥ sarvaṃ kariṣyāmi yad ūcur māṃ dvija'|rṣabhāḥ.
na śuṣkeṇa, na c' ārdreṇa, n' āśmanā na ca dāruṇā,
na śastreṇa, na c' âstreṇa, na divā, na tathā niśi
10.30 vadhyo bhaveyaṃ, vipr'|êndrāḥ, Śakrasya saha daivataiḥ.

The mighty *ásura* Vritra listened to the sages' words, and then, bowing his head, he replied to all the seers: 'I have listened thoroughly to everything that you and the *gan-dhárvas* had to say, illustrious lords, so now listen to me in return, sinless ones. How can there be a reconciliation between me and Shakra? How can friendship exist, gods, between our two magnificent powers?'

THE SAGES said:

'Peace between the good should be sought at least once. What must be later will be. One should not violate an alliance with a good man. Therefore, peace between the good should be sought. An alliance between the good is eternally strong. A wise man should give advice for profit in difficult circumstances. An alliance with a good man is of great benefit, and therefore the wise man would not kill the good man.
Indra is held in high esteem among good men and is the 10.25
abode of high-souled men. He is truthful, irreproachable, learned in law, and acutely resolute. So let eternal peace exist between you and Shakra. Have faith and don't plan anything else.'

SHALYA continued:

When the great glorious being heard the great sages' advice he replied to them: 'I must inevitably honor you noble ascetics. So let everything I say be done, gods, and if so, then I will do everything which the bull-like twiceborn have advised. But I am not to be killed by Shakra and the gods by 10.30
anything dry or wet, by rock or wood, nor by sword or any weapon, in the day or in the night, lords among seers. It is on these conditions that eternal peace with Shakra appeals

evaṃ me rocate sandhiḥ Śakreṇa saha nityadā.›
‹bāḍham ity› eva ṛṣayas tam ūcur, Bharata'|rṣabha.
evaṃ vṛtte tu sandhāne Vṛtraḥ pramudito 'bhavat.
yuktaḥ sad" âbhavac c' âpi Śakro harṣa|samanvitaḥ,
Vṛtrasya vadha|saṃyuktān upāyān anvacintayat.
chidr'|ânveṣī samudvignaḥ sadā vasati deva|rāṭ.
sa kadā cit samudr'|ânte samapaśyan mah"|âsuram,
sandhyā|kāla upāvṛtte muhūrte c' âti|dāruṇe,
tataḥ sañcintya bhagavān vara|dānaṃ mah"|ātmanaḥ,
10.35 ‹sandhy" êyaṃ vartate raudrā, na rātrir, divasaṃ na ca,
Vṛtraś c' âvaśya|vadhyo 'yaṃ mama sarva|haro ripuḥ.
yadi Vṛtraṃ na hanmy adya vañcayitvā mah"|âsuram
mahā|balaṃ mahā|kāyaṃ, na me śreyo bhaviṣyati.›
evaṃ sañcintayann eva Śakro, Viṣṇum anusmaran,
atha phenaṃ tad" âpaśyat samudre parvat'|ôpamam.
‹n' âyaṃ śuṣko, na c' ārdro 'yaṃ, na ca śastram idaṃ tathā.
enaṃ kṣepsyāmi Vṛtrasya; kṣaṇād eva naśiṣyati!›
sa|vajram atha phenaṃ taṃ kṣipraṃ Vṛtre nisṛṣṭavān;
praviśya phenaṃ taṃ Viṣṇur atha Vṛtraṃ vyanāśayat.
10.40 nihate tu tato Vṛtre diśo vitimir" âbhavan,
pravavau ca śivo vāyuḥ, prajāś ca jahṛṣus tathā.
tato devāḥ sa|gandharvā yakṣa|rakṣo|mah"|ôragāḥ,
ṛṣayaś ca mah"|Êndraṃ tam astuvan vividhaiḥ stavaiḥ.
namas|kṛtaḥ sarva|bhūtaiḥ, sarva|bhūtāny asāntvayat,
hatvā śatruṃ prahṛṣṭ'|ātmā, Vāsavaḥ saha daivataiḥ

to me.' And the sages replied 'Certainly,' bull of the Bharata race.

When the alliance was fixed, Vritra was pleased. But Shakra was constantly attentive, full of excitement, contemplating some means of carrying out Vritra's murder. The king of the gods lived incessantly agitated and watchful for any loophole. Then one time he caught sight of the great *ásura* on the sea-shore at the time of twilight, the juncture between night and day; and when that particularly frightful moment had come, the revered and high-souled lord
thought back on the favor he had been granted. 'Now that 10.35
inauspicious twilight has fallen, and it is neither day nor night, Vritra, my all-destroying enemy, must assuredly be killed. If I do not kill massive-bodied Vritra, the mighty great *ásura*, now, by being underhanded, then I will find no happiness.'

Thinking these things, and remembering Vishnu, Shakra then saw foam like a mountain on the sea. 'This is neither wet nor dry, and it is not a weapon. I will hurl this at Vritra and he will be destroyed instantly!' So he swiftly hurled the foam with his thunderbolt at Vritra, and Vishnu entered the foam and then destroyed Vritra.

When Vritra had been killed the sky became bright, a 10.40
kindly wind blew, and the living creatures were delighted. Then the gods and *gandhárva*s, *yaksha*s, *rákshasa*s, and the great serpents and sages praised great Indra with various hymns. Being worshipped by all creatures and soothing all creatures in return, Vásava, who was delighted in his soul now that he had killed his enemy, and who knew moral law,

Viṣṇuṃ tri|bhuvana|śreṣṭhaṃ pūjayām āsa dharma|vit.
tato hate mahā|vīrye Vṛtre deva|bhayaṅ|kare,
an|ṛten' âbhibhūto 'bhūc Chakraḥ parama|durmanā.
tri|śīrṣay" âbhibhūtaś ca sa pūrvaṃ brahma|hatyayā.
10.45 so 'ntam āśritya lokānāṃ naṣṭa|saṃjño vicetanaḥ,
na prājñāyata dev'|êndras tv abhibhūtaḥ sva|kalmaṣaiḥ.
praticchanno 'vasac c' âpsu, ceṣṭamāna iv' ôragaḥ.
tataḥ pranaṣṭe dev'|êndre brahma|hatyā|bhay'|ârdite,
bhūmiḥ pradhvasta|saṃkāśā, nirvṛkṣā, śuṣka|kānanā,
vicchinna|srotaso nadyaḥ, sarāṃsy an|udakāni ca,
saṃkṣobhaś c' âpi sattvānām an|āvṛṣṭi|kṛto 'bhavat.
devāś c' âpi bhṛśaṃ trastās, tathā sarve maha"|rṣayaḥ.
a|rājakaṃ jagat sarvam abhibhūtam upadravaiḥ.
tato bhīt" âbhavan devāḥ, ‹ko no rājā bhaved? iti.›
10.50 divi deva'|rṣayaś c' âpi deva|rāja|vinā|kṛtāḥ
na sma kaś cana devānāṃ rājye vai kurute matim.

ŚALYA uvāca:

11.1 ṚṢAYO 'TH' ÂBRUVAN sarve, devāś ca tri|div'|ēśvarāḥ,
‹ayaṃ vai Nahuṣaḥ śrīmān deva|rājye 'bhiṣicyatām,
tejasvī ca, yaśasvī ca, dhārmikaś c' âiva nityadā.›
te gatvā tv abruvan sarve, ‹rājā no bhava, pārthiva!›
sa tān uvāca Nahuṣo devān ṛṣi|gaṇāṃs tathā
pitṛbhiḥ sahitān, rājan, parīpsan hitam ātmanaḥ:

paid his respects along with the gods to Vishnu, the greatest being of the three worlds.

But once the powerful Vritra, who caused fear among the gods, was dead, Shakra was overcome by his own deceit and became terribly depressed. He had already been overwhelmed by his earlier brahmanicide of the three-headed
creature. So the lord of the gods, insensible and near un- 10.45
conscious, resorted to the end of the worlds, and he was unable to comprehend anything, overwhelmed as he was by his own sins. He lived hiding in the waters, thrashing like a snake.

Once the lord of the gods was ruined, tormented by his fear of brahmanicide, the earth looked withered and the forests were shriveled and treeless. The river currents were disrupted and lakes became dry. Hysteria developed among all living creatures as a result of the drought, and even the gods and all the great sages were thoroughly terrified. The entire kingless universe was overwhelmed by calamities. The
gods were fearful and said, 'Who should be our king?' The 10.50
gods and sages in heaven had become leaderless, and none of the gods set their mind on kingship.

SHALYA continued:

THEN ALL THE sages and the thirty gods, the lords of 11.1
heaven, said, 'Let the illustrious Náhusha here be consecrated as king of the gods. He is splendid, glorious, and perpetually virtuous.' So they all went to him and said: 'Become our king, lord!' But in an attempt to benefit himself, Náhusha said to gods and flocks of sages and ancestors in reply, my king:

‹dur|balo 'haṃ; na me śaktir bhavatāṃ paripālane.
balavān jāyate rājā, balaṃ Śakre hi nityadā.›
11.5 tam abruvan punaḥ sarve devā ṛṣi|purogamāḥ:
‹asmākaṃ tapasā yuktaḥ pāhi rājyaṃ tri|viṣṭape.
paraspara|bhayaṃ ghoram asmākaṃ hi, na saṃśayaḥ.
abhiṣicyasva, rāj'|êndra, bhava rājā tri|viṣṭape.
deva|dānava|yakṣāṇām, ṛṣīṇāṃ, rakṣasāṃ tathā,
pitṛ|gandhāava|bhūtānāṃ cakṣur|viṣaya|vartinām
teja ādāsyase paśyan, balavāṃś ca bhaviṣyasi.
dharmaṃ puras|kṛtya sadā sarva|lok'|âdhipo bhava.
brahma'|rṣīṃś c' âpi devāṃś ca gopāyasva tri|viṣṭape.›
abhiṣiktaḥ sa, rāj'|êndra, tato rājā tri|viṣṭape,
11.10 dharmaṃ puraskṛtya tadā, sarva|lok'|âdhipo 'bhavat.
su|durlabhaṃ varaṃ labdhvā, prāpya rājyaṃ tri|viṣṭape,
dharm'|ātmā satataṃ bhūtvā kām'|ātmā samapadyata.
dev'|ôdyāneṣu sarveṣu, Nandan'|ôpavaneṣu ca,
Kailāse, Himavat|pṛṣṭhe, Mandare, śveta|parvate
Sahye, Mahendre, Malaye, samudreṣu saritsu ca,
apsarobhiḥ parivṛto deva|kanyā|samāvṛtaḥ,
Nahuṣo deva|rājo 'tha krīḍan bahu|vidhaṃ tadā,
śṛṇvan divyā bahu|vidhāḥ kathāḥ śruti|mano|harāḥ,
vāditrāṇi ca sarvāṇi, gītaṃ ca madhura|svanam.
11.15 Viśvāvasur Nāradaś ca, gandharv'|âpsarasāṃ gaṇāḥ,
ṛtavaḥ ṣaṭ ca dev'|êndraṃ mūrtimanta upasthitāḥ;
mārutaḥ surabhir vāti mano|jñaḥ sukha|śītalaḥ.

'I am weak and unable to protect you. It is a powerful man who succeeds in becoming king, and the power is eternally Shakra's.' But all the gods and leading sages said to him 11.5
again: 'Govern the kingdom of heaven making use of our austerity. Our great fear of each other is certainly not in doubt. So be consecrated, lord of kings, and become king of heaven.

When gods, Dánavas, *yakshas*, sages, *rákshasas*, ancestors, *gandhárvas*, or spirits come in range of your vision, you will take their spendor just by looking at them, and so you shall become strong. Become lord of all worlds and always put law first. Defend the brahmin sages and gods of heaven like a herdsman!'

So he was consecrated as king of heaven, lord of kings,
and became lord of all worlds, putting the law first. But 11.10
once he had gained this blessing, near impossible to attain, of acquiring the kingdom of heaven, his soul became corrupted by lust, though he had previously always been virtuous-hearted. Náhusha, the king of the gods, played around in various ways, surrounded by the company of divine girls and *ápsaras*es in all the gardens of the gods, in Nándana's forest groves, on Mount Kailása, the far face of the Himálaya, Mount Mándara, the white hill Sahya, Mahéndra and Málaya, as well as in oceans and lakes.

He listened to various divine tales, pleasing to the mind and ear, as well as all musical instruments and mellifluous
songs. Vishva·vasu, Nárada, and throngs of *gandhárvas* and 11.15
*ápsaras*es as well as the six seasons incarnate attended the lord of the gods, and a charming, sweet-smelling, and pleasingly cool breeze blew.

evaṃ ca krīḍatas tasya Nahuṣasya dur|ātmanaḥ
saṃprāptā darśanaṃ devī Śakrasya mahiṣī priyā.
sa tām saṃdṛśya duṣṭ'|ātmā prāha sarvān sabhā|sadaḥ:
‹Indrasya mahiṣī devī kasmān māṃ n' ôpatiṣṭhati?
aham Indro 'smi devānāṃ, lokānāṃ ca tath" ēśvaraḥ.
āgacchatu Śacī mahyaṃ kṣipram adya niveśanam!›
tac chrutvā dur|manā devī Bṛhaspatim uvāca ha:
11.20 ‹rakṣa māṃ Nahuṣād, brahmaṃs,
tvām asmi śaraṇaṃ gatā.
sarva|lakṣaṇa|sampannaṃ,
brahmaṃs, tvaṃ māṃ prabhāṣase
deva|rājasya dayitām atyantaṃ sukha|bhāginīm,
a|vaidhavyena yuktāṃ c' âpy eka|patnīṃ pati|vratam.
uktavān asi māṃ pūrvam, ṛtāṃ tāṃ kuru vai giram.
n' ôkta|pūrvaṃ ca, bhagavan, vṛthā te kiñ cid, īśvara,
tasmād etad bhavet satyaṃ tvay" ôktaṃ, dvija|sattama!›
Bṛhaspatir ath' ôvāca Śakrāṇīṃ bhaya|mohitām:
‹yad ukt" âsi mayā, devi, satyaṃ tad bhavitā dhruvam.
drakṣyase deva|rājānam Indraṃ śīghram ih' āgatam.
11.25 na bhetavyaṃ ca Nahuṣāt, satyam etad bravīmi te;
samānayiṣye Śakreṇa na cirād bhavatīm aham.›
atha śuśrāva Nahuṣaḥ Śakrāṇīṃ śaraṇaṃ gatām
Bṛhaspater Aṅgirasaś; cukrodha sa nṛpas tadā.

ŚALYA uvāca:

12.1 KRUDDHAṂ TU Nahuṣaṃ dṛṣṭvā devā ṛṣi|purogamāḥ
abruvan deva|rājānaṃ Nahuṣaṃ ghora|darśanam:
‹deva|rāja, jahi krodhaṃ. tvayi kruddhe jagad, vibho,
trastaṃ s'|âsura|gandharvaṃ sa|kinnara|mah'|ôragam.

But while wicked-souled Náhusha was playing around in this manner, Shakra's beloved heavenly wife entered his view. Looking at her, the corrupt-souled god said to all his courtiers: 'Why doesn't Indra's divine wife wait on me? I am Indra, lord of gods and lord of worlds. Let Shachi quickly come to my house at once!'

When she heard him the goddess sadly said to Brihas·pati: 'Protect me from Náhusha, brahmin, for I have come 11.20
to you for refuge. You say that I am endowed with all auspicious marks, brahmin, that as the beloved of the king of the gods I possess eternal bliss, and that since I am a devoted and loyal wife to my husband I will not endure widowhood. This is what you told me in the past, so ensure your words remain true. You have never spoken anything vainly before, blessed lord, so your words should be true, greatest of the twiceborn!'

Brihas·pati said to Shakra's wife, who was thrown into confusion by her fear: 'Everything I told you, goddess, will assuredly come true. You will soon see Indra, the king of the gods, return here. There is nothing to be feared from 11.25
Náhusha, for I speak the truth. Not long from now I will re-unite you with Shakra.' But Náhusha had heard that Shakra's wife had sought refuge with Brihas·pati, son of Án-giras, and the king was furious.

SHALYA continued:

SEEING THAT Náhusha was angry, the gods and leading 12.1
sages spoke to the king of the gods, the frightful-looking Náhusha: 'King of the gods, curb your anger. When you are angry, my lord, the universe trembles with its *ásura*s,

jahi krodham imaṃ, sādho, na kupyanti bhavad|vidhāḥ.
parasya patnī sā devī. prasīdasva, sur'|ēśvara.
nirvartaya manaḥ pāpāt para|dār'|âbhimarśanāt!
deva|rājo 'si, bhadraṃ te! prajā dharmeṇa pālaya!›
12.5 evam ukto na jagrāha tad|vacaḥ kāma|mohitaḥ.
atha devān uvāc' êdaṃ Indraṃ prati sur'|âdhipaḥ:
‹Ahalyā dharṣitā pūrvam ṛṣi|patnī yaśasvinī
jīvato bhartur Indreṇa. sa vaḥ kiṃ na nivāritaḥ?
bahūni ca nṛśaṃsāni kṛtān' Îndreṇa vai purā,
vaidharmyāṇy upadhāś c' âiva. sa vaḥ kiṃ na nivāritaḥ?
upatiṣṭhatu devī mām, etad asyā hitaṃ param,
yuṣmākaṃ ca sadā, devāḥ, śivam evaṃ bhaviṣyati.›

DEVĀ ūcuḥ:

‹Indrāṇīm ānayiṣyāmo yath" êcchasi, divas|pate,
jahi krodham imaṃ, vīra, prīto bhava, sur'|ēśvara.›

ŚALYA uvāca:

12.10 ity uktvā taṃ tadā devā ṛṣibhiḥ saha, Bhārata,
jagmur Bṛhaspatiṃ vaktum Indrāṇīṃ c' â|śubhaṃ vacaḥ.
‹jānīmaḥ śaraṇaṃ prāptām Indrāṇīṃ tava veśmani,
datt'|âbhayāṃ ca, vipr'|êndra, tvayā, deva'|ṛṣi|sattama.
te tvāṃ devāḥ sa|gandharvā, ṛṣayaś ca, mahā|dyute,
prasādayanti c': Êndrāṇī Nahuṣāya pradīyatām.
Indrād viśiṣṭo Nahuṣo deva|rājo mahā|dyutiḥ,

*gandhárvas*, *kínnaras*, and great snakes. Excellent lord, curb this anger! Beings of your kind do not boil with rage. The goddess is another god's wife! Be gracious, lord of the gods. Turn your mind away from sin and from interfering with another person's wife! You are the king of the gods, bless you! Defend your subjects with righteousness!'

Though counseled, he did not take their advice, dis- 12.5
tracted with lust as he was. Instead the lord of the celestials proceeded to talk to the gods about Indra: 'Ahályа, the illustrious wife of the sage, was violated long ago by Indra while her husband was alive. So why did you not prevent him? In the past Indra committed numerous malicious and unjust deeds and frauds. Why did you not prevent him? Let the goddess serve me, for it would be to her ultimate advantage, and things will always turn out well for you too, gods.'

THE GODS replied:

'We will bring you Indráni if that is what you wish, lord of heaven. Curb this anger of yours, hero, and be glad, lord of the gods.'

SHALYA continued:

Once they had spoken in this manner, the gods and sages, 12.10
Bhárata, went to Brihas·pati to tell Indráni the bad news. They said, 'We know that Indráni has come to your house for protection, and that you have granted her an assurance of safety, lord of seers and greatest of gods and sages. The gods, *gandhárvas*, and sages beg you, great glorious being: let Indráni be handed over to Náhusha. Náhusha, the great

vṛṇotv imaṃ var'|ârohā bhartṛtve vara|varṇinī.›
evam ukte tu sā devī bāṣpam utsṛjya sa|svanam
uvāca rudatī dīnā Bṛhaspatim idaṃ vacaḥ:
12.15 ‹n' âham icchāmi Nahuṣaṃ patiṃ, deva'|ṛṣi|sattama!
śaraṇ'|āgat" âsmi te, brahmaṃs, trāyasva mahato bhayāt!›

BṚHASPATIR uvāca:

‹śaraṇ'|āgatāṃ na tyajeyam, Indrāṇi, mama niścayaḥ,
dharma|jñāṃ satya|śīlāṃ ca na tyajeyam, a|nindite.
n' â|kāryaṃ kartum icchāmi, brāhmaṇaḥ san viśeṣataḥ,
śruta|dharmā, satya|śīlo, jānan dharm'|ânuśāsanam.
n' âham etat kariṣyāmi; gacchadhvaṃ vai, sur'|ôttamāḥ.
asmiṃś c' ârthe purā gītaṃ Brahmaṇā śrūyatām idam:
«na tasya bījaṃ rohati roha|kāle,
na tasya varṣaṃ varṣati varṣa|kāle,
bhītaṃ prapannaṃ pradadāti śatrave.
na sa trātāraṃ labhate trāṇam icchan.
12.20 mogham annaṃ vindati c' âpy a|cetāḥ,
svargāl lokād bhraśyati naṣṭa|ceṣṭaḥ.
bhītaṃ prapannaṃ pradadāti yo vai,
na tasya havyaṃ pratigṛhṇanti devāḥ.
pramīyate c' âsya prajā hy a|kāle,
sadā vivāsaṃ pitaro 'sya kurvate,
bhītaṃ prapannaṃ pradadāti śatrave.
s'|Êndrā devāḥ praharanty asya vajram.»

glorious king of the gods, surpasses Indra, so let the flawlessly complexioned and shapely hipped lady choose him for her husband.'

Once they had spoken these words, the miserable goddess burst into loud sobs, and through her tears she addressed Brihas·pati in these words: 'I do not want Náhusha 12.15
for my husband, greatest of the gods and sages! I came for protection, brahmin, so protect me from great danger!'

BRIHAS·PATI said:

'I will not abandon a woman who has come to me for protection, Indráni. I am resolved on this point. I will not abandon a woman of truthful conduct who understands moral law, blameless lady. As a brahmin I do not want to commit an immoral act, especially since I have learned what righteousness is, am truthful in conduct, and know the precepts of law. I will not do it, so leave, most excellent gods. Listen to this song which Brahma sang in times gone by on this subject:

"Seed does not grow in spring, nor does rain fall in the monsoon for the man who hands over a terrified suppliant to their enemy. When he looks for protection, he will find no one to save him. The fool who hands over a terrified 12.20
suppliant finds his harvest unsuccessful. When dead he is ejected from heaven, and the gods will not accept his offerings. His descendants will die before their time, and his ancestors will make him an outcast for all time if he hands over a terrified suppliant to their enemy. The gods and Indra will hurl the thunderbolt at him."

etad evaṃ vijānan vai, na dāsyāmi Śacīm imām
Indrāṇīṃ viśrutāṃ loke Śakrasya mahiṣīṃ priyām.
asyā hitaṃ bhaved yac ca, mama c' âpi hitaṃ bhavet,
kriyatāṃ tat, sura|śreṣṭhā, na hi dāsyāmy ahaṃ Śacīm.›

ŚALYA uvāca:

atha devāḥ sa|gandharvā gurum āhur idaṃ vacaḥ:
‹kathaṃ su|nītaṃ nu bhaven, mantrayasva, Bṛhaspate.›

BṚHASPATIR uvāca:

12.25 ‹Nahuṣaṃ yācatāṃ devī kiṃ cit kāl'|ântaram śubhā
Indrāṇī, hitam etadd hi tath" âsmākaṃ bhaviṣyati.
bahu|vighnaḥ, surāḥ, kālaḥ; kālaḥ kālaṃ nayiṣyati.
garvito balavāṃś c' âpi Nahuṣo vara|saṃśrayāt.›

ŚALYA uvāca:

tatas tena tath" ôkte tu
prītā devās tath" âbruvan,
‹brahman, sādhv idam uktaṃ te.
hitaṃ sarvaṃ div'|âukasām
evam etad, dvija|śreṣṭha, devī c' êyaṃ prasādyatām!›
tataḥ samastā Indrāṇīṃ devāś c' Âgni|purogamāḥ
ūcur vacanam a|vyagrā lokānāṃ hita|kāmyayā:

DEVĀ ūcuḥ:

‹tvayā jagad idaṃ sarvaṃ dhṛtaṃ sthāvara|jaṅgamam.
eka|patny asi satyā ca, gacchasva Nahuṣaṃ prati
12.30 kṣipraṃ, tvām abhikāmaś ca vinaśiṣyati pāpa|kṛt
Nahuṣo, devi, Śakraś ca sur'|āiśvaryam avāpsyati.›
evaṃ viniścayaṃ kṛtvā Indrāṇī kārya|siddhaye,

Knowing this, I will not hand over Shachi Indráni here, famed throughout the world as the beloved wife of Shakra. Let what is beneficial both to her and to me be done, best of the gods, for I will not hand over Shachi.'

SHALYA continued:

The gods and *gandhárvas* spoke these words to the teacher: 'Brihas·pati, advise us on what would be a wise plan.'

BRIHAS·PATI replied:

'Let the beautiful goddess Indráni beg Náhusha for some 12.25
more time, for it will be advantageous to us as well. Time, gods, can cause numerous difficulties, but time inevitably brings one's destiny. Náhusha is conceited and powerful because he can rely on his largesse.'

SHALYA continued:

Then, when he had finished speaking in this manner, the gods were pleased and they said, 'Brahmin, you have spoken excellently. This plan will be of benefit to all heaven-dwellers, greatest of the twiceborn. May this goddess be placated!' Then the gods, led by Agni, collectively addressed these words to Indráni, in a reasoned manner, eager for the good of the world:

THE GODS said:

'You support the whole moving and stationary universe.
You are a true and devoted wife, so go to Náhusha quickly, 12.30
for that miscreant Náhusha who lusts after you will be destroyed, goddess, and Shakra will take back his lordship of the gods.' Indráni came to this conclusion, so she went

abhyagacchata sa|vrīḍā Nahuṣaṃ ghora|darśanam.
dṛṣṭvā tāṃ Nahuṣaś c' âpi vayo|rūpa|samanvitām,
samahṛṣyata duṣṭ'|ātmā, kām'|ôpahata|cetanaḥ.

ŚALYA uvāca:

13.1 ATHA TĀM ABRAVĪD dṛṣṭvā Nahuṣo deva|rāṭ tadā,
‹trayāṇām api lokānām aham Indraḥ, śuci|smite,
bhajasva māṃ, var'|ārohe, patitve, vara|varṇini.›
evam uktā tu sā devī Nahuṣeṇa pati|vratā
prāvepata bhay'|ôdvignā pravāte kadalī yathā.
praṇamya sā hi Brahmāṇaṃ śirasā tu kṛt'|âñjaliḥ,
deva|rājam ath' ôvāca
Nahuṣaṃ ghora|darśanam:
‹kālam icchāmy ahaṃ labdhuṃ
tvattaḥ kaṃ cit, sur'|ēśvara,
13.5 na hi vijñāyate Śakraḥ, kiṃ vā prāptaḥ, kva vā gataḥ.
tattvam etat tu vijñāya yadi na jñāyate, prabho,
tato 'haṃ tvām upasthāsye. satyam etad bravīmi te.›
evam uktaḥ sa Indrāṇyā Nahuṣaḥ prītimān abhūt.

NAHUṢA uvāca:

‹evaṃ bhavatu, su|śroṇi, yathā mām iha bhāṣase.
jñātvā c' āgamanaṃ kāryaṃ. satyam etad anusmareḥ.›
Nahuṣeṇa visṛṣṭā ca niścakrāma tataḥ śubhā
Bṛhaspati|niketaṃ ca sā jagāma yaśasvinī.
tasyāḥ saṃśrutya ca vaco devāś c' Âgni|purogamāḥ,
cintayām āsur ek'|âgrāḥ Śakr'|ârthaṃ, rāja|sattama.
13.10 deva|devena saṅgamya Viṣṇunā prabhaviṣṇunā,

bashfully to frightful-looking Náhusha, in order to achieve her task. And when wicked-souled Náhusha saw her, endowed with youth and beauty, he was delighted, corrupted in his mind by lust as he was.

SHALYA continued:

ONCE NÁHUSHA, the king of the gods, caught sight of 13.1
her, he said, 'I am the Indra of the three worlds, sweet-smiling goddess, so love me as though I were your husband, shapely hipped and flawlessly complexioned lady.' Spoken to in this manner by Náhusha, the goddess, who was loyal to her husband, trembled from fear as a banana tree sways in the wind. But bowing to Brahma, and putting her hands together at her head, she said to Náhusha, the terrifying-looking king of the gods:

'I would like some time from you, lord of the gods, since 13.5
it is not known what has happened to Shakra, or where he has gone. When the truth of the matter has been established, or if it cannot be discovered, lord, then I will indeed wait upon you. I give my word of honor.' And given this answer by Indráni, Náhusha was delighted.

NÁHUSHA replied:

'Very well, let it be as you told me, shapely hipped lady. But when you know you must come back. Remember your promise.' Dismissed by Náhusha, the beautiful and illustrious goddess left and went to Brihas·pati's home.

Once they had listened to what she had to say, the gods, led by Agni, reflected single-mindedly, set on Shakra's cause,
O greatest of kings. Meeting with Vishnu, the god of gods, 13.10
the supreme overlord, the eloquent but anxious gods spoke

ūcuś c' âinaṃ samudvignā vākyaṃ vākya|viśāradāḥ:
‹brahma|vadhy'|âbhibhūto vai Śakraḥ sura|gaṇ'|ēśvaraḥ.
gatiś ca nas tvaṃ, dev'|ēśa, pūrva|jo jagataḥ prabhuḥ!
rakṣ'|ârthaṃ sarva|bhūtānāṃ Viṣṇutvam upajagmivān.
tvad|vīrya|nihate Vṛtre Vāsavo brahma|hatyayā
vṛtaḥ, sura|gaṇa|śreṣṭha. mokṣaṃ tasya vinirdiśa.›
teṣāṃ tad vacanaṃ śrutvā devānāṃ, Viṣṇur abravīt,
‹mām eva yajatāṃ Śakraḥ; pāvayiṣyāmi vajriṇam.
puṇyena haya|medhena mām iṣṭvā Pāka|śāsanaḥ
13.15 punar eṣyati devānām Indratvam a|kuto|bhayaḥ.
sva|karmabhiś ca Nahuṣo nāśaṃ yāsyati dur|matiḥ.
kiṃ cit kālam idaṃ, devā, marṣayadhvam a|tandritāḥ.›
śrutvā Viṣṇoḥ śubhāṃ satyāṃ vāṇīṃ tām amṛt'|ôpamām,
tataḥ sarve sura|gaṇāḥ s'|ôpādhyāyāḥ saha'|ṛṣibhiḥ
yatra Śakro bhay'|ôdvignas, taṃ deśam upacakramuḥ.
tatr' âśva|medhaḥ su|mahān mah"|Êndrasya mah"|ātmanaḥ
vavṛte pāvan'|ârthaṃ vai brahma|haty"|âpaho, nṛpa.
vibhajya brahma|hatyāṃ tu vṛkṣeṣu ca nadīṣu ca,
parvateṣu pṛthivyāṃ ca, strīṣu c' âiva, Yudhiṣṭhira,
13.20 saṃvibhajya ca bhūteṣu, visṛjya ca sur'|ēśvaraḥ
vijvaro dhūta|pāpmā ca Vāsavo 'bhavad ātmavān.

to him in these words: 'Shakra, the lord of the heavenly hosts, is overcome by his brahmanicide. You are the first-born lord of the universe, and our refuge, lord of the gods! You undertook the role of Vishnu in order to protect all beings. When Vritra was destroyed by your power, Vásava became fixated by his brahmanicide, greatest of the hosts of gods. So indicate how he may find release.'

Once he had listened to what the gods had to say, Vishnu replied, 'Let Shakra make a sacrifice to me, and I will absolve the thunderbolt wielder. When the punisher of the
Daitya Paka has appeased me with a holy horse-sacrifice he 13.15
will once again return to the position of Indra over the gods, free of fear from any quarter. Wicked-minded Náhusha will reach his end by means of his own actions. But, gods, you must tolerate him for a while longer, remaining alert.'

Once they had listened to Vishnu's auspicious, truthful, and nectar-like speech, all the hosts of gods along with the teachers and sages departed to the place where Shakra was overwhelmed with fear. And it was there that high-souled mighty Indra's grandiose horse-sacrifice was performed in order to cleanse him by eradicating the brahmanicide, my king. So he distributed the brahmanicide among the trees,
rivers, mountains, earth, and women, Yudhi·shthira. And 13.20
once the lord of the gods had distributed and released his sin among living creatures, Vásava became free of his fever. He composed himself by dissolving his sin.

a|kampyam* Nahuṣaṃ sthānād dṛṣṭvā Bala|niṣūdanaḥ,
tejo|ghnaṃ sarva|bhūtānāṃ, vara|dānāc ca duḥ|saham,
tataḥ Śacī|patir devaḥ punar eva vyanaśyata,
a|dṛśyaḥ sarva|bhūtānāṃ kāl'|ākāṅkṣī cacāra ha.
pranaṣṭe tu tataḥ Śakre Śacī śoka|samanvitā,
‹hā Śakr'! êti› tadā devī vilalāpa su|duḥkhitā.
‹yadi dattaṃ, yadi hutaṃ, guravas toṣitā yadi,
eka|bhartṛtvam ev' âstu, satyaṃ yady asti vā mayi!
13.25 puṇyāṃ c' êmām ahaṃ divyāṃ pravṛttām uttar'|âyaṇe
devīṃ rātriṃ namasyāmi. sidhyatāṃ me mano|rathaḥ!›
prayatā ca Niśāṃ devīm upātiṣṭhata tatra sā;
prativratātvāt satyena s" ôpaśrutim ath' âkarot.
‹yatr' âste deva|rājo 'sau, taṃ deśaṃ darśayasva me.›
ity āh' ôpaśrutiṃ devīṃ: ‹satyaṃ satyena dṛśyatām.›

ŚALYA uvāca:

14.1 ATH' ÂINĀṂ RŪPIṆĪ sādhvīm upātiṣṭhad upaśrutiḥ
tāṃ vayo|rūpa|saṃpannāṃ dṛṣṭvā devīm upasthitām.
Indrāṇī saṃprahṛṣṭ'|ātmā
saṃpūjy' âinām ath' âbravīt,
‹icchāmi tvām ahaṃ jñātuṃ.
kā tvaṃ? brūhi, var'|ānane.›

When the slayer of Bala perceived that Náhusha could not be shaken from office, for he had removed the splendor of all creatures due to the gift he had been given, and so was unconquerable, Shachi's divine husband disappeared once again and roamed about invisible to all beings, waiting for the opportune moment.

But when Shakra disappeared this time, Shachi was overwhelmed with grief, and the wretchedly unhappy goddess wailed, 'Alas, Shakra! If I have been generous, if I have sacrificed, if I have pleased my teachers, and if the truth resides
within me, then I pray I remain a one-husband woman! I 13.25
will pay obeisance to this holy and divine Night passing on the day of the summer solstice. Let my heart's desire be fulfilled!'

So, ritually pure, she served the goddess Night, and, through her loyalty to her husband and her honesty, she produced an oracular voice. She said to the oracular goddess: 'Show me the place where the king of the gods resides. Let truth be seen through truth.'

SHALYA continued:

THE ORACULAR VOICE took corporeal form and waited 14.1
upon the excellent goddess, and when she noticed that a goddess endowed with youth and beauty was waiting upon her, joyful-souled Indráni honored her and said, 'I wish to know who you are, beautifully countenanced lady. Please tell me.'

UPAŚRUTIR uvāca:

‹upaśrutir ahaṃ, devi, tav' ântikam upāgatā.
darśanaṃ c' âiva saṃprāptā tava satyena, bhāvini.
pati|vratā ca, yuktā ca yamena niyamena ca,
darśayiṣyāmi te Śakraṃ devaṃ Vṛtra|niṣūdanam.
14.5 kṣipram anvehi, bhadraṃ te, drakṣyase sura|sattamam.›
tatas tāṃ prahitāṃ devīm Indrāṇī sā samanvagāt.
dev'|âraṇyāny atikramya, parvatāṃś ca bahūṃs tataḥ,
Himavantam atikramya uttaraṃ pārśvam āgamat.
samudraṃ ca samāsādya bahu|yojana|vistṛtam,
āsasāda mahā|dvīpaṃ nānā|druma|latā|vṛtam.
tatr' âpaśyat saro divyaṃ nānā|śakunibhir vṛtam,
śata|yojana|vistīrṇaṃ, tāvad ev' āyataṃ śubham.
tatra divyāni padmāni pañca|varṇāni, Bhārata,
ṣaṭ|padair upagītāni praphullāni sahasraśaḥ.
14.10 sarasas tasya madhye tu padminī mahatī śubhā
gaureṇ' ônnata|nālena padmena mahatā vṛtā.
padmasya bhittvā nālaṃ ca viveśa sahitā tayā.
bisa|tantu|praviṣṭaṃ ca tatr' âpaśyac chata|kratum
taṃ dṛṣṭvā ca su|sūkṣmeṇa rūpeṇ' âvisthitaṃ prabhum,
sūkṣma|rūpa|dharā devī babhūv', ôpaśrutiś ca sā.
Indraṃ tuṣṭāva c' Êndrāṇī viśrutaiḥ pūrva|karmabhiḥ;
stūyamānas tato devaḥ Śacīm āha puran|daraḥ:

THE ORACULAR VOICE said:

'I am an oracular voice, goddess, who has come before you and revealed myself through the power of your truth, beautiful lady. Since you are a devoted wife, endowed with self discipline and restraint, I will show you the god Shakra, the slayer of Vritra. Quickly follow me, my dear, and you 14.5
will see the best of the gods.'

Indráni followed the goddess once she had set out. Passing the forests of the gods and numerous mountains, she crossed Mount Himálaya and came to the north face. She came across a sea which stretched for many miles, and reached a great island which was covered with various trees and creepers. And there she saw a beautiful heavenly lake, teeming with birds of numerous breeds, nine hundred miles wide and equally expansive in length. There celestial lotuses of five hues bloomed in their thousands, serenaded by bees, Bhárata.

And in the middle of the lake there was a large and beau- 14.10
tiful lotus held in place by a long, upraised, yellowish lotus stalk. Having broken open the lotus stalk, she entered with Indráni. There she saw the god of a hundred sacrifices, who had climbed inside the lotus fibre. And seeing the lord in his tiny condition, the goddess and oracle took on tiny forms as well. Indráni complimented Indra on his famous achievements from the past, but being lauded, the city-destroying god said to Shachi:

‹kim artham asi saṃprāptā? vijñātaś ca kathaṃ tv aham?›
tataḥ sā kathayām āsa Nahuṣasya viceṣṭitam:
14.15 ‹Indratvaṃ triṣu lokeṣu prāpya vīrya|samanvitaḥ,
darp'|āviṣṭaś ca duṣṭ'|ātmā mām uvāca, śata|krato,
‹upatiṣṭh', êti› sa krūraḥ; kālaṃ ca kṛtavān mama.
yadi na trāsyasi, vibho, kariṣyati sa māṃ vaśe!
etena c' âhaṃ saṃprāptā drutaṃ, Śakra, tav' ântikam.
jahi raudraṃ, mahā|bāho, Nahuṣaṃ pāpa|niścayam!
prakāśay' ātman" ātmānam, daitya|dānava|sūdana!
tejaḥ samāpnuhi, vibho, deva|rājyaṃ praśādhi ca!›

ŚALYA uvāca:

15.1 EVAM UKTAḤ SA bhagavān Śacyā tāṃ punar abravīt,
‹vikramasya na kālo 'yaṃ. Nahuṣo balavattaraḥ.
vivardhitaś ca ṛṣibhir havya|kavyaiś ca, bhāvini.
nītim atra vidhāsyāmi, devi; tāṃ kartum arhasi.
guhyaṃ c' âitat tvayā kāryaṃ,
n' ākhyātavyaṃ, śubhe, kva cit.
gatvā Nahuṣam ekānte
bravīhi ca, su|madhyame:
‹ṛṣi|yānena divyena mām upaihi, jagat|pate,
evaṃ tava vaśe prītā bhaviṣyām', îti› taṃ vada.
15.5 ity uktvā deva|rājena patnī sā kamal'|ēkṣaṇā
‹evam astv ity› ath' ôktvā tu jagāma Nahuṣaṃ prati.
Nahuṣas tāṃ tato dṛṣṭvā sa|smito vākyam abravīt:
‹svāgataṃ te, var'|ārohe! kim karomi, śuci|smite?
bhaktaṃ māṃ bhaja, kalyāṇi! kim icchasi, manasvini?

'Why have you come here? And how did you find me?' So she told the tale of Náhusha's behavior: 'Full of power, he attained the position of Indra over the three worlds, but, god of a hundred sacrifices, the wicked-souled being was filled with arrogance and the cruel creature ordered me to serve him, even setting me a time limit. If you do not scare him into submission, my lord, then he will make me subject to his will! It is for this reason that I came before you without delay. Kill fierce and evil-intentioned Náhusha, long-armed god! Show yourself, slayer of the Daityas and Dánavas! Retrieve your splendor, my lord, and take control of the kingdom of the gods!' 14.15

SHALYA continued:

ADDRESSED IN THIS manner by Shachi, the lord spoke again, saying, 'This is not the time for strength. Náhusha is too strong. His power has grown by means of the sages performing sacrifices to the gods and ancestors, beautiful lady. I will devise a plan, goddess, and you ought to put it into action. It must be done secretly and must not be discussed anywhere, lovely lady. Go to Náhusha when he is alone and say this to him, slender-waisted woman: 'Come to me with a celestial, sage-driven carriage, O lord of the universe. On these terms I will gladly submit to your will.' 15.1

Given these instructions by the king of the gods, his lotus-eyed wife said, 'So it shall be,' and went to Náhusha. When Náhusha saw her, he smiled and said these words to her: 'Welcome, shapely hipped lady! What can I do for you, sweet-smiling goddess? Love me as I love you, pretty girl! What do you want, my clever girl? I will do whatever you 15.5

tava, kalyāṇi, yat kāryaṃ, tat kariṣye, su|madhyame.
na ca vrīḍā tvayā kāryā, su|śroṇi, mayi viśvaseḥ.
satyena vai śape, devi, kariṣye vacanaṃ tava.›

INDRĀṆY uvāca:

‹yo me kṛtas tvayā kālas, tam ākāṅkṣe, jagat|pate,
tatas tvam eva bhartā me bhaviṣyasi, sur'|âdhipa.
15.10 kāryaṃ ca hṛdi me yat tad, deva|rāj', âvadhāraya.
vakṣyāmi, yadi me, rājan, priyam etat kariṣyasi,
vākyaṃ praṇaya|saṃyuktaṃ, tataḥ syāṃ vaśa|gā tava.
Indrasya vājino, vāhā, hastino, 'tha rathās tathā,
icchāmy aham ath' â|pūrvaṃ vāhanaṃ te, sur'|âdhipa,
yan na Viṣṇor na Rudrasya n' âsurāṇāṃ na rakṣasām.
vahantu tvāṃ, mahā|bhāgā ṛṣayaḥ saṅgatā, vibho,
sarve śibikayā, rājann; etadd hi mama rocate.
n' âsureṣu na deveṣu tulyo bhavitum arhasi,
sarveṣāṃ teja ādatse svena vīryeṇa darśanāt.
15.15 na te pramukhataḥ sthātuṃ kaś cic chaknoti vīryavān!›

ŚALYA uvāca:

evam uktas tu Nahuṣaḥ prāhṛṣyata tadā kila.
uvāca vacanaṃ c' âpi sur'|êndras tām a|ninditām:

NAHUṢA uvāca:

‹a|pūrvaṃ vāhanam idaṃ tvay" ôktaṃ, vara|varṇini,
dṛḍhaṃ me rucitaṃ, devi. tvad|vaśo 'smi var'|ānane!
na hy alpa|vīryo bhavati yo vāhān kurute munīn!
ahaṃ tapasvī balavān bhūta|bhavya|bhavat|prabhuḥ.

want done, my pretty, slender-waisted lady. Don't be embarrassed, shapely hipped girl! Trust me. I swear by the truth, goddess, that I will do what you say.'

INDRÁNI replied:

'I am waiting for as much time as you allotted me, lord of the universe, and then you will become my husband, lord
of the gods. Consider my heart's desire, king of the gods. I 15.10
will tell you, king, if you will do me this favor. If you will do me this favor, king, then I shall talk to you affectionately and I will be yours to command.

Indra had horses to ride, and elephants and chariots, but I want an unprecedented carriage from you, lord of the gods, like nothing belonging to Vishnu, Rudra, or the *ásura*s or *rákshasa*s. Let all the illustrious sages carry you together in a palanquin, my lord, for that would please me, my king. You ought not to be equal to the *ásura*s and gods, for through your own power you take all their majesty with
a mere glimpse. No one has the strength to be able to stand 15.15
against you!'

SHALYA continued:

Náhusha was delighted by such advice, or so they say. The Indra of the gods replied to that blameless goddess in these words:

NÁHUSHA said:

'The carriage you suggest is certainly unparalleled, flawlessly complexioned lady, but it appeals to me a great deal, goddess. I am yours to control, gorgeously countenanced lady! He who uses sages as draft animals is by no means a being of little power! I am a mighty ascetic, and the lord

mayi kruddhe jagan na syān. mayi sarvaṃ pratiṣṭhitam,
deva|dānava|gandharvāḥ kinnar'|ôraga|rākṣasāḥ.
na me kruddhasya paryāptāḥ sarve lokāḥ, śuci|smite.
cakṣuṣā yaṃ prapaśyāmi tasya tejo harāmy aham.
15.20 tasmāt te vacanaṃ, devi, kariṣyāmi na saṃśayaḥ.
sapta'|rṣayo māṃ vakṣyanti, sarve brahma'|rṣayas tathā.
paśya māhātmya|yogaṃ me, ṛddhiṃ ca, vara|varṇini!›

ŚALYA uvāca:

evam uktvā tu tāṃ devīṃ, visṛjya ca var'|ānanām,
vimāne yojayitvā ca ṛṣīn niyamam āsthitān,
a|brahmaṇyo, bal'|ôpeto, matto mada|balena ca,
kāma|vṛttaḥ sa duṣṭ'|ātmā, vāhayām āsa tān ṛṣīn.
Nahuṣena visṛṣṭā ca Bṛhaspatim ath' âbravīt:
‹samayo 'lp'|âvaśeṣo me Nahuṣēṇ' êha yaḥ kṛtaḥ.
Śakraṃ mṛgaya śīghraṃ tvaṃ. bhaktāyāḥ kuru me dayām!›
‹bāḍham, ity› eva bhagavān Bṛhaspatir uvāca tām:
15.25 ‹na bhetavyaṃ tvayā, devi, Nahuṣād duṣṭa|cetasaḥ.
na hy eṣa sthāsyati ciraṃ, gata eṣa nar'|âdhamaḥ
a|dharmajño maha"|rṣīṇāṃ vāhanāc ca tataḥ, śubhe.
iṣṭiṃ c' âhaṃ kariṣyāmi vināśāy' âsya dur|mateḥ,
Śakraṃ c' âdhigamiṣyāmi.
mā bhais tvaṃ, bhadram astu te!›

of what was, what will be, and what is. If I were to become angry the universe would cease to exist. Everything is dependent upon me: gods, Dánavas, *gandhárva*s, *kínnara*s, snakes, and *rákshasa*s. All worlds cannot match my anger, sweet-smiling girl. I seize the majestic splendor of anyone
I cast my eye on. Therefore, have no doubt that I will do 15.20
what you say, goddess. The seven sages and the brahmin seers will all carry me. Behold my high-souled vehicle and success, flawlessly complexioned girl!'

SHALYA continued:

When he had finished speaking he dismissed the lovely-faced goddess. Then the unbrahmanical, mighty, lascivious, power-crazed, lust-ridden, and wicked-souled being yoked the sages, who maintained their restraint, to his chariot and rode the seers around.

But once Náhusha had dismissed her, Shachi said to Brihas·pati: 'Little time remains of the agreement which Náhusha made with me. Quickly, hunt for Shakra. Have pity on me—I love him!' Lord Brihas·pati replied to her:
'By all means. There is nothing for you to fear from wicked- 15.25
minded Náhusha, goddess. He will not remain in power much longer, since that wretched creature, who fails to abide by the constraints of morality, has become lost by using the great sages as his vehicle, beautiful lady. I will perform a sacrifice for the destruction of that evil-minded creature, and I will find Shakra. Do not be afraid. Blessings upon you!'

tataḥ prajvālya vidhivaj
juhāva paramaṃ haviḥ
Bṛhaspatir mahā|tejā deva|rāj'|ôpalabdhaye.
hutv" âgniṃ so 'bravīd, rājañ, ‹Chakram anviṣyatām, iti.›
tasmāc ca bhagavān devaḥ svayam eva hut'|âśanaḥ
strī|veṣam adbhutaṃ kṛtvā, tatr' âiv' ântar|adhīyata.
15.30 sa diśaḥ pradiśaś c' âiva, parvatāni vanāni ca,
pṛthivīṃ c' ântarikṣaṃ ca vicinty' âtha mano|gatiḥ,
nimeṣ'|ântara|mātreṇa Bṛhaspatim upāgamat.

AGNIR uvāca:

‹Bṛhaspate, na paśyāmi deva|rājam iha kva cit.
āpaḥ śeṣāḥ; sadā c' āpaḥ praveṣṭuṃ n' ôtsahāmy aham.
na me tatra gatir, brahman; kim anyat karavāṇi te?›
tam abravīd deva|gurur: ‹apo viśa, mahā|dyute!›

AGNIR uvāca:

‹n' āpaḥ praveṣṭuṃ śakṣyāmi! kṣayo me 'tra bhaviṣyati!
śaraṇaṃ tvāṃ prapanno 'smi. svasti te 'stu, mahā|dyute!
adbhyo 'gnir, brahmataḥ kṣatram, aśmano loham utthitam;
teṣāṃ sarvatra|gaṃ tejaḥ svāsu yoniṣu śāṃyati.›

BṚHASPATIR uvāca:

16.1 ‹TVAM, AGNE, sarva|devānāṃ
mukhaṃ tvam asi, havya|vāṭ.
tvam antaḥ sarva|bhūtānāṃ
gūḍhaś carasi sākṣivat.
tvām āhur ekaṃ kavayas tvām āhus tri|vidhaṃ punaḥ.

Then greatly majestic Brihas·pati kindled the fire, and in accordance with the custom he offered an excellent oblation in order to find the king of the gods. Having performed the sacrifice, my king, he said to Agni: 'Find Shakra.' So lord god Fire, the eater of oblations, appeared, having taken on
a marvelous female guise, and then disappeared. He inves- 15.30
tigated the directions, regions, mountains, forests, and the earth and sky, going where he pleased, and in the blink of an eye he returned to Brihas·pati.

AGNI said:

'Brihas·pati, I cannot see the king of the gods anywhere here. Only the waters are left, as always, for I am unable to enter the waters. That is not my path, brahmin, but is there anything else I can do for you?' The teacher of the gods said to him: 'Enter the water, great glorious being!'

AGNI said:

'I cannot enter the waters! It will be the end of me! I approach you as a suppliant for protection! Good luck, great glorious being! Fire came into existence from water, the kshatriya order from the brahmin, and copper from stone, but their universal splendor disappears in the presence of their origins.'

BRIHAS·PATI said:

'FIRE, YOU ARE the mouth of all gods; you are the car- 16.1
rier of the oblation. You move hidden within all creatures like a witness. The wise say you are one, yet again they say that you are a trinity. Were you to abandon this universe it would be destroyed in that very instant, oblation-eating

tvayā tyaktaṃ jagac c' êdaṃ sadyo naśyedd, hut'|âśana.
kṛtvā tubhyaṃ namo viprāḥ sva|karma|vijitāṃ gatim
gacchanti saha patnībhiḥ sutair api ca śāśvatīm.
tvam ev', Âgne, havya|vāhas, tvam eva paramaṃ haviḥ.
yajanti sattrais tvām eva yajñaiś ca param'|âdhvare.
16.5 sṛṣṭvā lokāṃs trīn imān, havya|vāha,
prāpte kāle pacasi punaḥ samiddhaḥ.
tvaṃ sarvasya bhuvanasya prasūtis
tvam ev', Âgne, bhavasi punaḥ pratiṣṭhā.
tvām, Agne, jala|dān āhur, vidyutaś ca manīṣiṇaḥ.
vahanti sarva|bhūtāni tvatto niṣkramya hetayaḥ.
tvayy āpo nihitāḥ sarvās, tvayi sarvam idaṃ jagat.
na te 'sty a|viditaṃ kiñ cit triṣu lokeṣu, Pāvaka.
sva|yoniṃ bhajate sarvo, viśasv' āpo '|viśaṅkitaḥ.
ahaṃ tvāṃ vardhayiṣyāmi brāhmair mantraiḥ sanātanaiḥ.›
evaṃ stuto havya|vāṭ sa bhagavān kavir uttamaḥ
Bṛhaspatim ath' ôvāca prītimān vākyam uttamam:
16.10 ‹darśayiṣyāmi te Śakraṃ, satyam etad bravīmi te.›

ŚALYA uvāca:

pravisy' āpas tato vahniḥ sa|samudrāḥ sa|palvalāḥ
āsasāda saras tac ca gūḍho yatra śata|kratuḥ.
atha tatr' âpi padmāni vicinvan, Bharata'|rṣabha,
apaśyat sa tu dev'|êndraṃ bisa|madhya|gataṃ tadā.
āgatya ca tatas tūrṇam tam ācaṣṭa Bṛhaspateḥ
anumātreṇa vapuṣā padma|tantv āśritaṃ prabhum.
gatvā deva'|rṣi|gandharvaiḥ sahito 'tha Bṛhaspatiḥ
purāṇaiḥ karmabhir devaṃ tuṣṭāva Bala|sūdanam.

Fire. Brahmins who have done you homage go to the eternal place won by their achievements, with their wives and sons. You, Fire, carry the oblation, and you are the ultimate oblation. It is you to whom they sacrifice with the sessions* and sacrifices at the highest sacrifice.

Having created the three worlds, oblation-carrying Fire, 16.5
you ignite and cook them when the time comes. You are the creator of this whole universe, Fire, and yet again you are its point of dissolution.* Wise men call you cloud and lightning, O Fire. The flames which shoot forth from you carry all creatures. All waters rest on you. This whole universe rests on you. There is nothing in the three worlds which is unknown to you, Fire. Everyone loves the source of their creation, so enter the waters without hesitation. I will cause you to grow in strength with eternal brahmic mantras.'

Once the oblation-carrying lord, the ultimate sage, was glorified in this manner, he was delighted and addressed
this most excellent speech to Brihas·pati: 'I tell you truly, I 16.10
will show you Shakra.'

SHALYA continued:

So the oblation carrier entered the waters, including oceans and pools, and then he entered the lake where the god of a hundred sacrifices was hiding. Investigating the lotuses there, bull of the Bharata race, he saw the lord of the gods who had retreated inside a fibre. So he returned to Brihas·pati at speed, and told him that the lord had adopted a tiny form and had taken refuge in a lotus fibre. So, accompanied by gods, sages, and *gandhárvas*, Brihas·pati glorified the Bala-slaying god for his past achievements.

‹mah"|âsuro hataḥ, Śakra, Namucir dāruṇas tvayā,
Śambaraś ca Balaś c' âiva tath" ôbhau ghora|vikramau.
16.15 śata|krato, vivardhasva, sarvān śatrūn niṣūdaya!
uttiṣṭha, Śakra, saṃpaśya deva'|rṣīṃś ca samāgatān!
mah"|êndra, dānavān hatvā lokās trātās tvayā, vibho.
apāṃ phenaṃ samāsādya Viṣṇu|tejo 'ti|bṛṃhitam
tvayā Vṛtro hataḥ pūrvaṃ, deva|rāja jagat|pate.
tvaṃ sarva|bhūteṣu śaraṇya īḍyas.
tvayā samaṃ vidyate n' êha bhūtam.
tvayā dhāryante sarva|bhūtāni, Śakra.*
tvaṃ devānāṃ mahimānaṃ cakartha.
pāhi sarvāṃś ca lokāṃś ca, mah"|Êndra, balam āpnuhi!›

evaṃ saṃstūyamānaś ca so 'vardhata śanaiḥ śanaiḥ,
svaṃ c' âiva vapur āsthāya babhūva sa bal'|ânvitaḥ.
abravīc ca guruṃ devo Bṛhaspatim avasthitam:
16.20 ‹kiṃ kāryam avaśiṣṭaṃ vo? hatas Tvāṣṭro mah"|âsuraḥ,
Vṛtraś ca su|mahā|kāyo yo vai lokān anāśayat.›

'You killed the great *ásura,* cruel Námuchi, Shakra, as well as Shámbara and Bala, both terrifyingly awesome in their prowess. God of a hundred sacrifices, grow and de- 16.15
stroy all your enemies! Get up, Shakra, and look at the gods and sages who have gathered! Great Indra, when you killed the Dánavas you saved the worlds, my lord. You killed Vritra, lord, by using the foam on the water empowered by Vishnu's splendor, O king of the gods and lord of the universe. You are the refuge of all creatures and should be worshipped as such. Your equal cannot be found in this world. All beings are supported by you, Shakra. You have formed the majesty of the gods. Protect all worlds and find your strength, great Indra!'

Praised in this way, he grew little by little, and when he had ascended to his own body he became imbued with power. The god said to the teacher Brihas·pati, as he stood beside him: 'What else is left that I need to do for you? The 16.20
great *ásura* Tvashtri has been killed, as has gigantic-bodied Vritra who was annihilating the worlds.'

BṚHASPATIR uvāca:

‹mānuṣo Nahuṣo rājā deva'|rṣi|gaṇa|tejasā
deva|rājyam anuprāptaḥ sarvān no bādhate bhṛśam.›

INDRA uvāca:

‹kathaṃ ca Nahuṣo rājyaṃ devānāṃ prāpa dur|labham?
tapasā kena vā yuktaḥ, kiṃ|vīryo vā, Bṛhaspate?›

BṚHASPATIR uvāca:

‹devā bhītāḥ Śakram akāmayanta
tvayā tyaktaṃ mahad Aindraṃ padaṃ tat.
tadā devāḥ pitaro 'tha' rṣayaś ca
gandharva|mukhyāś ca sametya sarve
gatv" âbruvan Nahuṣaṃ tatra, Śakra:
‹tvaṃ no rājā bhava bhuvanasya goptā!›
tān abravīn Nahuṣo, ‹n' âsmi śakta
āpyāyadhvaṃ tapasā tejasā mām!›
16.25 evam uktair vardhitaś c' âpi devai
rāj" âbhavan Nahuṣo ghora|vīryaḥ.
trailokye ca prāpya rājyaṃ maha"|rṣīn
kṛtvā vāhān yāti lokān dur|ātmā.
tejo|haraṃ dṛṣṭi|viṣaṃ su|ghoraṃ
mā tvaṃ paśyer Nahuṣaṃ vai kadā cit!
devāś ca sarve Nahuṣaṃ bhṛś'|ārtā
na paśyante gūḍha|rūpāś carantaḥ.›

BRIHAS·PATI said:

'The human King Náhusha has gained lordship over the gods by means of the splendor of the hosts of gods and sages, and he harasses us all terribly.'

INDRA replied:

'And how exactly did Náhusha manage to attain a prize so unattainable as the sovereignty of the gods? With what austerity is he endowed, or what power does he possess, Brihas·pati?'

BRIHAS·PATI said:

'When you abandoned your rank of great Indra, the gods were afraid and longed for a Shakra. So the gods, ancestors, sages, and eminent *gandhárvas* all gathered. Going to Náhusha, Shakra, they said: 'You be our king and protector of the world!' But Náhusha replied, 'I am not capable. So strengthen me with austerity and majesty!' At these 16.25
words the gods made him grow in strength, and Náhusha became a king of terrifying prowess. Now that he has assumed sovereignty over the three worlds, he makes great sages his vehicle, and the evil-souled being rides them over the worlds. His horrifying, poisonous glance steals power. Never look at Náhusha! Violently unhappy, all the gods are running in hidden forms so they do not see him.'

ŚALYA uvāca:

evaṃ vadaty Aṅgirasāṃ variṣṭhe
Bṛhaspatau, loka|pālaḥ Kuberaḥ,
Vaivasvataś c' âiva Yamaḥ purāṇo,
devaś ca Somo, Varuṇaś c' ājagāma.
te vai samāgamya mah"|Êndram ūcur:
‹diṣṭyā Tvāṣṭro nihataś c' âiva Vṛtraḥ,
diṣṭyā ca tvāṃ kuśalinam a|kṣataṃ ca
paśyāmo vai nihat'|ârim ca, Śakra!›
sa tān yathāvac ca hi loka|pālān
sametya vai prīta|manā mah"|Êndraḥ
uvāca c' âinān pratibhāṣya Śakraḥ
saṃcodayiṣyan Nahuṣasy' ântareṇa:
16.30 ‹rājā devānāṃ Nahuṣo ghora|rūpas;
tatra sāhyaṃ dīyatāṃ me bhavadbhir!›
te c' âbruvan, ‹Nahuṣo ghora|rūpo!
dṛṣṭī|viṣas tasya bibhīma, īśa!
tvaṃ ced rājānaṃ Nahuṣaṃ parājayes,
tato vayaṃ bhāgam arhāma, Śakra!›
Indro 'bravīd, ‹bhavatu. bhavān apāṃ|patir,
Yamaḥ, Kuberaś ca may" âbhiṣekam
saṃprāpnuvantv adya. sah' âiva daivatai
ripuṃ jayāma taṃ Nahuṣaṃ ghora|dṛṣṭim!›
tataḥ Śakraṃ jvalano 'py āha: ‹bhāgaṃ
prayaccha mahyaṃ, tava sāhyaṃ kariṣye!›
tam āha Śakro bhavit", Âgne, tav' âpi,
c' Êndr'|Âgnyor vai bhāga eko mahā|kratau.›

SHALYA continued:

While Brihas·pati, the greatest of Ángiras's race, was speaking, Kubéra the defender of the world, ancient Yama the son of Vivásvat, and the gods Soma and Váruna arrived. Gathered together they said to great Indra: 'How fortunate that Tvashtri and Vritra are dead, and how fortunate that we see you healthy and uninjured with your enemies dead, Shakra!' Delighted, great Indra joined those world-protectors, and Shakra addressed them in the appropriate manner, speaking so as to drive them away from Náhusha's influence:

'Horrifying-looking Náhusha is king of the gods, so grant 16.30
me your assistance in his destruction!' In reply they said, 'Náhusha is indeed horrifying-looking! His gaze is poison, and we are afraid, my lord! But if you were to defeat King Náhusha then we would deserve our share, Shakra!' Indra replied, 'So be it. May you, the lord of the waters, and Yama and Kubéra today obtain consecration along with me. With the gods we will defeat this enemy Náhusha of terrifying gaze!' But then the fire said to Shakra: 'Grant me a share too, and I will give you my assistance!' So Shakra replied, 'It will be for you also, O Fire: one portion for Indra and Fire during the great ritual.'

ŚALYA uvāca:

evaṃ sañcintya bhagavān mah"|Êndraḥ Pāka|śāsanaḥ
Kuberaṃ sarva|yakṣāṇāṃ dhanānāṃ ca prabhuṃ tathā,
Vaivasvataṃ pitṝṇāṃ ca, Varuṇaṃ c' âpy apāṃ tathā
ādhipatyaṃ dadau Śakraḥ sañcintya vara|das tathā.

ŚALYA uvāca:

17.1 ATHA SAṂCINTAYĀNASYA deva|rājasya dhīmataḥ
Nahuṣasya vadh'|ôpāyaṃ loka|pālaiḥ sad" âiva taiḥ
tapasvī tatra bhagavān Agastyaḥ pratyadṛśyata.
so 'bravīd arcya dev'|êndraṃ: ‹diṣṭyā vai vardhate bhavān
Viśvarūpa|vināśena Vṛtr'|âsura|vadhena ca!
diṣṭy" âdya Nahuṣo bhraṣṭo deva|rājyāt, Puran|dara!
diṣṭyā hat'|ârim paśyāmi bhavantaṃ, Bala|sūdana!›

INDRA uvāca:

‹svāgataṃ te, maha"|rṣe, 'stu! prīto 'haṃ darśanāt tava.
pādyam, ācamanīyaṃ, ca gām, arghyaṃ ca pratīccha me.›

ŚALYA uvāca:

17.5 pūjitaṃ c' ôpaviṣṭaṃ tam āsane muni|sattamam
paryapṛcchata dev'|ēśaḥ prahṛṣṭo brāḥmaṇa'|rṣabham:
‹etad icchāmi, bhagavan, kathyamānaṃ, dvij'|ôttama,
paribhraṣṭaḥ kathaṃ svargān Nahuṣaḥ pāpa|niścayaḥ!›

SHALYA continued:

After some thought, mighty Lord Indra, the punisher of Paka, granted sovereignty of all *yaksha*s and wealth to Kubéra, lordship of the ancestors to Yama the son of Vivásvat, and sovereignty of the waters to Váruna. So Shakra, the giver of gifts, decided.

SHALYA continued:

17.1 WHILE THE WISE king of the gods pondered incessantly with those world-protectors over a means to kill Náhusha, the ascetic Lord Agástya appeared, and after worshipping the king of the gods, he said to him: 'How fortunate that you prosper now Vishva·rupa, the creature of universal form, has been destroyed and the *ásura* Vritra is slaughtered! How fortunate that Náhusha has today been overthrown from lordship over the gods, Sacker of Cities! Thank goodness I behold you now with your enemies destroyed, slayer of Bala!'

INDRA replied:

'Welcome, great sage! I am pleased to see you. Accept my water for you feet, water to sip, a cow, and the proper reception for a guest.'

SHALYA continued:

17.5 When the greatest of sages had been honored and had taken a seat, the lord of the gods cheerfully questioned the bull among brahmins: 'Blessed and greatest of the twice-born, I want you to tell me how evil-intentioned Náhusha was toppled from heaven!'

AGASTYA uvāca:

‹śṛṇu, Śakra, priyaṃ vākyaṃ yathā rājā dur|ātmavān
svargād bhraṣṭo dur|ācāro Nahuṣo bala|darpitaḥ.
śram'|ārtāś ca vahantas taṃ Nahuṣaṃ pāpa|kāriṇam
deva'|rṣayo mahā|bhāgās tathā brahma'|rṣayo '|malāḥ
papracchur Nahuṣaṃ, deva, saṃśayaṃ, jayatāṃ vara:
«ya ime Brahmaṇā proktā mantrā vai prokṣaṇe gavām,
17.10 ete pramāṇaṃ bhavata, ut' āho n'? êti,» Vāsava.
Nahuṣo «n', êti» tān āha tamasa mūḍha|cetanaḥ.›

ṚṢAYA ūcuḥ:

‹a|dharme saṃpravṛttas tvaṃ dharmaṃ na pratipadyase.
pramāṇam etad asmākaṃ pūrvaṃ proktaṃ maha''|rṣibhiḥ!›

AGASTYA uvāca:

‹tato vivadamānaḥ sa munibhiḥ saha, Vāsava,
atha mām aspṛśan mūrdhni pāden' â|dharma|pīḍitaḥ.
ten' âbhūdd hata|tejāś ca niḥśrīkaś ca mahī|patiḥ.
tatas taṃ tamas'' āvignam avocaṃ bhṛśa|pīḍitam:
‹yasmāt pūrvaiḥ kṛtaṃ, rājan, brahma'|rṣibhir anuṣṭhitam
a|duṣṭaṃ* dūṣayasi, me yac ca mūrdhny aspṛśaḥ padā,
17.15 yac c' âpi tvam ṛṣīn, mūḍha, brahma|kalpān dur|āsadān,
vāhān kṛtvā vāhayasi, tena svargādd hata|prabhaḥ
dhvaṃsa, pāpa, paribhraṣṭaḥ kṣīṇa|puṇyo mahī|tale!
daśa varṣa|sahasrāṇi sarpa|rūpa|dharo mahān
vicariṣyasi pūrṇeṣu, punaḥ svargam avāpsyasi.›

AGÁSTYA replied:

'Well then, Shakra, listen to this welcome news of how wicked-souled and badly behaved King Náhusha, so proud of his strength, was toppled from heaven. Pained by exhaustion from carrying that miscreant Náhusha around, the illustrious divine sages and pure brahmic sages asked 17.10
Náhusha about a matter of debate, celestial Vásava, greatest of victors: "Are the brahmic mantras which are to be recited while sprinkling cows authoritative or not?" Náhusha, whose mind was fooled by darkness, told them that they were not.

THE SAGES said:

"You concern yourself with immorality and you do not practice correct conduct. We hold them as authoritative because they were said to be so by the great sages of the past!"

AGÁSTYA said:

While he was contesting the matter with the sages, Vásava, troubled by the transgression, he touched me on my head with his foot. Through this act the king was deprived of his majesty and glory. So I said to him, terribly oppressed and confused by darkness as he was: "Since you have defiled the pure Veda, set down by the ancients and practiced by brahmic sages, king, since you have touched my head with your foot, and since you have made unparalleled Brahma- 17.15
like sages into your vehicle and ridden them around, you fool, leave heaven, deprived of radiance, you evil creature, and fall to the surface of the earth with all your merit lost! There you will slither in the body of a huge snake for ten

evaṃ bhraṣṭo dur|ātmā sa deva|rājyād, arin|dama.
diṣṭyā vardhāmahe, Śakra, hato brāhmaṇa|kaṇṭakaḥ!
tri|viṣṭapaṃ prapadyasva, pāhi lokān, Śacī|pate,
jit'|êndriyo, jit'|âmitraḥ, stūyamāno maha"|rṣibhiḥ!›

ŚALYA uvāca:

17.20 tato devā bhṛśaṃ tuṣṭā, maha"|rṣi|gaṇa|saṃvṛtāḥ,
pitaraś c' âiva, yakṣāś ca, bhujagā, rākṣasās tathā,
gandharvā, deva|kanyāś ca, sarve c' âpsarasāṃ gaṇāḥ,
sarāṃsi, saritaḥ, śailāḥ, sāgarāś ca, viśām pate.
upāgamy' âbruvan sarve, ‹diṣṭyā vardhasi, śatru|han!
hataś ca Nahuṣaḥ pāpo diṣṭy" Âgastyena dhīmatā!
diṣṭyā pāpa|samācāraḥ kṛtaḥ sarpo mahī|tale!›

ŚALYA uvāca:

18.1 TATAḤ ŚAKRAḤ stūyamāno gandharv'|âpsarasāṃ gaṇaiḥ
Airāvataṃ samāruhya dvip'|êndraṃ lakṣaṇair yutam,
Pāvakaḥ su|mahā|tejā, maha"|rṣiś ca Bṛhaspatiḥ,
Yamaś ca, Varuṇaś c' âiva, Kuberaś ca dhan'|ēśvaraḥ,
sarvair devaiḥ parivṛtaḥ Śakro Vṛtra|niṣūdanaḥ
gandharvair apsarobhiś ca yātas tri|bhuvanaṃ prabhuḥ.

thousand years, and only when they are fulfilled will you once again attain heaven."

That is how the evil-souled creature was overthrown from sovereignty over the gods, subduer of your enemies. So, Shakra, luck has allowed us to prosper, for the thorn in the side of brahmins has been killed! Return to heaven with your senses controlled and your enemy defeated, and protect the worlds while being praised by great sages, husband of Shachi!'

SHALYA continued:

The gods were extremely pleased, and the flocks of great 17.20
sages, and the ancestors, *yakshas*, snakes, *rákshasas*, *gandhárvas*, heavenly maidens, and all the hosts of *ápsarases* as well as the lakes, rivers, mountains, and oceans, lord of men, were also delighted. They approached together and said in unison, 'It is by good fortune that you prosper, slayer of your enemies! What luck that wise Agástya disposed of evil Náhusha! How lucky it is that the miscreant has been transformed into a snake to writhe on the surface of the earth!'

SHALYA continued:

BEING CELEBRATED BY the flocks of *gandhárvas* and 18.1
*ápsarases*, Shakra climbed up onto Airávata, the auspiciously marked lord of elephants. Brightly majestic Fire and the great sage Brihas·pati were there, as were Yama, Váruna, and Kubéra the lord of wealth. So it was that surrounded by all the gods, *gandhárvas*, and *ápsarases*, Lord Shakra, the slayer of Vritra, returned to heaven.

sa sametya mah"|Êndrāṇyā deva|rājaḥ śata|kratuḥ
mudā paramayā yuktaḥ pālayām āsa deva|rāṭ.
18.5 tataḥ sa bhagavāṃs tatra Aṅgirāḥ samadṛśyata,
Atharva|veda|mantraiś ca dev'|êndraṃ samapūjayat.
tatas tu bhagavān Indraḥ saṃhṛṣṭaḥ samapadyata
varaṃ ca pradadau tasmai Atharvāṅgirase tadā:
‹Atharvāṅgiraso nāma vedo 'smin vai bhaviṣyati;
udāharaṇam etadd hi, yajña|bhāgaṃ ca lapsyase.›

evaṃ saṃpūjya bhagavān Atharvāṅgirasaṃ tadā
vyasarjayan, mahā|rāja, deva|rājaḥ śata|kratuḥ.
saṃpūjya sarvās tri|daśān ṛṣīṃś c' âpi tapo|dhanān
Indraḥ pramudito, rājan, dharmeṇ' âpālayat prajāḥ.
18.10 evaṃ duḥkham anuprāptam Indreṇa saha bhāryayā,
a|jñāta|vāsaś ca kṛtaḥ śatrūṇāṃ vadha|kāṅkṣayā.

n' âtra manyus tvayā kāryo yat kliṣṭo 'si mahā|vane
Draupadyā saha, rāj'|êndra, bhrātṛbhiś ca mah"|ātmabhiḥ.
evaṃ tvam api, rāj'|êndra, rājyaṃ prāpsyasi, Bhārata,
Vṛtraṃ hatvā yathā prāptaḥ Śakraḥ, Kaurava|nandana.
dur|ācāraś ca Nahuṣo, brahma|dviṭ, pāpa|cetanaḥ
Agastya|śāp'|âbhihato vinaṣṭaḥ śāśvatīḥ samāḥ.
evaṃ tava dur|ātmānaḥ śatravaḥ, śatru|sūdana,
kṣipraṃ nāśaṃ gamiṣyanti Karṇa|Duryodhan'|ādayaḥ!
18.15 tataḥ sāgara|paryantāṃ bhokṣyase medinīm imām
bhrātṛbhiḥ sahito, vīra, Draupadyā ca sah' ânayā!

Now that the god of a hundred sacrifices had been reunited with great Indráni, the king of the gods was filled
with utter bliss and governed as king of the gods. Then Lord 18.5
Ángiras appeared and worshipped the lord of the gods with spells from the Athárva Veda. Lord Indra was delighted and in return he granted a favor to Atharvángiras: 'This quotation in this Veda will be known as the Atharvángirasa from now on, and you will have your share of the sacrifice.'

Having celebrated Atharvángiras in this way, the blessed king of the gods, known for his hundred sacrifices, then dismissed him, great king. He also honored all thirty gods as well as the sages whose wealth lies in asceticism. So Indra cheerfully ruled his subjects with righteousness, my king.
And this is the story of how Indra and his wife suffered 18.10
misery, and how he even lived in hiding because of his desire to murder his enemies.

You should not be angry that you were tormented in the great forest with Dráupadi and your high-souled brothers, lord of kings. For you too will regain your kingdom, Bhárata, lord of kings, just as Shakra regained his when he killed Vritra, O descendant of Kuru. Badly behaved and evil-minded Náhusha, the enemy of all that is sacred, was struck down by Agástya's curse and lost for near eternity. And so too will your black-hearted enemies soon meet their destruction, slayer of your enemies, starting with Karna and
Duryódhana! Then you, your brothers, and Dráupadi here 18.15
will enjoy this earth encircled by oceans, my hero!

upākhyānam idaṃ Śakra|vijayaṃ Veda|saṃmitam
rājñā vyūḍheṣv anīkeṣu śrotavyaṃ jayam icchatā.
tasmāt saṃśrāvayāmi tvāṃ vijayaṃ, jayatāṃ vara.
saṃstūyamānā vardhante mah"|ātmāno, Yudhiṣṭhira.
kṣatriyāṇām a|bhāvo 'yaṃ, Yudhiṣṭhira, mah"|ātmanām
Duryodhan'|âparādhena Bhīm'|Ârjuna|balena ca.
ākhyānam Indra|vijayaṃ ya idaṃ niyataḥ paṭhet,
dhūta|pāpmā jita|svargaḥ paratr' êha ca modate.
18.20 na c' âri|jaṃ bhayaṃ tasya, n' â|putro vā bhaven naraḥ.
n' āpadaṃ prāpnuyāt kāñ cid, dīrgham āyuś ca vindati.
sarvatra jayam āpnoti, na kadā cit parājayam!»

VAIŚAMPĀYANA uvāca:

evam āśvāsito rājā Śalyena, Bharata'|rṣabha,
pūjayām āsa vidhivac Chalyaṃ dharma|bhṛtāṃ varaḥ.
śrutvā tu Śalya|vacanaṃ Kuntī|putro Yudhiṣṭhiraḥ
pratyuvāca mahā|bāhur Madra|rājam idaṃ vacaḥ:
«bhavān Karṇasya sārathyaṃ kariṣyati na saṃśayaḥ
tatra tejo|vadhaḥ kāryaḥ Karṇasy' Ârjuna|saṃstavaḥ!»

ŚALYA uvāca:

«evam etat kariṣyāmi, yathā māṃ saṃprabhāṣase;
yac c' ânyad api śakṣyāmi, tat kariṣyāmy ahaṃ tava.»

A king who desires victory, with his armies drawn up, should listen to this story of Shakra's victory; a tale of equal worth to the Veda. That is the very reason I am making sure you listen to this story of triumph, greatest of victors. High-souled men prosper when they are praised, Yudhi·shthira. But this war will prove to be the end of great-hearted warriors, Yudhi·shthira, and it will come to be through Duryódhana's transgression and the strength of Bhima and Árjuna.

If a man is self-disciplined and recites this tale of Indra's victory he will shake off his sins, win heaven, and be happy
in the next world as well as in the here and now. That man 18.20
will have no fear of enemies, nor will he fail to produce an heir. No disaster will befall him, and he will live a long life. He will have success in everything he does, and he will never be defeated!"

VAISHAMPÁYANA said:

Once Shalya had encouraged the king, bull of the Bharata race, the greatest of virtuous men honored Shalya as the law prescribed. And having listened to what Shalya had to say, Yudhi·shthira, the strong-armed son of Kunti, replied to the king of the Madras in these words: "There is no doubt that you will be Karna's charioteer. Karna's splendor must be thwarted by praise of Árjuna!"

SHALYA replied:

"I will do as you tell me, and what's more I will do anything else for you which is within my power."

VAIŚAMPĀYANA uvāca:

18.25 tatas tv āmantrya Kaunteyāñ Chalyo Madr'|âdhipas tadā
jagāma sa|balaḥ śrīmān Duryodhanam, arin|dama.

VAIŚAMPĀYANA uvāca:

19.1 YUYUDHĀNAS TATO vīraḥ Sātvatānāṃ mahā|rathaḥ
mahatā catur|aṅgeṇa balen' āgād Yudhiṣṭhiram.
tasya yodhā mahā|vīryā nānā|deśa|samāgatāḥ,
nana|praharaṇā vīrāḥ śobhayāñ cakrire balam.
paraśvadhair, bhindipālaiḥ, śūla|tomara|mudgaraiḥ,
parighair, yaṣṭibhiḥ, pāśaiḥ, karavālaiś ca nirmalaiḥ,
khaḍga|kārmuka|nirvyūhaiḥ, śaraiś ca vividhair api
taila|dhautaiḥ prakāśadbhiḥ sad" âśobhata vai balam.
19.5 tasya megha|prakāśasya sauvarṇaiḥ śobhitasya ca
babhūva rūpaṃ sainyasya meghasy' êva sa|vidyutaḥ.
akṣauhiṇī tu sā senā tadā Yaudhiṣṭhiraṃ balam
praviśy' ântar|dadhe, rājan, sāgaraṃ ku|nadī yathā.
tath" âiv' âkṣauhiṇīṃ gṛhya Cedīnām ṛṣabho balī
Dhṛṣṭaketur upāgacchat Pāṇḍavān a|mit'|âujasaḥ.
Māgadhaś ca Jayatseno Jārāsandhir mahā|balaḥ
akṣhauhiṇy' âiva sainyasya dharma|rājam upāgamat.
tath" âiva Pāṇḍyo, rāj'|êndra, sāgar'|ânūpa|vāsibhiḥ
vṛto bahu|vidhair yodhair Yudhiṣṭhiram uupāgamat.
19.10 tasya sainyam at'|îv' āsīt tasmin bala|samāgame
prekṣaṇīyataraṃ, rājan, su|veṣaṃ balavat tadā.

VAISHAMPÁYANA said:

Then, once Shalya, the king of the Madras, had taken his leave from the sons of Kunti, the eminent man left with his forces for Duryódhana, destroyer of your enemies. 18.25

VAISHAMPÁYANA said:

NEXT, YUYUDHÁNA, the great warrior hero of the Sát- 19.1
vatas, came to Yudhi·shthira with a massive four-flanked force of infantry, cavalry, chariots, and elephants. His warriors of mighty strength had gathered from various regions, and with their diverse weaponry the heroes made the army gleam. The force incessantly glimmered with axes, slingshots, lances, javelins, mallets, iron bludgeons, maces, chains, polished swords, scimitars, bows, helmets, as well as various types of arrows which were gleaming with the
oil rubbed into them. The army resembled a storm cloud 19.5
illuminated with golden flashes of lightning.

As the battalion entered Yudhi·shthira's forces it was absorbed, my king, as a stream is absorbed into an ocean. And so too Dhrishta·ketu, the powerful bull of the Chedis, took his battalion and went to join the Pándavas of immeasurable prowess. Mighty Jayat·sena of Mágadha, the son of Jara·sandha, also went to join the virtuous king with his battalion. Pandya too, lord of kings, surrounded by the many varied warriors who lived on the shore of the ocean, came to
join Yudhi·shthira. And his army was particularly impres- 19.10
sive to behold in the congregation of forces, my king, due to its strength and splendid uniform.

Drupadasy' âpy abhūt senā nānā|deśa|samāgataiḥ
śobhitā puruṣaiḥ śūraiḥ putraiś c' âsya mahā|rathaiḥ
tath" âiva rājā Matsyānāṃ Virāṭo vāhinī|patiḥ
pārvatīyair mahī|pālaiḥ sahitaḥ Pāṇḍavān iyāt.
itaś c' êtaś ca Pāṇḍūnāṃ samājagmur mah"|ātmanām
akṣauhiṇyas tu sapt' âitā vividha|dhvaja|saṅkulāḥ,
yuyutsamānāḥ Kurubhiḥ Pāṇḍavān samaharṣayan.
tath" âiva Dhārtarāṣṭrasya harṣaṃ samabhivardhayan
19.15 Bhagadatto mahī|pālaḥ senām akṣauhiṇīṃ dadau.
tasya Cīnaiḥ kirātaiś ca kāñcanair iva saṃvṛtam
babhau balam an|ādhṛṣyaṃ karṇikāra|vanaṃ yathā.
tathā Bhūriśravāḥ śūraḥ, Śalyaś ca, Kuru|nandana,
Duryodhanam upāyātāv akṣauhiṇyā pṛthak pṛthak.
Kṛtavarmā ca Hārdikyo Bhoj'|Ândha|Kukuraiḥ saha
akṣauhiṇy" âiva senāyā Duryodhanam upāgamat.
tasya taiḥ puruṣa|vyāghrair vana|mālā|dharair balam
aśobhata yathā mattair vanaṃ prakrīḍitair gajaiḥ.
Jayadratha|mukhāś c' ânye Sindhu|Sauvīra|vāsinaḥ
19.20 ājagmuḥ pṛthivī|pālāḥ kampayanta iv' âcalān.
teṣām akṣauhiṇī senā bahulā vibabhau tadā
vidhūyamāno vātena, bahu|rūpa iv' âmbudaḥ.
Sudakṣiṇaś ca Kāmbojo Yavanaiś ca Śakais tathā
upājagāma Kauravyam akṣauhiṇyā, viśām pate.
tasya senā|samāvāyaḥ śalabhānām iv' ābabhau,
sa ca samprāpya Kauravyaṃ tatr' âiv' ântar|dadhe tadā.

Drúpada brought an army gathered from various areas, radiant with brave men and his own mighty warrior sons. Viráta, king of the Matsyas and lord of his army, also came to the Pándavas, bringing with him mountainous chiefs. From all over, seven battalions, thronged with various banners, came to join the high-souled Pándavas, ready to fight against the Kurus, and by so doing they cheered the sons of Pandu.

But King Bhaga·datta likewise augmented Dhrita· 19.15
rashtra's joy by giving his battalion to him. His invincible army, packed with warriors from the mountains and lands in the north-east, was as stunning as a forest of *karnikára* flowers packed with golden *káñchana* plants. Brave Bhuri·shravas and Shalya joined Duryódhana with a battalion each, descendant of Kuru. Krita·varman and Hrídika, along with the Bhojas, Andhas, and Kúkuras, went to join Duryódhana with a single battalion of troops. And with its tiger-like men wearing garlands of forest flowers, the army shone as though it were a wood filled with playing elephants in rut.

Then came other kings of earth who lived by the Sindhu 19.20
and in Suvíra, led by Jayad·ratha, almost shaking the mountains. Their dense battalion resembled a motley-shaped rain cloud being driven by the wind. Kambója Sudákshina came to join the Kaurávya with one battalion, lord of men, along with the Greeks and Scythians. His assembled army resembled a swarm of locusts, but when it reached the Káuravan army it was subsumed by it.

tathā Māhiṣmatī|vāsī Nīlo nīl'|āyudhaiḥ saha
mahī|pālo mahā|vīryair dakṣiṇā|patha|vāsibhiḥ,
Āvantyau ca mahī|pālau mahā|bala|susaṃvṛtau
19.25 pṛthag akṣauhiṇībhyāṃ tāv abhiyātau Suyodhanam.
Kekayāś ca nara|vyāghrāḥ sodaryāḥ pañca pārthivā
saṃharṣayantaḥ Kauravyam akṣauhiṇyā samādravan.
tatas tatas tu sarveṣāṃ bhūmi|pānāṃ mah"|ātmanām
tisro 'nyāḥ samavartanta vāhinyo, Bharata'|rṣabha.
evam ekā|daś' āvṛttāḥ senā Duryodhanasya tāḥ
yuyutsamānāḥ Kaunteyān, nānā|dhvaja|samākulāḥ.
na Hāstinapure, rājann, avakāśo 'bhavat tadā
rājñāṃ sva|bala|mukhyānāṃ prādhāṇyen' âpi, Bhārata.
tataḥ pañca|nadaṃ c' âiva, kṛtsnaṃ ca Kuru|jāṅgalam,
19.30 tathā Rohitak'|âraṇyaṃ, maru|bhūmiś ca kevalā,
Ahicchatraṃ, Kālakūṭaṃ, Gaṅgā|kūlaṃ ca, Bhārata,
Vāraṇaṃ, Vāṭadhānaṃ ca, Yāmunaś c' âiva parvataḥ,
eṣa deśaḥ su|vistīṛnaḥ prabhūta|dhana|dhāṇyavān
babhūva Kauraveyāṇāṃ balen' âtīva saṃvṛtaḥ.
tatra sainyaṃ tathā|yuktaṃ dadarśa sa puro|hitaḥ
yaḥ sa Pāñcāla|rājena preṣitaḥ Kauravān prati.

King Nila who dwelled in Mahíshmati came with mighty heroes who lived in the wilderness of the south and bore dark weapons. The two kings of Avántya came to join Su- 19.25
yódhana, closely surrounded by a mighty force comprising of a battalion each. The five Kékayan tiger-like brother kings also rushed there with their battalion, pleasing the Kaurávya.

From all sides three other armies of all high-souled earth-lords came, O bull of the Bharata race. So, in all, eleven armies, thronging with various banners, turned to Duryódhana ready to fight the Kauntéyas. But there was not even enough space in Hástina·pura, my king, for the kings leading their own forces and their chief warriors, descendant of Bharata.

And so, the whole region of the five rivers, the Kuru
jungle, the Róhitaka forest, the entire desert, Ahi·chchátra, 19.30
Kala·kuta, the banks of the Ganges, descendant of Bharata, Várana, Vata·dhana, and the Yámuna mountains—this very extensive area, abounding in riches and crops, was completely brimming with the Kauravan army. And it was arranged in this manner that the priest, sent by the king of Pañchála to the Káuravas, saw the army.

# 20–21

# THE FIRST EMBASSY ARRIVES

VAIŚAMPĀYANA uvāca:

20.1 SA CA KAURAVYAM āsādya Drupadasya puro|hitaḥ
sat|kṛto Dhṛtarāṣṭreṇa, Bhīṣmeṇa Vidureṇa ca.
sarve kauśalyam uktv" ādau, pṛṣṭvā c' âivam an|āmayam
sarva|senā|praṇetṝṇāṃ madhye vākyam uvāca ha.
«sarvair bhavadbhir vidito rāja|dharmaḥ sanātanaḥ,
vāky'|ôpādāna|hetos tu vakṣyāmi vidite sati.
Dhṛtarāṣṭraś ca Pāṇḍuś ca sutāv ekasya viśrutau,
tayoḥ samānaṃ draviṇaṃ paitṛkaṃ, n' âtra saṃśayaḥ.
20.5 Dhṛtarāṣṭrasya ye putrāḥ, prāptaṃ taiḥ paitṛkaṃ vasu;
Pāṇḍu|putrāḥ kathaṃ nāma na prāptāḥ paitṛkaṃ vasu?
evaṃ gate Pāṇḍaveyair viditaṃ vaḥ purā yathā
na prāptaṃ paitṛkaṃ dravyaṃ Dhṛtarāṣṭreṇa saṃvṛtam,
prāṇ'|ântikair apy upāyaiḥ prayatadbhir an|ekaśaḥ
śeṣavanto na śakitā netuṃ vai Yama|sādanam.
punaś ca vardhitaṃ rājyaṃ sva|balena mah"|ātmabhiḥ,
chadman" âpahṛtaṃ kṣudrair Dhārtarāṣṭraiḥ sa|Saubalaiḥ!
tad apy anumataṃ karma yathā|yuktam anena vai!

VAISHAMPÁYANA continued:

ONCE DRÚPADA'S priest had approached the Kaurávya, he was treated well by Dhrita·rashtra, Bhishma, and Vídura. After he had told them of the health of all the Pándavas, and enquired after his hosts' well-being, he gave a speech in the midst of all the army generals. 20.1

"You all know the eternal code of kings, but though it is known, I will repeat it by way of introduction to my speech. Dhrita·rashtra and Pandu are known to be the sons of one and the same father, and there is no doubt that they had equal claim to their paternal property. Currently it is 20.5 Dhrita·rashtra's sons who have taken control of their ancestral inheritance, but how is it then that the sons of Pandu have not, in fact, inherited their paternal property?

This is how it stands, and you know how the Pándavas did not previously receive the substance of their inheritance as was set aside by Dhrita·rashtra. Their enemies have repeatedly tried various means, including attempted murder, but since they survived, the others have been unable to guide them to the house of Yama. Yet again, their kingdom prospered through those high-souled men's own strength, but it was taken from them deceitfully by the low-born sons of Dhrita·rashtra and Súbala! Dhrita·rashtra here even sanctioned this action in his usual manner!

vāsitāś ca mah"|âraṇye varṣāṇ' îha trayo|daśa.
20.10 sabhāyāṃ kleśitair vīraiḥ saha|bhāryais tathā bhṛśam,
araṇye vividhāḥ kleśāḥ saṃprāptās taiḥ su|dāruṇāḥ.
tathā Virāṭa|nagare, yony|antara|gatair iva,
prāptaḥ parama|saṃkleśo yathā pāpair mah"|ātmabhiḥ!
te sarvaṃ pṛṣṭhataḥ kṛtvā tat sarvaṃ pūrva|kilbiṣam
sām' âiva Kurubhiḥ sārdham icchanti Kuru|puṃgavāḥ.
teṣāṃ ca vṛttam ājñāya, vṛttaṃ Duryodhanasya ca,
anunetum ih' ârhanti Dhārtarāṣṭraṃ suhṛj|janāḥ.
na hi te vigrahaṃ vīrāḥ kurvanti Kurubhiḥ saha
a|vināśena lokasya kāṅkṣante Pāṇḍavāḥ svakam.
20.15 yaś c' âpi Dhārtarāṣṭrasya hetuḥ syād vigrahaṃ prati
sa ca hetur na mantavyo. balīyāṃsas tathā hi te!
akṣauhiṇyaś ca sapt' âiva Dharma|putrasya saṃgatāḥ
yuyutsamānāḥ Kurubhiḥ pratīkṣante 'sya śāsanam.
apare puruṣa|vyāghrāḥ sahasr'|âkṣauhiṇī|samāḥ
Sātyakir, Bhīmasenaś ca, yamau ca su|mahā|balau!
ekā|daś' âitāḥ pṛtanā ekataś ca samāgatāḥ
ekataś ca mahā|bāhur bahu|rūpī Dhanañjayaḥ!
yathā Kirīṭī sarvābhyaḥ senābhyo vyatiricyate,
evam eva mahā|bāhur Vāsudevo mahā|dyutiḥ.
20.20 bahulatvaṃ ca senānāṃ, vikramaṃ ca Kirīṭinaḥ,
buddhimattvaṃ ca Kṛṣṇasya buddhvā yudhyeta ko naraḥ?
te bhavanto yathā|dharmaṃ yathā|samayam eva ca
prayacchantu pradātavyaṃ. mā vaḥ kālo 'tyagād ayam!

So they lived in the great forest for thirteen years. Manifold, horrendously painful troubles befell those heroes in the forest after they and their wife had been so terribly tormented in the assembly. But it was in Viráta's city that they suffered such extreme distress that it was as if the high-souled men were in fact wicked, and born into another life! 20.10

But they have put all offences done to them in the past entirely behind them. The bull-like Kurus only want conciliation with their family. Their friends, who know how both they and Duryódhana behaved, ought to bring Dhrita·rashtra round to the idea. The heroes are not waging war with the Kurus, but the Pándavas just want to have what is theirs, avoiding the destruction of the world.

Whatever reason Dhartaráshtra gives for war, it should 20.15
not be believed. After all, the Pándavas are stronger! The son of Dharma has seven battalions gathered and ready to fight against the Kurus, just waiting for his command. And they have other tiger-like men who match a thousand legions, such as Sátyaki, Bhima·sena, and the hugely powerful twins! There may be eleven forces gathered on one side, but on the other is strong-armed and many-formed Dhanañ·jaya!

Diademed Kirítin surpasses all armies, just like strong-
armed, great, glorious Vasudéva. What man who under- 20.20
stood the extent of their armies, the prowess of Kirítin, and the intellect of Krishna, would fight against them? May you pay what is owed according to the system of morality and established custom. Don't let time pass you by!"

VAIŚAMPĀYANA uvāca:

21.1 TASYA TAD VACANAṂ śrutvā prajñā|vṛddho mahā|dyutiḥ
sampūjy' âinaṃ yathā|kālaṃ Bhīṣmo vacanam abravīt,
«diṣṭyā kuśalinaḥ sarve saha Dāmodareṇa te!
diṣṭyā sahāyavantaś ca, diṣṭyā dharme ca te ratāḥ.
diṣṭyā ca sandhi|kāmās te bhrātaraḥ Kuru|nandanāḥ!
diṣṭyā na yuddha|manasaḥ Pāṇḍavāḥ saha bāndhavaiḥ!
bhavatā satyam uktaṃ tu sarvam etan, na saṃśayaḥ;
atitīkṣṇaṃ tu te vākyaṃ brāhmaṇyād, iti me matiḥ.
21.5 a|saṃśayaḥ kleśitās te vane c' êha ca Pāṇḍavāḥ,
prāptāś ca dharmataḥ sarvaṃ pitur dhanam a|saṃśayam.
Kirīṭī balavān Pārthaḥ, kṛt'|âstraś ca mahā|rathaḥ.
ko hi Pāṇḍu|sutaṃ yuddhe viṣaheta Dhanañjayam,
api Vajra|dharaḥ sākṣāt, kim ut' ânye dhanur|bhṛtaḥ?
trayāṇām api lokānāṃ samartha, iti me matiḥ.»
Bhīṣme bruvati tad vākyaṃ dhṛṣṭam ākṣipya manyunā,
Duryodhanaṃ samālokya, Karṇo vacanam abravīt,
«na tatr' â|viditaṃ, brahman, loke bhūtena kena cit!
punar uktena kiṃ tena bhāṣitena punaḥ punaḥ?
21.10 Duryodhan'|ârthe Śakunir dyūte nirjitavān purā,
samayena gato 'raṇyaṃ Pāṇḍu|putro Yudhiṣṭhiraḥ.
sa taṃ samayam āśritya rājyaṃ n' êcchati paitṛkam,
balam āśritya Matsyānāṃ Pāñcālānāṃ ca mūrkhavat!

VAISHAMPÁYANA continued:

HAVING LISTENED to his speech, the great glorious Bhishma, advanced in wisdom, honored him and gave a speech to fit the occasion. 21.1

"How fortunate that they are all in good health along with Krishna Damódara! How fortunate that they have allies and take pleasure in lawful behavior. Thank heaven those brothers, the descendants of Kuru, are set on reconciliation! It is fortunate that the Pándavas and their family have not set their minds on battle!

There is no doubt that everything you have said is true, but to my mind your speech was too sharp, presumably
because you are a brahmin. It is not in question that the 21.5
Pándavas suffered in the forest as well as here, and there is no doubt that they have a lawful right to inherit their father's property. Kirítin, the son of Pritha, is a strong warrior, versed in weaponry. Who would be a match for Dhanañ·jaya, the son of Pandu, in battle, even if he were the wielder of thunderbolt incarnate, let alone other archers? He is the equal of the three worlds, or at least that is my opinion."

While Bhishma was speaking, Karna glanced at Duryódhana and resolutely challenged his words in anger, saying, "This is news to no one in this world, brahmin! Why
must it be repeated over and over again? Shákuni defeated 21.10
Yudhi·shthira, the son of Pandu, at a game of dice long ago for Duryódhana's sake, and so he went to the forest by the terms of the agreement. But he no longer wishes to abide by the agreement for his ancestral kingdom, and instead, in his stupidity, he is relying on the army of the Matsyas and Pañchálas!

Duryodhano bhayād, vidvan, na dadyāt pādam antataḥ!
dharmatas tu mahīṃ kṛtsnāṃ pradadyāc chatrave 'pi ca.
yadi kāṅkṣanti te rājyaṃ pitṛ|paitāmahaṃ punaḥ,
yathā|pratijñaṃ kālaṃ taṃ carantu vanam āśritāḥ!
tato Duryodhanasy' âṅke vartantām a|kuto|bhayāḥ.
a|dhārmikīṃ tu mā buddhiṃ maurkhyāt kurvantu kevalāt!
21.15 atha te dharmam utsṛjya yuddham icchanti Pāṇḍavāḥ,
āsādy' êmān Kuru|śreṣṭhān smariṣyanti vaco mama!»

BHĪṢMA uvāca:

«kiṃ nu, Rādheya, vācā te? karma tat smartum arhasi,
eka eva yadā Pārthaḥ ṣaḍ|rathāñ jitavān yudhi.
bahuśo jīyamānasya karma dṛṣṭaṃ tad" âiva te!
na ced evaṃ kariṣyāmo yad ayaṃ brāhmaṇo 'bravīt,
dhruvaṃ yudhi hatās tena bhakṣayiṣyāma pāṃsukān!»

VAIŚAMPĀYANA uvāca:

Dhṛtarāṣṭras tato Bhīṣmam anumānya prasādya ca,
avabhartsya ca Rādheyam, idaṃ vacanam abravīt:
«asmadd|hitaṃ vākyam idaṃ Bhīṣmaḥ Śāntanavo 'bravīt,
Pāṇḍavānāṃ hitaṃ c' âiva, sarvasya jagatas tathā.
21.20 cintayitvā tu Pārthebhyaḥ preṣayiṣyāmi Sañjayam.
sa bhavān pratiyātv adya Pāṇḍavān eva mā ciram.»
sa taṃ sat|kṛtya Kauravyaḥ preṣayām āsa Pāndavān.
sabhā|madhye samāhūya Sañjayaṃ vākyam abravīt:

Duryódhana will not budge an inch out of fear, wise man! If it were lawful he would hand over even the entire world to his enemy. If they want their paternal and ancestral kingdom back again, then let them abide by the agreement and wander in the forest for the stated time. Then let them remain at Duryódhana's side, free of fear from any quarter. But don't let them make unlawful decsions based on complete idiocy! If the Pándavas cast aside what is right and 21.15
want war, they will remember my words when they meet these greatest Kurus!"

BHISHMA replied:

"Who are you to say these things, Radhéya? You of all people ought to remember Partha's feat when he single-handedly defeated six chariot-warriors in battle. Your achievement then was to be repeatedly and resolutely defeated! If we do not do as this brahmin advises, we will certainly die at Árjuna's hand in battle and bite the dust!"

VAISHAMPÁYANA continued:

Dhrita·rashtra then assented and appeased Bhishma. He admonished Radhéya and said these words: "Bhishma, son of Shántanu, has given a speech which is not only to our advantage but also beneficial to the Pándavas and the entire
universe. Having given it some thought, I will send Sáñjaya 21.20
to the Parthas. But you, sir, should go back to the Pándavas now, without delay." So it was that once the Kaurávya had provided the proper hospitality, he sent him back to the Pándavas. Then he called Sáñjaya to the middle of the court and said this to him:

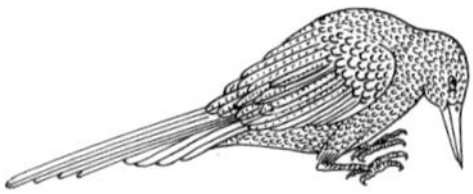

22–32

# SÁÑJAYA, THE SECOND ENVOY

DHṚTARĀṢṬRA uvāca:

22.1 «PRĀPTĀN ĀHUḤ, Sañjaya, Pāṇḍu|putrān
Upaplavye. tān vijānīhi gatvā.
Ajātaśatruṃ ca sabhājayethā:
‹diṣṭy" ānahya sthānam upasthitas tvam!›
sarvān vadeḥ, Sañjaya, svastimantaḥ
kṛcchraṃ vāsam a|tad|arhan niruṣya.
teṣāṃ śāntir vidyate 'smāsu śīghraṃ
mithy" ôpetānām upakāriṇāṃ satām.
n' âhaṃ kva cit, Sañjaya, Pāṇḍavānāṃ
mithyā|vṛttiṃ kāñ cana jātv apaśyam.
sarvā śriyaṃ hy ātma|vīryeṇa labdhāṃ
paryākārṣuḥ Pāṇḍavā mahyam eva.
doṣaṃ hy eṣāṃ n' âdhyagacchaṃ parīcchan
nityaṃ kañ cid yena garheya Pārthān.
dharm'|ârthābhyāṃ karma kurvanti nityaṃ,
sukha|priyā n' ânurudhyanti kāmāt.
22.5 gharmaṃ, śītaṃ, kṣut|pipāse tath" âiva,
nidrāṃ, tandrīṃ, krodha|harṣau, pramādam
dhṛtyā c' âiva prajñayā c' âbhibhūya
dharm'|ârtha|yogāt prayatanti Pārthāḥ.

DHRITA·RASHTRA said:

"THEY SAY THE sons of Pandu have reached Upa- 22.1
plávya, Sáñjaya. Go and inquire about them. Honor Ajáta·shatru, saying: 'How fortunate that you have come and stopped in this place!' Tell them all that they are blessed for having lived through their painful and undeserved exile, Sáñjaya. Peace between us will spring up quickly, for though they entered into the accord by being deceived, they are upright and good.

Sáñjaya, I have certainly never witnessed any dishonest behavior from the Pándavas. All the sons of Pandu won glory through their own heroism, and yet they were always deferential to me. I searched constantly but I could never discover a single fault with which I could reproach the Parthas. They always commit acts for virtue and profit, and though fond of joy, they are not overwhelmed by desire. They withstand heat and cold, and similarly withstand 22.5
hunger and thirst, sloth, sleep, anger, and joy and intoxication with wisdom and superiority. The Parthas strive for the practice of virtue and profit.

tyajanti mitreṣu dhanāni kāle
na saṃvāsāj jīryati teṣu maitrī.
yath"|ârha|mān'|ârtha|karā hi Pārthās,
teṣāṃ dveṣṭā n' âsty Ājamīḍhasya pakṣe,
anyatra pāpād viṣamān manda|buddher
Duryodhanāt kṣudratarāc ca Karṇāt.
teṣāṃ h' îmau hīna|sukha|priyāṇāṃ
mah"|ātmanāṃ saṃjanayato hi tejaḥ.
utthāna|vīryaḥ sukham edhamāno,
Duryodhanaḥ su|kṛtam manyate tat.
teṣāṃ bhāgaṃ yac ca manyeta bālaḥ
śakyaṃ hartuṃ jīvatāṃ Pāṇḍavānām!
yasy' Ârjunaḥ padavīṃ, Keśavaś ca,
Vṛkodaraḥ, Sātyako 'jātaśatroḥ,
Mādrī|putrau Sṛñjayāś c' âpi yānti,
purā yuddhāt sādhu tasya pradānam.
22.10 sa hy ev' âikaḥ pṛthivīṃ Savyasācī
Gāṇḍīva|dhanvā praṇuded ratha|sthaḥ,
tathā jiṣṇuḥ Keśavo 'py a|pradhṛṣyo
loka|trayasy' âdhipatir mah"|ātmā.
tiṣṭheta kas tasya martyaḥ purastād
yaḥ sarva|lokeṣu vareṇya ekaḥ,
parjanya|ghoṣān pravapan śar'|âughān
pataṅga|saṅghān iva śīghra|vegān?
diśaṃ hy udīcīm api c' ôttarān Kurūn
Gāṇḍīva|dhanv" âika|ratho jigāya.
dhanaṃ c' âiṣām āharat Savyasācī
sen"|ânugān Draviḍāṃś c' âiva cakre.
yaś c' âiva devān Khāṇḍave Savyasācī
Gāṇḍīva|dhanvā prajigāya s'|Êndrān!

They give away their money to friends as they please, and their friendship does not break with time. The sons of Pritha bestow advantages and honours according to merit, and they have no enemy in the family of Ajamídha—that is, apart from the wicked, disagreeable, and slow-witted Duryódhana, and Karna, the lowest of the low. Those two only serve to generate the splendor of those high-souled men whose pleasures and luxuries were taken from them. Duryódhana, bursting with energy and raised in luxury, thinks that he has acted correctly. But only a child would imagine that the Pándavas' share can be kept away from them for their whole lives!

Árjuna, Késhava, Vrikódara, and Sátyaka follow in Ajáta·shatru's footsteps, as do Madri's twin sons, and the Sríñjayas. Giving him his share before it comes to war would be best. The ambidextrous Gandíva-wielding archer stands 22.10
on his chariot and single-handedly drives the earth, and so too does triumphant, invincible Késhava, the high-souled lord of the three worlds. Which mortal man would stand before the single greatest person in all worlds, who scatters his clouds of arrows which boom like thunder and rush at speed like flocks of birds?

The Gandíva-wielding archer defeated the Northern region and the Northernmost Kurus on a single chariot. Ambidextrous Savya·sachin seized their property and made the Dravidians soldiers in his army. He is the ambidextrous Gandíva-archer who defeated the gods, led by Indra, at Khándava! That son of Pandu made an offering to the fire god and thereby augmented the fame and honor of the Pándavas.

upāharat Pāṇḍavo jāta|vedase
yaśo mānaṃ vardhayan Pāṇḍavānām.
gadā|bhṛtāṃ n' âsti samo 'tra Bhīmādd,
hasty|āroho n' âsti samaś ca tasya.
rathe 'rjunād āhur a|hīnam enaṃ,
bāhvor balen' âyuta|nāga|vīryam!
22.15 su|śikṣitaḥ kṛta|vairas tarasvī
dahet kṣudrāṃs tarasā Dhārtarāṣṭrān.
sad" âty|amarṣī na balāt sa śakyo
yuddhe jetuṃ Vāsaven' âpi sākṣāt.
su|cetasau balinau śighra|hastau
su|śikṣitau bhrātarau Phālgunena,
śyenau yathā pakṣi|pūgān rujantau,
Madrī|putrau śeṣayetāṃ na śatrūn.
etad balaṃ pūrṇam asmākam evaṃ
yat satyaṃ tān prāpya n' âst', îti manye.
teṣāṃ madhye vartamānas tarasvī
Dhṛṣṭadyumnaḥ Pāṇḍavānām ih' âikaḥ.
sah' âmātyaḥ Somakānāṃ prabarhaḥ
saṃtyakt'|ātmā Pāṇḍav'|ârthe śruto me.
Ajātaśatruṃ prasaheta ko 'nyo
yeṣāṃ sa syād agra|ṇīr Vṛṣṇi|siṃhaḥ?
sah' ôṣitaś carit'|ârtho vayaḥ|stho
Mātsyeyānām adhipo vai Virāṭaḥ
sa vai sa|putraḥ Pāṇḍav'|ârthe ca śaśvad,
Yudhiṣṭhire bhakta, iti śrutaṃ me.
22.20 avaruddhā rathinaḥ Kekayebhyo
mah"|êṣvāsā bhrātaraḥ pañca santi,
Kekayebhyo rājyam ākāṅkṣamāṇā
yuddh'|ârthinaś c' ânuvasanti Pārthān.

There is no mace-bearer to match Bhima, nor any elephant rider to equal him. They say he rivals Árjuna on a chariot, and the strength of his arms equals the power of ten thousand elephants! Well-trained and spirited, turned 22.15
hostile he would quickly burn the inferior Dhartaráshtras. Not even Vásava incarnate would be able to forcibly defeat this eternally and excessively truculent man in battle.

The clever, strong, swift-handed brothers, the twin sons of Madri, have been well trained by Phálguna, and just as a pair of eagles dash flocks of birds to pieces, so those two will not spare their enemies. So I reckon that our army, full as it is, will truly turn out to be nothing when it comes across them. For energetic Dhrishta·dyumna is among them, like one of the Pándavas. I have heard that the most excellent of the Sómakas is prepared to sacrifice his life for the Pándava's cause, along with his ministers. Who else could defeat Ajáta·shatru, whose leader is that Vrishni lion?

Viráta, the aged king of the Matsyas, and his sons have taken the Pándava's side forever, because the sons of Pandu lived with him and served him. In fact, I hear that he is Yudhi·shthira's close friend. The five brother warriors who 22.20
were banished from the Kékayans are great archers, and since they are eager to take the kingdom away from the Kékayans they live with the Parthas, keen for war. I hear that all the heroic earth-lords are gathered for the Pándava's cause and encamped. I also hear that those brave men are

sarvāṃś ca vīrān pṛthivī|patīnāṃ
samāgatān Pāṇḍav'|ârthe niviṣṭān
śūrān ahaṃ bhaktimataḥ śṛṇomi,
prītyā yuktān, saṃśritān dharma|rājam.
giry|āśrayā durga|nivāsinaś ca,
yodhāḥ pṛthivyāṃ kula|jāti|śuddhāḥ,
mlecchāś ca nān"|āyudha|vīryavantaḥ,
samāgatāḥ Pāṇḍav'|ârthe niviṣṭāḥ.
Pāṇḍyaś ca rājā samit'|Îndra|kalpo
yodha|pravīrair bahubhiḥ sametaḥ
samāgataḥ Pāṇḍav'|ârthe mah"|ātmā
loka|pravīro '|prativīrya|tejāḥ.
astraṃ Droṇād, Arjunād, Vāsudevāt,
Kṛpād, Bhīṣmād yena vṛtaṃ śṛṇomi,
yaṃ taṃ Kārṣṇi|pratimam āhur ekaṃ,
sa Sātyakiḥ Pāṇḍav'|ârthe niviṣṭaḥ.
22.25 upāśritāś Cedi|Karūṣakāś ca
sarv'|ôdyogair bhūmi|pālāḥ sametāḥ.
teṣāṃ madhye sūryam iv' ātapantaṃ,
śriyā vṛtaṃ Cedi|patiṃ jvalantam,
a|stambhanīyaṃ yudhi manyamāno,
jyāṃ karṣatāṃ śreṣṭhatamaṃ pṛthivyām,
sarv'|ôtsāhaṃ kṣatriyāṇāṃ nihatya
prasahya Kṛṣṇas tarasā mamarda.

loyal and have joined and entered the service of the king of virtue with pleasure.

Mountain soldiers and warriors who live in impassable areas, the nobly born and pure-line warriors on the earth, and mighty barbarians with diverse weaponry have gathered for the Pándava's cause and encamped. High-souled King Pandya, like Indra in battle, a leading hero of inescapable splendor in this world, has come with numerous hero warriors for the Pándava's cause. I hear that Sátyaki, who learned about weapons from Drona, Árjuna, Vasudéva, Kripa, and from Bhishma, Sátyaki who they say is the spitting image of Karshni, has settled on the Pándava's cause.

The Chedi and Karúshaka kings have gathered and gone 22.25
over to their side with all their resources. The one from among them who burned like the sun, the king of the Chedis who blazed, full of glory, a man considered unstoppable in battle, and the greatest of those who draw a bowstring on earth—that most energetic of kshatriyas was the man whom Krishna defeated, conquered, and energetically crushed.

yaśo|mānau vardhayan Pāṇḍavānāṃ
pur" âbhinac Chiśupālaṃ samīke*
yasya sarve vardhayanti sma mānaṃ
Karūṣa|rāja|pramukhā nar'|êndrāḥ.
tam a|sahyaṃ Keśavaṃ tatra matvā
Sugrīva|yuktena rathena Kṛṣṇam,
ke prādravaṃś Cedi|patiṃ vihāya,
siṃhaṃ dṛṣṭvā kṣudra|mṛgā iv' ânye.
yas taṃ pratīpas tarasā pratyudīyād
āśaṃsamāno dvai|rathe Vāsudevam
so 'śeta Kṛṣṇena hataḥ parāsur
vāten' êv' ônmathitaḥ karṇikāraḥ.
22.30 parākramaṃ me yad avedayanta
teṣām arthe, Sañjaya, Keśavasya,
anusmaraṃs tasya karmāṇi Viṣṇor,
Gāvalgaṇen', âdhigacchāmi śāntim.
na jātu tāñ chatrur anyaḥ saheta
yeṣāṃ sa syād agra|ṇīr Vṛṣṇi|siṃhaḥ!
pravepate me hṛdayaṃ bhayena
śrutvā Kṛṣṇāv eka|rathe sametau.
na ced gacchet saṅgaraṃ manda|buddhis,
tābhyāṃ labhec charma tadā suto me!
no cet Kurūn, Sañjaya, nirdahetām
Indrā|Viṣṇū daitya|senāṃ yath" âiva!
mato hi me Śakra|samo Dhanañjayaḥ
sanātano Vṛṣṇi|vīraś ca Viṣṇuḥ.

Augmenting the glory and honor of the Pándavas, Krishna long ago broke Shishu·pala in battle, Shishu·pala whose distinction all earth-lords, led by the king of Karú-shaka, inflated. But those men thought Késhava Krishna was unbeatable on his chariot yoked to Sugríva, so they ran away and left the king of the Chedis, just as feeble deer run when they see a lion. The king rose up with strength to face him, hoping to win a chariot duel against Vasudéva, but instead he fell dead, killed by Krishna, like a *karnikára* tree uprooted by the wind.

Since they told me about Késhava's prowess on behalf of 22.30
the Pándavas, Sáñjaya, and as I remember Vishnu's feats, I can find no peace, son of Gaválgana. No enemy would ever defeat those whose leader was the Vrishni lion! My heart trembled with fear when I heard that both Krishnas were to stand together on a single chariot. If my slow-witted son does not go to battle against them he may find some peace, but if he does then those two will burn the Kurus, Sáñjaya, just as Indra and Vishnu burned the army of Daityas! To my mind Dhanañ·jaya is Shakra's equal and the Vrishni hero is eternal Vishnu.

dharm'|ārāmo, hrī|niṣevas, tarasvī
Kuntī|putraḥ Pāṇḍavo 'jātaśatruḥ.
Duryodhanena nikṛto manasvī
no cet kruddhaḥ pradahed Dhārtarāṣṭrān!
n' âhaṃ tathā hy Arjunād, Vāsudevād,
Bhīmād v" âhaṃ, yamayor vā bibhemi,
22.35 yathā rājñaḥ krodha|dīptasya, sūta,
manyor ahaṃ bhītataraḥ sad" âiva!
mahā|tapā brahmacaryeṇa yuktaḥ
saṅkalpo 'yaṃ mānasas tasya siddhyet.
tasya krodhaṃ, Sañjay', âhaṃ samīke*
sthāne jānan, bhṛśam asmy adya bhītaḥ!
sa gaccha śīghraṃ prahito rathena
Pāñcāla|rājasya camū|niveśanam,
Ajātaśatruṃ kuśalaṃ sma pṛccheḥ
punaḥ punaḥ prīti|yuktaṃ vades tvam.
Janārdanaṃ c' âpi sametya, tāta,
mahā|mātraṃ vīryavatām udāram,
an|āmayaṃ mad|vacanena pṛccher:
‹Dhṛtarāṣṭraḥ Pāṇḍavaiḥ śāntim īpsuḥ.›
na tasya kiñ cid vacanaṃ na kuryāt
Kuntī|putro Vāsudevasya, sūta,
priyaś c' âiṣām ātma|samaś ca Kṛṣṇo
vidvāṃś c' âiṣāṃ karmaṇi nitya|yuktaḥ.

Ajáta·shatru, the energetic son of Kunti and Pandu, delights in virtue and practices modesty. This intelligent man was mistreated by Duryódhana. Pray god he does not burn the Dhartaráshtras in his fury! I am not as afraid of Árjuna
or Vasudéva, or Bhima, or the twins, as I am constantly 22.35
terrified, *suta*, of the fury of that king who blazes with anger! He is a great ascetic and disciplined with his Vedic studies, and his mind's purpose will be achieved. And knowing that his anger on the battlefield will be righteous, I am terribly afraid right now, Sáñjaya!

So, when sent, go quickly on your chariot to the king of Pañchála's army encampment, and ask after Ajáta·shatru's health over and over again, making sure your tone is full of affection. And when you meet Janárdana, my friend, that illustrious and most excellent of heroes, you should inquire about his health according to my instructions, and say to him: 'Dhrita·rashtra desires peace with the Pándavas.' There is nothing which the son of Kunti would not do if Vasudéva told him to, *suta*, for Krishna is as dear to them as their own selves, and in return that wise man is always devoted to what they do.

samānītān Pāṇḍavān, Sṛñjayāṃś ca,
Janārdanaṃ, Yuyudhānaṃ, Virāṭam,
22.40 an|āmayaṃ mad|vacanena pṛccheḥ
sarvās tathā Draupadeyāṃś ca pañca.
yad yat tatra prāpta|kālaṃ parebhyas
tvaṃ manyethā, Bhāratānāṃ hitaṃ ca,
tad bhāṣethāḥ, Sañjaya, rāja|madhye,
na mūrcchayed yan na ca yuddha|hetuḥ.»

VAIŚAMPĀYANA uvāca:

23.1 RĀJÑAS TU VACANAṂ śrutvā Dhṛtarāṣṭrasya Sañjayaḥ
Upaplavyaṃ yayau draṣṭuṃ Pāṇḍavān a|mit'|âujasaḥ.
sa tu rājānam āsādya Kuntī|putraṃ Yudhiṣṭhiram,
abhivādya tataḥ pūrvaṃ sūta|putro 'bhyabhāṣata:
Gāvalgaṇiḥ Sañjayaḥ sūta|sūnur
Ajātaśatrum avadat pratītaḥ:
«diṣṭyā, rājaṃs, tvām a|rogaṃ prapaśye
sahāyavantaṃ ca mah"|Êndra|kalpam!
an|āmayaṃ pṛcchati tv" Āmbikeyo
vṛddho rājā Dhṛtarāṣṭro manīṣī.
kac cid Bhīmaḥ kuśalī Pāṇḍav'|âgryo,
Dhanañjayas, tau ca Mādrī|tanūjau?
23.5 kac cit Kṛṣṇā Draupadī rāja|putrī,
satya|vratā vīra|patnī sa|putrā,
manasvinī yatra ca vāñcchasi tvam
iṣṭān kāmān, Bhārata, svasti|kāmaḥ?»

So when you meet the Pándavas all gathered together with the Sríñjayas, Janárdana, Yuyudhána, and Viráta, you 22.40
should ask after their health, according to my instructions, and also after the health of all five of Dráupadi's sons. And in the midst of the kings, say to them whatever you deem appropriate for the occasion as well as advantageous for the Bháratas, Sáñjaya, so long as it does not aggravate them and become a cause for war."

VAISHAMPÁYANA continued:

ONCE HE HAD heard King Dhrita·rashtra's orders, Sáñ- 23.1
jaya went to Upaplávya to see the boundlessly energetic Pándavas. He approached King Yudhi·shthira, the son of Kunti. First the *suta*'s son saluted him, and then he spoke.

Sáñjaya, son of the *suta* Gaválgana, addressed Ajáta·shatru unhesitatingly: "How fortunate that I see you, king, in good health, the image of mighty Indra, along with your companions! The wise, aged King Dhrita·rashtra, son of Ámbika, inquires after your health. Is Bhima, the leading Pándava, well? And what of Dhanañ·jaya and Madri's twin sons? How is princess Krishná Dráupadi, along with her 23.5
sons—loyal wife to her heroic husbands, the intelligent lady in whom you search for your hearts' desires, Bhárata, and for whom you wish good fortune?"

YUDHIṢṬHIRA uvāca:
«Gāvalgaṇe Sañjaya, svāgataṃ te!
priyāmahe te vayaṃ darśanena.
an|āmayaṃ pratijāne tav' âhaṃ
sah' ânujaiḥ kuśalī c' âsmi, vidvan.
cirād idaṃ kuśalaṃ Bhāratasya
śrutvā rājñaḥ Kuru|vṛddhasya, sūta,
manye sākṣād dṛṣṭam ahaṃ nar'|êndraṃ
dṛṣṭv" âiva tvāṃ, Sañjaya, prīti|yogāt.
pitā|maho naḥ sthaviro manasvī,
mahā|prājñaḥ sarva|dharm'|ôpapannaḥ,
sa Kauravyaḥ kuśalī, tāta, Bhīṣmo?
yathā|pūrvaṃ vṛttir asty asya kac cit?
kac cid rājā Dhṛtarāṣṭraḥ, sa|putro,
Vaicitravīryaḥ kuśalī mah"|ātmā?
mahā|rājo Bāhlikaḥ Prātipeyaḥ,
kac cid vidvān kuśalī, sūta|putra?
23.10 sa Somadattaḥ kuśalī, tāta, kac cid?
Bhūriśravāḥ, Satyasandhaḥ, Śalaś ca,
Droṇaḥ sa|putraś ca, Kṛpaś ca vipro,
mah"|êṣvāsāḥ kac cid ete 'py a|rogāḥ?
mahā|prajñāḥ, sarva|śāstr'|âvadātā,
dhanur|bhṛtāṃ mukhyatamāḥ pṛthivyām,
kac cin mānaṃ, tāta, labhanta ete?
dhanur|bhṛtaḥ kac cid ete 'py a|rogāḥ?*
sarve Kurubhyaḥ spṛhayanti, Sañjaya,
dhanur|dharā ye pṛthivyāṃ pradhānāḥ,
yeṣāṃ rāṣṭre nivasati darśanīyo
mah"|êṣvāsaḥ śīlavān Droṇa|putraḥ?
Vaiśyā|putraḥ kuśalī, tāta, kac cin

YUDHI·SHTHIRA replied:

"Welcome, Sáñjaya, son of Gaválgana! We are delighted to see you. I can confirm I am in good health; I am well, as are my brothers, wise man. It was a long time ago now that I last heard how the aged Kuru, King Bhárata, was doing, *suta*. I can believe I am looking at that lord of men himself when I look affectionately at you, Sáñjaya. How is our venerable, wise grandfather, who is so intelligent and endowed with every virtue? Is Kaurávya Bhishma in good health, young man? Is his character still the same as it always was?

Is high-souled King Dhrita·rashtra, son of Vichítra·virya, in good health along with his sons? And what about great King Báhlika, son of Pratípa—is that wise man well, son of a *suta*? Is Soma·datta in good shape, my friend? And 23.10
what about Bhuri·shravas, Satya·sandha, and Shala? How are Drona and his son doing? And what about the brahmin Kripa? Are all those great archers in fine fettle? Do those chief archers on earth, supremely wise and excellent in every science, receive due honor, my friend? And are those bowmen free of disease? Everyone envies the Kurus, Sáñjaya, because they are the foremost of bowmen on earth and Drona's handsome and virtuous archer son lives in their kingdom.

What of Yuyútsu, the son of a vaishya woman—is that highly intelligent prince in good health, young man? And

mahā|prājño rāja|putro Yuyutsuḥ?
Karno 'mātyaḥ kuśalī, tāta, kac cit,
Suyodhano yasya mando vidheyaḥ?
striyo vṛddhā Bhāratānāṃ jananyo,
mahānasyo dāsa|bhāryāś ca, sūta,
vadhvaḥ, putrā, bhāgineyā, bhaginyo,
dauhitrā vā kac cid apy a|vyalīkāḥ?
23.15 kac cid rājā brāhmaṇānāṃ yathāvat
pravartate pūrvavat, tāta, vṛttim?
kac cid dāyān māmakān Dhārtarāṣṭro
dvi|jātīnāṃ, Sañjaya, n' ôpahanti?
kac cid rājā Dhṛtarāṣṭraḥ sa|putra
upekṣate brāhmaṇ'|âtikramān vai,
svargasya kac cin na tathā vartma|bhūtām
upekṣate teṣu sad" âiva vṛttim?
etaj jyotiś c' ôttamaṃ jīva|loke
śuklaṃ prajānāṃ vihitaṃ vidhātrā,
te ced doṣaṃ na niyacchanti mandāḥ
kṛtsno nāśo bhavitā Kauravāṇām.
kac cid rājā Dhṛtarāṣṭraḥ sa|putro
bubhūṣate vṛttim amātya|varge?
kac cin na bhedena jijīviṣanti
suhṛd|rūpā dur|hṛdaiś c' āikamatyāt?

what of Karna, the minister whom the fool Suyódhana depends upon—is he well, my friend? What about the old ladies, the mothers of the Bháratas, the kitchen girls, and the wives of the slaves, *suta*, what about the daughters-in-law, sons, nephews, sisters, and grandsons—are they also keeping well?

Does the king continue his conduct towards the brah- 23.15
mins as before, young man? Dhartaráshtra hasn't taken away the gifts I gave to the twiceborn long ago, has he, Sáñjaya? Do King Dhrita·rashtra and his son overlook disrepect from brahmins but never overlook their livelihood, since they are the path to heaven? This is the supreme, bright light which the creator set up for creatures in the land of the living, and if the fools do not curb their sin then the result will be total destruction of the Kurus. Have King Dhrita·rashtra and his son arranged support for his group of ministers? They don't have enemies who wish to live in disharmony and who only pretend to be their friends because they have the same opinions, do they?

kac cin na pāpaṃ kathayanti, tāta,
te Pāṇḍavānāṃ Kuravaḥ sarva eva?
Droṇaḥ sa|putraś ca Kṛpaś ca vīro
n' âsmāsu pāpāni vadanti kac cit?
23.20 kac cid rājye Dhṛtarāṣṭraṃ sa|putraṃ
samety' āhur Kuravaḥ sarva eva?
kac cid dṛṣṭvā dasyu|saṃghān sametān
smaranti Pārthasya yudhāṃ praṇetuḥ?
maurvī|bhuj'|âgra|prahitān sma, tāta,
dodhūyamānena dhanur|dhareṇa
Gāṇḍīva|nunnān stanayitnu|ghoṣān
ajihma|gān kac cid anusmaranti?
na c' âpaśyaṃ kañ cid ahaṃ pṛthivyāṃ
yodhaṃ samaṃ v" âdhikam Arjunena,
yasy' âika|ṣaṣṭir niśitās tīkṣṇa|dhārāḥ
su|vāsasaḥ saṃmato hasta|vāpaḥ!
gadā|pāṇir Bhīmasenas tarasvī
pravepayañ chatru|saṅghān anīke,
nāgaḥ prabhinna iva naḍvaleṣu
caṅkramyate, kac cid enaṃ smaranti?
Mādrī|putraḥ Sahadevaḥ Kaliṅgān
samāgatān ajayad Dantakūre,
vāmen' âsyan dakṣiṇen' âiva yo vai,
mahā|balaṃ kac cid enaṃ smaranti?
23.25 purā jetuṃ Nakulaḥ preṣito 'yaṃ
Śibīṃs, Trigartān, Sañjaya, paśyatas te,
diśaṃ pratīcīṃ vaśam ānayan me,
Mādrī|sutaṃ kac cid enaṃ smaranti?
parābhavo Dvaita|vane ya āsīd
dur|maṃtrite ghoṣayātr"|āgatānām,

The Kurus don't all talk about any wrong-doing on the
Pándavas' part, do they, my friend? Drona, his son, and
the hero Kripa don't talk about sins of ours, do they? The 23.20
Kurus don't all discuss it when they meet Dhrita·rashtra
and his son in his kingdom, do they? When they see hordes of barbarians gathered together, do they remember Partha, the leader of warriors? Do they recall the straight-flying arrows attached by the hand to the bowstring, young man, that sounded like thunder when fired from Gandíva by the archer as he shakes violently? For I have not seen any warrior on earth to compare or surpass Árjuna, whose arrow-firing hand is the equivalent of sixty-one sharp-pointed, sharp-edged, well-feathered arrows!

Do they remember energetic Bhima·sena, mace in hand,
causing companies of his enemies to tremble within the
ranks, like a rutting elephant roaming among the reedbeds?
Do they remember mighty Saha·deva, the son of Madri,
who defeated the gathered Kalíngas at Danta·kura, shooting with his left and right arm? Do they remember Nákula, 23.25
son of Madri, who long ago was sent against the Shibis and Trigártans, and brought the western region under my control while you watched, Sáñjaya?

Do they perhaps remember the bloodshed at the Dvaita Forest, when they came for their ill-advised herdsmen procession, and Bhima·sena and Jaya released the fools who had

yatra mandāñ chatru|vaśaṃ prayātān
amocayad Bhīmaseno Jayaś ca,
ahaṃ paścād Arjunam abhyarakṣam;
Mādrī|putrau Bhīmaseno 'py arakṣat;
Gāṇḍīva|dhanvā śatru|saṅghān udasya
svasty" āgamat; kañ cid enaṃ smaranti?
na karmaṇā sādhun" âikena nūnaṃ
sukhaṃ śakyaṃ vai bhavat' îha, Sañjaya,
sarv'|ātmanā parijetuṃ vayaṃ cen
na śaknumo Dhṛtarāṣṭrasya putram?»

SAÑJAYA uvāca:

24.1 «YATH" ĀTTHA ME, Pāṇḍava, tat tath" âiva,
Kurūn, Kuru|śreṣṭha, janaṃ ca pṛcchasi.
an|āmayās, tāta, manasvinas te,
Kuru|śreṣṭhān pṛcchasi, Pārtha, yāṃs tvam.
santy eva vṛddhāḥ sādhavo Dhārtarāṣṭrāḥ*
santy eva pāpāḥ, Pāṇḍava, tasya viddhi,
dadyād ripubhyo 'pi hi Dhārtarāṣṭraḥ
kuto dāyāl lopayed brāhmaṇānām?
yad yuṣmākaṃ vartate 'sau na dharmyam
a|drugdheṣu drugdhavat, tan na sādhu.
mitra|dhruk syāt Dhṛtarāṣṭraḥ sa|putraḥ
yuṣmān dviṣan sādhu|vṛttān a|sādhuḥ.
na c' ânujānāti bhṛśaṃ ca tapyate.
śocaty antaḥ sthaviro, 'jātaśatro.
śṛṇoti hi brāhmaṇānāṃ sametya
mitra|drohaḥ pātakebhyo garīyān.
24.5 smaranti tubhyaṃ, nara|deva, saṃyuge,
yuddhe ca Jiṣṇoś ca yudhāṃ praṇetuḥ.
samutkṛṣṭe dundubhi|śaṅkha|śabde

walked right into enemy control? While I guarded Árjuna's back, and Bhima·sena defended the twin sons of Madri, the Gandíva bowman disposed of hordes of the enemy and came out successful! But surely at this point good relations cannot be salvaged by a single good deed, Sáñjaya, if we cannot with our whole hearts win over Dhrita·rashtra's son?"

SÁÑJAYA said:

"INDEED, PÁNDAVA, it is just as you say, but you ask about 24.1
the Kurus, greatest Kuru of all, and about their leaders. Those wise men, the most excellent Kurus about whom you enquired, are all in good health, Partha my friend. Know that there are good old men who serve Dhrita·rashtra, and there are also wicked men, Pándava, but since the Dhartaráshtra would even provide for his enemies, what reason would he have to rob wealth from the brahmins? Behaving unlawfully towards you and harassing the innocent is not proper. Dhrita·rashtra would be guilty of betraying their friends if, like his son, he wrongly hated you even though you are honorable in your conduct.

He does not excuse the wrongs done to you, and it distresses him terribly. The old man grieves inside, Ajáta·shatru. He gathers brahmins and hears from them that treachery
towards family is the most serious of sins. They do remem- 24.5
ber you, god among men, when they meet, and they remember Jishnu, the leader of warriors in battle. And they remember Bhima·sena, mace in hand, when the sounds of conches and drums are raised. They recall Madri's twin sons,

gadā|pāṇiṃ Bhīmasenaṃ smaranti.
Mādrī|sutau c' âpi raṇ'|āji|madhye
sarvā diśaḥ saṃpatantau smaranti,
senāṃ varṣantau śara|varṣair a|jasraṃ,
mahā|rathau samare duṣ|prakampau.
na tv eva manye puruṣasya, rājann,
an|āgataṃ jñāyate yad bhaviṣyam,
tvaṃ cet tathā sarva|dharm'|ôpapannaḥ
prāptaḥ kleśaṃ, Pāṇḍava, kṛcchra|rūpam.
tvam ev' âitat kṛcchra|gataś ca bhūyaḥ
samī|kuryāḥ prajñay", Âjātaśatro.
na kām'|ârthaṃ santyajeyur hi dharmaṃ
Pāṇḍoḥ sutāḥ sarva ev' Êndra|kalpāḥ.
tvam ev' âitat prajñay", Âjātaśatro,
samī|kuryā, yena śarm' āpnuyus te
Dhārtarāṣṭrāḥ, Pāṇḍavāḥ, Sṛñjayāś ca,
ye c' âpy anye sanniviṣṭā nar'|êndrāḥ.
yan māṃ bravīd Dhṛtarāṣṭro niśāyām,
Ajātaśatro, vacanaṃ pitā te
24.10 sah' âmātyaḥ saha|putraś ca, rājan,
sametya tāṃ vācam imāṃ nibodha.»

YUDHIṢṬHIRA uvāca:

25.1 «SAMĀGATĀḤ Pāṇḍavāḥ Sṛñjayāś ca,
Janārdano, Yuyudhāno, Virāṭaḥ,
yat te vākyaṃ Dhṛtarāṣṭr'|ânuśiṣṭaṃ,
Gāvalgaṇe, brūhi tat, sūta|putra.»

SAÑJAYA uvāca:

«Ajātaśatruṃ ca, Vṛkodaraṃ ca,
Dhanañjayaṃ, Mādravatī|sutau ca,

those great unshakeable warriors, who rush round in all directions in the middle of the battlefield, unremittingly raining downpours of arrows onto the army.

I believe that no one knows what a man's future will hold, king, if you, endowed with every virtue, found trouble and distress, Pándava. You will more than make up for the suffering you underwent, Ajáta·shatru, with your wisdom. None of the Indra-like sons of Pandu would ever fail morally for the sake of desire. It will be you, Ajáta·shatru, who will make up for the past with your wisdom so that the Dhartaráshtras, the Pándavas, the Sríñjayas, and the other
lords of men who have gathered will find protection. Now 24.10
listen to what Dhrita·rashtra told me at night when he met with his sons and ministers, king; listen to your father's words, Ajáta·shatru."

YUDHI·SHTHIRA said:

"THE PÁNDAVAS, Sríñjayas, Janárdana, Yuyudhána, and 25.1
Viráta have all gathered, and so, son of the *suta* Gaválgana, tell us what Dhrita·rashtra instructed you to say."

SÁÑJAYA said:

"Ajáta·shatru, wolf-bellied Bhima, Dhanañ·jaya, and Madri's twins, I salute you, and Vasudéva Shauri, as well as Yuyudhána, Chekitána, Viráta, and also the venerable king

āmantraye Vāsudevaṃ ca Śauriṃ,
Yuyudhānaṃ, Cekitānaṃ, Virāṭam,
Pañcālāṇām adhipaṃ c' âiva vṛddhaṃ,
Dhṛṣṭadyumnaṃ Pārṣataṃ Yājñasenim.
sarve vācaṃ śṛṇut' êmāṃ madīyāṃ
vakṣyāmi yāṃ bhūtim icchan Kurūṇām.
śamaṃ rājā Dhṛtarāṣṭro 'bhinandann
ayojayat tvaramāṇo rathaṃ me.
sa|bhrātṛ|putra|svajanasya rājñas
tad rocatāṃ. Pāṇḍavānāṃ śamo 'stu!
25.5 sarvair dharmaiḥ samupetās tu Pārthaḥ:
saṃsthānena, mārdaven' ārjavena.
jātāḥ kule hy, a|nṛśaṃsā, vadānyā,
hrī|niṣevāḥ, karmaṇāṃ niścaya|jñāḥ.
na yujyate karma yuṣmāsu hīnaṃ,
sattvaṃ hi vas tādṛśaṃ, bhīma|senāḥ!
udbhāsate hy añjana|binduvat tac
chubhre vastre yad bhavet kilbiṣaṃ vaḥ.
sarva|kṣayo dṛśyate yatra kṛtsnaḥ
pāp'|ôdayo nirayo 'bhāva|saṃsthaḥ,
kas tatra kuryaj jātu karma prajānan
parājayo yatra samo jayaś ca?
te vai dhanyā yaiḥ kṛtaṃ jñāti|kāryaṃ,
te vai putrāḥ, suhṛdo, bāndhavāś ca
upakruṣṭaṃ jīvitaṃ santyajeyur
yataḥ Kurūṇāṃ niyato vai bhavaḥ syāt.
te cet Kurūn anuśiṣy' âtha, Pārthā,
nirṇīya sarvān dviṣato nigṛhya,
samaṃ vas taj jīvitaṃ mṛtyunā syād,
yaj jīvadhvaṃ jñāti|vadhe na sādhu.

of the Pañchálas, and Dhrishta·dyumna Párshata Yajñaséni. All of you listen to what I have to say, for I will speak with the welfare of the Kurus as my aim.

King Dhrita·rashtra, rejoicing at the prospect of peace, quickly had me yoke my chariot. May this please the king and his brothers, sons, and kinsmen. Peace be with the Pándavas! You Parthas are endowed with every virtue: firmness, 25.5
gentleness, and sincerity. Born into a noble line, you are indeed kind and generous; you act with modesty and know how to make decisions to fit the situation. Bad behavior does not suit you, for you have such a true nature and terrifying armies! Any crime you commit would be as glaringly obvious as a drop of collyrium on an otherwise spotless garment. Who would do something which they knew meant total destruction, something which was clearly entirely a means to evil, hellish and conducive to destruction, and an act where victory would amount to the same as defeat?

Those who act to the advantage of their family are virtuous, and so your sons, friends, and relatives are virtuous, since they would forsake their lamented lives if it would bring about some fixed surety for the Kurus. If you, Parthas, punish the Kurus, leading off all your enemies and suppressing them, then your lives would be like death, for there is
no good in living when your family is slaughtered. Who 25.10
would be able to match and defeat you, even if he had the gods led by Indra with him, when Késhava is with you, as well as Chekitána, and Sátyaki, and you are defended by Párshata's arms?

25.10 ko hy eva yuṣmān saha Keśavena,
sa|Cekitānān Pārṣata|bāhu|guptān,
sa|Sātyakīn viṣaheta prajetuṃ,
labdhv" âpi devān sacivān sah'|Êndrān?
ko vā Kurūn Droṇa|Bhīṣm'|âbhiguptān,
Aśvatthāmnā, Śalya|Kṛp'|ādibhiś ca
raṇe vijetuṃ viṣaheta, rājan,
Rādheya|guptān saha bhūmi|pālaiḥ?
mahad balaṃ Dhārtarāṣṭrasya rājñaḥ,
ko vai śakto hantum a|kṣīyamāṇaḥ?
so 'haṃ jaye c' âiva parājaye ca
niḥśreyasaṃ n' âdhigacchāmi kiñ cit.
kathaṃ hi nīcā iva dauṣkuleyā
nirdharm'|ârthaṃ karma kuryuś ca Pārthāḥ?
so 'haṃ prasādya praṇato Vāsudevaṃ
Pañcālānām adhipaṃ c' âiva vṛddham.
kṛt'|âñjaliḥ śaraṇaṃ vaḥ prapadye.
kathaṃ svasti syāt Kuru|Sṛñjayānām?
na hy eva te* vacanaṃ Vāsudevo
Dhanañjayo vā jātu kiṃ cin na kuryāt.
25.15 prānān dadyād yācamānaḥ; kuto 'nyad?
etad, vidvan, sādhan'|ârthaṃ bravīmi:
etad rājño Bhīṣma|purogamasya
mataṃ yad vaḥ śāntir ih' ôttamā syāt.»

YUDHIṢṬHIRA uvāca:

26.1 «KĀṂ NU VĀCAṂ, Sañjaya, me śṛṇoṣi
yuddh'|âiṣiṇīṃ, yena yuddhād bibheṣi?
a|yuddhaṃ vai, tāta, yuddhād garīyaḥ.
kas tal labdhvā jātu yudhyeta, sūta?
a|kurvataś cet puruṣasya, Sañjaya,

Then again, who could stand against and conquer the Kurus, defended by Drona and Bhishma, with Ashvatthá-man, and led by Shalya and Kripa, my king, as well as Ra-dhéya protecting them along with the kings of the earth? King Dhartaráshtra has a mighty army, so who could destroy it without being himself destroyed? I do not find any great benefit that would emerge from either victory or defeat. But how could the Parthas do anything which is not for the sake of virtue, as if they were low-born and morally inadequate? I bow to Vasudéva and to the aged king of Pañchála, appeasing them. I fall at your feet with my hands folded for your protection. How can it turn out well for the Kurus and Sríñjayas? For there is absolutely nothing at all that Vasudéva or Dhanañ·jaya would not do at a word from
you. He would give his life if asked, so what else would he 25.15
refuse? Wise man, I will say this to finish: It is the decision of the king, accompanied by Bhishma, that there should be final peace with you."

YUDHI·SHTHIRA replied:

"WHAT WAR-MONGERING speech of mine have you heard, 26.1
Sáñjaya, for you to fear war? Peace is preferable to war, my friend! Who would fight if he had achieved peace, *suta*? If every wish desired in the heart of a man who does nothing came true, Sáñjaya, then I know for a fact that he would do nothing. What else is more flippant than war? Why would

sidhyet saṃkalpo manasā yaṃ yam icchet
na karma kuryād viditaṃ mam' âitad,
anyatra yuddhād bahu yal laghīyaḥ?
kuto yuddhaṃ jātu naro 'vagacchet?
ko daiva|śapto hi vṛṇīta yuddham?
sukh'|âiṣiṇaḥ karma kurvanti Pārthā
dharmad a|hīnaṃ, yac ca lokasya pathyam,
dharm'|ôdayaṃ sukham āśaṃsamānāḥ.
kṛcchr'|ôpāyaṃ tattvataḥ karma duḥkham,
sukhaṃ prepsur vijighāṃsuś ca duḥkham,
ya indriyāṇāṃ prīti|ras'|ânugāmī.
26.5 kām'|âbhidhyā sva|śarīraṃ dunoti
yayā pramukto na karoti duḥkham.
yath" êdhyamānasya samiddha|tejaso
bhūyo balaṃ vardhate pāvakasya,
kām'|ârtha|lābhena tath" âiva bhūyo,
na tṛpyate sarpiṣ" êv' âgnir iddhaḥ.
saṃpaśy' êmaṃ bhoga|cayaṃ mahāntaṃ
sah' âsmābhir Dhṛtarāṣṭrasya rājñaḥ!

a man ever go to war? Who but a man whose fate is cursed would choose war?

The Parthas wish for happiness but they act to fulfill the law and for the welfare of the world. They wish for happiness only by righteous means. But the man who happily makes himself a slave to the pleasurable sensation of his senses, wishing for happiness and preventing misery, in reality only commits an act of misery which is a means to
pain. Intent on pleasure one consumes one's own body, but 26.5
released from it one does not suffer misery. For just as a kindled fire will grow in power again if fuel is added, so too desire grows once it has achieved its goal, and like a fire kindled with clarified butter, it is not sated. Compare King Dhrita·rashtra's enormous multitude of indulgences to ours!

n' â|śreyān vā* īśvaro vigrahāṇāṃ,
n' â|śreyān vai gīta|śabdaṃ śṛṇoti.
n' â|śreyān vai sevate mālya|gandhān,
na c' âpy a|śreyān anulepanāni.
n' â|śreyān vai prāvārān saṃvivaste.
kathaṃ tv asmān saṃpraṇudet Kurubhyaḥ?
atr' âiva syād a|budhasy' âiva kāmaḥ,
prāyaḥ śarīre hṛdayaṃ dunoti.
svayaṃ rājā viṣama|sthaḥ pareṣu
sāmarthyam anvicchati, tan na sādhu
yath" ātmanaḥ paśyati vṛttam eva
tathā pareṣām api so 'bhyupaiti.
26.10 āsannam agniṃ tu nidāgha|kāle
gambhīra|kakṣe gahane visṛjya,
yathā vivṛddhaṃ vāyu|vaśena śocet
kṣemaṃ mumukṣuḥ śiśira|vyapāye.
prāpt'|āiśvaryo Dhṛtarāṣṭro 'dya rājā
lālapyate, Sañjaya, kasya hetoḥ?
pragṛhya dur|buddhim an|ārjave rataṃ
putraṃ mandaṃ mūḍham a|mantriṇaṃ tu.
an|āptavac c' āptatamasya vācaḥ
Suyodhano Vidurasy' âvamanya
sutasya rājā Dhṛtarāṣṭraḥ priy'|âiṣī,
saṃbudhyamāno viśate '|dharmam eva.
medhāvinaṃ hy artha|kāmaṃ Kurūṇāṃ
bahu|śrutaṃ vāgminaṃ śīlavantam
sa taṃ rājā Dhṛtarāṣṭraḥ Kurubhyo
na sasmāra Viduraṃ putra|kāmyāt.

The inferior man is not a victor in battles, nor does the inferior man listen to the sound of songs. The inferior man does not make use of fragrances and garlands, nor does the inferior man use unguents. The inferior man never wears fine clothes. How else could we have been driven from the Kurus? As a general rule, only a fool desires that which consumes the heart in his body. It is not right that the king expects the agreement of those who are in such a different situation from his own. He sees precisely the same treatment towards himself as he also practices towards others.

The man who starts a fire nearby in the dewy season when 26.10
it is really hot, in a dense forest of dead trees, will grieve when it spreads through the force of the wind and he is desperate to escape to safety. Now that he has attained power King Dhrita·rashtra wails, Sáñjaya—and why? Because he took ill-considered pleasure in moral crookedness and took the advice of his idiotic, foolish, and witless son. Unreliable Suyódhana disregarded most trustworthy Vídura's advice, and King Dhrita·rashtra, wishing to favor his son, became absorbed in lawlessness, and he knew perfectly well what he was doing. Out of love for his son over the Kurus, King Dhrita·rashtra was not mindful of Vídura, that intelligent, learned, eloquent, and moral man, who desired only profit for the Kurus.

mānaǀghnasy' âsau mānaǀkāmasya c' ērṣoḥ
samrambhiṇaś c' ârthaǀdharm'ǀâtigasya,
durǀbhāṣiṇo manyuǀvaś'ǀânugasya
kām'ǀātmano daurhṛdair bhāvitasya,
26.15 aǀneyasy' âǀśreyaso dīrghaǀmanyor
mitraǀdruhaḥ, Sañjaya, pāpaǀbuddheḥ,
sutasya rājā Dhṛtarāṣṭraḥ priy'ǀâiṣī
prapaśyamānaḥ prājahād dharmaǀkāmau.
tad" âiva me, Sañjaya, dīvyato 'bhūn
matiḥ, Kurūṇām āgataḥ syād aǀbhāvaḥ!
kāvyāṃ vācaṃ Viduro bhāṣamāṇo
na vindate yad Dhārtarāṣṭrāt praśaṃsām.
kṣattur yadā n' ânvavartanta buddhiṃ,
kṛcchraṃ Kurūn, sūta, tad" âbhyājagāma,
yāvat prajñām anvavartanta tasya,
tāvat teṣāṃ rāṣṭraǀvṛddhir babhūva.
tad arthaǀlubdhasya nibodha me 'dya
ye mantriṇo Dhārtarāṣṭrasya, sūta.
Duḥśāsanaḥ, Śakuniḥ, sūtaǀputro,
Gāvalgaṇe, paśya saṃmoham asya!
so 'haṃ na paśyāmi parīkṣamāṇaḥ
kathaṃ svasti syāt KuruǀSṛñjayānām,
ātt' āiśvaryo Dhṛtarāṣṭraḥ parebhyaḥ
pravrājite Vidure dīrghaǀdṛṣṭau.

That son is an envious destroyer of respect, who loves his own arrogance; an irascible man who transgresses law and profit. He is a foul-mouthed slave to his anger, a lust-ridden soul who promotes the wicked-hearted. He is dissident, in- 26.15
ferior, extremely agressive, and a wicked-minded traitor to his friends, Sáñjaya. This is the son whom Dhrita·rashtra wishes to favor, abandoning virtue and desire, though he saw the implications. When I was gambling, Sáñjaya, the thought occurred to me that calamity was upon the Kurus, as Vídura gave his inspired advice but found no praise from Dhartaráshtra.

For as long as they followed the advice of that assistant, *suta*, then the Kurus did not suffer. While they followed his wisdom their kingdom flourished. Now take in what I tell you, *suta*, about Dhartaráshtra's advisors, greedy for wealth. Duhshásana, Shákuni, and Karna the *suta*'s son: look at his stupidity, son of Gaválgana! I cannot see, for all my investigation, how the Kurus and Sríñjayas manage to prosper since Dhrita·rashtra took sovereignty from the others, and since far-sighted Vídura was sent into exile.

26.20 āśaṃsate vai Dhṛtarāṣṭraḥ sa|putro
mahā|rājyam a|sapatnaṃ pṛthivyām.
tasmin śamaḥ kevalaṃ n' ôpalabhyaḥ
sarvaṃ svakaṃ mad|gate manyate 'rtham.
yat tat Karṇo manyate pāraṇīyaṃ
yuddhe gṛhīt'|āyudham Arjunaṃ vai,
āsaṃś ca yuddhāni purā mahānti
kathaṃ Karṇo n' âbhavad dvīpa eṣām?
Karṇaś ca jānāti, Suyodhanaś ca,
Droṇaś ca jānāti, pitā|mahaś ca,
anye ca ye Kuravas tatra santi,
yath" Ârjunān n' âsty aparo dhanur|dharaḥ.
jānanty etat Kuravaḥ sarva eva,
ye c' âpy anye bhūmi|pālāḥ sametāḥ,
Duryodhane rājyam ih' âbhavad yathā
arin|dame Phālgune '|vidyamāne.
ten' ânubandhaṃ manyate Dhārtarāṣṭraḥ
śakyaṃ hartuṃ Pāṇḍavānāṃ mamatvam,
Kirīṭinā tāla|mātr'|āyudhena
tad veditā saṃyugaṃ tatra gatvā.
26.25 Gāṇḍīva|visphārita|śabdam ājāv
a|śṛṇvānā Dhārtarāṣṭrā dhriyante!
kruddhaṃ na ced īkṣate Bhīmasenaṃ
Suyodhano manyate siddham artham.
Indro 'py etan n' ôtsahet, tāta, hartum
aiśvaryaṃ no jīvati Bhīmasene
Dhanañjaye Nakule c' âiva, sūta,
tathā vīre Sahadeve sahiṣṇau!

Dhrita·rashtra and his son hope for the earth as one great 26.20
kingdom without any rival. In that case, total peace could not be achieved, since he thinks all the wealth is his own, with me out of the picture. If Karna thinks it practical to stand against Árjuna when he has taken up arms in battle, then how is it that Karna is not an island standing out among the great battles from days gone by? Karna knows, as well as Suyódhana, just as Drona and our grandfather know, as well as the other Kurus, that there is no other archer like Árjuna. All the Kurus and other assembled kings know that the kingdom only belonged to Duryódhana while Phálguna, the destroyer of his enemies, was absent.

So Dhartaráshtra thinks he can take wealth from the Pándavas which rightfully belongs to them, but Kirítin knows
this and goes to battle with his palm-tree-sized bow! The 26.25
Dhartaráshtras continue to survive only because they do not hear the sound of the Gandíva being drawn on the field of battle! Suyódhana thinks his aim has been achieved so long as he does not see furious Bhima·sena. Not even Indra would dare to take my power, my lad, while Bhima·sena, Dhanañ·jaya, Nákula, and the patient hero Saha·deva are still alive, *suta*!

sa ced etāṃ pratipadyeta buddhiṃ
vṛddho rājā saha putreṇa, sūta,
evaṃ raṇe Pāṇḍava|kopa|dagdhā
na naśyeyuḥ, Sañjaya, Dhārtarāṣṭrāḥ.
jānāsi tvaṃ kleśam asmāsu vṛttaṃ,
tvāṃ pūjayan, Sañjay', âhaṃ kṣameyam,
yac c' âsmākaṃ Kauravair bhūta|pūrvaṃ,
yā no vṛttir Dhārtarāṣṭre tad" āsīt.
ady' âpi tat tatra tath" âiva vartatāṃ:
śāntiṃ gamiṣyāmi yathā tvam āttha,
Indraprasthe bhavatu mam' âiva rājyaṃ,
Suyodhano yacchatu Bhārat'|âgryaḥ!»

SAÑJAYA uvāca:

27.1 «DHARMA|NITYĀ, Pāṇḍava, te viceṣṭā
loke śrutvā dṛśyate c' âpi, Pārtha,
mahāsrāvaṃ jīvitaṃ c' âpy a|nityaṃ
saṃpaśya tvaṃ, Pāṇḍava, mā vyanīnaśaḥ!
na ced bhāgaṃ Kuravo 'nyatra yuddhāt
prayaccheraṃs tubhyam, Ajātaśatro,
bhaikṣa|caryām Andhaka|Vṛṣṇi|rājye
śreyo manye na tu yuddhena rājyam.

If the old king and his son see sense, *suta*, then the Dhartaráshtras will not meet their destruction, scorched by the Pándavas' fury in battle, Sáñjaya. You know what pain we have suffered, how we were treated by the Káuravas in the past, and you know how we behaved towards Dhrita·rashtra's son in return, but out of respect to you, Sáñjaya, I forgive them. Even today we behave in the same way: I will arrive at peace just as you said, but let me have my kingdom in Indra·prastha, and let Suyódhana, the leader of the Bháratas, grant it to me!"

SÁÑJAYA replied:

"PÁNDAVA, YOUR behavior is heard to be ever-righteous 27.1
throughout the world, and it is borne out by what I have seen, Partha. But the great deluge of life is not eternal, and so, Pándava, considering this, do not destroy yourself! If the Kurus will not grant you your share, Ajáta·shatru, without resorting to war, then in my opinion, a life of begging in the kingdom of the Ándhaka Vrishnis would be better than winning your kingdom through war.

alpa|kālaṃ jīvitaṃ yan manuṣye
mahā|srāvaṃ nitya|duḥkhaṃ calaṃ ca,
bhūyaś ca tad yaśaso n' ânurūpaṃ
tasmāt pāpaṃ, Pāṇḍava, mā kṛthās tvam.
kāmā manuṣyaṃ prasajanta ete
dharmasya ye vighna|mūlaṃ, nar'|êndra.
pūrvaṃ naras tān matimān praṇighnan
loke praśaṃsāṃ labhate 'n|avadyām.
27.5 nibandhanī hy artha|tṛṣṇ" êha, Pārtha,
tām icchatāṃ bādhyate dharma eva.
dharmaṃ tu yaḥ pravṛṇīte sa buddhaḥ
kāme gṛdho hīyate 'rth'|ânurodhāt.
dharmaṃ kṛtvā karmaṇāṃ, tāta, mukhyaṃ
mahā|pratāpaḥ savit" êva bhāti.
hīno hi dharmeṇa mahīm ap' îmāṃ
labdhvā naraḥ sīdati pāpa|buddhiḥ.
vedo 'dhītaś, caritaṃ brahma|caryaṃ,
yajñair iṣṭaṃ, brāhmaṇebhyaś ca dattam,
paraṃ sthānaṃ manyamānena bhūya
ātmā datto varṣa|pūgaṃ sukhebhyaḥ.
sukha|priye sevamāno 'tivelaṃ
yog'|âbhyāse yo na karoti karma,
vitta|kṣaye hīna|sukho 'tivelaṃ
duḥkhaṃ śete kāma|vega|praṇunnaḥ.
evaṃ punar brahma|cary'|â|prasakto
hitvā dharmaṃ yaḥ prakaroty a|dharmam,
a|śraddadhat para|lokāya mūḍho
hitvā dehaṃ tapyate pretya mandaḥ.
27.10 na karmaṇāṃ vipraṇāśo 'sty amutra
puṇyānāṃ v" âpy atha vā pāpakānām.

A man's life is a brief deluge, permanently painful and
changeable, and is nothing compared to glory, so don't commit sin, Pándava. These desires cling to mankind and are the
root of obstacles to virtue, lord of men. The wise man who
fully destroys them gains praise in this world and no blame.
The thirst for material wealth is constricting, Partha, and 27.5
the virtue of those full of desire is destroyed. The man who
chooses virtue is wise, but the man who is greedy for his
desires is diminished by his fondness for material wealth.

When he puts virtue at the head of his actions, my friend, then he shines like the magnificently blazing sun. A wicked-minded man devoid of morality still sinks down even if he has attained the world. You have learned the Veda, practiced the duties of Brahman, performed sacrifices, and been generous to brahmins, and though more than aware that this is the highest position, you have given yourself over to pleasures for a succession of years. The man who excessively devotes himself to the indulgence of pleasure and does not act in the practice of discipline becomes excessively miserable when his wealth has been consumed; and, spurred on by the outburst of desire, he wallows in misery. And again, by not being devoted to the duties of Brahman, by avoiding virtue, he practices immorality; and the idiot who does not put his faith in a world beyond this one destroys his body, and when he has died the fool burns.

There is no annihilation of one's deeds in the next world, 27.10
regardless of whether they were holy or sinful. The good and
evil deeds go in front, and the doer follows behind. Your

pūrvaṃ kartur gacchati puṇya|pāpaṃ
paścāt tv enam anuyāty eva kartā.
nyāy'|ôpetaṃ brāhmaṇebhyo 'tha dattaṃ
śraddhā|pūtaṃ gandha|ras'|ôpapannam
anvāhāryeṣ' ûttama|dakṣiṇeṣu
tathā|rūpaṃ karma vikhyāyate te.
iha kṣetre kriyate, Pārtha, kāryaṃ
na vai kiñ cit kriyate pretya kāryam.
kṛtaṃ tvayā pāralaukyaṃ ca karma
puṇyaṃ mahat sadbhir atipraśastam.
jahāti mṛtyuṃ ca jarāṃ bhayaṃ ca,
na kṣut|pipāse manaso '|priyāṇi.
na kartavyaṃ vidyate tatra kiñ cid
anyatra vai c' êndriya|prīṇanādd hi.
evaṃ rūpaṃ karma|phalaṃ, nar'|êndra,
m" âtr' āvahaṃ hṛdayasya priyeṇa
sa krodha|jaṃ, Pāṇḍava, harṣa|jaṃ ca
lokāv ubhau mā prahāsīś cirāya.
27.15 antaṃ gatvā karmaṇāṃ mā prajahyāḥ
satyaṃ damaṃ c' ārjavam ānṛśaṃsyam
aśva|medhaṃ rāja|sūyaṃ tath" êjyāḥ
pāpasy' ântaṃ karmaṇo mā punar gāḥ.
tac ced evaṃ dveṣa|rūpeṇa, Pārthāḥ,
kariṣyadhvaṃ karma pāpaṃ cirāya,
nivasadhvaṃ varṣa|pūgān vaneṣu
duḥkhaṃ vāsaṃ, Pāṇḍavā, dharma eva?
a|pravrajye mā sma hitvā purastād
ātm'|âdhīnaṃ yad balaṃ hy etad āsīt?
nityaṃ ca vaśyāḥ sacivās tav' ême
Janārdano Yuyudhānaś ca vīraḥ.

acts are notoriously as pure as the correctly prepared food which is made holy by faith, endowed with fine fragrance, and given to brahmins at the most sincere ceremonies of liberality. Partha, everything that should be done is done here, in this field, for there is nothing which needs to be done once we have died. The holy deeds you have done, which were so greatly praised by the very wise, go to the world beyond.

One leaves death behind, as well as old age and fear. One rids oneself of hunger and thirst and things which displease the mind. There is nothing left that needs to be done in that place, other than pleasing one's senses. Those are the consequences of our actions, lord of men, which are born from anger and joy, Pándava, so don't act from your heart's
desire. Do not, Pándava, act out of anger or joy. Having got 27.15
to the end of your actions, don't throw away truth, control, sincerity, and kindness. You can perform the horse-sacrifice and the coronation sacrifice, but don't commit an act which takes you to the brink of evil.

So if you must commit an evil act of such hostility, Parthas, after all this time, why then, Pándavas, did you have to live in the forest for those successive years, in miserable exile, just because it was right? Why did you not mobilize the army which was loyal to your will long ago, without going into exile? Your friends Janárdana and Yuyudhána were always obedient to you. King Viráta of Matsya on his golden chariot along with his son and his warrior successors, as well as the kings you defeated in the past, would have gathered to join you.

Matsyo rājā rukma|rathaḥ sa|putraḥ
prahāribhiḥ saha putrair Virāṭaḥ
rājānaś ca ye vijitāḥ purastāt
tvām eva te saṃśrayeyuḥ samastāḥ.
mahā|sahāyaḥ pratapan bala|sthaḥ
puras|kṛto Vāsudev'|Ârjunābhyām,
varān haniṣyan dviṣato raṅga|madhye
vyaneṣyathā Dhārtarāṣṭrasya darpam.
27.20 balaṃ kasmād vardhayitvā parasya?
nijān kasmāt karśayitvā sahayan?
niruṣya kasmād varṣa|pūgān vaneṣu
yuyutsase, Pāṇḍava, hīna|kālam?
a|prājño vā, Pāṇḍava, yudhyamāno
'|dharma|jño vā bhūtim atho 'bhyupaiti
prajñāvān vā budhyamāno 'pi dharmaṃ
saṃstambhād vā so 'pi bhūtair apaiti.
n' â|dharme te dhīyate, Pārtha, buddhir,
na saṃrambhāt karma cakartha pāpam.
āttha kiṃ tat kāraṇaṃ yasya hetoḥ
prajñā|viruddhaṃ karma cikīrṣas' îdam?
a|vyādhi|jam kaṭukaṃ śīrṣa|rogaṃ
yaśo|muṣaṃ pāpa|phal'|ôdayaṃ vā,
satāṃ peyaṃ yan na pibanty a|santo,
manyuṃ, mahā|rāja, piba praśāmya.
pāp'|ânubandhaṃ ko nu taṃ kāmayeta,
kṣam" âiva jyāyasī n' ôta bhogāḥ,
yatra Bhīṣmaḥ Śāntanavo hataḥ syād
yatra Droṇaḥ saha|putro hataḥ syāt?

Blazing and powerful, with great allies and with Vasudéva and Árjuna in the lead, you would have killed the greatest of your enemies and damaged Dhartaráshtra's pride in the middle of the arena. Why have you increased your enemy's 27.20
army? Why have you diminished your own faction and allies? And why have you spent these successive years in the forests if you want to fight now, Pándava, when you have lost so much time? It is a foolish man who fights, son of Pandu, or a man who doesn't know what is right and so goes for prosperity, or a wise man who is well aware of the correct course but strays from what is good for him out of obstinacy.

But your thoughts are not set on immorality, Partha, nor do you commit sinful acts out of anger. So what is the cause for this motive of wanting to commit an act contrary to wisdom? A fierce headache which does not arise from a wound, and robs one of one's glory or is the means to evil consequences, is the temper which the good swallow down but the bad do not. Great king, swallow your anger and be calm. Since forgiveness is superior to praising luxuries, who would want a situation tied in with evil, where Bhishma, son of Shántanu, would be killed, and where Drona and his son would be dead?

27.25 Kṛpaḥ, Śalyaḥ, Saumadattir, Vikarṇo,
Viviṃśatiḥ, Karṇa|Duryodhanau ca—
etān hatvā kīdṛśaṃ tat sukhaṃ syād,
yad vindethās? tad anubrūhi, Pārtha.
labdhv" âp' îmāṃ pṛthivīṃ sāgar'|ântāṃ
jarā|mṛtyū n' âiva hi tvaṃ prajahyāḥ,
priy'|â|priye sukha|duḥkhe ca, rājann.
evaṃ vidvān n' âiva yuddhaṃ kuru tvam.
amātyānāṃ yadi kāmasya hetor
evaṃ yuktaṃ karma cikīrṣasi tvam,
apakrāmeḥ svaṃ pradāy' âiva teṣāṃ
mā gās tvaṃ vai deva|yānāt patho 'dya!»

YUDHIṢṬHIRA uvāca:

28.1 «A|SAṂŚAYAṂ, SAÑJAYA, satyam etad:
dharmo varaḥ karmaṇāṃ, yat tvam āttha.
jñātvā tu māṃ, Sañjaya, garhayes tvaṃ
yadi dharmaṃ yady a|dharmaṃ careyam.
yatr' â|dharmo dharma|rūpāṇi dhatte,
dharmaḥ kṛtsno dṛśyate '|dharma|rūpaḥ,
bibhrad dharmo dharma|rūpaṃ tathā ca
vidvāṃsas taṃ samprapaśyanti buddhyā.
evaṃ tath" âiv' āpadi liṅgam etad
dharm'|â|dharmau nitya|vṛttī bhajetām.
ādyaṃ liṅgaṃ yasya tasya pramāṇam
āpad|dharmaṃ, Sañjaya, taṃ nibodha.

When Kripa, Shalya, Soma·datta's son, Vikárna, Vivín-shati, Karna, and Duryódhana have been killed, what kind of pleasure will you find in it? Tell me that, Partha. Once you have taken the world to the ends of the ocean, you will still not have dispensed with old age and death, nor pleasant and unpleasant matters, nor happiness and misery, king. Since you know all this, don't wage war. If you want to do this because your ministers wish it, then you should run away, giving them all you have, but don't stray from the path that leads to the gods now!" 27.25

YUDHI·SHTHIRA responded:

"IT IS UNDOUBTEDLY true, Sáñjaya, that the greatest act is virtue, as you said. But you should only reproach me when you know whether what I practice is right or wrong, Sáñjaya. Wise men use their intelligence to discern cases where immorality bears the appearance of morality, where all virtue seems to have the form of lawlessness, or where virtue does indeed bear a virtuous appearance. In times of trouble, right and wrong, which are eternal in nature, assume each other's appearances. One should practice the duty one's position from birth dictates, but know, Sáñjaya, that in times of trouble one's duty alters. 28.1

luptāyāṃ tu prakṛtau yena karma
niṣpādayet tat parīpsed vihīnaḥ,
prakṛti|sthaś c' āpadi vartamāna,
ubhau garhyau bhavataḥ, Sañjay', êtau.

28.5 a|vināśam icchatāṃ brāhmaṇānāṃ
prāyaś|cittaṃ vihitaṃ yad vidhātrā
saṃpaśyethāḥ karmasu vartamānān
vikarma|sthan, Sañjaya, garhayes tvam.

manīṣiṇāṃ sattva|vicchedanāya
vidhīyate satsu vṛttiḥ sad" âiva,
a|brāhmaṇāḥ santi tu ye na vaidyāḥ,
sarv'|ôcchedaṃ sādhu manyeta tebhyaḥ.

tad|adhvānaḥ pitaro ye ca pūrve,
pitā|mahā ye ca, tebhyaḥ pare 'nye,
yajñ'|âiṣiṇo ye ca hi karma kuryur;
n' ânyaṃ tato nāstiko 'sm', îti manye.
yat kiñ can' êdaṃ vittam asyāṃ pṛthivyāṃ,
yad devānāṃ tri|daśānāṃ paraṃ yat,
Prājāpatyaṃ tri|divaṃ brahma|lokaṃ
n' â|dharmataḥ, Sañjaya, kāmayeyam.
dharm'|ēśvaraḥ kuśalo nītimāṃś c' âpy,
upāsitā brāhmaṇānāṃ manīṣī,

When one's normal livelihood is disrupted and one is
totally poverty-stricken, one should wish for other means
to carry out one's prescribed duties. Both the man of stable livelihood and the man in trouble, Sáñjaya, are culpable if they behave as though their circumstances are otherwise. The creator made restorative arrangements for brah- 28.5
mins who performed unprescribed duties, though they did
not wish for destruction, which means that in dire situa-
tions one may perform normally improper acts. You should
blame those whom you see busy in unprescribed actions in
normal circumstances, or those who practice their ordained
duties in times of trouble.

The conduct prescribed for strict brahmins is always prescribed for men who wish for wisdom in separating the true self from the false. As for those who are not brahmins, and are not trying to gain knowledge of the true self through Vedic study, they should observe the codes of conduct set down for them in every situation.

Our fathers and those before them, our grandfathers and
those others before them, as well as those who strove for
sacrifice and did their duty, set it this way, and so, in my
opinion, this is not a case where I am impious. Sáñjaya, I
do not unlawfully desire whatever wealth there is on this
earth, or the wealth of the thirty gods, or what is beyond
that, or for that matter Praja·pati's heaven, or the world of
Brahma. Krishna, the skilled lord of moral law, who is also
wise in statecraft, is the revered teacher of brahmins and
advises various mighty Bhojas and other royalty. So let the 28.10
great glorious Késhava tell me if I need to be blamed for

nānā|vidhāṃś c' âiva mahā|balāṃś ca
Rājanya|Bhojān anuśāsti Kṛṣṇaḥ.
28.10 yadi hy ahaṃ visṛjan sāma garhyo
niyudhyamāno yadi jahyāṃ sva|dharmam
mahā|yaśāḥ Keśavas tad bravītu;
Vāsudevas t' ûbhayor artha|kāmaḥ.
Śaineyo 'yaṃ, Cedayaś c', Ândhakāś ca,
Vārṣṇeya|Bhojāḥ, Kukurāḥ, Sṛñjayāś ca,
upāsīnā Vāsudevasya buddhiṃ,
nigṛhya śatrūn suhṛdo nandayanti.
Vṛṣṇy|Andhakā hy Ugrasen'|ādayo vai
Kṛṣṇa|praṇītāḥ sarva ev' Êndra|kalpāḥ.
manasvinaḥ satya|parāyaṇāś ca
mahā|balā Yādavā bhogavantaḥ.
Kāśyo Babhruḥ śriyam uttamāṃ gato
labdhvā Kṛṣṇaṃ bhrātaram īśitāram,
yasmai kāmān varṣati Vāsudevo.
grīṣm'|âtyaye megha iva prajābhyaḥ.
īdṛśo 'yaṃ Keśavas, tāta, vidvān
viddhi hy enaṃ karmaṇāṃ niścaya|jñam.
priyaś ca naḥ sādhutamaś ca Kṛṣṇo;
n' âtikrāme vacanaṃ Keśavasya.»

VĀSUDEVA uvāca:

29.1 «A|VINĀŚAṂ, SAÑJAYA, Pāṇḍavānām
icchāmy ahaṃ, bhūtim eṣāṃ, priyaṃ ca.
tathā rājño Dhṛtarāṣṭrasya, sūta,
samāśaṃse bahu|putrasya vṛddhim.
kāmo hi me, Sañjaya, nityam eva,
n' ânyad brūyāṃ, tān prati śāmyat' êti.
rājñaś ca hi priyam etac chṛṇomi

rejecting conciliation or if I go to war, jeopardizing my own virtue. For Vasudéva has both our interests at heart.

This Sátyaki, the descendant of Shini, and the Chedis, Ándhakas, Vrishnis, Bhojas, Kúkuras, and Sríñjayas abide by Vasudéva's opinion by restraining their enemies and pleasing their friends. The Vrishnis and Ándhakas, led by Ugra·sena, are all Indra-like men brought to us by Krishna. Those intelligent men are devoted to the truth, and the mighty Yádavas enjoy themselves. King Babhru of the Kashis has come into the greatest fortune now that he has taken Krishna as his brother and his master, for Vasudéva rained down all his wishes upon him, just like a cloud rains on the creatures once the summer has passed away. Késhava is the wise sort of man whom you should know, my friend, to be the arbiter of lawful or unlawful conduct. Since most excellent Krishna is our friend, I will not transgress Késhava's advice."

VASUDÉVA said:

"SÁÑJAYA, I WISH for the Pándavas' ascendancy and for 29.1
their prosperity and happiness. But, *suta*, I also hope that Dhrita·rashtra's kingdom and many sons will thrive. It has always been my desire, Sáñjaya, that there be peace; and I should tell them nothing else. I hear that it is something a king holds dear, and I believe that it is within the Pándavas' sights. But obviously the peaceful nature shown by the son of Pandu is extremely rare, Sáñjaya. Dhrita·rashtra and his

manye vai tat Pāṇḍavānāṃ samakṣam.
su|duṣkaras tatra śamo hi nūnaṃ
pradarśinaḥ, Sañjaya, Pāndavena.
yasmin gṛddho Dhṛtarāṣṭraḥ sa|putraḥ
kasmād eṣāṃ kalaho n' âvamūrcchet?
na tvaṃ dharmaṃ vicaraṃ, Sañjay', êha
mattaś ca jānāsi, Yudhiṣṭhirāc ca.
atho kasmāt, Sañjaya, Pāṇḍavasya
utsāhinaḥ, pūrayataḥ sva|karma,
29.5 yathā|khyātam āvasataḥ kuṭumbe
purā kasmāt sādhu vilopam āttha?
asmin vidhau vartamāne yathāvad
ucc'|âvacā matayo brāhmaṇānām.
karmaṇ" āhuḥ siddhim eke paratra,
hitvā karma vidyayā siddhim eke.
n' â|bhuñjāno bhakṣya|bhojyasya tṛpyed,
vidvān ap' îha vihitaṃ brāhmaṇānām.
yā vai vidyāḥ sādhayant' îha karma,
tāsāṃ phalaṃ vidyate n' êtarāsām.
tatr' êha vai dṛṣṭa|phalaṃ tu karma
pītv" ôdakaṃ śāmyati tṛṣṇay" ārtaḥ.
so 'yaṃ vidhir vihitaḥ karmaṇ" âiva
saṃvartate, Sañjaya, tatra karma.
tatra yo 'nyat karmaṇaḥ sādhu manyen,
moghaṃ tasy' ālapitaṃ dur|balasya.
karmaṇ" âmī bhānti devāḥ paratra,
karmaṇ" âiv' êha plavate mātari|śvā.
aho|rātre vidadhat karmaṇ' âiva
a|tandrito nityam udeti sūryaḥ.

sons have been greedy in this matter, and so is it odd that a quarrel over these things would drag on?

You know very well, Sáñjaya, that neither I nor Yudhi· 29.5
shthira ever stray from the law. And so why then, Sáñjaya, did you previously denigrate the energetic Pándava, the famous lord of his household who fulfills his own duty? In this matter various opinions exist among the brahmins. One school of thought says that one's actions bring success in the future, but some cast actions aside and say success follows knowledge. The brahmins know that someone who does not eat will not be satisfied merely by knowing about eating food.

So it is only knowledge leading to action which is found to bear fruit, rather than other kinds. The act itself has visible consequences; someone suffering from thirst is soothed when they have drunk water. Moral law is established as action, and the action is inherent to it, Sáñjaya. Therefore he who deems anything other than action to be desirable is a weak man who speaks in vain. The gods shine through action in the world beyond, and here on earth the wind blows through action. Indeed it is through action that the unwearied sun constantly rises and so establishes the day and night.

29.10 mās'|ârdha|māsān atha nakṣatra|yogān
a|tandritaś candramāś c' âbhyupaiti.
a|tandrito dahate Jātavedāḥ
samidhyamānaḥ karma kurvan prajābhyaḥ.
a|tandritā bhāram imaṃ mahāntaṃ
bibharti devī pṛthivī balena.
a|tandritāḥ śīghram apo vahanti
santarpayantyaḥ sarva|bhūtāni nadyaḥ.
a|tandrito varṣati bhūri|tejāḥ,
sannādayann antarikṣaṃ diśaś ca,
a|tandrito brahma|caryaṃ cacāra
śreṣṭhatvam icchan Bala|bhid devatānām.
hitvā sukhaṃ manasaś ca priyāṇi
tena Śakraḥ karmaṇā śraiṣṭyam āpa.
satyaṃ dharmaṃ pālayann a|pramatto
damaṃ titikṣāṃ samatāṃ priyaṃ ca
etāni sarvāṇy upasevamānaḥ
sa deva|rājyaṃ Maghavān prāpa mukhyam.
Bṛhaspatir brahma|caryaṃ cacāra,
samāhitaḥ saṃśit'|ātmā yathāvat,
29.15 hitvā sukhaṃ pratirudhy' êndriyāṇi,
tena devānām agamad gauravaṃ saḥ.
nakṣatrāṇi* karmaṇ" âmutra bhānti
rudr'|âdityā Vasavo 'th' âpi viśve
Yamo rājā Vaiśravaṇaḥ Kubero
gandharva|yakṣ'|âpsarasaś ca, sūta;
brahma|vidyāṃ brahma|caryaṃ kriyāṃ ca
niṣevamāṇā ṛṣayo 'mutra bhānti.

The untiring moon passes through the fortnights, 29.10
months, and conjunctions. Indomitable fire burns when
kindled, favoring living beings. The earth goddess unfail-
ingly bears this massive burden through her strength. The
indefatigable rivers quickly carry the waters and refresh all
creatures. The magnificently splendid slayer of Bala tirelessly pours down rain, fills the sky and directions with
thunder, and, eager for the position of greatest of the gods,
he practiced chaste austerities.

It was through action, forsaking happiness and the wishes
of his heart, that Shakra attained preeminence. By carefully defending the truth and moral law, by practicing control, endurance, equity, and pleasure, Mághavat attained
supremacy over the kingdom of heaven. Brihas·pati practiced his chaste asceticism, concentrating with his soul prepared accordingly, by forsaking happiness and keeping con- 29.15
trol over his senses. It was through this method that he
became the guru of the gods. It is through the acts of the
*rudras* and *adítyas*, as well as Vásava, the *vishvas*, King Yama,
Kubéra Váishravana, and the *gandhárvas*, *yakshas*, and *ápsarases*, that the constellations up there shine, *suta*. The sages
there in the other world shine by observing the sacred
knowledge, the duties of Brahman, and rituals.

jānann imaṃ sarva|lokasya dharmaṃ,
vipr'|êndrāṇāṃ, kṣatriyāṇāṃ, viśāṃ ca,
sa kasmāt tvaṃ jānatāṃ jñānavān san,
vyāyacchase, Sañjaya, Kaurav'|ârthe?
āmnāyeṣu nitya|saṃyogam asya
tath" âśva|medhe rāja|sūye ca viddhi;
saṃyujyate dhanuṣā varmaṇā ca
hasty|aśv'|ādyai ratha|śastraiś ca bhūyaḥ.
te ced ime Kauravāṇām upāyam
avagaccheyur a|vadhen' âiva Pārthāḥ,
dharma|trāṇaṃ puṇyam eṣāṃ kṛtaṃ syād,
ārye vṛtte Bhīmasenaṃ nigṛhya.
29.20 te cet pitrye karmaṇi vartamānā
āpadyeran diṣṭa|vaśena mṛtyum,
yathā|śaktyā pūrayantaḥ sva|karma,
tad apy eṣāṃ nidhanaṃ syāt praśastam.
ut' āho tvaṃ manyase śāmyam eva,
rājñāṃ yuddhe vartate dharma|tantram,
a|yuddhe vā vartate dharma|tantraṃ,
tath" âiva te vācam imāṃ śṛṇomi.
cāturvarṇyasya prathamaṃ vibhāgam
avekṣya tvaṃ, Sañjaya, svaṃ ca karma,
niśamy' âtho Pāṇḍavānāṃ ca karma
praśaṃsa vā, ninda vā, yā matis te.

Knowing that this is the correct principle for the whole world, whether they are lordly brahmins, kshatriyas, or vaishyas, why do you make such an effort for the Káurava's cause, Sáñjaya, when you possess the same knowledge as those in the know? Recognize the Pándava's constant devotion to sacred texts, as also to horse-sacrifice and consecration sacrifice. Then again, he is conversant with the bow and armor, as well as with elephants and horses and so on, and with chariots and weapons.

If the Parthas could find some means to their end which didn't involve slaughtering the Káuravas, then their holy task would be the protection of moral rectitude, and they
would confine Bhima·sena to noble behavior. But if when 29.20
performing their ancestral task, fulfilling their own duty to the best of their ability, they meet their death by the power of fate, then even their fall would be laudable.

And since you have an opinion about reconciliation, I want to hear you tell us whether you think the kings' responsibility to defend the law is accomplished in war, or whether defending the law is accomplished without war. First of all you should take the distribution of the four castes into consideration, Sáñjaya, as well as the duty of each, and when you have distinguished the Pándavas' duty, then either praise or blame them as you see fit.

adhīyīta brāhmaṇo vai, yajeta,
dadyād, īyāt tīrtha|mukhyāni c' âiva;
adhyāpayed, yājayec c' âpi yājyān,
pratigrahān vā vihitān pratīcchet.
tathā rājanyo rakṣaṇaṃ vai prajānāṃ,
kṛtvā dharmeṇ', â|pramatto 'tha dattvā,
yajñair iṣṭvā, sarva|vedān adhītya,
dārān kṛtvā puṇya|kṛd āvased gṛhān.
29.25 sa dharm'|ātmā dharmam adhītya puṇyam,
yadṛcchayā* vrajati Brahma|lokam;
vaiśyo 'dhītya kṛṣi|gorakṣa|paṇyair
vittaṃ cinvan pālayann a|pramattaḥ.
priyaṃ kurvan brāhmaṇa|kṣatriyāṇāṃ
dharma|śīlaḥ puṇya|kṛd āvased gṛhān.
paricaryā vandanaṃ brāhmaṇānāṃ,
n' âdhīyīta, pratiṣiddho 'sya yajñaḥ,
nity'|ôtthito bhūtaye '|tandritaḥ syād;
evaṃ smṛtaḥ śūdra|dharmaḥ purāṇaḥ.
etān rājā pālayann a|pramatto
niyojayan sarva|varṇān sva|dharme.
a|kām'|ātmā, sama|vṛttiḥ prajāsu,
n' â|dhārmikān anurudhyeta kāmān.
śreyāṃs tasmād yadi vidyeta* kaś cid
abhijñātaḥ sarva|dharm'|ôpapannaḥ,
sa taṃ draṣṭum anuśiṣyan prajānāṃ
na c' âitad budhyed iti tasminn a|sāduḥ.

A brahmin should learn, sacrifice, be generous, and go on pilgrimages to sacred bathing sites. He should teach and officiate as well for worthy sacrificers, and receive the established gifts. A kshatriya should provide protection for the citizens, act with virtue, be conscientiously generous, offer sacrifices, and learn all the Vedas. He should marry and govern his home, acting piously.

A vaishya who is virtuous in his soul and studies the rules 29.25
of piety can attain Brahma's world if, after completing his studies, he gains wealth by agriculture, hubandry, or business, and conscientiously preserves it. He should do favors for brahmins and kshatriyas and rule his household justly and piously. The ancient law for shudras is handed down as follows: a shudra should pay homage to the brahmins, but not study. Sacrifice is forbidden to him; instead he should tirelessly and constantly strive for his own welfare.

A king should carefully protect all of these castes, and assign them to their respective duties. His soul must be free of lust; he should behave consistently towards his citizens; he should not be fond of immoral pleasures. If some renowned man endowed with every virtue is found and discovered to be better than him, then he should instruct his subjects to see him—but a wicked king would not understand this.

yadā gr̥dhyet para|bhūtau nr̥śaṃso
vidhi|prakopād balam ādadānaḥ,
tato rājñām abhavad yuddham etat;
tatra jātaṃ varma śastraṃ dhanuś ca:
29.30 Indreṇ' âitad dasyu|vadhāya karma
utpāditaṃ varma śastraṃ dhanuś ca.
tatra puṇyaṃ dasyu|vadhena labhyate;
so 'yaṃ doṣaḥ Kurubhis tīvra|rūpaḥ,
a|dharma|jñair dharmam a|budhyamānaiḥ,
prādur bhūtaḥ, Sañjaya, sādhu tan na.
tatra rājā Dhr̥tarāṣṭraḥ sa|putro
dharmyaṃ haret Pāṇḍavānām a|kasmāt,
n' âvekṣante rāja|dharmaṃ purāṇaṃ
tad|anvayāḥ Kuravaḥ sarva eva.
steno hared yatra dhanaṃ hy a|dr̥ṣṭaḥ
prasahya vā yatra hareta dr̥ṣṭaḥ,
ubhau garhyau bhavataḥ, Sañjay', âitau.
kiṃ vai pr̥thaktvaṃ Dhr̥tarāṣṭrasya putre?
so 'yaṃ lobhān manyate dharmam etaṃ
yam icchati krodha|vaś'|ânugāmī.
bhāgaḥ punaḥ Pāṇḍavānāṃ niviṣṭas,
taṃ naḥ kasmād ādadīran pare vai?
29.35 asmin pade yudhyatāṃ no vadho 'pi
ślāghyaḥ; pitryaṃ para|rājyād viśiṣṭam.
etān dharmān Kauravāṇāṃ purāṇān
ācakṣīthāḥ, Sañjaya, rāja|madhye.
ete madān mr̥tyu|vaś'|âbhipannāḥ
samānītā Dhārtarāṣṭreṇa mūḍhāḥ.
idaṃ punaḥ karma pāpīya eva
sabhā|madhye paśya vr̥ttam Kurūṇām:

When a king becomes malicious, takes on power, and is greedy for someone else's property, he is open to destiny's fury. Then the result is war between kings. Armor, weapons, and the bow were created for this very circumstance: It was 29.30
Indra's work that created armor, weapons, and the bow, in order to slaughter the *dasyus*.

War was waged piously in the slaughter of the *dasyus*, so this particularly vicious-seeming fault which has been displayed by the Kurus, who do not understand morality and pay no heed to virtue, is not right. King Dhrita·rashtra and his son would take what is rightfully the Pándavas' without reason, and the entire Kuru lineage will give no thought to the legendary king of righteousness.

Regardless of whether it is a thief who steals wealth unseen, or whether someone steals publicly and violently, both are equally culpable, Sáñjaya. What is the exception in the case of Dhrita·rashtra's son? A slave to the power of his anger, he interprets that law as suits him, out of greed. The Pándavas' share has been earned once again, so why should others rob us of it? In this matter of war even our deaths 29.35
will be laudable, since inheritance surpasses invasion. Recite those ancient laws to the Káuravas in the midst of the kings, Sáñjaya.

The men who have gathered together with Dhartaráshtra from arrogance are idiots, overcome by the power of death. Look again at the worst deed committed in the midst of the court of the Kurus: Led by Bhishma, the Kurus looked the other way when the Pándavas' dear wife Dráupadi, an illus-

priyāṃ bhāryāṃ Draupadīṃ Pāṇḍavānāṃ
yaśasvinīṃ śīla|vṛtt'|ôpapannām
yad upaikṣanta Kuravo Bhīṣma|mukhyāḥ
kām'|ânugen' ôparuddhāṃ vrajantīm.
taṃ cet tadā te su|kumāra|vṛddhā
avārayiṣyan Kuravaḥ sametāḥ,
mama priyaṃ Dhṛtarāṣṭro 'kariṣyat;
putrāṇāṃ ca kṛtam asy' âbhaviṣyat!
Duḥśāsanaḥ prātilomyān nināya
sabhā|madhye śvaśurāṇāṃ ca Kṛṣṇām,
sā tatra nītā karuṇaṃ vyapekṣya
n' ânyaṃ kṣattur nātham avāpa kiñ cit.
29.40 kārpaṇyād eva sahitās tatra bhūpā
n' âśaknuvan prativaktuṃ sabhāyām.
ekaḥ kṣattā dharmyam artham bruvāṇo
dharma|buddhyā pratyuvāc' âlpa|buddhim.
a|buddhvā tvaṃ dharmam etaṃ sabhāyām
ath' êcchase Pāṇḍavasy' ôpadeṣṭum.
Kṛṣṇā tv etat karma cakāra śuddhaṃ
su|duṣkaraṃ tatra sabhāṃ sametya.
yena kṛcchrāt Pāṇḍavān ujjahāra
tath" ātmānaṃ naur iva sāgar'|âughāt.
yatr' âbravīt sūta|putraḥ sabhāyāṃ
Kṛṣṇāṃ sthitāṃ śvaśurāṇāṃ samīpe:
‹na te gatir vidyate, Yājñaseni,
prapadya dāsī Dhārtarāṣṭrasya veśma.
parājitās te patayo na santi
patiṃ c' ânyaṃ, bhāvini, tvaṃ vṛṇīṣva.›

trious lady endowed with virtuous conduct, was molested by a man enslaved to his lust while she was in seclusion. If the Kurus, old and young, who were gathered there had wanted to stop it, then Dhrita·rashtra would have pleased me with his behavior, and it would have been for the good of his sons as well!

Duhshásana led Krishná into the midst of the court of her fathers-in-law, contrary to all custom, and, brought there, she looked mournfully around, but found no other protector but Vídura the steward. It was their weakness 29.40
which prevented the kings gathered there from speaking out in the court. Only Vídura, the steward, with some thought for virtue, spoke correctly on the matter and replied to that brainless man. You did not give any consideration to moral law in the court, but now you want to lecture the son of Pandu!

It was Krishná, when she came to the assembly, who did the right thing, regardless of how very hard it was, and by doing so she helped the Pándavas and herself escape from disaster, like a boat from the ocean's floods. Karna, the *suta*'s son, spoke to Krishná in court, as she stood in front of her fathers-in-law, saying: 'You've no other option, Yajñaséni. Go as a slave to Dhartaráshtra's house. You do not have husbands any more, since they have been overthrown, so choose another husband, beautiful woman.'

yo Bībhatsor hṛdaye prauḍha* āsīd
    asthi cchindan marma|ghātī su|ghoraḥ
Karnāc charo vāṅ|mayas tigma|tejāḥ
    pratiṣṭhito hṛdaye Phālgunasya.
29.45 kṛṣṇ'|âjināni paridhitsamānān
    Duḥśāsanaḥ kaṭukāny abhyabhāṣat:
‹ete sarve ṣaṇḍha|tilā vinaṣṭāḥ
    kṣayaṃ gatā narakaṃ dīrgha|kālam!›
Gandhāra|rājaḥ Śakunir nikṛtyā
    yad abravīd dyūta|kāle sa Pārtham:
‹parājito Nakulaḥ* kiṃ tav' âsti
    Kṛṣṇayā tvaṃ dīvya vai Yājñasenyā!›
jānāsi tvaṃ, Sañjaya, sarvam etat
    dyūte vākyaṃ garhyam evaṃ yath" ôktam.
svayaṃ tv ahaṃ prārthaye tatra gantuṃ
    samādhātuṃ kāryam etad vipannam.
a|hāpayitvā yadi Pāṇḍav'|ârthaṃ,
    śamaṃ Kurūṇām api cec chakeyam,
puṇyaṃ ca me syāc caritaṃ mah"|ôdayam,
    mucyeraṃś ca Kuravo mṛtyu|pāśāt.
api me vācaṃ bhāṣamāṇasya kāvyāṃ,
    dharm'|ārāmām, arthavatīm, a|hiṃsrām
avekṣeran Dhārtarāṣṭrāḥ samakṣaṃ,
    māṃ ca prāptaṃ Kuravaḥ pūjayeyuḥ.

Karna's violent, vicious, horrifying, and gut-wrenching speech—an arrow of words—cut to the bone, and went straight to Bibhátsu Phálguna's heart and stuck there.
Duhshásana spoke to them, as they were all putting on their 29.45
black antelope skins, in these bitter words: 'You are all useless like barren sesame seeds, you are lost, going to your destruction in hell for a long time!' And Shákuni, the dishonest king of Gandhára, goaded Partha during the gambling match, saying: 'You have lost Nákula, your youngest brother, so what else do you have left? Gamble for Krishná Yajñaséni!'

You know all the reprehensible things that were said during the gambling, Sáñjaya. I wish to go there myself to repair the damage that needs to be resolved. If I am able to bring peace to the Kurus without harming the Pándavas' cause, then my achievement will be fair and extremely fortunate, and the Kurus will be saved from the noose of death. Dhrita·rashtra's followers will take what I say into consideration, for my words will be inspired, delightful with virtue, and full of meaning, without being harmful. The Kurus will honor me when I arrive.

29.50 ato 'nyathā rathinā Phālgunena
Bhīmena c' âiv' āhava|daṃśitena
parāsiktān Dhārtarāṣṭrāṃś ca viddhi
pradahyamānān karmaṇā svena pāpān.
parājitān Pāṇḍaveyāṃs tu vāco
raudrā rūkṣā bhāṣate Dhārtarāṣṭraḥ,
gadā|hasto Bhīmaseno '|pramatto
Duryodhanaṃ smārayitā hi kāle.
Suyodhano manyu|mayo mahā|drumaḥ;
skandhaḥ Karṇaḥ, Śakunis tasya śākhā;
Duḥśāsanaḥ puṣpa|phale samṛddhe,
mūlaṃ rājā Dhṛtarāṣṭro '|manīṣī.
Yudhiṣṭhiro dharma|mayo mahā|drumaḥ;
skandho 'rjuno, Bhīmaseno 'sya śākhā;
Mādrī|putrau puṣpa|phale samṛddhe,
mūlaṃ tv ahaṃ, brahma ca brāhmaṇāś ca.
vanaṃ rājā Dhṛtarāṣṭraḥ sa|putro
vyāghrās te vai, Sañjaya, Pāndu|putrāḥ.
mā vanaṃ chindhi sa|vyāghraṃ;
mā vyāghrān nīnaśo* vanāt.
29.55 nirvano vadhyate vyāghro nirvyāghraṃ chidyate vanam;
tasmād vyāghro vanaṃ rakṣed, vanaṃ vyāghraṃ ca pālayet.
latā|dharmā Dhārtarāṣṭrāḥ, śālāḥ, Sañjaya, Pāṇḍavāḥ;
na latā vardhate jātu mahā|drumam an|āśritā.

But if not, the wicked Dhartaráshtras will duly be thrown 29.50
down by Phálguna on his chariot and Bhima armed for war, and they will burn because of their own action. Dhartaráshtra addressed the defeated Pándavas with harsh and cruel words, but in time vigilant Bhima·sena will remind Duryódhana, mace in hand.

Suyódhana, composed of fury, is a great tree; Karna is the trunk; Shákuni, its branches; Duhshásana is in the lush flowers and fruit; and foolish King Dhrita·rashtra is the root. Yudhi·shthira, composed of virtue, is also a great tree; Árjuna is the trunk; Bhima·sena comprises its branches; Madri's sons flourish as the flowers and fruit; and the root consists of Brahman, brahmins, and me. King Dhrita·rashtra and his sons are the forest, and the sons of Pandu, Sáñjaya, are tigers.

Don't cut the forest down, because the tigers will die with it; but don't exterminate the tigers from the forest either. The tiger dies without the forest, and similarly the for- 29.55
est is cut down without the tiger. The tiger should protect the forest, and the forest should defend the tiger. The Dhartaráshtras are by nature creepers, Sáñjaya, and the Pándavas are *shala* trees; creepers, of course, do not grow without being supported by a great tree.

sthitāḥ śuśrūṣituṃ Pārthāḥ, sthitā yoddhum arin|damāḥ.
yat kṛtyaṃ Dhṛtarāṣṭrasya tat karotu nar'|âdhipaḥ,
sthitāḥ śame mah"|ātmānaḥ Pāṇḍavā dharma|cāriṇaḥ
yodhāḥ samarthās. tad, vidvann, ācakṣīthā yathā|tatham.»

SAÑJAYA uvāca:

30.1 «ĀMANTRAYE TVĀṂ, nara|deva|deva,
gacchāmy aham, Pāndava, svasti te 'stu.
kac cin na vācā vṛjinaṃ hi kiñ cid
uccāritaṃ me manaso 'bhiṣaṅgāt.
Janārdanaṃ, Bhīmasen'|Ârjunau ca,
Mādrī|sutau, Sātyakiṃ, Cekitānam
āmantrya gacchāmi. śivaṃ sukhaṃ vaḥ!
saumyena māṃ paśyata cakṣuṣā, nṛpāḥ.»

YUDHIṢṬHIRA uvāca:

«anujñātaḥ, Sañjaya, svasti gaccha.
na naḥ smarasy a|priyaṃ jātu, vidvan.
vidmaś ca tvāṃ te ca vayaṃ ca sarve
śuddh'|ātmānaṃ madhya|gataṃ sabhā|stham.
āpto dūtaḥ, Sañjaya, su|priyo 'si
kalyāṇa|vāk, śīlavāṃs tṛptimāṃś ca.
na muhyes tvaṃ, Sañjaya, jātu matyā,
na ca kruddhyer ucyamāno dur|uktaiḥ.

The Parthas are ready to obey, but those destroyers of their enemies are also ready to fight. Let King Dhrita·rashtra do what he has to. The virtue-practicing high-souled Pándavas are ready for peace, but equally they are warriors. Tell them precisely this, wise man."

SÁÑJAYA replied:

"I BID YOU FAREWELL, god among kings. I am leaving, 30.1
Pándava, so good luck to you. I hope I have committed no sin against you with my speech due to the inclination of my mind. Taking my leave of Janárdana, Bhima·sena and Árjuna, Madri's sons, Sátyaki, and Chekitána, I am going now. May kindly fortune and happiness be with you! Kings, look at me with affectionate eyes."

YUDHI·SHTHIRA said:

"Sáñjaya, you have been given leave, so go with our blessing. You never remember us unkindly, wise man. Everyone knows, us included, that you are a pure-souled man when you stand in court in the midst of all. Sáñjaya, you are a very pleasant messenger to receive. You are a beautiful speaker, a man of good conduct, and competent. Indeed your mind is well ordered, Sáñjaya, and you do not become angry when given negative replies.

30.5 na marma|gāṃ jātu vakt" âsi rūkṣāṃ,
n' ôpaśrutiṃ kaṭukāṃ n' ôta muktām.
dharm'|ārāmām arthavatīm a|hiṃsrām
etāṃ vācaṃ tava jānīma, sūta.
tvam eva naḥ priyatamo 'si dūta;
ih' āgacched Viduro vā dvitīyaḥ.
abhīkṣṇa|dṛṣṭo 'si purā hi nas tvaṃ,
Dhanañjayasy' ātma|samaḥ sakh" âsi!
ito gatvā, Sañjaya, kṣipram eva
upātiṣṭhethā brāhmaṇān ye tad|arhāḥ,
viśuddha|vīryāś, caraṇ'|ôpapannāḥ,
kule jātāḥ sarva|dharm'|ôpapannāḥ.
svādhyāyino brāhmaṇā bhikṣavaś ca
tapasvino ye ca nityā vaneṣu.
abhivādyā vai mad|vacanena vṛddhās
tath" êtareṣāṃ kuśalaṃ vadethāḥ.
puro|hitaṃ Dhṛtarāṣṭrasya rājñas
tath" ācāryān ṛtvijo ye ca tasya
taiś ca tvaṃ, tāta, sahitair yath" ârhaṃ
saṅgacchethāḥ kuśalen' âiva, sūta.
30.10 a|śrotriyā ye ca vasanti vṛddhā,
manasvinaḥ śīla|bal'|ôpapannāḥ,
āśaṃsanto 'smākam anusmaranto,
yathā|śakti dharma|mātrāṃ carantaḥ,
ślāghasva māṃ kuśalinaṃ sma tebhyo hy
an|āmayaṃ, tāta, pṛccher jaghanyam;
ye jīvanti vyavahāreṇa rāṣṭre,
ye pālayanto nivasanti rāṣṭre.

You do not say cruel things which cut deep, nor do you 30.5
let bitter reports escape your mouth. We know, *suta*, that your speech is delightfully virtuous, meaningful, and undamaging. You are our favorite messenger; besides you, Vídura may come here. We saw you constantly in the old days, and you are a friend of Dhanañ·jaya, as dear to him as his own self!

Once you have left here, Sáñjaya, visit worthy brahmins; pure and brave men, endowed with good conduct; men born into good families who are furnished with every virtue. Visit the particularly academic brahmins and mendicants, as well as ascetics who are always in the forests. Greet the elderly on my behalf, and enquire after the health of the others. Meet King Dhrita·rashtra's family priest as well as his teachers and sacrificers, my friend, and upon meeting them together as they deserve, ask after their health, *suta*.

Commend me to the wise old men, endowed with 30.10
strength and good conduct though they have not learned the Veda, who talk about us and remember us, and live as far as possible by the correct code, and first tell them I am well, then enquire after their well-being, my friend. Commend me to those who live in the kingdom through business, and those who dwell in the kingdom governing it.

ācārya iṣṭo naya|go vidheyo
Vedān abhīpsan brahma|caryaṃ cacāra
yo 'straṃ catuṣpāt punar eva cakre
Droṇaḥ prasanno 'bhivādyas tvay" âsau.
adhīta|vidyaś caraṇ'|ôpapanno
yo 'straṃ catuṣpāt punar eva cakre
gandharva|putra|pratimaṃ tarasvinaṃ
tam Aśvatthāmānaṃ kuśalaṃ sma pṛccheḥ.
Śāradvatasy' âvasathaṃ sma gatvā,
mahā|rathasy' ātma|vidāṃ varasya,
tvaṃ mām abhīkṣṇaṃ parikīrtayan vai
Kṛpasya pādau, Sañjaya, pāṇinā spṛśeḥ.
30.15 yasmin śauryam, ānṛśaṃsyaṃ tapaś ca,
prajñā, śīlaṃ, śruti|sattve dhṛtiś ca,
pādau gṛhītvā Kuru|sattamasya
Bhīṣmasya māṃ tatra nivedayethāḥ.
prajñā|cakṣur yaḥ praṇetā Kurūṇāṃ
bahu|śruto vṛddha|sevī manīṣī,
tasmai rājñe sthavirāy' âbhivādya
ācakṣīthāḥ, Sañjaya, mām a|rogam.
jyeṣṭhaḥ putro Dhṛtarāṣṭrasya mando,
mūrkhaḥ śaṭhaḥ, Sañjaya, pāpa|śīlaḥ,
praśāstā* vai pṛthivī yena sarvā,
Suyodhanaṃ kuśalaṃ, tāta, pṛccheḥ.

Pass on my regards to illustrious Drona, our favorite teacher, who is law-abiding despite his allegiance; who practiced chaste asceticism in his desire for the Vedas, who re-established the four-part weapon study, and who treats us graciously. You should ask after the health of Ashvatthá-man, who has studied and is a man of good conduct; who has re-established the four-part weapon study; an energetic man like the son of a *gandhárva.*

Once you've gone to Sharádvata's house you ought to touch Kripa's feet with your hand, Sáñjaya, while repeating my name to that great warrior, the greatest of those who understand the nature of the soul.

Taking him by the feet, mention me to Bhishma, the 30.15
greatest of the Kurus, in whom there is heroism, non-violence, austerity, wisdom, good conduct, true learning, and constancy. Greet the aged king, the very learned and intelligent guide of the Kurus, whose only sight is wisdom, and who cares for the old, and tell him that I am well. Sáñjaya my friend, ask after Dhrita·rashtra's eldest son, the idiot Suyódhana, the deceitful fool of evil conduct who now commands the entire world.

bhrātā kanīyān api tasya mandas,
tathā|śīlaḥ, Sañjaya, so 'pi śaśvat,
mah"|êṣvāsaḥ śūratamaḥ Kurūṇāṃ,
Duḥśāsanaḥ kuśalaṃ, tāta, vācyaḥ.
yasya kāmo vartate nityam eva
n' ânyac chamād Bhāratānām, iti sma,
sa Bāhlikānām ṛṣabho manīṣī
tvay" âbhivādyaḥ, Sañjaya, sādhu|śīlaḥ.
30.20 guṇair anekaiḥ pravaraiś ca yukto,
vijñānavān n' âiva ca niṣṭhuro yaḥ,
snehād a|marṣaṃ sahate sad" âiva
sa Somadattaḥ pūjanīyo mato me.
arhattamaḥ Kuruṣu Saumadattiḥ,
sa no bhrātā, Sañjaya, mat|sakhā ca,
mah"|êṣvāso rathinām uttamo 'rhaḥ,
sah'|âmātyaḥ kuśalaṃ tasya pṛccheḥ.
ye c' âiv' ânye Kuru|mukhyā yuvānaḥ,
putrāḥ, pautrā, bhrātaraś c' âiva ye naḥ,
yaṃ yam eṣāṃ manyase yena yogyaṃ,
tat tat procy' ân|āmayaṃ, sūta, vācyāḥ.
ye rājānaḥ Pāṇḍav'|āyodhanāya
samānītā Dhārtarāṣṭreṇa ke cit;
Vaśātayaḥ, Śālvakāḥ Kekayāś ca,
tath" Âmbaṣṭhā ye, Trigartāś ca mukhyāḥ
prācy'|ôdīcyā, dākṣiṇātyāś ca śūrās,
tathā pratīcyā, pārvatīyāś ca sarve,
a|nṛśaṃsāḥ śīla|vṛtt'|ôpapannās,
teṣāṃ sarveṣāṃ kuśalaṃ, sūta, pṛccheḥ.

You ought also to enquire after the health of his younger brother, the fool who is always just as badly behaved, Sáñjaya; the bravest mighty archer the Kurus possess—Duhshásana. Greet the wise and well-behaved bull of the Bahlíkas, Sáñjaya, whose wish has always been for nothing other than peace between the Bháratas. Soma·datta too, in my 30.20
opinion, deserves to be honored, for he is endowed with many excellent qualities, wise but not cruel, and always suppresses his impatience out of love.

Ask how Soma·datta's son is doing, that most worthy of the Kurus, the great archer and greatest of chariot warriors, the worthy man who is like our brother, Sáñjaya, and is my friend. Ask how his counselors are doing too. Then of course there are the other leading Kuru youths, our sons, grandsons, and brothers. *Suta*, ask after the health of each and every one of them, speaking by whatever means you see fit.

Whichever kings Dhartaráshtra has brought together for war against the Pándavas—Vashátis, Shálvakas, Kékayas, Ambáshthas, and the leading Tri·gartas, as well as brave men from the east, north, south, and west, and of course all the mountain heroes—ask after the health of all these kind men who are endowed with good conduct, *suta*.

30.25 hasty|ārohā, rathinaḥ sādinaś ca,
padātayaś c' ārya|saṅghā mahāntaḥ,
ākhyāya māṃ kuśalinaṃ sma nityam
an|āmayaṃ paripṛccheḥ samagrān.
tathā rājño hy, artha|yuktān amātyān,
dauvārikān, ye ca senāṃ nayanti,
āya|vyayaṃ ye gaṇayanti nityam,
arthāṃś ca ye mahataś cintayanti.
vṛndārakaṃ Kuru|madhyeṣv a|mūḍhaṃ,
mahā|prajñaṃ, sarva|dharm'|ôpapannam,
na tasya yuddhaṃ rocate vai kadā cid,
vaiśyā|putraṃ kuśalaṃ, tāta, pṛccheḥ.
nikartane, devane yo '|dvitīyaś;
chann'|ôpadhaḥ, sādhu|devī, mat'|âkṣaḥ,
yo dur|jayo deva|rathena saṃkhye,
sa Citrasenaḥ kuśalaṃ, tāta, vācyaḥ.
Gandhāra|rājaḥ Śakuniḥ pārvatīyo,
nikartane yo '|dvitīyo 'kṣa|devī,
mānaṃ kurvan Dhārtarāṣṭrasya, sūta,
mithyā|buddheḥ kuśalaṃ, tāta, pṛccheḥ.
30.30 yaḥ Pāṇḍavān eka|rathena vīraḥ
samutsahaty a|pradhṛṣyān vijetum,
yo muhyatāṃ mohayit" â|dvitīyo,
Vaikartanaḥ, kuśalaṃ tasya pṛccheḥ.

Tell the elephant riders, charioteers, and horsemen, and the huge masses of noble infantry, that I am in good health as always, then enquire after the well-being of each and every one. Do the same for the king's significant ministers, his door-keepers as well as those who lead the army, his accountants who constantly calculate income and expenditure, and the great men who consider his interests. 30.25

Enquire, my friend, after the health of Dhrita·rashtra's son by a vaishya woman; the most prominent sagacious man among the Kurus, a man of great wisdom, endowed with every virtue, who has never taken pleasure in war. Then, my friend, find out how Chitra·sena is doing; that man who has no equal in impoverishing men and gambling; a dice-obsessed, successful gambler whose tricks always remain undiscovered and who is near impossible to defeat in war with his divine chariot.

Then there is Shákuni, mountain king of Gandhára, unmatched at impoverishing people or as a gambler of dice; the man who fuels Dhartaráshtra's arrogance, *suta*. My friend, you should ask after that deceitful-minded man's health. You should also enquire after the well-being of Karna 30.30
Vaikártana, the hero who thinks he is able to defeat the invincible Pándavas with his single chariot; a man who is a matchless trickster of the already confused.

sa eva bhaktaḥ, sa guruḥ, sa bhartā,
sa vai pitā, sa ca mātā, suhṛc ca,
a|gādha|buddhir Viduro dīrgha|darśī,
sa no mantrī kuśalaṃ taṃ sma pṛccheḥ.
vṛddhāḥ striyo yāś ca guṇ'|ôpapannāḥ
jñāyante naḥ, Sañjaya, mātaras tāḥ,
tābhiḥ sarvābhiḥ sahitābhiḥ sametya
strībhir vṛddhābhir* abhivādaṃ vadethāḥ:
‹kac cit putrā, jīva|putrāḥ, su|samyag
vartante vo vṛttim a|nṛśaṃsa|rupāḥ?›
iti sm' ôktvā, Sañjaya, brūhi paścād,
‹Ajātaśatruḥ kuśalī sa|putraḥ.›
yā no bhāryāḥ, Sañjaya, vettha tatra,
tāsāṃ sarvāsāṃ kuśalaṃ, tāta, pṛccheḥ,
‹su|saṃguptāḥ surabhayo 'n|avadyāḥ
kac cid gṛhān āvasath'|â|pramattāḥ?
30.35 kac cid vṛttiṃ śvaśureṣu bhadrāḥ,
kalyāṇīṃ vartadhvam a|nṛśaṃsa|rūpām?
yathā ca vaḥ syuḥ patayo 'nukūlās
tathā vṛttim ātmanaḥ sthāpayadhvam?›
yā naḥ snuṣāḥ, Sañjaya, vettha tatra,
prāptāḥ kulebhyaś ca guṇ'|ôpapannāḥ,
‹prajāvatyo,› brūhi sametya tāś ca,
‹Yudhiṣṭhiro vo 'bhyavadat prasannaḥ!›
kanyāḥ svajethāḥ sadaneṣu, Sañjaya,
an|āmayaṃ mad|vacanena pṛṣṭvā,
‹kalyāṇā vaḥ santu patayo 'nukūlā
yūyaṃ patīnāṃ bhavat' ânukūlāḥ.›

Ask after the well-being of our counselor, the far-sighted and unfathomably intelligent Vídura, our devoted guru, master, father, mother, and friend. Meet all the old women, together with those who are known to be endowed with virtue, and those who are like mothers to us, Sáñjaya, and give them this message: 'Ladies with living sons, are your sons treating you entirely properly and kindly?' Say this, Sáñjaya, and tell them afterwards that Ajáta·shatru and his sons are in good health.

My friend, please ask after the well-being of all the women there who you know as our wives, saying, 'Are you well-defended, perfumed, and blameless, carefully attending to the household? Are you gracious in your behavior 30.35
towards your fathers-in-law? Do you live good and benign lives? Do you arrange your conduct in such a manner that your husbands would be pleased with you?'

When you meet the ladies you know to be our daughters-in-law there, Sáñjaya, who are endowed with virtue and from good families, say to them together: 'Mothers, Yudhi·shthira greets you kindly!' Embrace the girls in their homes, Sáñjaya, and enquire after their well-being in my words, 'May you have handsome husbands who are pleased with you, and may you yourselves be faithful to your husbands.'

alaṃ|kṛtā, vastravatyaḥ, su|gandhā,
a|bībhatsāḥ, sukhitā, bhogavatyaḥ,
laghu yāsāṃ darśanaṃ, vāk ca laghvī,
veśa|striyaḥ kuśalaṃ, tāta, pṛccheḥ.
dāsyaḥ syur yā, ye ca dāsāḥ Kurūṇāṃ,
tad|āśrayā bahavaḥ kubja|khañjāḥ,
ākhyāya māṃ kuśalinaṃ sma tebhyo 'py
an|āmayaṃ paripṛccher jaghanyam:
30.10 ‹kac cid vṛttiṃ vartate vai purāṇīṃ?
kac cid bhogān Dhārtarāṣṭro dadāti?›
aṅga|hīnān, kṛpaṇān, vāmanān vā
yān ānṛśaṃsyo Dhṛtarāṣṭro bibharti,
andhāṃś ca sarvān, sthavirāṃs tath" âiva,
hasty|ājīvā bahavo ye 'tra santi
ākhyāya māṃ kuśalinaṃ sma tebhyo 'py
an|āmayaṃ paripṛccher jaghanyam:
‹mā bhaiṣṭa duḥkhena ku|jīvitena
nūnaṃ kṛtaṃ para|lokeṣu pāpam.
nigṛhya śatrūn, suhṛdo 'nugṛhya,
vāsobhir annena ca vo bhariṣye.
santy eva me brāhmaṇebhyaḥ kṛtāni
bhāvīny atho no bata vartayanti!
tān paśyāmi yukta|rūpāṃs tath" âiva.
tām eva siddhiṃ śrāvayethā nṛpaṃ tam.›
ye c' â|nāthā dur|balāḥ sarva|kālam
ātmany eva prayatante 'tha mūḍhāḥ,
tāṃś c' âpi tvaṃ kṛpaṇān sarvath" âiva
asmad vākyāt kuśalaṃ, tāta, pṛccheḥ.

You ought also to ask how the courtezans are faring, my friend; those finely dressed, decorated, and beautifully perfumed women, who are appealing, happy, and furnished with luxury, and whose visits and conversation are fleeting.

Please tell the Kurus' slave girls and slaves, as well as those many lame and hump-backed people who rely on them, that I am in fine health, and ask how it's going for them in
their most wretched situation: 'Do you still make a living 30.40
as you used to? Does Dhartaráshtra give you some relief?'

You should also ask after those who have lost limbs, the poor, or the dwarves, whom Dhrita·rashtra benevolently supports, the blind and all the old people, as well as the many people whose only livelihood is through their hands, telling them first that I am doing well, and then asking how their health is in their terrible situation: 'Don't be afraid of the pain of a miserable life, which is surely the result of sin committed in a previous life. Once I have subdued my enemies and helped my friends, I will support you with clothing and food. I have blessings performed by the brahmins, and they will continue to be produced I am sure! I see that your bodies will one day be properly formed. Tell the king of your success when it comes.' My friend, you should ask after the health of the defenseless and weak, those who spend all their time trying to support themselves, and the fools unaware that there are people who are pitiable in every respect.

30.45 ye c' âpy anye saṃśritā Dhārtarāṣṭrān
nānā|digbhyo 'bhyāgatāḥ, sūta|putra,
dṛṣṭvā tāṃś c' âiv', ârhataś c' âpi sarvān,
saṃpṛcchethāḥ kuśalaṃ c' â|vyayaṃ ca.
evaṃ sarvān āgat'|âbhyāgatāṃś ca,
rājño dūtān sarva|digbhyo 'bhyupetān,
pṛṣṭvā sarvān kuśalaṃ tāṃś ca, sūta,
paścād ahaṃ kuśalī teṣu vācyaḥ.
na h' īdṛśāḥ santy apare pṛthivyāṃ
ye yodhakā Dhārtarāṣṭreṇa labdhaḥ.
dharmas tu nityo mama dharma eva
mahā|balaḥ śatru|nibarhaṇāya.
idaṃ punar vacanaṃ Dhārtarāṣṭraṃ
Suyodhanaṃ, Sañjaya, śrāvayethāḥ:
‹yas te śarīre hṛdayaṃ dunoti
kāmaḥ, Kurūn a|sapatno 'nuśiṣyām,
na vidyate yuktir etasya kā cin!
n' âivaṃ|vidhāḥ syāma, yathā priyaṃ te.
dadasva vā Śakra|purīṃ mam' âiva,
yudhyasva vā, Bhārata|mukhya vīra.› »

YUDHIṢṬHIRA uvāca:

31.1 «UTA SANTAM A|SANTAṂ vā, bālaṃ vṛddhaṃ ca, Sañjaya,
ut' â|bālaṃ balīyāṃsaṃ dhātā prakurute vaśe.
uta bālāya pāṇḍityaṃ, paṇḍitāy' ôta bālatām
dadāti sarvam īśānaḥ, purastāc chukram uccaran.
balam jijñāsamānasya ācakṣīthā yathā|tatham
atha mantraṃ mantrayitvā yāthātathyena hṛṣṭavat.

When you see the others who have taken refuge with 30.45
the Dhartaráshtras, coming from various directions, son of a *suta*, or when you see anyone worthy, ask all of them whether they are unchangingly healthy. Ask all the messengers who have come from every direction to see the king, as they arrive and visit, whether they are well, and afterwards tell them that I am in good shape. There are no other warriors on the earth like those Dhartaráshtra has found. However, righteousness is eternal, and righteousness is my great power for the destruction of my enemies.

Sáñjaya, repeat my final words to Suyódhana Dhartaráshtra: 'There is no justification for the desire that burns the heart inside your body to command the Kurus uncontested! Nor are we the sort of people who will do you any favors. Either give me Shakra·puri, the capital city of Indra·prastha, or fight, heroic leader of the Bháratas!'"

YUDHI·SHTHIRA continued:

"THE CREATOR IS in control whether someone is good or 31.1
evil, young or old, Sáñjaya, or weak or strong. The Lord bestows learning upon a child or childishness upon a teacher right from the start, as he pours out the seed. When questioned for information about our power, explain it precisely, since you have happily and truthfully consulted with us upon our resolve.

Gāvalgaṇe, Kurūn gatvā Dhṛtarāṣṭraṃ mahā|balam
abhivādy' ôpasaṅgṛhya tataḥ pṛccher an|āmayam.
31.5 brūyāś c' âinaṃ tvam āsīnaṃ Kurubhiḥ parivāritam:
‹tav' âiva, rājan, vīryeṇa sukhaṃ jīvanti Pāndavāḥ.
tava prasādād bālās te prāptā rājyam, arin|dama,
rājye tān sthāpayitv" âgre n' ôpekṣasva vinaśyataḥ.›
sarvam apy etad ekasya n' âlaṃ, Sañjaya, kasya cit.
‹tāta, saṃhatya jīvāmo, dviṣatām mā vaśaṃ gamaḥ!›
tathā Bhīṣmaṃ Śāntanavaṃ Bhāratānām pitā|maham
śiras" âbhivadethās tvaṃ mama nāma prakīrtayan.
abhivādya ca vaktavyas tato 'smākaṃ pitā|mahaḥ:
‹bhavatā Śantanor vaṃśo nimagnaḥ punar uddhṛtaḥ.
31.10 sa tvaṃ kuru tathā, tāta, sva|matena, pitā|maha,
yathā jīvanti te pautrāḥ prītimantaḥ paras|param.›
tath" âiva Viduraṃ brūyāḥ Kurūṇāṃ mantra|dhāriṇam:
‹a|yuddhaṃ, saumya, bhāṣasva hita|kāmo Yudhiṣṭhire.›
atha Duryodhanaṃ brūyā rāja|putram a|marṣaṇam
madhye Kurūṇām āsīnam anunīya punaḥ punaḥ:
‹a|pāpāṃ yad upaikṣas tvaṃ Kṛṣṇām etāṃ sabh"|āgatām
tad duḥkham atitikṣāma, mā vadhīṣma Kurūn, iti.
evaṃ pūrv'|âparān kleśān atitikṣanta Pāṇḍavāḥ
balīyāṃso 'pi santo yat, tat sarvaṃ Kuravo viduḥ.
31.15 yan naḥ pravrājayeḥ, saumya, ajinaiḥ prativāsitān,

Son of Gaválgana, once you have gone to the Kurus,
greeted the mighty Dhrita·rashtra, and embraced him, ask
whether he is well. Then, once he is seated, surrounded by 31.5
the Kurus, say to him: 'My king, the Pándavas live happily because of your strength. By your grace they attained a kingdom while still young, destroyer of your enemies, but since you established them in a kingdom at the beginning, you should not now look the other way as they are destroyed.' For no one man ought to own everything, Sáñjaya. 'Let us live together, sir. Don't succumb to the power of your enemies!'

In the same way greet Bhishma, son of Shántanu, the
grandfather of the Bháratas, bowing your head and men-
tioning my name. Once you have greeted him, you must
say to our grandfather: 'My lord, when Shántanu's lineage
was sinking, you elevated it once more. Now, father, do it 31.10
again, using your own judgment, grandfather, so that your grandchildren can live together pleasantly.'

Speak in the same way to Vídura, the Kurus' advisor, saying: 'Speak peaceful rather than war-mongering words, and be well-meaning towards Yudhi·shthira.' Then address intolerant Prince Duryódhana when he is sitting in the midst of the Kurus, repeatedly conciliating him, quoting us as saying:

'We will patiently bear the pain of having had to ignore the blameless Krishná when she was being led into the court, in order to prevent a massacre of the Kurus! The Pándavas have suffered other miseries in the past and managed to endure them, despite the fact that they were powerful enough to overcome them—all of which the Kurus

tad duḥkham atitikṣāma, mā vādhīṣma Kurūn iti.
yat sabhyāṃ* samatikramya Kṛṣṇāṃ keśēṣv adharṣayat
Duḥśāsanas te 'numate, tac c' âsmābhir upekṣitam.
ath' ôcitaṃ svakaṃ bhāgaṃ labhemahi, paran|tapa,
nivartaya para|dravyād buddhiṃ gṛddhāṃ, nara'|rṣabha!
śāntir evaṃ bhaved, rājan, prītiś c' âiva paras|param.
rājy'|âika|deśam api naḥ prayaccha śamam icchatām:
Avisthalaṃ, Vṛkasthalaṃ, Mākandīṃ, Vāraṇāvatam;
avasānaṃ bhavatv atra kiñ cid ekaṃ ca pañcamam.
31.20 bhrātṝṇāṃ dehi pañcānāṃ pañca|grāmān, Suyódhana!›
śāntir no 'stu, mahā|prājña, jñātibhiḥ saha, Sañjaya.
bhrātā bhrātaram anvetu pitā putreṇa yujyatām.
smayamānāḥ samāyāntu Pāñcālāḥ Kurubhiḥ saha.
a|kṣatān Kuru|Pāñcālān paśyeyam, iti kāmaye.
sarve su|manasas, tāta, śāmyāma, Bhārata'|rṣabha.
alam eva śamāy' âsmi, tathā yuddhāya, Sañjaya,
dharm'|ârthayor alaṃ c' âhaṃ, mṛdave dāruṇāya ca.»

VAIŚAMPĀYANA uvāca:

32.1 ANUJÑĀTAḤ PĀṆḌAVENA prayayau Sañjayas tadā
śāsanaṃ Dhṛtarāṣṭrasya sarvaṃ kṛtvā mah"|ātmanaḥ.
saṃprāpya Hāstinapuraṃ śīghram eva praviśya ca
antaḥ|puraṃ samāsthāya dvāḥ|sthaṃ vacanam abravīt:
«ācakṣva Dhṛtarāṣṭrāya, dvāḥ|stha, māṃ samupāgatam
sakāśāt Pāṇḍu|putrāṇāṃ Sañjayaṃ; mā ciraṃ kṛthāḥ.
jāgarti ced, abhivades tvaṃ hi, dvāḥ|stha,

know. Despite the fact that you banished us, excellent man, 31.15
clothed in antelope skin, we will endure the pain to prevent the slaughter the Kurus. We will also overlook the fact that Duhshásana marched into court and molested Krishná, grabbing her by the hair with your approval. But we must take our fair share, scorcher of your enemies, so turn your greedy mind away from other people's property, bull-like man! Then there will be peace, king, and mutual harmony. Give a single region of your kingdom to us, for we want peace: Avísthala, Vrika·sthala, Makándi, Varanávata, and let some boundary area be the fifth part. Give five 31.20
villages to five brothers, Suyódhana!'

So, may there be peace between us, wise Sáñjaya, and our relatives. Let brother follow brother, and let father be united with son. Let the Pañchálas join smilingly with the Kurus. It is my wish to see the Kurus and Pañchálas unharmed. We will all be cheerfully at peace, my friend, bull of the Bháratas. I am just as capable of peace as I am of war, Sáñjaya, and I am as capable of duty and profit as I am of gentleness and severity."

VAISHAMPÁYANA said:

ONCE HE HAD been instructed by the Pándava, Sáñjaya 32.1
left, for he had achieved everything high-souled Dhrita·rashtra had commanded. Having reached Hástina·pura, he quickly entered, and once he had come to the inner apartments, he said to the door-keeper: "Door-keeper, announce to Dhrita·rashtra at once that I, Sáñjaya, have returned from meeting the Pándavas. You should tell him if he's awake, door-keeper, for I would like to enter with the king's prior

praviśeyaṃ vidito bhūmi|pasya.
nivedyam atr' ātyayikaṃ hi me 'sti.»
dvāḥ|stho 'tha śrutvā nṛpatiṃ jagāda.

DVĀḤSTHA uvāca:

32.5 «Sañjayo 'yaṃ, bhūmi|pate, namaste.
didṛkṣayā dvāram upāgatas te.
prāpto dūtaḥ Pāṇḍavānāṃ sakāśāt.
praśādhi, rājan, kim ayaṃ karotu.»

DHṚTARĀṢṬRA uvāca:

«ācakṣva māṃ kuśalinaṃ kalpam asmai.
praveśyatāṃ; svāgataṃ Sañjayāya.
na c' âham etasya bhavāmy a|kalpaḥ,
sa me kasmād dvāri tiṣṭhec ca saktaḥ?»

VAIŚAMPĀYANA uvāca:

tataḥ praviśy', ânumate nṛpasya,
mahad veśma, prājña|śūr'|ārya|guptam,
siṃh'|āsana|sthaṃ pārthivam āsasāda
Vaicitravīryaṃ prāñjaliḥ sūta|putraḥ.

SAÑJAYA uvāca:

«Sañjayo 'haṃ, bhūmi|pate, namaste.
prāpto 'smi gatvā, nara|deva, Pāṇḍavān.
abhivādya tvāṃ Pāṇḍu|putro manasvī
Yudhiṣṭhiraḥ kuśalaṃ c' ânvapṛcchat.
sa te putrān pṛcchati prīyamāṇaḥ,
kac cit putraiḥ prīyase, naptṛbhiś ca,
tathā suhṛdbhiḥ, sacivaiś ca, rājan,
ye c' âpi tvām upajīvanti, taiś ca?»

knowledge. My message is urgent!" And when the door-keeper heard this, he went to the king.

THE DOOR-KEEPER said:

"Greetings, king. Sáñjaya is here. He has come to the 32.5
door and wants to see you. Your messenger has returned from meeting the Pándavas. Give orders, my king, as to what he should do."

DHRITA·RASHTRA replied:

"Tell him that I am well and able to receive him. Let Sáñjaya enter and bid him welcome. I have never yet been unable to see him, so why is he stuck standing at my door?"

VAISHAMPÁYANA said:

So, with the king's permission, the *suta*'s son entered the massive apartment guarded by wise and brave nobles, and with his hands folded he approached King Váichitravirya as he sat on his lion throne.

SÁÑJAYA said:

"I, Sáñjaya, bow to you, my king. I have returned after visiting the Pándavas, lord of men. Wise Yudhi·shthira, son of Pandu, sends his greetings to you and enquires after your health. He affectionately asks after your sons, and asks whether you are pleased with your sons and grandsons, and likewise with your friends and attendants, my king, as well as those whose livelihood depends upon you."

DHṚTARĀṢṬRA uvāca:

32.10 «abhinandya tvāṃ, tāta, vadāmi, Sáñjaya,
Ajātaśatruṃ ca sukhena Pārtham.
kac cit sa rājā kuśalī sa|putraḥ
sah' âmātyaḥ s'|ânujaḥ Kauravāṇām?»

SAÑJAYA uvāca:

«sah' âmātyaḥ kuśalī Pāṇḍu|putro;
bhūyaś c' âto yac ca te 'gre mano 'bhūt*
nirṇikta|dharm'|ârtha|karo manasvī,
bahu|śruto, dṛṣṭimān śīlavāṃś ca.
paro dharmāt Pāṇḍavasy' ānṛśaṃsasyaṃ;
dharmaḥ paro vitta|cayān mato 'sya.
sukha|priye dharma|hīne 'n|apārthe
na rudhyate, Bhārata, tasya buddhiḥ.
para|prayuktaḥ puruṣo viceṣṭate,
sūtra|protā dāru|may" îva yoṣā.
imaṃ dṛṣṭvā niyamaṃ Pāṇḍavasya
manye paraṃ karma daivaṃ manuṣyāt.
imaṃ ca dṛṣṭvā tava karma|doṣaṃ
pāp'|ôdarkaṃ, ghoram a|varṇa|rūpam,
yāvat paraḥ kāmayate 'tivelaṃ
tāvan naro 'yaṃ labhate praśaṃsām.
32.15 Ajātaśatrus tu vihāya pāpaṃ,
jīrṇāṃ tvacaṃ sarpa iv' â|samarthām,
virocate '|hārya|vṛttena vīro
Yudhiṣṭhiras tvayi pāpaṃ visṛjya.
hant' ātmanaḥ karma, nibodha, rājan,
dharm'|ârtha|yuktād ārya|vṛttād apetam!
upakrośaṃ c' êha gato 'si, rājan,
bhūyaś ca pāpaṃ prasajed amutra.

DHRITA·RASHTRA replied:

"I welcome and greet you, Sáñjaya my friend, and Ajáta·shatru Partha with pleasure. Are the king and his sons well? And how are his advisors and Káurava brothers?" 32.10

SÁÑJAYA continued:

"The son of Pandu and his advisors are well; in fact the wise, discerning, and highly learned man of good character is now more intent on practicing pure moral duty and profit than ever he was when you first knew him. In the Pándava's opinion non-violence surpasses moral duty and morality surpasses making money. His mind does not succumb to immoral and purposeless pleasure and joy, Bhárata.

A man is controlled by outside forces when he acts, just like a wooden puppet strung on strings; and having witnessed the Pándava's restraint, I believe that karma is the fate which surpasses man. I have seen your sinful deed of reprehensible horror with its evil consequence, and I believe a man of your sort only wins praise for as long as his enemy wishes to prolong the situation. Ajáta·shatru has renounced 32.15
evil, just as a snake casts off its useless, worn-out slough; the hero Yudhi·shthira shines with his unalterable conduct, and he heaps the sin on you.

Oh realize what you have done, my king! Your actions were devoid of noble conduct or any connection to duty and profit! You have come under criticism, my king, and this evil will follow you again to the next world. Without thought of them, but subservient to your son's will, you can

sa tvam arthaṃ saṃśayitaṃ vinā tair
āśaṃsase putra|vaś'|ânugo 'sya.
a|dharma|śabdaś ca mahān pṛthivyāṃ;
n' êdaṃ karma tvat|samaṃ, Bhārat'|âgrya.
hīna|prajño, dauṣkuleyo, nṛśaṃso,
dīrghaṃ vairī, kṣatra|vidyāsv a|dhīraḥ,
evaṃ|dharmān āpadaḥ saṃśrayeyur,
hīna|vīryo yaś ca bhaved a|śiṣṭaḥ.
kule jāto, balavān, yo yaśasvī,
bahu|śrutaḥ, sukha|jīvī, yat'|atmā,
dharm'|âdharmau grathitau yo bibharti;
sa hy asya diṣṭasya vaśād upaiti.
32.20 kathaṃ hi mantr'|âgrya|dharo manīṣī,
dharm'|ârthayor āpadi saṃpraṇetā,
evam uktaḥ sarva|mantrair a|hīno,
naro nṛśaṃsaṃ karma kuryād a|mūḍhaḥ?
tav' âp' îme* mantra|vidaḥ sametya
samāsate karmasu nitya|yuktāḥ;
teṣām ayaṃ balavān niścayaś ca
Kuru|kṣaye nirayo vyapādi.*
a|kālikaṃ Kuravo n' âbhaviṣyan
pāpena cet pāpam Ajātaśatruḥ
icchej jātu tvayi pāpaṃ visṛjya;
nindā c' êyaṃ tava loke 'bhaviṣyat.
kim anyatra viṣayād īśvarāṇāṃ
yatra Pārthaḥ para|lokaṃ sma draṣṭum
atyakrāmat sa tathā saṃmataḥ syān?
na saṃśayo, n' âsti manuṣya|kāraḥ.

only hope for a dubious profit. Word of your lawless act has spread far over the world; this act was not worthy of you, foremost of the Bháratas.

Catastrophes will flock to men of the following kinds: the man who lacks wisdom, the man who is ignobly born, the violent man who nurses grudges for too long, who is deficiently versed in warrior codes, who is untrained, and who lacks heroism. And it is certainly only through the power of fate that a man is born strong and illustrious, into a good family; that he lives well, that he is highly learned and self-disciplined, and that he bears ever-intertwined right and
wrong. For how can a wise man, given the greatest advice, 32.20
a guide to what is right and profitable in times of disaster, commit a cruel deed when he is unconfused and is not lacking counsel, but is supplied with every spell?

Your advisors have gathered and sit together, devoted to your affairs as always; they have come to a powerful decision; hell has broken loose in ruin and the Kurus' destruction. The Kurus would be destroyed in no time if Ajáta·shatru wished to fight evil with evil, while certainly pouring the sin onto you; the blame of the world would be directed towards you. What else is there but the dominion of the gods; the place beyond, to which Partha passed to see the next world and was greatly honored? Doubtless human actions are as nothing.

etān guṇān karma|kṛtān avekṣya,
bhāv'|âbhāvau, vartamānāv a|nityau,
Balir hi rājā, pāram a|vindamāno
n' ânyat kālāt kāraṇaṃ tatra mene.
32.25 cakṣuḥ|śrotre, nāsikā, tvak ca, jihvā
jñānasy' âitāny āyatanāni jantoḥ.
tāni prītāny eva tṛṣṇā|kṣay'|ânte;
tāny a|vyatho duḥkha|hīnaḥ praṇudyāt.
na tv eva manye puruṣasya karma
saṃvartate su|prayuktaṃ yathavat.
mātuḥ pituḥ karmaṇ" âbhiprasūtaḥ
saṃvardhate vidhivad bhojanena.
priy'|â|priye sukha|duḥkhe ca, rājan,
nindā|praśaṃse ca bhajanta eva.
paras tv enaṃ garhayate 'parādhe
praśaṃsate sādhu|vṛttaṃ tam eva.
sa tvāṃ garhe Bhāratānāṃ virodhād;
anto nūnaṃ bhavit" âyaṃ prajānām.
no ced idaṃ tava karm'|âparādhāt
Kurūn dahet Kṛṣṇa|vartm" êva kakṣam.
svam ek'|âiko jātu putrasya, rājan,
vaśaṃ gatvā sarva|loke, nar'|êndra;
kām'|ātmanaḥ ślāghano dyūta|kāle!
n' āgāḥ śamaṃ, paśya vipākam asya!
32.30 an|āptānāṃ saṃgrahāt tvaṃ, nar'|êndra,
tath" āptānāṃ nigrahāc c' âiva, rājan,
bhūmiṃ sphītāṃ durbalatvād an|antām
a|śaktas tvaṃ rakṣituṃ, Kauraveya.

King Bali examined the qualities of completed actions,
the existent and non-existent, the present and non-eternal;
but when he couldn't get to the bottom of it, he believed
the cause was nothing other than time. Eyes, ears, the nose, 32.25
skin, and the tongue are the seats of human knowledge.
When their thirsts are quenched they are pleased, and so
one should drive them on, controlling them, untroubled
and free from pain. Some disagree, arguing that a man's
action turns out properly if done well. For a child is born
through the mother and father's actions, and nourishment
duly causes the child to grow.

People are allotted pleasure and discomfort, happiness
and misery, my king, and praise and blame. One reproaches
the other when he has sinned, but praises him for good behavior. I blame you for the hostility between the Bháratas;
it will surely be the end of your descendants. I hope your
crime does not result in Árjuna consuming the Kurus, just
as black-trailed fire burns a forest. You, my king, are certainly the only man in the whole world who has fallen under the control of his son, lord of men. During the game of
dice you flattered that lust-ridden man! If we do not reach a
peaceful settlement, then behold the consequences of your
actions! By your kind treatment of the untrustworthy, lord 32.30
of men, and your suppression of the trustworthy, my king,
you are too weak to be able to protect your endless, rich
land.

anujñāto ratha|veg'|âvadhūtaḥ
 śrānto 'bhipadye śayanam, nṛ|siṃha.
prātaḥ śrotāraḥ Kuravaḥ sabhāyām
 Ajātaśatror vacanaṃ sametāḥ.»

DHṚTARĀṢṬRA uvāca:

«anujñāto 'sy, āvasathaṃ parehi,
 prapadyasva śayanam, sūta|putra.
prātaḥ śrotāraḥ Kuravaḥ sabhāyām
 Ajātaśatror vacanaṃ tvay" ôktam.»

I have been shaken by the speed of the chariot and I am exhausted; please allow me to go and lie down, lion-like king. The Kurus will hear what Ajáta·shatru had to say when they gather in court in the morning."

DHRITA·RASHTRA said:

"You have my permission. Run along home and go and lie down, son of a *suta*. The Kurus will hear you tell us what Ajáta·shatru had to say in the morning in court."

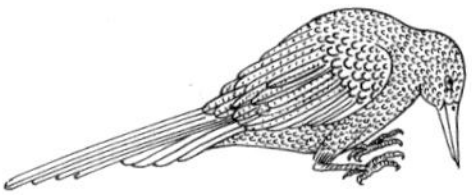

# 33–41
# VÍDURA'S TEACHINGS

VAIŚAMPĀYANA uvāca:

33.1 DVĀḤ|STHAM PRĀHA mahā|prājño
Dhṛtarāṣṭro mahī|patiḥ:
«Viduraṃ draṣṭum icchāmi.
tam ih' ānaya mā|ciram.»
prahito Dhṛtarāṣṭreṇa dūtaḥ kṣattāram abravīt:
«īśvaras tvāṃ mahā|rājo, mahā|prājña, didṛkṣati.»
evam uktas tu Viduraḥ prāpya rāja|niveśanam
abravīd: «Dhṛtarāṣṭrāya» dvāḥ|sthaṃ «māṃ prativedaya!»

DVĀḤSTHA uvāca:

«Viduro 'yam anuprāpto, rāj'|êndra, tava śāsanāt.
draṣṭum icchati te pādau. kiṃ karotu, praśādhi mām.»

DHṚTARĀṢṬRA uvāca:

33.5 «praveśaya mahā|prājñaṃ Viduraṃ dīrgha|darśinam
ahaṃ hi Vidurasy' âsya n' â|kalpo jātu darśane.»

DVĀḤSTHA uvāca:

«praviś' ântaḥ|puraṃ, kṣattar, mahā|rājasya dhīmataḥ,
‹na hi te darśane '|kalpo jātu› rāj" âbravīdd hi mām.»

VAIŚAMPĀYANA uvāca:

tataḥ praviśya Viduro Dhṛtarāṣṭra|niveśanam,
abravīt prāñjalir vākyaṃ cintayānaṃ nar'|âdhipam:
«Viduro 'haṃ, mahā|prājña, saṃprāptas tava śāsanāt.
yadi kiñ cana kartavyam; ayam asmi, praśādhi mām.»

VAISHAMPÁYANA continued:

Wise King Dhrita·rashtra said to his door-keeper: "I want to see Vídura. Bring him here quickly." So, sent by Dhrita·rashtra, the messenger said to the steward: "The lord, the great king, wishes to see you, wise man." Addressed in this manner, Vídura went to the king's apartment and said to the door-keeper: "Announce me to Dhrita·rashtra!" 33.1

THE DOOR-KEEPER said:

"Vídura has come, lord of kings, at your command. He wishes to see your feet. Tell me what he should do."

DHRITA·RASHTRA replied:

"Let highly intelligent, far-sighted Vídura enter. It is cer- 33.5
tainly never inconvenient to see him."

THE DOOR-KEEPER said:

"Enter the wise king's inner chambers, steward, for the king has told me that it is certainly never inconvenient to see you."

VAISHAMPÁYANA continued:

Once he had entered Dhrita·rashtra's apartment, Vídura folded his hands and spoke to the king, who was lost in thought: "It is me, Vídura, supremely wise man, and I have come here as you ordered. If there is anything I must do, then command me."

DHṚTARĀṢṬRA uvāca:

«Sañjayo, Vidura, prāpto garhayitvā ca māṃ gataḥ.
Ajātaśatroḥ śvo vākyaṃ sabhā|madhye sa vakṣyati.
33.10 tasy' âdya Kuru|vīrasya na vijñātaṃ vaco mayā.
tan me dahati gātrāṇi, tad akārṣīt prajāgaram.
jāgrato dahyamānasya śreyo yad anupaśyasi,
tad brūhi tvaṃ hi nas, tāta, dharm'|ârtha|kuśalo hy asi.
yataḥ prāptaḥ Sañjayaḥ Pāṇḍavebhyo,
na me yathāvan manasaḥ praśāntiḥ;
sarv'|êndriyāṇy a|prakṛtiṃ gatāni
‹kiṃ vakṣyat', îty› eva me 'dya pracintā.»

VIDURA uvāca:

«abhiyuktaṃ balavatā dur|balaṃ, hīna|sādhanam,
hṛta|svaṃ, kāminaṃ, coram āviśanti prajāgarāḥ.
kac cid etair mahā|doṣair na spṛṣṭo 'si, nar'|âdhipa?
kac cic ca para|vitteṣu gṛdhyan na paritapyase?»

DHṚTARĀṢṬRA uvāca:

33.15 «śrotum icchāmi te dharmyaṃ
paraṃ naiḥśreyasaṃ vacaḥ
asmin rāja'|ṛṣi|vaṃśe hi
tvam ekaḥ prājña|saṃmataḥ.»

VIDURA uvāca:

«rājā lakṣaṇa|sampannas trailokyasy' âdhipo bhavet
preṣyas te preṣitaś c' âiva, Dhṛtarāṣṭra, Yudhiṣṭhiraḥ,*
viparītataraś ca tvaṃ bhāga|dheyena saṃmataḥ
arciṣāṃ prakṣayāc c' âiva dharm'|ātmā dharma|kovidaḥ.
ānṛśaṃsyād, anukrośād, dharmāt, satyāt, parākramāt,

DHRITA·RASHTRA said:

"Vídura, Sáñjaya came here, and once he'd blamed me for the present predicament, he left. He will tell us what Ajáta·shatru had to say in the midst of court tomorrow. At the moment I have no idea what the Kuru hero's mes- 33.10
sage was. It burns my limbs, and it draws out my insomnia. Since you are skilled in what is right and profitable, tell me what you see as best for a sleepless and fevered man, my friend.

Ever since Sáñjaya returned from the Pándavas my mind has not been properly at peace; all my senses have gone into turmoil as I wonder now what he will say."

VÍDURA replied:

"Insomnia visits the weak man who is attacked by a stronger opponent, it visits the man who has lost his means, who has lost himself, and it visits a lover or a thief. You are not touched by these great evils, are you, lord of men? Do you burn because you covet another man's property?"

DHRITA·RASHTRA said:

"I want to hear what beneficial advice of ultimate righ- 33.15
teousness you have to offer. For in the lineage of royal sages you alone are honored as wise."

VÍDURA said:

"King Yudhi·shthira, possessed of the proper characteristics, should be lord of the three realms. He is obedient to you, and you abused his obedience by exiling him, Dhrita·rashtra. You are the exact opposite of that man. Your loss of sight means that you are deemed unworthy of a share of the inheritance, despite the fact that you are virtuous in

gurutvāt tvayi saṃprekṣya bahūn kleśāṃs titikṣate.
Duryodhane Saubale ca, Karṇe, Duḥśāsane tathā,
eteṣv aiśvaryam ādhāya kathaṃ tvaṃ bhūtim icchasi?

33.20 ātma|jñānaṃ, samārambhas, titikṣā, dharma|nityatā
yam arthān n' âpakarṣanti, sa vai paṇḍita ucyate.
niṣevate praśastāni, ninditāni na sevate;
a|nāstikaḥ, śraddadhāna, etat paṇḍita|lakṣaṇam.
krodho, harṣaś ca, darpaś ca, hrī|stambho, mānya|mānitā
yam arthān n' âpakarṣanti, sa vai paṇḍita ucyate.
yasya kṛtyaṃ na jānanti mantraṃ vā mantritaṃ pare,
kṛtam ev' âsya jānanti, sa vai paṇḍita ucyate.

yasya kṛtyaṃ na vighnanti śītam, uṣṇaṃ, bhayaṃ, ratiḥ,
samṛddhir, a|samṛddhir vā, sa vai paṇḍita ucyate.

33.25 yasya saṃsāriṇī prajñā dharm'|ârthāv anuvartate,
kāmād arthaṃ vṛṇīte yaḥ, sa vai paṇḍita ucyate.
yathā|śakti cikīrṣanti, yathā|śakti ca kurvate,
na kiñ cid avamanyante narāḥ paṇḍita|buddhayaḥ.

kṣipraṃ vijānāti ciraṃ śṛṇoti;
vijñāya c' ârthaṃ bhajate na kāmāt;
n' â|saṃpṛṣṭo vyupayuṅkte par'|ârthe;
tat prajñānaṃ prathamaṃ paṇḍitasya.

n' â|prāpyam abhivāñchanti, naṣṭaṃ n' êcchanti śocitum,
āpatsu ca na muhyanti narāḥ paṇḍita|buddhayaḥ.

your soul and skilled in moral law. Due to his benevolence, compassion, virtue, truth, strength, and the respect he observes towards you, he endures his many miseries. How can you wish for prosperity when you have invested power upon Duryódhana, Súbala's son, Karna, and Duhshásana?

It is the man whose self-knowledge, effort, endurance, 33.20
and eternal virtue do not drag down his goals, who is said to be wise. What distinguishes a wise man is his pursuit of laudable deeds and avoidance of reprehensible deeds. He is not unorthodox but has belief. The man whom anger, joy, greed, trumped-up modesty, or egotism cannot drag away from his purpose, is said to be wise. The man whose enemies do not know his intention, plan, or counsel, but merely know his actions, is said to be wise.

The man whose plans are not obstructed by cold, heat,
fear, love, wealth, or poverty, is said to be wise. The man 33.25
whose wise, transmigratory soul follows virtue and profit, and chooses profit over desire, is said to be wise. Wise-minded men want to do whatever they can, do do whatever they can, and do not spurn anything.

This is the foremost sign of a wise man: he understands quickly but listens at leisure, he cultivates his aim with knowledge rather than from lust, and he does not meddle in other people's business unless requested to. Wise-minded men do not long for the unattainable, they do not wish to grieve for what is lost, and they are not confused in times of disaster.

niścitya yaḥ prakramate, n' ântarvasati karmaṇaḥ,
a|vandhya|kālo, vaśy'|ātmā, sa vai paṇḍita ucyate.
33.30 ārya|karmaṇi rajyante, bhūti|karmāṇi kurvate,
hitaṃ ca n' âbhyasūyanti paṇḍitā, Bharata'|rṣabha.
na hṛṣyaty ātma|saṃmāne, n' âvamānena tapyate,
Gāṅgo hrada iv' â|kṣobhyo yaḥ, sa paṇḍita ucyate.
tattva|jñaḥ sarva|bhūtānāṃ, yoga|jñaḥ sarva|karmaṇām,
upāya|jño manuṣyāṇāṃ naraḥ paṇḍita ucyate.
pravṛtta|vāk, citra|katha, ūhavān, pratibhānavān,
āśu granthasya vaktā ca yaḥ, sa paṇḍita ucyate.
śrutaṃ prajñ"|ânugaṃ yasya, prajñā c' âiva śrut'|ânugā,
a|saṃbhinn'|ārya|maryādaḥ paṇḍit'|ākhyāṃ labheta saḥ.
33.35 a|śrutaś ca samunnaddho, daridraś ca mahā|manāḥ,
arthāś c' â|karmaṇā prepsur mūḍha ity ucyate budhaiḥ.
svam arthaṃ yaḥ parityajya par'|ârtham anutiṣṭhati,
mithy" ācarati mitr'|ârthe yaś ca, mūḍhaḥ sa ucyate.
a|kāmān kāmayati yaḥ, kāmayānān parityajet,
balavantaṃ ca yo dveṣṭi, tam āhur mūḍha|cetasam.
a|mitraṃ kurute mitraṃ, mitraṃ dveṣṭi hinasti ca,
karma c' ārabhate duṣṭaṃ, tam āhur mūḍha|cetasam.
saṃsārayati kṛtyāni, sarvatra vicikitsate,
ciraṃ karoti kṣipr'|ârthe, sa mūḍho, Bharata'|rṣabha.
33.40 śrāddhaṃ pitṛbhyo na dadāti, daivatāni na c' ârcati,
suhṛn|mitraṃ na labhate, tam āhur mūḍha|cetasam.

It is the man who acts upon his decision, who does not give up half way through, whose time is not unproductive, and who is self-disciplined, who is said to be wise. Wise men 33.30
are attracted to noble deeds, perform acts for wealth, but are not indignant at what is beneficial, bull of the Bharatas. The man who is not pleased when he is honored, nor burns when snubbed, but is as unruffled as a Ganges lake, is said to be wise.

The man who knows the true nature of all creatures, who knows the practice of all acts, and knows the means of all men, is said to be wise. The man whose speech is eloquent, whose conversation is varied, who comprehends and is quick-witted, and who can teach a text quickly, is said to be wise. The man whose learning serves his wisdom and whose wisdom serves his learning, and who does not breach the customs of the noble, would win the title of wise man.

The man who is not educated yet arrogant, a beggar yet 33.35
proud, and eager to attain his goal without work, is named a fool by wise men. The man who abandons his own goal, contributes to another man's goal, and behaves deceitfully on behalf of a friend, is said to be a fool. They call a man idiotic-minded if he longs for the undesirable, abandons the desirable, and hates the stronger man.

They call the man who treats his enemy like a friend, hates and harms his friend, and undertakes wicked deeds, idiotic-minded. Bull of the Bharatas, a fool broadcasts tasks which need to be done, questions everything, and takes ages to accomplish simple matters. They call a man idiotic- 33.40
minded if he does not give offerings to his ancestors, does not worship the gods, and does not take friends as allies.

an|āhūtaḥ praviśati, a|pṛṣṭo bahu bhāṣate,
a|viśvaste viśvasiti mūḍha|cetā nar'|âdhamaḥ.
paraṃ kṣipati doṣeṇa vartamānaḥ svayaṃ tathā,
yaś ca krudhyaty an|īśānaḥ, sa ca mūḍhatamo naraḥ.
ātmano balam a|jñāya dharm'|ârtha|parivarjitam
a|labhyam icchan naiṣkarmyān mūḍha|buddhir ih' ôcyate.

a|śiṣyaṃ śāsti yo, rājan, yaś ca śūnyam upāsate,
kad|aryaṃ bhajate yaś ca, tam āhur mūḍha|cetasam.
33.45 arthaṃ mahāntam āsādya, vidyām aiśvaryam eva vā,
vicaraty a|samunnaddho yaḥ, sa paṇḍita ucyate.

ekaḥ saṃpannam aśnāti, vaste vāsaś ca śobhanam
yo '|saṃvibhajya bhṛtyebhyaḥ, ko nṛśaṃsataras tataḥ?
ekaḥ pāpāni kurute, phalaṃ bhuṅkte mahā|janaḥ;
bhoktāro vipramucyante, kartā doṣeṇa lipyate.
ekaṃ hanyān, na vā hanyād iṣur mukto dhanuṣmatā;
buddhir buddhimat" ôtsṛṣṭā hanyād rāṣṭraṃ sa|rājakam.

ekayā dve viniścitya, trīṃś caturbhir vaśe kuru,
pañca jitvā, viditvā ṣaṭ, sapta hitvā sukhī bhava.
33.50 ekaṃ viṣa|raso hanti, śastreṇ' âikaś ca vadhyate;
sa|rāṣṭraṃ sa|prajaṃ hanti rājānaṃ mantra|viplavaḥ.
ekaḥ svādu na bhuñjīta, ekaś c' ârthān na cintayet,
eko na gacched adhvānaṃ, n' âikaḥ supteṣu jāgṛyāt.

An idiot, the lowest of men, enters when uninvited, speaks endlessly when unasked, and puts his trust in the cynical. The man who blames someone else, when in fact it was he who was acting wickedly, and gets angry without any authority, is the most idiotic of men. The man who, unaware of his own strength, wants to attain what is unattainable, devoid of moral law and profit, without doing any work, is said to be foolish-minded.

My king, they call a man idiotic-minded who teaches someone not his pupil, who serves a destitute man, and
who shares with the miserly. But the man who has gained a 33.45
great goal, knowledge, or power, and who wanders around without arrogance, is said to be wise.

Who is more malicious than the man who eats plentifully but alone, who dresses gloriously in his clothes, and who doesn't share with his dependants? It takes only one man to commit evil acts for people at large to suffer the consequences. Those who experience the results are free from guilt, but the perpetrator is polluted by blame. A single arrow fired by an archer may or may not kill, but intelligence used by an intelligent man could destroy a kingdom and its king.

Be happy by resolving upon two with one, bring three under your control with four, conquer five, understand the
six, and disregard seven. A poisonous draft kills one, and 33.50
one person dies by the sword, but disastrous advice kills the king along with his kingdom and subjects. One should not eat tasty food alone, nor should one deliberate matters on one's own. One should not go on a journey alone, or be the only one who wakes up when everyone else is sleeping.

ekam ev' â|dvitīyaṃ tad, yad, rājan, n' âvabudhyase,
satyaṃ svargasya sopānaṃ pār'|âvārasya naur iva.
ekaḥ kṣamāvatāṃ doṣo, dvitīyo n' ôpapadyate:
yad enaṃ kṣamayā yuktam a|śaktaṃ manyate janaḥ.
so 'sya doṣo na mantavyaḥ; kṣamā hi paramaṃ balam;
kṣamā guṇo hy a|śaktānāṃ, śaktānāṃ bhūṣaṇaṃ kṣamā.
33.55 kṣamā vaśī|kṛtir loke, kṣamayā kiṃ na sādhyate?
śānti|khaḍgaḥ kare yasya, kiṃ kariṣyati dur|janaḥ?
a|tṛṇe patito vahniḥ svayam ev' ôpaśāmyati;
a|kṣamāvān paraṃ doṣair ātmānaṃ c' âiva yojayet.
eko dharmaḥ paraṃ śreyaḥ, kṣam" âikā śāntir uttamā,
vidy" âikā paramā tṛptir, a|hiṃs" âika|sukh'|āvahā.
dvāv imau grasate bhūmiḥ, sarpo bila|śayān iva,
rājānaṃ c' â|viroddhāraṃ, brāhmaṇaṃ c' â|pravāsinam.
dve karmaṇī naraḥ kurvann asmiĩ loke virocate:
a|bruvan paruṣaṃ kiñ cid, a|sato 'n|arcayaṃs tathā.
33.60 dvāv imau, puruṣa|vyāghra, para|pratyaya|kāriṇau:
striyaḥ kāmita|kāminyo, lokaḥ pūjita|pūjakaḥ.
dvāv imau kaṇṭakau tīkṣṇau śarīra|pariśoṣiṇau:
yaś c' â|dhanaḥ kāmayate, yaś ca kupyaty an|īśvaraḥ.
dvāv eva na virājete viparītena karmaṇā:
gṛha|sthaś ca nirārambhaḥ, kāryavāṃś c' âiva bhikṣukaḥ.

The One without a second,* a being whom you, my king, do not understand, is truth; the stairway to heaven, like a ferry between two shores.

There is one and only one problem with the forgiving: people assume that a man who possesses forgiveness is incompetent. A man's forgiveness should not be considered a fault but his greatest strength. For while forgiveness is a quality of the incompetent, forgiveness is also the adornment of the competent. Forgiveness is a means of subjuga- 33.55
tion on earth, for what goal is not achieved through forgiveness? What can a wicked man do when he has the sword of peace in his hand? Just as fire subsides when it has fallen on the grassless ground, so the man who does not forgive his enemy yokes himself with sins. Virtue is the one greatest good, forgiveness the one ultimate peace, knowledge the one greatest insight, and non-violence the one path to happiness.

Just as a snake devours creatures that live in holes in the ground, so the earth devours these two: a king who does not fight, and a brahmin who does not go on pilgrimages. A man shines in this world by doing two things: not speaking unkindly, and not honoring anything wicked. These are the 33.60
two kinds of people who put all their faith in others, tiger-like man: women who love men because others love them, and those who honor men because others worship them.

These are the two sharp, thorn-like diseases that emaciate the body: a low man full of desire, and a powerless man who is angry. There are two sets of people whose unconventional behavior means they are not illuminated: a householder who abstains from all work, and a mendicant

dvāv imau puruṣau, rājan, svargasy' ôpari tiṣṭhataḥ:
prabhuś ca kṣamayā yukto, daridraś ca pradānavān.

nyāy'|āgatasya dravyasya boddhavyau dvāv atikramau:
a|pātre pratipattiś ca, pātre c' â|pratipādanam.

33.65 dvāv ambhasi niveṣṭavyau gale baddhvā dṛḍhāṃ śilām:
dhanavantam a|dātāraṃ, daridraṃ c' â|tapasvinam.
dvāv imau, puruṣa|vyāghra, sūrya|maṇḍala|bhedinau:
parivrāḍ yoga|yuktaś ca, raṇe c' âbhimukho hataḥ.

tray' ôpāyā manuṣyāṇāṃ śrūyante, Bharata'|rṣabha:
kanīyān, madhyamaḥ, śreṣṭha, iti› veda|vido viduḥ.
tri|vidhāḥ puruṣā, rājann: uttam'|âdhama|madhyamāḥ.
niyojayed yathāvat tāṃs tri|vidheṣv eva karmasu.
traya ev' â|dhanā, rājan: bhāryā, dāsas, tathā sutaḥ;
yat te samadhigacchanti, yasya te, tasya tad dhanam.

33.70 haraṇaṃ ca para|svānāṃ, para|dār'|âbhimarśanam,
suhṛdaś ca parityāgas trayo doṣāḥ kṣay'|āvahāḥ.
tri|vidhaṃ narakasy' êdaṃ dvāraṃ nāśanam ātmanaḥ:
kāmaḥ, krodhas, tathā lobhas. tasmād etat trayaṃ tyajet.
vara|pradānaṃ rājyaṃ ca putra|janma ca, Bhārata,
śatroś ca mokṣaṇaṃ kṛcchrāt trīṇi c' âikaṃ ca tat samam.
bhaktaṃ ca, bhajamānaṃ ca, ‹tav' âsm' îti› ca vādinam
trīn etāñ charaṇaṃ prāptān viṣame 'pi na saṃtyajet.

engaged in work. There are two sets of men, my king, who stand beyond heaven: a master endowed with forgiveness, and a beggar who is generous.

Wealth may be acquired correctly, but the following two actions must be understood as transgressions: giving it to an
unworthy man, and not giving it to a worthy man. There 33.65
are two kinds of people who should have a solid rock tied to their neck and be drowned: a rich man who is ungenerous, and a beggar who is not austere. There are two things, tiger-like man, which split the disk of the sun: someone who practices the discipline of renunciation, and someone who dies face forward in battle.

Bull of the Bharatas, there are said to be three states of men. Those who know the Veda know them as: inferior, middling, and greatest. There are three sorts of men, my king: the best, the worst, and the middling. One ought to match them properly to the three sorts of occupation. There are three groups who own no property, my king: wives, slaves, and sons; for whatever wealth they have passes to whoever owns them.

Theft of someone else's property, adultery with someone 33.70
else's wife, and abandoning a friend are the three sins which bring destruction. The door to hell and self-destruction has three forms: desire, anger, and greed. Therefore, avoid these three. The giving of a boon, a kingdom, and the birth of sons, Bhárata, are three things which are equal to one: release from the trouble of an enemy. One who reveres you, one who begs you, saying 'I am yours,' and one who has come to you for refuge are three people whom one should not abandon even in times of trouble.

catvāri rājñā tu mahā|balena
varjyāny āhuḥ, paṇḍitas tāni vidyāt;
alpa|prajñaiḥ saha mantraṃ na kuryān
na dīrgha|sūtrai, rabhasaiś, cāraṇaiś ca.
33.75 catvāri te, tāta, gṛhe vasantu
śriy" âbhijuṣṭasya gṛha|stha|dharme:
vṛddho jñātir, avasannaḥ kulīnaḥ,
sakhā daridro, bhaginī c' ân|apatyā.

catvāry āha, mahā|rāja, sādyaskāni Bṛhaspatiḥ
pṛcchate tri|daś'|Êndrāya. tān' îmāni nibodha me:
devatānāṃ ca saṃkalpam, anubhāvaṃ ca dhīmatām,
vinayaṃ kṛta|vidyānāṃ, vināśaṃ pāpa|karmaṇām.
catvāri karmāṇy abhayaṃ|karāṇi
bhayaṃ prayacchanty a|yathā|kṛtāni.
mān'|âgnihotram, uta māna|maunaṃ,
mānen' âdhītam, uta māna|yajñaḥ.

pañc'|âgnayo manuṣyeṇa paricaryāḥ prayatnataḥ:
pitā, māt", âgnir, ātmā ca, guruś ca, Bharata'|rṣabha.
33.80 pañc' âiva pūjayan loke yaśaḥ prāpnoti kevalam:
devān, pitṝn, manuṣyāṃś ca, bhikṣūn atithi|pañcamān.
pañca tv" ânugamiṣyanti yatra yatra gamiṣyasi:
mitrāṇy, a|mitrā, madhya|sthā, upajīvy'|ôpajīvinaḥ.
pañc' êndriyasya martyasya chidraṃ ced ekam indriyam,
tato 'sya sravati prajñā dṛteḥ pātrād iv' ôdakam.

They say, and a wise man would know, that there are four things that should be avoided by a powerful king: he should not take advice from men of little intelligence, procrastinators, violent men, or spies. My friend, may you pos- 33.75
sess good fortune, living by the duties of a householder, and may these four reside with you: an elderly relative, a wellborn man who has fallen on hard times, a poverty stricken friend, and a childless sister.

When asked by Indra, lord of the thirty gods, Brihas·pati replied that these four things can take immediate effect, great king. Learn them from me: the intention of the gods, the opinion of the wise, the training of the learned, and the destruction of miscreants. There are four things which create safety but which bestow fear when done improperly: an Agni·hotra sacrifice instituted through pride, proud silence, study through pride, and sacrifice done out of pride.

A man should take care of five fires with effort: one's father, one's mother, fire itself, oneself, and one's teacher, bull of the Bharatas. Only by worshipping these five does one 33.80
attain fame in this world: the gods, ancestors, men, mendicants, and guests are the fifth. Five things will go wherever you go, following you: friends, enemies, the indifferent, those upon whom you depend, and those who depend on you. If one of a mortal man's five senses has a hole, then the knowledge runs out, just as water leaks from a leather water bag.

ṣaḍ doṣāḥ puruṣeṇ' êha hātavyā bhūtim icchatā:
nidrā, tandrī, bhayaṃ, krodha, ālasyaṃ, dīrgha|sūtratā.
ṣaḍ imān puruṣo jahyād bhinnāṃ nāvam iv' ârṇave:
a|pravaktāram ācāryam, an|adhīyānam ṛtvijam,
33.85 a|rakṣitāraṃ rājānaṃ, bhāryāṃ c' â|priya|vādinīm,
grāma|kāmaṃ ca gopālaṃ, vana|kāmaṃ ca nāpitam.
ṣaḍ eva tu guṇāḥ puṃsā na hātavyāḥ kadā cana:
satyaṃ, dānam, an|ālasyam, an|asūyā, kṣamā, dhṛtiḥ.
arth'|āgamo, nityam a|rogitā ca,
priyā ca bhāryā priya|vādinī ca,
vaśyaś ca putro, 'rtha|karī ca vidyā
ṣaḍ jīva|lokasya sukhāni, rājan.
ṣaṇṇām ātmani nityānām aiśvaryaṃ yo 'dhigacchati
na sa pāpaiḥ kuto 'n|arthair yujyate vijit'|êndriyaḥ.
ṣaḍ ime ṣaṭsu jīvanti, saptamo n' ôpalabhyate:
caurāḥ pramatte jīvanti, vyādhiteṣu cikitsakāḥ,
33.90 pramadāḥ kāmayāneṣu, yajamāneṣu yājakāḥ,
rājā vivadamāneṣu, nityaṃ mūrkheṣu paṇḍitāḥ.
ṣaḍ imāni vinaśyanti muhūrtam an|avekṣaṇāt:
gāvaḥ, sevā, kṛṣir, bhāryā, vidyā, vṛṣala|saṃgatiḥ.

A man who wishes for prosperity should avoid these six faults: sleep, laziness, fear, anger, sloth, and procrastination. A man should abstain from these six as though they were a broken ship on the sea: a teacher who does not teach, a
priest who is not learned, a king who does not defend, a 33.85
nagging wife, a cowherd who longs for the village, and a barber who longs for the forest.

But there are also six virtues that a man should never avoid: truth, generosity, industry, politeness, forgiveness, and constancy. My king, reaching one's goals, constant health, an affectionate and kindly spoken wife, slaves, sons, and knowledge which brings profit, are the six pleasures of the world of the living. The man who achieves lordship over these eternal six within himself, and has his senses under control, will not meet evil or disadvantage from any quarter.

These six live off another six, but no seventh can be found:
thieves live off negligence, doctors live off the diseased, lust- 33.90
ful women live off lustful men, sacrificers off those who sacrifice, kings off the quarrelsome, and teachers always live off fools. These six are lost through a moment's carelessness: cattle, servants, the harvest, one's wife, knowledge, and a community of low born people.

ṣaḍ ete hy avamanyante nityaṃ pūrv'|ôpakāriṇam:
ācāryaṃ śikṣitāḥ śiṣyāḥ, kṛta|dārāś ca mātaram,
nārīṃ vigata|kāmās tu, kṛt'|ârthāś ca prayojakam,
nāvaṃ nistīrṇa|kāntārā, āturāś ca cikitsakam.

ārogyam ānṛṇyam a|vipravāsaḥ,
sadbhir manuṣyaiḥ saha saṃprayogaḥ,
sva|pratyay'|āvṛttir, a|bhīta|vāsaḥ
ṣaḍ jīva|lokasya sukhāni, rājan.

33.95 īrṣur, ghṛṇī, na saṃtuṣṭaḥ, krodhano, nitya|śaṅkitaḥ,
para|bhāgy'|ôpajīvī ca ṣaḍ ete nitya|duḥkhitāḥ.

sapta doṣāḥ sadā rājñā hātavyā vyasan'|ôdayāḥ,
prāyaśo yair vinaśyanti kṛta|mūlā ap' īśvarāḥ:
striyo, 'kṣā, mṛgayā, pānaṃ, vāk|pāruṣyaṃ ca pañcamam,
mahac ca daṇḍa|pāruṣyam, artha|dūṣaṇam eva ca.

aṣṭau pūrva|nimittāni narasya vinaśiṣyataḥ:
brāhmaṇān prathamaṃ dveṣṭi, brāhmaṇaiś ca virudhyate,
brāhmaṇa|svāni c' ādatte, brāhmaṇāṃś ca jighāṃsati,
ramate nindayā c' âiṣāṃ, praśaṃsāṃ n' âbhinanadati,
33.100 n' âinān smarati kṛtyeṣu, yācitaś c' âbhyasūyati.
etān doṣān naraḥ prājño budhyed, buddhvā visarjayet.

These six former benefactors are always treated contemptuously: so it is between students and teachers, married girls and their mothers, those whose desire has passed and their wives, those who have completed business transactions and their creditors, those who have crossed the wilderness and their vessel, as well as the sick and their doctors. Health, freedom from obligation, living in one's home country, contact with good men, living free from fear, and living according to one's own rules: these are the six pleasures of the
world of the living, my king. The envious man, passionate 33.95
man, discontented man, angry man, distrustful man, and the man who depends on hand-outs from others, are the six who are eternally miserable.

A king must always avoid the seven sins which are the means to ruin, and because of which, as a general rule, even firmly rooted kings perish: women, gambling, hunting, drinking, and insulting language as the fifth, as well as especially violent punishment, and putting wealth to bad use.

There are eight omens of a man's destruction: the first is his hatred of brahmins, next his fighting with brahmins, his theft of brahmins' property, his wanting to kill brahmins, the pleasure he takes in ridiculing them, his displeasure in
praising them, his failure to remember them in his affairs, 33.100
and his indignation when they entreat him. These are the faults which a wise man who makes use of his intelligence would be sensible to avoid.

aṣṭāv imāni harṣasya nava|nītāni, Bhārata,
vartamānāni dṛśyante tāny eva sva|sukhāny api:
samāgamaś ca sakhibhir, mahāṃś c' âiva dhan'|āgamaḥ,
putreṇa ca pariṣvaṅgaḥ, sannipātaś ca maithune,
samaye ca priy'|ālāpaḥ, sva|yūthyeṣu samunnatiḥ,
abhipretasya lābhaś ca, pūjā ca jana|saṃsadi.
aṣṭau guṇāḥ puruṣaṃ dīpayanti:
prajñā ca, kaulyaṃ ca, damaḥ, śrutaṃ ca,
parākramaś c', â|bahu|bhāṣitā ca,
dānaṃ yathā|śakti, kṛta|jñatā ca.
33.105 nava|dvāram idaṃ veśma, tri|sthūṇaṃ, pañca|sākṣikam,
kṣetra|jñ'|âdhiṣṭhitaṃ vidvān yo veda, sa paraḥ kaviḥ.
daśa dharmaṃ na jānanti,
Dhṛtarāṣṭra. nibodha tān:
mattaḥ, pramatta, unmattaḥ,
śrāntaḥ, kruddho, bubhukṣitaḥ,
tvaramāṇaś ca, lubdhaś ca, bhītaḥ, kāmī ca, te daśa;
tasmād eteṣu sarveṣu na prasajjeta paṇḍitaḥ.
atr' âiv' ôdāharant' îmam itihāsaṃ purātanam
putr'|ârtham asur'|êndreṇa gītaṃ c' âiva Sudhanvanā.

These eight are the *crème de la crème* of happiness, Bhárata, and are shown to bring one pleasure when practiced: meeting friends, a great arrival of wealth, hugging one's son, sex, pleasant discussions in meetings, elevation within one's own group, attaining what one desired, and honor in society. These eight virtues illuminate a man: wisdom, noble descent, control, learning, courage, not speaking too much, generosity according to one's means, and gratitude.

The wise man who understands the dwelling with nine 33.105
gates, three pillars, and five witnesses, which is controlled by the soul, is the ultimate sage. There are ten who do not know the law, Dhrita·rashtra. Learn them: the intoxicated, the idle, the mad, the tired, the angry, the hungry, the speedy, the greedy, the scared, and the tenth is the lustful man. Therefore, a wise man should not become connected to any of these. It is on this topic that the ancient story of Sudhánvan and the *ásura* lord Prahráda's debate for the sake of the latter's son is quoted.*

yaḥ kāma|manyū prajahāti rājā,
pātre pratiṣṭhāpayate dhanaṃ ca,
viśeṣa|vic, chrutavān, kṣipra|kārī,
taṃ sarva|lokaḥ kurute pramāṇam.
33.110 jānāti viśvāsayituṃ manuṣyān,
vijñāta|doṣeṣu dadhāti daṇḍam,
jānāti mātrāṃ ca, tathā kṣamāṃ ca,
taṃ tādṛśaṃ śrīr juṣate samagrā.
su|durbalaṃ n' âvajānāti kañ cid,
yukto ripuṃ sevate buddhi|pūrvam.
na vigrahaṃ rocayate bala|sthaiḥ,
kāle ca yo vikramate, sa dhīraḥ.
prāpy' āpadaṃ na vyathate kadā cid
udyogam anvicchati c' â|pramattaḥ.
duḥkhaṃ ca kāle sahate mah"|ātmā;
dhuran|dharas tasya jitāḥ sapatnāḥ.
an|arthakaṃ vipravāsaṃ gṛhebhyaḥ,
pāpaiḥ sandhiṃ, para|dār"|âbhimarśam,
dambhaṃ, stainyaṃ, paiśunaṃ, madya|pānaṃ
na sevate yaḥ, sa* sukhī sad" âiva.
na saṃrambheṇ' ārabhate tri|vargam,
ākāritaḥ śaṃsati tattvam eva,
na mitr'|ârthe rocayate vivādaṃ
sarvatra tādṛg labhate praśaṃsām.
33.115 na yo 'bhyasūyaty, anukampate ca,
na dur|balaḥ prātibhāvyaṃ karoti,
n' âtyāha kiñ cit, kṣamate vivādaṃ,
sarvatra tādṛg labhate praśamsām.

The king who renounces desire and anger and bestows his wealth on a deserving man, who is judicious, learned, and swift-acting, is the man whom the entire world takes as its standard. All good fortune will favor the sort of king 33.110
who knows how to encourage his people, enforces punishment on known criminals, knows his own measure, and is forgiving. He shows not even the slightest contempt for his weakest enemy, but, disciplined, he waits purposefully for an opportunity to use against his enemy. He does not delight in division with powerful men, but bravely attacks when the time is right.

When he meets with disaster he never trembles, but carefully seeks a way back through strenuous endeavor. The high-souled man withstands misery when it is his time. This burdened man's enemies are conquered. The man who does not resort to living abroad, far from home, to no advantage, nor mixes with wicked men, nor indulges in adultery, fraud, theft, wickedness, or alcoholism, is always happy.

The sort of man who does not arrogantly undertake his pursuit of the three aims of life, who recites the truth when questioned, and who does not take pleasure in quarrels even for the sake of a friend, receives praise in every society. The 33.115
man who does not grow indignant but is compassionate, who does not brew conflict when weak, nor talk too much in any way, but forgives quarrels, receives praise everywhere.

yo n' ôddhataṃ kurute jātu veṣaṃ,
na pauruṣeṇ' âpi vikatthate 'nyān,
na mūrcchitaḥ kaṭukāny āha kiñ cit,
priyaṃ sadā taṃ kurute jano hi.
na vairam uddīpayati praśāntaṃ,
na darpam ārohati, n' âstam eti,
na ‹dur|gato 'sm' îti› karoty a|kāryaṃ,
tam ārya|śīlaṃ param āhur āryāḥ.
na sve sukhe vai kurute praharṣaṃ,
n' ânyasya duḥkhe bhavati prahṛṣṭaḥ,
dattvā na paścāt kurute na tāpaṃ,
sa kathyate sat|puruṣ'|ārya|śīlaḥ.
deś'|ācārān, samayān, jāti|dharmān
bubhūṣate yaḥ, sa par'|âvara|jñaḥ,
sa yatra tatr' âbhigataḥ sad" âiva
mahā|janasy' âdhipatyaṃ karoti.
33.120 dambhaṃ, mohaṃ, matsaraṃ, pāpa|kṛtyaṃ,
rāja|dviṣṭaṃ, paiśunaṃ, pūga|vairaṃ,
matt'|ônmattair dur|janaiś c' âpi vādaṃ
yaḥ prajñāvān varjayet, sa pradhānaḥ.
dānaṃ, śaucaṃ*, daivataṃ, maṅgalāni,
prāyaś|cittān, vividhāl loka|vādān,
etāni yaḥ kurute naityakāni
tasy' ôtthānaṃ devatā rādhayanti.
samair vivāhaṃ kurute na hīnaiḥ,
samaiḥ sakhyaṃ vyavahāraṃ kathāṃ ca,
guṇair viśiṣṭāṃś ca puro dadhāti,
vipaścitas tasya nayāḥ su|nītāḥ.
mitaṃ bhuṅkte saṃvibhajy' āśritebhyo,
mitaṃ svapity a|mitaṃ karma kṛtvā,

People always hold dear the man who certainly doesn't put on an inflated facade, who doesn't boast about his manliness at all, who doesn't get agitated and speak abusively in any way. Noble men say the man of the noblest conduct is the man who doesn't ignite a peaceful situation, provoking hostility, who doesn't ascend arrogantly, who doesn't disappear like the setting sun, who does not do what one should not, using his misfortune as an excuse.

A good man of noble conduct is said to be someone who does not make a big fuss of his happiness during his happy times, nor take pleasure in another man's misery, nor feel regret after he has been generous. The man who understands both high important and low trivial matters, and who is intent on the customs of various places, traditions, and caste laws, will always gain lordship over the majority of people, wherever he goes.

The greatest wise man is he who renounces pride, folly, 33.120
envy, bad behavior, hatred towards the king, wickedness, widespread hostility, and conversation with drunk, mad, and bad people. The gods hand over a man for elevation if he practices generosity, purity, piety, auspicious rites, atonement, conversation with various people of the world, and the obligatory duties.

The man who marries within his own caste rather than below him, whose friendships, activities, and conversations are conducted among his equals, and who gives priority to those distinguished by their virtues, is sensible and his behavior is well-conducted. Disaster will avoid the man of disciplined soul who eats in moderation, sharing with those

dadāty a|mitreṣv api yācitaḥ saṃs,
tam ātmavantaṃ prajahaty an|arthāḥ.
cikīrṣitaṃ viprakṛtaṃ ca yasya,
n' ânye janāḥ karma jānanti kiñ cit,
mantre gupte samyag anuṣṭhite ca
n' âlpo 'py asya cyavate kaś cid arthaḥ.
33.125 yaḥ sarva|bhūta|praśame niviṣṭaḥ,
satyo, mṛdur, māna|kṛc, chuddha|bhāvaḥ,
atīva sa jñāyate jñāti|madhye
mahā|maṇir jātya iva prasannaḥ.
ya ātman" âpatrapate bhṛśaṃ naraḥ
sa sarva|lokasya gurur bhavaty uta;
ananta|tejāḥ su|manāḥ samāhitaḥ
sa tejasā sūrya iv' âvabhāsate.
vane jātāḥ śāpa|dagdhasya rājñaḥ
Pāṇḍoḥ putrāḥ pañca pañc'|Êndra|kalpāḥ
tvay" âiva bālā vardhitāḥ śikṣitāś ca,
tav' ādeśaṃ pālayanty, Āmbikeya!
pradāy' âiṣām ucitaṃ, tāta, rājyaṃ
sukhī putraiḥ sahito modamānaḥ,
na devānāṃ n' âpi ca mānuṣāṇāṃ
bhaviṣyasi tvaṃ tarkaṇīyo, nar'|êndra.»

DHṚTARĀṢṬRA uvāca:

34.1 «JĀGRATO DAHYAMĀNASYA yat kāryam anupaśyasi,
tad brūhi tvaṃ hi nas, tāta; dharm'|ârtha|kuśalo hy asi.
tvaṃ māṃ yathāvad, Vidura, praśādhi
prajñā|pūrvaṃ sarvam Ajātaśatroḥ
yan manyase pathyam, a|dīna|sattva,
śreyas|karaṃ, brūhi tad vai Kurūṇām.

who rely on him, who sleeps in moderation but works relentlessly, and who is generous even to his enemies when he is asked.

The man whose plan is kept completely secret and well-executed, and whose actions are never known by other men to be intended to cause harm, does not fail to achieve even his most trivial of aims. The man who is intent on the peace 33.125
of all creatures, and who is truthful, gentle, respectful, and pure-minded, is especially renowned among his kinsmen as a precious jewel, gracious to his caste. A man who is particularly modest about himself becomes the teacher of the whole world; boundlessly glorious, kindly disposed, and steadfast, he shines with his brilliance as though he were the sun.

The five forest-born and Indra-like sons of Pandu, who was scorched by his curse, were brought up and taught as your children, and they now wait for your orders, Ambikéya! By giving them their promised kingdom, my friend, you will be happy, rejoicing with your sons, and you will no longer be suspected by gods and mortals, lord of men."

DHRITA·RASHTRA said:

"TELL ME, MY friend, since you are skilled in moral law 34.1
and profit, what you think a sleepless and fevered man should do. Instruct me properly, Vídura, in your knowledge of what has happened, about everything that is fitting for Ajáta·shatru, flawless man, and tell me what you think will serve the Kurus best. Expecting and perceiving evil, I question you with a troubled soul: Tell me, sage, truthfully

pāp'|āśaṅkī pāpam ev' ânupaśyan
pṛcchāmi tvām vyākulen' ātman" âham:
kave, tan me brūhi sarvaṃ yathāvan
manīṣitaṃ sarvam Ajātaśatroḥ.»

VIDURA uvāca:

«śubhaṃ vā yadi vā pāpaṃ, dveṣyaṃ vā yadi vā priyam,
a|pṛṣṭas tasya tad brūyād yasya n' êcchet parābhavam.
34.5 tasmād vakṣyāmi te, rājan, hitaṃ yat syāt Kurūn prati;
vacaḥ śreyas|karaṃ dharmyaṃ bruvatas tan nibodha me.
mithy" ôpetāni karmāṇi siddheyur yāni, Bhārata,
an|upāya|prayuktāni, mā sma teṣu manaḥ kṛthāḥ.
tath" âiva yoga|vihitaṃ yat tu karma na sidhyati
upāya|yuktaṃ, medhāvī na tatra glapayen manaḥ.
anubandhān apekṣeta s'|ânubandheṣu karmasu,
saṃpradhārya ca kurvīta, na vegena samācaret.
anubandhaṃ ca saṃprekṣya, vipākaṃ c' âiva karmaṇām,
utthānam ātmanaś c' âiva dhīraḥ kurvīta vā, na vā.
34.10 yaḥ pramāṇaṃ na jānāti sthāne, vṛddhau, tathā kṣaye,
kośe, jana|pade, daṇḍe, na sa rājye 'vatiṣṭhate.
yas tv etāni pramāṇāni yath"|ôktāny anupaśyati,
yukto dharm'|ârthayor jñāne sa rājyam adhigacchati.
na rājyaṃ prāptam, ity eva vartitavyam a|sāṃpratam,
śriyaṃ hy a|vinayo hanti jarā rūpam iv' ôttamam.

and in its entirety, everything Ajáta·shatru wishes for in his plans."

VÍDURA replied:

"If one wishes to avoid someone's destruction, then one should tell them what one has to say, even if unasked, regardless of whether what one has to say is good or evil, or hateful or pleasant. Therefore, I will tell you, my king, since 34.5
I wish for what is beneficial to the Kurus. Listen to what I have to say, for it is both useful and compliant with moral law.

Bhárata, do not fix your mind on deeds which are accomplished through deceitful means and contrived without expediency. A wise man does not weary his mind when a properly planned and expedient act does not succeed. One ought to act by taking the competence of the agent, the nature of the act itself, and the act's purpose into consideration, for actions depend on these. One should not act rashly. By examining the consequence and result along with the act itself, as well as one's own effort, then one can resolutely act or not act.

The king who does not know what standard to use for 34.10
position, growth as well as loss, the treasury, his people, and punishment, will not remain in his kingship. The man who observes the standards just mentioned and is endowed with knowledge of virtue and profit, finds lordship. One should not do something improper in the belief that one's kingdom is secure, for misbehavior kills good fortune just as surely as old age kills great beauty.

bhakṣy'|ôttama|praticchannaṃ matsyo baḍiśam āyasam
lobh'|âbhipātī grasate, n' ânubandham avekṣate.
yac chakyaṃ grasituṃ grasyaṃ, grastaṃ pariṇamec ca yat,
hitaṃ ca pariṇāme yat, tad ādyaṃ bhūtim icchatā.
34.15 vanas|pater a|pakvāni phalāni pracinoti yaḥ,
sa n' āpnoti rasaṃ tebhyo, bījaṃ c' âsya vinaśyati.
yas tu pakvam upādatte kāle pariṇataṃ phalam,
phalād rasaṃ sa labhate, bījāc c' âiva phalaṃ punaḥ.
yathā madhu samadatte rakṣan puṣpāṇi ṣaṭ|padaḥ,
tadvad arthān manuṣyebhya ādadyād a|vihiṃsayā.
puṣpaṃ puṣpaṃ vicinvīta, mūla|cchedaṃ na kārayet,
mālā|kāra iv' ārāme, na yath" âṅgāra|kārakaḥ.
‹kin nu me syād idaṃ kṛtvā, kin nu me syād a|kurvataḥ?›
iti karmāṇi sañcintya kuryād vā puruṣo, na vā.
34.20 an|ārabhyā bhavanty arthāḥ ke cin nityaṃ tath" â|gatāḥ,
kṛtaḥ puruṣa|kāro hi bhaved yeṣu nirarthakaḥ.
prasādo niṣphalo yasya, krodhaś c' âpi nirarthakaḥ,
na taṃ bhartāram icchanti, ṣaṇḍhaṃ patim iva striyaḥ.
kāṃś cid arthān naraḥ prājño laghu|mūlān mahā|phalān
kṣipram ārabhate kartuṃ, na vighnayati tādṛśān.
ṛju paśyati yaḥ sarvaṃ cakṣuṣ" ânupibann iva,
āsīnam api tūṣṇīkam anurajyanti taṃ prajāḥ.
su|puṣpitaḥ syād a|phalaḥ, phalitaḥ syād dur|āruhaḥ,
a|pakvaḥ pakva|saṃkāśo na tu śīryeta karhi cit.
34.25 cakṣuṣā, manasā, vācā, karmaṇā ca catur|vidham

A fish rushes greedily and swallows an iron fish-hook cloaked with tasty food without thinking about the consequences. The man who seeks prosperity first seeks something edible, then food which could be digested once eaten, and once digested, food that would be beneficial. The man 34.15
who picks unripe fruit from a tree not only fails to get the juice, but also loses the seed. But the man who picks ripe fruit just as it ripens, gets the juice from the fruit, and also gets more fruit from its seeds.

Just as the bee takes the honey but protects the flowers, so one should take property from people without harming them. Pick flower after flower like a garland maker in a garden, but do not end up cutting the root like a charcoal burner. A man should think about whether or not he should act, saying to himself, 'What do I have to gain by doing this, and what do I have to gain by not doing it?'

There are some goals that should not be undertaken, 34.20
which will always be impossible, and human effort put into them will be wasted. People do not want a master whose favor is profitless and whose anger is unproductive, just as women do not want a eunuch for a husband. Other aims may turn out extremely fruitful despite the shortness of their roots, and so the wise man begins to do them quickly and does not obstruct such aims.

People are fond of the man who sees everything straight, as though drinking through his eyes, even when he is sitting silently. A tree may be fruitless but bursting with flowers, or abounding in fruit but hard to climb, but an unripe fruit which looks ripe will never break open. When someone ap- 34.25
peases the world in four ways—with the eye, mind, speech,

prasādayati yo lokaṃ, taṃ loko 'nuprasīdati.
yasmāt trasyanti bhūtāni, mṛga|vyādhān mṛgā iva,
sāgar'|ântām api mahīṃ labdhvā sa parihīyate.

pitṛ|paitāmahaṃ rājyaṃ prāptavān svena karmaṇā,
vāyur abhram iv' āsādya, bhraṃśayaty a|naye sthitaḥ.
dharmam ācarato rājñaḥ sadbhiś caritam āditaḥ
vasudhā vasu|saṃpūrṇā vardhate bhūti|vardhanī.
atha santyajato dharmam a|dharmaṃ c' ânutiṣṭhataḥ
pratisaṃveṣṭate bhūmir agnau carm' āhitaṃ yathā.

34.30 ya eva yatnaḥ kriyate para|rāṣṭra|vimardane,
sa eva yatnaḥ kartavyaḥ sva|rāṣṭra|paripālane.
dharmeṇa rājyaṃ vindeta, dharmeṇa paripālayet,
dharma|mūlāṃ śriyaṃ prāpya na jahāti, na hīyate.

apy unmattāt pralapato, bālāc ca parijalpataḥ
sarvataḥ sāram ādadyād, aśmabhya iva kāñcanam?
su|vyāhṛtāni, s'|ûktāni, su|kṛtāni tatas tataḥ
saṃcinvan dhīra āsīta, śil'|āhārī śilaṃ yathā.
gandhena gāvaḥ paśyanti, vedaiḥ paśyanti brāhmaṇāḥ,
cāraiḥ paśyanti rājānaś, cakṣurbhyām itare janāḥ.

and deed—then the world is satisfied with him. He may have attained the earth up to the boundary of the ocean, but if the creatures tremble before him like deer before hunters, then he is still destitute.

A man may gain his ancestral kingdom through his own achievement, but just as the wind dissolves a cloud, so he will lose his kingdom if he is engaged in bad policy. The fertile, wealth-filled earth will increase and develop the prosperity of a king who practices virtue as it has been practiced from the beginning by wise men. But just as an animal hide shrivels when placed on the fire, so the earth will do the same for the man who abandons moral law and is intent on immorality.

Just as much effort should be put into protecting one's 34.30
own kingdom as is put into laying waste to one's enemy's kingdom. If one obtains a kingdom through righteousness and defends it with righteousness, then one will neither lose the good fortune rooted in morality that one has gained, nor will one be abandoned by it.

Is there any real value in the ranting of a madman or the chatter of a child? It's like trying to get gold from stone. The self-possessed man collects good behavior, good sayings, and good deeds, just as a farmer gathers the ears of corn. Cattle see with smell, brahmins see with the Vedas, kings see through spies, and the rest of the people see with their eyes.

34.35 bhūyāṃsaṃ labhate kleśaṃ yā gaur bhavati dur|duhā,
atha yā su|duhā, rājan, n' âiva tāṃ vitudanty api.
yad a|taptaṃ praṇamati, na tat santāpayanty api;
yac ca svayaṃ nataṃ dāru, na tat saṃnāmayanty api.
etay" ôpamayā dhīraḥ sannameta balīyase,
Indrāya sa praṇamate, namate yo balīyase.

parjanya|nāthāḥ paśavo, rājāno mantri|bāndhavāḥ,
patayo bāndhavāḥ strīṇāṃ, brāhmaṇā veda|bāndhavāḥ.
satyena rakṣyate dharmo, vidyā yogena rakṣyate,
mṛjayā rakṣyate rūpaṃ, kulaṃ vṛttena rakṣyate.
34.40 mānena rakṣyate dhānyam, aśvān rakṣaty anukramaḥ,
abhīkṣṇa|darśanaṃ gāś ca, striyo rakṣyāḥ ku|celataḥ.

na kulaṃ vṛtta|hīnasya pramāṇam, iti me matiḥ;
anteṣv api hi jātānāṃ vṛttam eva viśiṣyate.
ya īrṣuḥ para|vitteṣu, rūpe, vīrye, kul'|ânvaye,
sukha|saubāgya|satkāre, tasya vyādhir an|antakaḥ.

a|kārya|karaṇād bhītaḥ, kāryāṇāṃ ca vivarjanāt,
a|kāle mantra|bhedāc ca, yena mādyen, na tat pibet.
vidyā|mado, dhana|madas, tṛtīyo 'bhijano madaḥ;
madā ete 'valiptānām, eta eva satāṃ damāḥ.
34.45 tāvan na tasya su|kṛtaṃ kiṃ cit kāryaṃ kadā cana,
manyante santam ātmānam a|santam api viśrutam.
gatir ātmavatāṃ santaḥ, santa eva satāṃ gatiḥ,

A cow which is difficult to milk suffers a great deal of pain, but they do not hurt a cow which is easy to milk, my king. People do not heat a substance which bends without being heated, nor do they bend wood which is bent all by itself. By this logic, the resolute man bows down to the stronger man, and he who bows to the stronger man therefore bows to Indra. 34.35

Cattle have the rain to serve as their protectors, kings' families are counselors, women's families are their husbands, and brahmins' families are the Veda. Law is protected by truth, knowledge is protected through discipline, beauty is protected by washing, and lineage is protected by behavior. Grain is preserved by keeping track of how much 34.40
of it one has, exercise keeps horses fit, cattle are protected by constant scrutiny, and women are protected by dressing modestly.

In my opinion a person's lineage is worthless if they have no courtesy, for even among the lowest strata of society courtesy is distinguished. The man who envies other people for their conduct, beauty, courage, family lineage, happiness, success, and favor, has an eternal sickness.

The man who is afraid of doing the wrong thing, afraid of avoiding what should be done, and afraid of a break in concentration at the wrong time, should not drink whatever makes him drunk. Those who are intoxicated get drunk on knowledge, on wealth, and thirdly on renown. These are the
very same restraints of the wise. But if the good man ever 34.45
fails to do something that needs doing properly, then the man who is renowned as bad considers himself good. The good man is the path of the ensouled, and the good man is

a|satāṃ ca gatiḥ santo, na tv a|santaḥ satāṃ gatiḥ.

jitā sabhā vastravatā, miṣṭ'|āśā gomatā jitā,
adhvā jito yānavatā, sarvaṃ śīlavatā jitam.
śīlaṃ pradhānaṃ puruṣe; tad yasy' êha praṇaśyati,
na tasya jīviten' ârtho, na dhanena, na bandhubhiḥ.
āḍhyānāṃ māṃsa|paramaṃ, madhyānāṃ goras'|ôttaram,
tail'|ôttaraṃ daridrāṇāṃ bhojanaṃ, Bharata'|rṣabha.

34.50 saṃpannataram ev' ânnaṃ daridrā bhuñjate sadā;
kṣut svādutāṃ janayati, sā c' āḍhyeṣu su|durlabhā.
prāyeṇa śrīmatāṃ loke bhoktuṃ śaktir na vidyate;
jīryanty api hi kāṣṭhāni daridrāṇāṃ, mahī|pate.
a|vṛttir bhayam antyānāṃ, madhyānāṃ maraṇād bhayam,
uttamānāṃ tu martyānām avamānāt paraṃ bhayam.

aiśvarya|mada|pāpiṣṭhā madāḥ pāna|mad'|ādayaḥ
aiśvarya|mada|matto hi n' āpatitvā vibudhyate.
indriyair indriy'|ârtheṣu vartamānair a|nigrahaiḥ
tair ayaṃ tāpyate loko nakṣatrāṇi grahair iva.

34.55 yo jitaḥ pañca|vargeṇa sahajen' ātma|karṣiṇā,
āpadas tasya vardhante śukla|pakṣa iv' ôḍu|rāṭ.

the path of the good. The good man is the path of the bad but the bad man is not the path of the good.

The court is won over by a well-dressed man, a cattle-owner wins the satisfaction of his desire for delicacies, the man with a vehicle conquers the road, but the man of good conduct wins everything. Good conduct is a man's most essential part; if he loses it in this world then he gets no profit from life, wealth, or his family. Meat is the chief food of the wealthy, cow's milk is by and large the food of the middle classes, and oil is the main constituent of a beggar's diet, bull of the Bharatas.

The poor always eat the more palatable food since hunger 34.50
makes it sweet, but this is hard to come by among the wealthy. It is generally found that the fortunate in the world do not have much appetite, but the poverty-stricken digest even wood, lord of earth. The fear of the lowest in society is to have no work, the fear of the middle classes is death, but the greatest fear of those highest in mortal society is contempt.

The worst type of intoxicated people are those who are drunk with power, rather than those merely drunk with alcohol and so on, for the power-obsessed do not wake up before they fall. This world is tormented by the senses, just as the stars are affected by the planets, when they are focused unrestrainedly upon their objects. Just as the moon, 34.55
the king of stars, waxes in the bright fortnight, so disasters develop for the man who is overpowered, with his soul being dragged around by his natural five senses.

a|vijitya yath" ātmānam amātyān vijigīṣate
a|mitrān v" â|jit'|âmātyaḥ so 'vaśaḥ parihīyate.
ātmānam eva prathamaṃ dveṣya|rūpeṇa yojayet,
tato 'mātyān a|mitrāṃś ca na moghaṃ vijigīṣate.
vaśy'|êndriyaṃ, jit'|ātmānaṃ, dhṛta|daṇḍaṃ vikāriṣu
parīkṣya|kāriṇaṃ dhīram atyantaṃ śrīr niṣevate.
rathaḥ śarīraṃ puruṣasya, rājann,
ātmā niyant", êndriyāṇy asya c' âśvāḥ
tair a|pramattaḥ kuśalī sad|aśvair
dāntaiḥ sukhaṃ yāti rath" îva dhīraḥ.
34.60 etāny a|nigṛhītāni vyāpādayitum apy alam
a|vidheyā iv' â|dāntā hayāḥ pathi ku|sārathim.
an|artham arthataḥ paśyann,
arthaṃ c' âiv' âpy an|arthataḥ,
indriyair a|jitair bālaḥ
su|duḥkhaṃ manyate sukham.
dharm'|ârthau yaḥ parityajya syād indriya|vaś'|ânugaḥ,
śrī|prāṇa|dhana|dārebhyaḥ kṣipraṃ sa parihīyate.
arthānām īśvaro yaḥ syād indriyāṇām an|īśvaraḥ,
indriyāṇām an|aiśvaryād aiśvaryād bhraśyate hi saḥ.
ātman" ātmānam anvicchen
mano|buddh'|îndriyair yataiḥ;
ātmā hy ev' ātmano bandhur,
ātm" âiva ripur ātmanaḥ.
34.65 bandhur ātm" ātmanas tasya, yen' âiv' ātm" ātmanā jitaḥ;
sa eva niyato bandhuḥ, sa eva niyato ripuḥ.

The man who wishes to conquer his ministers without controlling himself, or wants to control his enemies before his ministers are controlled, perishes in circumstances beyond his control. He should first discipline himself as though he were an enemy, and then it will be no idle wish to subdue his ministers and enemies. Good fortune cherishes the perfectly resolute king whose senses are controlled, who has disciplined himself, who brings punishment to the corrupt, and who acts after contemplation.

A man's body, my king, is like a chariot: The soul is the driver and the senses are the horses; the soul rides happily when he is skilled and undistracted by his excellent and
properly broken horses. Just as untrained and unbroken 34.60
horses can topple a bad charioteer to the road, so unrestrained senses are quite capable of causing disaster.

An infantile person with uncontrolled senses sees calamity in profit and profit in calam-ity, and so identifies great misery with happiness. The man who abandons virtue and profit would be a slave to the power of his senses, and is soon himself abandoned by good fortune, his life, wealth, and wife. A man with mastery over wealth, but not over his own senses, loses the power he does have because of his lack of control over his senses.

A man should seek his own soul with subdued heart, mind, and senses, since the soul is one's friend while at
the same time being one's enemy. The soul is the friend of 34.65
the man whose own soul is under control, inasmuch as he overpowers his soul by means of his soul; so one's friend is subdued just as one's enemy is subdued. Two large fish are

kṣudr'|âkṣeṇ' êva jālena jhaṣāv apihitāv urū;
kāmaś ca, rājan, krodhaś ca; tau prajñānaṃ vilumpataḥ.
samavekṣy' êha dharm'|ârthau
sambhārān yo 'dhigacchati,
sa vai saṃbhṛta|saṃbhāraḥ
satataṃ sukham edhate.
yaḥ pañc'|âbhyantarān śatrūn a|vijitya mano|mayān
jigīṣati ripūn anyān, ripavo 'bhibhavanti tam.
dṛśyante hi mah"|ātmāno badhyamānāḥ sva|karmabhiḥ
indriyāṇām an|īśatvād rājāno rājya|vibhramaiḥ.
34.70 a|santyāgāt pāpa|kṛtām a|pāpāṃs
tulyo daṇḍaḥ spṛśate miśra|bhāvāt,
śuṣkeṇ' ārdraṃ dahyate miśra|bhāvāt;
tasmāt pāpaiḥ saha sandhiṃ na kuryāt.
nijān utpatataḥ śatrūn pañca pañca prayojanān
yo mohān na nigṛhṇāti, tam āpad grasate naram.
an|asūy", ārjavaṃ, śaucaṃ, santoṣaḥ, priyavāditā,
damaḥ, satyam, an|āyāso na bhavanti dur|ātmanām.
ātma|jñānam, an|āyāsas, titikṣā, dharma|nityatā,
vāk c' âiva guptā, dānaṃ ca – n' âitāny antyeṣu, Bhārata.
ākrośa|parivādābhyāṃ vihiṃsanty a|budhā budhān.
vaktā pāpam upādatte, kṣamamāṇo vimucyate.
34.75 hiṃsā|balam a|sādhūnāṃ, rājñāṃ daṇḍa|vidhir balam,
śuśrūṣā tu balaṃ strīṇāṃ, kṣamā guṇavatāṃ balam.
vāk|saṃyamo hi, nṛpate, su|duṣkaratamo mataḥ;
arthavac ca vicitraṃ ca na śakyaṃ bahu bhāṣitum.
abhyāvahati kalyāṇaṃ vividhaṃ vāk su|bhāṣitā;

covered with a tight-meshed net; they are desire and anger, my king, and they destroy wisdom as fish break their net.

If one obtains wealth while keeping an eye on virtue and profit, then one wins eternal happiness, having now assembled what one had wished for. The man who does not subdue the five inner mental enemies, but still wants to destroy his other enemies, will end up being defeated by them. High-souled kings are seen to be restricted by their own actions, so vehement for lordship, because of their lack of control over their senses.

Equal punishment falls upon good men by their association with and by their failure to renounce the company 34.70
of miscreants, just as damp matter burns when it is mixed up with dry things; so one should not make associations with wicked men. Disaster swallows the man who does not suppress his five naturally rising enemies with their five purposes.

Absence of spite, sincerity, integrity, contentment, sweet speech, discipline, truth, and readiness do not exist within evil-hearted men. Self-awareness, ease, patience, eternal virtue, secret speech, and generosity do not reside in the lowest ranks of society, Bhárata. Idiots wish to harm the intelligent with accusations and abuse. The man who speaks evil is guilty, but the forgiving man is released of blame.

Wicked men's strength is violence, kings' strength is rule 34.75
through punishment, women's strength is obedience, and forgiveness is the strength of the virtuous. Controlling one's speech is considered by far the most difficult, my king, for it is not possible to say much which is both significant and

s" âiva dur|bhāṣitā, rājann, an|arthāy' ôpapadyate.
rohate sāyakair viddhaṃ vanaṃ paraśunā hatam;
vācā dur|uktaṃ bībhatsaṃ na saṃrohati vāk|kṣatam
karṇi|nālīka|nārācān nirharanti śarīrataḥ;
vāk|śalyas tu na nirhartuṃ śakyo, hṛdi|śayo hi saḥ.
34.80 vāk|sāyakā vadanān niṣpatanti,
yair āhataḥ śocati rātry|ahāni.
parasya n' â|marmasu te patanti.
tān paṇḍito n' âvasṛjet parebhyaḥ.
yasmai devāḥ prayacchanti puruṣāya parābhavam,
buddhiṃ tasy' âpakarṣanti so 'vācīnāni paśyati.
buddhau kaluṣa|bhūtāyāṃ vināśe pratyupasthite,
a|nayo naya|saṅkāśo hṛdayān n' âpasarpati.
s' êyaṃ buddhiḥ parītā te putrāṇāṃ, Bharata'|rṣabha,
Pāṇḍavānāṃ virodhena; na c' âinān avabuddhyase.
rājā lakṣaṇa|saṃpannas trailokyasy' âpi yo bhavet,
śiṣyas te, śāsitā so 'stu, Dhṛtarāṣṭra, Yudhiṣṭhiraḥ!
34.85 atīva sarvān putrāṃs te bhāgadheya|puraskṛtaḥ,
tejasā prajñayā c' âiva yukto, dharm'|ârtha|tattva|vit.
anukrośād ānṛśaṃsyād yo 'sau dharma|bhṛtāṃ varaḥ
gauravāt tava, rāj'|êndra, bahūn kleśāṃs titikṣati.»

varied. Varied speech, well spoken, brings good results, but badly spoken speech results in bad fortune, my king.

A forest filled with arrows and struck by axes still thrives, but the hideous wound made by abusive speech does not recover. Arrows, shafts, and iron darts are pulled out of the body, but the weapon of unkind words lies in the heart and cannot be removed.

The arrows of speech fly from the mouth, and when 34.80
struck by them a man grieves day and night. They do not fall wide of one's enemies' vulnerable spots. A wise man would not release them upon his enemies.

When the gods strive for a man's defeat, they take away his intelligence, so he looks to low deeds. When his intelligence has become muddy and his destruction is on the horizon, his bad policy, which appears to to him be good policy, does not leave his heart. Your sons' intelligence has lapsed, bull-like Bharata, because of their hostility towards the Pándavas, but you do not comprehend this.

Your pupil Yudhi·shthira, endowed with the auspicious markings, should be king of the three worlds, so let him be
the ruler, Dhrita·rashtra! He has been honored by destiny 34.85
beyond all your sons, since he is endowed with splendor and wisdom and knows the truth of moral law and profit. That greatest of those who uphold moral law has endured numerous miseries, lord of kings, out of compassion, kindness, and respect for you."

DHṚTARĀṢṬRA uvāca:

35.1 «BRŪHI BHŪYO, mahā|buddhe,
dharm'|ârtha|sahitaṃ vacaḥ.
śṛṇvato n' âsti me tṛptir;
vicitrāṇ' îha bhāṣase.»

VIDURA uvāca:

«sarva|tīrtheṣu vā snānaṃ, sarva|bhūteṣu c' ārjavam,
ubhe tv ete same syātām, ārjavaṃ vā viśiṣyate.
ārjavaṃ pratipadyasva putreṣu satataṃ, vibho,
iha kīrtiṃ parāṃ prāpya pretya svargam avāpsyasi.
yāvat kīrtir manuṣyasya puṇyā loke pragīyate,
tāvat sa, puruṣa|vyāghra, svarga|loke mahīyate.
35.5 atr' âpy udāharant' îmam itihāsaṃ purātanam,
Virocanasya saṃvādaṃ Keśiny|arthe Sudhanvanā:
svayaṃ|vare sthitā kanyā Keśinī nāma nāmataḥ,
rūpeṇ' â|pratimā, rājan, viśiṣṭa|pati|kāmyayā.
Virocano 'tha Daiteyas tadā tatr' ājagāma ha,
prāptum icchaṃs; tatas tatra daity'|êndraṃ prāha Keśinī:

DHRITA·RASHTRA said:

"SPEAK TO ME again, highly intelligent man, in words which conform to virtue and profit. I am not satisfied with listening to you, because you speak delightfully variedly." 35.1

VÍDURA replied:

"Bathing at all sacred fords and sincerity to all creatures are either of equal value, or maybe sincerity excels. Always practice honesty towards your sons, my lord, and you will attain the greatest glory on this earth, and once you have passed over you will gain heaven. For as long as his pious fame is celebrated in the human world, tiger-like man, a man is honored in heaven. This is the point on which peo- 35.5
ple cite the ancient legend of Viróchana's discussion with Sudhánvan for the sake of Késhini:

A girl, by the name of Késhini, stood at her *svayam·vara*,* unequaled in her beauty and in her wish for an excellent husband, my king. Viróchana, son of Diti, arrived there, wishing to win Késhini as his wife, and Késhini said to the lord of the Daityas:

KEŚINY uvāca:

‹kiṃ brāhmaṇāḥ svic chreyāṃso, Diti|jāḥ svid, Virocana?
atha kena sma paryaṅkaṃ Sudhanvā n' âdhirohati?›

VIROCANA uvāca:

‹Prājāpatyās tu vai śreṣṭhā vayaṃ, Keśini, sattamāḥ!
asmākaṃ khalv ime lokāḥ! ke devāḥ? ke dvijātayaḥ?›

KEŚINY uvāca:

35.10 ‹ih' âiv' āvāṃ pratīkṣāva upasthāne, Virocana.
Sudhanvā prātar āgantā; paśyeyaṃ vāṃ samāgatau.›

VIROCANA uvāca:

‹tathā, bhadre, kariṣyāmi, yathā tvaṃ, bhīru, bhāṣase.
Sudhanvānaṃ ca māṃ c' âiva prātar draṣṭ" âsi saṅgatau.›

VIDURA uvāca:

atītāyāṃ ca śarvaryām, udite sūrya|maṇḍale,
atha ājagāma taṃ deśaṃ Sudhanvā, rāja|sattama.
Virocano yatra, vibho, Keśinyā sahitaḥ sthitaḥ.
Sudhanvā ca samāgacchat Prāhrādiṃ Keśinīṃ tathā.
samāgataṃ dvijaṃ dṛṣṭvā
Keśinī, Bharata'|rṣabha,
pratyutthāy' āsanaṃ tasmai,
pādyam arghyaṃ dadau punaḥ.

KÉSHINI said:

'Are the brahmins or the sons of Diti better, Viróchana? Or, to put it another way, with which would Sudhánvan refuse to take a seat on a couch?'

VIRÓCHANA replied:

'Since we are descended from Praja·pati we are the best and greatest, Késhini! In fact these worlds are ours! Who are the gods? Who are the twiceborn?'

KÉSHINI said:

'We will wait here in the assembly, Viróchana. Sudhán- 35.10
van will arrive in the morning and I will see you both together.'

VIRÓCHANA replied:

'My dear, I will do as you say, timid lady. In the morning you will see both me and Sudhánvan together.'

VÍDURA continued:

When the star-spangled night was past and the disk of the sun was rising, Sudhánvan came to that place, greatest of kings. Viróchana stood there with Késhini, my lord, and Sudhánvan approached the son of Prahráda and Késhini. When Késhini saw the brahmin approaching, bull-like Bharata, she rose from her seat to greet him, and once again provided water for the feet and gave him the proper reception for a guest.

SUDHANV" ôvāca:

‹anvālabhe hiraṇ|mayaṃ, Prāhrāde, te var'|āsanam;
ekatvam upasaṃpanno; na tv āse 'haṃ tvayā saha.›

VIROCANA uvāca:

35.15 ‹tav' ârhate tu phalakaṃ, kūrcaṃ v" âpy, atha vā bṛsī,
Sudhanvan, na tvam arho 'si mayā saha samāsanam.›

SUDHANV" ôvāca:

‹pitā|putrau sah' āsītāṃ, dvau viprau, kṣatriyāv api,
vṛddhau vaiśyau ca, śūdrau ca; na tv anyāv itar'|êtaram.
pitā hi te samāsīnam upāsīt' âiva mām adhaḥ;
bālaḥ sukh'|âidhito gehe na tvaṃ kiñ cana budhyase.›

VIROCANA uvāca:

‹hiraṇyaṃ ca gav'|âśvaṃ ca yad vittam asureṣu naḥ,
Sudhanvan, vipaṇe tena praśnaṃ pṛcchāva, ye viduḥ!›

SUDHANV" ôvāca:

‹hiraṇyaṃ ca gav'|âśvaṃ ca tav' âiv' âstu, Virocana.
prāṇayos tu paṇaṃ kṛtvā praśnaṃ pṛcchāva, ye viduḥ!›

VIROCANA uvāca:

35.20 ‹āvāṃ kutra gamiṣyāvaḥ prāṇayor vipaṇe kṛte?
na tu deveṣv ahaṃ sthātā, na manuṣyeṣu karhi cit.›

SUDHÁNVAN said:

'I will accept the best golden seat from you, son of Prahráda, now that I have met you face to face, but I will not sit with you.'

VIRÓCHANA replied:

'A wooden bench or a bundle of grass or alternatively a 35.15
cushion would suit you, Sudhánvan, but you are not worthy to share a seat with me.'

SUDHÁNVAN said:

'A pair of brahmins, father and son, even two kshatriyas, and old vaishyas and shudras, sit together on the same seat, but no other pair are allowed to sit together. Your father is my inferior and even he gets up rather than share a seat with me, but you have grown up in luxury as a child in your home, and you understand nothing.'

VIRÓCHANA replied:

'Let us pose our query to those who know, with a wager of gold, cattle, and horses, and whatever wealth we *ásura*s possess, Sudhánvan!'

SUDHÁNVAN said:

'Keep your gold, and cattle and horses, Viróchana. Let us pose our query to those who know, making our lives the stake!'

VIRÓCHANA replied:

'Where will we go once we have bet our lives? I will never 35.20
stand before gods or humans!'

SUDHANV" ôvāca:
‹pitaraṃ te gamiṣyāvaḥ prāṇayor vipaṇe kṛte.
putrasy' âpi sa hetor hi Prahrādo n' ânṛtaṃ vadet.›

VIDURA uvāca:
evaṃ kṛta|paṇau kruddhau tatr' âbhijagmatus tadā
Virocana|Sudhanvānau, Prahrādo yatra tiṣṭhati.

PRAHRĀDA uvāca:
‹imau tau saṃpradṛśyete, yābhyāṃ na caritaṃ saha,
āśī|viṣāv iva kruddhāv eka|mārgāv ih' āgatau.
kiṃ vai sah' âiva caratho, na purā carathaḥ saha?
Virocan', âitat pṛcchāmi, kiṃ te sakhyaṃ Sudhanvanā?›

VIROCANA uvāca:
35.25 ‹na me Sudhanvanā sakhyaṃ; prāṇayor vipaṇāvahe.
Prahrāda, tattvaṃ pṛcchāmi, mā praśnam an|ṛtaṃ vadeḥ.›

PRAHRĀDA uvāca:
‹udakaṃ, madhu|parkaṃ c' âpy* ānayantu Sudhanvane.
brahmann, abhyarcanīyo 'si. śvetā gauḥ pīvarī|kṛtā.›

SUDHANV" ôvāca:
‹udakaṃ madhu|parkaṃ ca pathiṣv ev' ârpitaṃ mama;
Prahrāda, tvaṃ tu me tathyaṃ praśnaṃ prabrūhi pṛcchataḥ:
kiṃ brāhmaṇāḥ svic chreyāṃsa, ut' āho svid Virocanaḥ?›

SUDHÁNVAN said:

'Let's go to your father once we have bet our lives. For Prahráda would not lie, even for the sake of his son.'

VÍDURA said:

So, once they had made their wager, Viróchana and Sudhánvan, both furious, then set out for the place where Prahráda was staying.

PRAHRÁDA said:

'These two have never done anything together before, but now they can be seen in each other's company. They come here on a single road like a couple of enraged, poisonous snakes. Why are you traveling together when you have never traveled together in the past? I am asking you, Viróchana, why you have formed a friendship with Sudhánvan.'

VIRÓCHANA replied:

'I am not friendly with Sudhánvan, rather we have staked 35.25
our lives. So, Prahráda, I ask you a question truly. Do not give us a false answer.'

PRAHRÁDA said:

'Let them bring water or a honey offering for Sudhánvan. You should be honored, brahmin. A white cow has been fattened.'

SUDHÁNVAN replied:

'Water and the honey offerings were offered to me on the road, Prahráda, so please tell me the answer to the question you are asked: Who is better—brahmins or Viróchana?'

PRAHRĀDA uvāca:

‹putra eko mama, brahmaṃs, tvaṃ ca sākṣād ih' āsthitaḥ.
tayor vivadatoḥ praśnaṃ katham asmad|vidho vadet?›

SUDHANV" ôvāca:

‹gāṃ pradadyās tv aurasāya,
yad v" ânyat syāt priyaṃ dhanam;
dvayor vivadatos tathyaṃ
vācyaṃ ca, matimaṃs, tvayā.›

PRAHRĀDA uvāca:

35.30 ‹atha yo n' âiva prabrūyāt satyaṃ vā, yadi v" ân|ṛtam,
etat, Sudhanvan, pṛcchāmi; dur|vivaktā sma kiṃ vaset.›

SUDHANV" ôvāca:

‹yāṃ rātrim adhivinnā strī, yāṃ c' âiv' âkṣa|parājitaḥ,
yāṃ ca bhār'|âbhitapt'|âṅgo, dur|vivaktā sma tāṃ vaset.
nagare pratiruddhaḥ san bahir dvāre bubhukṣitaḥ,
amitrān bhūyasaḥ paśyed yaḥ sākṣyam anṛtaṃ vadet.
pañca paśv|anṛte hanti, daśa hanti gav'|ânṛte;
śatam aśv'|ânṛte hanti, sahasraṃ puruṣ'|ânṛte;
hanti jātān a|jātāṃś ca
hiraṇy'|ârthe 'nṛtaṃ vadan;
sarvaṃ bhūmy|anṛte hanti;
mā sma bhūmy|anṛtaṃ vadeḥ!›

PRAHRÁDA responded:

'Brahmin, this is my only son! But then there is the fact that you stand here in person. When you two quarrel over this question, how could someone in my position settle it?'

SUDHÁNVAN said:

'You should give a cow or whatever other precious wealth you have to your son, but you should speak the truth, wise one, when we quarrel.'

PRAHRÁDA replied:

'Well then, Sudhánvan, I ask you how a man who an- 35.30
swers wrongly could live, if he would not tell the truth or lie.'

SUDHÁNVAN said:

'The man who answers incorrectly would pass the night just as a neglected wife would spend it, or a man who has lost at dice, or a man whose body has been worn out from his burden. The man who gives false evidence is like the man who is banished from the city so stays outside the door, hungry and watching his numerous enemies. The man who lies about goats kills five, who lies about cattle kills ten, who lies about horses kills one hundred, and who lies about people kills one thousand. The man who tells lies for the sake of gold kills both the born and the unborn, and the man who lies about the earth kills everything, so don't tell lies about the earth!'

PRAHRĀDA uvāca:

35.35 ‹mattaḥ śreyān Aṅgirā vai, Sudhanvā tvad, Virocana;
māt” âsya śreyasī mātus; tasmāt tvaṃ tena vai jitaḥ.
Virocana, Sudhanv” âyaṃ prāṇānām īśvaras tava.
Sudhanvan, punar icchāmi tvayā dattaṃ Virocanam.›

SUDHANV” ôvāca:

‹yad dharmam avṛṇīthās tvaṃ, na kāmād an|ṛtaṃ vadīḥ,
punar dadāmi te putraṃ tasmāt, Prahrāda, dur|labham.
eṣa, Prahrāda, putras te mayā datto Virocanaḥ.
pāda|prakṣālanaṃ kuryāt kumāryāḥ sannidhau mama.›

VIDURA uvāca:

tasmād, rāj'|êndra, bhūmy|arthe
n' ân|ṛtaṃ vaktum arhasi.
mā gamaḥ sa|sut'|âmātyo
nāśaṃ putr'|ârtham abruvan.
35.40 na devā daṇḍam ādāya rakṣanti paśu|pālavat;
yaṃ tu rakṣitum icchanti, buddhyā saṃvibhajanti tam.
yathā yathā hi puruṣaḥ kalyāṇe kurute manaḥ,
tathā tath” âsya sarv'|ârthāḥ sidhyante n' âtra saṃśayaḥ.
n' âinaṃ chandāṃsi vṛjināt tārayanti
māyāvinaṃ māyayā vartamānam;
nīḍaṃ śakuntā iva jāta|pakṣāś,
chandāṃsy enaṃ prajahaty anta|kāle.
madya|pānaṃ, kalahaṃ, pūga|vairaṃ,
bhāryā|patyor antaraṃ, jñāti|bhedam,
rāja|dviṣṭaṃ, strī|puṃsayor vivādaṃ
varjyāny āhur, yaś ca panthāḥ praduṣṭaḥ.

PRAHRÁDA replied:

'Ángiras is better than me, Sudhánvan is better than you, 35.35
Viróchana, and his mother is better than yours, and so he has beaten you. Viróchana, Sudhánvan here owns your life. Sudhánvan, I would like you to return Viróchana's life to him once more.'

SUDHÁNVAN said:

'Since you chose to follow the law, and did not tell lies swayed by love, I will return your son to you, Prahráda; a scarce gift. I return your son Viróchana here to you, Prahráda. But he should wash my feet in full view of the princess.'

VÍDURA continued:

That is why, my king, you ought not to tell lies for the sake of land. Don't go to your destruction along with your charioteers and advisors by speaking in defense of your son.
The gods do not pick up a stick and protect like a herdsman; 35.40
instead they bestow wisdom upon the man whom they wish to protect. There is no doubt that all a man's aims are successful only to the degree that he sets his mind on what is virtuous.

Sacred hymns do not rescue a fraudster from disaster if he operates with deception. Just as birds whose wings have developed leave the nest, so sacred hymns desert him in the final moments. They say that intoxicating drinks should be avoided, as should quarrels, enmity towards large numbers of people, arguments between husband and wife, hatred towards the king, battles of the sexes, and corrupt paths.

sāmudrikaṃ, vaṇijaṃ cora|pūrvaṃ,
śalāka|dhūrtaṃ ca, cikitsakaṃ ca,
ariṃ ca, mitraṃ ca, kuśīlavaṃ ca;
n' âitān sākṣye tv adhikurvīta sapta.
35.45 mān'|âgnihotram, uta māna|maunaṃ,
mānen' âdhītam, uta māna|yajñaḥ;
etāni catvāry abhayaṅ|karāṇi
bhayaṃ prayacchanty a|yathā|kṛtāni.*
agāra|dāhī, gara|daḥ, kuṇḍ'|āśī, soma|vikrayo,
parva|kāraś ca, sūcī ca, mitra|dhruk, pāra|dārikaḥ,
bhrūṇa|hā, guru|talpī ca, yaś ca syāt pāna|po dvijaḥ,
atitīkṣṇaś ca, kākaś ca, nāstiko, veda|nindakaḥ,
sruva|pragrahaṇo, vrātyaḥ, kīnāśaś c' ātmavān api,
‹rakṣ', êty› uktaś ca yo hiṃsyāt, sarve brahma|habhiḥ samāḥ.
tṛṇ'|ôlkayā jñāyate jāta|rūpaṃ,
vṛttena bhadro, vyavahāreṇa sādhuḥ,
śūro bhayeṣv, artha|kṛcchreṣu dhīraḥ,
kṛcchreṣv āpatsu suhṛdaś c' ârayaś ca.
35.50 jarā rūpaṃ harati hi, dhairyam āśā
mṛtyuḥ prāṇān, dharma|caryām a|sūyā,
krodhaḥ śriyaṃ, śīlam anārya|sevā,
hriyaṃ kāmaḥ, sarvam ev' âbhimānaḥ.
śrīr maṅgalāt prabhavati, prāgalbhyāt saṃpravardhate,
dākṣyāt tu kurute mūlaṃ, saṃyamāt pratitiṣṭhati.

These seven people should not be appointed to give evidence: a palm reader, a merchant who was once a thief, a bird catcher, a doctor, an enemy, a friend, and an actor. There are four things which create safety but which bestow 35.45
fear when done improperly: an Agni·hotra sacrifice instituted through pride, proud silence, study through pride, and sacrifice done out of pride.

An arsonist, a poisoner, a pimp, a *soma* seller, an arrow maker, a spy, someone who hurts his friends, an adulterer, an abortionist, a cuckold in the teacher's bed, an alcoholic brahmin, someone who is too cruel, an insolent man, an atheist, a man who ridicules the Veda, one who takes everything for himself, a tramp, a self-possessed peasant, and the man who harms when begged to defend, are all equal to brahmin-murderers.

Gold is proven by a fire of hay, a good man by his behavior, a pious man by his conduct, a brave man in dangers, a resolute man in disastrous affairs, and friends and enemies in times of painful calamity. Old age steals one's 35.50
beauty, hope steals one's patience, death steals one's life, jealousy steals one's moral behavior, anger steals one's good fortune, servitude to the ignoble steals one's good conduct, desire robs one's modesty, and arrogance steals everything. Good fortune develops from welfare, grows from bold judgment, takes root from industry, and remains established with control.

aṣṭau guṇāḥ puruṣaṃ dīpayanti:
prajñā ca, kaulyaṃ ca, damaḥ, śrutaṃ ca,
parākramaś c', â|bahu|bhāṣitā ca,
dānaṃ yathā|śakti, kṛta|jñātā ca.
etān guṇāṃs, tāta, mah"|ânubhāvān
eko guṇaḥ saṃśrayate prasahya;
rājā yadā sat|kurute manuṣyaṃ.
sarvān guṇān eṣa guṇo vibhāti.
aṣṭau, nṛp', êmāni manuṣya|loke
svargasya lokasya nidarśanāni;
catvāry eṣām anvavetāni sadbhiś,
catvāri c' âiṣām anuyānti santaḥ.
35.55 yajño, dānam, adhyayanaṃ, tapaś ca,
catvāry etāny anvavetāni sadbhiḥ.
damaḥ, satyam, ārjavam, ānṛśaṃsyaṃ,
catvāry etāny anvavayanti santaḥ.
ijy'|âdhyayana|dānāni, tapaḥ, satyaṃ, kṣamā, ghṛṇā,
a|lobha, iti mārgo 'yaṃ dharmasy' âṣṭa|vidhiḥ smṛtaḥ.
tatra pūrva|catur|vargo dambh'|ârtham api sevyate;
uttaraś ca catur|vargo n' â|mah"|ātmasu tiṣṭhati.
na sā sabhā yatra na santi vṛddhā;
na te vṛddhā ye na vadanti dharmam,
n' âsau dharmo yatra na satyam asti,
na tat satyaṃ yac chalen' âbhyupetam.
satyaṃ, rūpaṃ, śrutaṃ, vidyā,
kaulyaṃ, śīlaṃ, balaṃ, dhanam,
śauryaṃ ca, citra|bhāṣyaṃ ca,
daś' ême svarga|yonayaḥ.

Eight virtues illuminate a man: wisdom, noble descent, control, learning, heroism, taciturnity, generosity according to one's means, and gratitude. These are mighty virtues, my friend, but one virtue unites them together—when a king behaves honorably towards a man. This is the virtue which illuminates all virtues.

My king, these eight are signs of the heavenly world in the world of men; four of them follow the good, and the
other four are sought by the good. Sacrifice, generosity, 35.55
study, and austerity are the four which follow along with the good, and self control, truth, sincerity, and non-violence are the four which the good seek.

This is passed down as the eight-fold path to virtue: honor, learning, generosity, austerity, truth, forgiveness, compassion, and a lack of greed. The first four comprise a group which can also be cultivated for the sake of deceit, but the second group of four does not reside in the mean-spirited.

Where there are no elders there is no court; where men do not speak moral law there are no elders. Where there is no morality there is no truth, and something endowed with deceit is not truth. The ten bases of regeneration in heaven are truth, beauty, learning, knowledge, noble descent, good conduct, strength, wealth, bravery, and varied speech.

35.60 pāpaṃ kurvan pāpa|kīrtiḥ pāpam ev' âśnute phalam;
puṇyaṃ kurvan puṇya|kīrtiḥ puṇyam atyantam aśnute.
tasmāt pāpaṃ na kurvīta puruṣaḥ śaṃsita|vrataḥ
pāpaṃ prajñāṃ nāśayati kriyamāṇaṃ punaḥ punaḥ.
naṣṭa|prajñaḥ pāpam eva nityam ārabhate naraḥ;
puṇyaṃ prajñāṃ vardhayati kriyamāṇaṃ punaḥ punaḥ.
puṇyaṃ kurvan puṇya|kīrtiḥ
puṇyaṃ sthanaṃ sma gacchati,
tasmāt puṇyaṃ niṣeveta
puruṣaḥ su|samāhitaḥ.
asūyako, dandaśūko, niṣṭhuro, vaira|kṛc, chaṭhaḥ,
sa kṛcchraṃ mahad āpnoti na cirāt pāpam ācaran.
35.65 an|asūyuḥ, kṛta|prajñaḥ, śobhanāny ācaran sadā
na kṛcchraṃ mahad āpnoti sarvatra ca virocate.
prajñām ev' āgamayati yaḥ prājñebhyaḥ, sa paṇḍitaḥ;
prājño hy avāpya dharm'|ârthau śaknoti sukham edhitum.
divasen' âiva tat kuryād, yena rātrau sukhaṃ vaset;
aṣṭa|māsena tat kuryād, yena varṣāḥ sukhaṃ vaset.
pūrve vayasi tat kuryād, yena vṛddhaḥ sukhaṃ vaset;
yāvaj|jīvena tat kuryād yena pretya sukhaṃ vaset.
jīrṇam annaṃ praśaṃsanti, bhāryāṃ ca gata|yauvanām,
śūraṃ vijita|saṅgrāmaṃ, gata|pāraṃ tapasvinam.

The man with a bad reputation who perpetrates evil gains 35.60
an evil reward, but the man with a reputation for piety who commits holy acts always reaps holy rewards. Therefore, the man whose conduct is praiseworthy would not perpetrate evil, since by committing evil acts over and over again he destroys his wisdom. The man whose wisdom is lost will always undertake wickedness. But by committing pious acts over and over again a man increases his wisdom. The man with a reputation for piety who commits pious deeds goes to a position of piety. Therefore, a man should cultivate piety with great concentration.

The jealous man, the malignant man, the harsh man, the quarrelsome man, and the fraudster soon meet great disaster by doing evil deeds. But the man who is free of jealousy, 35.65
the grateful man who always does glorious deeds, does not meet with great disaster. Instead he shines in all matters. The man who learns wisdom from the wise is himself a teacher, and when that wise man obtains moral law and profit, he is able to reach happiness.

During the day a man should do what will make him live happily at night, and during the eight dry months he should do what will make him live happily through the monsoon. In his first bloom of youth a man should do what will enable him to live happily when he is old, and for his whole life he should act in such a way that he will exist happily once he has passed to the next world. People praise food which has been digested, a wife whose youth has passed, a hero whose battles have been won, and an ascetic who has reached the highest limit.

35.70 dhanen' â|dharma|labdhena yac chidram apidhīyate,
a|saṃvṛtaṃ tad bhavati, tato 'nyad avadīryate.
gurur ātmavatāṃ śāstā, śāstā rājā dur|ātmanām;
atha pracchanna|pāpānāṃ śāstā Vaivasvato Yamaḥ.
ṛṣīṇāṃ ca, nadīnāṃ ca, kulānāṃ ca mah"|ātmanām
prabhavo n' âdhigantavyaḥ, strīṇāṃ duś|caritasya ca.
dvijāti|pūj"|âbhirato, dātā, jñātiṣu c' ārjavī,
kṣatriyaḥ śīla|bhāg, rājaṃś, ciraṃ pālayate mahīm.
suvarṇa|puṣpāṃ pṛthivīṃ cinvanti puruṣās trayaḥ:
śūraś ca, kṛtavidyaś ca, yaś ca jānāti sevitum.
35.75 buddhi|śreṣṭhāni karmāṇi bāhu|madhyāni, Bhārata,
tāni jaṅghā|jaghanyāni bhāra|pratyavarāṇi ca.
Duryodhane 'tha Śakunau, mūḍhe Duḥśāsane tathā,
Karṇe c' āiśvaryam ādhāya kathaṃ tvaṃ bhūtim icchasi?
sarvair guṇair upetās tu Pāṇḍavā, Bharata'|rṣabha.
pitṛvat tvayi vartante; teṣu vartasva putravat.»

VIDURA uvāca:

36.1 «ATR' ÂIV' ÔDĀHARANT' îmam itihāsaṃ purātanam
Ātreyasya ca saṃvādaṃ Sādhyānāṃ c', êti naḥ śrutam.
carantaṃ haṃsa|rūpeṇa maha"|rṣiṃ saṃśita|vratam
Sādhyā devā mahā|prājñaṃ paryapṛcchanta vai purā:

A hole concealed with immorally earned wealth will become uncovered and burst open. The guru is the governor of the self-possessed, the king is the chastiser of the wicked, and Yama Vaivásvata is the chastiser of those whose wickedness is hidden. The source of sages, rivers, and high-souled lineages cannot be found, nor the source of women's bad behavior. 35.70

A generous warrior engaged in honoring brahmins, who is honest to his relatives and who has his share of good conduct, my king, will defend the earth for a long time. Three kinds of men pluck the beautifully hued flowers of earth:
heroes, learned men, and men who know how to serve. Acts 35.75
of intelligence are the best, those of strength of arms are middling, Bhárata, acts of the legs are the worst, and acts of burden fall even below those.

How do you wish for prosperity when you have given power to the foolish Duryódhana, Shákuni, Duhshásana, and Karna? The Pándavas are endowed with every virtue, bull of the Bharatas. They behave towards you as if you were their father, so treat them like sons."

VÍDURA continued:

"THIS IS THE point of the ancient saying people quote, 36.1
which is passed down to us as the conversation between Atréya and the *sadhyas*. Long ago the *sadhya* gods questioned a very wise, great sage of laudable conduct, who happened to be in the form of a goose:

SĀDHYĀ ūcuḥ:

‹Sādhyā devā vayam ete, maha"|rṣe.
dṛṣṭvā bhavantaṃ na śaknumo 'numātum.
śrutena dhīro buddhimāṃs tvaṃ mato naḥ,
kāvyāṃ vācaṃ vaktum arhasy udārām.›

HAṂSA uvāca:

‹etat kāryam, a|marāḥ, saṃśrutaṃ me:
dhṛtiḥ, śamaḥ, satya|dharm'|ânuvṛttiḥ.
granthiṃ vinīya hṛdayasya sarvaṃ
priy'|âpriye c' ātma|samaṃ nayīta.
36.5 ākruśyamāno n' ākrośen; manyur eva titikṣataḥ
ākroṣṭāraṃ nirdahati, su|kṛtaṃ c' âsya vindati.›
n' ākrośī syān, n' âvamānī parasya,
mitra|drohī, n' ôta nīc'|ôpasevī,
na c' âbhimānī, na ca hīna|vṛtto;
rūkṣāṃ vācaṃ ruṣatīṃ varjayīta.
marmāṇy, asthīni, hṛdayaṃ tath" âsūn
rūkṣā vāco nirdahant' îha puṃsām.
tasmād vācaṃ ruṣatīṃ rūkṣa|rūpāṃ
dharm'|ārāmo nityaśo varjayīta.
arun|tudaṃ paruṣaṃ rūkṣa|vācaṃ,
vāk|kaṇṭakair vitudantaṃ manuṣyān
vidyād a|lakṣmīkatamaṃ janānāṃ;
mukhe nibaddhāṃ nirṛtiṃ vahantam.
paraś ced enam abhividhyeta bāṇair
bhṛśaṃ su|tīkṣṇair anal'|ârka|dīptaiḥ,
sa vidhyamāno 'py atidahyamāno
vidyāt kaviḥ su|kṛtaṃ me dadhāti.
36.10 yadi santaṃ sevati, yady a|santaṃ,
tapasvinaṃ, yadi vā stenam eva,

THE SADHYA GODS said:

'We are the *sadhya* gods, great sage. We have seen you but are unable to guess who you are. In our opinion you are steady in learning and wise, so you ought to say something inspired and eloquent.'

THE GOOSE replied:

'Immortals, I have learned what one must do: Be steady and peaceful, and practice truth and moral law, expelling all knots in the heart, and regard what is pleasant and unpleasant as equal to oneself. When being treated with abuse 36.5
don't think abusively, for the man who suffers it with patience will burn up the abuser and take the other man's merit.'

One should not be an abuser, despise one's enemy, betray a friend, or serve those low in the social hierarchy; one should not be arrogant or lack good behavior. Avoid cruel and offensive speech. Cruel speech burns a man's innards, bones, heart, and life. Therefore, the man who takes delight in moral law should always avoid offensive and cruelly formed speech. One should know that the tormenting, rough, and offensive-speaking man who stings men with thorny speech is the least fortunate of all men; he carries disaster upon his lips and mouth.

If an enemy severely wounds you with razor-sharp arrows that blaze like fire and the sun, the sage should know that though wounded and terribly scorched, the enemy bestows his merit on him. If one serves a good man or a bad man, or 36.10
if one serves an ascetic or thief, then, just as clothes become tainted by dye, so one becomes tainted by them.

vāso yathā raṅga|vaśaṃ prayāti,
tathā sa teṣāṃ vaśam abhyupaiti.
ativādaṃ na pravaden, na vādayed,
yo n' āhataḥ pratihanyān na ghātayet;
hantuṃ ca yo n' êcchati pāpakaṃ vai,
tasmai devāḥ spṛhayanty āgatāya.
a|vyāhṛtaṃ vyāhṛtāc chreya āhuḥ,
satyaṃ vaded vyāhṛtaṃ tad dvitīyam,
priyaṃ vaded vyāhṛtaṃ tat tṛtīyaṃ,
dharmyaṃ vaded vyāhṛtaṃ tac caturtham.
yādṛśaiḥ sanniviśate, yādṛśāṃś c' ôpasevate;
yādṛg icchec ca bhavituṃ, tādṛg bhavati pūruṣaḥ.
yato yato nivartate, tatas tato vimucyate;
nirvartanādd hi sarvato na vetti duḥkham aṇv api.
36.15 na jīyate c' ânujigīṣate 'nyān;
na vaira|kṛc c' â|pratighātakaś ca;
nindā|praśaṃsāsu sama|svabhāvo;
na śocate hṛṣyati n' âiva c' âyam.
bhāvam icchati sarvasya, n' â|bhāve kurute manaḥ,
satya|vādī, mṛdur, dānto yaḥ, sa uttama|pūruṣaḥ.
n' ân|arthakaṃ sāntvayati, pratijñāya dadāti ca,
randhraṃ parasya jānāti yaḥ, sa madhyama|pūruṣaḥ.
duḥ|śāsanas t' ûpahato 'bhiśasto,
n' âvartate manyu|vaśāt kṛta|ghnaḥ,
na kasya cin mitram atho dur|ātmā,
kalāś c' âitā adhamasy' êha puṃsaḥ.
na śraddadhāti kalyāṇaṃ parebhyo 'py ātma|śaṅkitaḥ,
nirākaroti mitrāṇi yo vai, so 'dhama|pūruṣaḥ.

The gods are eager for the arrival of a man who does not reply abusively to the man who abuses him, who would not force anyone else to either, who would not strike back when assaulted or force anyone else to either, and who doesn't wish to kill the villain who attacks him. They say that not speaking is better than speaking, secondly that one should speak the truth if one must speak, thirdly that one should speak pleasantly when speaking, and fourthly that one should speak in accordance with moral law when speaking. A man becomes like those with whom he associates and like those whom he serves; he becomes the kind of man he would wish to be.

One is released from whatever one abstains from. By abstaining from everything, one does not even know the minutest misery. Such a man is not defeated nor does he wish 36.15
to defeat others; he is not quarrelsome and does not strike back; he is egalitarian towards blame and praise; he does not grieve or rejoice. He is the greatest of men who wishes for the continuance of all, whose mind is not set on destruction, who is truthful, gentle, and disciplined.

The middling man is the one who does not conciliate a useless person, who gives as promised, and who knows his enemy's weakness. The signs of the lowest type of man are his inability to be controlled when injured or blamed, the fact that he will not abstain from the power of his rage, his ingratitude, his friendlessness, and his wicked soul. The worst man of all does not believe any good comes from others. He is suspicious even of himself and he shuns his friends.

36.20 uttamān eva seveta, prāpta|kāle tu madhyamān,
adhamāṃs tu na seveta ya icched bhūtim ātmanaḥ.
prāpnoti vai cittam a|sad|balena
nity'|ôtthānāt prajñayā pauruṣeṇa;
na tv eva samyag labhate praśaṃsāṃ,
na vṛttam āpnoti mahā|kulānām.»

DHṚTARĀṢṬRA uvāca:
«mahā|kulebhyaḥ spṛhayanti devā
dharm'|ârtha|nityāś ca bahu|śrutāś ca.
pṛcchami tvāṃ, Vidura, praśnam etam:
bhavanti vai kāni mahā|kulāni?»

VIDURA uvāca:
«tapo, damo, brahma|cittaṃ, vitānāḥ,
puṇyā vivāhāḥ, satat'|ânna|dānam—
yeṣv ev' âite sapta guṇā vasanti,
samyag|vṛttās tāni mahā|kulāni.
yeṣāṃ na vṛttaṃ vyathate na yoniś,
citta|prasādena caranti dharmam,
ye kīrtim icchanti kule viśiṣṭāṃ
tyakt'|ânṛtās tāni mahā|kulāni.
36.25 an|ijyayā, ku|vivāhair, vedasy' ôtsādanena ca
kulāny a|kulatāṃ yānti, dharmasy' âti|krameṇa ca.
deva|dravya|vināśena, brahma|sva|haraṇena ca
kulāny a|kulatāṃ yānti, dharmasy' âti|krameṇa ca.
brāhmaṇānāṃ paribhavāt parīvādāc ca, Bhārata
kulāny a|kulatāṃ yānti, nyās'|âpaharaṇena ca.
kulāni samupetāni gobhiḥ, puruṣato, 'rthataḥ
kula|saṃkhyāṃ na gacchanti yāni hīnāni vṛttataḥ.
vṛttatas tv a|vihīnāni kulāny alpa|dhanāny api

The man who wishes for prosperity for himself should serve the best men, and when the occasion calls for it middling men, but he should not serve the basest. A man can gain wealth through force of wickedness, constant effort, intelligence, and valor, but he does not win complete praise, nor attain to the conduct of the great lineages." 36.20

DHRITA·RASHTRA said:

"The gods, those of eternal law and profit, and the very learned, envy great families. I ask you, Vídura, this question: Which families are great lineages?"

VÍDURA replied:

"The great lineages are those of proper conduct within which the seven virtues of austerity, self-discipline, Vedic study, oblations, piety, good marriage, and perpetual food-donation dwell. The great lineages are those in which neither conduct nor the womb fails, in which they practice morality through the purity of their behavior, and which desire special renown for their line, abandoning deceit.

It is by failure to sacrifice, degrading marriage, putting aside the Veda, and transgressing moral law that families descend and become low. Families descend by destroying the goods the gods deserve, by confiscating brahmins' property, and by transgressing moral law. Contempt for brahmins, slander of brahmins, and plundering wealth that was entrusted to them, ensure that families slip down in hierarchy, Bhárata. Families which lack proper conduct do not rise to the title of great lineage even if they own cattle, wealth, and men. However, families which do not lack proper conduct 36.25

kula|saṃkhyāṃ ca gacchanti, karṣanti ca mahad yaśaḥ.
36.30 vṛttam yatnena saṃrakṣed; vittam eti ca yāti ca;
a|kṣīṇo vittataḥ kṣīṇo, vṛttatas tu hato hataḥ.
gobhiḥ, paśubhir, aśvaiś ca, kṛṣyā ca su|samṛddhayā
kulāni na prarohanti, yāni hīnāni vṛttataḥ.
mā naḥ kule vaira|kṛt kaś cid astu;
rāj'|âmātyo mā para|sv'|âpahārī,
mitra|drohī naikṛtiko 'nṛtī vā,
pūrv'|âśī vā pitṛ|dev'|âtithibhyaḥ
yaś ca no brāhmaṇān hanyād, yaś ca no brāhmaṇān dviṣet,
na naḥ sa samitiṃ gacched, yaś ca no nirvapet kṛṣim.
tṛṇāni, bhūmir, udakaṃ, vāk caturthī ca sūnṛtā—
satām etāni geheṣu n' ôcchidyante kadā cana;
36.35 śraddhayā parayā, rājann, upanītāni sat|kṛtim
pravṛttāni, mahā|prājña, dharmiṇāṃ puṇya|karmiṇām.
sūkṣmo 'pi bhāraṃ, nṛpate, syandano vai
śakto voḍhuṃ, na tath" ânye mahī|jāḥ,
evaṃ yuktā bhāra|sahā bhavanti
mahā|kulīnā, na tath" ânye manuṣyāḥ.
na tan mitraṃ, yasya kopād bibheti,
yad vā mitraṃ śaṅkiten' ôpacaryam;
yasmin mitre pitar' îv' âśvasīta,
tad vai mitraṃ; saṅgatān' îtarāṇi.
yaḥ kaś cid apy a|saṃbaddho mitra|bhāvena vartate,
sa eva bandhus, tan mitraṃ, sā gatis, tat par'|âyaṇam.

do attain the title of great lineage and reap great fame, even if they possess little wealth.

One should defend proper conduct with effort, for wealth 36.30
comes and goes, but when one's good conduct fails then one is destroyed and lost. Families which lack proper conduct do not rise by merely having cattle, goats, horses, or an abundant harvest.

May there be no quarrel in our family, may no royal minister steal other people's property, be treacherous towards friends, dishonest or deceitful, or eat before the ancestors, gods, and guests. Whoever among us would kill a brahmin, hate a brahmin, or practice agriculture, should have no association with us.

There are four things which are never lacking in the homes of good men: straw as a cushion, the ground to sit on, water to wash with, and a kind word as the fourth.
The hospitality and courteous behavior of law-abiding and 36.35
pious-acting men are presented with complete faith, my wise king. Just as even a small *syándana* tree, my king, can bear a great weight which other trees cannot, so the men of great lineages are able to bear great loads, even when already burdened, which other men cannot.

A man is not one's friend if one fears his fury or if one treats him with suspicion; but the friend from whom one can take comfort as though he were one's father is a true friend. Others are mere acquaintances. Anyone who behaves like a friend though he is unrelated, is in fact a family member, a friend, a refuge, and one's last resort. The man of changeable opinions who fails to wait upon his elders and

cala|cittasya vai puṃso vṛddhān an|upasevataḥ
pāriplava|mater nityam a|dhruvo mitra|saṃgrahaḥ.
36.40 cala|cittam, an|ātmānam, indriyāṇāṃ vaś'|ânugam
arthāḥ samabhivartante, haṃsāḥ śuṣkaṃ saro yathā.
a|kasmād eva kupyanti, prasīdanty a|nimittataḥ;
śīlam etad a|sādhūnām, abhraṃ pāriplavaṃ yathā.
sat|kṛtāś ca kṛt'|ârthāś ca mitrāṇāṃ na bhavanti ye,
tān mṛtān api kravy'|âdāḥ kṛta|ghnān n' ôpabhuñjate.
arthayed eva mitrāṇi sati v" âsati vā dhane;
n' ân|arthayan prajānāti mitrāṇāṃ sāra|phalgutām.
santāpād bhraśyate rūpaṃ, santāpād bhraśyate balam,
santāpād bhraśyate jñānaṃ, santāpād vyādhim ṛcchati.
36.45 an|avāpyaṃ ca śokena, śarīraṃ c' ôpatapyate,
abhitrāś ca prahṛṣyanti, mā sma śoke manaḥ kṛthāḥ.
punar naro mriyate jāyate ca,
punar naro hīyate vardhate ca;
punar naro yācati yācyate ca,
punar naraḥ śocati śocyate ca.
sukhaṃ ca duḥkhaṃ ca, bhav'|âbhavau ca,
lābh'|â|lābhau, maraṇaṃ jīvitaṃ ca
paryāyaśaḥ sarvam ete spṛśanti,
tasmād dhīro na ca hṛṣyen na śocet.
calāni h' îmāni ṣaḍ indriyāṇi,
teṣāṃ yad yad vardhate yatra yatra,
tatas tataḥ sravate buddhir asya,
chidr'|ôda|kumbhād iva nityam ambhaḥ.»

has an irresolute mind, will always be irresolute at making friends.

Wealth leaves the changeable-minded man who has no 36.40
control over himself and is a slave to his senses, just as geese leave a dry lake. The conduct of wicked men is like an inconstant cloud; they grow angry without cause, or become soothed without reason. Beasts of prey will not eat the bodies of ungrateful men who have not treated their friends properly or made them successful. One should ask favors of friends regardless of whether one is rich or poor, for one does not learn whether one's friends are good or bad without asking.

Anguish destroys beauty, anguish destroys strength, anguish destroys wisdom, and anguish causes disease. Nothing 36.45
is gained through grief; the body burns and one's enemies rejoice, so don't let your mind turn to grief.

A man repeatedly dies and is born, a man repeatedly sinks and prospers, a man repeatedly asks and is asked, a man repeatedly grieves and is grieved for. Happiness and misery, prosperity and adversity, gain and detriment, and life and death periodically touch everyone, and so the steadfast man should neither rejoice nor grieve. These six senses are fluctuating; wherever any of them turns, a man's judgment flows out just as water always flows out of a cracked water-jar."

DHṚTARĀṢṬRA uvāca:

«tanu|ruddhaḥ śikhī rājā mithy" ôpacarito mayā
mandānāṃ mama putrāṇāṃ yuddhen' ântaṃ kariṣyati.
36.50 nity'|ôdvignam idaṃ sarvaṃ; nity'|ôdvignam idaṃ manaḥ.
yat tat padam an|udvignaṃ, tan me vada, mahā|mate.»

VIDURA uvāca:

«n' ânyatra vidyā|tapasor, n' ânyatr' êndriya|nigrahāt,
n' ânyatra lobha|santyāgāc chāntiṃ paśyāmi te, 'n|agha.
buddhyā bhayaṃ praṇudati, tapasā vindate mahat,
guru|śuśrūṣayā jñānaṃ, śāntiṃ yogena vindati.
an|āśritā dāna|puṇyaṃ, deva|puṇyam an|āśritāḥ,
rāga|dveṣa|vinirmuktā vicarant' îha mokṣiṇaḥ.
sv|adhītasya, su|yuddhasya, su|kṛtasya ca karmaṇaḥ,
tapasaś ca su|taptasya tasy' ânte sukham edhate.
36.55 sv|āstīrṇāni śayanāni prapannā,
na vai bhinnā jātu nidrāṃ labhante,
na strīṣu, rājan, ratim āpnuvanti,
na māgadhaiḥ stūyamānā na sūtaiḥ.
na vai bhinnā jātu caranti dharmaṃ,
na vai sukhaṃ prāpnuvant' îha bhinnāḥ,
na vai bhinnā gauravaṃ prāpnuvanti,
na vai bhinnāḥ praśamaṃ rocayanti.
na vai teṣāṃ svadate pathyam uktaṃ,
yoga|kṣemaṃ kalpate n' âiva teṣām;
bhinnānāṃ vai, manuj'|êndra, par'|âyaṇaṃ
na vidyate kiñ cid anyad vināśāt.

DHRITA·RASHTRA said:

"The king is a flame of fire. I smothered that fire by treating him deceitfully, but he will bring my idiotic sons to an end in battle. This whole situation is constantly depress- 36.50
ing. My mind is always depressed. Great, wise man, tell me something which isn't depressing."

VÍDURA said:

"I see no peace for you, sinless man, beyond knowledge and austerity, subduing the senses, or the renunciation of greed. One dispels fear with knowledge, finds something great through austerity, finds knowledge through obedience to one's guru, and finds peace through self-discipline. Those who desire release wander here, unreliant on the piety of generosity, unreliant on the piety of the gods, and free from love and hatred. Once well-performed study, well-performed battle, well-perfomed acts, and well-performed austerities are finished, happiness grows.

Men who have broken family ties cannot fall asleep de- 36.55
spite the fact that they have well-spread beds, nor, my king, can they find any pleasure in women, nor when being praised by panegyrists or bards. Those who have broken family ties certainly do not follow moral law, nor do they find happiness. Those who have broken family ties do not gain any respect, nor do they enjoy rest. Proper advice is not welcome to those who have broken family ties. Acquisition and preservation is not of interest to them, and they can find no other final resort than death, lord of men.

sampannaṃ goṣu saṃbhāvyaṃ,
saṃbhāvyaṃ brāhmaṇe tapaḥ,
saṃbhāvyaḥ cāpalaṃ strīṣu,
saṃbhāvyaṃ jñātito ’|bhayam.*
tantavo ”pyāyitā nityaṃ tanavo bahulāḥ samāḥ
bahūn bahutvād āyāsān sahant’, îty upamā satām.
36.60 dhūmāyante vyapetāni, jvalanti sahitāni ca,
Dhṛtarāṣṭr’, ôlmukān’ îva jñātayo, Bharata’|rṣabha.
brāhmaṇesu ca ye śūrāḥ, strīṣu, jñātiṣu, goṣu ca,
vṛntād iva phalaṃ pakvaṃ, Dhṛtaraṣṭra, patanti te.
mahān apy eka|jo vṛkṣo balavān su|pratiṣṭhitaḥ
prasahya eva vātena sa|skandho marditum kṣaṇāt.
atha ye sahitā vṛkṣāḥ saṃghaśaḥ su|pratiṣṭhitāḥ,
te hi śīghratamān vātān sahante ’nyonya|saṃśrayāt
evaṃ manuṣyam apy ekaṃ guṇair api samanvitam
śakyaṃ dviṣanto manyante, vāyur drumam iv’ âika|jam.
36.65 anyonya|samupaṣṭambhād anyony’|âpāśrayeṇa ca
jñātayaḥ saṃpravardhante saras’ îv’ ôtpalāny uta.
a|vadhyā brāhmaṇā, gāvo, jñātayaḥ, śiśavaḥ, striyaḥ,
yeṣāṃ c’ ânnāni bhuñjīta, ye ca syuḥ śaraṇ’|āgatāḥ.
na manuṣye guṇaḥ kaś cid, rājan, sadhanatām ṛte,
an|āturatvād, bhadraṃ te, mṛta|kalpā hi rogiṇaḥ.
a|vyādhi|jaṃ, kaṭukaṃ śīrṣa|rogaṃ
pāp’|ânubandhaṃ, paruṣaṃ, tīkṣṇam, uṣṇam;
satāṃ peyaṃ yan na pibanty a|santo,
manyuṃ, mahā|rāja, piba praśāmya.
rog’|ârditā na phalāny ādriyante,

Just as milk is found in cows, austerity in a brahmin, and fickleness in women, so security is found among relatives. The comparison good men cite to illustrate their point is that the abundance of vast numbers of intertwined fibres always allows them to bear many burdens, though the individual fibres may be thin. Relatives are like firebrands, 36.60
Dhrita·rashtra; separately they merely smoke, but together they blaze, bull of the Bharatas.

Men who overpower brahmins, women, relatives, and cattle, fall as though they were ripe fruit falling from its stalk, Dhrita·rashtra. Even a solitary, massive, powerful, and highly stable tree and its trunk can be instantaneously and ferociously ravaged by a gale-force wind. But then, crowds of trees, firmly rooted together, can withstand the fastest winds, relying upon each other. So men are hostile to an individual man, even if he possesses virtues, and consider him a feasible target, just as the wind considers a solitary tree. Relatives prosper by supporting each other and rely- 36.65
ing on one another, just like lotuses on a lake.

Brahmins, cattle, relatives, children, women, those whose food you have eaten, and those who have come for protection, mustn't be killed. No virtue is found within a man without wealth, my king, other than health, bless you, for the sick are like the dead. Rage is a fierce headache, born of no illness, which is piercing, sharp, and hot, and its outcome is evil. The good swallow it down but the wicked do not, so, great king, swallow down your rage and be calm. Those afflicted with disease do not care about consequences, nor do they grasp the truth of any of the objects of their

na vai labhante viṣayeṣu tattvam.
duḥkh'|ôpetā rogiṇo nityam eva;
na budhyante dhana|bhogān na saukhyam.
36.70 purā hy uktaṃ n' âkaros tvaṃ vaco me
dyūte jitāṃ Draupadīṃ prekṣya, rājan:
‹Duryodhanaṃ vāray', êty akṣavatyāṃ!
kitavatvaṃ paṇḍitā varjayanti.›
na tad balaṃ yan mṛdunā virudhyate.
sūkṣmo dharmas tarasā sevitavyaḥ;
pradhvaṃsinī krūra|samāhitā śrīr;
mṛdu|prauḍhā gacchati putra|pautrān.
Dhārtarāṣṭrāḥ Pāṇḍavān pālayantu,
Pāṇḍoḥ sutās tava putrāṃś ca pāntu.
ek'|âri|mitrāḥ Kuravo hy eka|kāryā
jīvantu, rājan, sukhinaḥ samṛddhāḥ.
meḍhī|bhūtaḥ Kauravāṇāṃ tvam adya,
tvayy' âdhīnaṃ Kuru|kulam, Ājamīḍha.
Pārthān bālān vana|vāsa|prataptān
gopāyasva, svaṃ yaśas, tāta, rakṣan.
sandhatsva tvaṃ, Kaurava, Pāṇḍu|putrair,
mā te 'ntaraṃ ripavaḥ prārthayantu.
satye sthitās te, nara|deva, sarve
Duryodhanaṃ sthāpaya tvaṃ, nar'|êndra!»

senses. The sick are always in misery; they do not comprehend the pleasures of wealth or happiness.

Long ago, during the gambling, watching Dráupadi being won, you did not act on the advice I gave you, king. 36.70
'Stop Duryódhana from gambling with dice! Wise men avoid gambling,' I told you. It is not strength if it obstructs gentleness. A subtle law should be energetically cultivated. Good fortune held together by ferocity is merely transitory, but a gentle and confident fortune will go on to the sons and grandsons. Let the Dhartaráshtras defend the Pándavas, and the sons of Pandu should defend your sons in return. Let the Kurus live harmoniously and prosperously, with the same enemies and friends and the same aim, my king.

You are the central point of the Káuravas now, Ajamídha, and the Kuru lineage is reliant on you. Guard the Partha children who have suffered in their forest exile, and by so doing, my friend, protect your own reputation. Join the Káuravas with the sons of Pandu to prevent your enemies looking for your weakness. They are all intent on the truth, god among men, so restrain Duryódhana, lord of men!"

VIDURA uvāca:

37.1 «SAPTA|DAŚ' ÊMĀN, rāj'|êndra,
Manuḥ Svāyaṃbhuvo 'bravīt,
Vaicitravīrya, puruṣān
ākāśaṃ muṣṭibhir ghnataḥ,
dānav'|êndrasya ca dhanur a|nāmyaṃ namato 'bravīt,
atho marīcinaḥ pādān a|grāhyān gṛhṇatas tathā.
yaś c' â|śiṣyaṃ śāsti vai, yaś ca tuṣyed,
yaś c' âtivelaṃ bhajate dviṣantam,
striyaś ca yo rakṣati, bhadram astu te,*
yaś c' â|yācyaṃ yācate katthate vā;
yaś c' âbhijātaḥ prakaroty a|kāryaṃ,
yaś c' â|balo balinā nitya|vairī,
a|śraddadhānāya ca yo bravīti,
yaś c' â|kāmyaṃ kāmayate, nar'|êndra;
37.5 vadhv" âvahāsaṃ śvaśuro manyate yo,
vadhvā vasann a|bhayo māna|kāmaḥ,
para|kṣetre nirvapati yaś ca bījaṃ,
striyaṃ ca yaḥ parivadate 'tivelam;
yaś c' âpi labdhvā ‹na smarām', îti› vādī,
dattvā ca yaḥ katthati yācyamānaḥ,
yaś c' â|sataḥ sattvam upānayīta:
etān nayanti nirayaṃ pāśa|hastāḥ.
yasmin yathā vartate yo manuṣyas,
tasmiṃs tathā vartitavyaṃ, sa dharmaḥ;
māy"|ācāro māyayā vartitavyaḥ
sādhv|ācāraḥ sādhunā pratyupeyaḥ.
jarā rūpaṃ harati hi, dhairyam āśā,

VÍDURA continued:

"MANU, SON OF the self-created power, said these are the seventeen types of men, lord of kings, son of Vichítra·virya, who try to beat at the air with their fists, who try to bend the unbendable bow belonging to the lord of the Dánavas, or equally try to catch the elusive rays of the sun: 37.1

There is the one who teaches the unteachable, the one who is content, the one who is excessively subservient to his enemy, the one who guards women—good luck to you there!—the one who asks what should not be asked, the one who boasts, the one who, though of noble birth, does what should not be done, the one who though weak always quarrels with someone strong, the one who tries to convince the man who does not believe him, the one who
desires what he should not desire, lord of men, the father- 37.5
in-law who thinks jokes are appropriate with his daughter-in-law, the man who is so foolhardy as to expect respect when living with his daughter-in-law, the man who sows his seed in another man's field, the man who excessively slanders a woman, the man who says 'I don't remember' once he has taken something, the man who boasts about being begged when he has given, and the man who adduces goodness from evil: these men are guided to hell by their envoys, noose in hand.

The law dictates that a man must be treated in the manner he behaves. So an illusionist should be treated with deception, and well-behaved people should be treated well. Old age steals beauty, hope steals patience, death steals life, jealousy steals moral behavior, desire steals modesty, serv-

mṛtyuḥ prāṇān, dharma|caryām asūyā,
kāmo hriyaṃ, vṛttam an|ārya|sevā,
krodhaḥ śriyaṃ, sarvam ev' âbhimānaḥ.»*

DHṚTARĀṢṬRA uvāca:
«śat'|āyur uktaḥ puruṣaḥ sarva|vedeṣu vai yadā,
n' āpnoty atha ca tat sarvam āyuḥ ken' êha hetunā?»

VIDURA uvāca:
37.10 «atimāno 'tivādaś ca, tath" â|tyāgo, nar'|âdhipa,
krodhaś c', ātma|vidhitsā ca, mitra|drohaś ca, tāni ṣaṭ.
eta ev' âsayas tīkṣṇāḥ kṛntanty āyūṃṣi dehinām;
etāni mānavān ghnanti, na mṛtyur, bhadram astu te.
viśvastasy' âiti yo dārān, yaś c' âpi guru|talpa|gaḥ,
vṛṣalī|patir dvijo yaś ca, pānapaś c' âiva, Bhārata,
ādeśa|kṛd, vṛtti|hantā, dvijānāṃ preṣakaś ca yaḥ,
śaraṇ'|āgata|hā c' âiva sarve brahma|haṇaḥ samāḥ.
etaiḥ sametya kartavyaṃ prāyaścittam, iti śrutiḥ.
gṛhīta|vākyo, naya|vid, vadānyaḥ,
śeṣ'|ânna|bhoktā, hy a|vihiṃsakaś ca,
n' ân|artha|kṛt, tyakta|kaliḥ,* kṛta|jñaḥ,
satyo, mṛduḥ svargam upaiti vidvān.

ing ignoble people steals one's own good conduct, anger steals good fortune, and arrogance steals everything."

DHRITA·RASHTRA said:

"Since a man's life is said to be one hundred years in all the Vedas, what is the reason that one does not get the whole span?"

VÍDURA replied:

"Lord of men, excessive arrogance, excessive talking, a 37.10
lack of renunciation, anger, selfishness, and treachery towards friends are the six sharp swords which determine the life of embodied creatures: these are what kill humans—not death. So best of luck to you.

The man who sleeps with the wives of a man who trusts him, the man who defiles his teacher's bed, the brahmin who marries a low-caste woman or who is an alcoholic, Bhárata, the man who destroys brahmins' means of subsistance when following orders, as well as the man sending him, and the man who kills someone who has come to him for protection, are all equal to brahmin-murderers. It is passed down that a penitentiary act must be performed when one has associated with such people. The man who accepts advice, the man who understands policy, the man who is munificent, the man who only eats what is left over after he has given a share to the gods and ancestors, the man who harms no one, the man who does not do anything to anyone's disadvantage, the man who has abandoned discord, and the man who is grateful, truthful, gentle, and wise, goes to heaven.

37.15 su|labhāḥ puruṣā, rājan, satataṃ priya|vādinaḥ,
a|priyasya tu pathyasya vaktā śrotā ca dur|labhaḥ.
yo hi dharmaṃ samāśritya, hitvā bhartuḥ priy'|âpriye,
a|priyāṇy āha pathyāni, tena rājā sahāyavān.
tyajet kul'|ârthaṃ puruṣaṃ, grāmasy' ârthe kulaṃ tyajet,
grāmaṃ jana|padasy' ârthe, ātm'|ârthe pṛthivīṃ tyajet.
āpad|arthe dhanaṃ rakṣed, dārān rakṣed dhanair api,
ātmānaṃ satataṃ rakṣed, dārair api dhanair api.
dyūtam etat purā|kalpe dṛṣṭaṃ vaira|karaṃ nṛṇām,
tasmād dyūtaṃ na seveta hāsy' ârtham api buddhimān.

37.20 uktaṃ mayā dyūta|kāle 'pi, rājan,
n' êdaṃ yuktaṃ vacanaṃ, Prātipeya,
tad" āuṣadhaṃ pathyam iv' âturasya
na rocate tava, Vaicitravīrya.
kākair imāṃś citra|barhān mayūrān
parājayethāḥ Pāṇḍavān Dhārtarāṣṭraiḥ,
hitvā siṃhān kroṣṭukān gūhamānaḥ,
prāpte kāle śocitā tvaṃ, nar'|êndra.

yas, tāta, na krudhyati sarva|kālaṃ
bhṛtyasya bhaktasya hite ratasya,
tasmin bhṛtyā bhartari viśvasanti,
na c' âinam āpatsu parityajanti.
na bhṛtyānāṃ vṛtti|saṃrodhanena
rājyaṃ dhanaṃ sañjighṛkṣed a|pūrvam,

My king, men who will tell you what you want to hear are always easy to come by, but a man who listens and gives you unpleasant but appropriate advice is hard to find. A king has a true friend in someone who relies on moral law, avoiding the likes and dislikes of his master, and gives the correct advice, even if it is unpleasant. One should abandon a man for the sake of a family, abandon a family for the sake of a village, abandon a village for the sake of one's subjects, and abandon the earth for the sake of one's soul. One should protect one's wealth against disaster, protect one's wives at the cost of wealth, and always protect oneself even if it be at the cost of both one's wives and one's wealth. Long ago it was observed that gambling creates hostility between men, and so a wise man would not cultivate gambling, even if only for fun. 37.15

I told you, king, at the time of the gambling, that it was not proper, son of Pratípa, but just as a sick man dislikes his wholesome herbal medicine, so you, son of Vichitra·virya, were not pleased. You overthrew those bright-tailed peacock Pándavas with the crow Dhartaráshtras. Passing over lions, you protect jackals, and when the time comes you will grieve for it, lord of men. 37.20

Servants, my friend, trust a master who is not constantly angry with a servant who loyally cares for his welfare, and they do not desert him in times of trouble. One should not wish to rise to unparalleled royal wealth by restricting the servants wages, since even affectionate ministers abandon their master when they are deceived and exploited and when their privileges are taken away. First calculating everything that needs doing, one should keep the wage in check

tyajanti hy enaṃ vañcitā vai viruddhāḥ
snigdhā hy amātyāḥ parihīna|bhogāḥ.
kṛtyāni pūrvaṃ parisaṃkhyāya sarvāṇy
āya|vyayau c' ânurūpāṃ ca vṛttim
saṃgṛhṇīyād anurūpān sahāyān;
sahāya|sādhyāni hi duṣ|karāṇi.

37.25 abhiprāyaṃ yo viditvā tu bhartuḥ
sarvāṇi kāryāṇi karoty a|tandrī,
vaktā hitānām, anurakta, āryaḥ,
śakti|jña ātm" êva hi so 'nukampyaḥ.
vākyaṃ tu yo n' âdriyate 'nuśiṣṭaḥ,
pratyāha yaś c' âpi niyujyamānaḥ,
prajñ"|âbhimānī, pratikūla|vādī,
tyājyaḥ sa tādṛk tvaray" âiva bhṛtyaḥ.
a|stabdham, a|klībam, a|dīrgha|sūtraṃ,
s'|ânukrośaṃ, ślakṣṇam, a|hāryam anyaiḥ,
a|roga|jātīyam, udāra|vākyaṃ
dūtaṃ vadanty aṣṭa|guṇ'|ôpapannam.
na viśvāsāj jātu parasya gehe
gacchen naraś cetayāno vikāle,
na catvare niśi tiṣṭhen nigūḍho,
na rāja|kāmyāṃ yoṣitaṃ prārthayīta.

so that it corresponds to one's income and expenditure, and get oneself some suitable assistants, since even difficult matters can be achieved by one's assistants.

The man who knows his master's wish and relentlessly 37.25
does his chores, who gives advantageous advice, is devoted, noble, and knows his own capabilities, should be sympathized with as though he were a second self. The sort of servant who has been instructed but does not heed his master's words, who talks back when given orders, or who thinks he is clever and contradicts you, should be dispensed with quickly.

They say that a messenger should be endowed with eight virtues: modesty, manliness, promptness, compassion, gentleness, total honesty, complete health, and eloquent speech. A thoughtful man would certainly not trust that he could enter someone else's house at an inappropriate time, nor stand hidden at the crossroads at night, nor proposition a woman fit for a king.

na nihnavam mantra|gatasya gacchet
saṃsṛṣṭa|mantrasya ku|saṃgatasya,
na ca brūyān ‹n' āśvasimi tvay', îti,›
sa|kāraṇaṃ vyapadeśaṃ tu kuryāt.
37.30 ghṛṇī, rājā, puṃś|calī, rāja|bhṛtyaḥ,
putro, bhrātā, vidhavā, bāla|putrā,
senā|jīvī c', ôddhṛta|bhūtir eva;
vyavahāreṣu varjanīyāḥ syur ete.
aṣṭau guṇāḥ puruṣaṃ dīpayanti:
prajñā ca, kaulyam ca, śrutaṃ, damaś ca,
parākramaś c', â|bahu|bhāṣitā ca,
dānaṃ yathā|śakti, kṛta|jñātā ca.
etān guṇāṃs, tāta, mah"|ânubhāvān
eko guṇaḥ saṃśrayate prasahya:
rājā yadā sat|kurute manuṣyaṃ.
sarvān guṇān eṣa guṇo bibharti.*
guṇā daśa snāna|śīlaṃ bhajante:
balaṃ, rūpaṃ, svara|varṇa|praśuddhiḥ,
sparśaś ca, gandhaś ca, viśuddhatā ca,
śrīḥ, saukumāryaṃ, pravarāś ca nāryaḥ.
guṇāś ca ṣaṇ mita|bhuktaṃ bhajante:
ārogyam, āyuś ca, balaṃ, sukhaṃ ca,
an|āvilaṃ c' âsya bhavaty apatyaṃ,
na c' âinam ādyūna, iti kṣipanti.
37.35 a|karma|śīlaṃ ca, mah"|âśanaṃ ca,
loka|dviṣṭaṃ, bahu|māyaṃ, nṛśaṃsam,
a|deśa|kāla|jñam, an|iṣṭa|veṣam:
etān gṛhe na prativāsayeta.
kadaryam, ākrośakam, a|śrutaṃ ca,
van'|âukasaṃ, dhūrtam, a|mānya|māninam,

One should not go against the decision a man has come to if he keeps bad company and asks advice from all he meets. One should not say 'I do not trust you,' but one
should make up some reason or excuse. These people should 37.30
be exempt from one's commerce: a violent man, a king, a prostitute, a royal servant, one's son or brother, a widow, someone with young children, a soldier, or someone whose power is on the rise.

Eight virtues illuminate a man: wisdom, noble birth, learning, self control, heroism, taciturnity, generosity according to one's means, and gratitude. These are mighty virtues, my friend, but one virtue unites them: when a king behaves honorably towards a man. This is the virtue which supports all virtues.

Ten virtues adorn the man who is bathing: strength, beauty, purity of voice, purity of complexion, touch, smell, cleanliness, good fortune, tenderness, and beautiful women. Six virtues adorn the man who eats in moderation: health, long life, strength, happiness, a clear future for his descendants, and no one accusing him of greed.

One should not put these people up in one's house: a 37.35
man who does no work, a glutton, someone hated by the whole world, a man of numerous tricks, a cruel man, a man with no understanding of the proper time and place, and a man of inappropriate dress. One should definitely not ask anything of these people even if suffering grievously: a miser, an abusive man, a man of no learning, someone who lives in the forest, a fraudster, a man who honors those who

niṣṭhūriṇaṃ, kṛta|vairaṃ, kṛta|ghnam:
 etān bhṛś'|ārto 'pi na jātu yācet.
saṃkliṣṭa|karmāṇam, atipramādaṃ,
 nity'|ânṛtaṃ c', â|dṛḍha|bhaktikaṃ ca,
visṛṣṭa|rāgaṃ, paṭu|māninaṃ c' âpy:
 etān na seveta nar'|âdhamān ṣaṭ.
sahāya|bandhanā hy arthāḥ, sahāyāś c' ârtha|bandhanāḥ;
anyonya|bandhanāv etau vin" ânyonyaṃ na sidhyataḥ.
 utpādya putrān, an|ṛṇāṃś ca kṛtvā,
 vṛttiṃ ca tebhyo 'nuvidhāya kāñ cit,
sthāne kumārīḥ pratipādya sarvā,
 araṇya|saṃstho 'tha munir bubhūṣet.
37.40 hitaṃ yat sarva|bhūtānām, ātmanaś ca sukh'|āvaham,
tat kuryād īśvaro, hy etan mūlaṃ sarv'|ârtha|siddhaye.
vṛddhiḥ, prabhāvas, tejaś ca, sattvam, utthānam eva ca,
vyavasāyaś ca yasya syāt, tasy' â|vṛtti|bhayaṃ kutaḥ?
 paśya doṣān Pāṇḍavair vigrahe tvaṃ,
 yatra vyatheyur api devāḥ sa|Śakrāḥ:
putrair vairaṃ, nityam udvigna|vāso,
 yaśaḥ|praṇāśo, dviṣataś ca harṣaḥ.
Bhīṣmasya kopas, tava c' âiv', Êndra|kalpa,
 Droṇasya, rājñaś ca Yudhiṣṭhirasya
utsādayel lokam imaṃ pravṛddhaḥ
 śveto grahas tiryag iv' āpatan khe.

deserve no respect, a cruel man, a cantankerous man, or an ungrateful man.

One should not serve these six lowest of the low: a man who does everything with difficulty, a man who is totally insane, a constant liar, a man who is not firm in his allegiance to a god, a man whose feelings of goodwill have deserted him, or a man of intense pride. Profits are inextricably linked to the assistant, and assistants are linked to profits; they are linked together and achieve nothing without each other.

Once a man has had sons, freed them of debts, arranged some kind of living for them, and given away all his daughters in marriage to men in good positions, he should live in
the forest and want to be a sage. A lord should do what is 37.40
beneficial to all beings and bring about happiness for himself, for this is the root upon which the success of all profit relies. If a man has prosperity, power, splendor, truth, effort, and determination, then how could he fear that he would have no means of living?

See the sins inherent in your quarrel with the Pándavas, at whom even the gods and Shakra tremble: strife with your sons, a life of constant anxiety, your good reputation in tatters, and your enemies delighted. If the fury of Bhishma, Drona, and King Yudhi·shthira were roused, O Indra-like man, then it would annihilate this world as though it were a white comet shooting across the sky.

tava putra|śataṃ c' âiva, Karṇaḥ, pañca ca Pāṇḍavāḥ
pṛthivīm anuśāseyur akhilāṃ sāgar'|âmbarām.
37.45 Dhārtarāṣṭrā vanaṃ, rājan, vyāghrāḥ Pāṇḍu|sutā matāḥ.
mā vanaṃ chindhi sa|vyāghraṃ! mā vyāghrā nīnaśan vanāt!
na syād vanam ṛte vyāghrān, vyāghrā na syur ṛte vanam.
vanaṃ hi rakṣyate vyāghrair, vyāghrān rakṣati kānanam.
na tath" êcchanti kalyāṇān pareṣāṃ vedituṃ guṇān,
yath" âiṣāṃ jñātum icchanti nairguṇyaṃ pāpa|cetasaḥ.
arthaṃ siddhiṃ parām icchan dharmam ev' āditaś caret,
na hi dharmād apaity arthaḥ, svarga|lokād iv' âmṛtam.
yasy' ātmā virataḥ pāpāt, kalyāṇe ca niveśitaḥ,
tena sarvam idaṃ buddhaṃ prakṛtir vikṛtiś ca yā.
37.50 yo dharmam arthaṃ kāmaṃ ca yathā|kālaṃ niṣevate,
dharm'|ârtha|kāma|saṃyogaṃ so 'mutr' êha ca vindati.
saṃniyacchati yo vegam utthitaṃ krodha|harṣayoḥ
sa śriyo bhājanaṃ, rājan, yaś c' āpatsu na muhyati.
balaṃ pañca|vidhaṃ nityaṃ puruṣāṇāṃ nibodha me:
yat tu bāhu|balaṃ nāma, kaniṣṭhaṃ balam ucyate;
amātya|lābho, bhadraṃ te, dvitīyaṃ balam ucyate;
tṛtīyaṃ dhana|lābhaṃ tu balam āhur manīṣiṇaḥ;
yat tv asya saha|jaṃ, rājan, pitṛ|paitāmahaṃ balam,
abhijāta|balaṃ nāma tac caturthaṃ balam smṛtam;
37.55 yena tv etāni sarvāṇi saṅgṛhītāni, Bhārata,

Your hundred sons, Karna, and the five Pándavas, can
rule the whole earth, up to the boundary of the ocean. My 37.45
king, the Dhartaráshtras are a forest, and the sons of Pandu
are thought of as its tigers. Don't chop down the forest along
with the tigers! Don't force the tigers out of the forest! There
would be no forest except with tigers and there would be no
tigers except with the forest. The forest is protected by the
tigers and the forest protects the tigers.

Wicked-minded men do not wish to know their enemies'
good virtues as much as they want to know their faults.
Someone who wishes for the greatest success of his aim
should act virtuously right from the start, for profit does
not diverge from virtue, just as ambrosia does not leave the
realm of heaven. The man whose soul has given up wickedness and is intent on goodness, knows everything—both
origin and consequence.

The man who practices virtue, profit, and desire, each at 37.50
the appropriate time, finds here and in the next world the
fusion of virtue, profit, and desire. The man who restrains
the violent rise of anger and joy, my king, is good luck's
vessel, and he is not confused in times of trouble.

Learn from me: there are always five kinds of strength
that men possess, and that which is called strength of arms
is said to be the least important. The second strength is said
to be the acquisition of advisors—good luck to you there!
The wise say the third strength is the acquisition of wealth.
The fourth strength is recorded as being called the strength
of noble birth, which is an inborn strength, passed down
from father and grandfather, my king. The greatest strength 37.55

yad balānāṃ balaṃ śreṣṭhaṃ, tat prajñā|balam ucyate.
mahate yo 'pakārāya narasya prabhaven naraḥ,
tena vairaṃ samāsajya ‹dūra|stho 'sm', îti› n' āśvaset.
strīṣu, rājasu, sarpeṣu, sv'|âdhyāye, prabhu|śatruṣu,*
bhogeṣv, āyuṣi viśvāsaṃ kaḥ prājñaḥ kartum arhati?
prajñā|śareṇ' âbhihatasya jantoś
cikitsakāḥ santi na c' āuṣadhāni;
na homa|mantrā, na ca maṅgalāni,
n' âtharvaṇā, n' âpy agadāḥ su|siddhāḥ.
sarpaś c', âgniś ca, siṃhaś ca, kula|putraś ca, Bhārata,
n' âvajñeyā manuṣyeṇa; sarve hy ete 'titejasaḥ.
37.60 agnis tejo mahal loke gūḍhas tiṣṭhati dāruṣu;
na c' ôpayuṅkte tad dāru, yāvan n' ôddīpyate paraiḥ.
sa eva khalu dārubhyo yadā nirmathya dīpyate,
tad dāru ca vanaṃ c' ânyan nirdahaty āśu tejasā.
evam eva kule jātāḥ pāvak'|ôpama|tejasaḥ
kṣamāvanto nirākārāḥ kāṣṭhe 'gnir iva śerate.
latā|dharmā tvaṃ sa|putraḥ; śālāḥ Pāṇḍu|sutā matāḥ;
na latā vardhate jātu mahā|drumam an|āśritā.
vanaṃ, rājaṃs, tava putro, 'mbikeya,
siṃhān vane Pāṇḍavāṃs, tāta, viddhi
siṃhair vihīnaṃ hi vanaṃ vinaśyet
siṃhā vinaśyeyur ha' rte vanena.»

of all, by which all the others are embraced, is said to be the strength of wisdom, Bhárata.

Once one has begun a quarrel with a man who could cause great misfortune for a fellow human being, one should not feel safe, thinking, 'I'm far away.' Which wise man ought to have confidence in women, kings, snakes, his own learning, powerful enemies, pleasures, and long life? For the man who has been wounded by the arrow of wisdom there are no doctors and no herbal remedies; neither oblation-spells, blessings, nor even magical priests or medicines can make it better. A man should not despise snakes, fires, lions, or the son of a noble lineage, Bhárata, for all these are extremely powerful.

Fire is a mighty energy in the world which lies dormant 37.60
and hidden in wood, but it does not use it, so long as it is not kindled by other pieces. But then when it is rubbed together with sticks, it blazes and quickly burns not only the wood but also the forest and the rest with its splendor. Similarly, men born into a noble lineage have a fire-like brilliance. They are forgiving, do not make a fuss, and are as patient as fire in wood.

You and your son are like creepers, whereas the sons of Pandu are considered *shala* trees; the creeper certainly does not grow without relying on the great tree. King Ambikéya, you and your sons are the forest, but, my friend, the Pándavas are the lions in the forest: a forest bereft of lions perishes, but the lions perish without the forest."

VIDURA uvāca:

38.1 «ŪRDHVAM PRĀṆĀ hy utkrāmanti yūnaḥ sthavira āyati;
pratyutthān' âbhivādābhyāṃ punas tān pratipadyate.
pīṭhaṃ datvā sādhave 'bhyāgatāya,
ānīy' âpaḥ, parinirṇijya pādau,
sukhaṃ pṛṣṭvā, prativedy ātma|saṃsthāṃ,
tato dadyād annam avekṣya dhīraḥ.
yasy' ôdakaṃ madhu|parkaṃ ca gāṃ ca
na mantra|vit pratigṛhṇāti gehe
lobhād bhayād atha kārpaṇyato vā,
tasy' ân|arthaṃ jīvitam āhur āryāḥ.
cikitsakaḥ, śalya|kart", âvakīrṇī,
stenaḥ, krūro, madya|po, bhrūṇa|hā ca,
senā|jīvī, śruti|vikrāyakaś ca
bhṛśaṃ priyo 'py atithir n'|ôdak'|ârhaḥ.
38.5 a|vikreyaṃ lavaṇaṃ, pakvam annaṃ,
dadhi, kṣīraṃ, madhu, tailaṃ ghṛtaṃ ca,
tilā, māṃsaṃ, phala|mūlāni, śākaṃ,
raktaṃ, vāsaḥ, sarva|gandhā, guḍāś ca.
a|roṣaṇo yaḥ, sama|loṣṭh'|âśma|kāñcanaḥ,
prahīṇa|śoko, gata|sandhi|vigrahaḥ,
nindā|praśaṃs"|ôparataḥ priy'|âpriye,
tyajann udāsīnavad eṣa bhikṣukaḥ.
nīvāra|mūl'|êṅguda|śāka|vṛttiḥ,
su|saṃyat'|ātm", âgni|kāryeṣu codyaḥ,
vane vasann atithiṣv a|pramatto
dhuran|dharaḥ puṇya|kṛd eṣa tāpasaḥ.

VÍDURA continued:

"WHEN AN OLD man approaches, the spirits of a young 38.1
man soar up in the air; but when he rises to greet him, he catches them again. When a good man arrives, the resolute man should give him a stool, bring water, wash his feet, ask after his welfare, and inform him of his own situation, then watchfully give him food. Noble men say that a man's life is useless if someone who knows mantras does not, in his house, accept his water, honey and milk offerings, and a cow, either because of his greed or fear, or his weak-spiritedness. A doctor, an arrow maker, an unchaste man, a thief, a cruel man, an alcoholic, an abortionist, a soldier, and a man who trades the Veda are not worthy of the guest water, even if they are a dear friend.

A brahmin should not sell salt, cooked food, sour milk, 38.5
milk, honey, sesame oil, clarified butter, sesame seeds, meat, fruit and roots, vegetables, dye, clothes, any perfumes, or sugar. A man is a mendicant if he is not inclined to anger, for whom clay, stone, and gold are the same, who avoids grief, has passed beyond friendship and separation, is indifferent to praise and blame, has abandoned what is pleasant and unpleasant, and is neutral. The man whose sustenance is wild rice, roots, nuts, and vegetables, whose soul is well controlled, a man driven to his fire duties, who lives in the woods carefully attending to his guest duties, is a leading and pious-acting ascetic.

apakṛtya buddhimato, ‹dūra|stho ’sm’, îti› n’ āśvaset;
dīrghau buddhimato bāhū, yābhyāṃ hiṃsati hiṃsitaḥ.
na viśvased a|viśvaste, viśvaste n’ âtiviśvaset;
viśvāsād bhayam utpannaṃ mūlāny api nikṛntati.
38.10 an|īrṣur gupta|dāraś ca, saṃvibhāgī, priayṃ|vadaḥ,
ślakṣṇo, madhura|vāk strīṇāṃ, na c’ āsāṃ vaśa|go bhavet.
pūjanīyā, mahā|bhāgāḥ, puṇyāś ca, gṛha|dīptayaḥ,
striyaḥ śriyo gṛhasy’ ôktās, tasmād rakṣyā viśeṣataḥ.
pitur antaḥ|puraṃ, dadyān mātur dadyan mahānasam,
goṣu c’ ātma|samaṃ dadyāt, svayam eva kṛṣiṃ vrajet.
bhṛtyair vāṇijya|cāraṃ ca, putraiḥ seveta ca dvijān.
adbhyo ’gnir, brahmataḥ kṣatram,
aśmano loham utthitam:
teṣāṃ sarvatra|gaṃ tejaḥ
svāsu yoniṣu śāmyati.
nityaṃ santaḥ kule jātāḥ pāvak’|ôpama|tejasaḥ;
38.15 kṣamāvanto nirākārāḥ kāṣṭhe ’gnir iva śerate.*
yasya mantraṃ na jānanti bāhyāś c’ âbhyantarāś ca ye,
sa rājā sarvataś cakṣuś ciram aiśvaryam aśnute.
kariṣyan na prabhāṣeta, kṛtāṇy eva tu darśayet,
dharma|kāma’|ârtha|kāryāṇi, tathā mantro na bhidyate.
giri|pṛṣṭham upāruhya, prāsādaṃ vā raho gataḥ
araṇye niḥśalāke vā, tatra mantro ’bhidhīyate.

The man who has insulted a wise man should not be
heartened by telling himself, 'I am far away.' The wise man's
arms are long and he will harm you with them if he has
been hurt. One should not trust the distrusted man, nor
should one trust the trusted man too far, for the danger
which arises from putting too much trust in others cuts
one's very roots. One should not be envious, but one should 38.10
protect one's wife, share with others, and be kindly spoken,
polished, and sweetly spoken towards women, without becoming a slave to them.

Women deserve honor, are highly illustrious, holy, light
up the home, and are said to be a house's good fortune, so
protect them in particular. One should entrust the women's
quarters to the father, the kitchen to the mother, and the
cattle to someone one considers one's equal, but one should
do the plowing oneself. A man should cultivate his business
of trade through his servants, and serve brahmins by means
of his son.

Fire arises from water, warriordom from brahmindom,
and iron from rock: their all-pervading splendor is calmed
before their origins. Men born into a noble family always
have fire-like splendor; they are forgiving, do not make a 38.15
fuss, and are as patient as fire in wood. The king whose
counsel no one outside or inside knows, but who has eyes
everywhere, will stay in power for a long time.

He should act, but not speak of his actions, and he should reveal his acts—which conform to virtue, desire, and profit—only once they are done, so that the secrecy of his counsel is not broken. He should compose his plans once he has climbed to the top of a mountain, or concealed at the top

n' â|suhṛt paraṃ mantraṃ, Bhārat', ârhati veditum,
a|paṇḍito v" âpi suhṛt, paṇḍito v" âpy an|ātmavān.
n' â|parīkṣya mahī|pālaḥ kuryāt sacivam ātmanaḥ;
38.20 amātye hy artha|lipsā ca, mantra|rakṣaṇam eva ca.
kṛtāni sarva|kāryāṇi yasya pāriṣadā viduḥ
dharme c', ârthe ca, kāme ca, sa rājā rāja|sattamaḥ;
gūḍha|mantrasya nṛpates tasya siddhir a|saṃśayam.
a|praśastāni kāryāṇi yo mohād anutiṣṭhati
sa teṣāṃ viparibhraṃśād bhraśyate jīvitād api.
karmāṇāṃ tu praśastānām anuṣṭhānaṃ sukh'|āvaham
teṣām ev' ân|anuṣṭhānaṃ paścāt|tāpa|karaṃ matam.
an|adhītya yathā vedān na vipraḥ śrāddham arhati,
evam a|śruta|ṣāḍguṇyo na mantraṃ śrotum arhati.
38.25 sthāna|vṛddhi|kṣaya|jñasya ṣāḍguṇya|vidit'|ātmanaḥ
an|avajñāta|śīlasya sv'|âdhīnā pṛthivī, nrpa.
a|mogha|krodha|harṣasya svayaṃ kṛtv" ânvavekṣiṇaḥ
ātma|pratyaya|kośasya vasu|d" âiva vasun|dharā.
nāma|mātreṇa tuṣyeta chatreṇa ca mahī|patiḥ;
bhṛtyebhyo visṛjed arthān, n' âikaḥ sarva|haro bhavet.

of a lofty building, or in a lonely wilderness. A man who is not one's friend ought not to know one's ultimate plan, Bhárata, nor, for that matter, should a friend if he is not learned, nor even a learned man if he lacks self-discipline.

A king should not make someone his own advisor without having proven him, for the acquisition of profit and 38.20
the protection of plans rests on a minister. The greatest of kings is the king whose members of court only know all his plans, conforming to virtue, profit, and desire, once already carried out; success is assured for the king whose plans are secret.

The man who carries out censurable activities through folly will lose even his life due to their failure. Carrying out laudable activities results in happiness, but failing to carry them out creates regretful thoughts later on. Just as no brahmin who has not studied the Vedas deserves the memorial offerings, so someone who has not learned the six measures of royal policy does not deserve to hear the royal counsel.

The world is in the power of the man who understands 38.25
position, increase, and decrease, whose soul is aware of the six measures of royal policy, and whose behavior is not condemned, my king. A country grants wealth if it has a king whose anger and joy are productive, who inspects what has been done himself, and who has a full understanding of his treasury. A king should be satisfied with his mere title and his royal parasol, should disperse wealth to his servants, and should not take everything for himself alone.

brāhmaṇaṃ brāhmaṇo veda, bhartā veda striyaṃ tathā,
amātyaṃ nṛpatir veda, rājā rājānam eva ca.
na śatrur vaśam āpanno moktavyo vadhyatāṃ gataḥ;
nyag|bhūtvā paryupāsīta, vadhyaṃ hanyād bale sati;
a|hatādd hi bhayaṃ tasmāj jāyate na|cirād iva.
38.30 daivateṣu prayatnena, rājasu brāhmaṇeṣu ca
niyantavyaḥ sadā krodho vṛddha|bāl'|ātureṣu ca.
nirarthaṃ kalahaṃ prājño varjayen mūḍha|sevitam,
kīrtiṃ ca labhate loke, na c' ân|arthena yujyate.
prasādo niṣphalo yasya, krodhaś c' âpi nirarthakaḥ,
na taṃ bhartāram icchanti ṣaṇḍhaṃ patim iva striyaḥ.
na buddhir dhana|lābhāya, na jāḍyam a|samṛddhaye;
loka|paryāya|vṛtt'|ântaṃ prājño jānāti n' êtaraḥ.
vidyā|śīla|vayo|vṛddhān buddhi|vṛddhāṃś ca, Bhārata,
dhan'|âbhijāta|vṛddhāṃś ca nityaṃ mūḍho 'vamanyate.
38.35 an|ārya|vṛttam, a|prājñam, asūyakam, a|dhārmikam
an|arthāḥ kṣipram āyānti, vāg|duṣṭaṃ krodhanaṃ tathā.
a|visaṃvādanaṃ, dānaṃ, samayasy' â|vyatikramaḥ
āvartayanti bhūtāni, samyak praṇihitā ca vāk.
a|visaṃvādako, dakṣaḥ, kṛta|jño, matimān, ṛjuḥ
api saṃkṣīṇa|kośo 'pi labhate parivāraṇam.
dhṛtiḥ, śamo, damaḥ, śaucaṃ, kāruṇyaṃ, vāg a|niṣṭhurā,
mitrāṇāṃ c' ân|abhidrohaḥ sapt' âitāḥ samidhaḥ śriyaḥ.

Brahmin understands brahmin, a husband understands his wife, a king understands his minister, and a king understands another king. An enemy who ought to be killed should not be released when he has come over to your side; for when he is humbled he honors his enemy, but at full strength he would kill him. If he is not killed he will become dangerous before long.

Anger against the gods, kings, brahmins, the elderly, chil- 38.30
dren, and the sick, should always be curbed with effort. The wise man should avoid the fruitless disputes which are cherished by fools, for then he will win fame in this world and not be shackled with any disaster. People do not want a master whose favor is profitless and whose anger is unproductive, just as women do not want a eunuch for a husband.

Intelligence is not necessarily the way to acquiring wealth, nor is stupidity necessarily the way to failure; the wise man, but no other, knows the end result of the course of conduct in this world. The fool always despises those who have prospered by knowledge, conduct, or age, by intelligence,
or by wealth or lineage, Bhárata. Calamities quickly befall 38.35
the man whose conduct is ignoble, who is without wisdom, who is envious, who does not conform to moral law, or who is foul-mouthed and angry.

Agreement, generosity, honoring a treaty, and prudent speech bring all creatures to one's side. A sincere, industrious, grateful, intelligent, and honest man wins a retinue, even if his treasury is depleted. Resolve, peace, self-control, purity, compassion, gentle speech, and faithfulness to friends are, together, the kindling sticks of fortune.

a|saṃvibhāgī, duṣṭ'|ātmā, kṛta|ghno, nirapatrapaḥ,
tādṛṅ nar'|âdhipo loke varjanīyo, nar'|âdhipa.
38.40 na ca rātrau sukhkaṃ śete, sa|sarpa iva veśmani,
yaḥ kopayati nirdoṣaṃ sa|doṣo 'bhyantaraṃ janam.
yeṣu duṣṭeṣu doṣaḥ syād yoga|kṣemasya, Bhārata,
sadā prasādanaṃ teṣāṃ devatānām iv' ācaret.

ye 'rthāḥ strīṣu samāyuktāḥ, pramatta|patiteṣu ca,
ye c' ân|arthe samāsaktāḥ, sarve te saṃśayaṃ gatāḥ.
yatra strī, yatra kitavo, bālo yatr' ânuśāsitā,
majjanti te '|vaśā, rājan, nadyām aśma|plavā iva.
prayojaneṣu ye saktā na viśeṣeṣu, Bhārata,
tān ahaṃ paṇḍitān manye, viśeṣā hi prasaṅginaḥ.
38.45 yaṃ praśaṃsanti kitavā, yaṃ praśaṃsanti cāraṇāḥ,
yaṃ praśamsanti bandhakyo, na sa jīvati mānavaḥ.

hitvā tān param'|êṣvāsān Pāṇḍavān a|mit'|âujasaḥ,
āhitaṃ, Bhārat', āiśvaryaṃ tvayā Duryodhane mahat.
taṃ drakṣyasi paribhraṣṭaṃ tasmāt tvam a|cirād iva,
aiśvarya|mada|saṃmūḍhaṃ Baliṃ loka|trayād iva.»

DHṚTARĀṢṬRA uvāca:

39.1 «AN|ĪŚVARO 'YAṂ puruṣo bhav'|âbhave,
sūtra|protā dāru|may" îva yoṣā;
dhātrā tu diṣṭasya vaśe kṛto 'yaṃ.
tasmād vada tvaṃ, śravaṇe dhṛto 'ham.»

The kind of king who does not share, who is wicked in his very soul, ungrateful, and shameless, should be avoided
in this world, lord of men. Just like a man sleeping in a 38.40
house full of snakes, the man who angers the blameless in his house when he is in fact himself to blame, does not sleep happily at night. One should always propitiate those who could damage one's welfare when they are hostile, as though they were the gods, Bhárata.

All property entrusted to women and careless husbands, as well as that entrusted to an unproductive man, has an uncertain future. Wherever a woman, a gambler, or a child governs, my king, men sink, powerless to prevent it, like a raft made of stone in a river. I consider men who are attached to the overall design and not the specific details to
be wise, Bhárata, for the details are contingent. The man 38.45
whom gamblers, thieves, and courtezans praise is not really alive.

Ignoring those boundlessly energetic Pándava archers, Bhárata, you have invested mighty power upon Duryódhana. Therefore, you will soon watch as he falls just as Bali, made idiotic by his intoxication with power, fell from the three worlds."

DHRITA·RASHTRA said:

"A MAN IS NOT master of his life and death, but like a 39.1
wooden puppet strung on strings. The creator has made him subject to the power of fate—so speak, for I am intent on listening to you."

VIDURA uvāca:

«a|prāpta|kālaṃ vacanaṃ Bṛhaspatir api bruvan
labhate buddhy|avajñānam avamānaṃ ca, Bhārata.
priyo bhavati dānena priya|vādena c' âparaḥ,
mantra|mūla|balen' ânyo; yaḥ priyaḥ priya eva saḥ.
dveṣyo na sādhur bhavati, na medhāvī, na paṇḍitaḥ;
priye śubhāni kāryāṇi, dveṣye pāpāni c' âiva ha.
39.5 uktaṃ mayā jāta|mātre 'pi, rājan:
‹Duryodhanaṃ tyaja putraṃ tvam ekam.
tasya tyāgāt putra|śatasya vṛddhir,
asy' â|tyāgāt putra|śatasya nāśaḥ.›
na vṛddhir bahu mantavyā yā vṛddhiḥ kṣayam āvahet;
kṣayo 'pi bahu mantavyo yaḥ kṣayo vṛddhim āvahet.
na sa kṣayo, mahā|rāja, yaḥ kṣayo vṛddhim āvahet;
kṣayaḥ sa tv iha mantavyo yaṃ labdhvā bahu nāśayet.
samṛddhā guṇataḥ ke cid bhavanti, dhanato 'pare;
dhana|vṛddhān guṇair hīnān, Dhṛtarāṣṭra, vivarjaya.»

DHṚTARĀṢṬRA uvāca:

«sarvaṃ tvam āyatī|yuktaṃ bhāṣase prājña|saṃmatam,
na c' ôtsahe sutaṃ tyaktuṃ; yato dharmas tato jayaḥ.»

VÍDURA continued:

"By speaking inappropriately even Brihas·pati gained contempt for his intelligence, and disrespect, Bhárata. One man becomes favored through his generosity, another through his pleasing speech, and another through the strength of his roots and spells, but whoever is naturally pleasing is also held dear. A hated man is not good, clever, or learned. Pure activities are inherent to the loved and wicked deeds to the hated.

I even told you when he was born, king: abandon Dur- 39.5
yódhana, this one son, for by abandoning him your hundred sons will have prosperity. If you fail to abandon him, your hundred sons will meet with destruction.

Success that brings loss with it should not be considered a great success, and loss that brings success with it should also not be considered a great loss. It is no loss, great king, which brings prosperity with it, but it should be considered a loss if it destroys a great deal more. Some people are abundantly furnished with virtue, while others are successful in wealth; avoid those who are prosperous in monetary terms but lack virtue, Dhrita·rashtra."

DHRITA·RASHTRA said:

"Everything you say is proper for the future and respected by the wise, but I dare not abandon my son, for where there is moral law there is also victory."

VIDURA uvāca:

39.10 «atīva guṇa|sampanno na jātu vinay'|ânvitaḥ
su|sūkṣmam api bhūtānām upamardam upekṣate.
par'|âpavāda|niratāḥ para|duḥkh'|ôdayeṣu ca
paraspara|virodhe ca yatante satat'|ôtthitāḥ.
sa|doṣaṃ darśanaṃ yeṣāṃ saṃvāse su|mahad bhayam;
arth'|ādāne mahān doṣaḥ, pradāne ca mahad bhayam.

ye vai bhedana|śīlās tu, sa|kāmā, nistrapāḥ, śaṭhaḥ,
ye pāpā iti vikhyātāḥ, saṃvāse parigarhitāḥ,
yuktāś c' ânyair mahā|doṣair ye narās, tān vivarjayet.
nivartamāne sauhārde prītir nīce praṇaśyati,
39.15 yā c' âiva phala|nirvṛttiḥ, sauhṛde c' âiva yat sukham.
yatate c' âpavādāya yatnam ārabhate kṣaye
alpe 'py apakṛte mohān na śāntim adhigacchati.

tādṛśaiḥ saṅgataṃ nīcair nṛśaṃsair a|kṛt'|ātmabhiḥ
niśamya nipuṇaṃ buddhyā vidvān dūrād vivarjayet.
yo jñātim anugṛhṇāti daridraṃ, dīnam, āturam,
sa putra|paśubhir vṛddhiṃ śreyaś c' ân|antyam aśnute.
jñātayo vardhanīyās tair ya icchanty ātmanaḥ śubham;
kula|vṛddhiṃ ca, rāj'|êndra, tasmāt sādhu samācara.
śreyasā yokṣyase, rājan, kurvāṇo jñāti|satkriyām.

VÍDURA continued:

"A man who is particularly furnished with virtue and possesses propriety will notice even the smallest injury to creatures. People who take pleasure in insulting others are always striving for advantage in other people's misery and endeavor for success by beginning disputes among themselves. The mere sight of these people is objectionable and association with them is extremely dangerous; accepting benefits from them is very risky, and giving to them is also highly dangerous. 39.10

One should avoid shameless and willing fraudsters of loose conduct who are reported to be wicked, whose association is forbidden, and who are endowed with other enormous faults. When a friendship comes to an end, the
base man's affection is lost, as are the fruits which devel- 39.15
oped and the happiness that existed within the friendship. He is eager to abuse him and makes an effort to destroy him, even if the injury done to himself was small, and he finds no peace from his folly.

A wise man will observe matters precisely and with intelligence, and keep the company of such base and noxious men with no self-discipline at a distance. The man who takes in a begging relative who is wretched and sick, will gain an increase in his sons and livestock as well as unending glory. Those who wish for their own good should always help their relatives prosper. So ensure the success of your lineage, lord of kings, and equip yourself with glory, my king, by acting properly towards your relatives.

39.20 viguṇā hy api saṃrakṣyā jñātayo, Bharata'|rṣabha,
kiṃ punar guṇavantas te tvat prasād'|âbhikāṅkṣiṇaḥ?
prasādaṃ kuru vīrāṇāṃ Pāṇḍavānāṃ, viśām pate:
dīyantāṃ grāmakāḥ ke cit teṣāṃ vṛtty|artham, īśvara,
evaṃ loke yaśaḥ prāptaṃ bhaviṣyati, nar'|âdhipa.

vṛddhena hi tvayā kāryaṃ putrāṇāṃ, tāta, śāsanam;
mayā c' âpi hitaṃ vācyaṃ viddhi māṃ tvadd|hitaiṣṇam.
jñātibhir vigrahas, tāta, na kartavyaḥ śubh'|ârthinā;
sukhāni saha bhojyāni jñātibhir, Bharata'|rṣabha.
saṃbhojanaṃ, saṃkathanaṃ, saṃprītiś ca paras|param
jñātibhiḥ saha kāryāṇi, na virodhaḥ kadā cana.
39.25 jñātayas tārayant' îha, jñātayo majjayanti ca;
su|vṛttās tārayant' îha, dur|vṛttā majjayanti ca.

su|vṛtto bhava, rāj'|êndra, Pāṇḍavān prati, māna|da,
a|dharṣaṇīyaḥ śatrūṇāṃ tair vṛtas tvaṃ bhaviṣyasi.
śrīmantaṃ jñātim āsādya yo jñātir avasīdati
digdha|hastaṃ mṛga iva, sa enas tasya vindati.

paścād api, nara|śreṣṭha, tava tāpo bhaviṣyati;
tān vā hatān sutān v" âpi śrutvā, tad anucintaya.
yena khaṭvāṃ samārūḍhaḥ paritapyeta karmaṇā,
ādāv eva na tat kuryād a|dhruve jīvite sati.
39.30 na kaś cin n' âpanayate pumān anyatra Bhārgavāt;
śeṣa|saṃpratipattis tu buddhimatsv eva tiṣṭhati.

Even relatives of no virtue ought to be protected, bull- 39.20
like Bharata, so how much more are those virtuous men,
who long for your favor, owed? Grant your favor to those
heroic Pándavas, lord of earth; allow some villages to be
given to them for their subsistance, lord, and you will win
fame in this world, lord of men.

My friend, you must take control of your sons, for you
are old. Know that what I say is to your benefit and that
I wish you only the best. The man who aims for what is
good should not quarrel with relatives, but should share his
pleasures and luxuries with them, bull of the Bharatas. They
should share meals and conversation and feel affection towards each other, but no quarrels should be undertaken between relatives. Relatives either rescue or drown each other 39.25
in this world; the men of good conduct rescue their relatives, while those of wicked conduct drown them.

Be a man of good conduct towards the Pándavas, lord
of kings, granter of honor, and then, when surrounded by
them, you will be unbeatable. If a man sinks down before
his prosperous relative like a deer before a hunter, then the
wealthy relative takes on the other's sins.

It will bring you grief later, best of men, when you hear
that the Pándavas or your sons have been killed, so think
about it. Life is unstable, and so right from the start one
should not rise on the back of a villainous act that will
cause regret. No man but a Bhárgava does not deviate from 39.30
morality, but the intelligent possess awareness of the consequences.

Duryodhanena yady etat pāpaṃ teṣu purā kṛtam,
tvayā tat kula|vṛddhena pratyāneyaṃ, nar'|ēśvara.
tāṃs tvaṃ pade pratiṣṭhāpya loke vigata|kalmaṣaḥ
bhaviṣyasi, nara|śreṣṭha, pūjanīyo manīṣiṇām.
su|vyāhṛtāni dhīrāṇāṃ phalataḥ paricintya yaḥ
adhyavasyati kāryeṣu, ciraṃ yaśasi tiṣṭhati.
a|samyag upayuktaṃ hi jñānaṃ su|kuśalair api
upalabhyaṃ c' â|viditaṃ, viditaṃ c' ân|anuṣṭhitam.
39.35 pāp'|ôdaya|phalaṃ vidvān yo n' ārabhati, vardhate;
yas tu pūrva|kṛtaṃ pāpam avimṛśy' ânuvartate.
so 'ny'|âgha|paṅke dur|medhā viṣame vinipātyate,
mantra|bhedasya ṣaṭ prājño dvārāṇ' îmāni lakṣayet,
artha|santati|kāmaś ca rakṣed etāni nityaśaḥ:
madaṃ, svapnam, a|vijñānam, ākāraṃ c' ātma|saṃbhavam,
duṣṭ'|âmātyeṣu viśrambhaṃ, dūtāc c' â|kuśalād api.
dvārāṇy etāni yo jñātvā saṃvṛṇoti sadā, nṛpa,
39.40 tri|varg'|ācaraṇe yuktaḥ, sa śatrūn adhitiṣṭhati.
na vai śrutam a|vijñāya vṛddhān an|upasevya vā
dharm'|ârthau vedituṃ śakyau Bṛhaspati|samair api.
naṣṭaṃ samudre patitaṃ, naṣṭaṃ vākyam a|śṛṇvati,
an|ātmani śrutaṃ naṣṭaṃ, naṣṭaṃ hutam an|agnikam.

If Duryódhana committed some sin against them in the past, then you should put it right, for you are the family elder, lord of men. If you set them up in their proper station in this world, then you will become freed from your sins, best of men, and be respected by the wise.

The man who reflects on the sensible words of steadfast men on the subject of consequences, and who considers what he should do accordingly, will retain his good reputation for a long time. Even the wisdom taught by the extremely learned is not perfect, for things can be taken in but not fully comprehended, and things which are properly
understood are not put into practice. The wise man who 39.35
does not cling to the means and results of evil will flourish, and the man who ignores the evil he committed in the past repeats it.

The stupid man falls into a terrible mire because of his other sins, but the wise man ought to recognize these six doors through which counsel can be breached, and against which the man who desires a succession of gains should always guard: lust, sleep, ignorance, wearing his heart on his sleeve, reliance on wicked ministers, and an unskilled messenger. The man who understands these doors always
chooses wisely, my king, and, intent on practicing aims 39.40
conforming to the triad of virtue, profit, and desire, he surpasses his enemies.

Even men like Brihas·pati cannot understand virtue and profit without knowledge of the Veda and without paying attention to their elders. Advice given to someone who does not listen is as lost as something that falls into the sea, the Veda is lost on someone who has no self-discipline, and an

matyā parīkṣya medhāvī, buddhyā sampādya c' â|sakṛt,
śrutvā dṛṣṭv" âtha vijñāya prājñair maitrīṃ samācaret.
a|kīrtiṃ vinayo hanti, hanty an|arthaṃ parākramaḥ,
hanti nityaṃ kṣamā krodham, ācāro hanty a|lakṣaṇam.
paricchadena, kṣatreṇa, veśmanā, paricaryayā
39.45 parīkṣeta kulaṃ, rājan, bhojan'|ācchādanena ca.
upasthitasya kāmasya prativādo na vidyate
api nirmukta|dehasya; kāma|raktasya kiṃ punaḥ?
prājñ'|ôpasevinaṃ, vaidyaṃ,
dhārmikaṃ, priya|darśanam,
mitravantaṃ, su|vākyaṃ ca
suhṛdaṃ paripālayet;
duṣ|kulīnaḥ kulīno vā maryādāṃ yo na laṅghayet,
dharm'|âpekṣī, mṛdur, hrīmān sa kulīna|śatād varaḥ.
yayoś cittena vā cittaṃ nibhṛtaṃ nibhṛtena vā
sameti prajñayā prajñā, tayor maitrī na jīryati.
dur|buddhim a|kṛta|prajñaṃ channaṃ kūpaṃ tṛṇair iva
39.50 vivarjayīta medhāvī; tasmin maitrī praṇaśyati.
avalipteṣu mūrkheṣu raudra|sāhasikeṣu ca
tath" âiv' âpeta|dharmeṣu
na maitrīm ācared budhaḥ;
kṛta|jñaṃ, dhārmikaṃ, satyam,
a|kṣudraṃ, dṛḍha|bhaktikam,
jit'|êndriyaṃ, sthitaṃ sthityāṃ mitram a|tyāgi c' êṣyate.

oblation is lost when not made over a fire. A clever person conducts friendships with wise men once he has examined good advice in his mind and repeatedly made use of his intelligence, hearing, sight, and knowledge.

Propriety destroys disgrace, courage overcomes adversity,
forgiveness always destroys anger, and good behavior over- 39.45
comes bad omens. My king, one should examine a family by their finery, power, home, devotion, and by their food and clothes. No refusal is found when something desirable is on offer, even from someone who is released from their bodily desires; so then what about the man who is devoted to his desires?

One should protect a friend who practices wisdom, who is learned in the Veda, abides by moral law, is handsome, has friends, and is eloquent. Regardless of how noble or ignoble his birth, he would not transgress; he observes morality, is gentle, modest, and is greater than a hundred nobly born men. The friendship between two men whose behavior, secrets, or wisdom mesh, does not break.

A clever man would avoid an unintelligent person who 39.50
has developed no wisdom as he would avoid a hole concealed by grass, for that man's friendship dissolves. The wise man would not conduct a friendship with arrogant men, idiots, men of fierce violence, or men whose virtue has gone, but he wishes for a friend who is grateful, abides by moral constraints, is truthful rather than mean-hearted, resolutely loyal, whose senses are under control, who is faithful, virtuous in his conduct, and does not abandon his friend.

indriyāṇām an|utsargo mṛtyunā na viśīṣyate;
atyartham punar utsargaḥ sādayed daivatān api.
mārdavaṃ sarva|bhūtānām, an|asūyā, kṣamā, dhṛtiḥ—
āyuṣyāni budhāḥ prāhur, mitrāṇāṃ c' â|vimānanā.
apanītaṃ su|nītena yo 'rthaṃ pratyāninīṣa,te
39.55 matim āsthāya su|dṛḍhāṃ, tad a|kāpuruṣa|vratam.
āyatyāṃ pratikāra|jñas tadātve dṛḍha|niścayaḥ
atīte kārya|śeṣa|jño naro 'rthair na prahīyate.
karmaṇā manasā vācā yad abhīkṣṇaṃ niṣevate,
tad ev' âpaharaty enaṃ, tasmāt kalyāṇam ācaret.
maṅgal'|ālambhanaṃ, yogaḥ, śrutam, utthānam, ārjavam—
bhūtim etāni kurvanti, satāṃ c' âbhīkṣṇa|darśanam.
a|nirvedaḥ śriyo mūlaṃ, lābhasya ca śubhasya ca;
mahān bhavaty a|nirviṇṇaḥ, sukhaṃ c' ân|antyam aśnute.
n' âtaḥ śrīmattaraṃ kiñ cid anyat pathyatamaṃ matam,
39.60 prabhaviṣṇor yathā, tāta, kṣamā sarvatra sarvadā.
kṣamed a|śaktaḥ sarvasya śaktimān dharma|kāraṇāt;
arth'|ân|arthau samau yasya, tasya nityaṃ kṣamā hitā.
yat sukhaṃ sevamāno 'pi dharm'|ârthābhyāṃ na hīyate,
kāmaṃ tad upaseveta na mūḍha|vratam ācaret.

The withdrawal of the senses is like death; their excessive license would destroy even the gods. Wise men say that gentleness towards all creatures, as well as a lack of envy, forgiveness, constancy, and respect for one's friends bring long life. The man who wants to rearrange a badly conducted aim with a well-conducted one by employing great 39.55
firmness of mind, displays manly resolve.

The man who understands how to counteract the future behaves resolutely in the present, and the man who understands the consequences of his tasks will not be separated from his wealth. Since a man gets carried away by the things he continually cultivates in his actions, mind, and words, he ought therefore to practice what is good. Depending on what is auspicious, endurance, learning, manliness, sincerity, and constant observation of good men bring prosperity. The root of gain and prosperity is not becoming depressed about one's fortune; the man who does not become downcast is powerful and will attain eternal happiness.

Nothing else is considered more fortunate or more beneficial, my friend, than a powerful man's forgiveness in every 39.60
situation and place. A powerless man should forgive everything, and a powerful man should forgive for reasons of righteousness. If profit and loss are the same to him, then his forgiveness will always be resolute. The man who cultivates happiness without becoming separated from moral duty and profit, should cultivate what he desires but should not practice subservience to fools.

duḥkh'|ārteṣu, pramatteṣu, nāstikeṣv, alaseṣu ca
na śrīr vasaty a|dānteṣu, ye c' ôtsāha|vivarjitāḥ.
ārjavena naraṃ yuktam ārjavāt sa|vyapatrapam
a|śaktaṃ manyamānās tu dharṣayanti ku|buddhayaḥ.
atyāryam, atidātāram, atiśūram, ativratam
prajñ"|âbhimāninaṃ c' âiva śrīr bhayān n' ôpasarpati.
39.65 na c' âtiguṇavatsv eṣā, n' âtyantaṃ nir,guṇeṣu ca,
n' âiṣa guṇān kāmayate, nairguṇyān n' ânurajyate.
unmattā gaur iv' ândhā śrīḥ kva cid ev' âvatiṣṭhate.
agnihotra|phalā vedāḥ, śīla|vṛtta|phalaṃ śrutam,
rati|putra|phalā nārī, datta|bhukta|phalaṃ dhanam.
a|dharm'|ôpārjitair arthair yaḥ karoty aurdhvadehikam,
na sa tasya phalaṃ pretya bhuṅkte 'rthasya dur|āgamāt.
kāntāre, vana|durgeṣu, kṛcchrāsv, āpatsu, saṃbhrame,
udyateṣu ca śastreṣu
n' âsti sattvavatāṃ bhayam.
utthānaṃ, saṃyamo, dākṣyam,
a|pramādo, dhṛtiḥ, smṛtiḥ,
39.70 samīkṣya ca samārambho – viddhi mūlaṃ bhavasya tu.
tapo balaṃ tāpasānāṃ, brahma brahma|vidāṃ balam,
hiṃsā balam a|sādhūnāṃ, kṣamā guṇavatāṃ balam.
aṣṭau tāny a|vrata|ghnāni: āpo, mūlaṃ, phalaṃ, payaḥ,
havir, brāhmaṇa|kāmyā ca, guror vacanam, auṣadham.

Good fortune does not reside in those afflicted by misery, the careless, those without faith, the lazy, the uncontrolled, and those who avoid risks. Wicked-minded men treat a man contemptuously if he is endowed with sincerity and is bashful out of honesty, for they imagine he is powerless. Fear prevents good fortune from creeping up on the man who is excessively noble, excessively generous, excessively brave, the man of excessive vows, or the man who
takes pride in his wisdom. Success does not reside in those 39.65
who are excessively virtuous, nor in those who are always without virtue; she does not desire virtues, but she is not fond of a total lack of virtue either. Lady luck is disorderly and abides wherever she feels, like a blind cow.

Agni·hotra offerings are the fruits of the Veda, good behavior is the fruit of learning, love and sons are the fruits of women, and gifts and food are the fruits of wealth. The man who performs offerings for the dead with immorally gained wealth, does not enjoy the fruits of his labor in the next world on account of the evil way he acquired his wealth. The courageous have nothing to fear in the desert, in an impassable forest, in disasters and calamities, in confusion, or among drawn weapons.

Know these as the roots of prosperity: effort, discipline, 39.70
dexterity, vigilance, resolve, learning, and enterprise after investigation. Austerity is the strength of ascetics, the Brahman is the strength of those who understand the Brahman, violence is the strength of evil men, and forgiveness is the strength of the virtuous. These eight things do not destroy a vow: water, roots, fruit, milk, oblations, brahmins' wishes, the advice of one's teacher, and medicine.

na tat parasya sandadhyāt pratikūlaṃ yad ātmanaḥ:
saṃgraheṇ' âiṣa dharmaḥ syāt, kāmād anyaḥ pravartate.
a|krodhena jayet krodham, a|sādhuṃ sādhunā jayet,
jayet kadaryaṃ dānena, jayet satyena c' ân|ṛtam.
strī|dhūrtake, 'lase, bhīrau, caṇḍe, puruṣa|mānini,
39.75 caure, kṛta|ghne viśvāso na kāryo, na ca nāstike.
abhivādana|śīlasya nityaṃ vṛddh'|ôpasevinaḥ
catvāri saṃpravardhante: kīrtir, āyur, yaśo, balam.

atikleśena ye 'rthāḥ syur, dharmasy' âtikrameṇa vā,
arer vā praṇipātena, mā sma teṣu manaḥ kṛthāḥ.
a|vidyaḥ puruṣaḥ śocyaḥ, śocyaṃ maithunam a|prajam,
nirāhārāḥ prajāḥ śocyāḥ, śocyaṃ rāṣṭram a|rājakam.
adhvā jarā dehavatāṃ, parvatānāṃ jalaṃ jarā,
a|saṃbhogo jarā strīṇāṃ, vāk|śalyaṃ manaso jarā.

an|āmnāya|malā vedā, brāhmaṇasy' â|vrataṃ malam,
39.80 malaṃ pṛthivyā Bāhlīkāḥ, puruṣasy' ânṛtaṃ malam,
kautūhala|malā sādhvī, vipravāsa|malāḥ striyaḥ,
suvarṇasya malaṃ rūpyaṃ, rūpyasay' âpi malaṃ trapu,
jñeyaṃ trapu|malaṃ sīsaṃ, sīsasy' âpi malaṃ malam.
na svapnena jayen nidrāṃ, na kāmena jayet striyaḥ,
n' êndhanena jayed agniṃ, na pānena surāṃ jayet.
yasya dāna|jitaṃ mitraṃ, śatravo yudhi nirjitāḥ,
anna|pāna|jitā dārāḥ, sa|phalaṃ tasya jīvitam.

One should not direct towards someone else what is unpleasant to oneself: this would be a succinct version of moral duty. Another form of virtue emerges from desire. One should defeat anger with forbearance, wickedness with what is good, avarice with generosity, and lies with the truth. 39.75
One should not put faith in a woman, a cheat, a lazy man, a coward, a violent man, someone who boasts of their prowess, a thief, an ungrateful man, or an atheist. These four increase in the man who constantly practices respectful greetings and cares for the elderly: good reputation, long life, fame, and strength.

Don't set your mind on aims which involve too much pain, transgression of moral duty, or sycophancy before one's enemy. A man without knowledge should be lamented, as should the childless couple, starving subjects, and a kingless realm. A journey ages the embodied, rain ages mountains, lack of sex ages women, and cruel speech ages the mind.

Failure to pass them down sullies the Vedas, failure to
observe vows sullies a brahmin, the Bahlíkas sully the earth 39.80
and deceit sullies a man, curiosity sullies a good woman and staying away from home sullies women, silver sullies gold, tin sullies silver, lead is known to sully tin, and dirt sullies lead. One should not overcome sloth with sleep, women with lust, fire by kindling it, or wine by drinking. The man who wins a friend through generosity, wins enemies in battle, and wins wives with food and drink, has a fruitful life.

sahasriṇo 'pi jīvanti, jīvanti śatinas tathā,
Dhṛtarāṣṭra, vimuñc' êcchāṃ; na kathañ cin na jīvyate.
39.85 ‹yat pṛthivyāṃ vrīhi|yavaṃ, hiraṇyaṃ, paśavaḥ, striyaḥ,
n' âlam ekasya tat sarvam, iti› paśyan na muhyati.
rājan, bhūyo bravīmi tvāṃ putreṣu samam ācara,
samatā yadi te, rājan, sveṣu Pāṇḍu|suteṣu vā.»

VIDURA uvāca:

40.1 «YO 'BHYARCITAḤ sadbhir a|sajjamanaḥ
karoty arthaṃ śaktim a|hāpayitvā,
kṣipraṃ yaśas taṃ samupaiti santam;
alaṃ prasannā hi sukhāya santaḥ.
mahāntam apy artham a|dharma|yuktaṃ
yaḥ santyajaty an|apākṛṣṭa eva,
sukhaṃ su|duḥkhāṇy avamucya śete,
jīrṇāṃ tvacaṃ sarpa iv' âvamucya.
an|ṛte ca samutkarṣo, rāja|gāmi ca paiśunam,
guroś c' âlīka|nirbandhaḥ samāni brahma|hatyayā.
asūy"|âika|padaṃ mṛtyur, ativādaḥ śriyo vadhaḥ.
a|śuśrūṣā, tvarā, ślāghā vidyāyāḥ śatravas trayaḥ.
40.5 ālasyaṃ mada|mohau ca, cāpalaṃ goṣṭhir eva ca,
stabdhatā c' âbhimānitvaṃ, tathā tyāgitvam eva ca,
ete vai sapta doṣāḥ syuḥ sadā vidy"|ârthināṃ matāḥ.
sukh'|ârthinaḥ kuto vidyā? n' âsti vidy'|ârthinaḥ sukham.
sukh'|ârthī vā tyajed vidyāṃ, vidy'|ârthī vā tyajet sukham.

Men who have thousands live just the same as those who have hundreds, Dhrita·rashtra, so let go of your desire, for
there is no way that one cannot live. The man who observes 39.85
the saying, 'All the rice, barley, gold, cattle, and women in the world are not enough for one man,' does not get confused. My king, I tell you again: you treat your sons fairly if you treat your own sons and Pandu's sons with equality."

VÍDURA continued:

"FAME QUICKLY finds the good man who is respected by 40.1
the wise without being proud and carries out his aim without overstepping his own limits, for the good, when gracious towards someone, can certainly bring him happiness. The man who abandons even great profit if it is connected to immorality, and turns away from it, sleeps happily, released from great miseries, just as a snake casts off its worn-out slough.

A lie, self-advancement, bringing slander before the king, back-stabbing, and displeasing obstinacy before one's guru are equal to brahmanicide. A single word of envy is death, and excessive disputes murder good fortune. Disobedience,
speed, and boasting are the three enemies of wisdom. Sloth, 40.5
lust, confusion, restlessness, arrogance, conceit, and resignation are always considered to be the seven faults of those whose aim is wisdom. How can the hedonist have wisdom when the man whose goal is wisdom has no pleasure? Either the hedonist should abandon wisdom, or the man whose goal is wisdom should abandon happiness.

n' âgnis tṛpyati kāṣṭhānāṃ, n' āpagānāṃ mah"|ôdadhiḥ,
n' ântakaḥ sarva|bhūtānāṃ, na puṃsāṃ vāma|locanā.
āśā dhṛtiṃ hanti, samṛddhim antakaḥ,
krodhaḥ śriyaṃ hanti, yaśaḥ kadaryatā,
a|pālanaṃ hanti paśūṃś ca, rājann,
ekaḥ kruddho brāhmaṇo hanti rāṣṭram.
ajāś ca, kāṃsyaṃ, rajataṃ ca nityaṃ,
madhv, ākarṣaḥ, śakuniḥ, śrotriyaś ca,
vṛddho jñātir, avasannaḥ kulīna—
etāni te santu gṛhe sad" âiva.
40.10 aj'|ôkṣā, candanaṃ, vīṇā, ādarśo, madhu|sarpiṣī,
viṣam'|āudumbaraṃ, śaṅkhaḥ, svarṇa|nābho, 'tha rocanā
gṛhe sthāpayitavyāni dhanyāni Manur abravīt,
deva|brāhmaṇa|pūj"|ârtham, atithīnāṃ ca, Bhārata.
idaṃ ca tvāṃ sarva|paraṃ bravīmi
puṇyaṃ padaṃ, tāta, mahā|viśiṣṭam:
na jātu kāmān, na bhayān, na lobhād
dharmaṃ jahyāj jīvitasy' âpi hetoḥ.
nityo dharmaḥ, sukha|duḥkhe tv a|nitye,
jīvo nityo, hetur asya tv a|nityaḥ,
tyaktv" â|nityaṃ pratitiṣṭhasva nitye.
santuṣya tvaṃ; toṣa|paro hi lābhaḥ.
mahā|balān paśya mah"|ânubhāvān,
praśāsya bhūmiṃ dhana|dhānya|pūrṇām,
rājyāni hitvā vipulāṃś ca bhogān
gatān nar'|êndrān vaśam antakasya.
40.15 mṛtaṃ putraṃ duḥkha|puṣṭaṃ manuṣyā
utkṣipya, rājan, sva|gṛhān nirharanti.
taṃ mukta|keśāḥ karuṇaṃ rudantaś,*
citā|madhye kāṣṭham iva kṣipanti.

Fire is never satisfied with wood, nor is the ocean sated by its tributaries. Death is not sated with all creatures, nor a lovely-eyed lady with men. Hope kills resolve, death kills success, anger kills good fortune, avarice kills fame, and poor protection kills livestock, my king, but a single angry brahmin destroys a kingdom.

In one's house one should always have goats, copper,
silver, honey, attractions, a bird, a priest, an elderly relative, and a nobly born man who has fallen into depression.
Manu said that a goat, bull, sandalwood, a musical instru- 40.10
ment, a mirror, honey and ghee, copper, a conch shell, an
ammonite, and red dye should be put aside in the house as
auspicious items in order to honor the gods, brahmins, and
guests, Bhárata.

I give you this sacred advice, particularly distinguished, which surpasses all else, my friend: do not destroy your morality out of lust, fear, greed, or even for the sake of your life. Moral duty is eternal, but happiness and misery are transitory. Life is eternal but the agent bodies are not, so, having abandoned the transitory, concentrate on the eternal. Be satisfied, for satisfaction is the greatest profit.

Look at the powerful and magnanimous kings who governed the earth, full of wealth and benefits, but losing their
realms and abundant luxuries fell under the power of death.
People lift their dead son, once nourished at great pains, and 40.15
carry him out of their house, my king, weeping for him in
their distress, with their hair flowing in disarray, and throw
him onto the middle of the funeral pyre as though he were a
piece of wood. Another man enjoys the dead man's wealth,
and the birds and fire eat his body parts.

anyo dhanaṃ preta|gatasya bhuṅkte,
vayāṃsi c' âgniś ca śarīra|dhātūn.
dvābhyām ayaṃ saha gacchaty amutra:
puṇyena pāpena ca veṣṭyamānaḥ.
utsṛjya vinivartante jñātayaḥ suhṛdaḥ sutāḥ,
a|puṣpān a|phalān vṛkṣān yathā, tāta, patatriṇaḥ,
agnau prāstaṃ tu puruṣaṃ karm' ânveti svayaṃ kṛtam.
tasmāt tu puruṣo yatnād dharmaṃ saṃcinuyāc chanaiḥ.
asmāl lokād ūrdhvam, amuṣya c' âdho,
mahat tamas tiṣṭhati hy andha|kāram.
tad vai mahā|mohanam indriyāṇāṃ
budhyasva, mā tvāṃ pralabheta, rājan.
40.20 idaṃ vacaḥ śakṣyasi ced yathāvan
niśamya sarvaṃ pratipattum eva,
yaśaḥ paraṃ prāpsyasi jīva|loke,
bhayaṃ na c' âmutra na c' êha te 'sti.
ātmā nadī, Bhārata, puṇya|tīrthā,
saty'|ôdakā dhṛti|kūlā day"|ōrmiḥ;
tasyāṃ snātaḥ pūyate puṇya|karmā,
puṇyo hy ātmā, nityam a|lobha eva.
kāma|krodha|grāhavatīṃ pañc'|êndriya|jalāṃ nadīm
nāvaṃ dhṛti|mayīṃ kṛtvā janma|durgāṇi santara.
prajñā|vṛddhaṃ, dharma|vṛddhaṃ sva|bandhuṃ,
vidyā|vṛddhaṃ, vayasā c' âpi vṛddham
kāry'|â|kārye pūjayitvā, prasādya
yaḥ saṃpṛcchen, na sa muhyet kadā cit.
dhṛtyā śiśn'|ôdaraṃ rakṣet, pāṇipādaṃ ca cakṣuṣā,
cakṣuḥ|śrotre ca manasā, mano vācaṃ ca karmaṇā.

He goes to the other world accompanied by two things: his merit and sin. Relatives, friends, and sons dispose of him and turn away just as birds leave trees which do not fruit or flower, my friend, but the deeds he has done follow the man who has been thrown in the fire. Therefore, a man should accumulate virtue slowly and with effort. Know that above this world, and below the next world, there is a vast, blinding darkness which causes great confusion to the sesnes. Do not aim for it, my king.

If you are able to do everything properly, just as you have 40.20
learned it, then you will gain the highest reputation in the world of the living and have nothing to fear either here or in the next world. One's soul is a river, Bhárata, one's merit constitues the bathing places, its waters are truth, its banks are resolve, its waves are compassion; the man of pious actions who bathes in it is purified, for the soul is pure and eternally without desire.

Having constructed a boat made of steady resolve, cross the river whose waters consist of the five senses and swarm with the predators of desire and anger, even crossing the tricky swells of rebirth. The man who would honor and propitiate his elderly relative, advanced in wisdom, virtue, and knowledge, and ask what ought to be done and what ought not to be done, will never be confused. One should protect one's penis and belly with steady resolve, one's hands and feet with one's eyes, one's eyes and ears with the mind, and one's mind and speech with one's action.

40.25 nity'|ôdakī, nitya|yajñ'|ôpavītī,
nitya|svādhyāyī, patit'|ânna|varjī,
satyaṃ bruvan gurave, karma kurvan
na brāhmaṇaś cyavate brahma|lokāt.
adhītya vedān, parisaṃstīrya c' âgnīn,
iṣṭvā yajñaiḥ, pālayitvā prajāś ca,
go|brāhmaṇ'|ârthaṃ śastra|pūt'|ântar'|ātmā
hataḥ saṃgrāme kṣatriyaḥ svargam eti.
vaiśyo 'dhītya, brāhmaṇān kṣatriyāṃś ca
dhanaiḥ kāle saṃvibhajy' āśritāṃś ca,
tretā|pūtaṃ dhūmam āghrāya puṇyaṃ,
pretya svarge divya|sukhāni bhuṅkte.
brahma, kṣatraṃ, vaiśya|varṇaṃ ca śūdraḥ
krameṇ' âitān nyāyataḥ pūjayānaḥ
tuṣṭeṣv eteṣv a|vyatho dagdha|pāpas
tyaktvā dehaṃ svarga|sukhāni bhuṅkte.
cāturvarṇyasy' âiṣa dharmas tav' ôkto,
hetuṃ c' ânubruvato me nibodha.
kṣātrād dharmādd hīyate Pāṇḍu|putras;
taṃ tvaṃ, rājan, rāja|dharme niyuṅkṣva.»

DHṚTARĀṢṬRA uvāca:

40.30 «evam etad yathā tvaṃ mām anuśāsasi nityadā;
mam' âpi ca matiḥ, saumya, bhavaty evaṃ yath" āttha mām.
sā tu buddhiḥ kṛt" âpy evaṃ Pāṇḍavān prati me sadā
Duryodhanaṃ samāsādya punar viparivartate.
na diṣṭam abhyatikrāntuṃ śakyaṃ bhūtena kena cit;
diṣṭam eva dhruvaṃ manye, pauruṣaṃ tu nirarthakam.»

The brahmin who always sips water, who always wears his sacred thread, always studies well, avoids food that has fallen to the ground, speaks the truth to his guru, and performs his duties, does not fall from Brahma's realm. The kshatriya who studies the Veda, kindles fires, performs sacrifices, and defends his subjects, but who dies in battle, purifying his inner soul with weapons drawn in the cause of cattle and brahmins, will go to heaven. The vaishya who has studied and has distributed his wealth among the brahmins and kshatriyas as well as those who rely upon him at the proper time, and who has smelt the holy smoke of the three pure fires, goes to heaven when he dies, and enjoys divine pleasures. The shudra who properly honors the brahmin, kshatriya, and vaishya castes in their proper hierarchy, so long as they are satisfied, will enjoy heavenly pleasures when he gives up his body, and be untroubled, for his sin has been burned up. 40.25

I have told you the moral obligations of the four castes for a reason, so learn from me when I address you. The son of Pandu is being taken from his kshatriyan duty, so, my king, reuinte him with his kingly moral obligation."

DHRITA·RASHTRA said:

"It is indeed just as you always teach, and my mind agrees with what you tell me, excellent man. My reason always sways towards the Pándavas, but whenever I meet Duryódhana it turns away again. No living creature can exceed his fate. I believe that fate is set and human exertion is pointless." 40.30

DHṚTARĀṢṬRA uvāca:

41.1 «AN|UKTAṂ YADI te kiñ cid vācā, Vidura, vidyate,
tan me śuśrūṣato brūhi; vicitrāṇi hi bhāṣase.»

VIDURA uvāca:

«Dhṛtarāṣṭra, kumāro vai yaḥ purāṇaḥ sanātanaḥ,
Sanatsujātaḥ provāca, ‹mṛtyur n' âst', îti› Bhārata.
sa te guhyān prakāśāṃś ca sarvān hṛdaya|saṃśrayān
pravakṣyati, mahā|rāja, sarva|buddhimatāṃ varaḥ.»

DHṚTARĀṢṬRA uvāca:

«kiṃ tvaṃ na veda tad bhūyo, yan me brūyāt sanātanaḥ?
tvaṃ eva, Vidura, brūhi, prajñā|śeṣo 'sti cet tava.»

VIDURA uvāca:

41.5 «śūdra|yonāv ahaṃ jāto, n' âto 'nyad vaktum utsahe,
kumārasya tu yā buddhir, veda tāṃ śāśvatīm aham.
brāhmīṃ hi yonim āpannaḥ su|guhyam api yo vadet,
na tena garhyo devānāṃ, tasmād etad bravīmi te.»

DHṚTARĀṢṬRA uvāca:

«bravīhi, Vidura, tvaṃ me purāṇaṃ taṃ sanātanam,
katham etena dehena syād ih' âiva samāgamaḥ?»

DHRITA·RASHTRA said:

"IF THERE IS anything you have left unsaid, Vídura, then tell me. I wish to hear it, for you speak charmingly." 41.1

VÍDURA replied:

"Dhrita·rashtra Bhárata, the ancient and eternal youth known as Sanat·sujáta* has said that death does not exist. The greatest of creatures of intelligence, great king, will reveal to you all the hidden and manifest doubts which dwell in your heart."

DHRITA·RASHTRA said:

"Do you not also know what that eternal man would tell me, Vídura? Tell me if you have any remaining wisdom to impart."

VÍDURA replied:

"I am born from a shudra womb and so I do not dare say 41.5
anything else, though I do know the young man's wisdom is without limit. The man who was born from a brahmin-caste womb is not restrained by the gods, even if he speaks of something extremely secret, and that is why I say this to you."

DHRITA·RASHTRA said:

"Vídura, communicate with the ancient and eternal youth on my behalf, so that somehow I can meet him with this body and in this place."

VAIŚAMPĀYANA uvāca:

cintayām āsa Viduras tam ṛṣiṃ śaṃsita|vratam;
sa ca tac cintitaṃ jñātvā darśayām āsa, Bhārata.
sa c' âinaṃ pratijagrāha vidhi|dṛṣṭena karmaṇā.
sukh'|ôpaviṣṭaṃ viśrāntam ath' âinaṃ Viduro 'bravīt:
41.10 «bhagavan, saṃśayaḥ kaś cid Dhṛtarāṣṭrasya mānasaḥ,
yo na śakyo mayā vaktuṃ. tvam asmai vaktum arhasi.
yaṃ śrutv" âyaṃ manuṣy'|êndraḥ sarva|duḥkh'|âtigo bhavet
lābh'|âlābhau, priya|dveṣyau, yath" âinaṃ na jar"|ântakau
viṣaheran, bhay'|âmarṣau, kṣut|pipāse, mad'|ôdbhavau,
a|ratiś c' âiva, tandrī ca, kāma|krodhau, kṣay'|ôdayau.»

VAISHAMPÁYANA said:

Vídura concentrated on the sage of laudable vows, and, understanding that he was being meditated upon, he appeared, Bhárata. Vídura received him with an act revealed in the prescribed rules, and when he was sitting happily and was rested, Vídura said:

"Lord, there is doubt in Dhrita·rashtra's mind which I 41.10
cannot explain, so you ought to explain it to him. When he has heard it, that lord of men may be beyond all misery, acquisition and loss, affection and hatred, so that old age and death do not overpower him, nor fear and impatience, hunger and thirst, intoxication and power, discontent and exhaustion, desire and anger, nor destruction and creation."

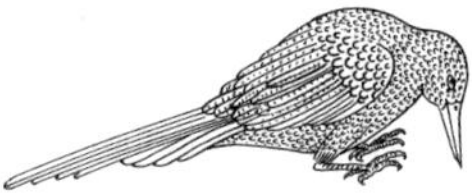

# 42–46
# SANAT·SUJÁTA'S TEACHINGS

VAIŚAMPĀYANA uvāca:

42.1 TATO RĀJĀ Dhṛtarāṣṭro manīṣī
sampūjya vākyaṃ Vidur'|ēritaṃ tat
Sanatsujātaṃ rahite mah"|ātmā
papraccha buddhiṃ paramāṃ bubhūṣan.

DHṚTARĀṢṬRA uvāca:

«Sanatsujāta, yad idaṃ śṛṇomi,
‹na mṛtyur ast', îti› tava pravādam;
dev'|âsurā hy ācaran brahma|caryam
a|mṛtyave; tat kataran nu satyam?»

SANATSUJĀTA uvāca:

«apṛcchaḥ karmaṇā yac ca, mṛtyur n' âst' îti c' âparam.
śṛṇu me bruvato, rājan, yath" âitan, mā viśaṅkithāḥ.
ubhe satye, kṣatriy', âitasya viddhi;
mohān mṛtyuḥ saṃmato 'yaṃ kavīnām!
pramādaṃ vai mṛtyum ahaṃ bravīmi;
tath" â|pramādam amṛtatvaṃ bravīmi.
42.5 pramādād vai asurāḥ parābhavan,
na pramādād Brahma|bhūtā bhavanti.
n' âiva mṛtyur vyāghra iv' âtti jantūn
na hy asya rūpam upalabhyate hi.
Yamaṃ tv eke mṛtyum ato 'nyam āhur;
ātm'|âvasannam a|mṛtaṃ brahma|caryam.
pitṛ|loke rājyam anuśāsti devaḥ,
śivaḥ śivānām, a|śivo '|śivānām.
āsyād eṣa niḥsarate narāṇāṃ
krodhaḥ, pramādo, lobha|rūpaś ca mṛtyuḥ.
ahaṃ|gaten' âiva caran vimārgān
na c' ātmano yogam upaiti kaś cit.

VAISHAMPÁYANA said:

THE WISE AND high-souled King Dhrita·rashtra re- 42.1
spected what Vídura had said, and in secret questioned Sanat·sujáta, wishing to attain the ultimate wisdom.*

DHRITA·RASHTRA said:

"Sanat·sujáta, I have heard that you claim death does not exist; but the gods and *ásura*s performed the duties of Brahman specifically for immortality, so which is true?"

SANAT·SUJÁTA replied:

"Some believe that death can be avoided through action, and others that death does not exist. You asked which is correct, so listen to me as I explain it to you, king, so that you don't misjudge. Both are true, warrior, according to this rule: sages think that death results from folly! I tell you death is carelessness; so I tell you immortality is vigilance.

The *ásura*s were overcome by carelessness, but the gods 42.5
who have attained the nature of Brahman have done so from vigilance. Death is not like a tiger that eats men; its form is not perceived. Some believe death is Yama, but they speak out of ignorance. Immortality is the practice of Brahman deep in the soul. That god, Yama, rules the kingdom in the world of ancestors, kind to the kind but harsh to the harsh.

It is he who dispatches death among men as fury, as carelessness, and in the form of confusion. Anyone who follows an evil course, led by his own pride, does not attain discipline over his soul. Those who are confused act on their impulses, pass away to the next world, and then fall again.

te mohitās tad|vaśe vartamānā
itaḥ pretās tatra punaḥ patanti;
tatas tān devā anuviplavante,
ato mṛtyur maraṇ'|ākhyām upaiti.
karm'|ôdaye karma|phal'|ânurāgās
tatr' ânu te yānti, na taranti mṛtyum.
sad|artha|yogān avagamāt samantāt
pravartate bhoga|yogena dehī.
42.10 tad vai mahā|mohanam indriyāṇāṃ;
mithy"|ârtha|yogasya gatir hi nityā.
mithy"|ârtha|yog'|âbhihat'|ântar'|ātmā
smarann upāste viṣayān samantāt.
abhidhyā vai prathamaṃ hanti lokān,
kāma|krodhāv anugṛhy' āśu paścāt.
ete bālān mṛtyave prāpayanti;
dhīrās tu dhairyeṇa taranti mṛtyum.
yo 'bhidhyāyann utpatitān nihanyād,
an|ādareṇ' â|pratibudhyamānaḥ;
n' âinaṃ mṛtyur Mṛtyur iv' âtti bhūtvā;
evaṃ vidvān yo vinihanti kāmān.
kām'|ânusārī puruṣaḥ kāmān anu vinaśyati;
kāmān vyudasya dhunute yat kiñ cit puruṣo rajaḥ.
tamo '|prakāśo bhūtānāṃ, narako 'yaṃ pradṛśyate,
muhyanta iva dhāvanti gacchantaḥ śvabhravat sukham.

The gods, as one's senses, follow after these people, and so ignorance comes to be called death.

Men who long for the fruit of their acts follow them, go to heaven, and then reap the fruits of their acts, but do not cross beyond death. An embodied man is caught in this cycle because he does not comprehend his oneness with Brahman, and is devoted to pleasures in all respects.
This, indeed, is the source of enormous confusion of the 42.10
senses; for by engaging in false matters, a man's cycle of rebirth becomes eternal. The inner soul, when destroyed by the practice of false goals, remembers only the objects of the senses and is completely enslaved by them.

Longing is the first to kill men, and desire and anger swiftly assist thereafter, bringing these foolish men to death; but the resolute pass beyond death with fortitude. The man who pays no attention to his desires and treats them with indifference would destroy them as they arise, and then the ignorance that is death, becoming Yama, as it were, cannot devour this wise man. Those who know this strike down their desires.

The man who follows his desires is destroyed as he chases his desires. The man who has rid himself of his desires liberates himself from any passion. The dim gloom of desire seems like hell for living creatures, for they become bewildered by it, and they rush to their destruction as though they were drunken men running into potholes in the road.

42.15 a|mūḍha|vṛtteḥ puruṣasy' êha kuryāt
kiṃ vai mṛtyus, tārṇa iv' âsya vyāghraḥ?
a|manyamānaḥ, kṣatriya, kiñ cid anyan
n' âdhīyīta nirṇudann iv' âsya c' āyuḥ.
sa krodha|lobhau mohavān antar'|ātmā*
sa vai mṛtyus tvac|charīre ya eṣaḥ.
evaṃ mṛtyuṃ jāyamānaṃ viditvā
jñāne tiṣṭhan na bibhet' îha mṛtyoḥ.
vinaśyate viṣaye tasya mṛtyur,
mṛtyor yathā viṣayaṃ prāpya martyaḥ.»

DHṚTARĀṢṬRA uvāca:
«yān ev' āhur ijyayā sādhu|lokān,
dvijātīnāṃ puṇyatamān, sanātanān,
teṣāṃ par'|ârthaṃ kathayant' îha Vedā;
etad vidvān n' ôpaiti; kathaṃ nu karma?»

SANATSUJĀTA uvāca:
«evaṃ hy a|vidvān upayāti tatra,
tatr' ârtha|jātaṃ ca vadanti Vedāḥ.
anīha āyāti paraṃ par'|ātmā,
prayāti mārgeṇa nihatya mārgān.»

DHṚTARĀṢṬRA uvāca:
«ko 'sau niyuṅkte tam a|jaṃ purāṇaṃ?
sa ced idaṃ sarvam anukrameṇa,
kiṃ v" âsya kāryam atha vā sukhaṃ ca?
tan me, vidvan, brūhi sarvaṃ yathāvat.»

What could death do to a man whose conduct is not confused by desire in this world? It is like a grass tiger. Warrior, if desire, which is essentially ignorance, is to be destroyed, then no desire should be entertained at all. Your inner soul is confused by anger and greed; this is death inside your body. Knowing that this is how death comes into being, the man who stands in knowledge does not fear death. When the object desired by his senses is destroyed, then so too is his death. A mortal man dies when he reaches the territory of death, just as death itself dies when sensual enjoyments are eliminated." 42.15

DHRITA·RASHTRA said:

"The Vedas say that the highest aim aims at those good and most holy eternal realms which are accessible for the twiceborn through sacrifice; so why should a wise man not practice actions?"

SANAT·SUJÁTA replied:

"The man without wisdom does indeed go where the Vedas say there is happiness and rebirth, but the dispassionate man, becoming the supreme soul, goes beyond those realms and advances by this path, dismissing other paths."

DHRITA·RASHTRA said:

"Who commands the Unborn and Ancient one? If it is that which is everything in succession, then what is its task or happiness? Tell me the whole matter truthfully, wise one."*

SANATSUJĀTA uvāca:

42.20 «doṣo mahān atra vibheda|yoge hy
anādi|yogena bhavanti nityāḥ.
tath" âsya n' ādhikyam apaiti kiñ cid;
anādi|yogena bhavanti puṃsaḥ.
ya etad vā bhagavān sa nityo
vikāra|yogena karoti viśvam,
tathā ca tac chaktir iti sma manyate
tath" ârtha|yoge ca bhavanti Vedāḥ.»

DHṚTARĀṢṬRA uvāca:

«ye 'smin dharmān n' ācarant' îha ke cit,
tathā dharmān ke cid ih' ācaranti;
dharmaḥ pāpena pratihanyate svid,
ut' āho dharmaḥ pratihanti pāpam?»

SANATSUJĀTA uvāca:

ubhayam eva tatr' ôpayujyate
phalaṃ dharmasy' âiv' êtarasya ca.
tasmin sthitau v" âpy ubhayaṃ hi nityaṃ.
jñānena vidvān pratihanti siddham.
tath" ânyathā puṇyam upaiti dehī,
tathā|gataṃ pāpam upaiti siddham.
42.25 gatv" ôbhayaṃ karmaṇā yujyate sthiraṃ,
śubhasya pāpasya sa c' âpi karmaṇā,
dharmeṇa pāpaṃ praṇudat' îha vidvān

SANAT·SUJÁTA replied:

"It is a great error to assume that two essentially separate principles—one of control and one of being controlled—are one and the same. The eternal individual selves* exist in union with beginningless Brahman. This does not diminish the supremacy of the Unborn and Ancient one; men exist in union with that which has no beginning, namely the supreme soul of Brahman.* The supreme Lord is eternal and creates the universe by transformation, which is nothing other that trickery. This is considered to be his power, and the Vedas are the significant authority on this creation of the universe." 42.20

DHRITA·RASHTRA said:

"There are some people in this world who do not practice their moral duties, and then there are those here who do practice them. Is law destroyed by evil, or does law destroy evil?"

SANAT·SUJÁTA replied:

"The fruit of moral law and the other, namely inaction, are both employed in gaining emancipation. Both are permanently established as such in this world. The wise man achieves success with knowledge, namely inaction, but the material-minded man achieves merit in a different manner, namely through action, though he achieves a success
tainted with evil as a result. Having achieved the rewards 42.25
of both virtue and vice, which are transitory, the man of action is once again firmly connected to action by his previous deeds of good and evil, whereas the man of action who

dharmo balīyān, iti tasya siddhiḥ.»

DHṚTARĀṢṬRA uvāca:

«yān ih' āhuḥ svasya dharmasya lokān
dvijātīnāṃ puṇyakṛtāṃ sanātanān,
teṣāṃ kramān kathaya, tato 'pi c' ânyān;
n' âitad, vidvan, vettum icchāmi karma.»

SANATSUJĀTA uvāca:

«yeṣāṃ vrate 'tha vispardhā, bale balavatām iva,
te brāhmaṇā itaḥ pretya Brahma|loka|prakāśakāḥ.
yeṣāṃ dharme ca vispardhā, teṣāṃ taj jñāna|sādhanam.
te brāhmaṇā ito muktāḥ svargaṃ yānti tri|viṣṭapam.
tasya samyak samācāram āhur Veda|vido janāḥ;
n' âinaṃ manyeta bhūyiṣṭhaṃ bāhyam ābhyantaraṃ janam.
42.30 yatra manyeta bhūyiṣṭhaṃ, prāvṛṣ' îva tṛṇ'|ôlapam,
annaṃ pānaṃ brāhmaṇasya, taj jīven n' ânusañjvaret.
yatr' â|kathayamānasya prayacchaty a|śivaṃ bhayam,
atiriktam iv' â|kurvan, sa śreyān, n' êtaro janaḥ.
yo vā kathayamānasya hy ātmānaṃ n' ânusañjvaret,
brahma|svaṃ n' ôpabhuñjīta, tad annaṃ saṃmataṃ satām.

possesses wisdom dispels evil in this world with his virtue. Since virtue is stronger, it is the man of action's success."

DHRITA·RASHTRA said:

"Tell me, in succession, about those eternal worlds they say can be attained through the virtue of piously acting twiceborn men, and then also about others, for I do not want to know about actions, wise one."

SANAT·SUJÁTA replied:

"Those brahmins who rival each other in vows, the way strong men rival each other in strength, illuminate the realm of Brahman once they have passed over to that world. Those brahmins who compete in pious sacrifice and Vedic rites, by which they reach the limit of their wisdom, are released from this world and go to the gods' heaven. People who know the Veda say that practicing the due rites is correct; but one should not hold a man who concerns himself with external matters in too high a regard, even though he does so for the sake of his inner self, rather than for any worldly gains.

A brahmin should live wherever he believes there is an 42.30
abundant supply of suitable food and drink, like water on grass and shrubs in the rainy season, and where he will not be troubled. The man who holds his tongue, refraining from boasting when in the face of hostility and danger, and does not do anything unnecessary, is the better man, and no other. Food which belongs to the man who would not be troubled within himself when before a boastful man, and who does not consume the property of brahmins, is highly regarded among the strict.

yathā svaṃ vāntam aśnāti śvā vai nityam a|bhūtaye,
evaṃ te vāntam aśnanti sva|vīryasy' ôpasevanāt.
‹nityam a|jñāta|caryā me, iti› manyeta brāhmaṇaḥ
jñātīnāṃ tu vasan madhye; taṃ vidur brāhmaṇaṃ budhāḥ.
42.35 ko hy an|antaram ātmānaṃ brāhmaṇo hantum arhati,
nirliṅgam, a|calaṃ, śuddhaṃ, sarva|dvaita|vivarjitam?
tasmādd hi kṣatriyasy' âpi Brahmā vasati paśyati.
yo 'nyathā santam ātmānam anyathā pratipadyate,
kiṃ tena na kṛtaṃ pāpaṃ caureṇ' ātm'|âpahāriṇā?
a|śrāntaḥ syād, an|ādātā, saṃmato, nirupadravaḥ,
śiṣṭo na śiṣṭavat sa syād brāhamaṇo Brahma|vit kaviḥ.
an|āḍhyā mānuṣe vitte,
āḍhyā daive tathā kratau,
te dur|dharṣā duṣ|prakampyās;
tān vidyād Brahmaṇas tanum.
42.40 sarvān sv|iṣṭa|kṛto devān vidyād ya iva kaś cana,
na samāno brāhmaṇasya tasmin prayatate svayam.
yam a|prayatamānaṃ tu mānayanti sa mānitaḥ,
na mānyamāno manyeta, na mānyam abhisañjvaret.

Just as a dog eats whatever it has just retched up and invariably suffers for it, so by worshipping their own prowess, men too devour nothing but their own vomit. Wise men know a brahmin as a true brahmin if, when living among his family, he thinks to himself, 'May my righteous actions
always remain undiscovered.' Indeed, what other brahmin 42.35
deserves to know* the supreme eternal soul which is indefinable, unmoving, pure, and evades all duality?

Therefore, even a kshatriya can see Brahman living within him. On the other hand, if a man understands his soul to be something other than what it really is, what evil does that thief who steals his own self not commit? A brahmin should be unflagging, should not accept gifts, should be respected, free of danger, and should be educated but seem not to be, so that he may become a sage who truly understands Brahman.

Those who are not rich in human wealth, but who are rich in divine opulence and judgment, are inviolable and immovable; one should know them as the embodiment of
Brahman. Whoever knows all the gods and performs proper 42.40
sacrifices to them is not the equal of a brahmin who knows Brahman, nor even is that god for whom the man exerts himself. People respect the man who makes no effort with action, but, though highly respected, he would not consider himself highly respected, nor would he be troubled if he were not respected.

‹lokaḥ sva|bhāva|vṛttir hi nimeṣ'|ônmeṣavat sadā;
vidvāṃso mānayant' îha› iti manyeta mānitaḥ.
a|dharma|nipuṇā mūḍhā loke māyā|viśāradāḥ
na mānyaṃ mānayiṣyanti mānyānām avamāninaḥ.
na vai mānaṃ ca maunaṃ ca sahitau vasataḥ sadā
ayaṃ hi loko mānasya asau maunasya tad viduḥ.
42.45 śrīḥ sukhasy' êha saṃvāsaḥ, sā c' âpi paripanthinī;
brāhmī su|dur|labhā śrīr hi prajñā|hīnena, kṣatriya.
dvārāṇi tasy' êha vadanti santo
bahu|prakārāṇi, durādharāṇi:
saty'|ārjave, hrīr, dama|śauca|vidyā,
yathā na moha|pratibodhanāni.»

DHṚTARĀṢṬRA uvāca:

43.1 «KASY' ÂIṢA maunaḥ, kataran nu maunaṃ?
prabrūhi, vidvann, iha mauna|bhāvam.
maunena vidvān uta yāti maunaṃ?
kathaṃ, mune, maunam ih' ācaranti?»

The respected man would think: 'The world acts according to its own nature, and just as naturally as men always blink, so it is only natural that wise men pay me respect in this world.' Fools skilled in deceit, and with a talent for immorality in this world, do not want to honor a man who should be respected, but instead always treat the man who deserves respect with contempt. Respect and silent asceticism never co-exist. Know that this is a world of admiration, but that the next is a world of silent asceticism.

In this world, good fortune is the abode of happiness 42.45
through admiration, though it is also a hindrance to real bliss; but Brahman's prosperity is extremely difficult to acquire for a man without wisdom, warrior. They say there are many doors that lead to it in this world, but that they are hard to sustain: truth, sincerity, modesty, control, purity, and knowledge, undertaken in such a way so as not to spread confusion."

DHRITA·RASHTRA said:

"WHO POSSESSES silent asceticism, and which of the two 43.1
kinds is right—restraint of speech, or restraint of all the senses? Tell me, wise one, the true reality of silent asceticism in this world. Can a wise man reach true silent asceticism—namely Brahman—through human silent asceticism? How do people practice silent asceticism in this world, sage?"

SANATSUJĀTA uvāca:

«yato na Vedā manasā sah' âinam
anupraviśanti, tato 'tha maunam.
yatr' ôtthito Veda|śabdas tath" âyaṃ,
sa tanmayatvena vibhāti, rājan.»

DHṚTARĀṢṬRA uvāca:

«Ṛco, Yajūṃṣi yo veda, Sāmavedaṃ ca veda yaḥ,
pāpāni kurvan pāpena lipyate, kiṃ na lipyate?»

SANTASUJĀTA uvāca:

«n' âinaṃ Sāmāny, Ṛco v" âpi, na Yajūṃṣy a|vicakṣaṇam
trāyante karmaṇaḥ pāpān. na te mithyā bravīmy aham.
43.5 na cchandāṃsi vṛjināt tārayanti
māyāvinaṃ māyayā vartamānam.
nīḍaṃ śakuntā iva jāta|pakṣāś
chandāṃsy enaṃ prajahaty anta|kāle.»

DHṚTARĀṢṬRA uvāca:

«na ced Vedā vinā dharmaṃ trātuṃ śaktā, vicakṣaṇa,
atha kasmāt pralāpo 'yaṃ brāhmaṇānāṃ sanātanaḥ?»

SANATSUJĀTA uvāca:

«tasy' âiva nām'|ādi|viśeṣa|rūpair
idaṃ jagad bhāti, mah"|ânubhāva.
nirdiśya samyak pravadanti Vedās,
tad viśva|vairūpyam udāharanti.
tad artham uktaṃ tapa etad ijyā,

SANAT·SUJÁTA replied:

"Since memorizing the Vedas does not penetrate Brahman, Brahman is pure silent austerity. Brahman is that about which the words of the Veda are uttered, and Brahman is that which shines through and with the Veda, my king. That from which the Vedic 'Om' and this mundane speech arise is illuminated as the word, my king."

DHRITA·RASHTRA said:

"Does the man who knows the Rig and Yajur Vedas as well as the Sama Veda become tainted with evil when he commits wicked acts, or not?"

SANAT·SUJÁTA replied:

"The Sama, Rig, or Yajur Vedas do not protect the man who has not restrained his senses—and is therefore ignorant—if he commits evil. I am not speaking vainly. Sacred 43.5
hymns do not save the hypocrite who behaves hypocritically from sin. Just as birds leave the nest when their wings have developed, so too sacred hymns desert him in the end."

DHRITA·RASHTRA said:

"If the Vedas are unable to save a man without morality, restrained one, then why do the brahmins always rave that the Vedas can destroy sins?"

SANAT·SUJÁTA replied:

"This universe, which springs from the supreme soul, is illuminated firstly through names, as well as through characteristics and appearances, magnanimous man. The Vedas point to entirely the same conclusion and affirm it, illustrating the difference of the supreme soul, rather than identi-

tābhyām asau puṇyam upaiti vidvān.
puṇyena pāpaṃ vinihatya paścāt
sañjāyate jñāna|vidīpit'|ātmā.
jñānena c' ātmānam upaiti vidvān
ath' ânyathā varga|phal'|ânukāṅkṣī
asmin kṛtaṃ tat parigṛhya sarvam
amutra bhuṅkte punar eti mārgam.
43.10 asmil̃ loke tapas taptaṃ, phalam anyatra bhujyate;
brāhamaṇānām ime lokā dhātve tapasi tiṣṭhatām.»

DHṚTARĀṢṬRA uvāca:
«kathaṃ samṛddham a|samṛddhaṃ
tapo bhavati kevalam?
Sanatsujāta, tad brūhi,
yathā vidyāma tad vayam.»

SANATSUJĀTA uvāca:
«niṣkalmaṣaṃ tapas tv etat kevalaṃ paricakṣate;
etat samṛddham apy ṛddhaṃ tapo bhavati kevalam.
tapo|mūlam idaṃ sarvaṃ, yan māṃ pṛcchasi, kṣatriya,
tapasā Veda|vidvāṃsaḥ paraṃ tv a|mṛtam āpnuyuḥ.»

fying it and the universe as one and the same. It is said that asceticism and sacrifices are performed with this goal of attaining the supreme soul in mind, and it is through these that a wise man achieves merit. Destroying sin with piety, he later gains understanding, and his soul is illuminated with knowledge. The wise man reaches the supreme soul through knowledge, but if he longs for the group of materialistic rewards, clinging to everything he achieved in this world, he reaps the rewards in the next world, but inevitably returns to the same course again, for they are merely transitory. The man who has no control over his soul enjoys 43.10
the rewards of asceticism performed in this world in the next, but for those brahmins who do have control over their souls and who are intent on austerity, even this world yields rewards."

DHRITA·RASHTRA said:

"How is it that the same austerity is either very successful or entirely unsuccessful? Sanat·sujáta, tell me so that I may understand."

SANAT·SUJÁTA replied:

"Asceticism which is entirely sinless is acknowledged to be successful, for it wins emancipation, whereas asceticism which is tainted with sin is thought to be unsuccessful. Everything you ask me, warrior, is at the root of asceticism, for it is through asceticism that wise men understand the Veda, and therefore Brahman, and attain the ultimate immortality."

DHṚTARĀṢṬRA uvāca:

«kalmaṣaṃ tapaso brūhi; śrutaṃ niṣkalmaṣaṃ tapaḥ,
Sanatsujāta, yen' êdaṃ vidyāṃ guhyaṃ sanātanam.»

SANATSUJĀTA uvāca:

43.15 «krodh'|ādayo dvā|daśa yasya doṣās,
tathā nṛśaṃsāni daśa|tri, rājan,
dharm'|ādayo dvādaś' âite pitṝṇāṃ
śāstre guṇā ye viditā dvijānām.
krodhaḥ, kāmo, lobha|mohau, vidhitsā,
kṛp"|âsūye, māna|śokau, spṛhā ca,
īrṣyā, jugupsā ca, manuṣya|doṣā
varjyāḥ sadā dvā|daś' âite narāṇām.
ek' âikaḥ paryupāste ha manuṣyān, manuja'|rṣabha,
lipsamāno 'ntaraṃ teṣāṃ mṛgāṇām iva lubdhakaḥ.
vikatthanaḥ, spṛhayālur, manasvī,
bibhrat kopaṃ, capalo, '|rakṣaṇaś ca,
etān pāpāḥ ṣaṇ narāḥ pāpa|dharmān
prakurvate n' ôta santaḥ su|durge.
saṃbhoga|saṃvid, viṣamo, 'timānī,
datt'|ânutāpī, kṛpaṇo balīyān,
varga|praśaṃsī, vanitāsu dveṣṭā,
ete pare sapta nṛśaṃsa|vargāḥ.
43.20 dharmaś ca, satyaṃ ca, damas, tapaś ca,
a|mātsaryaṃ, hrīs, titikṣ", ân|asūyā,
yajñaś ca, dānaṃ ca, dhṛtiḥ, śrutaṃ ca
vratāni vai dvā|daśa brāhmaṇasya.

DHRITA·RASHTRA said:

"I have heard about sinless asceticism, so tell me about impure asceticism. For through this knowledge I may gain the eternal secret, Sanat·sujáta."

SANAT·SUJÁTA replied:

"The impure asceticism has twelve faults, beginning with 43.15
anger and so on, and thirteen cruelties, my king; and the other, pure asceticism, has the twelve virtues, beginning with moral law and so on, which are known to the twice-born from the texts of their ancestors. Anger, lust, greed, foolishness, selfishness, pity, discontent, pride, grief, envy, jealousy, and disgust are the twelve human sins which men should always avoid. Each and every one surrounds a man, bull-like man, searching for his weaknesses, just as a hunter lurks around deer.

Six men—a boastful man, an envious man, a man who uses his cleverness to humiliate others, a man who nurses his anger, a changeable man, and a man who does not protect those whom he ought—will subvert law and practice wickedness. They are not good now, nor will they be in the far future. The hedonist, the hostile man, the excessively proud man, the man who feels regret after generosity, the miser who taxes his subjects too heavily, the man who praises his own side, and the misogynist are the seven classified as cruel.

Morality, truth, control, austerity, indifference, modesty, 43.20
patience, absence of spite, sacrifice, generosity, resolve, and learning are a brahmin's twelve vows. The man who is amply endowed with these twelve could control this whole

yas tv etebhyaḥ prabhaved dvā|daśabhyaḥ,
 sarvām ap' îmāṃ pṛthivīṃ sa śiṣyāt.
tribhir dvābhyām ekato v" ârthito yas,
 tasya ‹svam ast', îti› sa veditavyaḥ.
damas tyāgo '|pramādaś ca—eteṣv amṛtam āhitam.
tāni satya|mukhāny āhur brāhmaṇā ye manīṣiṇaḥ.

damo hy aṣṭā|daśa|guṇaḥ: pratikūlaṃ kṛt'|âkṛte,
an|ṛtaṃ c', âbhyasūyā ca, kām'|ârthau ca, tathā spṛhā,
krodhaḥ, śokas, tathā tṛṣṇā, lobhaḥ, paiśunyam eva ca,
matsaraś ca, vihiṃsā ca, paritāpas, tath" âratiḥ,
43.25 apasmāraś c', âtivādas, tathā saṃbhāvan" ātmani—
etair vimukto doṣair yaḥ sa dāntaḥ sadbhir ucyate.

mado 'ṣṭā|daśa|doṣaḥ syāt; tyāgo bhavati ṣaḍ|vidhaḥ;
viparyayāḥ smṛtā ete mada|doṣā udāhṛtāḥ.
śreyāṃs tu ṣaḍ|vidhas tyāgas; tṛtīyo duṣkaro bhavet;
tena duḥkhaṃ taraty eva bhinnaṃ tasmin jitaṃ kṛte.
śreyāṃs tu ṣaḍ|vidhas tyāgaḥ; śriyaṃ prāpya na hṛṣyati;
iṣṭa|pūrtaṃ dvitīyaṃ syān nitya|vairāgya|yogataḥ.
kāma|tyāgaś ca, rāj'|êndra, sa tṛtīya iti smṛtaḥ;
apy a|vācyaṃ vadanty etaṃ; sa tṛtīyo guṇaḥ smṛtaḥ,
43.30 tyaktair dravyair yad bhavati, n' ôpayuktaiś ca kāmataḥ,
na ca dravyais tad bhavati, n' ôpayuktaiś ca kāmataḥ.

world. Alternatively a man who is furnished with one, two, or three should be known as someone of divine wealth. Acquiring immortality depends upon these: control, renunciation, and diligence. Wise brahmins say that these are led by the truth.

Self-control is made up of eighteen virtues. But opposition to what is or is not done, deceit, discontent, lust, greed for profit, envy, anger, grief, avidity, greed, back-stabbing,
jealousy, harm, sorrow, dissatisfaction, forgetfulness, talk- 43.25
ing too much, and having a high opinion of oneself are the faults which the strict say a controlled man is free from.

Those were the eighteen faults of pride, but there are six forms of renunciation, the opposite of which are handed down and named as the faults of pride. The six forms of renunciation are best. The third could be difficult, but it is through this one that one overcomes misery. Once this is achieved, even the state of division is overcome. The six forms of renunciation are best: the first is that one should not rejoice when one has good luck; the second is the discipline of constant aversion to accumulating merit; and the third, lord of kings, is handed down as renouncing desire. This virtue of renunciation which is recalled as the third
should only be called a virtue when all objects of enjoyment 43.30
are renounced without being first enjoyed, and should not be referred to as such when the renunciation comes after the objects of desire have been attained, nor when renunciation is adopted only after one is no longer capable of enjoying them.

na ca karmasv a|siddheṣu duḥkhaṃ tena ca na glapet,
sarvair eva guṇair yukto dravyavān api yo bhavet.
a|priye ca samutpanne vyathāṃ jātu na gacchati.
iṣṭān putrāṃś ca dārāṃś ca na yāceta kadā cana.
arhate yācamānāya pradeyaṃ tac chubhaṃ bhavet.
a|pramādī bhaved etaiḥ, sa c' âpy aṣṭa|guṇo bhavet:
satyaṃ, dhyānaṃ, samādhānaṃ,
codyaṃ, vairāgyam eva ca,
a|steyaṃ, brahma|caryaṃ ca,
tath" â|saṃgraham eva ca.
43.35 evaṃ doṣā madasy' ôktās; tān doṣān parivarjayet.
tathā tyāgo '|pramādaś ca, sa c' âpy aṣṭa|guṇo mataḥ.
aṣṭau doṣāḥ pramādasya; tān doṣān parivarjayet
indriyebhyaś ca pañcabhyo, manasaś c' âiva, Bhārata.
atīt'|ân|āgatebhyaś ca mukty|upetaḥ sukhī bhavet.
saty'|ātmā bhava, rāj'|êndra, satye lokāḥ pratiṣṭhitāḥ,
tāṃs tu satya|mukhān āhuḥ; satye hy a|mṛtam āhitam.

One should not feel misery when one's activities fail, nor should one be exhausted by that misery, even if one happens to be endowed with every virtue and wealth. In this way, when something unpleasant occurs one certainly won't feel anguish. One should never ask favors of those one loves, of sons, or of wives. One should give to a deserving suppliant, for it results in good fortune. By these methods one becomes diligent in self-knowledge, and this also has eight virtues: they are truth, meditation, the ability to join arguments, inviting criticism, indifference to worldly pleasures, not stealing, practicing abstinence, and not accepting gifts.

Equally there are the faults associated with pride which 43.35
have been revealed; one should avoid those faults. Just as renunciation and attention to self-knowledge are thought to have eight virtues, so negligence has eight faults associated with it; one should avoid these sins. Bhárata, the man who has reached release from his five senses, from his mind, as well as from what has passed and what has yet to come, will be happy. Be truthful in your soul, lord of kings, for the worlds are established upon truth. They say that men whose chief attribute is truth attain immortality based on truth.

nivṛtten' âiva doṣeṇa tapo|vratam ih' ācaret.
etad dhātṛ|kṛtaṃ vṛttaṃ satyam eva satāṃ vratam.
doṣair etair viyuktas tu guṇair etaiḥ samanvitaḥ;
etat samṛddham atyarthaṃ tapo bhavati kevalam.
43.40 yan māṃ pṛcchasi, rāj'|êndra, saṃkṣepāt prabravīmi te
etat pāpa|haraṃ puṇyaṃ janma|mṛtyu|jar"|âpaham.»

DHṚTARĀṢṬRA uvāca:

«ākhyāna|pañcamair Vedair bhūyiṣṭhaṃ kathyate janaḥ;
tathā c' ânye catur|Vedās, tri|Vedāś ca tath" âpare.
dvi|Vedāś c', âika|Vedāś c' âpy; an|ṛcaś ca tath" âpare.
teṣāṃ tu kataraḥ sa syād, yam ahaṃ veda vai dvijam?»

SANATSUJĀTA uvāca:

«ekasya Vedasy' âjñānād Vedās te bahavaḥ kṛtāḥ;
satyasy' âikasya, rāj'|êndra, satye kaś cid avasthitaḥ.
evaṃ Vedam a|vijñāya ‹prājño 'ham, iti› manyate;
dānam, adhyayanaṃ, yajño lobhād etat pravartate.
43.45 satyāt pracyavamānānāṃ saṅkalpaś ca tathā bhavet,
tato yajñaḥ pratāyeta satyasy' âiv' ādhāraṇāt
manas" ânyasya bhavati, vāc" ânyasy' âtha karmaṇā.
saṅkalpa|siddhaḥ puruṣaḥ saṅkalpān adhitiṣṭhati.
a|naibhṛtyena c' âitasya dīkṣita|vratam ācaret;
nām' âitad dhātu|nirvṛttaṃ satyam eva satāṃ param.

One should practice vows of asceticism in this world while fleeing from sin. It was arranged by the creator that truthful conduct should be the vow of good men. Asceticism which is free of those sins but endowed with those virtues, will turn out entirely prosperous and successful.
You asked me, lord of kings, and I have told you in con- 43.40
densed form about piety which removes evil and keeps rebirth, death, and old age at bay."

DHRITA·RASHTRA said:

"For the most part people are said to hold that there are five Vedas when story is added on; others claim there are four Vedas, others that there are three, others two, and others still that there is only one Veda; and some do not hold with any Veda at all. So which of these should I recognize as a brahmin?"

SANAT·SUJÁTA replied:

"Out of ignorance of the one Veda numerous Vedas have been made from the single truth, lord of kings, but some follow the real truth that is Brahman. Thinking he is wise, in his ignorance of the Veda a man practices generosity, study,
and sacrifice out of his desire for reward. Those who deviate 43.45
from the truth of Brahman have corresponding intentions and so rely on Vedic texts and perform sacrifices. For some this is done with the mind, for some through words, and for others through action. The man who stands by his intentions of attaining Brahman through truth, achieves his intentions. However, one should practice vows of silence, such as the *díkshita* vows, when one's intention cannot be carried out due to one's lack of knowledge of the self. In

jñānaṃ vai nāma pratyakṣaṃ, parokṣaṃ jāyate tapaḥ.
vidyād bahu paṭhantaṃ tu dvijaṃ vai bahu|pāṭhinam.
tasmāt, kṣatriya, mā maṃsthā jalpiten' âiva vai dvijam.
ya eva satyān n' âpaiti, sa jñeyo brāhmaṇas tvayā.

43.50 chandāṃsi nāma, kṣatriya, tāny Atharvā
purā jagau maha"|rṣi|saṅgha eṣaḥ.
chando|vidas te, ya uta n' âdhīta|vedā,
na veda|vedyasya vidur hi tattvam.
chandāṃsi nāma, dvipadāṃ variṣṭha,
svacchanda|yogena bhavanti tatra.
chando|vidas tena ca tān adhītya
gatā na vedasya na vedyam āryāḥ?
na vedānāṃ veditā kaś cid asti,
kaś cit tv etān budhate v" âpi, rājan,
yo veda vedān, na sa veda vedyaṃ;
satye sthito yas tu, sa veda vedyam.

fact the word *díkshita* originates from a root which means 'to vow to religiously observe.' As for good men with knowledge of the self, the truth that is Brahman is their highest goal.

A name reveals the fruits of knowledge, and asceticism gives birth to secret fruits. One should know a brahmin who merely reads a great deal as merely well-read. Therefore, warrior, don't consider someone a true brahmin on account of his prattling. Rather, you should only acknowledge him as a true brahmin if he does not deviate from the truth.

Warrior, long ago Athárvan recited the things we call 43.50
hymns at a gathering of great sages. Those who understand the hymns are not only men who study the Veda, for these may not grasp the truth that is Brahman within the Veda. Best of men, the hymns are men's means of finding Brahman through independent effort. Those who merely grasp the sacrifices in the Vedas cannot be considered men who understand the hymns. But haven't the noble men who have gone to those who do understand the Vedas, attained the object knowable through the Vedas? No one understands the Vedas, or perhaps there is someone who understands them, king, but the man who just knows the Vedas does not understand what should be understood, and does not comprehend the reality that is contained within them. However, the man who relies on truth understands the truth within, that is, Brahman.

na vedānāṃ veditā kaś cid asti;
vedyena vedaṃ na vidur na vedyam.
yo veda vedaṃ, sa ca veda vedyaṃ;
yo veda vedyaṃ, na sa veda satyam.
yo veda vedān, sa ca veda vedyaṃ;
na taṃ vidur veda|vido na vedāḥ;
tatha 'pi vede na vidanti vedam
ye brāhmaṇā veda|vido bhavanti.
43.55 dhām'|âṃśa|bhāgasya tathā hi vedā,
yathā ca śākhā hi mahī|ruhasya,
saṃvedane c' âiva yath" āmananti,
tasmin hi satye param'|ātmano 'rthe.

abhijānāmi brāhmaṇaṃ vyākhyātāraṃ vicakṣaṇam,
yaś chinna|vicikitsaḥ sa vyācaṣṭe sarva|saṃśayān.
n' âsya paryeṣaṇaṃ gacchet prācīnaṃ, n' ôta dakṣiṇam,
n' ârvācīnaṃ, kutas tiryaṅ, n' â|diśaṃ tu kathañ cana;
tasya paryeṣaṇaṃ gacchet pratyarthiṣu kathañ cana;
a|vicinvann imaṃ vede tapaḥ paśyati taṃ prabhum.
tūṣṇīṃ|bhūta, upāsīta, na ceṣṭen manas" âpi ca,
upāvartasva tad Brahma antar'|ātmani viśrutam.

There is no way one can gain true knowledge except through the means of knowing one's self. But one cannot know the self and what is not the self by means of the mind. The man who does understand the self also understands what is not the self—the truth is contained within it, but the man who merely knows what is not the self does not understand the truth. The man who knows the proofs also knows what is to be proven, but neither the Vedas themselves nor those who have learned them could truly understand the truth of what the thing to be proven really is. Despite this, the brahmins who don't understand the truth of the Veda within the Veda, do gain some knowledge of the
hidden Brahman through the Veda. Just as tree branches are 43.55
used as tools to locate the position of a star,* so in this goal of truth the Vedas are used to indicate the highest aspect of the supreme soul.

The person I recognize as a true brahmin is the self-controlled man whose own doubts have vanished and who dispels all others' doubts with his explanation. One will not come across what one's soul is searching for in the east, south, west, this way, horizontally, nor by going in no direction at all. Something of what he is looking for may occasionally come to he who regards this body as the self. Only the ascetic who is beyond even the comprehension in the Veda can see the supreme soul. Be silent, concentrate. One should not move even in one's mind, but turn to Brahman who is known to abide in your inner soul.

43.60 maunān na sa munir bhavati, n' âraṇya|vasanān muniḥ;
sva|lakṣaṇaṃ tu yo veda, sa muniḥ śreṣṭha ucyate.
sarv'|ârthānāṃ vyākaraṇād vaiyākaraṇa ucyate;
tan mūlato vyākaraṇaṃ vyākarot' îti tat tathā.
pratyakṣa|darśī lokānāṃ sarva|darśī bhaven naraḥ;
satye vai brāhmaṇas tiṣṭhaṃs tad|vidvān sarva|vid bhavet.
dharm'|ādiṣu sthito 'py evaṃ, kṣatriya, Brahma paśyati,
vedānāṃ c' ânupūrvyeṇa. etad buddhyā bravīmi te.»

DHṚTARĀṢṬRA uvāca:

44.1 «SANATSUJĀTA, YĀM imāṃ parāṃ tvaṃ
brāhmīṃ vācaṃ vadase viśva|rūpām,
parāṃ hi kāmena su|durlabhāṃ kathāṃ,
prabrūhi me vākyam idaṃ, kumāra.»

SANATSUJĀTA uvāca:

«n' âitad Brahma tvaramāṇena labhyaṃ,
yan māṃ pṛcchann atihṛṣyasy atīva.
buddhau vilīne manasi pracintyā
vidyā hi sā brahma|caryeṇa labhyā.»

DHṚTARĀṢṬRA uvāca:

«atyanta|vidyām iti yat sanātanīṃ
bravīṣi tvaṃ brahma|caryeṇa siddhām.
an|ārabhyāṃ vasat' îha kārya|kāle
kathaṃ Brāhmaṇyam amṛtatvaṃ labheta?»

A man does not become a sage from mere silence, nor from living in the woods; the sage is said to be one who knows the true definition of himself and so is the greatest of all. A grammarian is said to be a man who deciphers analysis from roots because of his grammatical analysis of all meanings. The man who sees the different worlds clearly, sees everything. The brahmin is the one who relies upon truth, understands Brahman, and so knows everything. Even a warrior will see Brahman if he is intent on moral virtue and so on as indicated in the Veda. I tell you this with certainty." 43.60

DHRITA·RASHTRA said:

"SANAT·SUJÁTA, THIS speech you are giving about Brahman and the forms that lead to Brahman is excellent, so give me rare instruction which transcends desire, young man." 44.1

SANAT·SUJÁTA replied:

"This Brahman, which you ask me about with such excessive excitement, cannot be attained by a man who rushes. This knowledge must be considered in a mind of unified will, which is focused on the self, not worldly objects, and it must be attained through the practice of Brahman."

DHRITA·RASHTRA said:

"You say that the eternal knowledge of Brahman is perpetual and is achieved through the practice of Brahman. No effort need be undertaken in terms of physical tasks when it is sought, for it exists here in the mind. So how can one gain Brahman's immortality?"

SANATSUJĀTA uvāca:

«a|vyakta|vidyām abhidhāsye purāṇīṃ;
buddhyā ca teṣāṃ brahma|caryeṇa siddhām.
yāṃ prāpy' âinaṃ martya|lokaṃ tyajanti,
yā vai vidyā guru|vṛddheṣu nityā.»

DHṚTARĀṢṬRA uvāca:

44.5 «brahma|caryeṇa yā vidyā
śakyā veditum añjasā,
tat kathaṃ brahma|caryaṃ syād?
etad, brahman, bravīhi me.»

SANATSUJĀTA uvāca:

«ācārya|yonim iha ye praviśya
bhūtvā garbhe brahma|caryaṃ caranti.
ih' âiva te śāstra|kārā bhavanti,
prahāya dehaṃ paramaṃ yānti yogam.
asmiṁl loke vai jayant' îha kāmān
brāhmīṃ sthitiṃ hy anutitikṣamāṇāḥ
ta ātmānaṃ nirharant' îha dehān,
muñjād iṣīkām iva sattva|saṃsthāḥ.
śarīram etau kurutaḥ pitā mātā ca, Bhārata,
ācārya|śāstā yā jātiḥ, sā puṇyā, s" â|jar'|â|marā.
yaḥ prāvṛṇoty a|vitathena varṇān,
ṛtaṃ kurvann, amṛtaṃ saṃprayacchan,
taṃ manyeta pitaraṃ mātaraṃ ca;
tasmai na druhyet kṛtam asya jānan.
44.10 guruṃ śiṣyo nityam abhivādayīta,
sv'|âdhyāyam icchec chucir a|pramattaḥ;

SANAT·SUJÁTA replied:

"The ancient knowledge is, as you say, imperceptible, though it resides within people's minds; but it is realized through their intelligence and the practice of Brahman. Once they attain it, men abandon the world of the dead. This knowledge always abides in venerable teachers."

DHRITA·RASHTRA said:

"Tell me what the practice of Brahman entails, brah- 44.5
min, through which knowledge of Brahman can quickly be known."

SANAT·SUJÁTA replied:

"Men who enter their teachers' wombs, as it were, by entering into their homes as students, and who practice Brahman while existing like a fetus, become the physical manifestations of scripture, and abandoning their bodies they go to union with the supreme soul. Those men in this world who are endowed with goodness, who overcome their desires, patiently enduring for the sake of the state of Brahman, extract their soul from their body as though it were a reed from the rushes. The body is made by one's father and mother, Bhárata, but the birth which springs from one's teacher's commands is holy, without old age, and immortal.

One should think of the man who cloaks all castes with truth, behaves properly, and bestows immortality, as one's father and mother, and bearing in mind what he has
achieved, one should do him no harm. A pupil should al- 44.10
ways greet his teacher honorably, be intent on his own study, and remain pure and attentive; he should not behave with

mānaṃ na kuryān, n' ādadhīta roṣam.
eṣa prathamo brahma|caryasya pādaḥ.
śiṣya|vṛtti|kramen' âiva vidyām āpnoti yaḥ śuciḥ,
brahma|carya|vratasy' âsya prathamaḥ pāda ucyate.
ācāryasya priyaṃ kuryāt prāṇair api, dhanair api,
karmaṇā, manasā, vācā: dvitīyaḥ pāda ucyate.
samā gurau yathā vṛttir, guru|patnyāṃ tath" ācaret,
tat|putre ca tathā kurvan: dvitīyaḥ pāda ucyate.
ācāryeṇ' ātma|kṛtaṃ vijānan,
jñātvā c' ârthaṃ, ‹bhavito 'sm' îty anena,›
yan manyate taṃ prati hṛṣṭa|buddhiḥ,
sa vai tṛtīyo brahma|caryasya pādaḥ.
44.15 n' ācāryasy' ân|apākṛtya pravāsaṃ
prājñaḥ kurvīta, n' âitad ‹ahaṃ karomi,›
it' îva manyeta, na bhāṣayeta;
sa vai caturtho brahma|caryasya pādaḥ.
kālena pādaṃ labhate tath" ârthaṃ,
tataś ca pādaṃ guru|yogataś ca;
utsāha|yogena ca pādam ṛcchec;
chāstreṇa pādaṃ ca tato 'bhiyāti.
dharm'|ādayo dvā|daśa yasya rūpam,
anyāni c' âṅgāni, tathā balaṃ ca,
ācārya|yoge phalat', îti c' āhur,
brahm'|ârtha|yogena ca brahma|caryam.
evaṃ pravṛtto yad upālabheta vai
dhanam, ācāryāya tad anuprayacchet.
satāṃ vṛttiṃ bahu|guṇām evam eti;
guroḥ putre bhavati ca vṛttir eṣā.

arrogance, nor turn to anger. This is the first pillar of practicing Brahman. A pure man attains knowledge of Brahman by keeping to the course of a pupil's conduct: this is said to be the first pillar of the vow of practicing Brahman.

With action, mind, and speech, he should do whatever his teacher wishes, using even his life and wealth: this is said to be the second pillar. He should employ the same conduct towards his teacher's wife and son as he does towards his teacher: this is said to be the second pillar.

Bearing in mind everything his teacher has done for him, as well as understanding his purpose in doing it, he should think, 'He made me what I am,' with a joyful mind: this is
the third pillar of practicing Brahman. He should not fail to 44.15
repay his teacher for the time he has spent abroad with him, and a wise man should not say, 'I am doing this as a gift,' or even think it: this is the fourth pillar of practicing Brahman. He obtains the first pillar of his goal of knowledge of Brahman with time, the second is achieved through the discipline of the teacher, the third he gains by the use of perseverence, and he reaches the last pillar through scripture.

They say that practice of Brahman is achieved by effort towards the goal of Brahman, and is made of twelve virtues beginning with moral law and so on; that the yoga actions are the limbs and yoga meditation is the strength; and that it bears fruit in the teacher's discipline. Whatever wealth he earns in this life he should offer to his teacher, for this livelihood multiplies for good men. This is the conduct he should adopt towards his teacher's son as well. Living in this manner, he prospers in every sense in this world, for he has numerous sons and firm success; every region and corner

evaṃ vasan sarvato vardhat' îha,
bahūn putrān labhate ca pratiṣṭhām;
varṣanti c' âsmai pradiśo diśaś ca;
vasanty asmin brahma|carye janāś ca.

44.20 etena brahma|caryeṇa devā devatvam āpnuvan,
ṛṣayaś ca mahā|bhāgā brahma|lokaṃ manīṣiṇaḥ.
gandharvāṇām anen' âiva rūpam apsarasām abhūt,
etena brahma|caryeṇa sūryo 'py ahnāya jāyate.
ākāṅkṣy'|ârthasya saṃyogād rasa|bhed'|ârthinām iva
evaṃ hy ete samājñāya tādṛg bhāvaṃ gatā ime.
ya āśrayet pāvayec c' âpi, rājan,
sarvaṃ śarīraṃ tapasā tapyamānaḥ,
etena vai bālyam atyeti vidvān,
mṛtyuṃ tathā sa jayaty anta|kāle.
antavantaḥ, kṣatriya, te jayanti
lokān janāḥ karmaṇā nirmalena.
Brahm' âiva vidvāṃs tena c' âbhyeti sarvam;
n' ânyaḥ panthā ayanāya vidyate.»

DHṚTARĀṢṬRA uvāca:

44.25 «ābhāti śuklam iva, lohitam iv' âtho,
kṛṣṇam, ath' āñjanaṃ, kādravaṃ vā?
sad Brahmaṇaḥ paśyati yo 'tra vidvān,
kathaṃ rūpaṃ tad a|mṛtam a|kṣaraṃ padam?»

of the world rain down wealth upon him, and people live with him to join him in the practice of Brahman.

It was by means of this performance of Brahman that the gods attained their divinity, and that wise and illustrious sages attained the world of Brahman. It was through this method that the *gandhárvas*' and *ápsaras*es' beauty came about, and through this performance of Brahman that even the sun took birth and began his daily course. Just as men searching for the philosopher's stone are filled with delight when they have reached the desired result after their efforts, so these celestial creatures I have just mentioned find similar joy in perceiving their desired results. 44.20

The man who lies down and purges his whole body, king, being consumed by his austerity, will indeed abandon foolishness by this method and become wise, and finally he will conquer death. Warrior, men conquer only limited worlds by means of their virtuous acts, but wise men reach the entire Brahman by the method I have explained; no other path to this course exists."*

DHRITA·RASHRA said:

"Does Brahman appear to be white, red, black, dark, or russet?* What appearance and mark of that immortal and unalterable Brahman does a wise brahmin see?" 44.25

SANATSUJĀTA uvāca:

«n' ābhāti* śuklam iva, lohitam iv' âtho,
kṛṣṇam, āyasam, arka|varṇam.
na pṛthivyāṃ tiṣṭhati, n' ântarikṣe,
n' âitat samudre salilaṃ bibharti.
na tārakāsu, na ca vidyud|āśritaṃ,
na c' âbhreṣu dṛśyate rūpam asya;
na c' âpi vāyau, na ca devatāsu,
n' âitac candre dṛśyate, n' ôta sūrye.
n' âiva' ṛkṣu tan, na yajuḥṣu, n' âpy atharvasu,
na dṛśyate vai vimaleṣu sāmasu,
Rathantare Bārhadrathe v" âpi, rājan,
Mahāvrate n' âiva dṛśyed dhruvaṃ tat.
a|pāraṇīyaṃ, tamasaḥ parastāt,
tad antako 'py eti vināśa|kāle;
aṇīyo rūpaṃ, kṣura|dhārayā samaṃ,
mahac ca rūpaṃ tad vai parvatebhyaḥ.
44.30 sā pratiṣṭhā, tad amṛtaṃ, lokās, tad Brahma, tad yaśaḥ;
bhūtāni jajñire tasmāt, pralayaṃ yānti tatra hi.
an|āmayaṃ tan mahad udyataṃ yaśo;
vāco vikāraṃ kavayo vadanti.
yasmin jagat sarvam idaṃ pratiṣṭhitaṃ
ye tad vidur, a|mṛtās te bhavanti.»

SANATSUJĀTA uvāca:

45.1 «ŚOKAḤ, KRODHAŚ CA, lobhaś ca, kāmo, mānaḥ, parāsutā,
īrṣyā, moho, vidhitsā ca, kṛp", âsūyā, jugupsutā,
dvā|daś' âite mahā|doṣā manuṣya|prāṇa|nāśanāḥ.
ek' âikam ete, rāj'|êndra, manuṣyān paryupāsate.
yair āviṣṭo naraḥ pāpaṃ mūḍha|saṃjño vyavasyati.

SANAT·SUJÁTA replied:

"Brahman does not appear as though it were white, red, black, iron-hued, or the color of the sun. Nothing to match it exists on earth or in the heavens, nor is its match to be found within the waves of the sea. It does not exist within the stars, it does not reside within lightning, nor can its beauty be seen in clouds; it is not revealed within the wind, nor within the gods, nor the moon or sun. It is not revealed in hymns, nor in prayers, nor in spells or pure chants,* nor even in Rathántara or Barhad·ratha chants, king, and one would certainly not perceive it by means of the Maha·vrata chant.

Impassable and beyond darkness—even death is subsumed within it at the time of destruction. Its form is keener than a razor's edge, and yet at the same time as vast as mountains. It is the basis, the immortal, the worlds, the Brahman, 44.30
and the glory; creatures take birth from it and so reach their dissolution within it. Huge, it defies defects and is elevated glory. Sages claim that the only example of its transformation is the speech used to describe it. This whole universe is established within it, and those who come to understand it become immortal."

SANAT·SUJÁTA continued:

"GRIEF, ANGER, GREED, lust, arrogance, excessive sloth, 45.1
envy, idiocy, self-interest, pity, displeasure, and abhorrence are the twelve major sins which destroy human life. Each and every one, lord of kings, surrounds men. When a man is burdened with them he decides upon evil with idiotic reasoning.

spṛhayālur, ugraḥ puruṣo, vā vadānyaḥ,
krodhaṃ bibhran, manasā vai vikatthī,
nṛśaṃsa|dharmāḥ ṣaḍ ime janā vai
prāpy' âpy arthaṃ n' ôta sabhājayante.
saṃbhoga|saṃvid, viṣamo, 'timānī,
dattvā vikatthī, kṛpaṇo, dur|balaś ca,
bahu|praśaṃsī, vanitā|dviṭ sad" âiva,
sapt' âiv' ôktāḥ pāpa|śīlā nṛśaṃsāḥ.*
45.5 dharmaś ca, satyaṃ ca, tapo, damaś ca,
a|mātsaryaṃ, hrīs, titikṣ", ân|asūyā,
dānaṃ, śrutaṃ c' âiva, dhṛtiḥ, kṣamā ca,
mahā|vratā dvā|daśa brāhmaṇasya.
yo n' âitebhyaḥ pracyaved dvā|daśabhyaḥ,
sarvām ap' îmāṃ pṛthivīṃ sa śiṣyāt;
tribhir, dvābhyām, ekato v" ârthito yo,
n' âsya svam ast', îti ca veditavyam.*
damas, tyāgo, 'th' â|pramāda, ity eteṣv amṛtaṃ sthitam;
etāni Brahma|mukhyānāṃ brāhmaṇānāṃ manīṣiṇām.
sad v" â|sad vā parīvādo brāhmaṇasya na śasyate;
te vai syur naraka|prasthā,* ya evaṃ kurvate janāḥ.
mado 'ṣṭā|daśa|doṣaḥ sa syāt purā yo 'prakīrtitaḥ:
loka|dveṣyaṃ, prātikūlyam, abhyasūyā, mṛṣā vacaḥ,
45.10 kāma|krodhau, pāratantryaṃ, parivādo, 'tha paiśunam,
artha|hānir, vivādaś ca, mātsaryaṃ, prāṇi|pīḍanam,
īrṣyā, modo, 'tivādaś ca, saṃjñā|nāśo, 'bhyasūyitā;
tasmāt prājño na mādyeta, sadā hy etad vigarhitam.

The man who is greedy, who is fierce, and who is slanderous, the man who nurses anger, the man who bears grudges, and the man who boasts comprise the six men of cruel practices who do not honor others when they come into money. The hedonist, the hostile man, the excessively arrogant man, the man who boasts when generous, the wretchedly weak man, the man who praises himself too much, and the constant misogynist are said to be the seven types of cruel men of sinful conduct.

A sense of morality, truth, austerity, control, indifference 45.5
to desire, modesty, patience, freedom from spite, generosity, learning, resolve, and forgiveness are the twelve great vows of a brahmin. The man who does not deviate from these twelve could even govern this whole world. The man who possesses three, two, or even one of these would never believe that any property is his alone.

Control, renunciation, and attention are thought to be the bases upon which immortality is established; these are the virtues of wise brahmins who are focused primarily on Brahman. Right or wrong, it is not approved of for a brahmin to speak badly of others. Men who do this have a home in hell.

There are eighteen sins associated with pride which have not yet been mentioned: hatred of the world, unpleasant-
ness, envy, deceitful speech, lust, anger, dependence on oth- 45.10
ers, slander, back-stabbing, loss of wealth, quarreling, jealousy, cruelty to animals, spite, conceited joy, abusive language, breaking treaties, and indignant anger. Therefore a wise man should not be proud, for it is always forbidden.

sauhṛde vai ṣaḍ guṇā veditavyāḥ.

priye hṛṣyanty, a|priye ca vyathante;

syād ātmanaḥ su|ciraṃ yācate yo

dadāty a|yācyam api deyaṃ khalu syāt,

iṣṭān putrān, vibhavān, svāṃś ca dārān

abhyarthitaś c' ârhati śuddha|bhāvaḥ

tyakta|dravyaḥ saṃvasen n' êha kāmād:

bhuṅkte karma sv'|āśiṣaṃ bādhate ca.

dravyavān guṇavān evaṃ tyāgī bhavati sāttvikaḥ.

pañca bhūtāni pañcabhyo nivartayati tādṛśaḥ.

45.15 etat samṛddham apy ūrdhvaṃ tapo bhavati kevalam;

sattvāt pracyavamānānāṃ saṅkalpena samāhitam.

yato yajñāḥ pravardhante satyasy' âiv' âvarodhanāt,

manas" ânyasya bhavati, vāc" ânyasy', âtha karmaṇā.

saṅkalpa|siddhaṃ puruṣam a|saṅkalpo 'dhitiṣṭhati,

brāhmaṇasya viśeṣeṇa. kiñ c' ânyad api me śṛṇu.

adhyāpayen mahad etad yaśasyaṃ:

vāco vikārāḥ kavayo vadanti.

asmin yoge sarvam idaṃ pratiṣṭhitaṃ;

ye tad vidur a|mṛtās te bhavanti.

There are known to be six virtues to friendship. Friends take joy in one another's affection, and they become miserable in hostility. When someone asks for something which has been dear to his heart for a very long time, then a friend would definitely grant it, even if it is something which strictly speaking one shouldn't ask for. When asked, a pure-natured friend ought to give even his dear sons, his wealth, and his own wives. But someone who's given away his estate shouldn't go to live with an old friend because he fancies it; he should restrain his longings and reap the benefit of his own deed.

The rich and virtuous man becomes pure by being a renouncer. Such a man restrains his five existing senses from
their five objects. When this restraint flourishes properly, it 45.15
becomes pure asceticism and can win bliss, whereas knowledge can lead to success even here; but those who have deviated, and so cannot attain knowledge, acquire this asceticism because of their resolve to attain bliss hereafter in heaven. By procuring the truth from which sacrifices increase, one man can sacrifice with his mind, another with his words, and yet another with his actions. The truth that is Brahman exists within the man who knows Brahman with characteristics, yet more so in the man who knows Brahman free of characteristics. Listen to something else I have to say as well.

One should teach this great and glorious knowledge: sages claim its only variations are the words used to describe it. Everything is established upon this discipline, and those who understand it become immortal. A man cannot

na karmaṇā su|kṛten' âiva, rājan,
satyaṃ jayej, juhuyād vā, yajed vā
n' âitena bālo '|mṛtyum abhyeti, rājan,
ratiṃ c' âsau na labhaty anta|kāle.
45.20 tūṣṇīm eka upāsīta, ceṣṭeta manas" âpi na;
tathā saṃstuti|nindābhyāṃ prīti|roṣau vivarjayet.
atr' âiva tiṣṭhan, kṣatriya, Brahm" āviśati paśyati,
vedeṣu c' ânupūrvyeṇa; etad, vidvan, bravīmi te.»

SANATSUJĀTA uvāca:

46.1 «YAT TAC CHUKRAM mahaj jyotir,
dīpyamānaṃ mahad yaśaḥ,
tad vai devā upāsate;
tasmāt sūryo virājate;
yoginas taṃ prapaśyanti bhagavantaṃ sanātanam.
śukrād Brahma prabhavati, Brahma śukreṇa vardhate;
tac chukraṃ jyotiṣāṃ madhye '|taptaṃ tapati tāpanam;
yoginas taṃ prapaśyanti bhagavantaṃ sanātanam.
āpo 'tha adbhyaḥ salilasya madhye,
ubhau devau śiśrayāte 'ntarikṣe,
a|tandritaḥ savitur vivasvān
ubhau bibharti pṛthivīṃ divaṃ ca;
yoginas taṃ prapaśyanti bhagavantaṃ sanātanam.
ubhau ca devau, pṛthivīṃ divaṃ ca,
diśaḥ śukro, bhuvanaṃ bibharti.
tasmād diśaḥ saritaś ca sravanti;
tasmāt samudrā vihitā mahāntāḥ;
yoginas taṃ prapaśyanti bhagavantaṃ sanātanam.
46.5 cakre rathasya tiṣṭhanto, dhruvasy' âvyaya|karmaṇaḥ,
ketumantaṃ vahanty aśvās taṃ divyam a|jaraṃ divi;
yoginas taṃ prapaśyanti bhagavantaṃ sanātanam.

win the truth of Brahman through actions, king, no matter how well-performed, or by pouring oblations or sacrificing; a fool will not attain immortality by these means, king, nor will he gain happiness in the end. One should sit 45.20
alone in silence, remaining motionless even in one's mind, and avoid delight and rage at praise and blame respectively. Remaining this way, warrior, a man enters and sees Brahman as indicated within the Veda. Learned man, this is the esoteric teaching I give you."

SANAT·SUJÁTA continued:

"THE YOGINS SEE the eternal blessed Lord; that bright 46.1
great seed of pure knowledge, the great blazing glory which the gods revere and from which the sun shines. The yogins see the eternal blessed Lord; the seed of joy's self from which Brahman is revealed, the seed with which Brahman grows, the seed inside luminous bodies which makes cold matter burn with splendor.

Water from water in the midst of the sea, both of the deities that recline in the sky, the rouser's untiring sun supports both earth and sky; the yogins see this eternal and blessed Lord. The seed supports both gods, the earth and the sky, and the regions of space, and the universe. From the seed the directions and rivers flow and the vast oceans are formed; the yogins see this eternal and blessed Lord.

The yogins see the eternal and blessed Lord of unchang- 46.5
ing acts, bright, divine, and ageless in the sky, to whom the man of wisdom is drawn, led by the horses of the senses through the region of consciousness, tied to the chariot

na sādṛśye tiṣṭhati rūpam asya,
na cakṣuṣā paśyati kaś cid enam,
manīṣay" âtho manasā hṛdā ca;
ya enaṃ vidur a|mṛtās te bhavanti;
yoginas taṃ prapaśyanti bhagavantaṃ sanātanam.
dvā|daśa|pūgāṃ saritaṃ pibanto deva|rakṣitām
madhv īkṣantaś ca te tasyāḥ sañcarant' îha ghorām;
yoginas taṃ prapaśyanti bhagavantaṃ sanātanam.
tad ardha|māsaṃ pibati sañcitya bhramaro madhu;
īśānaḥ sarva|bhūteṣu havir bhūtam akalpayat;
yoginas taṃ prapaśyanti bhagavantaṃ sanātanam.
hiraṇya|parṇam aśvattham abhipadya hy a|pakṣakāḥ,
te tatra pakṣiṇo bhūtvā prapatanti yathā|diśam;
yoginas taṃ prapaśyanti bhagavantaṃ sanātanam.
46.10 pūrṇāt pūrṇāny uddharanti, pūrṇāt pūrṇāni cakrire,
haranti pūrṇāt pūrṇāni, pūrṇam ev' âvaśiṣyate;
yoginas taṃ prapaśyanti bhagavantaṃ sanātanam.
tasmād vai vāyur āyātas, tasmiṃś ca prayataḥ sadā,
tasmād agniś ca somaś ca, tasmiṃś ca prāṇa ātataḥ,
sarvam eva tato vidyāt; tat tad vaktuṃ na śaknumaḥ;
yoginas taṃ prapaśyanti bhagavantaṃ sanātanam.
apānaṃ girati prāṇaḥ, prāṇaṃ girati candramāḥ,
ādityo girate candram, ādityaṃ girate paraḥ;
yoginas taṃ prapaśyanti bhagavantaṃ sanātanam.
ekaṃ pādaṃ n' ôtkṣipati salilādd haṃsa uccaran;

wheels which represent the acts of past lives, while the car is the body, doomed to destruction. No match for his beauty exists, no one can behold him with the naked eye, but those who come to know him through intelligence, the mind, and the heart become immortal; the yogins see this eternal and blessed Lord.

Men drink from the terrifying twelve-part river,* which is guarded by the gods and flows from that seed, and seeing charm within it they roam along it; the yogins see the eternal and blessed Lord. The bee drinks the fortnightly honey it has accumulated;* the master, who permeates the entire universe, has arranged for it to be a fit oblation for all creatures; the yogins see the eternal and blessed Lord.

Birds without wings come to the golden-leafed fig tree, but they fly in whichever direction they please when they have developed their wings;* the yogins see the eternal and
blessed Lord. They raise the full universe from the fullness 46.10
that is Brahman, and make the full from the fullness that is Brahman; they take the full from the fullness that is Brahman, and yet what remains is full; the yogins see the eternal and blessed Lord.

The wind takes its source from it, and eternally ends in it. Fire and *soma* develop from it, and life is drawn out within it. Everything is known through it, but we are unable to define it; the yogins see the eternal and blessed Lord.

Breath swallows *apána*, the downward-flowing vital air, and the moon swallows breath. The sun swallows the moon, and the ultimate body swallows the sun; the yogins see the eternal and blessed Lord. The swan does not raise one foot

taṃ cet santatam ūrdhvāya na mṛtyur n' âmṛtaṃ bhavet;
yoginas taṃ prapaśyanti bhagavantaṃ sanātanam.

46.15 aṅguṣṭha|mātraḥ puruṣo 'ntar'|ātmā
liṅgasya yogena sa yāti nityam;
tam īśam īḍyam anukalpam ādyaṃ
paśyanti mūḍhā na virājamānam;
yoginas taṃ prapaśyanti bhagavantaṃ sanātanam.
a|sādhanā v" âpi sa|sādhanā vā,
samānam etad dṛśyate mānuṣeṣu;
samānam etad amṛtasy' êtarasya
muktās tatra madhva utsaṃ samāpuḥ;
yoginas taṃ prapaśyanti bhagavantaṃ sanātanam.
ubhau lokau vidyayā vyāpya yāti
tadā hutaṃ c' â|hutam agni|hotram.
mā te brāhmī laghutām ādadhīta,
prajñānaṃ syān nāma dhīrā labhante;
yoginas taṃ prapaśyanti bhagavantaṃ sanātanam.
evaṃ rūpo mah"|ātmā sa pāvakaṃ puruṣo giran,
yo vai taṃ puruṣaṃ veda, tasy' êh' ârtho na riṣyate;
yoginas taṃ prapaśyanti bhagavantaṃ sanātanam.

when it rises up—as the four-footed supreme soul comprised of waking, dreaming, deep sleep, and *turíya*—out of the waters of the ocean of worldly matters, for if it did then it would incessantly continue to the heights, and there would be neither death nor immortality; the yogins see the eternal and blessed Lord.

A man's inner soul, measuring a mere thumb's width, 46.15
moves about constantly through contact with characteristic things such as the vital airs, the will, the intellect, and the ten senses. Fools do not see the governing lord who is worthy of praise, omnipotent, and the cause of all things; the yogins see the eternal and blessed Lord. There are those who have mastered themselves and those who have not, but the eternal soul is equally visible in all men. However, equally manifest though the eternal soul may be in he who has won immortality and he who has not, only those who have freed themselves attain the fountain of honey wine; the yogins see the eternal blessed Lord.

Once one has reached the stage of pervading both worlds through knowledge, the world of the soul and its opposite, then oblations to the fire can either be performed or not, as one wishes. Don't make yourself trivial, holy man, for it is men of constancy who obtain him whose name is wisdom; the yogins see the eternal and blessed Lord. This person of high-spirited form swallows fire, and the man who knows this person will not fail in his aims in this world; the yogins see the eternal and blessed Lord.

yaḥ sahasraṃ sahasrāṇāṃ pakṣān santatya saṃpatet,
madhyame madhya āgacched, api cet syān mano|javaḥ;
yoginas taṃ prapaśyanti bhagavantaṃ sanātanam.

46.20 na darśane tiṣṭhati rūpam asya,
paśyanti c' âinaṃ su|viśuddha|sattvāḥ.
hito manīṣī manasā na tapyate;
ye pravrajeyur, a|mṛtās te bhavanti;
yoginas taṃ prapaśyanti bhagavantaṃ sanātanam.
guhanti sarpā iva gahvarāṇi
sva|śikṣayā svena vṛttena martyāḥ;
teṣu pramuhyanti janā vimūḍhā,
yath" âdhvānaṃ mohayante bhayāya;
yoginas taṃ prapaśyanti bhagavantaṃ sanātanam.
‹n' âhaṃ sad" â|sat|kṛtaḥ syāṃ na mṛtyur
na c' â|mṛtyur a|mṛtaṃ me kutaḥ syāt?›
saty'|ânṛte satya|samāna|bandhe
sataś ca yonir a|sataś c' âika eva;
yoginas taṃ prapaśyanti bhagavantaṃ sanātanam.
na sādhunā n' ôta a|sādhunā v" â|
samānam etad dṛśyate mānuṣeṣu;
samānam etad amṛtasya vidyād;
evaṃ yukto madhu tad vai parīpset;
yoginas taṃ prapaśyanti bhagavantaṃ sanātanam.
n' âsy' âtivādā hṛdayaṃ tāpayanti,
n' ân|adhītaṃ n' â|hutam agni|hotram;
mano brāhmī laghutām ādadhīta,

If one stretched out thousands of thousands of wings and flew off, even if one were as swift as thought, then one would merely reach the centermost spirit in the middle—one could never find its limit, for it is without end;
the yogins see the eternal and blessed Lord. His form does 46.20
not exist within the range of mere sight, and only the extremely pure and true see him. A clever and kind-minded man does not suffer pain in his mind, and those who renounce the world become immortal; the yogins see the eternal and blessed Lord.

Just as snakes hide in dense thickets, so too mortals hide behind their learning and conduct. They fool only the foolish, and cause them to stray from the proper course and into danger; the yogins see the eternal and blessed Lord. An emancipated man of this kind thinks: 'I would never fail to exist, so there would never be death. So where could any hindrance to my immortality come from?' Both truth and deceit are equally bound to the truth, and existence and non-existence are similarly bound to their source; the yogins see the eternal and blessed Lord.

The knower of Brahman is not affected by good or bad actions, but among normal men good and bad actions do not produce the same results. One should know the knower of Brahman as equal to the ambrosia of immortality, and then, once one is practicing the means to Brahman as already described, one would long to attain the honey-sweet essence of Brahman; the yogins see the eternal and blessed Lord. Abuse does not cause pain to the heart of the man who understands Brahman, nor does a lack of learning, nor unperformed oblations. Let the mind practice Brahman's

prajñāṃ c' âsmai nāma dhīrā labhante;
yoginas taṃ prapaśyanti bhagavantaṃ sanātanam.
46.25 evaṃ yaḥ sarva|bhūteṣu ātmānam anupaśyati
anyatr' ânyatra yukteṣu, kiṃ sa śocet tataḥ param?
yath" ôdapāne mahati sarvataḥ saṃplut'|ôdake,
evaṃ sarveṣu vedeṣu ātmānam anujānataḥ.
aṅguṣṭha|mātraḥ puruṣo mah"|ātmā
na dṛśyate 'sau hṛdi saṃniviṣṭaḥ
a|jaś, caro divā|rātram, a|tandritaś ca;
sa taṃ matvā kavir āste prasannaḥ.
aham eva smṛto mātā, pitā putro 'smy ahaṃ punaḥ;
ātm" âham api sarvasya, yac ca n' âsti, yad asti ca.
pitā|maho 'smi sthaviraḥ, pitā putraś ca, Bhārata,
mam' âiva yūyam ātma|sthā, na me yūyaṃ, na vo vayam.
46.30 ātm" âiva sthānaṃ, mama janma c' ātmā;
ota|proto 'ham a|jara|pratiṣṭhaḥ.
a|jaś, caro divā|rātram, a|tandrito 'haṃ;
māṃ vijñāya kavir āste prasannaḥ.
aṇor aṇīyān, su|manāḥ, sarva|bhūteṣu jāgrati,
pitaraṃ sarva|bhūteṣu puṣkare nihitaṃ viduḥ.»

lightness, for men of constancy attain him whose name is wisdom; the yogins see the eternal and blessed Lord.

So why should the man who recognizes himself in all 46.25
creatures, as they busy themselves each in their own manner, grieve any longer? A man who understands the soul has as much use for the entirety of the Veda as he does for a large well when everything is flooded with water.* The high-souled person who measures a mere thumb's width cannot be seen abiding in one's heart. It moves incessantly, unborn, day and night, and the sage who concentrates on it sits calmly.

I am traditionally held to be mother, father, son, and myself. I am also the soul of everything which exists and does not.* I am the ancient grandfather, father, and son, Bhárata. I reside in my soul and in yours, but you are not mine, and I am not yours.

My soul is the foundation and my soul is birth. I ex- 46.30
ist without age, interwoven into the fabric of the universe. Unborn, I move ceaselessly night and day, and it is when he comes to know me that a sage sits calmly. More subtle than the subtle, benevolent, waking in all creatures, men know me as the father placed in the blue lotus-like heart within all creatures."

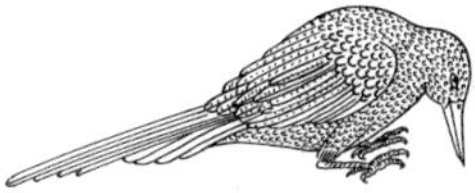

# 47–71

# THE KURUS' DEBATE

VAIŚAMPĀYANA uvāca:

47.1 EVAṂ SANATSUJĀTENA Vidureṇa ca dhīmatā
sārdhaṃ kathayato rājñaḥ sā vyatīyāya śarvarī.
tasyāṃ rajanyāṃ vyuṣṭāyāṃ rājānaḥ sarva eva te
sabhām āviviśur hṛṣṭāḥ sūtasy' ôpadidṛkṣayā.
śuśrūṣamāṇāḥ pārthānāṃ vāco dharm'|ârtha|saṃhitāḥ
Dhṛtarāṣṭra|mukhāḥ sarve yayū rāja|sabhāṃ śubhām.

sudh"|âvadātāṃ, vistīrṇāṃ, kanak'|âjira|bhūṣitām,
candra|prabhāṃ, su|rucirāṃ, siktāṃ candana|vāriṇā,
47.5 rucirair āsanaiḥ stīrṇāṃ kāñcanair dāravair api,
aśma|sāra|mayair, dāntaiḥ, sv|āstīrṇaiḥ s'|ôttara|cchadaiḥ.

Bhīṣmo, Droṇaḥ, Kṛpaḥ, Śalyaḥ,
Kṛtavarmā, Jayadrathaḥ,
Aśvatthāmā, Vikarṇaś ca,
Somadattaś ca Bāhlikaḥ,
Viduraś ca mahā|prājño, Yuyutsuś ca mahā|rathaḥ,
sarve ca sahitāḥ śūrāḥ pārthivā, Bharata'|rṣabha,
Dhṛtarāṣṭraṃ puras|kṛtya viviśus tāṃ sabhāṃ śūbhām,
Duḥśāsanaś, Citrasenaḥ, Śakuniś c' âpi Saubalaḥ,
Durmukhho, Duḥsahaḥ, Karṇa, Ulūko, 'tha Viviṃśatiḥ
Kuru|rājaṃ puras|kṛtya Duryodhanam a|marṣaṇam.

VAISHAMPÁYANA said:

SO THE NIGHT WAS spent in discussion between the king, Sanat·sujáta, and the wise Vídura. When night turned to dawn, all the kings happily entered the assembly hall, hoping to see the *suta*. They all went, led by Dhrita·rashtra, into the gleaming royal assembly, keen to listen to the moral and profitable speeches of the kings. 47.1

The extensive court was decorated with white stucco and adorned with gold. It gleamed brilliantly like the moon, and it was sprinkled with sandalwood water and strewn 47.5
with beautiful thrones of wood, gold, exquisite marble, and ivory, amply covered with the finest throws.

Bhishma, Drona, Kripa, Shalya, Krita·varman, Jayad·ratha, Ashvattháman, Vikárna, Soma·datta Báhlika, wise Vídura, and the great warrior Yuyútsu, all brave kings, gathered together, bull-like Bharata, and entered the gleaming court, making sure Dhrita·rashtra was at their head. Duhshásana, Chitra·sena, Shákuni Sáubala, Dúrmukha, Dúhsaha, Karna, Ulúka, and Vivínshati also entered, with Duryódhana, the intolerant Kuru king, at the front.

47.10 viviśus tāṃ sabhāṃ, rājan, sūrāḥ, Śakra|sado yathā.
āviśadbhis tadā, rājan, śūraiḥ parigha|bāhubhiḥ
śuśubhe sā sabhā, rājan, siṃhair iva girer guhā.
te praviśya mah"|ēṣvāsāḥ sabhāṃ sarve mah"|âujasaḥ
āsanāni vicitrāṇi bhejire sūrya|varcasaḥ.
āsana|stheṣu sarveṣu teṣu rājasu, Bhārata,
dvāḥ|stho nivedayām āsa sūta|putram upasthitam:
«ayaṃ sa ratha āyāti yo 'yāsīt Pāṇḍavān prati;
dūto nas tūrṇaṃ āyātaḥ Saindhavaiḥ sādhu|vāhibhiḥ.»
upeyāya sa tu kṣipraṃ rathāt praskandya kuṇḍalī;
praviveśa sabhāṃ pūrṇāṃ mahī|pālair mah"|ātmabhiḥ.

SAÑJAYA uvāca:

47.15 «prāpto 'smi Pāṇḍavān gatvā, taṃ vijānīta, Kauravāḥ.
yathā|vayaḥ Kurūn sarvān pratinandanti Pāṇḍavāḥ.
abhivādayanti vṛddhāṃś ca, vayasyāṃś ca vayasyavat,
yūnaś c' âbhyavadan Pārthāḥ pratipūjya yathā|vayaḥ.
yath" âhaṃ Dhṛtarāṣṭreṇa śiṣṭaḥ pūrvam ito gataḥ
abruvaṃ Pāṇḍavān gatvā, tan nibodhata, pārthivāḥ.»

DHṚTARĀṢṬRA uvāca:

48.1 «PṚCCHĀMI TVĀṂ, Sañjaya, rāja|madhye,
kim abravīd vākyam a|dīna|sattvaḥ
Dhanañjayas, tāta, yudhāṃ praṇetā,
dur|ātmanāṃ jīvita|cchin mah"|ātmā.»

So they entered the assembly hall, my king, as though they were the gods entering Shakra's home. And the court shone, my lord, with those heroes with arms like iron bars, as though, my king, it were a mountain cave filled with lions. Once all those powerfully energetic archers had entered the hall then, glorious as the sun, they took their beautifully decorated seats. And when those kings were all seated, Bhárata, the door-keeper announced that the *suta*'s son had returned: 47.10

"The chariot which went to the Pándavas has come back. Our messenger has returned quickly with his excellent Sáindhava horses." The earringed man himself quickly got up, dismounted from his chariot, and entered the the hall full of high-souled kings.

SÁÑJAYA said:

"Káuravas, know that I have returned from visiting the Pándavas. They send their greetings to all the Kurus according to their age. The Parthas salute their elders as well as their friends and contemporaries, and they greet their juniors with the honor their years deserve. So then, kings, find out what I have to tell you now that I have returned from visiting that place, having been previously commanded by Dhrita·rashtra." 47.15

DHRITA·RASHTRA said:

"I ASK YOU, Sáñjaya, in the middle of this royal gathering: what did Dhanañ·jaya of unimpaired goodness, the leader in battle, the high-souled annihilator of black-hearted men's lives, have to say, my friend?" 48.1

SAÑJAYA uvāca:
«Duryodhano vācam imāṃ śṛṇotu,
yad abravīd Arjuno yotsyamānaḥ
Yudhiṣṭhirasy' ânumate mah"|ātmā
Dhanañjayaḥ śṛṇvataḥ Keśavasya.
anvatrasto,* bāhu|vīryaṃ vidāna,
upahvare Vāsudevasya dhīraḥ,
avocan māṃ yotsyamānaḥ Kirīṭī:
‹madhye brūyā Dhārtarāṣṭraṃ Kurūṇām
saṃśṛṇvatas tasya dur|bhāṣiṇo vai
dur|ātmanaḥ sūta|putrasya, sūta,
yo yoddhum āśaṃsati māṃ sad" âiva,
manda|prajñaḥ, kāla|pakvo, 'timūḍhaḥ.
48.5 ye vai rājānaḥ Pāṇḍav'|āyodhanāya
samānītāḥ, śṛṇvatāṃ c' âpi teṣāṃ,
yathā samagraṃ vacanaṃ may" ôktaṃ
sah' âmātyaṃ śrāvayethā nṛpaṃ tat.›
yathā nūnaṃ deva|rājasya devāḥ
śuśrūṣante vajra|hastasya sarve,
tath" âśṛṇvan Pāṇḍavāḥ Sṛñjayāś ca
Kirīṭinā vācam uktāṃ samarthām!
ity abravīd Arjuno yotsyamāno
Gāṇḍīva|dhanvā lohita|padma|netraḥ:
‹na ced rājyaṃ muñcati Dhārtarāṣṭro
Yudhiṣṭhirasy' Ājamīḍhasya rājñaḥ,
asti nūnaṃ karma kṛtaṃ purastād
a|nirviṣṭaṃ pāpakaṃ Dhārtarāṣṭraiḥ!
yeṣāṃ yuddhaṃ Bhīmasen'|Ârjunābhyāṃ,
tath" Âśvibhyāṃ, Vāsudevena c' âiva,
Śaineyena dhruvam ātt'|āyudhena,

SÁÑJAYA replied:

"Let Duryódhana hear what Árjuna, high-souled Dhanañ·jaya, who is ready to fight, had to say with Yudhi·shthira's permission and within earshot of Késhava. Unhesitating and sure of his own strength, resolute in the close presence of Vasudéva, Kirítin, who is quite prepared to fight, said to me: 'Tell Dhartaráshtra in the midst of the Kurus, *suta*, within earshot of that wicked-hearted and insulting *suta*'s son, who is always itching to fight me, foolish-minded and idiotic man that is he, that his time is up. And also re- 48.5
peat everything I say, so that the king and his ministers can hear it, along with those kings who have gathered to fight the Pándavas.'

Surely those Pándavas and Sríñjayas listened to Kirítin's significant speech just as all the gods listen to their thunderbolt-wielding king! Eager for battle, Árjuna, the Gandíva archer with red lotus-like eyes, said:

'If Dhartaráshtra does not release the kingdom to Yudhi·shthira Ajamídha, then surely there is unsettled business to come with the Dhartaráshtras to pay for the evil things they have done!

If Dhrita·rashtra's son plans to fight in a battle with 48.10
Bhima and Árjuna, involving the twins, Vasudéva, the grandson of Shini when he has taken up weapons, Dhrishta·dyumna, Shikhándin, and Indra-like Yudhi·shthira who

Dhṛṣṭadyumnen', âtha Śikhaṇḍinā ca,
Yudhiṣṭhiren' Êndra|kalpena c' âiva,
yo 'padhyānān nirdahed gāṃ divaṃ ca.
48.10 taiś ced yoddhuṃ manyate Dhārtarāṣṭro,
nirvṛtto 'rthaḥ sakalaḥ Pāṇḍavānām!
mā tat kārṣīḥ Pāṇḍavasy' ârtha|hetor,
upaihi yuddhaṃ, yadi manyase tvam!
yāṃ tāṃ vane duḥkha|śayyām avātsīt
pravrājitaḥ Pāṇḍavo dharma|cārī,
apnotu tāṃ duḥkhatarām an|arthām
antyāṃ śayyāṃ Dhārtarāṣṭraḥ parāsuḥ!
hriyā, jñānena, tapasā, damena,
śauryeṇ' ârtho, dharma|guptyā, dhanena,
a|nyāya|vṛttiḥ Kuru|Pāṇḍaveyān
adhyātiṣṭhad Dhārtarāṣṭro dur|ātmā,
māy"|ôpadhaḥ praṇipāt'|ārjavābhyāṃ,
tapo|damābhyāṃ, dharma|guptyā, balena,
satyaṃ bruvan pratipanno nṛpo nas
titikṣamāṇaḥ kliśyamāno 'tivelam.
yadā jyeṣṭhaḥ Pāṇḍavaḥ saṃśit'|ātmā
krodhaṃ yat taṃ varṣa|pūgān su|ghoram
avasraṣṭā Kuruṣ' ûdvṛtta|cetās,
tadā yuddhaṃ Dhārtarāṣṭro 'nvatapsyat!
48.15 kṛṣṇa|vartm" êva jvalitaḥ samiddho
yathā dahet kakṣam agnir nidāghe,
evaṃ dagdhā Dhārtarāṣṭrasya senāṃ
Yudhiṣṭhiraḥ krodha|dīpto 'nvavekṣya!
yadā draṣṭā Bhīmasenaṃ ratha|sthaṃ,
gadā|hastaṃ, krodha|viṣaṃ vamantam,
a|marṣaṇaṃ Pāṇḍavaṃ bhīma|vegaṃ,

could scorch earth and heaven with a mere mental curse, then it seems that the Pándavas' whole aim is achieved! Don't draw back for the son of Pandu's sake, but start the war if you prefer it!

The law-abiding son of Pandu went into exile in the forest and found a bed of misery, so may Dhartaráshtra find a more wretched and unfortunate bed to be his last as he dies! Wicked-souled Dhartaráshtra has governed the Kurus and Pándavas behaving unlawfully, but our king has behaved with modesty, wisdom, austerity, control, courage, with wealth protected by morality, and, though deceived, with humble obeisance and honesty, asceticism, discipline, and strength defended by virtue. He speaks the truth and has overcome it all by being patient and enduring his excessive suffering.

When the eldest Pándava, whose soul has been sharpened in readiness and whose mind is agitated, pours the terrible anger he has been brewing for these successive years
on the Kurus, then Dhartaráshtra will regret his war! Just as 48.15
a kindled, black-trailed fire consumes a dead forest in the summer, so inflamed Yudhi·shthira, blazing with anger, will consume Dhartaráshtra's army with a mere glance!

When he sees Bhima·sena, the impatient and terribly violent son of Pandu, standing on his chariot, mace in hand, spewing out venom in his anger, then Dhartaráshtra will repent of his war! When he sees Bhima·sena in full armor at

tadā yuddhaṃ Dhārtarāṣṭro 'nvatapsyat.
sen"|âgra|gaṃ daṃśitaṃ Bhīmasenaṃ
sv|ālakṣaṇaṃ, vīra|haṇaṃ pareṣām,
ghnantaṃ camūm antaka|sannikāśaṃ,
tadā smartā vacanasy' âtimānī!
yadā draṣṭā Bhīmasenena nāgān
nipātitān giri|kūṭa|prakāśān,
kumbhair iv' âsṛg vamato bhinna|kumbhāṃs,
tadā yuddhaṃ Dhārtarāṣṭro 'nvatapsyat!
mahā|siṃho gāva iva praviśya
gadā|pāṇir Dhārtarāṣṭān upetya
yadā Bhīmo bhīma|rūpo nihantā,
tadā yuddhaṃ Dhārtarāṣṭro 'nvatapsyat!
48.20 mahā|bhaye vīta|bhayaḥ kṛt'|âstraḥ
samāgame śatru|bal'|âvamardī,
sakṛd rathen' â|pratimān rath'|âugān
padāti|saṅghān gaday" âbhinighnan,
śaikyena nāgāṃs tarasā vigṛhṇan
yadā chettā Dhārtarāṣṭrasya sainyam,
chindan vanaṃ paraśun" êva śūras,
tadā yuddhaṃ Dhārtarāṣṭro 'nvatapsyat!
tṛṇa|prāyaṃ jvalanen' êva dagdhaṃ
grāmaṃ yathā Dhārtarāṣṭrān samīkṣya,
pakvaṃ sasyaṃ vaidyuten' êva dagdhaṃ,
parāsiktaṃ vipulaṃ svaṃ bal'|âugham
hata|pravīraṃ, vimukhaṃ, bhay'|ārtaṃ,
parāṅ|mukhaṃ, prāyaśo '|dhṛṣṭa|yodham
śastr'|ârciṣā Bhīmasenena dagdhaṃ,
tadā yuddhaṃ Dhārtarāṣṭro 'nvatapsyat!
upāsaṅgād uddharan* dakṣiṇena

the head of the army, that killer of enemy heroes who is easy to spot as he slaughters the army, resembling Death himself, then arrogant Duryódhana will remember these words! When he sees the elephants like mountain peaks brought down by Bhima·sena, with blood oozing from their shattered skulls like water from jars, then Dhartaráshtra will regret his war!

When terrifying-looking Bhima falls upon Dhrita·rashtra's troops and kills them, mace in hand, like a lion entering a cattle-pen, then Dhartaráshtra will repent of his war! When that hero, skilled in weapons and undaunted 48.20
in great danger, for whom floods of chariots are no match when he has but one, crushes the enemy force in battle, destroying hordes of infantry with his mace, swiftly seizing elephants with his lasso, and chopping down Dhartaráshtra's army as though cutting down a forest with an axe, then Dhartaráshtra will regret his war!

When he sees the forces of Dhrita·rashtra burned like a village of straw huts consumed by fire, or like ripe corn burned by lightning, and his own extensive masses of forces rendered useless—the heroes dead, the rest fleeing, afflicted by fear, avoiding the enemy, made up for the most part of cowardly fighters, scorched by Bhima·sena's fiery weapon—then Dhartaráshtra will regret his war!

When the versatile and greatest of warriors, Nákula, dexterously shoots more than a hundred arrows from his quiver

parahśatān* Nakulaś citra|yodhī
yadā rath'|âgryo rathinaḥ pracetā,
tadā yuddhaṃ Dhārtarāṣṭro 'nvatapsyat!
48.25 sukh'|ôcito duḥkha|śayyāṃ vaneṣu
dīrghaṃ kālaṃ Nakulo yām aśeta,
āśī|viṣaḥ kruddha iv' ôdvaman viṣaṃ,
tadā yuddhaṃ Dhārtarāṣṭro 'nvatapsyat!
tyakt'|ātmānaḥ pārthiv'|āyodhanāya
samādiṣṭā dharma|rājena, sūta,
rathaiḥ śubhraiḥ sainyam abhidravanto
dṛṣṭvā paścāt tapsyate Dhārtarāṣṭraḥ.
śiśūn kṛt'|âstrān a|śiśu|prakāśān
yadā draṣṭā Kauravaḥ pañca śūrān,
tyaktvā prāṇān Kauravān ādravantas,
tadā yuddhaṃ Dhārtarāṣṭro 'nvatapsyat!
yadā gat'|ôdvāham, a|kūjan'|âkṣaṃ,
suvarṇa|tāraṃ ratham ātatāyī
dāntair yuktaṃ Sahadevo 'dhirūḍhaḥ,
śirāṃsi rājñāṃ kṣepsyate mārgaṇ'|âughaiḥ.
mahā|bhaye saṃpravṛtte ratha|sthaṃ
vivartamānaṃ samare kṛt'|âstram
sarvā diśaḥ sampatantaṃ samīkṣya,
tadā yuddhaṃ Dhārtarāṣṭro 'nvatapsyat!
48.30 hrī|niṣevo, nipuṇaḥ, satya|vādī,
mahā|balaḥ, sarva|dharm'|ôpapannaḥ,
Gāndhārim ārcchaṃs tumule kṣipra|kārī
kṣeptā janān Sahadevas tarasvī.
yadā draṣṭā Draupadeyān mah"|êṣūn
śūrān kṛt'|âstrān ratha|yuddha|kovidān
āśī|viṣān ghora|viṣān iv' āyatas,

and cuts down warriors, then Dhartaráshtra will regret his war! Nákula, accustomed to luxury, had to sleep on that 48.25
miserable bed in the forest for such a long time, spitting poison like an enraged snake, so Dhartaráshtra will regret his war!

Dhrita·rashtra's son will grieve in the future when he witnesses the Pándavas renouncing their own lives in the attack upon kings, as directed by Yudhi·shthira, the king of virtue, *suta*, overrunning his army with their gleaming chariots. When the Káurava sees the five young heroes, who appear anything but infantile in their skills with weapons, abandoning their lives as they attack the Káuravas, then Dhartaráshtra will regret his war!

When he sees that Saha·deva, bow drawn, has mounted his golden-starred chariot, the wheels of which turn noiselessly, yoked with broken-in horses, and sees him scatter the heads of kings with hosts of arrows, stationed on his chariot in battle, in the midst of great danger all around, flying in all directions and attacking, expertly trained with weapons, then Dhartaráshtra will regret this war! Practicing 48.30
modesty, skilled, truthful, mightily strong, endowed with every virtue, the swift-acting and fierce Saha·deva will scatter the soldiers as he attacks Duryódhana in the tumult.

When he sees Dráupadi's heroic, mighty archer sons, experts in weaponry and skilled in chariot battles, approaching like horrifyingly poisonous serpents, then Dhartaráshtra will regret this war! When Abhimányu, the destroyer

tadā yuddhaṃ Dhārtarāṣṭro 'nvatapsyat!
yad" Âbhimanyuḥ para|vīra|ghātī
śaraiḥ parān megha iv' âbhivarṣan
vigāhitā Kṛṣṇa|samaḥ kṛt'|âstras,
tadā yuddhaṃ Dhārtarāṣṭro 'nvatapsyat!
yadā draṣṭā bālam a|bāla|vīryaṃ
dviṣac|camūṃ mṛtyum iv' ôtpatantam
Saubhadram Indra|pratimaṃ kṛt'|âstraṃ,
tadā yuddhaṃ Dhārtarāṣṭro 'nvatapsyat!
Prabhadrakāḥ śīghratarā yuvāno
viśāradāḥ siṃha|samāna|vīryāḥ
yadā kṣeptāro Dhārtarāṣṭrān, sa|sainyāṃs
tadā yuddhaṃ Dhārtarāṣṭro 'nvatapsyat!
48.35 vṛddhau Virāṭa|Drupadau mahā|rathau
pṛthak camūbhyām abhivartamānau
yadā draṣṭārau Dhārtarāṣṭrān sa|sainyāṃs,
tadā yuddhaṃ Dhartarāṣṭro 'nvatapsyat!
yadā kṛt'|âstro Drupadaḥ pracinvan
śirāṃsi yūnāṃ samare ratha|sthaḥ
kruddhaḥ śaraiś chetsyati cāpa|muktais,
tadā yuddhaṃ Dhārtarāṣṭro 'nvatapsyat!
yadā Virāṭaḥ para|vīra|ghātī
mamattare śatru|camūṃ praveṣṭā
Matsyaiḥ sārdham a|nṛśaṃsa|rūpais,
tadā yuddhaṃ Dhārtarāṣṭro 'nvatapsyat!
jyeṣṭhaṃ Mātsyam a|nṛśaṃs'|ārya|rūpaṃ
Virāṭa|putraṃ rathinaṃ purastāt
yadā draṣṭā daṃśitaṃ Pāṇḍav'|ârthe,
tadā yuddhaṃ Dhārtarāṣṭro 'nvatapsyat!
raṇe hate Kauravāṇāṃ pravīre

of enemy heroes, rains down arrows upon his enemies as though he were a cloud, and plunges in, as expert as Krishna with weapons, then Dhartaráshtra will regret this war! When he sees Subhádra's boy, far from childish in prowess, fly at the enemy force like Death itself, as skilled with weapons as Indra, then Dhartaráshtra will regret this war!

When those extraordinarily fast and experienced Prabhádraka youths, with the prowess of lions, scatter the sons of Dhrita·rashtra and their army, then Dhartaráshtra will regret this war! When those two venerable mighty warriors, 48.35
Viráta and Drúpada, each attacking with their forces, see Dhrita·rashtra's sons and their army, then Dhartaráshtra will regret this war! When the skilled weaponsman Drúpada stands on his chariot, mows down the enemy, and cuts off the heads of young men in battle in his fury with arrows fired from his bow, then Dhartaráshtra will regret this war! When Viráta, the destroyer of enemy heroes, bursts into the hordes of the enemy where it is strongest with his admirable looking Matsyans, then Dhartaráshtra will regret the war!

When he sees Viráta's son, the eldest Matsyan, whose appearance is admirable and noble, the chariot warrior at the front, in full armor for Pándava's cause, then Dhartaráshtra will regret this war! Once the son of Shántanu, the leading hero of the Káuravas, is killed in battle by Shikhándin, then I'm telling you truly and without any hesitation that our enemies will certainly not survive. When the armored 48.40

Śikhaṇḍinā sattame Śāntanū|je
na jātu naḥ śatravo dhārayeyur,
a|saṃśayaṃ satyam etad bravīmi.
48.40 yadā Śikhaṇḍī rathinaḥ pracinvan
Bhīṣmaṃ rathen' âbhiyātā varūthī,
divyair hayair avamṛdnan rath'|âughāṃs,
tadā yuddhaṃ Dhārtarāṣṭro 'nvatapsyat!
yadā draṣṭā Sṛñjayānām anīke
Dhṛṣṭadyumnaṃ pramukhe rocamānam,
astraṃ yasmai guhyam uvāca dhīmān
Droṇas, tadā tapsyati Dhārtarāṣṭraḥ.
yadā sa senā|patir a|prameyaḥ
parāmṛdnann iṣubhir Dhārtarāṣṭrān
Droṇaṃ raṇe śatru|saho 'bhiyātā,
tadā yuddhaṃ Dhārtarāṣṭro 'nvatapsyat!
hrīmān, manīṣī, balavān, manasvī,
sa lakṣmīvān Somakānāṃ prabarhaḥ,
na jātu taṃ śatravo 'nye saheran
yeṣāṃ sa syād agra|ṇīr Vṛṣṇi|siṃhaḥ!
idaṃ ca brūyā, «mā vṛṇīṣv'! êti» loke
yuddhe '|dvitīyaṃ sacivaṃ ratha|stham.
Śiner naptāraṃ pravṛṇīma Sātyakiṃ
mahā|balaṃ, vīta|bhayaṃ, kṛt'|âstram.
48.45 mah"|ôrasko, dīrgha|bāhuḥ, pramāthī,
yuddhe '|dvitīyaḥ, param'|âstra|vedī
Śiner naptā tāla|mātr'|āyudho 'yaṃ,
mahā|ratho, vīta|bhayaḥ, kṛt'|âstraḥ.
yadā Śinīnām adhipo may" ôktaḥ
śaraiḥ parān megha iva pravarṣan
pracchādayiṣyaty ari|hā yodha|mukhyāṃs,

warrior Shikhándin mows down the enemy and comes at Bhishma with his chariot, grinding the hosts of warriors with his divine horses, then Dhartaráshtra will regret this war!

When he sees Dhrishta·dyumna enjoying himself at the head of the army of the Sríñjayas, the man to whom wise Drona told the secret weapon, then Dhartaráshtra will suffer! When that unfathomable commander of the army, who can withstand his enemies, crushes his enemies, the Dhartaráshtras, with arrows, and charges at Drona in battle, then Dhartaráshtra will regret this war!

No enemy could overcome those who have that modest, wise, strong, intelligent, blessed, and most excellent of the Sómakas, the Vrishni lion, as their leader! Tell Duryódhana this as well: "Don't choose him for yourself!" For we choose Sátyaki as our companion, second to no one in battle or in the world, the grandson of Shini, a fearless mighty warrior
who is an expert in weapons. Broad-chested, long-armed, a 48.45
destoyer without compare in battle, trained in the greatest weapons, this grandson of Shini has a weapon as large as a palm tree. He is a great and undaunted warrior who is an expert with weapons.

When I tell him to, the Shini leader, the slaughterer of his enemies, will shower his enemies with arrows like a cloud covering the leading warriors, and then Dhartaráshtra will regret this war! When about to fight, that high-souled,

tadā yuddhaṃ Dhārtarāṣṭro 'nvatapsyat!
yadā dhṛtiṃ kurute yotsyamānaḥ
sa dīrgha|bāhur dṛḍha|dhanvā mah"|ātmā,
siṃhasy' êva gandham āghrāya gāvaḥ,
sañceṣṭante śatravo 'smād raṇ'|âgre.
sa dīrgha|bāhur dṛḍha|dhanvā mah"|ātmā
bhindyād girīn, saṃharet sarva|lokān,
astre kṛtī, nipuṇaḥ, kṣipra|hasto,
divi sthitaḥ sūrya iv' âbhibhāti.
citraḥ, sūkṣmaḥ, su|krto Yādavasya
astre yogo, Vṛṣṇi|siṃhasya bhuyan;
yathā|vidhaṃ yogam āhuḥ praśastaṃ
sarvair guṇaiḥ Sātyakis tair upetaḥ.
48.50 hiraṇ|mayaṃ śveta|hayaiś caturbhir
yadā yuktaṃ syandanaṃ Mādhavasya
draṣṭā yuddhe Sātyaker Dhārtarāṣṭras,
tadā tapsyaty a|kṛt'|ātmā sa mandaḥ.
yadā rathaṃ hema|maṇi|prakāśaṃ,
śvet'|âśva|yuktaṃ, vānara|ketum, ugram
dṛṣṭvā mam' âpy āsthitaṃ Keśavena,
tadā tapsyaty a|kṛt'|ātmā sa mandaḥ!
yadā maurvyās tala|niṣpeṣam ugraṃ,
mahā|śabdaṃ, vajra|niṣpeṣa|tulyam
vidhūyamānasya mahā|raṇe mayā
sa Gāṇḍivasya śroṣyati manda|buddhiḥ,
tadā mūḍho Dhṛtarāṣṭrasya putras
taptā yuddhe dur|matir duḥ|sahāyaḥ,
dṛṣṭvā sainyaṃ bāṇa|varṣ'|ândhakāre
prabhajyantaṃ go|kulavad raṇ'|âgre.
balāhakād uccarataḥ su|bhīmān

long-armed, solid archer hardens his resolve and then, as though they were cattle catching the scent of a lion, his enemies on the front line of battle rush around in panic.

That long-armed, high-souled, solid archer could split mountains and annihilate all worlds, for he is an experienced and quick-handed master of weapons and blazes like the sun fixed in the sky. That descendant of Yadu, the Vrishni lion, practices an acute and flexible discipline in weaponry. Indeed Sátyaki is endowed with every skill in the discipline of weapons, which men praise.

When that undisciplined fool sees Sátyaki Mádhava's 48.50
golden chariot yoked with four white horses in battle, then Dhartaráshtra will suffer! And again, when that undisciplined fool sees my chariot shining with gold and jewels, yoked with white horses and the formidable monkey banner, and driven by Késhava, then he will suffer!

When that idiotic-minded man hears the mighty and formidable crack of Gandíva's bowstring, like a rumble of a thunderbolt as I twang it in the great battle, then Dhrita·rashtra's evil-minded and evil-associating fool of a son will be scorched in battle, as he watches his army being fractured in the blinding rain of arrows, like a herd of cattle, at the front line of battle.

When he sees me firing excellent bone-splitting and gut-piercing arrows of fearsome appearance, like sparks of light-

vidyut|sphuliṅgān iva ghora|rūpān,
sahasra|ghnān dviṣatāṃ saṅgareṣu,
asthi|cchido, marma|bhidaḥ, su|puṅkhān,
48.55 yadā draṣṭā jyā|mukhād bāṇa|saṅghān
Gāṇḍīva|muktān āpatataḥ śit'|âgrān,
hayān gajān varmiṇaś c' ādadānāṃs,
tadā yuddhaṃ Dhārtarāṣṭro 'nvatapsyat!
yada mandaḥ para|bāṇān vimuktān
mam' êṣubhir hriyamāṇān pratīpam
tiryag vidhyac chidyamānān pṛṣatkais,
tadā yuddhaṃ Dhārtarāṣṭro 'nvatapsyat!
yadā vipāṭhā mad|bhuja|vipramuktā,
dvijāḥ phalān' îva mahī|ruh'|âgrāt,
pracetāra uttam'|âṅgāni yūnāṃ,
tadā yuddhaṃ Dhārtarāṣṭro 'nvatapsyat!
yadā draṣṭā patataḥ syandanebhyo,
mahā|gajebhyo 'śva|gatān su|yodhanān,
śarair hatān, pātitāṃś c' âiva raṅge,
tadā yuddhaṃ Dhārtarāṣṭro 'nvatapsyat!
a|saṃprāptān astra|pathaṃ parasya
yadā draṣṭā naśyato Dhārtarāṣṭrān,
a|kurvataḥ karma yuddhe samantāt,
tadā yuddhaṃ Dhārtarāṣṭro 'nvatapsyat!

ning shooting forth from a fierce storm cloud, which kill thousands of my enemies in the conflicts; when he sees 48.55
swarms of sharp-pointed arrows released from the bowstring of Gandíva as they fly, taking out horses, elephants, and armored men, then Dhartaráshtra will regret this war!

When the fool sees that my shafts shame the arrows shot by the enemy into retreating, or sees them split when pierced obliquely by my arrows, then Dhartaráshtra will regret this war! When the arrows fired by my arms pluck off young men's heads, just as birds pluck fruit from the top of a large tree, then Dhartaráshtra will regret this war!

When he sees his good fighters fall from their chariots, the mighty elephants and the horses they were riding hit and toppled by my arrows in battle, then Dhartaráshtra will regret this war! When he sees his brothers, the sons of Dhrita·rashtra, destroyed all around him without even getting their enemy within range of their weapons and without having achieved any feat in battle, then Dhartaráshtra will regret this war!

48.60 padāti|saṅghān ratha|saṅghān samantād,
vyātt'|ānanaḥ kāla iv' ātat'|êṣuḥ,
praṇotsyāmi jvalitair bāṇa|varṣaiḥ
śatrūṃs, tadā tapsyati manda|buddhiḥ.
sarvā diśaḥ saṃpatatā rathena
rajo|dhvastaṃ Gāṇḍivena prakṛttam
yadā draṣṭā sva|balaṃ saṃpramūḍhaṃ,
tadā paścāt tapsyati manda|buddhiḥ.
kān|dig|bhūtaṃ, chinna|gātraṃ, visaṃjñaṃ
Duryodhano drakṣyati sarva|sainyam,
hat'|âśva|vīr'|âgrya|narendra|nāgaṃ,
pipāsitaṃ, śrānta|patraṃ, bhay'|ārtam,
ārta|svaraṃ, hanyamānaṃ, hataṃ ca,
vikīrṇa|keś'|âsthi|kapāla|saṅgham,
Prajāpateḥ karma yath" ârtha|niṣṭhitaṃ,
tadā dṛṣṭvā tapsyati manda|buddhiḥ!
yadā rathe Gāṇḍivaṃ, Vāsudevaṃ,
divyaṃ śaṅkhaṃ Pāñcajanyaṃ, hayāṃś ca,
tūṇāv a|kṣayyau, Devadattaṃ ca, māṃ ca
dṛṣṭvā yuddhe Dhārtarāṣṭro 'nvatapsyat!
48.65 udvartayan dasyu|saṅghān sametān,
pravartayan yugam anyad yug'|ânte,
yadā dhakṣyāmy agnivat Kauraveyāṃs,
tadā taptā Dhṛtarāṣṭraḥ sa|putraḥ!

That idiotic-minded man will suffer when I open my 48.60
mouth wide, like the end of time to all those with bows stretched to kill, and repel the enemy hosts of infantry and masses of chariots all around with fiery showers of arrows. When he sees his own army turned utterly bewildered by Gandíva, and covered in the dust raised by my chariot as it flies in all directions, the foolish-minded man will regret his actions, but too late!

When Duryódhana sees his entire army wondering which way to turn, broken-limbed and unconscious, with his horses, leading heroes, kings, and elephants dead, thirsty, with exhausted horses, and afflicted by fear, and when he sees them crying in pain, dead or about to die, a mass of skulls, bones, and hair strewn about, as though Praja·pati's work was unfinished, then that foolish-minded man will suffer!

When he sees Gandíva, Vasudéva, his divine conch Pañ-chajánya, and my horses, as well as my pair of everlasting quivers, Deva·datta, and of course me on my chariot in battle, then Dhartaráshtra will have regrets! When I break up 48.65
the hordes of barbarians who have gathered, and set another age in motion at the end of this one, then I will set the Káuravas alight as though I were a fire, and Dhrita·rashtra and his son will be consumed!

sa|bhrātā vai, saha|sainyaḥ, sa|bhṛtyo,
bhraṣṭ'|āiśvaryaḥ, krodha|vaśo, 'lpa|cetāḥ,
darpasy' ânte nihato vepamānaḥ
paścān mandas tapsyati Dhārtarāṣṭraḥ.
pūrv'|āhṇe māṃ kṛta|japyaṃ kadā cid
vipraḥ provāc' ôdak'|ânte mano|jñam:
«kartavyaṃ te duṣ|karaṃ karma, Pārtha,
yoddhavyaṃ te śatrubhiḥ, Savyasācin.
Indro vā te harivān vajra|hastaḥ
purastād yātu samare 'rīn vinighnan,
Sugrīva|yuktena rathena vā te
paścāt Kṛṣṇo rakṣatu Vāsudevaḥ.»
vavre c' âhaṃ vajra|hastān mah"|Êndrād
asmin yuddhe Vāsudevaṃ sahāyam.
sa me labdho dasyu|vadhāya Kṛṣṇo,
manye c' âitad vihitaṃ daivatair me.
48.70 a|yudhyamāno manas" âpi yasya
jayaṃ Kṛṣṇaḥ puruṣasy' âbhinandet,
evaṃ sarvān sa vyatīyād amitrān
s'|Êndrān devān – mānuṣe n' âsti cintā.

That fool Dhartaráshtra, a slave to his rage and a man of little sense, will suffer in the future with his brothers, his army, and his sons, when he has lost his power, when he is smitten and trembling and his pride is finally at an end! Early in the day, when I had finished my prayers and finished my ablutions, a brahmin spoke pleasantly to me: "Partha, you have a difficult task ahead of you, for you must fight with your enemies, Savya·sachin. Let Indra, thunderbolt in hand, go before you with his bay horses, killing your enemies in battle, or let Krishna Vasudéva guard the rear wih Sugríva yoked to his chariot."

I chose Vasudéva as my companion over great Indra, thunderbolt in hand, in this fight. I gained Krishna as an ally to kill the *dasyus*, though I believe that it was arranged
for me by the gods. The man for whom Krishna approves 48.70
victory, would indeed overpower all his enemies even if he doesn't actually fight, and even if his enemies were the gods headed by Indra—and that is without even giving a thought to humans!

sa bāhubhyāṃ sāgaram uttitīrṣen,
mah"|ôdadhiṃ salilasy' â|prameyam,
tejasvinaṃ Kṛṣṇam atyanta|śūraṃ
yuddhena yo Vāsudevaṃ jigīṣet!
giriṃ ya icchet tu talena bhettuṃ,
śil'|ôccayaṃ śvetam atipramāṇam,
tasy' âiva pāṇiḥ sa|nakho viśīryen,
na c' âpi kiñ cit sa gires tu kuryāt!
agniṃ samiddhaṃ śamayed bhujābhyāṃ,
candraṃ ca sūryaṃ ca nivārayeta,
hared devānām amṛtaṃ prasahya,
yuddhena yo Vāsudevaṃ jigīṣet!
yo Rukmiṇīm, eka|rathena Bhojān
utsādya, rājñaḥ samare prasahya
uvāha bhāryāṃ yaśasā jvalantīṃ,
yasyāṃ jajñe Raukmiṇeyo mah"|ātmā.
48.75 ayaṃ Gāndhārāṃs tarasā saṃpramathya,
jitvā putrān Nagnajitaḥ samagrān
baddhaṃ mumoca vinadantaṃ prasahya
Sudarśanaṃ vai devatānāṃ lalāmam.
ayaṃ kapāṭena jaghāna Pāṇḍyaṃ,
tathā Kaliṅgān Dantakūre mamarda,
anena dagdhā varṣa|pūgān vi|nāthā
Vārāṇasī nagarī saṃbabhūva.

The man who wishes to defeat Vasudéva, the splendid and limitlessly heroic Krishna, by fighting him, may as well wish to cross the vast and unfathomable ocean using merely the power of his arms! A man who wishes to split an immense white mountain heaped with rocks, using only the palm of his hand, would shatter his hand and nails, but wouldn't dent the mountain one bit! The man who wishes to defeat Vasudéva in battle may as well try to put out a kindled fire with his arms, remove the moon and sun, or violently steal the gods' immortal ambrosia!

On a single chariot he violently annihilated the Bhoja kings in battle and carried off Rúkmini, blazing with glory, to be his wife, and she bore high-souled Ráukmini Pradyúmna to him. Having swiftly oppressed the Gandháras 48.75
he defeated Nágnajit's gathered sons, and forcibly released the gods' eminent friend Sudárshana while he cried out. This is the man who killed King Pandya by striking him with his chest, and crushed the Kalíngas at Danta·kura, so that the city of Varánasi remained without a protector for a series of years once he had burned it.

yaṃ sma yuddhe manyate 'nyair a|jeyaṃ,
tam Ekalavyaṃ nāma Niṣāda|rājam
vegen' âiva śailam abhihatya Jambhaḥ
śete sa Kṛṣṇena hataḥ parāsuḥ.
tath" Ôgrasenasya sutaṃ su|duṣṭaṃ
Vṛṣṇy|Andhakānāṃ madhya|gataṃ sabhā|stham
apātayad Baladeva|dvitīyo,
hatvā dadau c' Ôgrasenāya rājyam.
ayaṃ Saubhaṃ yodhayām āsa kha|sthaṃ
vibhīṣaṇaṃ māyayā Śālva|rājam;
Saubha|dvāri pratyagṛhṇāc chata|ghnīṃ
dorbhyāṃ; ka enaṃ viṣaheta martyaḥ?
48.80 Prāgjyotiṣaṃ nāma babhūva durgaṃ
puraṃ ghoram asurāṇām a|sahyam.
mahā|balo Narakas tatra bhaumo
jahār' Âdityā maṇi|kuṇḍale śubhe.
na taṃ devāḥ saha Śakreṇa śekuḥ
samāgatā yudhi mṛtyor a|bhītāḥ,
dṛṣṭvā ca taṃ vikramaṃ Keśavasya,
balaṃ, tath" âiv' âstram a|vāraṇīyam,
jānanto 'sya prakṛtiṃ Keśavasya
nyayojayan dasyu|vadhāya Kṛṣṇam.
sa tat karma pratiśuśrāva duṣ|karam
aiśvaryavān siddhiṣu Vāsudevaḥ.

The man who was thought by others to be invincible in battle, the king of the Nishádas, named Eka·lavya, lay dead, killed by Krishna, as too did Jambha, violently struck on the mountain. He brought down and killed Ugra·sena's extremely wicked son as he stood in the assembly, having gone into the midst of the Vrishnis and Ándhakas with Bala·deva as his second, and then he gave the kingdom back to Ugra·sena. This man fought sky-dwelling Saubha the bullying Shalvan king with magic, and at Saubha's door he caught the weapon, the murderer of a hundred, in his arms, so which mortal can withstand him?

Then there was the far-off, horrifying, and unassailable 48.80
city of the *ásuras*, called Prag·jyótisha, where the mighty Náraka, the son of earth, stole Áditi's beautiful jewelled earrings. The gods and Shakra found themselves incapable when they gathered for the fight, unafraid of death, but they saw Késhava's prowess, his strength, and his unrestrainable weapon, and they understood Késhava's nature, so they appointed Krishna to the murder of the *dasyus*. He obeyed and carried out that difficult task, for Vasudéva held power over matters of success.

Nirmocane ṣaṭ sahasrāṇi hatvā,
saṃcchidya pāśān sahasā kṣur'|ântān,
Muraṃ hatvā vinihaty' âugha|rakṣo,
Nirmocanaṃ c' âpi jagāma vīraḥ.
tatr' âiva ten' âsya babhūva yuddhaṃ
mahā|balen' âtibalasya Viṣṇoḥ;
śete sa Kṛṣṇena hataḥ parāsur
vāten' êva mathitaḥ karṇikāraḥ.
48.85 āhṛtya Kṛṣṇo maṇi|kuṇḍale te,
hatvā ca bhaumaṃ Narakaṃ Muraṃ ca,
śriyā vṛto, yaśasā c' âiva vidvān
pratyājagām' â|pratima|prabhāvaḥ.
asmai varāṇy adadaṃs tatra devā
dṛṣṭvā bhīmaṃ karma kṛtaṃ raṇe tat.
«śramaś ca te yudhyamānasya na syād,
ākāśe c' āpsu ca te kramaḥ syāt,
śastrāṇi gātre na ca te kramerann!»
ity êva Kṛṣṇaś ca tataḥ kṛt'|ârthaḥ.
evaṃ|rūpe Vāsudeve '|prameye
mahā|bale guṇa|saṃpat sad" âiva.
tam a|sahyaṃ Viṣṇum an|anta|vīryam
āśaṃsate Dhārtarāṣṭro vijetum!
sadā hy enaṃ tarkayate dur|ātmā,
tac c' âpy ayaṃ sahate 'smān samīkṣya.
paryāgataṃ mama Kṛṣṇasya c' âiva
yo manyate kalahaṃ saṃprasahya
śakyaṃ hartuṃ Pāṇḍavānāṃ mamatvaṃ,
tad veditā saṃyugaṃ tatra gatvā!

At Nirmóchana he killed six thousand, forcefully cutting the razor-edged chains, and, killing and slaughtering Mura and hordes of *rákshasas*, the hero entered Nirmóchana. So it was there that the battle between the mighty creature and the more powerful Vishnu took place. He lay dead, killed by Krishna like a *karnikára* flower shaken by the wind. So, hav- 48.85
ing retrieved the jewelled earrings and killed the earth's son Náraka as well as Mura, wise Krishna of matchless power returned endowed with good fortune and glory.

When the gods saw the terrifying feat he had achieved in battle, they granted him favors: "You shall feel no exhaustion when you fight, your course shall be in the sky and in water, and no weapons will pierce your limbs!" Krishna was then satisfied: this is the form of matchless and powerful Vasudéva in which virtue and success reside eternally.

This is the invincible Vishnu of endless prowess that Dhartaráshtra expects to defeat! His wicked soul always dwells on this, but Krishna endures even this by taking us into consideration. If he thinks that he has the power to create a quarrel which will get between me and Krishna, and that he will be able to take away the Pándavas' wealth as well as mine, then he'll learn a thing or two when he comes to battle!

48.90 namas|kṛtvā Śāntanavāya rājñe,
Droṇāy' âtho saha|putrāya c' âiva,
Śāradvatāy' â|pratidvandvine ca,
yotsyāmy ahaṃ rājyam abhīpsamānaḥ!
dharmen' āptaṃ nidhanaṃ tasya manye,
yo yotsyate Pāṇḍavaiḥ pāpa|buddhiḥ.
mithya glahe nirjitā vai nṛśaṃsaiḥ
saṃvatsarān vai dvā|daśa rāja|putrāḥ,
vāsaḥ kṛcchro vihitaś c' âpy araṇye,
dīrghaṃ kālaṃ c' âikam a|jñāta|varṣam.
te hi kasmāj jīvatāṃ Pāṇḍavānāṃ
nandiṣyante Dhārtarāṣṭrāḥ pada|sthāḥ?
te ced asmān yudhyamānān yajeyur,
devair mah"|Êndra|pramukhaiḥ sahāyaiḥ,
dharmād a|dharmaś carito garīyāṃs,
tato dhruvaṃ n' âsti kṛtaṃ ca sādhu.
na ced imaṃ puruṣaṃ karma|baddhaṃ,
na ced asmān manyate 'sau viśiṣṭān,
āśaṃse 'haṃ Vāsudeva|dvitīyo
Duryodhanaṃ s'|ânubandhaṃ nihantum!

Having paid homage to the royal son of Shántanu, as 48.90
well as to Drona, and his son, and to unrivaled Sharádvata, I want to take back the kingdom and I will fight for it! I believe the law will be laid down on whichever wicked-minded man fights against the Pándavas, for we princes were defeated by trickery in the gambling by cruel men, and have lived as instructed in misery in the forest for twelve years—a long time—as well as one year unknown. So why now should the sons of Dhrita·rashtra wish to rejoice at the fact that the Pándavas are alive when they have filled our shoes?

If as we fight against them they should defeat us, with the gods led by great Indra as their allies, then immorality will turn out to be worth more than morality, and it is certain that no good is achieved. If he believes that a man is not bound to his actions, and that we Pándavas are nothing special, then I hope to kill Duryódhana and his cronies with Vasudéva as my second!

48.95 na ced idaṃ karma, nar'|êndra, bandhyaṃ,
na ced bhavet su|kṛtaṃ niṣphalaṃ vā,
idaṃ ca tac c' âbhisamīkṣya nūnaṃ
parājayo Dhāratrāṣṭrasya sādhuḥ.
pratyakṣaṃ vaḥ, Kuravo, yad bravīmi,
yudhyamānā Dhārtarāṣṭrā na santi.
anyatra yuddhāt, Kuravo, yadi syur,
na yuddhe vai śeṣa ih' âsti kaś cit.
hatvā tv ahaṃ Dhārtarāṣṭrān sa|Karṇān
rājyaṃ Kurūṇām avajetā samagram,
yad vaḥ kāryaṃ tat kurudhvaṃ yathā|svam
iṣṭān dārān ātma|bhogān bhajadhvam.
apy evaṃ no brāhmaṇāḥ santi vṛddhā,
bahu|śrutāḥ, śīlavantaḥ, kulīnāḥ,
sāṃvatsarā, jyotiṣi c' âbhiyuktā,
nakṣatra|yogeṣu ca niścaya|jñāḥ.
ucc'|âvacaṃ daiva|yuktaṃ rahasyaṃ,
divyāḥ praśnā, mṛga|cakrā, muhūrtāḥ,
kṣayaṃ mahāntaṃ Kuru|Sṛñjayānāṃ
nivedayante, Pāṇḍavānāṃ jayaṃ ca.
48.100 yathā hi no manyate 'jātaśatruḥ
saṃsiddh'|ârtho dviṣatāṃ nigrahāya,
Janārdanaś c' âpy a|parokṣa|vidyo
na saṃśayaṃ paśyati Vṛṣṇi|siṃhaḥ.
ahaṃ tath" âiva khalu bhāvi|rūpaṃ
paśyāmi buddhyā svayam a|pramattaḥ
dṛṣṭiś ca me na vyathate purāṇī:
saṃyudhyamānā Dhārtarāṣṭrā na santi.

And if action is not bound to men, lord of men, and there 48.95
is no reward or lack of it, then surely, with my sights set upon it, the destruction of Dhartaráshtra is correct. Kurus, I am telling you the obvious: the followers of Dhrita·rashtra will not live if they go to battle; the Kurus may survive if they choose an alternative to war, but in battle no one will be left. When I have killed the Dhartaráshtras and Karna then I will win back the united kingdom of the Kurus. So do what you must, as you wish, and enjoy your dear wives and pleasures of the soul.

We also have venerable brahmins of great learning, good conduct, and noble birth, trained as almanac makers and astrologers, men who understand the purposes held within the constellations and conjuctions. They foretell the high and low mysteries attached to fate, divine inquiries, the zodiac, moments, and the destruction and great end of the Kurus and Sríñjayas and the victory of the Pándavas.

Ajáta·shatru believes our goal of suppressing our enemies 48.100
is already achieved, and Janárdana, the Vrishni lion, who understands what is hidden, also sees no doubt. I too, in fact, see the shape of the future, vigilant in my mind. My ancient sight is not impaired: the Dhartaráshtras will not survive the war.

an|ālabdhaṃ jṛmbhati Gāṇḍivaṃ dhanur,
an|āhatā kampati me dhanur|jyā,
bāṇāś ca me tūṇa|mukhād visṛtya
muhur muhur gantum uśanti c' âiva.
khaḍgaḥ kośān niḥsarati prasanno,
hitv" êva jīrṇām uragas tvacaṃ svām.
dhvaje vāco raudra|rūpā bhavanti:
«kadā ratho yokṣyate te, Kirīṭin?»
gomāyu|saṅghāś ca nadanti rātrau,
rakṣāṃsy atho niṣpatanty antarikṣāt,
mṛgāḥ, śṛgālāḥ, śiti|kaṇṭhāś ca kākā,
gṛdhrā, bakāś c' âiva, tarakṣavaś ca,
48.105 suvarṇa|patrāś ca patanti paścād
dṛṣṭvā rathaṃ śveta|haya|prayuktam.
ahaṃ hy ekaḥ pārthivān sarva|yodhān
śarān varṣan mṛtyu|lokaṃ nayeyam.
samādadānaḥ pṛthag astra|mārgān,
yath" âgnir iddho gahanaṃ nidāghe,
sthūṇā|karṇaṃ Pāśupataṃ mah"|âstraṃ
Brāhmaṃ c' âstraṃ yac ca Śakro 'py adān me,
vadhe dhṛto vegavataḥ pramuñcan
n' âhaṃ prajāḥ kiñ cid ih' âvaśiṣye
śāntiṃ lapsye paramo hy, eṣa bhāvaḥ
sthiro mama: brūhi, Gāvalgaṇe, tān!

Gandíva, my bow, yawns without being touched, and my bowstring trembles without being struck. My arrows spill out from the mouth of my quiver, desperate to fly off at every moment. My bright sword glides from its sheath like a snake casting off its worn-out skin. There are horrid voices in my banner, saying: "When will your chariot be yoked, Kirítin?"

At night groups of jackals howl, *rákshasas* fly down from the sky, and deer, jackals, dark necked crows, vultures,
cranes, and hyenas appear. Golden-winged birds fly behind 48.105
my chariot yoked with white horses when they see it. I will single-handedly lead all those warrior kings to the world of the dead by showering my arrows.

Setting each of my weapons on their course—the pillar-eared, mighty weapon of Pashu·pati, the Brahma weapon, and that which Shakra gave to me—I, resolved upon slaughter and releasing my forceful shafts, will leave no creature alive in this world, like a kindled fire burning a dense wood in summer; and I will find peace. This is indeed my chief and firm intention. Tell them that, son of Gaválgana!

ye vai jayyāḥ samare, sūta, labdhvā
devān ap' Îndra|pramukhān sametān,
tair manyate kalahaṃ saṃprasahya,
sa Dhārtarāṣṭraḥ paśyata moham asya!
vṛddho Bhīṣmaḥ Śāntanavaḥ, Kṛpaś ca,
Droṇaḥ sa|putro, Viduraś ca dhīmān,
ete sarve yad vadante tad astu:
āyuṣmantaḥ Kuravaḥ santu sarve.› »

VAIŚAMPĀYANA uvāca:

49.1 SAMAVETEṢU SARVEṢU teṣu rājasu, Bhārata,
Duryodhanam idaṃ vākyaṃ Bhīṣmaḥ Śāntanavo 'bravīt:
«Bṛhaspatiś c' Ôśanā ca Brahmāṇaṃ paryupasthitau.
marutaś ca sah' Êndreṇa, Vasavaś c' Âgninā saha,
ādityāś c' âiva, sādhyāś ca, ye ca sapta|ṛṣayo divi,
Viśvāvasuś ca gandharvaḥ, śubhāś c' âpsarasāṃ gaṇāḥ.
namas|kṛty' ôpajagmus te loka|vṛddhaṃ pitā|maham,
parivārya ca viśv'|ēśaṃ paryāsata div'|âukasaḥ.
49.5 teṣāṃ manaś ca tejaś c' âpy ādadānāv iv' âujasā
pūrva|devau vyatikrāntau Nara|Nārāyaṇāv ṛṣī.
Bṛhaspatis tu papraccha Brahmāṇaṃ, ‹kāv imāv, iti,
bhavantaṃ n' ôpatiṣṭhete? tau naḥ śaṃsa, pitā|maha.›

BRAHM' ôvāca:

‹yāv etau pṛthivīṃ dyāṃ ca bhāsayantau tapasvinau,
jvalantau rocamānau ca, vyāpy'|âtitau mahā|balau,
Nara|Nārāyaṇāv etau, lokāl lokaṃ samāsthitau,
ūrjitau svena tapasā, mahā|sattva|parākramau.
etau hi karmaṇā lokaṃ nandayām āsatur dhruvam,
dvidhā bhūtau mahā|prajñau

Dhartaráshtra thinks he can withstand a quarrel with those who cannot be defeated in battle, *suta*, even if taken on by the gods together, led by Indra—behold his idiocy! Elderly Bhishma the son of Shántanu, Kripa, Drona and his son, and wise Vídura have all said it, so let it be: may all the Kurus be long-lived!'"

VAISHAMPÁYANA said:

ONCE ALL THE kings were assembled, O Bhárata, Bhish- 49.1
ma, son of Shántanu, said these words to Duryódhana:

"Brihas·pati and Úshanas once waited on Brahma. The Maruts and Indra, the Vasus with Agni, the *adítyas*, the *sadhyas*, and the seven sages in the sky as well as the *gandhárva* Vishva·vasu and hosts of beautiful *ápsarases* paid homage to their grandfather, the elder of the world, and approached him. Once they had surrounded the lord of the universe, the sky-dwellers sat around him.

Then the two ancient gods, the sages Nara and Naráyana, 49.5
left, and it was as if they were taking the minds and splendor of the gods with their energy. Brihas·pati asked Brahma: 'Who are these two who do not wait upon you? Instruct us, grandfather.'

BRAHMA replied:

'These two mightily powerful ascetics who illuminate the earth and heaven, blazing and shining, both pervading and surpassing, are Nara and Naráyana, who abide in this realm having come from the other. They are endowed with strength and noble prowess through their asceticism. These two certainly bring joy to the world through their deeds, but they are a dichotomy; wise in the statutes of Brahman

viddhi, brahman, paraṃ|tapau,
asurāṇāṃ vināśāya
deva|gandharva|pūjitau.›

VAIŚAMPĀYANA uvāca:

49.10 jagāma Śakras tac chrutvā yatra tau tepatus tapaḥ,
sārdhaṃ deva|gaṇaiḥ sarvair Bṛhaspati|purogamaiḥ.
tadā dev'|âsure yuddhe bhaye jāte div'|âukasām
ayācata mah"|ātmānau Nara|Nārāyaṇau varam.
tāv abrūtāṃ, ‹vṛṇīṣv'! êti› tadā, Bharata|sattama,
ath' âitāv abravīc Chakraḥ, ‹sahyaṃ naḥ kriyatām iti.›
tatas tau Śakram abrūtāṃ, ‹kariṣyāvo yad icchasi.›
tābhyāṃ ca sahitaḥ Śakro vijigye daitya|dānavān.
Nara Indrasya saṅgrāme hatvā śatrūn paran|tapaḥ
Paulomān Kālakhañjāṃś ca sahasrāṇi śatāni ca.
49.15 eṣa bhrānte rathe tiṣṭhan bhallen' âpāharac chiraḥ
Jambhasya grasamānasya, tadā hy Arjuna āhave.
eṣa pāre samudrasya Hiraṇyapuram ārujat,
jitvā ṣaṣṭiṃ sahasrāṇi Nivātakavacān raṇe.
eṣa devān sah' Êndreṇa jitvā para|purañ|jayaḥ
atarpayan mahā|bāhur Arjuno Jātavedasam.
Nārāyaṇas tath" âiv' âtra bhūyaso 'nyān jaghāna ha.
evam etau mahā|vīryau, tau paśyata samāgatau,
Vāsudev'|Ârjunau vīrau samavetau mahā|rathau
Nara|Nārāyaṇau devau pūrva|devāv, iti śrutiḥ,
49.20 a|jeyau mānuṣe loke s'|Êndrair api sur'|âsuraiḥ.
eṣa Nārāyaṇaḥ Kṛṣṇaḥ, Phālgunaś ca Naraḥ smṛtaḥ.
Nāryāyaṇo Naraś c' âiva sattvam ekaṃ dvidhā kṛtam.

but also scorchers of their enemies, they are worshipped by gods and *gandhárvas* alike for their destruction of the *ásuras*.'

VAISHAMPÁYANA continued:

When he heard this, Shakra, along with all the hosts of 49.10
the gods led by Brihas·pati, went to the place where those two performed their austerities. Since fear had arisen in heaven because of the war between the gods and the *ásuras* at that time, they asked high-souled Nara and Naráyana for a favor. Those two said, 'Choose!' And then, best of the Bharatas, Shakra replied, 'Give us help.' So those two then said, 'We will do what you want.' And together with these two, Shakra defeated the Daityas and Dánavas.

Nara, scorcher of his foe, killed hundreds of thousands
of Paulómas and Kala·khañjas in Indra's battle. Standing on 49.15
his chariot as it rolled along, Árjuna plucked off Jambha's head with an arrow in the battle as he was swallowing him up. This man demolished Hiránya·pura on the shore of the ocean after he defeated sixty thousand Niváta·kávachas in battle. This victor over enemy cities beat the gods and Indra, and then long-armed Árjuna satisfied Agni. Naráyana also killed many others there.

See how these two mighty heroes have returned together. It is said that the heroes Vasudéva and Árjuna, the great warriors who have come together, are the ancient gods Nara
and Naráyana. They are both invincible in the human 49.20
world, even against the gods and *ásuras* with Indra. Krishna is recorded as being Naráyana, and Phálguna as Nara. Naráyana and Nara are one in reality, but are made into

etau hi karmaṇā lokān aśnuvāte 'kṣayān dhruvān.
tatra tatr' âiva jāyete yuddha|kāle punaḥ punaḥ.
tasmāt ‹karm' âiva kartavyam, iti› h' ôvāca Nāradaḥ;
etadd hi sarvam ācaṣṭa Vṛṣṇi|cakrasya veda|vit.

śaṅkha|cakra|gadā|hastaṃ yadā drakṣyasi Keśavam,
paryādadānaṃ c' âstrāṇi bhīma|dhanvānam Arjunam,
sanātanau mah"|ātmānau Kṛṣṇāv eka|rathe sthitau,
Duryodhana, tadā, tāta, smart" âsi vacanaṃ mama.
49.25 no ced ayam a|bhāvaḥ syāt Kurūṇāṃ pratyupasthitaḥ!
arthāc ca, tāta, dharmāc ca tava buddhir upaplutā.

na ced grahīṣyase vākyaṃ, śrot" âsi su|bahūn hatān;
tav' âiva hi mataṃ sarve Kuravaḥ paryupāsate.
trayāṇām eva ca mataṃ tattvam eko 'numanyase:
Rāmeṇa c' âiva śaptasya Karṇasya, Bharata'|rṣabha.
dur|jāteḥ sūta|putrasya Śakuneḥ Saubalasya ca,
tathā kṣudrasya pāpasya bhrātur Duḥśāsanasya ca.»

KARṆA uvāca:

«n' âivam āyuṣmatā vācyaṃ, yan mām' âttha, pitā|maha,
kṣatra|dharme sthito hy asmi sva|dharmād an|apeyivān.
49.30 kiṃ c' ânyan mayi dur|vṛttaṃ, yena māṃ parigarhase?
na hi me vṛjinaṃ kiñ cid Dhārtarāṣṭrā viduḥ kva cit.
n' ācaraṃ vṛjinaṃ kiñ cid Dhārtarāṣṭrasya nityaśaḥ;
ahaṃ hi Pāṇḍavān sarvān haniṣyāmi raṇe sthitān.
prāg|viruddhaiḥ śamaṃ sadbhiḥ kathaṃ vā kriyate punaḥ?
rājño hi Dhṛtarāṣṭrasya sarvaṃ kāryaṃ priyaṃ mayā,
tathā Duryodhanasy' âpi; sa hi rājye samāhitaḥ.»

two. These two have certainly attained the indestructible worlds through their actions, but they are reborn here and there again and again when it is time for war. That is why Nárada said, 'The task must be done,' for that man who knows the Veda told everything to the circle of Vrishnis.

When you see Késhava holding his conch, discus, and mace in hand, and the dreaded archer Árjuna taking hold of his weapons, both high-souled and everlasting Krishnas standing on one chariot, then, Duryódhana, my friend, you will remember what I have said. If only this calamity were 49.25
not standing over the Kurus! But your mind, my friend, has veered from profit and moral law.

If you do not take my advice then you will hear that a great many have died, for it is your opinion that all the Kurus respect. You approve as truth the opinion of only three men: Karna, cursed by Rama, bull-like Bharata, the lowborn son of a *suta*; Shákuni, Súbala's son; and your wicked and base brother Duhshásana."

KARNA said:

"Don't say such things about me, long-lived grandfather, for I abide by a warrior's duty without departing from my own moral duty. What other bad behavior exists within me 49.30
for which you abuse me? The Dhartaráshtras know of no deceit of mine anywhere. I have never done any wrong to Dhartaráshtra, though I will kill all the Pándavas as they stand in battle. How can the wise make peace once again with those who have been wronged in the past? I do whatever is dear to King Dhrita·rashtra and of course to Duryódhana, since he is entrusted with the kingdom."

VAIŚAMPĀYANA uvāca:

Karṇasya tu vacaḥ śrutvā Bhīṣmaḥ Śāntanavaḥ punaḥ
Dhṛtarāṣṭraṃ, mahā|rāja, saṃbhāṣy' êdaṃ vaco 'bravīt:
«yad ayaṃ katthate nityaṃ, ‹hant" âhaṃ Pāṇḍavān, iti›
n' âyaṃ kal" âpi saṃpūrṇā Pāṇḍavānāṃ mah"|ātmanām.
49.35 an|ayo yo 'yam āgantā putrāṇāṃ te dur|ātmanām,
tad asya karma jānīhi sūta|putrasya dur|mateḥ.
etam āśritya putras te manda|buddhiḥ Suyodhanaḥ
avāmanyata tān vīrān deva|putrān arin|damān.
kiṃ c' âpy etena tat karma kṛta|pūrvaṃ su|duṣkaram,
tair yathā Pāṇḍavaiḥ sarvair ek' âikena kṛtaṃ purā?
dṛṣṭvā Virāṭa|nagare bhrātaraṃ nihataṃ priyam
Dhanañjayena vikramya, kim anena tadā kṛtam?
sahitān hi Kurūn sarvān abhiyāto Dhanañjayaḥ,
pramathya c' âcchinad vāsaḥ. kim ayaṃ proṣitas tadā?
49.40 gandharvair ghoṣa|yātrāyāṃ hriyate yat sutas tava,
kva tadā sūta|putro 'bhūd ya idānīṃ vṛṣāyate?
nanu tatr' âpi Bhīmena, Pārthena ca mah"|ātmanā,
yamābhyām eva saṃgamya gandharvās te parājitāḥ?
etāny asya mṛṣ" ôktāni bahūni, Bharata'|rṣabha,
vikatthanasya, bhadraṃ te, sadā dharm'|ârtha|lopinaḥ»

Bhīṣmasya tu vacaḥ śrutvā Bhāradvājo mahā|manāḥ
Dhṛtarāṣṭram uvāc' êdaṃ rāja|madhye 'bhipūjayan:
«yad āha Bharata|śreṣṭho Bhīṣmas, tat kriyatāṃ, nṛpa,
na kāmam artha|lipsūnāṃ vacanaṃ kartum arhasi.
49.45 purā yuddhāt sādhu manye Pāṇḍavaiḥ saha saṃgatam.

VAISHAMPÁYANA said:

When he had heard what Karna had to say, Bhishma the son of Shántanu then addressed Dhrita·rashtra, great king, saying this:

"This man constantly boasts that he will kill the Pándavas, but he isn't worth a fraction of the high-souled Pándavas. The disaster approaching your wicked-souled sons is 49.35
the work of this bad-minded son of a *suta*—know that.

Your slow-witted son, Suyódhana, relies on this man and has nothing but contempt for those heroic, foe-destroying sons of gods. What enormously difficult task has this man achieved in the past to match the past achievements of each and every one of the Pándavas? When he saw his own dear brother heroically killed in Viráta's city by Dhanañ·jaya, what did he do?

In fact, it was Dhanañ·jaya who charged all the assembled Kurus, harassed them, and cut off their clothes—was this man on vacation then? When your son was taken by the 49.40
*gandhárvas* at the herdsmen festival, where was this *suta*'s son who struts around like a bull now? Surely even in that instance it was Bhima, high-souled Partha, and the twins who met and defeated the *gandhárvas*? This man who always deviates from moral law and profit tells a great many lies, bull-like Bharata, bless you."

When the great-minded son of Bharad·vaja heard Bhishma's speech, he addressed Dhrita·rashtra in the midst of the kings, honoring him: "My king, do what Bhishma the best of the Bharatas has recommended, for you ought not to act upon the advice of those who are out for their

yad vākyam Arjunen' ôktaṃ Sañjayena niveditam,
sarvaṃ tad api jānāmi, kariṣyati ca Pāṇḍavaḥ,
na hy asya triṣu lokeṣu sadṛśo 'sti dhanur|dharaḥ!»

an|ādṛtya tu tad vākyam arthavad Droṇa|Bhīṣmayoḥ
tataḥ sa Sañjayaṃ rājā paryapṛcchata Pāṇḍavān.
tad" âiva Kuravaḥ sarve nirāśā jīvite 'bhavan,
Bhīṣma|Droṇau yadā rājā na samyag anubhāṣate.

DHṚTARĀṢṬRA uvāca:

50.1 «KIM ASAU PĀṆḌAVO rājā Dharma|putro 'bhyabhāṣata,
śrutv" êha bahulāḥ senāḥ prīty|arthaṃ naḥ samāgatāḥ?
kim asau ceṣṭate, sūta, yotsyamāno Yudhiṣṭhiraḥ?
ke v" âsya bhrātṛ|putrāṇāṃ paśyanty ājñ"|ēpsavo mukham?
ke svid enaṃ vārayanti, yuddhāc ‹chāmy' êti› vā punaḥ,
nikṛtyā kopitaṃ mandair dharma|jñaṃ dharma|cāriṇam?»

SAÑJAYA uvāca:

«rājño mukham udīkṣante Pāñcālāḥ Pāṇḍavaiḥ saha
Yudhiṣṭhirasya, bhadraṃ te, sa sarvān anuśāsti ca.
50.5 pṛthag bhūtāḥ Pāṇḍavānāṃ Pāñcālānāṃ ratha|vrajāḥ
āyāntam abhinandanti Kuntī|putraṃ Yudhiṣṭhiram.
nabhaḥ sūryam iv' ôdyantaṃ Kaunteyaṃ dīpta|tejasam
Pāñcālāḥ pratinandanti, tejo|rāśim iv' ôditam.

own advantage. I believe it would be correct for negotiation with the Pándavas to come before war. I know that the son of Pandu will do all that Árjuna said and Sáñjaya made known to us, for that archer has no match in the three worlds!" 49.45

But the king did not respect Drona and Bhishma's significant words, and instead questioned Sáñjaya about the Pándavas. So it was that all the Kurus lost any hope of saving their lives when the king did not reply to Bhishma and Drona properly.

DHRITA·RASHTRA said:

"WHAT DID THE royal Pándava, son of Dharma, say when 50.1
he heard that numerous armies had gathered to please us? How is Yudhi·shthira behaving, *suta*, now he is ready to fight? Which of his brothers and sons are looking to his face, keen for his commands? Who tries to steer him away from war or tells him to make peace again, as the man of righteous conduct who understands moral law remains angry about the deceit and angry with fools?"

SÁÑJAYA replied:

"The Pañchálas and the Pándavas look to the face of King
Yudhi·shthira, bless you, and he commands them all. The 50.5
hosts of Pándava and Pañchála chariots separately and together salute Yudhi·shthira, son of Kunti, when he approaches. The Pañchálas pay their respects to the Kauntéya, who blazes with splendor like the sun breaking out from behind the clouds, and who rises like the torrent of light.

ā gopāl'|âvipālebhyo nandamānaṃ Yudhiṣṭhiram*
Pāñcālāḥ, Kekayā, Matsyāḥ pratinandanti Pāṇḍavam.
brāhmaṇyo, rāja|putryaś ca, viśāṃ duhitaraś ca yāḥ,
krīḍantyo 'bhisamāyānti Pārthaṃ sannaddham īkṣitum.»

DHṚTARĀṢṬRA uvāca:

«Sañjay', âcakṣva yen' âsmān Pāṇḍavā abhyayuñjata
Dhṛṣṭadyumnasya sainyena Somakānāṃ balena ca.»

VAIŚAMPĀYANA uvāca:

50.10 Gāvalgaṇis tu tat pṛṣṭaḥ sabhāyāṃ Kuru|saṃsadi
niḥśvasya su|bhṛśaṃ dīrghaṃ, muhuḥ sañcintayann iva.
tatr' â|nimittato daivāt sūtaṃ kaśmalam āviśat.
tad" ācacakṣe Viduraḥ sabhāyāṃ rāja|saṃsadi:
«Sañjayo 'yaṃ, mahā|rāja, mūrcchitaḥ patito bhuvi.
vācaṃ na sṛjate kāñ cidd hīna|prajño 'lpa|cetanaḥ!»

DHṚTARĀṢṬRA uvāca:

«apaśyat Sañjayo nūnaṃ Kuntī|putrān mahā|rathān,
tair asya puruṣa|vyāghrair bhṛśam udvejitaṃ manaḥ.»

VAIŚAMPĀYANA uvāca:

Sañjayaś cetanāṃ labdhvā pratyāśvasy' êdam abravīt
Dhṛtarāṣṭraṃ, mahā|rāja, sabhāyāṃ Kuru|saṃsadi:

Even cowherds and shepherds rejoice in Yudhi·shthira, and the Pañchálas, Kékayas, and Matsyas pay their respects to the son of Pandu. Brahmin-caste women, princesses, and the daughters of ordinary subjects come together to play so they can watch the Partha in his battle armor."

DHRITA·RASHTRA said:

"Sáñjaya, tell me about Dhrishta·dyumna's army and the force of Sómakas that the Pándavas have drawn up against us."

VAISHAMPÁYANA said:

Asked this in the hall where the Kurus were assembled, 50.10
the son of Gaválgana sighed very deeply for some time, and appeared to be giving it consideration for a while. Then, unaccountably, as fate would have it, the *suta* fell into a faint, and Vídura spoke in the court, in the assembly of kings, saying: "Sáñjaya here has fainted and fallen to the floor, great king. He is unconscious, senseless, and isn't saying a word!"

DHRITA·RASHTRA said:

"Surely Sáñjaya's mind was greatly afflicted by beholding those mighty tiger-like warrior sons of Kunti."

VAISHAMPÁYANA said:

But Sáñjaya regained his senses and breathing again, and he said to Dhrita·rashtra, great king, in the court of the Kuru assembly:

SAÑJAYA uvāca:

50.15 «dṛṣṭavān asmi, rāj'|êndra, Kuntī|putrān mahā|rathān
Matsya|rāja|gṛh'|āvāsa|nirodhen' âvakarśitān.
śṛṇu yair hi, mahā|rāja, Pāṇḍavā abhyayuñjata.
Dhṛṣṭadyumnena vīreṇa yuddhe vas te 'bhyayuñjata,
yo n' âiva roṣān, na bhayān, na lobhān, n' ârtha|kāraṇāt,
na hetu|vādād dharm'|ātmā satyaṃ jahyāt kadā cana,
yaḥ pramāṇaṃ, mahā|rāja, dharme dharma|bhṛtāṃ varaḥ,
Ajātaśatruṇā tena Pāṇḍavā abhyayuñjata.

yasya bāhu|bale tulyaḥ pṛthivyāṃ n' âsti kaś cana,
yo vai sarvān mahī|pālān vaśe cakre dhanur|dharaḥ,
yaḥ Kāśīn, Aṅga|Magadhān, Kaliṅgāṃś ca yudh" âjayat,
50.20 tena vo Bhīmasenena Pāṇḍavā abhyayuñjata,
yasya vīryeṇa sahasā catvāro bhuvi Pāṇḍavāḥ
niḥsṛtya jatu|gehād vai, Hiḍimbāt puruṣ'|âdakāt,
yaś c' âiṣām abhavad dvīpaḥ Kuntī|putro Vṛkodaraḥ.

Yājñasenīm atho yatra Sindhu|rājo 'pakṛṣṭavān,
tatr' âiṣām abhavad dvīpaḥ Kuntī|putro Vṛkodaraḥ.
yaś ca tān saṅgatān sarvān Pāṇḍavān Vāraṇāvate
dahyato mocayām āsa, tena vas te 'bhyayuñjata.
Kṛṣṇāyāṃ caratā prītiṃ yena Krodhavaśā hatāḥ
praviśya viṣamaṃ ghoraṃ parvataṃ Gandhamādanam,
50.25 yasya nāg'|âyutair vīryaṃ bhujayoḥ sāram arpitam,
tena vo Bhīmasenena Pāṇḍavā abhyayuñjata!

Kṛṣṇa|dvitīyo vikramya tuṣṭy|arthaṃ Jātavedasaḥ
ajayad yaḥ purā vīro yudhyamānaṃ Puran|daram;
yaḥ sa sākṣān mahā|devaṃ giri|śaṃ śūla|pāṇinam
toṣayām āsa yuddhena deva|devam Umā|patim;

SÁÑJAYA said:

"I have seen, lord of kings, the great warrior sons of Kunti 50.15
dragged down by the imprisonment of living in the house of
the king of Matsya. Hear, great king, whom the Pándavas
have drawn up against you! They will fight you in battle
with the hero Dhrishta·dyumna. The Pándavas will fight
you with Ajáta·shatru, the virtuous-souled man who never
abandons the truth through anger, fear, greed, or for the
sake of wealth or excuses, who is the measure of morality,
great king, and the best of those who uphold moral law.

The Pándavas will fight you with Bhima·sena, the man 50.20
who has no equal in the strength of his arms on this earth,
the archer who has subjugated all kings, the warrior who has
defeated the Kashis, the Angas, Mágadhas, and Kalíngas; by
whose prowess the four Pándavas quickly escaped from the
lac house and from Hidímba the cannibal; the son of Kunti,
Vrikódara, who was those men's refuge.

They will fight you with Vrikódara, the son of Kunti, who
was the others' refuge when the king of Sindhu had dragged
off Yajñaséni, and who released the Pándavas when they
were all being burned together at Varanávata. The Pándavas 50.25
will fight you with Bhima·sena who killed the Krodha·
vashas as a favor for Krishná when he entered the terrifying
and rugged Gandha·mádana mounain, and in whose arms
reside the strength and power of ten thousand elephants!

The Pándavas will fight against you in battle with Víjaya, the hero who long ago defeated the Sacker of Cities in combat, attacking with Krishna as his second, in order to appease Agni; who in battle actually satisfied Shiva, the great god who dwells in the mountains, trident in hand, the

yaś ca sarvān vaśe cakre loka|pālān dhanur|dharaḥ
tena vo Vijayen' âjau Pāṇḍavā abhyayuñjata.
yaḥ pratīcīṃ diśaṃ cakre vaśe mleccha|gaṇ'|āyutām,
sa tatra Nakulo yoddhā citra|yodhī vyavasthitaḥ.
50.30 tena vo darśanīyena vīreṇ' âtidhanurbhṛtā
Mādrī|putreṇa, Kauravya, Pāṇḍavā abhyayuñjata.
yaḥ Kāśīn, Aṅga|Magadhān, Kaliṅgāṃś ca yudh" âjayat,
tena vaḥ Sahadevena Pāṇḍavā abhyayuñjata;
yasya vīryeṇa sadṛśāś catvāro bhuvi mānavāḥ
Aśvatthāmā, Dhṛṣṭaketū, Rukmī, Pradyumna eva ca;
tena vaḥ Sahadevena yuddhaṃ, rājan, mah"|âtyayam,
yavīyasā nṛ|vīreṇa Mādrī|nandi|kareṇa ca.
tapaś cacāra yā ghoraṃ Kāśi|kanyā purā satī,
Bhīṣmasya vadham icchantī prety' âpi, Bharata'|rṣabha,
50.35 Pāñcālasya sutā jajñe daivāc ca sa punaḥ pumān,
strī|puṃsoḥ, puruṣa|vyāghra, yaḥ sa veda guṇ'|â|guṇān,
yaḥ Kaliṅgān samāpede Pāñcālyo yuddha|durmadaḥ,
Śikhaṇḍinā vaḥ, Kuravaḥ, kṛt'|âstren' âbhyayuñjata.
yaṃ yakṣaḥ puruṣaṃ cakre Bhīṣmasya nidhan'|êcchayā,
mah"|êṣvāsena raudreṇa Pāṇḍavā abhyayuñjata.
mah"|êṣvāsā rāja|putrā bhrātaraḥ pañca Kekayāḥ
āmukta|kavacāḥ śūrās, taiś ca vas te 'bhyayuñjata.
yo dīrgha|bāhuḥ kṣipr'|âstro dhṛtimān satya|vikramaḥ,
tena vo Vṛṣṇi|vīreṇa Yuyudhānena saṅgaraḥ.
50.40 ya āsīc charaṇaṃ kāle Pāṇḍavānāṃ mah"|ātmanām,
raṇe tena Virāṭena bhavitā vaḥ samāgamaḥ.

god of gods, husband to Uma; the archer who brought all earthly kings under his control.

The Pándavas will fight you, Kaurávya, with Madri's son, 50.30
Nákula, the handsome hero and excellent archer, established as the versatile warrior who brought the western region under his control, subjugating hordes of barbarians.

The Pándavas will fight you with Saha·deva, the warrior who defeated the Kashis, Angas, Mágadhas, and Kalíngas; the hero who is matched by only four men on earth, Ashvattháman, Dhrishta·ketu, Rukmin, and Pradyúmna; Saha·deva who makes battle highly dangerous, my king, the youngest hero who brought joy to Madri.

Kurus, they will fight you with Shikhándin, expert in 50.35
weapons, who performed terrible acts of asceticism long ago as the daughter of Kashi, who wished for Bhishma's murder in the next life, bull-like Bharata, and who was born as the daughter of Pañchála and then again as a man, as fate would have it, so that he understood the virtues of the female and the male, tiger-like man. Full of lust for war, the Pañchályan prince destroyed the Kalíngas. The Pándavas will fight you with the fierce expert archer whom a *yaksha* turned into a man because he wished for Bhishma's destruction.

They will fight you with those five, brave, armored Kékaya brothers, the great archer princes. The war will be against long-armed Yuyudhána, the Vrishni hero, swift with his weapons, resolute, and truly valiant. You will encounter 50.40
Viráta in battle, the man who was for a time a refuge for those high-souled Pándavas.

yaḥ sa Kāśi|patī rājā Vārāṇasyāṃ mahā|rathaḥ,
sa teṣām abhavad yoddhā, tena vas te 'bhyayuñjata.
śiśubhir dur|jayaiḥ saṅkhye Draupadeyair mah"|ātmabhiḥ
āśīviṣa|sama|sparśaiḥ Pāṇḍavā abhyayuñjata.
yaḥ Kṛṣṇa|sadṛśo vīrye, Yudhiṣṭhira|samo dame,
ten' Âbhimanyunā saṅkhye Pāṇḍavā abhyayuñjata.
yaś c' âiv' â|pratimo vīrye Dhṛṣṭaketur mahā|yaśā,
duḥ|sahaḥ samare kruddhaḥ Śaiśupālir mahā|rathaḥ,
50.45 tena vaś Cedi|rājena Pāṇḍavā abhyayuñjata,
akṣauhiṇyā parivṛtaḥ Pāṇḍavān yo 'bhisaṃśritaḥ.
yaḥ saṃśrayaḥ Pāṇḍavānāṃ, devānām iva Vāsavaḥ,
tena vo Vāsudevena Pāṇḍavā abhyayuñjata.
tathā Cedi|pater bhrātā Śarabho, Bharata'|rṣabha,
Karakarṣeṇa sahitas, tābhyāṃ vas te abhyayuñjata.
Jārāsandhiḥ, Sahadevo, Jayatsenaś ca tāv ubhau
yuddhe '|pratirathe vīrau Pāṇḍav'|ârthe vyavasthitau.
Drupadaś ca mahā|tejā, balena mahatā vṛtaḥ,
tyakt'|ātmā Pāṇḍav'|ârthāya yotsyamāno vyavasthitaḥ.
50.50 ete c' ânye ca bahavaḥ prācy'|ôdīcyā mahī|kṣitaḥ
śataśo yān upāśritya dharma|rājo vyavasthitaḥ.»

DHṚTARĀṢṬRA uvāca:

51.1 «SARVA ETE mah"|ôtsāhā ye tvayā parikīrtitāḥ,
ekatas tv eva te sarve sametā Bhīma ekataḥ.
Bhīmasenādd hi me bhūyo bhayaṃ sañjāyate mahat,
kruddhād, a|marṣaṇāt, tāta, vyāghrād iva mahā|ruroḥ.
jāgarmi rātrayaḥ sarvā dīrgham uṣṇaṃ ca niḥśvasan,
bhīto Vṛkodarāt, tāta, siṃhāt paśur iv' âparaḥ.

They will fight you with the lord of Kashi, the great warrior king in Varánasi who has become their allied fighter. The Pándavas will fight you with the high-souled young sons of Dráupadi, near invincible in battle, whose touch is like that of a poisonous snake. The Pándavas will fight you in battle with Abhimányu, the equal of Krishna in prowess and the equal of Yudhi·shthira in control.

The Pándavas will fight you with the king of the Chedis, 50.45
the mighty warrior, great glorious Dhrishta·ketu, son of Shishu·pala, matchless in heroism, furious and invincible in battle, surrounded by a battalion, devoting himself to the Pándavas. The sons of Pandu will fight you with Vasudéva, who is their refuge just as Vásava is the refuge of the gods.

They will fight you with Shárabha, brother of the king of Chedi, bull-like Bharata, along with Kara·karsha. Saha·deva, son of Jara·sandha, and Jayat·sena, unequaled heroes in battle, have both decided upon the Pándavas' cause. Drúpada of great splendor, surrounded by his massive force, is resolved to fight for the Pándavas' cause and lay down his
life. Relying upon these and numerous other hundreds of 50.50
kings from the east and north, the king of virtue is waiting."

DHRITA·RASHTRA said:

"EVERYONE YOU have mentioned is extremely powerful, 51.1
but Bhima alone can match each and every one together. My great fear of furious, impatient Bhima·sena completely overwhelms me, my friend, like an antelope's fear of a tiger. I stay awake every night breathing heavily and hotly for a long time, afraid of Vrikódara, my son, just as a weaker animal fears a lion.

na hi tasya mahā|bāhoḥ Śakra|pratima|tejasaḥ
sainye 'smin pratipaśyāmi ya enaṃ viṣahed yudhi.
51.5 a|marṣaṇaś ca Kaunteyo, dṛḍha|vairaś ca Pāṇḍavaḥ,
a|narma|hāsī, s'|ônmādas, tiryak|prekṣī, mahā|svanaḥ.
mahā|vego, mah"|ôtsāho, mahā|bāhur, mahā|balaḥ,
mandānāṃ mama putrāṇāṃ yuddhen' ântaṃ kariṣyati.
urugrāha|gṛhītānāṃ gadāṃ bibhrad Vṛkodaraḥ
Kurūṇām ṛṣabho yuddhe daṇḍa|pāṇir iv' ântakaḥ.
aṣṭ'|âsrim āyasīṃ ghorāṃ gadāṃ kāñcana|bhūṣaṇām
manas" âhaṃ prapaśyāmi, brahma|daṇḍam iv' ôdyatam.
yathā mṛgāṇāṃ yūtheṣu siṃho jāta|balaś caret,
māmakeṣu tathā Bhīmo baleṣu vicariṣyati!
51.10 sarveṣāṃ mama putrāṇāṃ sa ekaḥ krūra|vikramaḥ
bahv|āśī vipratīpaś ca bālye 'pi rabhasaḥ sadā.
udvepate me hṛdayaṃ, ye me Duryodhan'|ādayaḥ
bālye 'pi tena yudhyanto vāraṇen' êva marditāḥ.
tasya vīryeṇa saṅkliṣṭā nityam eva sutā mama;
sa eva hetur bhedasya Bhīmo bhīma|parākramaḥ.
grasamānam anīkāni nara|vāraṇa|vājinām
paśyām' îv' âgrato Bhīmaṃ krodha|mūrchitam āhave.
astre Droṇ'|Ârjuna|samaṃ, vāyu|vega|samaṃ jave,
mah"|ēśvara|samaṃ krodhe, ko hanyād Bhīmam āhave?
51.15 Sañjay', ācakṣva me śūraṃ Bhīmasenam a|marṣaṇam!
atilābhaṃ tu manye 'haṃ, yat tena ripu|ghātinā
tad" âiva na hatāḥ sarve putrā mama manasvinā,
yena bhīma|balā yakṣā rākṣasāś ca purā hatāḥ!

Indeed, I do not see anyone in this army who could withstand that long-armed man whose splendor equals Shakra's
in a fight. The impatient son of Kunti and Pandu is a man of 51.5
firm valor who does not laugh at jokes, but furious, glancing obliquely, he makes a huge amount of noise. Incredibly
forceful, powerful, long-armed, and mighty, he will put an
end to my dull-witted sons with battle.

Vrikódara, the bull of the Kurus, bearing his mace down
upon my sons, caught up in a far-reaching disaster, will be
like Death himself wielding his stick in battle. In my mind I
see that horrifying eight-cornered iron mace gleaming with
gold like a brahmin's staff upraised in a curse. Just as a
mighty lion moves among the herds of animals, so Bhima
will wander among my troops!

This one, an obstinate man of insatiable appetite and 51.10
pitiless prowess, has always been violent towards all my sons
since his childhood. He made my heart tremble when Duryódhana and the others were crushed as though by an elephant when they fought him in their childhood. My sons
were always tarnished by his courage, and Bhima of fearful
prowess is the reason for the break between us.

I can almost see Bhima at the front, swallowing armies
of men, elephants, and horses, when his anger is roused in
battle. He is Drona and Árjuna's equal in weapons, matches
the force of the wind in speed, and is the mighty lord's equal
in fury, so who could kill Bhima in war? Sáñjaya, tell me 51.15
about the intolerant hero Bhima·sena! It was very lucky, in
my opinion, that all my sons were not killed by that spirited enemy-slaughterer who long ago destroyed fearsomely
strong *yaksha*s and *rákshasa*s!

kathaṃ tasya raṇe vegaṃ mānuṣaḥ prasahiṣyati?
na sa jātu vaśe tasthau mama bālye 'pi, Sañjaya.
kiṃ punar mama duṣ|putraiḥ kliṣṭaḥ samprati Pāṇḍavaḥ?
niṣṭhuro, roṣaṇo 'tyarthaṃ, bhajyet' âpi na saṃnamet.
tiryak|prekṣī, saṃhata|bhrūḥ, kathaṃ śāmyed Vṛkodaraḥ?
śūras, tath" â|prati|balo, gauras, tāla iv' ônnataḥ,
pramāṇato Bhīmasenaḥ prādeśen' âdhiko 'rjunāt.
51.20 javena vājino 'tyeti, balen' âtyeti kuñjarān,
a|vyakta|jalpī, madhv|akṣo madhyamaḥ Pāṇḍavo balī.
iti bālye śrutaḥ pūrvaṃ mayā Vyāsa|mukhāt purā,
rūpato vīryataś c' âiva yāthātathyena Pāṇḍavaḥ.
āyasena sa daṇḍena rathān nāgān narān hayān
haniṣyati raṇe kruddho, raudraḥ, krūra|parākramaḥ.
a|marṣī nitya|saṃrabdho Bhīmaḥ praharatāṃ varaḥ
mayā, tāta, pratīpāni kurvan pūrvaṃ vimānitaḥ.
niṣkarṇām, āyasīṃ, sthūlāṃ, su|pārśvāṃ kāñcanīṃ gadām
śata|ghnīṃ, śata|nirhrādāṃ kathaṃ śakṣyanti me sutāḥ?
51.25 a|pāram, a|plav'|â|gādhaṃ samudraṃ śara|vedhanam
Bhīmasenam ayaṃ durgaṃ, tāta, mandās titīrṣavaḥ.
krośato me na śṛṇvanti bālāḥ paṇḍita|māninaḥ,
viṣamaṃ na hi manyante prapātaṃ madhu|darśinaḥ.
saṃyugaṃ ye gamiṣyanti nara|rūpeṇa mṛtyunā,
niyataṃ c' ôditā dhātrā siṃhen' êva mahā|mṛgāḥ.

How could any man stand up to him in battle? Even as a child, Sáñjaya, he was not in my control, so how could I control the Pándava now, when he has been made to suffer by my wicked sons? The severe and excessively passionate man may even break but not bend. Glancing obliquely, knotted-browed, how could Vrikódara become calm?

Brave, matchlessly strong, beautiful in complexion, and tall like a palm-tree, Bhima·sena is a span taller than Árjuna. He surpasses horses in speed and elephants in strength. The 51.20
powerful, middle-born son of Pandu speaks incoherently and has eyes the hue of honey. In truth, I heard it from Vyasa's mouth long ago that the Pándava was precisely the same in strength and form even as a child.

When angry, the fierce son of Pandu, a man of vicious prowess, will destroy chariots, elephants, men, and horses with his iron mace in battle. Intolerant and constantly angry Bhima, the best of boxers, has been told off in the past for doing outrageous things, my son. How will my sons be able to withstand his straight, iron, bulky, well-sided, and golden mace, which kills hundreds and resounds a hundred times?

Fools, my son, wish to cross that distant, shoreless, un- 51.25
navigably deep ocean of piercing arrows that is Bhima·sena. These children think they are wise and do not listen to me when I am angry. They see only the honey and do not consider the dangerous pitfalls. Those who go to battle with death in human form are destined for destruction by the creator, just as antelopes before a lion.

śaikyāṃ, tāta, catuṣ|kiṣkuṃ, ṣaḍ|āstrim, a|mit'|âujasam,
prahitāṃ, duḥkha|saṃsparśāṃ katham śakṣyanti me sutā?
gadāṃ bhrāmayatas tasya, bhindato hasti|mastakān,
sṛkkiṇī lelihānasya, bāṣpam utsṛjato muhuḥ,
51.30 uddiśya nāgān patataḥ, kurvato bhairavān ravān,
pratīpaṃ patato mattān, kuñjarān pratigarjataḥ,
vigāhya ratha|mārgeṣu, varān uddiśya nighnataḥ,
agneḥ prajvalitasy' êva, api mucyeta me prajā?
vīthīṃ kurvan mahā|bāhur, drāvayan mama vāhinīm,
nṛtyann iva gadā|pāṇir yug'|ântaṃ darśayiṣyati.
prabhinna iva mātaṅgaḥ prabhañjan puṣpitān drumān,
pravekṣyati raṇe senāṃ putrāṇāṃ me Vṛkodaraḥ.
kurvan rathān vipuruṣān, visārathi|haya|dhvajān,
ārujan puruṣa|vyāghro rathinaḥ sādinas tathā,
51.35 Gaṅgā|vega iv' ânūpāṃs, tīra|jān vividhān drumān,
prabhaṅkṣyati raṇe senāṃ putrāṇāṃ mama, Saṇjaya!
diśo nūnaṃ gamiṣyanti Bhīmasena|bhay'|ârditāḥ
mama putrāś ca bhṛtyāś ca, rājānaś c' âiva, Sañjaya.
yena rājā mahā|vīryaḥ praviśy' ântaḥ|puraṃ purā
Vāsudeva|sahāyena Jarāsandho nipātitaḥ.
kṛtsn" êyaṃ pṛthivī devī Jarāsandhena dhīmatā
Māgadh'|êndreṇa balinā vaśe kṛtvā pratāpitā.
Bhīṣma|pratāpāt Kuravo, nayen' Ândhaka|Vṛṣṇayaḥ,
yan na tasya vaśe jagmuḥ, kevalaṃ daivam eva tat.

My friend, how will my sons be able to withstand that six-cornered mace of immeasurable power, four cubits long, the touch of which is misery, when it is hurled from its sling? When he is waving his mace, breaking elephants' heads, licking the corners of his mouth, constantly streaming tears, aiming for and falling upon elephants, producing 51.30
terrifying bellows, falling on the furious elephants against him and answering their trumpeting, diving into the paths of chariots, and aiming for and killing my best men, will any of my children escape him as he blazes like a fire?

The long-armed man will create a path and make my army flee, as though dancing, mace in hand, and he will show us the end of our age. Vrikódara will penetrate my sons' army just as an elephant with split temples breaks down flowering trees. Ridding the chariots of their warriors, and ridding them of charioteers, horses, and banners, that tiger-like man, tearing down charioteers and riders, will rout my sons' army in battle, just as the force of the 51.35
Ganges shatters the various water-loving trees which grown on the banks, Sáñjaya!

Surely my sons, dependants, and kings will spread out in all directions, afflicted with fear of Bhima·sena, Sáñjaya. This is the man by whom the powerful King Jara·sandha was brought low, when he once entered his inner apartments with Vasudéva as his accomplice. This entire, divine earth had been brought under the control of cunning Jara·sandha, the powerful lord of Mágadha, and tormented by him. It was entirely through their good luck that the Kurus, by the brilliance of Bhishma, and the Ándhakas and Vrishnis, through their policy, did not fall under his power.

51.40 sa gatvā Pāṇḍu|putreṇa tarasā bāhu|śālinā
an|āyudhena vīreṇa nihataḥ. kiṃ tato 'dhikam?
dīrgha|kāla|samāsaktaṃ viṣam āśī|viṣo yathā,
sa mokṣyati raṇe tejaḥ putreṣu mama, Sañjaya!
mah"|Êndra iva vajreṇa dānavān deva|sattamaḥ,
Bhīmaseno gadā|pāṇiḥ sūdayiṣyati me sutān.
a|viṣahyam, an|āvāryaṃ, tīvra|vega|parākramam
paśyām' îv' âtitāmr'|âkṣam āpatantaṃ Vṛkodaram.
a|gadasy' âpy a|dhanuṣo, virathasya vivarmaṇaḥ,
bāhubhyāṃ yudhyamānasya kas tiṣṭhed agrataḥ pumān?
51.45 Bhīṣmo, Droṇaś ca vipro 'yaṃ, Kṛpaḥ Śāradvatas tathā,
jānanty ete yath" âiv' âhaṃ vīrya|jñas tasya dhīmataḥ.
ārya|vrataṃ tu jānantaḥ, saṅgar'|ântaṃ vidhitsavaḥ,
senā|mukheṣu sthāsyanti māmakānāṃ nara'|rṣabhāḥ.
balīyaḥ sarvato diṣṭaṃ puruṣasya viśeṣataḥ;
paśyann api jayaṃ teṣāṃ na niyacchāmi yat sutān.
te purāṇaṃ mah"|êṣvāsā mārgam Aindraṃ samāsthitāḥ
tyakṣyanti tumule prāṇān rakṣantaḥ pārthivaṃ yaśaḥ.
yath" âiṣāṃ māmakās, tāta, tath" âiṣāṃ Pāṇḍavā api
pautrā Bhīṣmasya, śiṣyāś ca Droṇasya ca Kṛpasya ca.
51.50 ye tv asmad|āśrayaṃ kiñ cid dattam iṣṭaṃ ca, Sañjaya,
tasy' âpacitim āryatvāt kartāraḥ sthavirās trayaḥ.

Pandu's long-armed son went quickly and though he was 51.40
unarmed, he killed him. What beats that?

Just as a snake releases the poison that it has stored up for so long, so he will release his splendor upon my sons in battle, Sáñjaya! Just as mighty Indra, the greatest of the gods, put an end to the Dánavas with his thunderbolt, so Bhima·sena, mace in hand, will put an end to my sons. I see the irresistable Vrikódara of sharp, forceful prowess, against whom there is no protection, flying towards us with bright red eyes. Even if he were without his mace or bow, chariotless and unarmored and fighting with bare fists, what man would stand against him?

Bhishma, the brahmin Drona, and Kripa Sharádvata 51.45
know just as I do about the prowess of that intelligent man. Those bull-like men, who understand the noble vow, wish to bring an end to the war and will stand in the vanguard of my troops. Fate is stronger than everything—men in particular—and even though I see their victory, I will not restrain my sons.

The great archers setting out on the ancient path to Indra will abandon their lives in the tumult, defending their earthly fame. Both my own sons and the Pándavas are held in equal esteem by these men, my friend, for they are all grandsons of Bhishma and pupils of Drona and Kripa.
Whatever favors we have granted to them, Sáñjaya, their 51.50
nobility ensures they will repay us.

ādadānasya śastraṃ hi kṣatra|dharmaṃ parīpsataḥ
nidhanaṃ kṣatriyasy' ājau varam ev' āhur uttamam.
sa vai śocāmi sarvān vai ye yuyutsanti Pāṇḍavaiḥ.
vikruṣṭaṃ Vidureṇ' ādau tad etad bhayam āgatam.
na tu manye vighātāya jñānaṃ duḥkhasya, Sañjaya,
bhavaty atibalaṃ hy etaj jñānasy' âpy upaghātakam.
ṛṣayo hy api nirmuktāḥ paśyanto loka|saṃgrahān
sukhair bhavanti sukhinas, tathā duḥkhena duḥkhitāḥ.
51.55 kiṃ punar moham āsaktas tatra tatra sahasradhā,
putreṣu, rājya|dāreṣu, pautreṣv, api ca bandhuṣu?
saṃśaye tu mahaty asmin kiṃ nu me kṣamam uttaram?
vināśaṃ hy eva paśyāmi Kurūṇām anucintayan.
dyūta|pramukham ābhāti Kurūṇāṃ vyasanaṃ mahat;
manden' āiśvarya|kāmena lobhāt pāpam idaṃ kṛtaṃ.
manye paryāya|dharmo 'yaṃ kālasy' âtyanta|gāminaḥ.
cakre pradhir iv' āsakto n' âsya śakyaṃ palāyitum.
kin nu kuryāṃ? kathaṃ kuryāṃ?
kva nu gacchāmi, Sañjaya?
ete naśyanti Kuravo
mandāḥ kāla|vaśaṃ gatāḥ.
51.60 a|vaśo 'haṃ tadā, tāta, putrāṇāṃ nihate śate.
śroṣyāmi ninadaṃ strīṇāṃ! kathaṃ māṃ maraṇaṃ spṛśet?
yathā nidāghe jvalanaḥ samiddho
dahet kakṣaṃ vāyunā codyamānaḥ,
gadā|hastaḥ Pāṇḍavo vai tath" âiva
hantā madīyān sahito 'rjunena.»

They say that death on the battlefield is the greatest boon for a warrior who has taken up weapons and wishes to achieve his warrior duty. I grieve for all who will fight against the Pándavas. That danger which Vídura predicted at the beginning has now arrived. Sáñjaya, I do not believe that knowledge destroys misery, but instead that when it is excessively powerful, it is misery that obliterates knowledge.

Even the dispassionate sages who watch the welfare of the universe are made happy by its joys, or miserable by its
pains. So how much more will I grieve, who am foolishly 51.55
attached to a thousand things: my sons, queens, grandsons, and relatives? On the eve of such great danger, what great ability do I possess to endure it? I even see the destruction of the Kurus in my thoughts.

The Kurus' disastrous predicament became apparent at the time of the gambling; this sin was committed by that fool who, in his greed, lusts for power. I believe this is the law of the circularity of time which continues forever. I am attached to the wheel just like its rim, and so am unable to escape it.

What should I do, and how should I do it? Where shall I go, Sáñjaya? The foolish Kurus will be destroyed, for their
time is up and they are powerless to prevent it. So, then, I 51.60
am powerless, my friend, in the hundred deaths of my sons. I will hear the cries of the women! How may death touch me? Just as a kindled blaze in summer consumes the dead wood when assisted by the wind, so the son of Pandu, mace in hand, will be the murderer of my sons, accompanied by Árjuna."

DHṚTARĀṢṬRA uvāca:

52.1 «YASYA VAI N' ânṛtā vācaḥ kadā cid anuśuśruma,
trailokyam api tasya syād, yoddhā yasya Dhanañjayaḥ!
tasy' âiva ca na paśyāmi yudhi Gāṇḍīva|dhanvanaḥ,
a|niśaṃ cintayāno 'pi, yaḥ pratīyād rathena tam.
asyataḥ karṇi|nālīkān mārgaṇān hṛdaya|cchidaḥ
pratyetā na samaḥ kaś cid yudhi Gāṇḍīva|dhanvanaḥ!

Droṇa|Karṇau pratīyātāṃ yadi vīrau nara'|rṣabhau,
kṛt'|âstrau, balināṃ śreṣṭhau, samareṣv a|parājitau,
52.5 mahān syāt saṃśayo loke, na tv asti vijayo mama.
ghṛṇī Karṇaḥ pramādī ca, ācāryaḥ sthaviro guruḥ;
samartho balavān Pārtho dṛḍha|dhanvā jita|klamaḥ;
bhavet su|tumulaṃ yuddhaṃ sarvaśo 'py a|parājayaḥ.

sarve hy astra|vidaḥ śūrāḥ, sarve prāptā mahad yaśaḥ,
api sarv'|âmar'|āiśvaryaṃ tyajeyur, na punar jayam!
vadhe nūnaṃ bhavec chāntis tayor vā, Phālgunasya ca;
na tu hant" Ârjunasy' âsti; jetā c' âsya na vidyate.
manyus tasya kathaṃ śāmyen, mandān prati ya utthitaḥ?
anye 'py astrāṇi jānanti, jīyante ca jayanti ca;
52.10 ekānta|vijayas tv eva śrūyate Phālgunasya ha!

DHRITA·RASHTRA continued:

"THE MAN WHO has never uttered a deceitful word, and 52.1
who has Dhanañ·jaya as his warrior, may own even the three worlds! I ponder the matter incessantly but see no one who could mount his chariot and stand against the Gandíva archer in battle. No one is a match for the Gandíva archer and could go against him in battle when he shoots arrows, shafts, and darts that pierce the heart!

If Drona and Karna, those heroic, bull-like men, went against him, with their expert weapons training, and those two most powerful of the powerful were not destroyed in
battle, then there would be great uncertainty in this world, 52.5
but the victory would still not be mine. Karna is passionate and careless, and the teacher is elderly and influential, but powerful and energetic Partha, the firm bowman, is a match for both. The battle would be extremely fierce, but there would be no defeat on any side.

Indeed, all are brave experts with weapons, who have won great fame. Even if they were to renounce power over all the immortals they would not abandon victory! Surely peace will only exist with the death of those two or the death of Phálguna. However, Árjuna's killer does not exist; his defeat is not possible. How may his fury that has risen against my foolish sons be quelled? There are others who understand weapons and are either defeated or victorious, but of 52.10
Phálguna we hear exclusively about his victory!

trayas|triṃśat samāhūya Khāṇḍave 'gnim atarpayat.
jigāya ca surān sarvān; n' âsya vidmaḥ parājayam.
yasya yantā Hṛṣīkeśaḥ śīla|vṛtta|samo yudhi,
dhruvas tasya jayas, tāta, yath" Êndrasya jayas tathā.
Kṛṣṇāv eka|rathe yat tāv, adhijyaṃ Gāṇḍivaṃ dhanuḥ,
yugapat trīṇi tejāṃsi sametāny anuśuśruma.
n' âiv' âsti no dhanus tādṛṅ, na yoddhā na ca sārathiḥ;
tac ca mandā na jānanti Duryodhana|vaś'|ânugāḥ!
śeṣayed aśanir dīpto vipatan mūrdhni, Sañjaya,
52.15 na tu śeṣaṃ śarās, tāta, kuryur astāḥ Kirīṭinā.
api c' âsyann iv' ābhāti nighnann iva Dhanañjayaḥ,
uddharann iva kāyebhyaḥ śirāṃsi śara|vṛṣṭibhiḥ.
api bāṇa|mayaṃ tejaḥ pradīptam iva sarvataḥ
Gāṇḍīv'|ôtthaṃ dahed ājau putrāṇāṃ mama vāhinīm.
api sārathya|ghoṣeṇa bhay'|ārtā Savyasācinaḥ
vitrastā bahudhā senā Bhāratī pratibhāti me.
yathā kakṣaṃ mahān agniḥ pradahet sarvataś caran,
mah"|ârcir anil'|ôddhatas tadvad dhakṣyati māmakān!
yad" ôdvaman niśitān bāṇa|saṅghāṃs
tān ātatāyī samare Kirīṭī
sṛṣṭo 'ntakaḥ sarva|haro vidhātrā
yathā bhavet, tadvad a|pāraṇīyaḥ.
52.20 yadā hy abhīkṣṇaṃ su|bahūn prakārān
śrot" âsmi tān āvasathe Kurūṇām,
teṣāṃ samantāc ca tathā raṇ'|âgre
kṣayaḥ kil' âyaṃ Bharatān upaiti!»

He challenged the thirty-three gods as their equal, and sated Agni at Khándava. He defeated all the gods, and I know of no defeat he has suffered. Victory is assured in battle for the man whose charioteer is Hrishi·kesha, his equal in proper conduct, just as victory is assured for Indra, my friend. It is rumored that the two Krishnas and the strung bow Gandíva are on a single chariot, and these three glorious powers are gathered together. We, on the other hand, don't have such a bow, warrior, or charioteer, but these fools, who are slaves to Duryódhana's will, do not understand this!

Even a blazing lightning-strike to the head would leave something, Sáñjaya, but arrows shot by Kirítin leave noth- 52.15
ing, my friend. It is as if Dhanañ·jaya is shooting, blazing, killing, and plucking heads from bodies with his showers of arrows even now. The blazing splendor comprised of his arrows shot in all directions from Gandíva would consume my sons' army on the battlefield.

Even now the diverse Bháratan army seems terrified to me, afflicted by fear of Savya·sachin's rattling chariot-prowess. Just as a great fire consumes a dead wood, moving in all directions as the huge flames are enhanced by the wind, so he will destroy my sons!

When Kirítin has his bow drawn in battle and expels masses of sharpened arrows, he will become invincible Death, the destroyer of all, as brought forth by the creator.
When I constantly hear of the great number of omens in 52.20
the Kurus' homes, or all around them and at the beginning of battle, then destruction will indeed come upon the Bharatas!"

DHṚTARĀṢṬRA uvāca:

53.1 «YATH" ÂIVA Pāṇḍavāḥ sarve parākrāntā, jigīṣavaḥ,
tath" âiv' âbhisarās teṣāṃ tyakt'|ātmāno, jaye dhṛtāḥ.
tvam eva hi parākrāntān ācakṣīthāḥ parān mama:
Pañcālān, Kekayān, Matsyān, Māgadhān, Vatsa|bhūmipān.
yaś ca s'|Êndrān imāl̃ lokān icchan kuryād vaśe balī,
sa sraṣṭā jagataḥ Kṛṣṇaḥ Pāṇḍavānāṃ jaye dhṛtaḥ.
samastām Arjunād vidyāṃ Sātyakiḥ kṣipram āptavān,
Śaineyaḥ samare sthātā bījavat pravapan śarān.
53.5 Dhṛṣṭadyumnaś ca Pāñcālyaḥ krūra|karmā mahā|rathaḥ
māmakeṣu raṇaṃ kartā baleṣu param'|âstra|vit.
Yudhiṣṭhirasya ca krodhād, Arjunasya ca vikramāt,
yamābhyāṃ, Bhīmasenāc ca bhayaṃ me, tāta, jāyate.
a|mānuṣaṃ manuṣy'|êndrair jālaṃ vitatam antarā;
na me sainyās tariṣyanti, tataḥ krośāmi, Sañjaya!
darśanīyo, manasvī ca, lakṣmīvān, brahma|varcasī,
medhāvī, sukṛta|prajño, dharm'|ātmā Pāṇḍu|nandanaḥ.
mitr'|âmātyaiḥ su|saṃpannaḥ, saṃpanno yuddha|yojakaiḥ,
bhrātṛbhiḥ śvaśurair vīrair upapanno mahā|rathaiḥ;
53.10 dhṛtyā ca puruṣa|vyāghro, naibhṛtyena ca Pāṇḍavaḥ
a|nṛśaṃso, vadānyaś ca, hrīmān, satya|parākramaḥ.
bahu|śrutaḥ, kṛt'|ātmā ca, vṛddha|sevī, jit'|êndriyaḥ,
taṃ sarva|guṇa|saṃpannaṃ, samiddham iva pāvakam,
tapantam abhi ko mandaḥ patiṣyati pataṅgavat?
Pāṇḍav'|âgnim an|āvāryaṃ mumūrṣur naṣṭa|cetanaḥ.

DHRITA·RASHTRA continued:

"JUST AS ALL the Pándavas are bold and wish for victory, 53.1
so too their allies are renouncing their lives, resolved upon victory. You have, in fact, mentioned my energetic enemies: the Pañchálas, Kékayas, Matsyas, Mágadhas, and the kings of Vatsa. Krishna, the creator of the universe, the powerful man who could bring these worlds and Indra under his control if he so wished, is set on the Pándavas' victory.

Sátyaki, grandson of Shini, who quickly attained the entire science of weaponry from Árjuna, will stand in battle,
sowing arrows as though they were seeds. Dhrishta·dyumna, 53.5
the Pañchála prince, a great warrior of vicious deeds who knows the highest weapons, will bring war to my forces. Fear of Yudhi·shthira's anger, Árjuna's prowess, the twins, and Bhima·sena overwhelms me, my son. I lament, Sáñjaya, for my armies, for when the Indra-like men spread their inhuman net of arrows among them, they will not survive!

The descendant of Pandu is handsome, intelligent, and fortunate, possesses divine splendor, is learned, has well-formed wisdom, and a virtuous soul. He is well furnished with friends and advisors, possesses warriors and horses, and is endowed with heroic, powerful warrior brothers and
fathers-in-law. That tiger-like Pándava is furnished with re- 53.10
solve and silence, is mild, liberal, modest, and truly valiant.

He is highly learned, self-controlled, respectful to his elders, and has his senses under control, so which fool will fly at that man endowed with every virtue who blazes like a kindled fire, like a moth to the flame? A senseless man who does not avoid the Pándava fire has a death wish. The

tanur uddhaḥ śikhī rājā mithy" ôpacarito mayā
mandānāṃ mama putrāṇāṃ yuddhen' ântaṃ kariṣyati!
tair a|yuddhaṃ sādhu manye, Kuravas, tan nibodhata:
yuddhe vināśaḥ kṛtsnasya kulasya bhavitā dhruvam.
53.15 eṣā me paramā buddhir yayā śāmyati me manaḥ.
yadi tv a|yuddham iṣṭaṃ vom vayaṃ śāntyai yatāmahe.
na tu naḥ kliśyamānānām upekṣeta Yudhiṣṭhiraḥ,
jugupsati hy a|dharmeṇa mām êv' ôddiśya kāraṇam.»

SAÑJAYA uvāca:

54.1 «EVAM ETAN, mahā|rāja, yathā vadasi, Bhārata:
yuddhe vināśaḥ kṣatrasya Gāṇḍīvena pradṛśyate.
idaṃ tu n' âbhijānāmi tava dhīrasya nityaśaḥ;
yat putra|vaśam āgacches tattva|jñaḥ Savyasācinaḥ.
n' âiṣa kālo, mahā|rāja, tava śaśvat kṛt'|āgasaḥ;
tvayā hy ev' āditaḥ Pārthā nikṛtā, Bharata'|rṣabha.
pitā śreṣṭhaḥ suhṛd yaś ca samyak praṇihit'|ātmavān,
āstheyaṃ hi hitaṃ tena na drogdhā gurur ucyate.
54.5 ‹idaṃ jitam! idaṃ labdham! iti› śrutvā parājitān
dyūta|kāle, mahā|rāja, smayase sma kumāravat.
paruṣāṇy ucyamānāṃś ca purā Pārthān upekṣase,
kṛtsnaṃ rājyaṃ jayant', îti prapātaṃ n' ânupaśyasi.

king is a flame of fire. I smothered that fire by treating him deceitfully, but he will bring an end to my idiotic sons in battle!

I think it best to avoid war, so listen to this, Kurus: war will certainly result in the annihilation of the entire line.
This is my final decision on the matter, and if we follow it 53.15
my mind will be soothed. If war doesn't please you then let us aim for peace. Yudhi·shthira will not ignore us in our distress, for he is disgusted by the immorality of the situation and points at me as its cause."

SÁÑJAYA replied:

"GREAT BHÁRATA king, it is indeed just as you say: the de- 54.1
struction of warriors in war can be seen to be achieved by means of the Gandíva. I can never understand why, when you are wise and know the truth about Savya·sachin, you submit to the power of your son. It is too late to worry now, great king, for your sins have been incessant and you denigrated the Parthas right from the start, bull of the Bharatas.

The best father and friend, whose soul is completely resolute, should practice what is beneficial for his children, but
an ill-wisher is not called a teacher. At the time of the gam- 54.5
bling, great king, you childishly mocked them when you heard they'd been beaten, saying: 'We've won it! We've got it!' Back then you overlooked the fact that the Parthas had been spoken to rudely because you knew your sons had won the entire kingdom, but you failed to notice your fall.

pitryam rājyam, mahā|rāja, Kuravas te sa|jāṅgalāḥ;
atha vīrair jitām urvīm akhilām pratyapadyathāḥ.
bāhu|vīry'|ârjitā bhūmis tava Pārthair niveditā;
‹may" êdam kṛtam, ity› eva manyase, rāja|sattama!
grastān gandharva|rājena majjato hy a|plave 'mbhasi
āninaya punaḥ Pārthaḥ putrāṃs te, rāja|sattama.
54.10 kumāravac ca smayase dyūte vinikṛteṣu yat
Pāṇḍaveṣu vane, rājan, pravrajatsu punaḥ punaḥ.
pravarṣataḥ śara|vrātān Arjunasya śitān bahūn
apy arṇavā viśuṣyeyuḥ; kiṃ punar māṃsa|yonayaḥ?
asyatāṃ Phālgunaḥ śreṣṭho Gāṇḍīvaṃ dhanuṣāṃ varam,
Keśavaḥ sarva|bhūtānām āyudhānāṃ Sudarśanam,
vānaro rocamānaś ca ketuḥ ketumatāṃ varaḥ.
evam etāni sa|ratho bahūn śveta|hayo raṇe
kṣapayiṣyati no, rājan, kāla|cakram iv' ôdyatam.
tasy' âdya vasudhā, rājan, nikhilā, Bharata'|rṣabha,
54.15 yasya Bhīm'|Ârjunau yodhau; sa rājā, rāja|sattama.
tathā Bhīma|hata|prāyāṃ majjantīṃ tava vāhinīm
Duryodhana|mukhā dṛṣṭvā kṣayaṃ yāsyanti Kauravāḥ.
na Bhīm'|Ârjunayor bhītā lapsyante vijayaṃ, vibho,
tava putrā, mahā|rāja, rājānaś c' ânusāriṇaḥ.
Matsyās tvām adya n' ârcanti, Pañcālāś ca sa|Kekayāḥ,
Śālveyāḥ, Śūrasenāś ca sarve tvām avajānate;
Pārthaṃ hy ete gatāḥ sarve vīrya|jñās tasya dhīmataḥ.

Your ancestral kingdom, great monarch, comprises the Kuru lands and the jungles, but through those heroes you gained the whole earth. The Parthas entrusted the earth to you, which they had won by the strength of their arms, but now you believe it was your own achievement, greatest of kings! The Parthas led back your sons when they were being swallowed by the king of the *gandhárvas*, sinking in water
without a boat, greatest of kings. You childishly mocked 54.10
them time and time again during the gambling when they were being mistreated, and when the Pándavas left for the forest, my king. When even seas dry up before Árjuna, as he rains down his numerous swarms of sharp arrows, then how much more quickly will men born of flesh?

Phálguna is the greatest of archers, Gandíva the greatest of bows, Késhava the greatest of all creatures, Sudárshana the greatest of weapons, and the splendid monkey banner is the greatest of all banners. With these numerous items the white-horsed man and his chariot will destroy us in battle, my king, like the raised wheel of time. The entire world,
bull-like Bharata king, now belongs to the king whose war- 54.15
riors are Bhima and Árjuna, O greatest of kings.

So the Káuravas, led by Duryódhana, will go to their destruction, watching your army drowning, the majority killed by Bhima. Then, terrified of Bhima and Árjuna, my lord, your sons, great sovereign, as well as the kings and their followers, will not want to try for victory. As it stands now, the Matsyas, Pañchálas, and Kékayas do not honor you, the Shalvéyas and all the Shura·senas treat you with contempt, and all these peoples have gone over to Partha, for they understand the heroism of that wise man. In fact,

bhaktyā hy asya virudhyante tava putraiḥ sad" âiva te.
an|arhān eva tu vadhe dharma|yuktān vikarmaṇā
54.20 yo 'kleśayat Pāṇḍu|putrān, yo vidveṣṭy adhun" âpi vai,
sarv'|ôpāyair niyantavyaḥ s'|ânugaḥ pāpa|pūruṣaḥ
tava putro, mahā|rāja, n' ânuśuśocitum arhasi.
dyūta|kāle mayā c' ôktaṃ Vidureṇa ca dhīmatā.
yad idaṃ te vilapitaṃ Pāṇḍavān prati, Bhārata,
an|īśen' êva, rāj'|êndra, sarvam etan nirarthakam.»

DURYODHANA uvāca:

55.1 «NA BHETAVYAṂ, mahā|rāja, na śocyā bhavatā vayam;
samarthāḥ sma parān jetuṃ balinaḥ samare, vibho.
vane pravrājitān Pārthān yad" āyān Madhsūdanaḥ
mahatā bala|cakreṇa para|rāṣṭr'|âvamardinā,
Kekayā, Dhṛṣṭaketuś ca, Dhṛṣṭadyumnaś ca Pārṣataḥ,
rājānaś c' ânvayuḥ Pārthān bahavo 'nye 'nuyāyinaḥ.
Indraprasthasya c' â|dūrāt samājagmur mahā|rathāḥ,
vyagarhayaṃś ca saṅgamya bhavantaṃ Kurubhiḥ saha.
55.5 te Yudhiṣṭhiram āsīnam ajinaiḥ prativāsitam
Kṛṣṇa|pradhānāḥ saṃhatya paryupāsanta, Bhārata.
pratyādānaṃ ca rājyasya kāryam ūcur nar'|âdhipāḥ
bhavataḥ s'|ânubandhasya samucchedaṃ cikīrṣavaḥ.

it is due to their devotion to him that they always quarrel with your sons.

The wicked man who caused the sons of Pandu to suffer through his evil behavior, despite the fact that they adhere to moral law and do not deserve to die, that man who hates them even now—your son, great king—should be restrained by all means possible, along with his followers. You should not even grieve for him. But I warned you during the gambling match, as did wise Vídura! All this wailing over the Pándavas now, Bhárata, as though you were helpless in the matter, achieves nothing, lord of kings." 54.20

DURYÓDHANA said:

"THERE IS NOTHING to fear, great king, nor should you lament for us, for we are powerful and quite capable of defeating our enemies in battle, my lord. Madhu·súdana approached the Parthas when they were living in the forest, with his vast circle of forces which had crushed enemy kingdoms, and the Kékayan kings, Dhrishta·ketu, and Dhrishta·dyumna Párshata came, while many other kings also followed the Parthas. 55.1

The mighty warriors gathered close to Indra·prastha and joining together they abused you and the Kurus. Led by 55.5
Krishna, they combined and attended upon Yudhi·shthira as he dwelled upon a seat covered with antelope skin, Bhárata. Those kings told him he should take back his kingdom and they wanted to bring about the destruction of you and your relatives.

śrutvā c' âivaṃ may" ôktās tu Bhīṣma|Droṇa|Kṛpās tadā
jñāti|kṣaya|bhayād, rājan, bhītena, Bharata'|rṣabha:
«‹na te* sthāsyanti samaye Pāṇḍavā, iti› me matiḥ.
samucchedaṃ hi naḥ kṛtsnaṃ Vāsudevaś cikīrṣati.
ṛte ca Vidurāt sarve yūyaṃ vadhyā matā mama.
Dhṛtarāṣṭras tu dharma|jño na vadhyaḥ Kuru|sattamaḥ.
55.10 samucchedaṃ ca kṛtsnaṃ naḥ kṛtvā, tāta, Janārdanaḥ
eka|rājyaṃ Kurūṇāṃ sma cikīrṣati Yudhiṣṭhire.
tatra kiṃ prāpta|kālaṃ naḥ? praṇipātaḥ? palāyanam?
prāṇān vā saṃparityajya pratiyudhyāmahe parān?
pratiyuddhe tu niyataḥ syād asmākaṃ parājayaḥ;
Yudhiṣṭhirasya sarve hi pārthivā vaśa|vartinaḥ.
virakta|rāṣṭrāś ca vayaṃ, mitrāṇi kupitāni naḥ,
dhik|kṛtāḥ pārthivaiḥ sarvaiḥ, sva|janena ca sarvaśaḥ.
praṇipāte na doṣo 'sti; sandhir naḥ śāśvatīḥ samāḥ.
pitaraṃ tv eva śocāmi prajñā|netraṃ jan'|âdhipam,
55.15 mat|kṛte duḥkham āpannaṃ, kleśaṃ prāptam an|antakam.
kṛtaṃ hi tava putraiś ca pareṣām avarodhanam
mat|priy'|ârthaṃ pur" âiv', âitad viditaṃ te, nar'|ôttama.
te rājño Dhṛtarāṣṭrasya s'|âmātyasya mahā|rathāḥ
vairaṃ pratikariṣyanti kul'|ôcchedena Pāṇḍavāḥ.›
tato Droṇo 'bravīd, Bhīṣmaḥ, Kṛpo, Drauṇiś ca, Bhārata,
matvā māṃ mahatīṃ cintām āsthitaṃ vyathit'|êndriyam:

When I heard this I was afraid, and told it to Bhishma, Drona, and Kripa, fearing the destruction of my family, sovereign bull of the Bharatas, saying:

'I believe the Pándavas will not abide by the agreement. Vasudéva wishes for our complete annihilation. In my opinion you will all die, with the exception of Vídura. Dhrita·rashtra knows what is right and that greatest of the Kurus
must not be killed. Once he has achieved our total destruc- 55.10
tion, my friend, Janárdana will want to make the single kingdom of the Kurus Yudhi·shthira's property.

Our time is up, but what should we do? Bow before them? Escape? Or abandon our lives fighting against our enemies? If we retaliate in battle our defeat would be certain, for all the kings have fallen under Yudhi·shthira's control. Our kingdom is indifferent to us, our friends are offended by us, and we are reproached on all sides by every king and even our own relatives. Surrender is not a sin, for men in our position always make peace.

I grieve however for my father, lord of his people; the
man whose only sight is wisdom. He is burdened with mis- 55.15
eries of my making, and has met with an eternal calamity. In fact, as you knew long ago, best of men, your sons hindered the others in order to please me. The great warrior Pándavas will repay the hostility done to them by destroying King Dhrita·rashtra's line and his advisors.'

Then Drona, Bhishma, Kripa, and Drona's son, O Bhárata, realizing that my mind was dwelling on this a great deal, and that my senses were troubled, said:

‹abhidrugdhāḥ pare cen no, na bhetavyaṃ, paran|tapa,
a|samarthāḥ pare jetum asmān yudhi samāsthitān.
ek'|âikaśaḥ samarthāḥ smo vijetuṃ sarva|pārthivān;
āgacchantu, vineṣyāmo darpam eṣāṃ śitaiḥ śaraiḥ!

55.20 pur" âikena hi Bhīṣmeṇa vijitāḥ sarva|pārthivāḥ
mṛte pitary atikruddho rathen' âikena, Bhārata.
jaghāna su|bahūṃs teṣāṃ saṃrabdhaḥ Kuru|sattamaḥ;
tatas te śaraṇaṃ jagmur Devavratam imaṃ bhayāt.
sa Bhīṣmaḥ su|samartho 'yam asmābhiḥ sahito raṇe
parān vijetuṃ, tasmāt te vyetu bhīr, Bharata'|rṣabha.›

ity eṣāṃ niścayo hy āsīt tat kāle 'mita|tejasām,
purā pareṣāṃ pṛthivī kṛtsn" āsīd vaśa|vartinī.
asmān punar amī n' âdya samarthā jetum āhave;
chinna|pakṣāḥ pare hy adya, vīrya|hīnāś ca Pāṇḍavāḥ.
55.25 asmat|saṃsthā ca pṛthivī vartate, Bharata'|rṣabha,
ek'|ârthāḥ sukha|duḥkheṣu samānītāś ca pārthivāḥ.

apy agniṃ praviśeyus te, samudraṃ vā, paran|tapa,
mad|arthaṃ pārthivāḥ sarve. tad viddhi, Kuru|sattama.
unmattam iva c' âpi tvāṃ prahasant' îha duḥkhitam
vilapantaṃ bahu|vidhaṃ, bhītaṃ para|vikatthane.
eṣāṃ hy ek'|âikaśo rājñāṃ samarthaḥ Pāṇḍavān prati
ātmānaṃ manyate sarvo. vyetu te bhayam āgatam.
jetuṃ samagrāṃ senāṃ me Vāsavo 'pi na śaknuyāt
hantum akṣayya|rūp" êyaṃ Brahmaṇo 'pi svayaṃ|bhuvaḥ!

'If enemies should oppress us then we have nothing to fear, scorcher of the enemy, for our enemies are unable to defeat us when we are arrayed for battle. Each of us is capable of conquering all kings single-handedly, so let them come and we will destroy their arrogance with sharp arrows!

Long ago Bhishma single-handedly defeated all the kings 55.20
on one chariot, for he was incensed when his father had died, Bhárata. The greatest of the Kurus killed a great many in his fury until in their terror they went to Deva·vrata for peace. Bhishma here is more than capable of defeating your enemies in battle when accompanied by us. So dispel you fear, bull of the Bharatas.'

That was the decision those immeasurably splendid men made at the time long ago, when the whole earth was under the control of their enemies. But now they are not capable of defeating us in battle, for the enemy forces are divided
and the Pándavas have lost their valor. The earth now rests 55.25
on us, bull of the Bharatas, and the kings who have been brought together are of one purpose in joy and misery.

For my sake all these kings would walk into the fire or the ocean, scorcher of the foe. Understand this, greatest of the Kurus. They laugh at you in your present misery, as though you're mad; they laugh at your various, terrified lamentations while you praise your enemy! Every one of these kings is alone a match for the Pándavas, and every one of them believes himself to be, so rid yourself of the fear that has taken hold of you. Even Vásava himself would not be able to defeat my assembled army, and even self-created Brahma of imperishable form could not kill them, were he so inclined!

55.30 Yudhiṣṭhiraḥ puraṃ hitvā pañca grāmān sa yācati,
bhīto hi māmakāt sainyāt, prabhāvāc c' âiva me, vibho!
samarthaṃ manyase yac ca Kuntī|putraṃ Vṛkodaram,
tan mithyā; na hi me kṛtsnaṃ prabhāvaṃ vetsi, Bhārata.
mat|samo hi gadā|yuddhe pṛthivyāṃ n' âsti kaś cana.
n' āsīt kaś cid atikrānto, bhavitā na ca kaś cana!

yukto duḥkh'|ôṣitaś c' âhaṃ vidyā|pāra|gatas tathā,
tasmān na Bhīmān n' ânyebhyo bhayaṃ me vidyate kva cit.
‹Duryodhana|samo n' âsti gadāyām, iti› niścayaḥ
Saṃkarṣaṇasya, bhadraṃ te, yat tad" âinam upāvasam.
55.35 yuddhe Saṃkarṣaṇa|samo, balen' âbhyadhiko bhuvi.
gadā|prahāraṃ Bhīmo me na jātu viṣahed yudhi!
ekaṃ prahāraṃ yaṃ dadyāṃ Bhīmāya ruṣito, nṛpa,
sa ev' âinaṃ nayed ghoram kṣipraṃ Vaivasvata|kṣayam!

iccheyaṃ ca gadā|hastaṃ, rājan, draṣṭuṃ Vṛkodaram!
su|ciraṃ prārthito hy eṣa mama nityaṃ mano|rathaḥ.
gadayā nihato hy ājau mayā Pārtho Vṛkodaraḥ
viśīrṇa|gātraḥ pṛthivīṃ parāsuḥ prapatiṣyati.
gadā|prahār'|âbhihato Himavān api parvataḥ
sakṛn mayā vidīryeta giriḥ śata|sahasradhā!
55.40 sa c' âpy etad vijānāti, Vāsudev'|Ârjunau tathā,
‹Duryodhana|samo n' âsti gadāyām, iti› niścayaḥ.
tat te Vṛkodaram ayaṃ bhayaṃ vyetu mah"|āhave;
vyapaneṣyāmy ahaṃ hy enaṃ. mā, rājan, vimanā bhava.

Yudhi·shthira has abandoned the city and asks for only five villages because he is afraid of my army and my power, my lord! You have false ideas about Vrikódara Kauntéya's capability, but you don't really comprehend my full power, Bhárata. There is no one on earth to match me in mace warfare. No one has ever surpassed me nor will anyone surpass me! 55.30

By practice and continuous pain I have reached the highest pinnacle of the science, and so I have no fear of Bhima or anyone else. When I applied myself to his service, Sankárshana's decision was that 'Duryódhana has no equal in mace technique,' bless you. In battle I am Sankárshana's equal, 55.35
but in strength I am superior to anyone on earth. Bhima will certainly not withstand the strike of my mace in battle! I will plant a single strike on Bhima in my fury, king, and it will soon lead him to the horrifying house of Vaivásvata!

I would love to see Vrikódara, mace in hand, my king! I have longed for this for a very long time. It has been my constant wish. Struck by my mace on the battlefield, Vrikódara Partha will fall to the ground dead, his limbs smashed in. Even Mount Himálaya would smash into hundreds of thousands of pieces if I hit it just once with a strike of the mace! He knows just as well as Vasudéva and Árjuna that 55.40
the final word is, 'Duryódhana has no equal in mace technique.' Let your fear of Vrikódara in the great battle disappear, for I will destroy him. Don't be upset, my king.

tasmin mayā hate kṣipram Arjunaṃ bahavo rathāḥ
tulya|rūpā, viśiṣṭāś ca kṣepsyanti, Bharata'|rṣabha.
Bhīṣmo, Droṇaḥ, Kṛpo, Drauṇiḥ,
Karṇo, Bhūriśravās tathā,
Prāgjyotiṣ'|âdhipaḥ, Śalyaḥ,
Sindhu|rājo Jayadrathaḥ—
ek' âika eṣāṃ śaktas tu hantuṃ, Bhārata, Pāṇḍavān.
sametās tu kṣaṇen' âitān neṣyanti Yama|sādanam.
samagrā pārthivī senā Pārtham ekaṃ Dhanañjayam
55.45 kasmād a|śaktā nirjetum? iti hetur na vidyate.
śara|vrātais tu Bhīṣmeṇa śataśo nicito '|vaśaḥ
Droṇa|Drauṇi|Kṛpaiś c' âiva gantā Pārtho Yama|kṣayam.
pitā|maho 'pi Gāṅgeyaḥ Śāntanor adhi, Bhārata,
brahma'|rṣi|sadṛśo jajñe devair api su|duḥsahaḥ.
na hantā vidyate c' âpi, rājan, Bhīṣmasya kaś cana
pitrā hy uktaḥ prasannena, ‹n' â|kāmas tvaṃ mariṣyasi.›
brahma'|rṣeś ca Bharadvājād Droṇo droṇyām ajāyata.
Droṇāj jajñe, mahā|rāja, Drauṇiś ca param'|âstravit.
Kṛpaś c' ācārya|mukhyo 'yaṃ maha"|rṣer Gautamād api
55.50 śara|stamb'|ôdbhavaḥ, śrīmān, a|vadhya, iti me matiḥ.
a|yoni|jās trayo hy ete – pitā, mātā ca, mātulaḥ
Aśvatthāmno, mahā|rāja, sa ca śūraḥ sthito mama.

When I have killed him, numerous warriors of equal and indeed superior form will quickly destroy Árjuna, O bull of the Bharatas. Bhishma, Drona, Kripa, Drona's son, Karna, Bhuri·shravas, the king of Prag·jyótisha, Shalya, and Jayad·ratha the king of Sindhu are each capable of killing the Pándavas single-handedly, Bhárata. Together, they will instantly send those men to Yama's dwelling. There is no 55.45
reason why the assembled army of kings should be unable to defeat Dhanañ·jaya Partha on his own.

The Partha will be made powerless and go to Yama's realm, sent by the swarms of hundreds of arrows fired by Bhishma, Drona, Drona's son, and Kripa. Our grandfather Gangéya, sired by Shántanu, was born the equal of a brahmin sage, Bhárata, and is near invincible even to the gods. There is no one who could kill Bhishma, king, for his father graciously promised him, 'You will not die unless you want to.'

Drona was born from the brahmin sage Bharad·vaja in a wooden trough. Drona's son, Ashvattháman, was born 55.50
from Drona, mighty lord, with knowledge of the highest weapons. Kripa, this leading teacher, was born from a reed stalk from the mighty sage Gáutama. In my opinion this illustrious man cannot be killed. The three—Ashvattháman's father, mother, and uncle—were none of them born from the womb, and Ashvattháman, great king, stands as my hero.

sarva ete, mahā|rāja, deva|kalpā mahā|rathāḥ
Śakrasy' âpi vyathāṃ kuryuḥ saṃyuge, Bharata'|rṣabha.
n' âiteṣām Arjunaḥ śakta ek' âikaṃ prativīkṣitum.
sahitās tu nara|vyāghrā haniṣyanti Dhanañjayam!
Bhīṣma|Droṇa|Kṛpāṇāṃ ca tulyaḥ Karṇo mato mama.
anujñātaś ca Rāmeṇa, ‹mat|samo 's' îti,› Bhārata.
kuṇḍale rucire c' āstāṃ Karṇasya saha|je śubhe;
55.55 te Śacy|arthaṃ mah"|Êndreṇa yācitaḥ sa paraṃ|tapaḥ,
a|moghayā, mahā|rāja, śaktyā parama|bhīmayā.
tasya śakty" ôpagūḍhasya kasmāj jīved Dhanañjayaḥ?
vijayo me dhruvaṃ, rājan, phalaṃ pāṇāv iv' āhitam,
abhivyaktaḥ pareṣāṃ ca kṛtsno bhuvi parājayaḥ!
ahnā hy ekena Bhīṣmo 'yaṃ prayutaṃ hanti, Bhārata,
tat|samāś ca mah"|êṣvāsā Droṇa|Drauṇi|Kṛpā api!
saṃśaptakānāṃ vṛndāni kṣatriyāṇāṃ, paraṃ|tapa,
‹Arjunaṃ vayam, asmān vā nihanyāt kapi|ketanaḥ
taṃ c' âlam.› iti manyante Savyasāci|vadhe dhṛtāḥ
55.60 pārthivāḥ sa bhavāṃs tebhyo hy a|kasmād vyathate katham?
Bhīmasene ca nihate ko 'nyo yudhyeta, Bhārata?
pareṣāṃ tan mam' ācakṣva yadi vettha, paraṃ|tapa!
pañca te bhrātaraḥ sarve Dhṛṣṭadyumno 'tha Sātaykiḥ,
pareṣāṃ sapta ye, rājan, yodhāḥ sāraṃ balaṃ matam;
asmākaṃ tu viśiṣṭā ye Bhīṣma|Droṇa|Kṛp'|ādayaḥ:
Drauṇir, Vaikartanaḥ Karṇaḥ, Somadatto 'tha Bāhlikaḥ,
Prāgjyotiṣ'|âdhipaḥ, Śalya, Āvantyau ca, Jayadrathaḥ,

All these men, mighty monarch, are warriors who match the gods and would oppress even Shakra in battle, bull of the Bharatas. Not even Árjuna can look at these men individually. Together those tiger-like men will kill Dhanañ·jaya!

To my mind Karna is the equal of Bhishma, Drona, and Kripa. Bhárata, Rama agreed, telling him: 'You are my equal.' Karna was born wearing those gleaming, beautiful earrings, and great Indra begged the enemy-scorcher for 55.55
them for Shachi's sake, in exchange for the unfailing, most terrifying spear, great monarch. When he is embraced by the spear how could Dhanañ·jaya survive? Victory is assuredly mine, king, just like the fruit resting in my hand, and the complete defeat of our enemies on earth is manifest!

Bhishma here kills ten thousand in one day, Bhárata! These great archers, Drona, his son, and Kripa, match him as well. The swarms of mercenary soldiers and warriors, O scorcher of your enemy, claim, 'Either we will kill Árjuna or that monkey-bannered man will kill us.' The kings who are intent on Savya·sachin's death believe that they are a match 55.60
for those men, so why are you needlessly anxious? When Bhima·sena has been killed, who else will fight, Bhárata?

Tell me this about my enemies if you know, scorcher of the enemy! All five brothers with Dhrishta·dyumna and Sátyaki—these seven fighters, my king, are considered to be the army's strength, but our most distinguished warriors are Bhishma, Drona, Kripa, and so on: Drona's son, Vaikártana Karna, Soma·datta Báhlika, the king of Prag·jyótisha, Shalya, the king of Avántya, Jayad·ratha, Duhshásana, Dúrmukha, and Dúhsaha, lord of earth, as well as Shrutáyus,

Duḥśāsano, Durmukhaś ca, Duḥsahaś ca, viśām pate,
Śrutāyuś, Citrasenaś ca, Purumitro, Viviṃśatiḥ,
55.65 Śalo, Bhūriśravāś c' âiva, Vikarṇaś ca tav' ātma|jaḥ.
akṣauhiṇyo hi me, rājan, daś' âikā ca samāhṛtāḥ;
nyūnāḥ pareṣāṃ—sapt' âiva—kasmān me syāt parājayaḥ?
‹balaṃ triguṇato hīnaṃ yodhyaṃ,› prāha Bṛhaspatiḥ;
parebhyas triguṇā c' êyaṃ mama, rājann, anīkinī.
guṇa|hīnaṃ pareṣāṃ ca bahu paśyāmi, Bhārata,
guṇ'|ôdayaṃ bahu|guṇam ātmanaś ca, viśām pate.
etat sarvaṃ samajñāya bal'|âgryaṃ mama, Bhārata,
nyūnatāṃ Pāṇḍavānāṃ ca na mohaṃ gantum arhasi!»
ity uktvā Sañjayaṃ bhūyaḥ paryapṛcchata, Bhārata,
vivitsuḥ prāpta|kālāni jñātvā para|purañ|jayaḥ.

DURYODHANA uvāca:

56.1 «AKṢAUHIṆĪḤ SAPTA labdhvā rājabhiḥ saha, Sañjaya,
kiṃ svid icchati Kaunteyo yuddha|prepsur Yudhiṣṭhiraḥ?»

SAÑJAYA uvāca:

«atīva mudito, rājan, yuddha|prepsur Yudhiṣṭhiraḥ,
Bhīmasen'|Ârjunau c' ôbhau, yamāv api na bibhyataḥ.
rathaṃ tu divyaṃ Kaunteyaḥ sarvā vibhrājayan diśaḥ
mantraṃ jijñāsamānaḥ san Bibhatsuḥ samayojayat.
tam apaśyāma sannaddhaṃ meghaṃ vidyud|yutaṃ yathā;
samantāt samabhidhyāya hṛṣyamāṇo 'bhyabhāṣata:
56.5 ‹pūrva|rūpam idaṃ paśya—vayaṃ jeṣyāma, Sañjaya!›
Bībhatsur māṃ yath" ôvāca tath" âvaimy aham apy uta.»

Chitra·sena, Puru·mitra, Vivínshati, Shala, Bhuri·shravas, and your son Vikárna. 55.65

I have gathered eleven battalions, my lord, but the enemy has fewer—only seven, so how could I be defeated? Brihas·pati said, 'An army whose size is a third less than your own should be fought,' and my army is a third bigger than the enemy's, king. I see the enemy's numerous lack of advantages, Bhárata, in contrast with my army's numerous advantages and beneficial points, lord of earth. Understanding the total strength of my forces, Bhárata, as well as the Pándavas' deficiency, you ought not to sink into confusion!"

Having spoken in this manner the conqueror of enemy cities questioned Sáñjaya again, Bhárata, since he wished to know more, understanding the opportunities before him.

DURYÓDHANA said:

"NOW THAT HE has gathered seven battalions and their kings, Sáñjaya, what does Yudhi·shthira, son of Kunti, wish to do, as he aims for war?" 56.1

SÁÑJAYA replied:

"Yudhi·shthira is preparing for war exceedingly happily, my king, and Bhima·sena, Árjuna, and the twins are unafraid. Bibhátsu, son of Kunti, has yoked his celestial chariot, illuminating all directions as he experiments with his spells. We saw him armored, looking like a brilliant flashing storm cloud and completely lost in thought; he then
cheerfully said, 'Look at this omen—we will win, Sáñjaya!' 56.5
This is what Bibhátsu told me and I know it's true."

DURYODHANA uvāca:

«praśaṃsasy abhinandaṃs tān
Pārthān akṣa|parājitān.
Arjunasya rathe, brūhi,
katham aśvāḥ, kathaṃ dhvajāḥ.»

SAÑJAYA uvāca:

«Bhaumanaḥ saha Śakreṇa bahu|citraṃ, viśām pate,
rūpāṇi kalpayām āsa Tvaṣṭā dhātā sadā, vibho.
dhvaje hi tasmin rūpāṇi cakrus te deva|māyayā
mahā|dhanāni, divyāni, mahānti ca, laghūni ca.
Bhīmasen'|ânurodhāya Hanūmān Mārut'|ātmajaḥ
ātma|pratikṛtiṃ tasmin dhvaja āropayiṣyati.

56.10 sarvā diśo yojana|mātram antaraṃ
sa tiryag ūrdhvaṃ ca rurodha vai dhvajaḥ;
na saṃsajjaty asau tarubhiḥ saṃvṛto 'pi,
tathā hi māyā vihitā Bhaumanena.
yath" ākāśe Śakra|dhanuḥ prakāśate,
na c' âika|varṇaṃ, na ca vedmi kiṃ nu tat,
tathā dhvajo vihito Bhaumanena,
bahv|ākāraṃ dṛśyate rūpam asya.
yath" âgni|dhūmo divam eti ruddhvā,
varṇān bibhrat taijasāṃś citra|rūpān,
tathā dhvajo vihito Bhaumanena—
na ced bhāro bhavitā n' ôta rodhaḥ.

DURYÓDHANA said:

"You applaud and praise the Parthas who were defeated at dice. Tell me what horses and what banner Árjuna has on his chariot."

SÁÑJAYA replied:

"Bháumana, the creator and architect, and Shakra, my lord, always fashioned beautiful items of varied hue, lord of earth. Through divine illusion they fitted those magnificent, immensely precious, celestial, and large yet delicate objects to his banner. Hánuman, son of the Wind god, will superimpose his own insignia upon this banner to oblige Bhima·sena.

His flag obscures all directions, horizontally and verti- 56.10
cally, measuring a league in span. It does not cling even when surrounded by trees, for such was the magic conjured by Bháumana. Just as Shakra's rainbow gleams in the sky with its manifold hues—something we cannot explain—so the flag was created by Bháumana, its form appearing in many guises. Just as smoke issues from a fire and rises to the heavens, forming various shapes iridescent with gleaming colors, so the flag was created by Bháumana—there will be nothing dragging it down, and no obstruction.

śvetās tasmin vāta|vegāḥ sad|aśvā
divyā yuktāś, Citrarathena dattāḥ.
bhuvy antarikṣe divi vā, nar'|êndra,
yeṣāṃ gatir hīyate n' âtra sarvā.
śataṃ yat tat pūryate nitya|kālaṃ
hataṃ hataṃ, datta|varaṃ purastāt.
tathā rājño danta|varṇā bṛhanto
rathe yuktā bhānti tad|vīrya|tulyāḥ.
ṛkṣa|prakhyā Bhīmasenasya vāhā
rathe vāyos tulya|vegā babhūvuḥ.
56.15 kalmāṣ'|âṅgās tittiri|citra|pṛṣṭhā
bhrātrā dattāḥ prīyatā Phālgunena,
bhrātur vīrasya svais turaṅgair viśiṣṭā,
mudā yuktāḥ Sahadevaṃ vahanti.
Mādrī|putraṃ Nakulaṃ tv Ājamīḍhaṃ
mah"|Êndra|dattā harayo vāji|mukhyāḥ
samā vāyor, balvantas, tarasvino
vahanti vīraṃ, Vṛtra|śatruṃ yath" Êndram.
tulyāṃś c' âibhir vayasā vikrameṇa
mahā|javāś citra|rūpāḥ sad|aśvāḥ
Saubhadr'|ādīn Draupadeyān kumārān
vahanty aśvā deva|dattā bṛhantaḥ.»

DHṚTARĀṢṬRA uvāca:

57.1 «KĀṂS TATRA, Sañjay', âpaśyaḥ prīty|arthena samāgatān,
ye yotsyante Pāṇḍav'|ârthe putrasya mama vāhinīm?»

His excellent horses are swift as the wind, divinely trained gifts from Chitra·ratha. Their entire course, lord of men, be it on earth, in the ether, or in heaven, is unimpeded. They will remain one hundred in number for all time, even if one or the other dies—this is an ancient boon that was granted. The king too has large, glistening, ivory-hued horses yoked to his chariot to match his own valor. The horses yoked to Bhima·sena's chariot resemble bears, and their speed matches that of the wind.

When the piebald horses with backs of as varied hues as 56.15
partridges, which were given by his dear brother Phálguna and are superior to the horses of his hero brother, are yoked to his chariot, they happily carry Saha·deva. Excellent stallions, gifts from mighty Indra, which match the wind for strength and speed, carry Nákula, son of Madri and descendant of Aja·midha, the hero like Indra, enemy to Vritra. Large and wonderful, god-given, variously colored horses of enormous speed which match them in velocity and valor convey Saubhádra's and Dráupadi's princely sons."

DHRITA·RASHTRA said:

"SÁÑJAYA, WHO did you see gathered in that place, come 57.1
for reasons of affection to fight my son's army for the Pándavas' cause?"

SAÑJAYA uvāca:
«mukhyam Andhaka|Vṛṣṇīnām
apaśyaṃ Kṛṣṇam āgatam,
Cekitānaṃ ca tatr' âiva,
Yuyudhānaṃ ca Sātyakim.
pṛthag akṣauhiṇībhyāṃ tu Pāṇḍavān abhisaṃśritau
mahā|rathau samākhyātāv ubhau puruṣa|māninau.
akṣauhiṇy" âtha Pāñcālyo daśabhis tanayair vṛtaḥ
Satyajit|pramukhair vīrair Dhṛṣṭadyumna|purogamaiḥ
57.5 Drupado vardhayan mānaṃ Śikhaṇḍi|paripālitaḥ
upāyāt sarva|sainyānāṃ praticchādya tadā vapuḥ.
Virāṭaḥ saha putrābhyāṃ Śaṅkhen' âiv' Ottareṇa ca,
Sūryadatt'|ādibhir vīrair Madirākṣa|purogamaiḥ
sahitaḥ pṛthivī|pālo bhrātṛbhis tanayais tathā
akṣauhiṇy" âiva sainyānāṃ vṛtaḥ Pārthaṃ samāśritaḥ.
Jārāsandhir Māgadhaś ca, Dhṛṣṭaketuś ca Cedi|rāṭ,
pṛthak pṛthag anuprāptau pṛthag akṣauhiṇī|vṛtau.
Kekayā bhrātaraḥ pañca sarve lohitaka|dhvajāḥ
akṣauhiṇī|parivṛtāḥ Pāṇḍavān abhisaṃśritāḥ.
57.10 etān etāvatas tatra tān apaśyaṃ samāgatān,
ye Pāṇḍav'|ârthe yotsyanti Dhārtarāṣṭrasya vāhinīm.
yo veda mānuṣaṃ vyūhaṃ, daivaṃ, gāndharvam, āsuram,
sa tatra senā|pramukhe Dhṛṣṭadyumno mahā|rathaḥ.
Bhīṣmaḥ Śāṃtanavo, rājan, bhāgaḥ kḷptaḥ Śikhaṇḍinaḥ.
taṃ Virāṭo 'nusaṃyātā sārdhaṃ Matsyaiḥ prahāribhiḥ.
jyeṣṭhasya Pāṇḍu|putrasya bhāgo Madr'|âdhipo balī,
tau tu tatr' âbruvan ke cid, ‹viṣamau no matāv, iti.›
Duryodhanaḥ saha|sutaḥ, sārdhaṃ bhrātṛ|śatena ca,
prācyāś ca dākṣiṇātyāś ca Bhīmasenasya bhāgataḥ.

SÁÑJAYA replied:

"I saw Krishna arrive as the leader of the Ándhaka Vrishnis, as well as Chekitána and Yuyudhána Sátyaki. These
two renowned and mighty warriors, who pride themselves
on their manliness and have devoted themselves to the Pándavas, have each brought a battalion with them. Drúpada, 57.5
the king of Pañchála, came defended by Shikhándin when
he had supplied all his armies, surrounded by his ten hero
sons led by Sátyajit and headed by Dhrishta·dyumna, and
a full battalion thereby augmented the Pándavas' pride.

King Viráta came with his sons, Shankha and Úttara, with the heroes Surya·datta and so on, led by Madiráksha together with his brothers and sons, and joined Partha surrounded by the battalion of his armies.

The Mághadan son of Jara·sandha, and Dhrishta·ketu, king of the Chedis, each arrived surrounded by a battalion. All five crimson-bannered Kékayan brothers have joined the Pándavas, surrounded by their battalion.

These comprise the number of people whom I saw gath- 57.10
ered to fight Dhartaráshtra's army for the Pándavas' cause.
Dhrishta·dyumna, the mighty warrior who understands the
military arrays of men, gods, *gandhárva*s, and *ásura*s, will be
the leader of their army.

Bhishma, son of Shántanu, has been apportioned to Shikhándin as his share to kill in battle, and Viráta along with his Matsyan spearmen will go with him. The mighty king of the Madras has been assigned to the eldest son of Pandu, though some people said they considered them to be an unequal pairing. Duryódhana, his sons, his hundred brothers,

57.15 Arjunasya tu bhāgena Karṇo Vaikartano mataḥ,
Aśvatthāmā, Vikarṇaś ca, Saindhavaś ca Jayadrathaḥ.
a|śakyāś c' âiva ye ke cit pṛthivyāṃ śūra|māninaḥ,
sarvāṃs tān Arjunaḥ Pārthaḥ kalpayām āsa bhāgataḥ.
mah"|êṣvāsā rāja|putrā bhrātaraḥ pañca Kekayāḥ
Kekayān eva bhāgena kṛtvā yotsyanti saṃyuge.
teṣām eva kṛto bhāgo Mālavāḥ, Śālvakās tathā,
Trigartānāṃ c' âiva mukhyau, yau tau saṃśaptakāv iti.
Duryodhana|sutāḥ sarve, tathā Duḥśāsanasya ca,
Saubhadreṇa kṛto bhāgo, rājā c' âiva Bṛhadbalaḥ.
57.20 Draupadeyā mah"|êṣvāsāḥ suvarṇa|vikṛta|dhvajāḥ
Dhṛṣṭadyumna|mukhā Droṇam abhiyāsyanti, Bhārata.
Cekitānaḥ Somadattaṃ dvairathe yoddhum icchati;
Bhojaṃ tu Kṛtavarmāṇaṃ Yuyudhāno yuyutsati.
Sahadevas tu Mādreyaḥ śūraḥ saṅkrandano yudhi
svam aṃśaṃ kalpayām āsa śyālaṃ te Subal'|ātmajam.
Ulūkaṃ c' âiva Kaitavyaṃ ye ca Sārasvatā guṇāḥ,
Nakulaḥ kalpayām āsa bhāgaṃ Mādravatī|sutaḥ.
ye c' ânye pārthivā, rājan, pratyudyāsyanti saṅgare,
samāhvānena tāṃś c' âpi Pāṇḍu|putrā akalpayan.
57.25 evam eṣām anīkāni pravibhaktāni bhāgaśaḥ.
yat te kāryaṃ sa|putrasya, kriyatāṃ tad a|kālikam.»

and the eastern and southern kings were assigned as Bhima·sena's lot.

Karna Vaikártana, Ashvattháman, Vikárna, and Sindh 57.15
Jayad·ratha comprise Árjuna's lot, but Árjuna Partha also took as his share all those on earth who are invincible and pride themselves on their bravery.

The five Kékayan brother princes ensured they had the Kékayas as their lot to fight in the battle. The Málavas, the Shálvakas, and the two leaders of the Tri·gartas who had taken a warrior's oath to kill or die, also comprised their share.

All Duryódhana and Duhshásana's sons fall under the
lot of the son of Subhádra and King Brihad·bala. Bhárata, 57.20
Dráupadi's mighty archer sons, whose flags are embellished with gold, will attack Drona, led by Dhrishta·dyumna.

Chekitána wants to fight Soma·datta in single-chariot combat, and Yuyudhána will fight the Bhoja Krita·varman. Saha·deva, son of Madri, the brave warrior who bellows in battle, has taken as his share Súbala's son, his brother-in-law. Nákula, son of Mádravati, took as his share Ulúka Kaitávya and the Sarásvata groups.

And as for the other kings who will attack in battle, my
lord, the sons of Pandu will allot them by challenge. This is 57.25
how their armies have been divided into lots, so now you and your son's job is to take the necessary steps without delay."

DHṚTARĀṢṬRA uvāca:

«na santi sarve putrā me mūḍhā, dur|dyūta|devinaḥ,
yeṣāṃ yuddhaṃ balavatā Bhīmena raṇa|mūrdhani.
rājānaḥ pārthivāḥ sarve prokṣitāḥ kāla|dharmaṇā
Gāṇḍīv'|âgniṃ pravekṣyanti pataṅgā iva pāvakam.
vidrutāṃ vāhinīṃ manye kṛta|vairair mah"|ātmabhiḥ.
tāṃ raṇe ke 'nuyāsyanti prabhagnāṃ Pāṇḍavair yudhi?
sarve hy atirathāḥ, śūrāḥ, kīrtimantaḥ, pratāpinaḥ,
sūrya|pāvakayos tulyās tejasā, samitiñ|jayāḥ.
57.30 yeṣāṃ Yudhiṣṭhiro netā, goptā ca Madhusūdanaḥ,
yodhau ca Pāṇḍavau vīrau Savyasāci|Vṛkodarau,
Nakulaḥ, Sahadevaś ca, Dhṛṣṭadyumnaś ca Pārṣataḥ,
Sātyakir, Drupadaś c' âiva, Dhṛṣṭaketuś ca s'|ânujaḥ,
Uttamaujāś ca Pāñcālyo, Yudhāmanyuś ca, Durjayaḥ,
Śikhaṇḍī, Kṣatradevaś ca, tathā Vairāṭir Uttaraḥ,
Kāśayaś, Cedayaś c' âiva, Matsyāḥ, sarve ca Sṛñjayāḥ,
Virāṭa|putro Babhruś ca, Pāñcālāś ca, Prabhadrakāḥ;
yeṣām Indro 'py a|kāmānāṃ na haret pṛthivīm imām,
vīrāṇāṃ raṇa|dhīrāṇāṃ, ye bhindyuḥ parvatān api!
57.35 tān sarva|guṇa|sampannān a|manuṣya|pratāpinaḥ
krośato mama duṣ|putro yoddhum icchati, Sañjaya!»

DURYODHANA uvāca:

«ubhau sva eka|jātīyau, tath" ôbhau bhūmi|gocarau.
atha kasmāt Pāṇḍavānām ekato manyase jayam?
pitā|mahaṃ ca, Droṇaṃ ca, Kṛpaṃ, Karṇaṃ ca, Durjayam,
Jayadrathaṃ, Somadattam, Aśvatthāmānam eva ca,
su|tejaso mah"|êṣvāsān Indro 'pi sahito 'maraiḥ

DHRITA·RASHTRA said:

"All my foolish, devious gambler sons will die when they fight against powerful Bhima at the front of battle. All the kings and monarchs, consecrated by death, the law of time, will rush to the fire of Gandíva like moths to the flame. I imagine the army put to flight by those high-souled men taking their revenge. Who will follow the army to battle when it will be shattered by the the Pándavas in combat?

They really are valiant, famous, blazing warriors; victors
in battle who match the sun and fire with their splendor.
Their guide is Yudhi·shthira, their protector is Madhu· 57.30
súdana, and their warriors are the heroic Savya·sachin and
Vrikódara, the sons of Pandu. Then there's Nákula, Saha·
deva, Dhrishta·dyumna Párshata, Sátyaki, Drúpada,
Dhrishta·ketu along with his son, Uttamáujas from Pañchála, Yudha·manyu, Dúrjaya, Shikhándin, Kshatra·deva,
Viráta's son Úttara, the Kashis, the Chedis, as well as all the
Matsyans and Sríñjayas, Viráta's son Babhru, the Pañchálas,
and the Prabhádrakas; these are heroes, firm in battle, who
could even split mountains, from whom even Indra could
not take earth if they were unwilling! These are the men of 57.35
inhuman splendor, endowed with every virtue, whom my
wicked son wishes to fight in his rage, Sáñjaya!"

DURYÓDHANA said:

"Both sides are the same species, in as much as we both inhabit the earth, so why do you only imagine that the Pándavas will gain victory? Even Indra with the immortals is incapable of defeating the magnificent mighty archers grandfather, Drona, Kripa, Karna, Dúrjaya, Jayad·ratha, Soma·

a|śaktaḥ samare jetuṃ; kiṃ punas, tāta, Pāṇḍavāḥ?
sarve ca pṛthivī|pālā mad|arthe, tāta, Pāṇḍavān
āryāḥ, śastra|bhṛtaḥ, śūrāḥ, samarthāḥ pratibādhitum.
57.40 na māmakān Pāṇḍavās te samarthāḥ prativīkṣitum!
parākrānto hy ahaṃ Pāṇḍūn sa|putrān yoddhum āhave!
mat|priyaṃ pārthivāḥ sarve ye cikīrṣanti, Bhārata,
te tān āvārayiṣyanti, aiṇeyān iva tantunā.
mahatā ratha|vaṃśena śara|jālaiś ca māmakaiḥ
abhidrutā bhaviṣyanti Pāñcālāḥ Pāṇḍavaiḥ saha.»

DHṚTARĀṢṬRA uvāca:

«unmatta iva me putro vilapaty eṣa, Sañjaya!
na hi śakto raṇe jetuṃ dharma|rājaṃ Yudhiṣṭhiram!
jānāti hi yathā Bhīṣmaḥ Pāṇḍavānāṃ yaśasvinām
balavattāṃ sa|putrāṇāṃ dharma|jñānāṃ mah"|ātmanām.
57.45 yato n' ārocayad ayaṃ vigrahaṃ tair mah"|ātmabhiḥ.
kiṃ tu Sañjaya, me brūhi punas teṣāṃ viceṣṭitam.
kas tāṃs tarasvino bhūyaḥ sandīpayati Pāṇḍavān,
arciṣmato mah"|êṣvāsān, haviṣā pāvakān iva?»

SAÑJAYA uvāca:

«Dhṛṣṭadyumnaḥ sad" âiv' âitān sandīpayati, Bhārata,
‹yudhyadhvam! iti, mā bhaiṣṭa yuddhād, Bharata|sattamāḥ.
ye ke cit pārthivās tatra Dhāratrāṣṭreṇa saṃvṛtāḥ
yuddhe samāgamiṣyanti tumule śastra|saṅkule.
tān sarvān āhave kruddhān s'|ânubandhān samāgatān
aham ekaḥ samādāsye, timir matsyān iv' ôdakāt!

datta, and Ashvattháman in battle, so how much harder would it be, father, for the Pándavas?

All these brave, noble, weapon-bearing earth-lords are capable of beating back the Pándavas for my sake, father, but the sons of Pandu are not fit to look upon my troops! 57.40
In fact, I am powerful enough to fight the Pándavas and their sons in battle! All these kings want to do something to please me, Bhárata, and they will obstruct those men as if hemming in black antelope with a cord. The Pañchálas and Pándavas will be attacked by my enormous host of chariots and by showers of arrows."

DHRITA·RASHTRA said:

"Sáñjaya, my son is babbling like a madman! He is not able to defeat Yudhi·shthira, the king of righteousness, in battle! Bhishma does, in fact, know the strength of the famed, high-souled Pándavas who understand what is right, and he knows the strength of their sons. This is why I am 57.45
not pleased at the prospect of conflict with these high-souled men. Sáñjaya, tell me again about their behavior. Who is causing the energetic Pándavas, those resplendent archers, to blaze still more, just as oblations inflame fires?"

SÁÑJAYA replied:

"Dhrishta·dyumna always inflames them, Bhárata, saying, 'Fight! Don't be afraid of war, best of the Bharatas! No matter which kings Dhartaráshtra surrounds himself with and brings to the tumultuous battle, thronged with weapons, I will single-handedly remove them all as they rage in battle congregated with their kinsmen, just as a whale feasts on fish in the sea! I will even hold back Bhishma, Drona, 57.50

57.50 Bhīṣmaṃ, Droṇaṃ, Kṛpaṃ, Karṇaṃ,
Drauṇiṃ, Śalyaṃ, Suyodhanam—
etāṃś c' âpi nirotsyāmi,
vel" êva makar'|ālayam!›

tathā bruvantaṃ dharm'|ātmā prāha rājā Yudhiṣṭhiraḥ:
‹tava dhairyaṃ ca vīryaṃ ca Pāñcālāḥ Pāṇḍavaiḥ saha
sarve samadhirūḍhāḥ sma. saṅgrāmān naḥ samuddhara!
jānāmi tvāṃ, mahā|bāho, kṣatra|dharme vyavasthitam,
samartham ekaṃ paryāptaṃ Kauravāṇāṃ vinigrahe.
purastād upayātānāṃ Kauravāṇāṃ yuyutsatām
bhavatā yad vidhātavyaṃ, tan naḥ śreyaḥ, paran|tapa!

saṅgrāmād apayātānāṃ bhagnānāṃ śaraṇ'|âiṣiṇām
57.55 pauruṣaṃ darśayan śūro yas tiṣṭhed agrataḥ pumān,
krīṇīyāt taṃ sahasreṇa, iti nītimatāṃ matam.
sa tvaṃ śūraś ca, vīraś ca, vikrāntaś ca, nara'|rṣabha,
bhay'|ārtānāṃ paritrātā saṃyugeṣu, na saṃśayaḥ.›

evaṃ bruvati Kaunteye dharm'|ātmani Yudhiṣṭhire
Dhṛṣṭadyumna uvāc' êdaṃ māṃ vaco gata|sādhvasam:

‹sarvān jana|padān, sūta, yodhā Duryodhanasya ye,
sa|Bāhlikān Kurūn brūyāḥ, Prātipeyān, Śaradvataḥ,
sūta|putraṃ, tathā Droṇaṃ saha|putraṃ, Jayadratham,
Duḥśāsanaṃ, Vikarṇaṃ ca, tathā Duryodhanaṃ nṛpam,
Bhīṣmaṃ ca brūhi gatvā tvam, āśu gaccha ca mā ciram:
57.60 «Yudhiṣṭhiraḥ sādhun" âiv' âbhyupeyo,
mā vo vadhīd Arjuno deva|guptaḥ!
rājyaṃ daddhvaṃ dharma|rājasya tūrṇaṃ;
yācadhvaṃ vai Pāṇḍavaṃ loka|vīram!

Kripa, Karna, Drona's son, Shalya, and Suyódhana, just as the shore withstands the sea, home to monsters!'

When he talks like this, virtuous-souled King Yudhi·shthira says to him: 'The Pañchálas and Pándavas are all convinced of your resolve and courage. Rescue us from war! I am aware, long-armed man, that you abide by a warrior's duty and that you alone are capable of restraining the Káuravas. When the Kurus stand in front of us, about to fight, then whatever you accomplish will be to our benefit, scorcher of your foe!

Those who understand policy believe that the brave man 57.55
who stands at the front, displaying his prowess while others flee from battle, ranks broken, seeking protection, should be bought at a price of a thousand men. You are brave, valiant, and courageous, bull-like man. There is no doubt that you are the savior of those afflicted by fear in times of combat.'

When Yudhi·shthira, the virtuous-souled son of Kunti, had said this, Dhrishta·dyumna, unperturbed, said these words to me:

'*Suta*, go quickly and don't delay. Tell all the people who comprise Duryódhana's warriors, along with the Bahlíkas, Kurus, Pratipéyas, Sharádvata, Karna the *suta*'s son, Drona and his son, and Jayad·ratha, Duhshásana, Vikárna, King Duryódhana, and Bhishma:

"Some good man must approach Yudhi·shthira, lest di- 57.60
vinely protected Árjuna destroy you! Quickly give back the king of moral law's kingdom and beg mercy from the Pándava hero of the world! There is no warrior here on earth to suitably match Savya·sachin, the truly valiant son of Pandu.

n' âitādṛśo hi yodho 'sti pṛthivyām iha kaś cana,
yathā|vidhiḥ Savyasācī Pāṇḍavaḥ satya|vikramaḥ.
devair hi saṃbhṛto divyo ratho Gāṇḍīva|dhanvanaḥ.
na sa jeyo manuṣyeṇa, mā sma kṛddhvaṃ mano yudhi.»› »

DHṚTARĀṢṬRA uvāca:

58.1 «KṢATRA|TEJĀ, brahma|cārī kaumārād api Pāṇḍavaḥ;
tena saṃyugam eṣyanti mandā vilapato mama.
Duryodhana, nivartasva yuddhād, Bharata|sattama,
na hi yuddhaṃ praśaṃsanti sarv'|âvastham, arin|dama!
alam ardhaṃ pṛthivyās te sah' âmātyasya jīvitum.
prayaccha Pāṇḍu|putrāṇāṃ yath" ôcitam, arin|dama!
etadd hi Kuravaḥ sarve
manyante dharma|saṃhitam,
yat tvaṃ praśāntiṃ manyethāḥ
Pāṇḍu|putrair mah"|ātmabhiḥ.
58.5 aṅg' êmāṃ samavekṣasva, putra, svām eva vāhinīm
jāta eṣa tav' âbhāvas; tvaṃ tu mohān na budhyase.
na tv ahaṃ yuddham icchāmi, n' âitad icchati Bāhlikaḥ,
na ca Bhīṣmo, na ca Droṇo, n' Âśvatthāmā, na Sañjayaḥ,
na Somadatto, na Śalo, na Kṛpo yuddham icchati,
Satyavrataḥ, Purumitro, Jayo, Bhūriśravās tathā!
yeṣu saṃpratitiṣṭeyuḥ Kuravaḥ pīḍitāḥ paraiḥ,
te yuddhaṃ n' âbhinandanti tat tubhyaṃ, tāta, rocatām.
na tvaṃ karoṣi kāmena; Karṇaḥ kārayitā tava,
Duḥśāsanaś ca pāp'|ātmā, Śakuniś c' âpi Saubalaḥ.»

The divine chariot that belongs to the Gandíva archer is kept safe by the gods. He cannot be defeated by a mortal man, so don't set your mind on battle.'"'

DHRITA·RASHTRA said:

"THE SON OF Pandu has a warrior's splendor and has practiced sacred duties since his youth, but the fools want to go to battle with this man despite my wailing. Duryódhana, turn away from war, greatest of the Bharatas, for men do not praise war in any circumstance, tamer of your enemies! 58.1

Half the earth is enough for you and your ministers to live on. Offer the sons of Pandu what they deserve, enemy-tamer! Indeed, all the Kurus think it conforms with moral duty that you consider peace with the high-souled Pándavas. Look at your army, my son. It has developed into 58.5
your annihilation, but in your folly you do not comprehend it.

I do not want to fight, nor does Báhlika, nor Bhishma, Drona, Ashvattháman, or Sáñjaya, nor do Soma·datta, Shala, or Kripa wish for war, or Satya·vrata, Puru·mitra, Jaya, or Bhuri·shravas! The men upon whom the Kurus rely when oppressed by their enemies do not approve of war. May you find it acceptable, my son. You are not even doing this because you want to, but because Karna and wicked-souled Duhshásana and Shákuni, son of Súbala, compel you."

DURYODHANA uvāca:

58.10 «n' âhaṃ bhavati na Droṇe, n' Âśvatthāmni, na Sañjaye,
na Bhīṣme, na ca Kāmboje, na Kṛpe, na ca Bāhlike,
Satyavrate, Purumitre, Bhūriśravasi vā punaḥ,
anyeṣu vā tāvakeṣu bhāraṃ kṛtvā samāhvayam!
aham ca, tāta, Karṇaś ca raṇa|yajñaṃ vitatya vai
Yudhiṣṭhiraṃ paśuṃ kṛtvā dīkṣitau, Bharata'|rṣabha;
ratho vedī, sruvaḥ khaḍgo, gadā sruk, kavacaṃ sadaḥ,
cāturhotraṃ ca dhuryā me, śarā darbhā, havir yaśaḥ.
ātma|yajñena, nṛpate, iṣṭvā Vaivasvataṃ raṇe,
vijitya ca sameṣyāvo hat'|âmitrau, śriyā vṛtau!
58.15 ahaṃ ca, tāta, Karṇaś ca, bhrātā Duḥśāsanaś ca me—
ete vayaṃ haniṣyāmaḥ Pāṇḍavān samare trayaḥ.
ahaṃ hi Pāṇḍavān hatvā praśāstā pṛthivīm imām,
māṃ vā hatvā Pāṇḍu|putrā bhoktāraḥ pṛthivīm imām.
tyaktaṃ me jīvitaṃ, rājyaṃ, dhanaṃ sarvaṃ ca, pārthiva,
na jātu Pāṇḍavaiḥ sārdhaṃ vaseyam aham, Acyuta!
yāvadd hi sūcyās tīkṣṇāyā vidhyed agreṇa, māriṣa,
tāvad apy a|parityājyaṃ bhūmer naḥ Pāṇḍavān prati!»

DHṚTARĀṢṬRA:

«sarvān vas, tāta, śocāmi; tyakto Duryodhano mayā;
ye mandam anuyāsyadhvaṃ yāntaṃ Vaivasvata|kṣayam.
58.20 rurūṇām iva yūtheṣu vyāghrāḥ praharatāṃ varāḥ,
varān varān haniṣyanti sametā yudhi Pāṇḍavāḥ.
pratīpam iva me bhāti Yuyudhānena Bhāratī,

DURYÓDHANA replied:

"I am the one making the challenge and so the burden is not on Drona, Ashvattháman, Sáñjaya, Bhishma, Kambója, Kripa, Báhlika, Satya·vrata, Puru·mitra, Bhuri·shravas, or again on any other of your men! 58.10

Father, Karna and I are consecrated to perform this battle sacrifice, making Yudhi·shthira the animal victim, bull-like Bharata, with a chariot for an altar, a sword for a ladle, a mace for a large ladle to pour the libation, armor for the sacrificial enclosure, my four horses as the priests, my arrows as the *darbha* grass, and my fame as the oblation of clarified butter. Having offered ourselves as sacrifice to Vaivásvata in battle, my king, we will return in victory, cloaked with glory and with our enemies dead!

I, Karna, and my brother Duhshásana, father—we three will kill the Pándavas in battle. Once I have killed the Pándavas, I will govern this earth, or if they kill me then the sons of Pandu will enjoy this earth. I would rather abandon my life, my kingdom, and all my wealth, eternal king, than live together with the Pándavas! Not even as much land as one could cover with the sharp point of a needle, worthy man, will we relinquish to the Pándavas!" 58.15

DHRITA·RASHTRA said:

"My sons, I disown Duryódhana, but I grieve for all of you who will follow this fool as he walks straight into Vaivásvata's home. Like tigers among herds of antelope, the Pándavas, greatest of warriors, will gather together in war and kill the best and greatest among you. It's an unpleasant thought, but I imagine the Bharatan army as a woman, who 58.20

vyastā sīmantinī, grastā, pramṛṣṭā dīrgha|bāhunā.
sampūrṇam pūrayan bhūyo
dhanam Pārthasya Mādhavaḥ
Śaineyaḥ samare sthātā
bījavat pravapañ śarān
senā|mukhe prayuddhānām Bhīmaseno bhaviṣyati;
tam sarve saṃśrayiṣyanti prākāram a|kuto|bhayam.
yadā drakṣyasi Bhīmena kuñjarān vinipātitān,
viśīrṇa|dantān, giry|ābhān, bhinna|kumbhān, sa|śoṇitān,
58.25 tān abhiprekṣya saṃgrāme viśīrṇān iva parvatān,
bhīto Bhīmasya saṃsparśāt, smart" âsi vacanasy me.
nirdagdhaṃ Bhīmasenena sainyaṃ ratha|haya|dvipam,
gatim agner iva prekṣya, smart" âsi vacanasya me!
mahad vo bhayam āgāmi, na cec chāmyatha Pāṇḍavaiḥ;
gadayā Bhīmasenena hatāḥ śamam upaiṣyatha!
mahā|vanam iva cchinnaṃ yadā drakṣyasi pātitam
balaṃ Kurūṇāṃ Bhīmena, tadā smart" âsi me vacaḥ!»

VAIŚAMPĀYANA uvāca:

etāvad uktvā rājā tu sarvāṃs tān pṛthivī|patīn
anubhāṣya, mahārāja, punaḥ papraccha Sañjayam:

will be torn apart, tormented, and crushed by long-armed Yuyudhána.

Increasing Partha's wealth of force yet more, though already full to the brim, Mádhava the grandson of Shini will stand in battle, scattering arrows as though sowing seeds. Bhima·sena will be at the head of the army of warriors, and they will all rely on him as though he were a secure defensive wall. When you see the mountain-like elephants felled by Bhima with their shattered tusks, their temples cut open,
and drenched in blood, when you see them in battle like 58.25
shattered mountains, you will be afraid of Bhima's touch and you will remember what I said.

When you see your army of chariots, horses, and elephants consumed by Bhima·sena and looking as decimated as the path of a fire, then you will remember what I said! If you do not make peace with the Pándavas then great danger will come upon you, and only when killed by Bhima·sena's mace will you find any peace! When you see the force of the Kurus toppled by Bhima as though a mighty forest was being felled, then you will remember what I said!"

VAISHAMPÁYANA said:

When the king had spoken in this manner to all the kings of earth, he spoke once more to Sáñjaya, great king, and asked:

DHṚTARĀṢṬRA uvāca:

59.1 «YAD ABRŪTĀṂ mah"|ātmānau Vāsudeva|Dhanañjayau,
tan me brūhi, mahā|prājña, śuśrūṣe vacanaṃ tava.»

SAÑJAYA uvāca:

«śṛṇu, rājan, yathā dṛṣṭau mayā* Kṛṣṇa|Dhanañjayau,
ūcatuś c' âpi yad vīrau, tat te vakṣyāmi, Bhārata.
pād'|âṅgulīr abhiprekṣan prayato 'haṃ kṛt'|âñjaliḥ
śuddh'|ântaṃ prāviśaṃ, rājann, ākhyātuṃ nara|devayoḥ.
n' âiv' Âbhimanyur, na yamau taṃ deśam abhiyānti vai,
yatra Kṛṣṇau ca Kṛṣṇā ca, Satyabhāmā ca bhāminī.
59.5 ubhau madhv|āsava|kṣībāv, ubhau candana|rūṣitau,
sragviṇau, vara|vastrau tau, divy'|ābharaṇa|bhūṣitau.
n'|âika|ratna|vicitraṃ tu kāñcanaṃ mahad āsanam
vividh'|āstaraṇ'|ākīrṇaṃ, yatr' āsātām arin|damau.
Arjun'|ôtsaṅga|gau pādau Keśavasy' ôpalakṣaye,
Arjunasya ca Kṛṣṇāyāṃ, Satyāyāṃ ca mah"|ātmanaḥ.
kāñcanaṃ pāda|pīṭhaṃ tu Pārtho me prādiśat tadā;
tad ahaṃ pāṇinā spṛṣṭvā tato bhūmāv upāviśam.
ūrdhva|rekhā|talau pādau Pārthasya śubha|lakṣaṇau
pāda|pīṭhād apahṛtau tatr' âpaśyam ahaṃ śubhau.

DHRITA·RASHTRA said:

"WHAT DID high-souled Vasudéva and Dhanañ·jaya say? 59.1
Tell me, extraordinarily wise man, for I want to hear what you have to say."

SÁÑJAYA replied:

"Listen then, my king, for I will tell you, Bhárata, how Krishna and Dhanañ·jaya appeared, as well as what those two heroes said.

Looking down at my toes, I bowed with my hands folded together, and entered the holy sanctuary of those two god-like men, my king, in order to talk to them. Abhimányu and the twins do not go to the place where the two Krishnas, Krishná, and passionate Satya·bhama reside. Those two 59.5
were both intoxicated with sweet liquor, both annointed with sandalwood paste, both wearing garlands, exquisitely dressed, and adorned with celestial ornaments. There was a huge golden throne decorated with numerous jewels and covered with multi-colored cushions upon which those enemy-scorchers were sitting.

I saw that Késhava's feet were in Árjuna's lap, while high-souled Árjuna's feet were resting on Krishná and Satya·bhama. Partha then pointed me to a golden footstool, so I touched it with my hand and then sat on the foor. I saw splendid, auspicious markings of straight lines traveling up on the soles of Partha's feet as he took them away from the footstool.

59.10 śyāmau, bṛhantau, taruṇau, śāla|skandhāv iv' ôdgatau,
ek'|āsana|gatau dṛṣṭvā bhayaṃ māṃ mahad āviśat.
Indra|Viṣṇu|samāv etau mand'|ātmā n' âvabuddhyate
saṃśrayād Droṇa|Bhīṣmābhyāṃ, Karṇasya ca vikatthanāt.
nideśa|sthāv imau yasya, mānasas tasya setsyate
saṅkalpo dharma|rājasya, niścayo me tad" âbhavat.

sat|kṛtaś c' ânna|pānābhyām, āsīno labdha|satkriyaḥ,
añjaliṃ mūrdhni sandhāya tau sandeśam acodayam.
dhanur|guṇa|kiṇ'|âṅkena pāṇinā śubha|lakṣaṇam
pādam ānamayan Pārthaḥ Keśavaṃ samacodayat.
59.15 Indra|ketur iv' ôtthāya sarv'|ābharaṇa|bhūṣitaḥ
Indra|vīry'|ôpamaḥ Kṛṣṇaḥ saṃviṣṭo mām abhāṣata.

vācaṃ sa vadatāṃ śreṣṭho hlādinīṃ vacana|kṣamām,
trāsinīm Dhārtarāṣṭrāṇāṃ, mṛdu|pūrvāṃ, su|dāruṇām.
vācaṃ tāṃ vacan'|ârhasya śikṣ'|âkṣara|samanvitām
aśrauṣam aham iṣṭ'|ârthāṃ, paścādd hṛdaya|hāriṇīm.»

VĀSUDEVA uvāca:

‹Sañjay', êdaṃ vaco brūyā Dhṛtarāṣṭraṃ manīṣiṇam
Kuru|mukhyasya Bhīṣmasya Droṇasy' âpi ca śṛṇvataḥ,
āvayor vacanāt, sūta, jyeṣṭhān apy abhivādayan,
yavīyasaś ca kuśalaṃ paścāt pṛṣṭv" âivam uttaram.

When I saw those two large, dark-hued, youthful men 59.10
like tall *shala* tree-trunks, sitting together on one seat, great fear overtook me. That idiotic-souled man does not comprehend that they are like Indra and Vishnu because he relies on Drona and Bhishma, and because of Karna's boasting. It then occurred to me that the king of virtue's intention and decision would indeed be achieved if these two abided by his commands and were bound to his mind's desire.

Met with hospitality, I sat treated well with food and drink, and, putting my hands together at my head, I conveyed your message. Partha bent down to remove Késhava's auspiciously marked foot with his hand, which bore the
scars of the bowstring, and he urged him to speak. Krishna, 59.15
equal to Indra in valor, decorated with every ornamentation, sat rising high like Indra's flag, and spoke to me.

The words which that greatest of speakers uttered were comforting and appropriate in meaning, but though full of sweetness they were also terrifying and extremely harsh towards the Dhartaráshtras. I listened to the words that he alone was worthy to utter, which were properly pronounced and achieved their aim, but which were ultimately heartbreaking.

VASUDÉVA said:

'Sáñjaya, tell wise Dhrita·rashtra this message within earshot of Bhishma, the leading Kuru, and Drona, once you have greeted the elders at our request, *suta*, and afterwards enquired after the health of the younger members of court:

59.20 «yajadhvaṃ vividhair yajñair viprebhyo datta|dakṣiṇāḥ,
putrair dāraiś ca modadhvaṃ; mahad vo bhayam āgatam!
arthāṃs tyajata pātrebhyaḥ, sutān prāpnuta kāma|jān,
priyaṃ priyebhyaś carata; rājā hi tvarate jaye!»
ṛṇam etat pravṛddhaṃ me hṛdayān n' âpasarpati,
yad «Govind'! êti» cukrośa Kṛṣṇā māṃ dūra|vāsinam.
tejo|mayaṃ dur|ādharṣaṃ Gāṇḍīvaṃ yasya kārmukam,
mad|dvitīyena ten' êha vairaṃ vaḥ Savyasācinā.
mad|dvitīyaṃ punaḥ Pārthaṃ kaḥ prārthayitum icchati,
yo na kāla|parīto v" âpy, api sākṣāt Puraṃ|daraḥ?
59.25 bāhubhyām udvahed bhūmiṃ, dahet kruddha imāḥ prajāḥ,
pātayet tri|divād devān, yo 'rjunaṃ samare jayet.
dev'|âsura|manuṣyeṣu, yakṣa|gandharva|bhogiṣu
na taṃ paśyāmy ahaṃ yuddhe Pāṇḍavaṃ yo 'bhyayād raṇe.
yat tad Virāṭa|nagare śrūyate mahad adbhutam,
ekasya ca bahūnāṃ ca paryāptaṃ tan nidarśanam!
ekena Pāṇḍu|putreṇa Virāṭa|nagare yadā
bhagnāḥ palāyata diśaḥ, paryāptaṃ tan nidarśanam!
balaṃ, vīryaṃ ca, tejaś ca, śīghratā, laghu|hastatā,
a|viṣādaś ca, dhairyaṃ ca Pārthān n' ânyatra vidyate.›
59.30 ity abravīdd Hṛṣīkeśaḥ Pārtham uddharṣayan girā,
garjan samaya|varṣ" îva gagane Pāka|śāsanaḥ.
Keśavasya vacaḥ śrutvā Kirīṭī śveta|vāhanaḥ
Arjunas tan mahad vākyam abravīd roma|harṣaṇam.»

"Offer various sacrifices, give fees to brahmins, and make the most of your sons and wives, for great danger approaches you. Relinquish your wealth to worthy men, have sons who are born out of love, and do favors for those you care about, for the king hastens to victory!" 59.20

Krishná cried out "Go·vinda!" to me when I was living far away. My debt to her swelled, and does not retreat from my heart. This is why I am here as second to Savya·sachin, the man who wields the Gandíva bow, invincible and made of splendor, with whom you have your quarrel.

What man, unless his time has expired, wants to attack Partha when I am his second, even if he were the Sacker of
Cities? He could carry the earth in his arms, he could burn 59.25
the creatures in anger, and he could topple the gods from heaven, so who could defeat Árjuna in battle? I see no one among gods, *ásura*s, men, *yaksha*s, *gandhárva*s, or serpents who could take on the son of Pandu in battle.

The great wonder recounted of what happened at Viráta's city, when one fought against many, is ample evidence! The time when Pandu's son single-handedly broke his enemy and forced them to flee is more than enough proof! In no one other than the Partha can that force, valor, splendor, speed, dexterity, courage, and resolve be found.'

So Hrishi·kesha spoke, pleasing the Partha with his 59.30
praise, thundering like the punisher of Paka in the sky during the rainy season. And when he had heard Késhava's speech, white-horsed, diademed Árjuna spoke great hair-raising words."

VAIŚAMPĀYANA uvāca:

60.1 SAÑJAYASYA VACAḤ śrutvā prajñā|cakṣur jan'|ēśvaraḥ
tataḥ saṅkhyātum ārebhe tad vaco guṇa|doṣataḥ.
prasaṅkhyāya ca saukṣmyeṇa guṇa|doṣān vicakṣaṇaḥ
yathāvan mati|tattvena jaya|kāmaḥ sutān prati,
bal'|âbalaṃ viniścitya yāthātathyena buddhimān,
śaktiṃ saṅkhyātum ārebhe tadā vai manuj'|âdhipaḥ,
deva|mānuṣayoḥ śaktyā tejasā c' âiva Pāṇḍavān,
Kurūn śakty" âlpatarayā, Duryodhanam ath' âbravīt:
60.5 «Duryodhan', êyaṃ cintā me śaśvan na vyupaśāmyati.
satyaṃ hy etad ahaṃ manye pratyakṣaṃ, n' ânumānataḥ:
ātmajeṣu paraṃ snehaṃ sarva|bhūtāni kurvate,
priyāṇi c' âiṣāṃ kurvanti yathā|śakti hitāni ca.
evam ev' ôpakartṝṇāṃ prāyaśo lakṣayāmahe:
icchanti bahulaṃ santaḥ pratikartuṃ mahat priyam.
Agniḥ sācivya|kartā syāt Khāṇḍave tat|kṛtaṃ smaran
Arjunasy' âpi bhīme 'smin Kuru|Pāṇḍu|samāgame.
jāti|gṛdhy'|âbhipannāś ca Pāṇḍavānām anekaśaḥ
Dharm'|ādayaḥ sameṣyanti samāhūtā div'|âukasaḥ.
60.10 Bhīṣma|Droṇa|Kṛp'|ādīnāṃ bhayād aśani|sannibham
rirakṣiṣantaḥ saṃraṃbhaṃ gamiṣyant', îti me matiḥ.
te devaiḥ sahitāḥ Pārthā na śakyāḥ prativīkṣitum
mānuṣeṇa nara|vyāghrā vīryavanto 'stra|pāragāḥ.

VAISHAMPÁYANA said:

WHEN THE LORD of the people, a man of wise vision, had heard what Sáñjaya had to say, he began to calculate the benefits and disadvantages of his words. By subtle and clear-sighted calculation of the pros and cons with proper judgment, the sagacious and intelligent man, who desired victory for his sons, precisely weighed up the strengths and weaknesses, and then the lord of men began to work out the capabilities of each side. Since the Pándavas had human and divine power and glory, whereas the Kurus had little strength, he said to Duryódhana: 60.1

"Duryódhana, my constant anxiety does not cease. I believe it is truly obvious rather than being conjecture: All creatures feel the greatest love for their children and do whatever will please and benefit them to the best of their ability. Similarly, we notice a general pattern with benefactors: good men frequently wish to return favors and do what their benefactors wish. 60.5

So Agni, recalling what was done for him at Khándava, will also give his assistance to Árjuna in the terrible conflict between the Kurus and Pándavas. Hosts of celestials in great numbers led by Dharma, full of love for their children, will
gather on the side of the Pándavas when invoked. In my 60.10
opinion, wishing to protect them, out of fear of Bhishma, Drona, Kripa, and so on, they will reach lightning-like fury. A mere mortal can't even look at the tiger-like, valiant, and weapons-expert Parthas when they are accompanied by the gods.

dur|āsadaṃ yasya divyaṃ Gāṇḍīvaṃ dhanur uttamam,
dāruṇau c' â|kṣayau divyau śara|pūrṇau mah"|êṣudhī,
vānaraś ca dhvajo divyo niḥsaṅgo dhūmavad|gatiḥ,
rathaś ca catur|antāyāṃ yasya n' âsti samaḥ kṣitau,
mahā|megha|nibhaś c' âpi nirghoṣaḥ śrūyate janaiḥ,
mah"|âśani|samaḥ śabdaḥ śātravāṇāṃ bhayaṅ|karaḥ,
60.15 yaṃ c' âti|mānuṣaṃ vīrye kṛtsno loko vyavasyati,
devānām api jetāraṃ yaṃ viduḥ pārthivā raṇe.
śatāni pañca c' âiv' êṣūn yo gṛhṇan n' âiva dṛśyate,
nimeṣ'|ântara|mātreṇa muñcan, dūraṃ ca pātayan.
yam āha Bhīṣmo, Droṇaś ca, Kṛpo, Drauṇis tath" âiva ca,
Madra|rājas tathā Śalyo, madhya|sthā ye ca mānavāḥ,
yuddhāy' âvasthitaṃ Pārthaṃ pārthivair atimānuṣaiḥ
a|śakyaṃ nara|śārdūlaṃ parājetum arin|damam;
kṣipaty ekena vegena pañca bāṇa|śatāni yaḥ,
sadṛśaṃ bāhu|vīryeṇa Kārtavīryasya Pāṇḍavam
60.20 tam Arjunaṃ mah"|êṣvāsaṃ,
Mahendr'|Ôpendra|vikramam,
nighnantam iva paśyāmi
vimarde 'smin mah"|āhave!
ity evaṃ cintayan kṛtsnam aho|rātrāṇi, Bhārata,
a|nidro niḥsukhaś c' âsmi Kurūṇāṃ śama|cintayā.
kṣay'|ôdayo 'yaṃ su|mahān Kurūṇāṃ pratyupasthitaḥ,
asya cet kalahasy' ântaḥ śamād anyo na vidyate.
śamo me rocate nityaṃ Pārthais, tāta, na vigrahaḥ;
Kurubhyo hi sadā manye Pāṇḍavān śaktimattarān.»

The man who owns the invincible, divine, and greatest bow, Gandíva, who has Váruna's couple of frightful, inexhaustible, celestial quivers always full of arrows, whose celestial monkey-banner moves with the unobstructed path of smoke, whose chariot has no match in the four corners of the earth, the rattling of which men hear as the thundering of a mighty storm-cloud, and the great thundering
clatter of which brings fear to his enemies, is the man whom 60.15
the entire world has decided has superhuman prowess, and whom the kings know as the conqueror even of gods in battle.

He is the man who takes up five hundred arrows invisibly to the naked eye, releases them in the blink of an eye, and sends them flying a great distance. He is the foe-scorching, tiger-like Partha, whom Bhishma, Drona, Kripa, Drona's son, the king of the Madras, Shalya, and the non-committal kings say cannot be defeated even by superhuman leaders when he stands ready for war. He is the man who shoots five hundred shafts in a single volley, the Pándava who matches
Kartavírya in the strength of his arms, the great archer Ár- 60.20
juna, with the prowess of mighty Indra and Upéndra—this is the man whom I can almost see now, slaughtering in this great crushing battle!

This is what I think of day and night, Bhárata, and I don't sleep or have any pleasure with this worry about the Kurus. The great means of the Kurus' destruction is imminent unless peace can be found to end this quarrel. Peace with the Parthas always pleases me, my son, but not war, for I believe the Pándavas will always be more powerful than the Kurus."

VAIŚAMPĀYANA uvāca:

61.1 PITUR ETAD vacaḥ śrutvā Dhārtarāṣṭro ’tyamarṣaṇaḥ
ādhāya vipulaṃ krodhaṃ punar ev’ êdam abravīt:
«a|śakyā deva|sacivāḥ Pārthāḥ syur, iti yad bhavān
manyate, tad bhayaṃ vyetu bhavato, rāja|sattama.
a|kāma|dveṣa|saṃyogāl lobhād drohāc ca, Bhārata,
upekṣayā ca bhāvānāṃ devā devatvam āpnuvan.
iti Dvaipāyano Vyāso, Nāradaś ca mahā|tapāḥ,
Jāmadagnyaś ca Rāmo naḥ kathām akathayat purā.
61.5 n’ âiva mānuṣavad devāḥ pravartante kadā cana,
kāmāt, krodhāt, tathā lobhād, dveṣāc ca, Bharata’|rṣabha.
yadā hy Agniś ca Vāyuś ca, Dharma, Indro, ’śvināv api
kāma|yogāt pravarteran, na Pārthā duḥkham āpnuyuḥ.
tasmān na bhavatā cintā kāry” âiṣā syāt kathañ cana;
daiveṣv apekṣakā hy ete śaśvad bhāveṣu, Bhārata.
atha cet kāma|saṃyogād dveṣo lobhaś ca lakṣyate
deveṣu, daiva|prāmāṇyān n’ âiṣāṃ tad vikramiṣyati.
may” âbhimantritaḥ śaśvaj Jātavedāḥ praśāmyati,
didhakṣuḥ sakalāl̃ lokān parikṣipya samantataḥ.
61.10 yad vā paramakaṃ tejo yena yuktā div’|âukasaḥ,
mam’ âpy an|upamaṃ bhūyo devebhyo viddhi, Bhārata.
vidīryamāṇāṃ vasu|dhāṃ, girīṇāṃ śikharāṇi ca
lokasya paśyato, rājan, sthāpayāmy abhimantraṇāt.
cetan’|â|cetanasy’ âsya jaṅgama|sthāvarasya ca
vināśāya samutpannam ahaṃ ghoraṃ mahā|svanam,
aśma|varṣaṃ ca, vāyuṃ ca śamayām’ îha nityaśaḥ

VAISHAMPÁYANA uvāca:

ONCE HE HAD heard his father's words, the extremely impatient Dhartaráshtra became enormously angry and spoke again, saying: 61.1

"If you think the Parthas are invincible because they have help from the gods, then let your fear disappear, greatest of kings. Bhárata, the gods attain divinity through their apathy to love, hate, greed, and anger, and by their indifference to all beings. This is what Vyasa Dvaipáyana, the great ascetic Nárada, and Rama the son of Jamad·agni told us long ago.

The gods never behave in a human manner out of desire, 61.5
anger, greed, or hatred, bull of the Bharatas. In fact, if Agni, Vayu, Dharma, Indra, and the Ashvins were to act out of the bonds of love, then the Parthas would not have suffered their misery. Therefore, you shouldn't be at all anxious, for they are eternally concerned with divine matters, Bhárata.

If hatred or greed can be discerned among the gods through attachment to desire, then through their divine authority it will not progress. Agni is always soothed when I cast spells over him, even when he blazes all around and
wishes to burn the worlds in their entirety. The splendor 61.10
with which heaven is endowed is certainly great, but know, Bhárata, that mine is without compare, greater even than that of the gods.

If the earth herself were to split asunder and mountain peaks were to fall, then I could halt them with my formulas as the world looks on. With the universe looking on, out of my eternal compassion for living creatures I will always put an end to terrifying and loud thundering hurricane winds

jagataḥ paśyato 'bhīkṣṇaṃ bhūtānām anukampayā!
stambhitāsv apsu gacchanti mayā ratha|padātayaḥ!
dev'|âsurāṇāṃ bhāvānām aham ekaḥ pravartitā!
61.15 akṣauhiṇībhir yān deśān yāmi kāryeṇa kena cit,
tatr' âśvā me pravartante, yatra yatr' âbhikāmaye!
bhayānakāni viṣaye vyāl'|ādīni na santi me,
mantra|guptāni bhūtāni na hiṃsanti bhayaṅ|karāḥ!
nikāma|varṣī parjanyo, rājan, viṣaya|vāsinām,
dharmiṣṭhāś ca prajāḥ sarvā, ītayaś ca na santi me.
Aśvināv, atha Vāyv|Agnī, Marudbhiḥ saha Vṛtra|ha,
Dharmaś c' âiva mayā dviṣṭān n' ôtsahante 'bhirakṣitum!
yadi hy ete samarthāḥ syur mad|dviṣas trātum añjasā,
na sma trayo|daśa samāḥ Pārthā duḥkham avāpnuyuḥ!
61.20 n' âiva devā, na gandharvā, n' âsurā, na ca rākṣasāḥ
śaktās trātuṃ mayā dviṣṭaṃ; satyam etad bravīmi te.
yad abhidhyāmy ahaṃ śaśvac
chubhaṃ vā yadi v" â|śubham,
n' âitad vipanna|pūrvaṃ me
mitreṣv ariṣu c' ôbhayoḥ.
bhaviṣyat' îdam, iti vā yad bravīmi, paran|tapa,
n' ânyathā bhūta|pūrvaṃ ca! satya|vāg, iti māṃ viduḥ.
loka|sākṣikam etan me māhātmyaṃ dikṣu viśrutam;
āśvāsan'|ârthaṃ bhavataḥ proktaṃ, na ślāghayā, nṛpa.
na hy ahaṃ ślāghano, rājan, bhūta|pūrvaḥ kadā cana;
a|sad|ācaritaṃ hy etad yad ātmānaṃ praśaṃsati.

which cause avalanches, and which bring about the destruction of both the self-aware and the unaware, as well as the mobile and static!

When I make the waters freeze over then chariots and infantry can travel over it! I alone am the instigator of the gods' and *ásuras*' affairs! My horses carry me to whichever 61.15
regions I travel, with my armed forces, on whatever business; they carry me wherever I desire! There are no terrifying snakes and so on in my territory, nor do scary monsters harm the creatures who are protected by my incantations!

The clouds rain whenever those who live in my realm wish, king. All my citizens are completely law-abiding and no plagues befall them. The Ashvins, Vayu, Agni, and the slayer of Vritra along with the Maruts as well as Dharma would not dare to defend those I hate! If they were capable of protecting my enemies with their strength, then the Parthas would not have lived in misery for thirteen years!
I tell you honestly: neither gods, *gandhárva*s, *ásura*s, nor 61.20
*rákshasa*s can protect someone I despise.

Regardless of whether it is good or bad, whatever I set my heart on, for friends and enemies alike, is always fulfilled and never miscarries. When I say something will happen, scorcher of the enemy, it doesn't turn out otherwise! Men know that I speak the truth. King, I speak of my magnificence, which is renowned and observed by the world, to console you rather than merely to boast. I have never boasted before, my lord, for it is the behavior of the wicked to praise oneself.

61.25 Pāṇḍavāṃś c' âiva, Matsyāṃś ca, Pāñcālān Kekayaiḥ saha
Sātyakiṃ, Vāsudevaṃ ca śrot" âsi vijitān mayā.
saritaḥ sāgaraṃ prāpya yathā naśyanti sarvaśaḥ,
tath" âiva te vinaṅkṣyanti mām āsādya sah'|ânvayāḥ!
parā buddhiḥ, paraṃ tejo, vīryaṃ ca paramaṃ mama,
parā vidyā, paro yogo mama tebhyo viśiṣyate.
pitā|mahaś ca, Droṇaś ca, Kṛpaḥ, Śalyaḥ, Śalas tathā
astreṣu yat prajānanti, sarvaṃ tan mayi vidyate.»
ity uktvā Sañjayaṃ bhūyaḥ paryapṛcchata, Bhārata,
jñātva yuyutsoḥ kāryāṇi prāpta|kālam arin|damaḥ.

VAIŚAMPĀYANA uvāca:

62.1 tathā tu pṛcchantam atīva Pārthaṃ
Vaicitravīryaṃ tam a|cintayitvā,
uvāca Karṇo Dhṛtarāṣṭra|putraṃ
praharṣayan saṃsadi Kauravāṇām:
«mithyā pratijñāya mayā yad astraṃ
Rāmāt kṛtaṃ Brahma|mayaṃ purastāt,
vijñāya ten' âsmi tad" âivam uktas:
‹ten' ânta|kāle '|pratibhāsyat' îti.›*
mah"|âparādhe hy api yan na tena
maha"|rṣiṇ" âhaṃ guruṇā ca śaptaḥ,
śaktaḥ pradagdhuṃ hy api tigma|tejāḥ
sa|sāgarām apy avaniṃ maha"|rṣiḥ.
prasāditaṃ hy asya mayā mano 'bhūc
chuśrūṣayā svena ca pauruṣeṇa.
tad asti c' âstraṃ mama s'|âvaśeṣaṃ;
tasmāt samartho 'smi, mam' âiṣa bhāraḥ.

You will hear that I have defeated the Pándavas, Matsyas, Pañchálas, and the Kékayas, as well as Sátyaki and Vasudéva. Just as rivers are completely annihilated when they reach the ocean, so too will they and their followers be destroyed when they come across me! My supreme intelligence, supreme splendor, supreme heroism, supreme knowledge, and supreme discipline distinguish me as superior to them. Whatever my grandfather, Drona, Kripa, Shalya, and Shala know about weapons can also be found in me." 61.25

When he had said this, Bhárata, the enemy-tamer once again interrogated Sáñjaya to find out what Yudhi·shthira, ready for war, was up to, and when his opportunity would come.

VAISHAMPÁYANA said:

Without giving any consideration to the son of Vichítra·virya, who was asking questions about the Partha, Karna spoke to Dhrita·rashtra's son, raising spirits in the assembly of the Káuravas: 62.1

"When Rama discovered long ago that I had duplicitously attained the Brahma weapon from him, he warned me: 'In the final moment, when you come to fire, the missile will fail to materialize in your mind.'

Even for such a great offence I was not seriously cursed by that great sage and teacher, even though the mighty sage of passionate splendor is capable of burning the earth and its oceans. In fact, I later conciliated his mind through obedience and manliness, and the weapon still remains within me. So I am equal to this task and this burden is mine.

62.5 nimeṣa|mātrāt tam ṛṣeḥ prasādam
avāpya Pāñcāla|Karūṣa|Matsyān,
nihatya Pārthān saha putra|pautrair
lokān ahaṃ śastra|jitān prapatsye.
pitā|mahas tiṣṭhatu te samīpe,
Droṇaś ca, sarve ca nar'|êndra|mukhyāḥ,
yathā pradhānena balena gatvā
Pārthān haniṣyāmi; mam' âiṣa bhāraḥ!»
evaṃ bruvantaṃ tam uvāca Bhīṣmaḥ:
«kiṃ katthase, kāla|parīta|buddhe?
na, Karṇa, jānāsi yathā pradhāne
hate hatāḥ syur Dhṛtarāṣṭra|putrāḥ?
yat Khāṇḍavaṃ dāhayatā kṛtaṃ hi
Kṛṣṇa|dvitīyena Dhanañjayena,
śrutv" âiva tat karma niyantum ātmā
yuktas tvayā vai saha bāndhavena!
yāṃ c' âpi śaktiṃ tridaś'|âdhipas te
dadau mah"|ātmā bhagavān mah"|Êndraḥ,
bhasmī|kṛtāṃ tāṃ samare viśīrṇāṃ
cakr'|āhatāṃ drakṣyasi Keśavena.
62.10 yas te śaraḥ sarpa|mukho vibhāti
sad" âgrya|mālyair mahitaḥ prayatnāt,
sa Pāṇḍu|putr'|âbhihataḥ śar'|âughaiḥ;
saha tvayā yāsyati, Karṇa, nāśam.
Bāṇasya Bhaumasya ca, Karṇa, hantā
Kirīṭinaṃ rakṣati Vāsudevaḥ
yas tvādṛśānāṃ ca varīyasāṃ ca
hantā ripūṇāṃ tumule pragāḍhe.»

Now that I have won the sage's favor, in the blink of an 62.5
eye I will kill the Pañchálas, Karúshas, Matsyas, and Parthas along with their sons and grandsons, and then I will present to you the worlds I have won by my weapons. Let grandfather, Drona, and all the leading lords of men stay back with you, for I will advance with my essential force and kill the Parthas. This is my burden!"

While he was saying these things, Bhishma spoke up, saying to him: "Why are you boasting? Your mind is going as you near your end. Do you not understand, Karna, that once the chief is dead, then Dhrita·rashtra's sons would all be killed? Just hearing how Khándava was burned by Dhanañ·jaya with Krishna as his second, ought to restrain you and your faction from this act!

You will see your spear, given to you by the thirty gods and high-souled and mighty Lord Indra, shattered by Késhava's discus, turned to dust, and broken in battle. Your 62.10
shining, snake-mouthed arrow, which you always take the effort to celebrate with excellent garlands, will be destroyed by the swarms of arrows shot by the son of Pandu. It will go to its destruction with you, Karna. Vasudéva, the killer of Bana and Bhauma, protects Kirítin, the crowned hero, Karna, and he destroys enemies who are at least your equal if not stronger in the crowded tumult."

KARṆA uvāca:
«a|saṃśayaṃ Vṛṣṇi|patir yath" ôktas,
tathā ca bhūyāṃś ca tato mah"|ātmā,
ahaṃ yad uktaḥ paruṣaṃ tu kiñ cit,
pitā|mahas tasya phalaṃ śṛṇotu!
nyasyāmi śastrāṇi, na jātu saṅkhye
pitā|maho drakṣyati māṃ sabhāyām.
tvayi praśānte tu mama prabhāvaṃ
drakṣyanti sarve bhuvi bhūmi|pālāḥ!»

VAIŚAMPAYANA uvāca:
ity evam uktvā sa mahā|dhanuṣmān
hitvā sabhāṃ svaṃ bhavanaṃ jagāma.
Bhīṣmas tu Duryodhanam eva, rājan,
madhye Kurūṇāṃ prahasann uvāca:
62.15 «satya|pratijñaḥ kila sūta|putras!
tathā sa bhāraṃ viṣaheta kasmāt?
vyūhaṃ prativyūhya, śirāṃsi bhittvā
loka|kṣayaṃ paśyata Bhīmasenāt.
‹Āvantya|Kāliṅga|Jayadratheṣu,
Cedi|dhvaje tiṣṭhati, Bāhlike ca,
ahaṃ haniṣyāmi sadā pareṣāṃ
sahasraśaś c' âyutaśaś ca yodhān!›
yad" âiva Rāme bhagavaty a|nindye
brahma bruvāṇaḥ kṛtavāṃs tad astram,
tad" âiva dharmaś ca tapaś ca naṣṭaṃ
Vaikartanasy' âdhama|pūruṣasya!»

KARNA replied:

"Without doubt, the high-souled lord of the Vrishnis is just as you say, and in fact even more powerful, but I will say something in reply to your unkind words, and let grandfather hear the result of that! I will lay down my weapons, and grandfather will no longer see me in battle but only in court! Only when you are dead—quietened once and for all—will all the kings on earth witness my power!"

VAISHAMPÁYANA continued:

When the mighty archer had said his piece, he left court and went back to his own apartment, but Bhishma only laughed, my king, and spoke to Duryódhana in the midst of the Kurus:

"The *suta*'s son is indeed true to his word! How will he be 62.15
capable of carrying out his promised burdens now? Watch the destruction of the worlds spring from Bhima·sena as he cuts off head after head, when he has drawn up his forces in opposition.

'While Avántya, Kalínga, Jayad·ratha, Chedi·dhvaja, and Báhlika stand by, I will incessantly kill enemy warriors by the thousands and tens of thousands!'—or so he boasted! When he told blameless Lord Rama that he was a brahmin and attained that weapon, Vaikártana, the lowest of men, lost his moral virtue and austerity!"

VAIŚAMPĀYANA uvāca:

tath" ôkta|vākye, nṛpat'|îndra, Bhīṣme,
nikṣipya śastrāṇi gate ca Karṇe
Vaicitravīryasya suto 'lpa|buddhir
Duryodhanaḥ Śāntanavaṃ babhāṣe:

DURYODHANA uvāca:

63.1 «SADṚŚĀNĀṂ manuṣyeṣu sarveṣāṃ tulya|janmanām
katham ek'|ântatas teṣāṃ Pārthānāṃ manyase jayam?
vayaṃ ca te 'pi tulyā vai vīryeṇa ca parākramaiḥ,
samena vayasā c' âiva, prātibhena, śrutena ca,
astreṇa, yoga|yuktyā* ca, śīghratve, kauśale tathā.
sarve sma sama|jātīyāḥ, sarve mānuṣa|yonayaḥ.
pitā|maha, vijānīṣe Pārtheṣu vijayaṃ katham?
n' âhaṃ bhavati, na Droṇe, na Kṛpe, na ca Bāhlike,
63.5 anyeṣu ca nar'|êndreṣu parākramya samārabhe.
ahaṃ, Vaikartanaḥ Karṇo, bhrātā Duḥśāsanaś ca me
Pāṇḍavān samare pañca haniṣyāmaḥ śitaiḥ śaraiḥ.
tato, rājan, mahā|yajñair vividhair bhūri|dākṣiṇaiḥ
brāhmaṇāṃs tarpayiṣyāmi, gobhir, aśvair, dhanena ca.
yadā parikariṣyanti aiṇeyān iva tantunā
a|taritrān iva jale bāhubhir māmakā raṇe,
paśyantas te parāṃs tatra ratha|nāga|samākulān,
tadā darpaṃ vimokṣyanti Pāṇḍavāḥ sa ca Keśavaḥ!»

VAISHAMPÁYANA said:

When Bhishma had said these things, lord of kings, and Karna had set down his weapons and left, Duryódhana, Vaichítravírya's son of little intelligence, said to the son of Shántanu:

DURYÓDHANA said:

"WHY DO YOU think victory will exclusively belong to the Parthas? They are born the same as all men! We are also the same in strength and prowess, we are of the same age, have the same intuitive knowledge, learning, weapons, practice in discipline, and are equal in dexterity and skill. We are all the same species, all born from human wombs, so, grandfather, how can you know that victory will belong to the Parthas? 63.1

I will not rely on you, or Drona, Kripa, Báhlika, or any other kings for my prowess. Karna Vaikártana, my brother Duhshásana, and I will kill the five Pándavas in battle with our sharp arrows. Then, king, I will content the brahmins with various mighty sacrifices and their fees, as well as with cattle, horses, and wealth. 63.5

When my troops drag them down in battle as though they were antelope surrounded by hunters with rope, or men with no helmsman on the sea, and the Pándavas see their enemies, thronged with chariots and elephants, then they and Késhava will renounce their arrogance!"

VIDURA uvāca:

«iha niḥśreyasaṃ prāhur vṛddhā niścita|darśinaḥ;
brāhmaṇasya viśeṣeṇa damo dharmaḥ sanātanaḥ.
63.10 tasya dānaṃ, kṣamā, siddhir yathāvad upapadyate,
damo, dānaṃ, tapo, jñānam, adhītaṃ c' ânuvartate.
damas tejo vardhayati, pavitraṃ dama uttamam.
vipāpmā vṛddha|tejās tu puruṣo vindate mahat.
kravy'|âdbhya iva bhūtānām a|dāntebhyaḥ sadā bhayam,
yeṣāṃ ca pratiṣedh'|ârthaṃ kṣatraṃ sṛṣṭaṃ svayaṃ|bhuvā.
āśrameṣu caturṣv āhur damam ev' ôttamaṃ vratam.
tasya liṅgaṃ pravakṣyāmi, yeṣāṃ samudayo damaḥ:
kṣamā, dhṛtir, a|hiṃsā ca, samatā, satyam, ārjavam,
indriy'|âbhijayo, dhairyaṃ, mārdavaṃ, hrīr, a|cāpalam,
63.15 a|kārpaṇyam, a|saṃrambhaḥ, santoṣaḥ, śraddadhānatā;
etāni yasya, rāj'|êndra, sa dāntaḥ puruṣaḥ smṛtaḥ.
kāmo, lobhaś ca, darpaś ca, manyur, nidrā, vikatthanam,
māna, īrṣyā ca, śokaś ca – n' âitad dānto niṣevate.
a|jihmam, a|śaṭhaṃ, śuddham – etad dāntasya lakṣaṇam.
a|lolupas, tath" âlp'|ēpsuḥ, kāmānām a|vicintitā,
samudra|kalpaḥ puruṣaḥ – sa dāntaḥ parikīrtitaḥ.
su|vṛttaḥ, śīla|sampannaḥ, prasann'|ātm", ātmavid, budhaḥ,
prāpy' êha loke saṃmānaṃ su|gatiṃ pretya gacchati.

VÍDURA said:

"The elders who understand certainties say that nothing is better in this world than restraint, and in particular it is
the eternal virtue of a brahmin. The man whose restraint 63.10
follows liberality, austerity, knowledge, and study will produce generosity, forgiveness, and success accordingly. Restraint increases one's splendor and is the ultimate means of purification. Free from suffering, with one's splendor enhanced, a man finds true greatness in Brahman.

Creatures always fear those without control, just as if they were flesh-eating *rákshasas*, and it was for the sake of repelling these men that the self-existent created the warrior caste. Men say that restraint is the highest possible vow for the four periods of religious life, but I claim that the mark of restraint is the combination of these characteristics: forgiveness, resolve, non-violence, impartiality, truth, sincerity, control over the senses, fortitude, leniency, modesty, constancy, magnanimity, mildness, contentment, and 63.15
faith. The restrained man is considered to have these, lord of kings.

The man of restraint does not cultivate desire, greed, arrogance, pride, sleep, boasting, self-conceit, envy, or grief. Honesty, sincerity, and purity are the marks of a restrained man. The man who is free from desire, who wants little and disregards matters of lust—the man who is as calm as the sea is celebrated as restrained. The man of good conduct, endowed with proper behavior, pure-souled, wise, and self-knowing, attains respect in this world here, and reaches bliss in the next.

a|bhayaṃ yasya bhūtebhyaḥ, sarveṣām a|bhayaṃ yataḥ,
sa vai pariṇata|prajñaḥ prakhyāto manuj'|ôttamaḥ.
63.20 sarva|bhūta|hito maitras tasmān n' ôdvijate janaḥ,
samudra iva gambhīraḥ prajñā|tṛptaḥ praśāmyati.
karmaṇ" ācaritaṃ pūrvaṃ sadbhir ācaritaṃ ca yat,
tad ev' āsthāya modante dāntāḥ śama|parāyaṇāḥ.

naiṣkarmyaṃ vā samāsthāya jñāna|tṛpto, jit'|êndriyaḥ,
kāl'|ākāṅkṣī caraṃ loke brahma|bhūyāya kalpate.
śakunīnām iv' ākāśe padaṃ n' âiv' ôpalabhyate,
evaṃ prajñāna|tṛptasya muner vartma na dṛśyate.
utsṛjy' âiva gṛhān yas tu mokṣam ev' âbhimanyate,
lokās tejo|mayās tasya kalpante śāśvatā divi.»

VIDURA uvāca:

64.1 «ŚAKUNĪNĀM IH' ârthāya pāśaṃ bhūmāv ayojayat
kaś cic chākunikas, tāta, pūrveṣām iti śuśruma.
tasmiṃs tau śakunau baddhau yugapat saha|cāriṇau.
tāv upādāya taṃ pāśaṃ jagmatuḥ kha|carāv ubhau.
tau vihāya samākrāntau dṛṣṭvā śākunikas tadā
anvadhāvad a|nirviṇṇo yena yena sma gacchataḥ.

tathā tam anudhāvantaṃ mṛgayuṃ śakun'|ârthinam
āśrama|stho muniḥ kaś cid dadarś' âtha kṛt'|āhnikaḥ.
64.5 tāv antarikṣa|gau śīghram anuyāntaṃ mahī|caram
ślokeṅ' ânena, Kauravya, papraccha sa munis tadā:
‹vicitram idam āścaryaṃ, mṛga|han, pratibhāti me,

The man of fully developed wisdom, who has no fear of other creatures and whom no creatures fear, is renowned
as the greatest of men. A friend who benefits every living 63.20
thing so that no man comes to any harm, who is deep like the ocean and satisfied with his wisdom, remains calm. Restrained men whose behavior follows the practices of strict men from ages past, and whose final resort is peace, rejoice in this world.

Alternatively, the man who is satisfied with his wisdom and whose senses are controlled, withdraws from action, and hoping for his time to finish, he moves in this world, preparing for his transformation into Brahman. Just as the tracks of birds in the sky cannot be discerned, so the course of a sage who is satisfied because of his wisdom cannot be seen. By letting go of the worlds he seized, and concentrating on release, splendid and eternal worlds await him in heaven."

VÍDURA continued:

"MY SON, WE have heard the story from our elders of a 64.1
bird catcher who set his trap on the ground to catch birds. Two companion birds were caught in the trap, but taking the trap with them both birds went flying into the sky. When the bird catcher saw them rocketing into the sky, he ran after them in the direction they had gone, undismayed.

A certain sage, living in a hermitage, who had performed his morning duties, saw the hunter running in pursuit to
catch the birds, giving chase, running over the ground while 64.5
the pair of birds flew fast through the air, so the sage then questioned him with this verse, Kaurávya: 'It strikes me as

plavamānau hi khalcarau padātir anudhāvasi!›

SĀKUNIKA uvāca:

‹pāśam ekam ubhāv etau sahitau harato mama;
yatra vai vivadiṣyete, tatra me vaśam eṣyataḥ!›

VIDURA uvāca:

tau vivādam anuprāptau śakunau mṛtyu|sandhitau
vigṛhya ca su|durbuddhī pṛthivyāṃ sannipetatuḥ.
tau yudhyamānau saṃrabdhau mṛtyu|pāśa|vaś'|ânugau
upasṛty' â|parijñāto jagrāha mṛga|hā tadā.
64.10 evaṃ ye jñātayo 'rtheṣu mitho gacchanti vigraham,
te '|mitra|vaśam āyānti, śakunāv iva vigrahāt.
sambhojanaṃ, saṅkathanaṃ,
saṃpraśno, 'tha samāgamaḥ—
etāni jñāti|kāryāṇi,
na virodhaḥ kadā cana.
ye sma kāle su|manasaḥ sarve vṛddhān upāsate,
siṃha|guptam iv' âraṇyam a|pradhṛṣyā bhavanti te.
ye 'rthaṃ santatam āsādya dīnā iva samāsate,
śriyaṃ te saṃprayacchanti dviṣadbhyo, Bharata'|rṣabha.
dhūmāyante vyapetāni, jvalanti sahitāni ca,
Dhṛtarāṣṭr', ôlmukān' îva jñātayo, Bharata'|rṣabha.
64.15 idam anyat pravakṣyāmi yathā dṛṣṭaṃ girau mayā.
śrutvā tad api, Kauravya, yathā śreyas, tathā kuru.
vayaṃ kirātaiḥ sahitā gacchāmo girim uttaram,
brāhmaṇair deva|kalpaiś ca, vidyā|jambhaka|vārtikaiḥ.
kuñja|bhūtaṃ giriṃ sarvam abhito Gandhamādanam
dīpyamān'|âuṣadhi|gaṇaṃ siddha|gandharva|sevitam.

strange and curious, hunter, that you pursue a couple of sky-roaming birds on foot!'

THE BIRD CATCHER replied:

'Together those two are stealing my only trap, but wherever they start quarrelling, I'll get them!'

VÍDURA continued:

When those two birds, destined to die, started arguing,
aggressive and extremely dim-witted, they fell to the
ground. As they fought in their fury, still slaves to the power
of that death trap, the hunter turned up and seized them
unnoticed. So you see, relatives who come to blows with 64.10
each other over possessions fall under the power of their
enemies, just as those two birds fell because of their enmity.

Relatives should eat together, talk together, inquire into subjects together, and travel together, but they should never quarrel. When they are well-minded and wait on their elders, they become as unapproachable as a forest guarded by lions. But those who have gathered lasting wealth but behave as though they were paupers, offer good fortune to their enemies, bull of the Bharatas. Relatives are like firebrands, Dhrita·rashtra, which smoke when separated, but blaze when together, bull of the Bharatas.

I will tell you something else which I saw on a moun- 64.15
tain, and once you have heard that too, Kaurávya, then do
what is best. We were going together to the northern mountain with mountain tribesmen and god-like brahmins who
explained their knowledge of charms. The entire Gandha·
mádana mountain was overgrown with plants on all faces,

tatr' âpaśyāma vai sarve madhu pītaka|mākṣikam
maru|prapāte viṣame niviṣṭaṃ, kumbha|sammitam,
āśī|viṣai rakṣyamāṇaṃ, Kubera|dayitaṃ bhṛśam.
yat prāpya puruṣo martyo 'py a|maratvaṃ nigacchati,
64.20 a|cakṣur labhate cakṣur, vṛddho bhavati vai yuvā,
iti te kathayanti sma brāhmaṇā jambha|sādhakāḥ.
tataḥ kirātās tad dṛṣṭvā prārthayanto, mahī|pate,
vineśur viṣame tasmin sa|sarpe giri|gahvare.
tath" âiva tava putro 'yaṃ pṛthivīm eka icchati;
madhu paśyati, sammohāt prapātaṃ n' ânupaśyati.
Duryodhano yoddhu|manāḥ samare Savyasācinā;
na ca paśyāmi tejo 'sya vikramaṃ vā tathā|vidham.
ekena ratham āsthāya pṛthivī yena nirjitā,
Bhīṣma|Droṇa|prabhṛtayaḥ santrastāḥ sādhu|yāyinaḥ
64.25 Virāṭa|nagare bhagnāḥ; kiṃ tatra tava dṛśyatām.
pratīkṣamāṇo yo vīraḥ kṣamate vīkṣitaṃ tava.
Drupado, Matsya|rājaś ca, saṃkruddhaś ca Dhanañjayaḥ
na śeṣayeyuḥ samare vāyu|yuktā iv' âgnayaḥ.
aṅke kuruṣva rājānaṃ, Dhṛtarāṣṭra, Yudhiṣṭhiram
yudhyator hi dvayor yuddhe n' âik'|ântena bhavej jayaḥ.»

species of luminescent medicinal plants, and was frequented by *siddhas* and *gandhárvas*.

There we all saw a jar's worth of yellow bee's honey set upon a rocky, uneven precipice. The honey was particularly cherished by Kubéra, and so it was guarded by poisonous snakes. The man who reaches it gains immortality even if he is a mortal, the blind regain their sight, and the elderly 64.20
become young again, or so the brahmins, who were skilled in charms, told us.

The mountain tribesmen saw it and wanted to take it, lord of earth, but they were destroyed on that rocky, snake-infested, inpenetrable mountain ledge. Similarly your son here wants the earth for himself alone. He sees the honey, but in his idiocy he does not notice the impending fall. Duryódhana wishes to fight against Savya·sachin, the ambidextrous warrior, in battle, but I do not see similarly matched qualities of splendor or prowess in him.

Árjuna conquered the earth standing on a single chariot, 64.25
and at Viráta's city the excellent drivers, led by Bhishma and Drona, were terrified and the ranks were broken. Let what happened there be a lesson to you. That hero is forgiving and waits, looking to your face for a sign of your plans. Drúpada, the king of Matsya, and furious Dhanañ·jaya will leave none alive in battle, as though they were fires inflamed by the wind. Dhrita·rashtra, take King Yudhi·shthira to your lap, for in a battle between the two sides there will by no means be victory for either."

DHṚTARĀṢṬRA uvāca:

65.1 «DURYODHANA, vijānīhi yat tvāṃ vakṣyāmi, putraka.
utpathaṃ manyase mārgam, an|abhijña iv' âdhva|gaḥ.
pañcānāṃ Pāṇḍu|putrāṇāṃ yat tejaḥ prajihīrṣasi,
pañcānām iva bhūtānāṃ mahatāṃ loka|dhāriṇām.
Yudhiṣṭhiraṃ hi Kaunteyaṃ paraṃ dharmam ih' āsthitam
parāṃ gatim a|saṃpretya na tvaṃ jetum ih' ârhasi.

Bhīmasenaṃ ca Kaunteyaṃ, yasya n' âsti samo bale,
raṇ'|ântakaṃ tarjayase, mahā|vātam iva drumaḥ.
65.5 sarva|śastra|bhṛtāṃ śreṣṭhaṃ, Meruṃ śikhariṇām iva,
yudhi Gāṇḍīva|dhanvānaṃ ko nu yudhyeta buddhimān?
Dhṛṣṭadyumnaś ca Pāñcālyaḥ kam iv' âdya na śātayet
śatru|madhye śarān muñcan deva|rāḍ aśanīm iva?
Sātyakiś c' âpi dur|dharṣaḥ saṃmato 'ndhaka|Vṛṣṇiṣu
dhvaṃsayiṣyati te senāṃ Pāṇḍaveya|hite rataḥ.

yaḥ punaḥ pratimānena trīn lokān atiricyate,
taṃ Kṛṣṇaṃ puṇḍarīk'|âkṣaṃ ko nu yudhyeta buddhimān?
ekato hy asya dārāś ca, jñātayaś ca sa|bāndhavāḥ,
ātmā ca, pṛthivī c' êyam, ekataś ca Dhanañjayaḥ!
65.10 Vāsudevo 'pi dur|dharṣo yat'|ātmā yatra Pāṇḍavaḥ;
a|viṣahyaṃ pṛthivy" âpi tad balaṃ yatra Keśavaḥ.

DHRITA·RASHTRA said:

"DURYÓDHANA, MY boy, consider what I am about to say 65.1
to you. Like a traveler who doesn't know the way, you believe the wrong road to be the right one. The energy of the five sons of Pandu, which you wish to destroy, is as great as that of the five elements which support the world. You are not able to defeat Yudhi·shthira, son of Kunti, the best of those who abide by moral law in this world, without following the final path and dying.

You threaten Bhima·sena, son of Kunti, who has no equal in battle and is like death himself in conflict, as ineffectu-
ally as a tree threatening a mighty hurricane. Which man of 65.5
intelligence would fight the Gandíva archer in battle, when he is the greatest of all who wield weapons just as Meru is the greatest of mountains? Whom could Dhrishta·dyumna Pañchálya not extinguish as he fires his arrows in the midst of the enemy like the king of the gods hurling his thunderbolt? Sátyaki too is near unconquerable and held in high regard among the Ándhaka Vrishnis. He is attached to the Pándavas' cause and so will destroy your army.

Then again, which wise man would fight lotus-eyed Krishna, who by comparison surpasses the three worlds? On the one hand Krishna has wives, relatives and kinsmen, himself, and this earth, and to balance them on the other
he has Dhanañ·jaya! Vasudéva, invincible and disciplined 65.10
in his soul, is found where the Pándava is found; the army which cannot even be borne by the earth herself is where Késhava is found.

tiṣṭha, tāta, satāṃ vākye suhṛdām artha|vādinām.
vṛddhaṃ Śāntanavaṃ Bhīṣmaṃ titikṣasva pitā|maham,
māṃ ca bruvāṇaṃ śuśrūṣa Kurūṇām artha|darśinam.
Droṇaṃ, Kṛpaṃ, Vikarṇaṃ ca, mahā|rājaṃ ca Bāhlikam,
ete hy api, yath" âiv' âhaṃ, mantum arhasi tāṃs tathā;
sarve dharma|vido hy ete, tulya|snehāś ca, Bhārata.
yat tad Virāṭa|nagare saha bhrātṛbhir agrataḥ
utsṛjya gāḥ su|saṃtrastaṃ balaṃ te samaśīryata,
65.15 yac c' âiva nagare tasmin śrūyate mahad adbhutam
ekasya ca bahūnāṃ ca paryāptaṃ tan nidarśanam!
Arjunas tat tath" âkārṣīt, kiṃ punaḥ sarva eva te?
sa|bhrātṝn abhijānīhi, vṛttyā taṃ pratipādaya!»

VAIŚAMPĀYANA uvāca:

66.1 EVAM UKTVĀ mahā|prājño Dhṛtarāṣṭraḥ Suyodhanam,
punar eva mahā|bhāgaḥ Sañjayaṃ paryapṛcchata:
«brūhi, Sañjaya, yac cheṣaṃ Vāsudevād an|antaram,
yad Arjuna uvāca tvāṃ; paraṃ kautūhalaṃ hi me!»

SAÑJAYA uvāca:

«Vāsudeva|vacaḥ śrutvā Kuntī|putro Dhanañjayaḥ
uvāca kāle dur|dharṣo Vāsudevasya śṛṇvataḥ:

My son, abide by good men's advice, for they are your friends and speak profitably. Endure your aged grandfather Bhishma, son of Shántanu, and obey the commands I give you, for I see what is good for the Kurus. You ought to honor Drona, Kripa, Vikárna, and the mighty King Báhlika as you honor me, for they are like me, and they also all understand moral obligation and love you as I do, Bhárata.

The very fact that at Viráta's city, in your presence, your army and your brothers relinquished the cattle in their total terror and were routed, supports my advice. The incredibly 65.15
astounding story we have heard of one man battling against many at that city is clear evidence! Árjuna overpowered you all in this way, so how much worse will it be when all the Pándavas are united? Recognize them as your brothers and provide them with a livelihood here!"

VAISHAMPÁYANA uvāca:

WHEN DHRITA·RASHTRA of deep wisdom had spoken in 66.1
this way to Suyódhana, the illustrious man again questioned Sáñjaya, saying: "Sáñjaya, tell me what else Árjuna said after Vasudéva had finished, for my curiosity is endless!"

SÁÑJAYA replied:

"Once unconquerable Dhanañ·jaya, the son of Kunti, had heard Vasudéva's words, he then spoke within Vasudéva's hearing, saying:

‹pitā|mahaṃ Śāntanavaṃ, Dhṛtarāṣṭraṃ ca, Sañjaya,
Droṇaṃ, Kṛpaṃ ca, Karṇaṃ ca, mahā|rājaṃ ca Bāhlikam,
66.5 Drauṇiṃ ca, Somadattaṃ ca, Śakuniṃ c' âpi Saubalam,
Duḥśāsanaṃ, Śalaṃ c' âiva, Purumitraṃ, Viviṃśatim,
Vikarṇaṃ, Citrasenaṃ ca, Jayatsenaṃ ca pārthivam,
Vind'|Ânuvindāv Āvantyau, Durmukhaṃ c' âpi Kauravam,
Saindhavaṃ, Duḥsahaṃ c' âiva, Bhūriśravasam eva ca,
Bhagadattaṃ ca rājānaṃ, Jalasandhaṃ ca pārthivam,
ye c' âpy anye pārthivās tatra yoddhuṃ
samāgatāḥ Kauravāṇāṃ priy'|ârtham,
mumūrṣavaḥ Pāṇḍav'|âgnau pradīpte,
samānītā Dhārtarāṣṭreṇa hotum,
yathā|nyāyaṃ kauśalaṃ vandanaṃ ca
samāgatā mad|vacanena vācyāḥ.
idaṃ brūyāḥ, Sañjaya, rāja|madhye
Suyodhanaṃ pāpa|kṛtāṃ nidhānam,
66.10 a|marṣaṇaṃ dur|matiṃ rāja|putraṃ,
pāp'|ātmānaṃ Dhārtarāṣṭraṃ su|lubdham,
sarvaṃ mam' âitad vacanaṃ samagraṃ
sah' âmātyaṃ, Sañjaya, śrāvayethāḥ.›
evaṃ pratiṣṭhāpya Dhanañjayo māṃ
tato 'rthavad dharmavac c' âpi vākyam
provāc' êdaṃ Vāsudevaṃ samīkṣya
Pārtho dhīmāl lohit'|ânt'|āyat'|âkṣaḥ:
‹yathā śrutaṃ te vadato mah"|ātmano
Madhu|pravīrasya vacaḥ samāhitam,
tath" âiva vācyaṃ bhavatā hi mad|vacaḥ
samāgateṣu kṣiti|peṣu sarvaśaḥ:
«śar'|âgni|dhūme ratha|nemi|nādite
dhanuḥ|sruveṇ' âstra|bala|prasāriṇā

'Sáñjaya, when my grandfather, the son of Shántanu, as well as Dhrita·rashtra, Drona, Kripa, Karna, the mighty
King Báhlika, Drona's son, Soma·datta, Shákuni Sáubala, 66.5
Duhshásana, Shala, Puru·mitra, Vivínshati, Vikárna, Chitra·sena, King Jayat·sena, Vinda and Anuvínda, the two lords of Avánti, as well as Káurava Dúrmukha, Sáindhava Dúhsaha, and Bhuri·shravas, as well as King Bhaga·datta and King Jala·sandha and the other kings who have gathered to fight in order to please the Káuravas, and who will die brought together by Dhartaráshtra to be sacrificed as an offering in the blazing fire of the Pándavas, are congregated, then at my request greet them in proper order, enquiring after their health and paying them honor.

Then, Sáñjaya, in the midst of the kings, say this to Suyódhana, the treasure of miscreants, the impatient, wicked- 66.10
minded, and evil-souled prince, the excessively greedy son of Dhrita·rashtra—and make sure that he and his ministers hear everything I have to say in its entirety, Sáñjaya.'

Having begun in this manner, Dhanañ·jaya then spoke words which were full of significance and morality, and the wide-eyed, wise Partha glanced at Vasudéva with his red eyes, saying:

'You have heard the well-organized words of the high-souled leader of the Madhus, and so you must tell those kings when they are assembled on all sides that I too say the same thing, and also tell them: "All carefully endeavor together so that an oblation need not be made in the sacrifice of great battle, made smoky by the fire of our arrows, resounding with chariot wheels in place of spells, and with

yathā na homaḥ kriyate mahā|mṛdhe,
sametya sarve prayatadhvam ādṛtāḥ!
na cet prayacchadhvam a|mitra|ghātino
Yudhiṣṭhirasy' âṃśam abhīpsitaṃ svakam,
nayāmi vaḥ s'|âśva|padāti|kuñjarān
diśaṃ pitṝṇām a|śivāṃ śitaiḥ śaraiḥ.»›
66.15 tato 'ham āmantrya tadā Dhanañjayaṃ,
catur|bhujaṃ c' âiva namasya satvaraḥ,
javena saṃprāpta ih', âmara|dyute,
tav' ântikaṃ prāpayituṃ vaco mahat.»

VAIŚAMPĀYANA uvāca:

67.1 DURYODHANE Dhārtarāṣṭre tad vaco n' âbhinandati,
tūṣṇīṃ bhūteṣu sarveṣu samuttasthur nara'|rṣabhāḥ.
utthiteṣu, mahā|rāja, pṛthivyāṃ sarva|rājasu,
rahite Sañjayaṃ rājā paripraṣṭuṃ pracakrame,
āśaṃsamāno vijayaṃ teṣāṃ putra|vaś'|ânugaḥ,
ātmanaś ca pareṣāṃ ca, Pāṇḍavānāṃ ca niścayam.

DHṚTARĀṢṬRA uvāca:

«Gāvalgaṇe, brūhi naḥ sāra|phalgu,
sva|senāyāṃ yāvad ih' âsti kiñ cit.
tvaṃ Pāṇḍavānāṃ nipuṇaṃ vettha sarvaṃ;
kim eṣāṃ jyāyaḥ kimu teṣāṃ kanīyaḥ?
67.5 tvam etayoḥ sāra|vit sarva|darśī,
dharm'|ârthayor nipuṇo niścayajñaḥ.
sa me pṛṣṭaḥ, Sañjaya, brūhi sarvaṃ
yudhyamānāḥ katare 'smin na santi?»

the arrows shooting forth from the armed forces as the ladle! If you do not bestow upon Yudhi·shthira, the murderer of his enemies, what is his desired share, then I will send you with your horses, infantry, and elephants away to the dangerous realm of the ancestors with my sharp arrows."'

66.15 I then bid farewell to Dhanañ·jaya, quickly bowed to four-armed Krishna, and swiftly came here to bring this great message before you, king of immortal majesty."

VAISHAMPÁYANA said:

67.1 SINCE DURYÓDHANA, son of Dhrita·rashtra, did not acknowledge his words, and everyone else remained silent, the bull-like men stood up to leave. Once all the kings on earth had risen from their seats, great sovereign, the king began to question Sáñjaya in private, for that slave to his son's wishes hoped for victory for his side, and so he continued asking questions in order to come to a decision about himself, the others, and the Pándavas.

DHRITA·RASHTRA said:

"Son of Gaválgana, tell me whether our own army has the upper or lower hand, as it stands now. You know precisely the situation with the Pándavas in great detail, so in what ways do they have the advantage and in what ways do they fall behind? You are aware of the good points of either 67.5 side and you see everything, being precisely aware of the decisions of moral duty and profit. So tell me everything I ask, Sáñjaya, which of us will not survive as we fight in this war?"

SAÑJAYA uvāca:

«na tvāṃ brūyāṃ rahite jātu kiñ cid,
asūyā hi tvāṃ praviśeta, rājan.
ānayasva pitaraṃ mahā|vrataṃ,
Gāndhārīṃ ca mahiṣīm, Ājamīḍha.
tau te 'sūyāṃ vinayetāṃ, nar'|êndra,
dharma|jñau tau, nipuṇau, niścaya|jñau.
tayos tu tvāṃ sannidhau tad vadeyaṃ
kṛtsnaṃ mataṃ Keśava|Pārthayor yat.»

VAIŚAMPĀYANA uvāca:

ity uktena ca Gāndhārī, Vyāsaś c' âtr' ājagāma ha,
ānītau Vidureṇ' êha sabhāṃ śīghraṃ praveśitau.
|tatas tan matam ājñāya Sañjayasy', ātmajasya ca,
abhyupetya mahā|prājñaḥ Kṛṣṇa|Dvaipāyano 'bravīt:

VYĀSA uvāca:

67.10 «saṃpṛcchate Dhṛtarāṣṭrāya, Sañjaya,
ācakṣva sarvaṃ yāvad eṣo 'nuyuṅkte.
sarvaṃ yāvad vettha tasmin yathāvad
yāthātathyaṃ Vāsudeve 'rjune ca.»

SAÑJAYA uvāca:

68.1 «ARJUNO VĀSUDEVAŚ ca dhanvinau param'|ârcitau
kāmād anyatra sambhūtau, sarva|bhāvāya sammitau.
vyām'|ântaraṃ samāsthāya yathā|muktaṃ manasvinaḥ
cakraṃ tad Vāsudevasya māyayā vartate, vibho.
s'|âpahnavaṃ Kauraveṣu, Pāṇḍavānāṃ su|sammatam,
sār'|â|sāra|balaṃ jñātuṃ tejaḥ|puñj'|âvabhāsitam.

SÁÑJAYA replied:

"I will certainly not tell you anything in private, for you will be filled with displeasure, my king. Ajamídha, bring in your father of mighty vows and your queen Gandhári. Those two will rid you of your indignation, lord of kings, for they are both conversant with moral duty, shrewd, and find the truth of matters. I will tell you Késhava's and Partha's entire plan, but only when those two are present."

VAISHAMPÁYANA continued:

So, being addressed in this way, Dhrita·rashtra had Gandhári and Vyasa brought in, and, led there by Vídura, they quickly entered the court. Understanding what was on Sáñjaya's mind and on the mind of his son, the highly wise Krishna Dvaipáyana came up and said:

VYASA said:

"Sáñjaya, tell Dhrita·rashtra everything he asked, just as he commanded you. Truthfully tell everything that you know in this matter about Vasudéva and Árjuna." 67.10

SÁÑJAYA replied:

"ÁRJUNA AND VASUDÉVA, the most highly honored archers, have willingly been born in other forms, and are equal to all existence. Intelligent Vasudéva's discus is five cubits in width, can be thrown as far as the wielder wishes, and operates through illusion, my lord. It is concealed from the Káuravas, but very highly regarded by the Pándavas, and as it shines with its masses of splendor, it is the means to discover the strengths and weaknesses of the Pándavas' army. 68.1

Narakam̩, Śambaram̩ c' âiva,
Kam̩sam̩, Caidyam̩ ca Mādhavaḥ
jitavān ghora|saṅkāśān
krīḍann iva mahā|balaḥ.
68.5 pṛthivīm̩ c' ântarikṣam̩ ca, dyām̩ c' âiva puruṣ'|ôttamaḥ
manas" âiva viśiṣṭ'|ātmā nayaty ātma|vaśam̩ vaśī.
bhūyo bhūyo hi yad, rājan, pṛcchase Pāṇḍavān prati,
sār'|â|sāra|balam̩ jñātum̩, tat samāsena me śṛṇu:
ekato vā jagat kṛtsnam, ekato vā Janārdanaḥ;
sārato jagataḥ kṛtsnād atirikto Janārdanaḥ.
bhasma kuryāj jagad idam̩ manas" âiva Janārdanaḥ;
na tu kṛtsnam̩ jagac chaktam̩ bhasma kartum̩ Janārdanam.
yataḥ satyam̩, yato dharmo, yato hrīr, ārjavam̩ yataḥ,
tato bhavati Govindo. yataḥ Kṛṣṇas tato jayaḥ.
68.10 pṛthivīm̩ c' ântarikṣam̩ ca, divam̩ ca puruṣ'|ôttamaḥ
viceṣṭayati bhūt'|ātmā krīḍann iva Janārdanaḥ.
sa kṛtvā Pāṇḍavān satram̩ lokam̩ sam̩mohayann iva,
a|dharma|niratān mūḍhān dagdhum icchati te sutān.
kāla|cakram̩, jagac|cakram̩, yuga|cakram̩ ca Keśavaḥ
ātma|yogena bhagavān parivartayate 'niśam.
kālasya ca hi mṛtyoś ca, jaṅgama|sthāvarasya ca
īśate bhagavān ekaḥ, satyam etad bravīmi te.
īśann api mahāyogī sarvasya jagato Hariḥ
karmāṇy ārabhate kartum̩, kīnāśa iva vardhanaḥ.
68.15 tena vañcayate lokān māyā|yogena Keśavaḥ;
ye tam eva prapadyante na te muhyanti mānavāḥ.»

The mighty Mádhava defeated the horrifying-looking
Náraka, Shámbara, Kansa, and the king of the Chedis as
though he were playing. This supreme person, the mas- 68.5
ter whose soul is of especial distinction, brings the earth,
air, and sky under his control by his will. Again and again
you ask about the Pándavas, my king, so you can discover
the strengths and weaknesses of their army, so listen to my
summary:

If on the one hand you have the entire universe, and on the other Janárdana, then on balance Janárdana surpasses the entire universe in his nature. Janárdana could turn this universe to ash with merely his will, but the whole universe is not able to turn Janárdana to ash.

Where there is truth, where there is morality, where there
is modesty and sincerity, there is Go·vinda. Where Krishna
is, there is victory. Janárdana, the supreme person, the soul 68.10
of living creatures, makes the world, air, and sky go round,
as though he were playing.

Using the Pándavas as his cover, seemingly deceiving, he wishes to burn up your foolish sons who take pleasure in lawlessness. Blessed Lord Késhava incessantly turns the wheel of time, the wheel of the universe, and the wheel of the ages, through harnessing his own soul. I tell you truthfully, the blessed lord single-handedly governs time and death, as well as mobile and static matter.

Although Hari, the great ascetic, governs the whole
world, he still undertakes tasks just like a poor man who
thrives by working the land. Késhava deceives the worlds 68.15
by his practice of illusion, but men who attain him will not
be bewildered."

DHṚTARĀṢṬRA uvāca:

69.1 «KATHAṂ TVAṂ Mādhavaṃ vettha
sarva|loka|mah"|ēśvaram?
katham enaṃ na ved' âhaṃ?
tan mam' ācakṣva, Sañjaya.»

SAÑJAYA uvāca:

«śṛṇu, rājan. na te vidyā; mama vidyā na hīyate.
vidyā|hīnas tamo|dhvasto n' âbhijānāti Keśavam.
vidyayā, tāta, jānāmi tri|yugaṃ Madhu|sūdanam
kartāram a|kṛtaṃ devaṃ, bhūtānāṃ prabhav'|âpyayam.»

DHṚTARĀṢṬRA uvāca:

«Gāvalgaṇe, 'tra kā bhaktir yā te nityā Janārdane,
yayā tvam abhijānāsi tri|yugaṃ Madhu|sūdanam?»

SAÑJAYA uvāca:

69.5 «māyāṃ na seve, bhadraṃ te, na vṛthā dharmam ācare;
śuddha|bhāvaṃ gato bhaktyā śāstrād vedmi Janārdanam.»

DHṚTARĀṢṬRA uvāca:

«Duryodhana, Hṛṣīkeśaṃ prapadyasva Janārdanam!
āpto naḥ Sañjayas, tāta, śaraṇaṃ gaccha Keśavam!»

DHRITA·RASHTRA said:

"TELL ME HOW it is that you know that Mádhava is the great lord of all worlds, and how it is that I do not know this, Sáñjaya." 69.1

SÁÑJAYA replied:

"Listen, my lord. You do not have knowledge, though mine is not lacking. You do not recognize Késhava because you lack knowledge and are obscured by darkness. Through this knowledge, my friend, I recognize the slayer of Madhu as the one who appears in the first three ages, the creator who is himself not created, the divine source and dissolution of all creation."

DHRITA·RASHTRA said:

"Son of Gaválgana, what is your eternal devotion to Janárdana by which you recognize the slayer of Madhu as he who has existed through the three ages?"

SÁÑJAYA replied:

"I do not cultivate illusion, bless you, nor do I practice morality lightly, but rather I have become pure-spirited through my devotion, and I recognize Janárdana from the ancient texts." 69.5

DHRITA·RASHTRA said:

"Duryódhana, throw yourself on the mercy of Janárdana Hrishi·kesha! Sáñjaya is our trustworthy authority, my son, so go to Késhava for protection!"

DURYODHANA uvāca:

«bhagavān Devakī|putro lokāṃś cen nihaniṣyati,
pravadann Arjune sakhyaṃ, n' âhaṃ gacche 'dya Keśavam.»

DHṚTARĀṢṬRA uvāca:

«avāg, Gāndhāri, putras te gacchaty eṣa su|durmatiḥ,
īrṣur, dur|ātmā, mānī ca, śreyasāṃ vacan'|âtigaḥ!»

GĀNDHĀRY uvāca:

«aiśvarya|kāma, duṣṭ'|ātman, vṛddhānāṃ śāsan'|âtiga,
aiśvarya|jīvite hitvā, pitaraṃ māṃ ca, bāliśa,
69.10 vardhayan dur|hṛdāṃ prītiṃ, māṃ ca śokena vardhayan,
nihato Bhīmasenena smart" âsi vacanaṃ pituḥ!»

VYĀSA uvāca:

«priyo 'si, rājan, Kṛṣṇasya, Dhṛtarāṣṭra, nibodha me.
yasya te Sañjayo dūto yas tvāṃ śreyasi yokṣyate.
jānāty eṣa Hṛṣīkeśaṃ purāṇaṃ yac ca vai param,
śuśrūṣamāṇam aikāgryaṃ mokṣyate mahato bhayāt.
Vaicitravīrya, puruṣāḥ krodha|harṣa|samāvṛtāḥ,
sitā bahu|vidhaiḥ pāśair; ye na tuṣṭāḥ svakair dhanaiḥ,
Yamasya vaśam āyānti kāma|mūḍhāḥ punaḥ punaḥ,
andha|netrā yath" âiv' ândhā nīyamānāḥ sva|karmabhiḥ.
69.15 eṣa ek'|âyanaḥ panthā yena yānti manīṣiṇaḥ,
taṃ dṛṣṭvā mṛtyum atyeti, mahāṃs tatra na sajjati.»

DURYÓDHANA replied:

"Even if the blessed son of Dévaki were to destroy the worlds, proclaiming his friendship towards Árjuna, then I still would not go to Késhava now."

DHRITA·RASHTRA said:

"Gandhári, your excessively wicked-minded son is envious, black-souled, and arrogant! He violates the advice of his betters, and his downfall is assured!"

GANDHÁRI said:

"You wicked-souled, power-lusting transgressor of your elders' orders, who abandons power, life, your father, and
me, you fool, who increases the joy of your enemies while 69.10
augmenting my grief, you will remember your father's words when Bhima·sena is killing you!"

VYASA said:

"King Dhrita·rashtra, you are dear to Krishna, so listen to me. Sáñjaya is your messenger and he will bend to you, for you are his better. He knows the ancient and ultimate Hrishi·kesha, and if you listen to him intently he will save you from great danger.

Vaichítravírya, men are beset with anger and joy, and fettered with various kinds of traps; they are not satisfied with their own wealth. They fall into Yama's power time and time again when confused by desires, and are led by their own actions as though they were the blind being led by the blind.
The path by which the wise travel is the only path to Brah- 69.15
man, and when he sees it then the great man transcends death and is not stuck there."

DHṚTARĀṢṬRA uvāc:

«aṅga, Sañjaya, me śaṃsa panthānam a|kuto|bhayam,
yena gatvā Hṛṣīkeśaṃ prāpnuyāṃ siddhim uttamām.»

SAÑJAYA uvāca:

«n' â|kṛt'|ātmā kṛt'|ātmānaṃ jātu vidyāj Janārdanam;
ātmanas tu kriy"|ôpāyo n' ânyatr' êndriya|nigrahāt.
indriyāṇām udīrṇānāṃ kāma|tyāgo '|pramādataḥ;
a|pramādo '|vihiṃsā ca jñāna|yonir a|saṃśayam.
indriyāṇāṃ yame yatto bhava, rājann, a|tandritaḥ;
buddhiś ca te mā cyavatu, niyacch' âināṃ yatas tataḥ.
69.20 etaj jñānaṃ vidur viprā dhruvam indriya|dhāraṇam;
etaj jñānaṃ ca panthāś ca yena yānti manīṣiṇaḥ.
a|prāpyaḥ Keśavo, rājann, indriyair a|jitair nṛbhiḥ.
āgam'|âdhigamād yogād vaśī tattve prasīdati.»

DHṚTARĀṢṬRA uvāca:

70.1 «BHŪYO ME puṇḍarīk'|âkṣaṃ, Sañjay', ācakṣva pṛcchataḥ.
nāma|karm'|ârtha|vit, tāta, prāpnuyāṃ puruṣ'|ôttamam.»

SAÑJAYA uvāca:

«śrutaṃ me Vāsudevasya nāma|nirvacanaṃ śubham
yāvat tatr' âbhijāne 'ham a|prameyo hi Keśavaḥ.

DHRITA·RASHTRA said:

"Sáñjaya, please tell me of the path which holds no fear, by which I will reach Hrishi·kesha and attain ultimate success."

SÁÑJAYA replied:

"A man who has no control over his soul can certainly not know Janárdana, for his soul is disciplined. One's actions are not a means to this end if one does not suppress one's senses. It is beyond doubt that the renunciation of desire for the excitement of the senses, careful attention, and vigilant non-violence is the womb of knowledge. Be untiringly in control of your senses, king; don't let your mind wander, but restrain it from this and that distraction.

Brahmins know that constant firmness with one's senses 69.20
is wisdom. This is the wisdom and the path by which wise men travel. Késhava cannot be attained by men with undisciplined senses. The man who is under his own control finds relaxation in the truth, through study of sacred texts and the practice of discipline."

DHRITA·RASHTRA said:

"TELL ME ONCE more, Sáñjaya, since I am asking you, 70.1
about the lotus-eyed one. By understanding the significance of his names and deeds, my friend, I may reach the supreme person."

SÁÑJAYA replied:

"I have heard the holy and blameless names of Vasudéva and so I will explain as much as I know, for Késhava is indeed beyond our scope.

vasanāt sarva|bhūtānāṃ, vasutvād, deva|yonitaḥ
Vāsudevas tato vedyo; bṛhattvād Viṣṇur ucyate.
maunād, dhyānāc ca, yogāc viddhi, Bhārata, Mādhavam.
sarva|tattva|mayatvāc ca Madhu|hā Madhu|sūdanaḥ.
70.5 kṛṣir bhū|vācakaḥ śabdo, ṇaś ca nirvṛti|vācakaḥ;
Viṣṇus tad|bhāva|yogāc ca Kṛṣṇo bhavati śāśvataḥ.
puṇḍarīkaṃ paraṃ dhāma nityam a|kṣayam a|vyayam;
tad|bhāvāt Puṇḍarīk'|âkṣo. dasyu|trāsāj Janārdanaḥ.
yataḥ sattvān na cyavate, yac ca sattvān na hīyate,
sattvataḥ Sātvatas tasmād. ārṣabhād Vṛṣabhekṣaṇaḥ.
na jāyate janitr" âyam; Ajas tasmād anīka|jit.
devānāṃ sva|prakāśatvād damād Dāmodaro vibhuḥ.
harṣāt, sukhāt, sukh'|āiśvaryādd Hṛṣīkeśatvam aśnute.
bāhubhyāṃ rodasī bibhran mahā|bāhur iti smṛtaḥ.
70.10 adho na kṣīyate jātu yasmāt, tasmād Adhokṣajaḥ.
narāṇām ayanāc c' âpi tato Nārāyaṇaḥ smṛtaḥ.

Because he wraps himself around all creatures, because of his wealth, and because he is the source of the gods, he is known as Vasudéva; and he is called Vishnu because of his great size that pervades everything. Bhárata, know him as Mádhava on account of his austerity, his meditation, and his discipline. He is Madhu·súdana because he killed the *ásura* Madhu, and because he comprises the essential part of all twenty-four truths.

The word *krish* expresses existence and the word *na* ex- 70.5
presses tranquility, and so Vishnu became eternal Krishna because he combines both of these. He is called Pundarikáksha, the lotus-eyed one, from the word *pundaríka*, because the lotus is the highest eternal and everlasting dwelling, and the word *aksha* implies his indestructibility. He is Janárdana because he brings terror to enemies of the gods.

He is Sátvata, since he does not deviate from or lack the quality of *sattva*, or energy. He is called Vrishabhékshana from the words *vríshabha*, implying the Veda, and *íkshana*, implying eyes. So he is the one whose eyes are the Veda, or alternatively the one who can be seen through the Veda. The conqueror of armies is known as Aja—unborn—because no father gave him birth. He is omnipresent Damódara because he shines among the gods by his own self-existent splendor and has control over himself.

He has attained the title of Hrishi·kesha from the words *hrishíka*, meaning joy, and *isha*, meaning the six divine attributes.* So he encapsulates both of these. He is recalled as long-armed because he bears heaven and earth in his
arms. He is Adhókshaja because he never weakens and falls 70.10

pūraṇāt, sadanāc c âpi tato 'sau Puruṣottamaḥ,
a|sataś ca sataś c' âiva sarvasya prabhav'|âpyayāt.
sarvasya ca sadā jñānāt sarvam etaṃ pracakṣate.
satye pratitiṣṭhitaḥ Kṛṣṇaḥ, satyam atra pratiṣṭhitam
satyāt satyaṃ tu Govindas tasmāt Satyo 'pi nāmataḥ.
Viṣṇur vikramaṇād, devo jayanāj Jiṣṇur ucyate;
śāśvatatvād Anantaś ca, Govindo vedanād gavām.
a|tattvaṃ kurute tattvaṃ, tena mohayate prajāḥ.
70.15 evaṃ|vidho dharma|nityo bhagavān Madhu|sūdanaḥ;
āgantā hi mahā|bāhur ānṛśaṃsy'|ârtham a|cyutaḥ.»

DHṚTARĀṢṬRA uvāca:

71.1 «CAKṢUṢMATĀṂ vai spṛhayāmi, Sañjaya,
draksyanti ye Vāsudevaṃ samīpe,
bibhrājamānaṃ vapuṣā pareṇa,
prakāśayantaṃ pradiśo diśaś ca;
īrayantaṃ bhāratīṃ Bhāratānām,
abhyarcanīyāṃ śaṅkarīṃ Sṛñjayānām,
bubhūṣadbhir grahaṇīyām a|nindyāṃ,
parāsūnām a|grahaṇīya|rūpām;
samudyantaṃ Sātvatam eka|vīraṃ,
praṇetāram ṛṣabhaṃ Yādavānām,
nihantāraṃ kṣobhaṇaṃ śātravāṇāṃ,
muñcantaṃ ca dviṣatāṃ vai yaśāṃsi.

low. He is recorded as being Naráyana because he is the refuge of men.

He is called Purushóttama because he is the ancient home, the existent and the non-existent, the souce and consummation of everything. He always knows everything and so is given the title Sarva: everything. Krishna abides in truth and truth abides in him, and Go·vinda is truth beyond truth, and therefore he has the name Satya: truth.

The god is called Vishnu because of his prowess, Jishnu because of his victory, Anánta because of his imperishability, and Go·vinda because of his knowledge of cattle. He makes the unreal real, and by so doing bewilders creatures.
This is the kind of being he is. Eternally moral, the blessed 70.15
slayer of Madhu, the long-armed imperishable being, will certainly come in order to avoid violence."

DHRITA·RASHTRA said:

"SÁÑJAYA, I ENVY those who have their sight, for they 71.1
will see Vasudéva near them, scorching everything with his supreme beauty, illuminating all directions, and uttering words which must be honored by the Bháratas and are auspicous to the Sríñjayas; faultless words which should be taken in by those want to live, but appear unacceptable to those who will die. He is the unique hero of the Sátvatas, the leading bull of the Yádavas, the killer and agitator of enemies who will free his enemies of their fame, and he is coming to us.

drasṭāro hi Kuruvas taṃ sametā
mah"|ātmānaṃ, śatra|haṇaṃ, vareṇyam,
bruvantaṃ vācam a|nṛśaṃsa|rūpāṃ,
Vṛṣṇi|śreṣṭhaṃ mohayantaṃ madīyān.
71.5 ṛṣiṃ sanātanatamaṃ vipaścitaṃ,
vācaḥ samudraṃ, kalaśaṃ yatīnām,
Ariṣṭanemiṃ Garuḍaṃ su|parṇaṃ,
Hariṃ prajānāṃ, bhuvanasya dhāma,
sahasra|śīrṣaṃ puruṣaṃ purāṇam,
an|ādi|madhy'|ântam, ananta|kīrtim,
śukrasya dhātāram, a|jaṃ ca nityaṃ:
paraṃ pareṣāṃ śaraṇaṃ prapadye.
trailokya|nirmāṇa|karaṃ, janitraṃ
dev'|âsurāṇām atha nāga|rakṣasām,
nar'|âdhipānāṃ viduṣāṃ pradhānam,
Indr'|ânujaṃ taṃ śaraṇaṃ prapadye.»

The Kurus will gather and watch that excellent, high-souled enemy-killer, the greatest of the Vrishnis, as he speaks words of non-violence and confuses my sons. The most 71.5
eternal and learned seer, the ocean of speech, the jar of ascetics, the excellent- winged Gáruda Aríshta·nemi, the lord of creatures and abode of the universe, the ancient, thousand-headed person, without beginning, middle, or end, the man of unending glory, the unborn but eternal placer of the seed: this is the greatest of the great, whom I supplicate for protection. This is the creator of the three worlds, the father of the gods and *ásura*s, the snakes and the *rákshasa*s—the leader of wise kings, Indra's brother, whom I supplicate for protection."

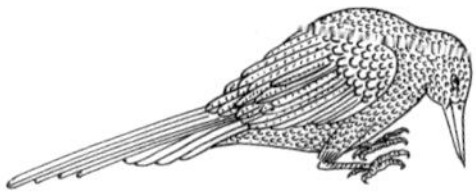

72–83

# THE BLESSED LORD'S VISIT

VAIŚAMPĀYANA uvāca:

72.1 SAÑJAYE PRATIYĀTE tu dharma|rājo Yudhiṣṭhiraḥ
abhyabhāṣata Dāśārham ṛṣabhaṃ sarva|Sātvatām:
«ayaṃ sa kālaḥ saṃprāpto mitrāṇāṃ, mitra|vatsala,
na ca tvad anyaṃ paśyāmi yo na āpatsu tārayet.
tvāṃ hi, Mādhava, saṃśritya* nirbhayā mogha|darpitam
Dhārtarāṣṭraṃ sah'|âmātyaṃ svayaṃ samanuyuṅkṣmahe.
yathā hi sarvāsv āpatsu pāsi Vṛṣṇīn, arin|dama,
tathā te Pāṇḍavā rakṣyāḥ; pāhy asmān mahato bhayāt.»

ŚRĪ BHAGAVĀN uvāca:

72.5 «ayam asmi, mahā|bāho, brūhi yat te vivakṣitam.
kariṣyāmi hi tat sarvaṃ yat tvaṃ vakṣyasi, Bhārata.»

YUDHIṢṬHIRA uvāca:

«śrutaṃ te Dhārtarāṣṭrasya sa|putrasya cikīrṣitam.
etadd hi sakalaṃ, Kṛṣṇa, Sañjayo māṃ yad abravīt.
tan mataṃ Dhṛtarāṣṭrasya so 'sy' ātmā vivṛt'|ântaraḥ.
yath" ôktaṃ dūta ācaṣṭe; vadhyaḥ syād anyathā bruvan.
a|pradānena rājyasya śāntim asmāsu mārgati
lubdhaḥ pāpena manasā carann a|samam ātmanaḥ.
yat tad dvā|daśa varṣāṇi vaneṣu hy uṣitā vayam
chadmanā śaradaṃ c' âikāṃ Dhṛtarāṣṭrasya śāsanāt,
72.10 ‹sthātā naḥ samaye tasmin Dhṛtarāṣṭra, iti,› prabho,
n' āhāsma samayaṃ, Kṛṣṇa, tadd hi no brāhmaṇā viduḥ!
gṛddho rājā Dhṛtarāṣṭraḥ sva|dharmaṃ n' ânupaśyati;
vaśyatvāt, putra|gṛddhitvān mandasy' ânveti śāsanam.

VAISHAMPÁYANA said:

ONCE SÁÑJAYA HAD left, Yudhi·shthira, the king of righteousness, said to Dashárha, the bull of all Sátvatas: "The time for friends has come, our affectionate friend, and I see no one else but you who could help us get through our troubles. By relying on you, Mádhava, we have asked for what is ours from Dhartaráshtra and his ministers, unafraid, for his arrogance is fruitless. Just as you protect the Vrishnis in all calamities, scorcher of the foe, the Pándavas must also be protected, so defend us from great danger." 72.1

THE BLESSED LORD replied:

"I am here, long-armed man, so tell me what you want 72.5
to say, and I will do everything you advise, Bhárata."

YUDHI·SHTHIRA said:

"You heard what Dhartaráshtra and his sons want to do. Sáñjaya told me everything Dhrita·rashtra is thinking, Krishna, and his soul was revealed inside Sáñjaya. A messenger speaks just as he is told, and if what he says deviates then he should be killed. Dhrita·rashtra strives for peace with us without returning our kingdom, for he is greedy and acts with a wicked mind, employing double standards towards himself and towards us.

We lived in the forests for twelve years and one more year
in disguise on Dhrita·rashtra's orders, since we believed that 72.10
Dhrita·rashtra would abide by the agreement, my lord. We did not break the agreement, Krishna, and the brahmins certainly know it! Greedy King Dhrita·rashtra does not perceive his own duty, but follows the orders of his idiotic son, because he loves him and is in his power. The king abides by

Suyodhana|mate tiṣṭhan rāj" âsmāsu, Janārdana,
mithyā carati lubdhaḥ san, caran hi priyam ātmanaḥ.
ito duḥkhataraṃ kiṃ nu, yad ahaṃ mātaraṃ tataḥ
saṃvidhātuṃ na śaknomi, mitrāṇāṃ vā, Janārdana?

Kāśibhiś, Cēdi|Pāñcālair, Matsyaiś ca, Madhu|sūdana,
bhavatā c' âiva nāthena pañca grāmā vṛtā mayā:

72.15 Avisthalaṃ, Vṛkasthalaṃ, Mākandī, Vāraṇāvatam,
avasānaṃ ca, Govinda, kañ cid ev' âtra pañcamam.

‹pañca nas, tāta, dīyantāṃ grāmā vā nagarāṇi vā,
vasema sahitā yeṣu; mā ca no Bharatā naśan.›
na ca tān api duṣṭ'|ātmā Dhārtarāṣṭro 'numanyate,
svāmyam ātmani matv" âsāv. ato duḥkhataraṃ nu kim?

kule jātasya vṛddhasya para|vitteṣu gṛdhyataḥ
lobhaḥ prajñānam āhanti, prajñā hanti hatā hriyam.
hrīr hatā bādhate dharmaṃ, dharmo hanti hataḥ śriyam,
śrīr hatā puruṣaṃ hanti, puruṣasy' â|dhanaṃ vadhaḥ.

72.20 a|dhanādd hi nivartante jñātayaḥ, suhṛdo, dvijāḥ,
a|puṣpād a|phalād vṛkṣād yathā, Kṛṣṇa, patatriṇaḥ.
etac ca maraṇaṃ, tāta, yan mattaḥ patitād iva
jñātayo vinivartante, preta|sattvād iv' âsavaḥ.

Suyódhana's decisions, Janárdana, treating us improperly, and the covetous man acts to his own advantage. What is more wretched than the fact that I am unable to provide for my mother or friends, Janárdana?

With the Kashis, Chedis, Pañchálas, Matsyas, and you, slayer of Madhu, as my protector, I asked for five villages:
Avísthala, Vrika·sthala, Makándi, Varanávata, and any other 72.15
as a fifth, Go·vinda.

I said, 'Let five villages or towns be granted to us, father, where we could live together so we can prevent the destruction of the Bharatas.' Wicked-souled Dhartaráshtra would not even consent to that, for he believes that dominion is his. What is more wretched than that?

When a man born and raised in a noble family covets other people's possessions, his greed destroys his wisdom, and once his wisdom is destroyed then it ruins his shame. When shame is dead it puts an end to morality, and once morality is dead it kills one's good fortune. When good fortune is dead it kills the man, for poverty is a man's downfall.

Friends, relatives, and brahmins turn away from a 72.20
poverty-stricken man, just as birds fly from a fruitless, flowerless tree, Krishna. This is death, my friend: relatives turn away from me as though I had fallen, just as vital breath leaves the man who has truly died.

n' âtaḥ pāpīyasīṃ kāñ cid avasthāṃ Śambaro 'bravīt,
yatra n' âiv' âdya na prātar bhojanaṃ pratidṛśyate.
dhanam āhuḥ paraṃ dharmaṃ, dhane sarvaṃ pratiṣṭhitam.
jīvanti dhanino loke, mṛtā ye tv a|dhanā narāḥ.
ye dhanād apakarṣanti
naraṃ sva|balam āsthitāḥ,
te dharmam arthaṃ kāmaṃ ca
pramathnanti, naraṃ ca tam.

72.25 etām avasthāṃ prāpy' âike maraṇaṃ vavrire janāḥ;
grāmāy' âike, vanāy' âike, nāśāy' âike pravavrajuḥ.
unmādam eke puṣyanti, yānty anye dviṣatāṃ vaśam,
dāsyam eke ca gacchanti pareṣām artha|hetunā.

āpad ev' âsya maraṇāt puruṣasya garīyasī;
śriyo vināśas tadd hy asya nimittaṃ dharma|kāmayoḥ,
yad asya dharmyaṃ maraṇaṃ śāśvataṃ loka|vartma tat
samantāt sarva|bhūtānāṃ; na tad atyeti kaś cana.

na tathā bādhyate, Kṛṣṇa, prakṛtyā nirdhano janaḥ,
yathā bhadrāṃ śriyaṃ prāpya tayā hīnaḥ sukh'|âidhitaḥ.
72.30 sa tad" ātm'|âparādhena saṃprāpto vyasanaṃ mahat
s'|Êndrān garhayate devān, n' ātmānaṃ ca kathañ cana.
na c' âsya sarva|śāstrāṇi prabhavanti nibarhaṇe.
so 'bhikrudhyati bhṛtyānāṃ, suhṛdaś c' âbhyasūyati.
tat tadā manyur ev' âiti, sa bhūyaḥ saṃpramuhyati.
sa moha|vaśam āpannaḥ krūraṃ karma niṣevate.

Shámbara said that there is no worse situation than seeing that there is no food for today or tomorrow. They say that wealth is the final law, and that everything relies on wealth. The rich live in this world, and the poor men are dead. Those who rely on their own strength to rob a man of his wealth, destroy his law, profit, and pleasure along with the man himself.

When they have got themselves in such a situation, some 72.25
people choose death. Some go to a village, some to the forest, and some to their own destruction. Some foster insanity, others fall under the control of their enemies, and some go into slavery, serving others, and all because of wealth.

The destruction of one's good fortune is a more serious disaster than death for a man; for it is the cause of law and pleasure, whereas death is a natural law and the eternal way of the world, a universal event for all creatures, and no one escapes it.

A man who is poor by nature is not as tormented, Krishna, as a man who has attained good fortune and then
lost it when his happiness was on the rise. When he then 72.30
falls on extremely hard times through no one's fault but his own, he blames Indra and the gods, but never himself. Not even all the sacred texts can remove his misery. He flies into tempers with his servants and is indignant to his friends. Then fury takes over and confuses him again. And once he is under the power of folly, he cultivates cruel deeds.

pāpa|karmatayā c' âiva saṅkaraṃ tena puṣyati.
saṅkaro narakāy' âiva, sā kāṣṭhā pāpa|karmaṇām.
na cet prabudhyate, Kṛṣṇa, narakāy' âiva gacchati;
tasya prabodhaḥ prajñ" âiva; prajñā|cakṣus tariṣyati.
72.35 prajñā|labhe hi puruṣaḥ śāstrāṇy ev' ânvavekṣate;
śāstra|niṣṭhaḥ punar dharmaṃ; tasya hrīr aṅgam uttamam.
hrīmān hi pāpaṃ pradveṣṭi, tasya śrīr abhivardhate;
śrīmān sa yāvad bhavati, tāvad bhavati pūruṣaḥ.
dharma|nityaḥ, praśānt'|ātmā, kārya|yoga|vahaḥ sadā
n' â|dharme kurute buddhiṃ, na ca pāpe pravartate.
a|hrīko vā vimūḍho vā n' âiva strī na punaḥ pumān;
n' âsy' âdhikāro dharme 'sti; yathā śūdras tath" âiva saḥ.
hrīmān avati devāṃś ca, pitṝn, ātmānam eva ca;
ten' â|mṛtatvaṃ vrajati; sā kāṣṭhā puṇya|karmaṇām.
72.40 tad idaṃ mayi te dṛṣṭaṃ pratyakṣaṃ, Madhu|sūdana,
yathā rājyāt paribhraṣṭo vasāmi vasatīr imāḥ.
te vayaṃ na śriyaṃ hātum alaṃ nyāyena kena cit,
atra no yatamānānāṃ vadhaś ced, api sādhu tat.
tatra naḥ prathamaḥ kalpo yad vayaṃ te ca, Mādhava,
praśāntāḥ śama|bhūtāś ca śriyaṃ tām aśnuvīmahi.
tatr' âiṣā paramā kāṣṭhā raudra|karma|kṣay'|ôdayā,
yad vayaṃ Kauravān hatvā tāni rāṣṭrāṇy avāpnumaḥ.

Through miscreancy he also furthers the intermingling of different castes. This integration leads to hell and is the highest limit of those who commit evil. If he doesn't come to his senses then he goes to hell, Krishna. Knowledge is his awareness, and only with the sight of wisdom will he get
through his troubles. For upon obtaining wisdom, a man 72.35
looks to the sacred texts, and once he is grounded in the texts, he looks to moral duty. His sense of shame is his most important limb.

A man with a sense of shame despises evil, and his good fortune increases. One is only a man to the extent that one is a fortunate man. Constantly virtuous, calm in his soul, and always bearing the labor of what is necessary, he does not turn his mind to immorality, nor is he intent on evil. A shameless and foolish person is neither a woman nor again are they a man. They have no authority in morality and are worth as little as a shudra. A man with shame satisfies the gods, the ancestors, and himself, and through this he goes to immortality, the final stage of those who commit pure acts.

You can see this clearly in me, slayer of Madhu, how I 72.40
have lived all this time deprived of my kingdom. There is no way that we can give up our good fortune, but if we should strive for it only to find death, then so be it. Our first alternative, Mádhava, is to regain our fortune living peacably and equitably with them. But our last resort will result in a terrible act of destruction, and once we have killed the Káuravas we will get our lands back.

ye punaḥ syur a|sambaddhā an|āryāḥ, Kṛṣṇa, śatravaḥ
teṣām apy a|vadhaḥ kāryaḥ, kiṃ punar ye syur īdṛśāḥ
72.45 jñātayaś c' âiva bhūyiṣṭhāḥ, sahāyā guravaś ca naḥ!
teṣāṃ vadho 'tipāpīyān; kiṃ nu yuddhe 'sti śobhanam?
pāpaḥ kṣatriya|dharmo 'yaṃ; vayaṃ ca kṣatra|bandhavaḥ;
sa naḥ sva|dharmo dharmo vā; vṛttir anyā vigarhitā.

śūdraḥ karoti śuśrūṣāṃ; vaiśyā vai paṇya|jīvikāḥ;
vayaṃ vadhena jīvāmaḥ; kapālaṃ brāhmaṇair vṛtam.
kṣatriyaḥ kṣatriyaṃ hanti, matsyo matsyena jīvati,
śvā śvānaṃ hanti, Dāśārha; paśya dharmo yathā|gataḥ.

yuddhe, Kṛṣṇa, kalir nityaṃ; prāṇāḥ sīdanti saṃyuge.
balaṃ tu nītim ādhāya yudhye jaya|parājayau.
72.50 n' ātma|cchandena bhūtānāṃ
jīvitaṃ maraṇaṃ tathā;
n' âpy a|kāle sukhaṃ prāpyaṃ,
duḥkhaṃ v" âpi, Yad'|ûttama.
eko hy api bahūn hanti, ghnanty ekaṃ bahavo 'py uta;
śūraṃ kā|puruṣo hanti, a|yaśasvī yaśasvinam.
jayo n' âiv' ôbhayor dṛṣṭo, n' ôbhayoś ca parājayaḥ.
tath" âiv' âpacayo dṛṣṭo vyapayāne kṣaya|vyayau.

sarvathā vṛjinaṃ yuddhaṃ. ko ghnan na pratihanyate?
hatasya ca, Hṛṣīkeśa, samau jaya|parājayau.
parājayaś ca maraṇān, manye, n' âiva viśiṣyate;
yasya syād vijayaḥ, Kṛṣṇa, tasy' âpy apacayo dhruvam.
72.55 antato dayitaṃ ghnanti ke cid apy apare janāḥ,
tasy' âṅga|bala|hīnasya putrān bhrātṝn a|paśyataḥ;

Since even enemies who are unrelated and ignoble, Krishna, should not be murdered, how much more does this hold true for men such as these, who are mostly our 72.45
relatives, friends, and teachers! Their murder is particularly wicked, but then what is there that shines out as glorious in war? This is the evil duty of a warrior. We are bound to the warrior code and this law is our own personal obligation, for any other behavior is prohibited.

The shudra acts in obedience, the vaishya lives through commerce, we live by murder, and the begging bowl is the brahmins' livelihood. Warrior kills warrior, fish live on fish, dog kills dog. Dashárha, see the law as it comes to us.

In war, Krishna, there is always strife, and lives slip away in battle. Strength forces policy, but victory and defeat are made in battle. The life and death of living creatures does 72.50
not rely on the will of the individual, and one can find neither happiness nor misery when the time for it is not at hand, best of the Yadus. One man can kill many or many men could kill one. A coward could kill a hero and an unknown could kill a famous man. There cannot be victory for both sides, nor can there be defeat for both. But the loss on both sides may be equal. Destruction and loss befall the man who flees.

War is entirely disastrous, for which killer is not killed? Victory and defeat are the same to a dead man, Hrishi·kesha. I do not believe there is any distinction between defeat and death. The man who gains victory will certainly also meet his downfall, Krishna. In the end, some other 72.55
men will kill someone he cares for, and when he has really

nirvedo jīvite, Kṛṣṇa, sarvataś c' ôpajāyate.

ye hy eva dhīrā hrīmanta āryāḥ karuṇa|vedinaḥ,
ta eva yuddhe hanyante; yavīyān mucyate janaḥ.
hatv" âpy anuśayo nityaṃ parān api, Janārdana,
anubandhaś ca pāpo 'tra, śeṣaś c' âpy avaśiṣyate;
śeṣo hi balam āsādya na śeṣam anuśeṣayet.
sarv'|ôcchede ca yatate vairasy' ânta|vidhitsayā.
jayo vairaṃ prasṛjati, duḥkham āste parājitaḥ.
72.60 sukhaṃ praśāntaḥ svapiti hitvā jaya|parājayau;
jāta|vairaś ca puruṣo duḥkhaṃ svapiti nityadā,
a|nirvṛttena manasā, sa|sarpa iva veśmani.
utsādayati yaḥ sarvaṃ yaśasā, sa vimucyate;
a|kīrtiṃ sarva|bhūteṣu śāśvatīṃ sa niyacchati.

na hi vairāṇi śāmyanti dīrgha|kāla|dhṛtāny api.
ākhyātāraś ca vidyante, pumāṃś ced vidyate kule.
na c' âpi vairaṃ vaireṇa, Keśava, vyupaśāmyati;
haviṣ" âgnir yathā, Kṛṣṇa, bhūya ev' âbhivardhate.
ato 'nyathā n' âsti śāntir; nityam antaram antataḥ;
72.65 antaraṃ lipsamānānām ayaṃ doṣo nirantaraḥ.

lost his strength and no longer sees his sons and brothers, disgust for living will completely overwhelm him, Krishna.

In fact, the firm, modest, noble, and compassionate are the ones who die in war, but the lesser men escape. There is always regret when one has killed, even if they are enemies, Janárdana. The consequences are evil for the surviving victors, for those who survive on the losing side gather their strength in order to leave none of their enemies alive. In an attempt to put an end to the entire dispute, people try to annihilate everyone. Victory brews hatred, for the defeated man lives miserably.

The peaceful man sleeps happily, for he renounces both 72.60
victory and defeat; whereas the man who causes hostility always sleeps uneasily, with an anxious mind, as though there were a snake in his room. The man who destroys everything is deprived of glory and ensures his eternal disgrace among all creatures.

Quarrels which have seethed for a long time do not just die down. For if a single man remains in his line, there are people who will tell him about it. One quarrel cannot be extinguished by another dispute either, Késhava. Instead, it only becomes stronger, just as a fire grows greater still with the oblation, Krishna. So, peace can never exist in any way other than total annihilation, for there is always a weakness
in the end which one or the other side can exploit. This is 72.65
the eternal problem for people who try to find their enemies' weakness.

pauruṣeyo hi balavān ādhir hṛdaya|bādhanaḥ;
tasya tyāgena vā śāntir, maraṇen' âpi vā bhavet.
atha vā mūla|ghātena dviṣatāṃ, Madhu|sūdana,
phala|nirvṛttir iddhā syān, na nṛśaṃsataraṃ bhavet.
yā tu tyāgena śāntiḥ syāt, tad ṛte vadha eva saḥ,
saṃśayāc ca samucchedād dviṣatām ātmanas tathā.

na ca tyaktuṃ tad icchāmo, na c' êcchāmaḥ kula|kṣayam;
atra yā praṇipātena śāntiḥ, s' âiva garīyasī.
sarvathā yatamānānām, a|yuddham abhikaṅkṣatām,
sāntve pratihite yuddhaṃ prasiddhaṃ n' â|parākramaḥ.
72.70 pratighātena sāntvasya dāruṇaṃ saṃpravartate.

tac chunām iva sampāte paṇḍitair upalakṣitam:
lāṅgūla|cālanaṃ, kṣveḍā, prativāco, vivartanam,
danta|darśanam, ārāvas, tato yuddhaṃ pravartate.
tatra yo balavān, Kṛṣṇa, jitvā so 'tti tad āmiṣam;
evam eva manuṣyeṣu; viśeṣo n' âsti kaś cana.

sarvathā tv etad ucitaṃ; dur|baleṣu balīyasām
an|ādaro virodhaś ca; praṇipātī hi dur|balaḥ.
pitā, rājā ca, vṛddhaś ca sarvathā mānam arhati,
tasmān mānyaś ca pūjyaś ca Dhṛtarāṣṭro, Janārdana.
72.75 putra|snehaś ca balavān Dhṛtarāṣṭrasya, Mādhava,
sa putra|vaśam āpannaḥ praṇipātaṃ prahāsyati.

The man who is assured of his own manliness is troubled in his heart as though by a powerful pain, and he can only find peace by renouncing it, or in death. Or alternatively, slayer of Madhu, destruction of the very root of one's enemies may yield the rewards of great prosperity, but it would be too cruel. Peace through our renunciation of our kingdom is death without actually dying, because the risk of the utter destruction of both our enemies and ourselves still remains.

We do not wish to renounce our claim, but nor do we wish for the destruction of a whole line. Peace by surrender is the preferred method. Men who strive in every way for peace do not desire war, but when conciliation fails, war is
inevitable, and that is not the time for a lack of valor. When 72.70
conciliation breaks down, horrible events follow.

Teachers have observed the same behavior in a pack of dogs: wagging tails leads to barking, return barking, then retreat, baring of fangs, howling, and finally a fight. Then the stronger one wins and eats the meat, Krishna. So it is with men: there is no difference.

This is the way it goes every time; the strong show contempt for the weak, then begin hostilities, and finally the weak party surrenders. A father, a king, and elderly man deserve respect in all circumstances, and so Dhrita·rashtra
should be respected and honored, Janárdana. But Dhrita· 72.75
rashtra's love for his son is powerful, Mádhava, and while under his son's control he will reject surrender.

tatra kiṃ manyase, Kṛṣṇa, prāpta|kālam an|antaram?
katham arthāc ca dharmāc ca na hīyema hi, Mādhava?
īdṛśe 'tyartha|kṛcchre 'smin kam anyaṃ, Madhu|sūdana,
upasaṃpraṣṭum arhāmi tvām ṛte, puruṣ'|ôttama?
priyaś ca, priya|kāmaś ca, gati|jñaḥ sarva|karmaṇām;
ko hi, Kṛṣṇ', âsti nas tvādṛk sarva|niścaya|vit suhṛt?»

VAIŚAMPĀYANA uvāca:

evam uktaḥ pratyuvāca dharma|rājaṃ Janārdanaḥ:
«ubhayor eva vām arthe yāsyāmi Kuru|saṃsadam.
72.80 śamaṃ tatra labheyaṃ ced yuṣmad artham a|hāpayan,
puṇyaṃ me su|mahad, rājaṃś, caritaṃ syān mahā|phalam.
mocayeyaṃ mṛtyu|pāśāt saṃrabdhān Kuru|Sṛñjayān,
Pāṇḍavān Dhārtarāṣṭrāṃś ca, sarvāṃ ca pṛthivīm imām.»

YUDHIṢṬHIRA uvāca:

«na mam' âitan mataṃ, Kṛṣṇa,
yat tvaṃ yāyāḥ Kurūn prati.
Suyodhanaḥ s'|ûktam api
na kariṣyati te vacaḥ.
sametaṃ pārthivaṃ kṣatraṃ Duryodhana|vaś'|ânugam;
teṣāṃ madhy'|âvataraṇaṃ tava, Kṛṣṇa, na rocaye.
na hi naḥ prīṇayed dravyaṃ, na devatvaṃ, kutaḥ sukham,
na ca sarv'|âmar'|āiśvaryaṃ tava droheṇa, Mādhava.»

What do you think, Krishna, now that the time is nigh? How can we prevent the loss of our aim and virtue, Mádhava? In such a painful matter as this, whom else besides you, slayer of Madhu, should I consult, supreme person? For who else is so dear to us and wishes us well? Who understands the course of all actions? What friend like you do we really have, Krishna, who understands all decisions?"

VAISHAMPÁYANA said:

Spoken to in this manner, Janárdana replied to the king of righteousness, saying: "I will go to the Kuru court for
the sake of you both. If I can assure peace wihout harming 72.80
your cause, then I will gain enormous purity, king, and the the act will have important results. I will release the furious Kurus, Sríñjayas, Pándavas, and Dhartaráshtras, as well as this whole earth, from the chains of death."

YUDHI·SHTHIRA replied:

"I do not agree, Krishna, that you should go to the Kurus, for Suyódhana will not accept what you have to say, regardless of how well you speak. Kingly warriordom is gathered there, enslaved to Duryódhana's wishes, and I am not pleased with the idea of you rushing off into their midst, Krishna. Nothing could console us—not wealth, divinity, happiness, or even power over all immortals—if you were offended, Mádhava."

ŚRĪ BHAGAVĀN uvāca:

72.85 «jānāmy etāṃ, mahā|rāja, Dhārtarāṣṭrasya pāpatām.
a|vācyās tu bhaviṣyāmaḥ sarva|loke mahī|kṣitām.
na c' âpi mama paryāptāḥ sahitā sarva|pārthivāḥ
kruddhasya saṃyuge sthātuṃ, siṃhasy' êv' êtare mṛgāḥ.
atha cet te pravarteta mayi kiñ cid a|sāmpratam,
nirdaheyaṃ Kurūn sarvān, iti me dhīyate matiḥ.
na jātu gamanaṃ, Pārtha, bhavet tatra nirarthakam;
artha|prāptiḥ kadā cit syād antato v" âpy a|vācyatā.»

YUDHIṢṬHIRA uvāca:

«yat tubhyaṃ rocate, Kṛṣṇa, svasti! prāpnuhi Kauravān.
kṛt'|ârthaṃ svastimantaṃ tvāṃ drakṣyāmi punar āgatam!
72.90 Viṣvaksena, Kurūn gatvā Bharatān śamayan, prabho,
yathā sarve su|manasaḥ saha syāma su|cetasaḥ.
bhrātā c' âsi, sakhā c' âsi, Bībhatsor mama ca priyaḥ.
sauhṛden' â|viśaṅkyo 'si. svasti! prāpnuhi bhūtaye!
asmān vettha, parān vettha, vetth' ârthān, vettha bhāṣitum;
yad yad asmadd|hitaṃ, Kṛṣṇa, tat tad vācyaḥ Suyodhanaḥ.
yady a|dharmeṇa saṃyuktam upapadyedd hitaṃ vacaḥ,
tat tat, Keśava, bhāṣethāḥ, sāntvaṃ vā yadi v" êtarat.»

ŚRĪ BHAGAVĀN uvāca:

73.1 «SAÑJAYASYA ŚRUTAṂ vākyaṃ, bhavataś ca śrutaṃ mayā.
sarvaṃ jānāmy abhiprāyaṃ teṣāṃ ca bhavataś ca yaḥ.
tava dharm'|āśritā buddhis, teṣāṃ vair'|āśrayā matiḥ.
yad a|yuddhena labhyeta, tat te bahu|mataṃ bhavet.
na c' âivaṃ naiṣṭhikaṃ karma kṣatriyasya, viśām pate,

THE BLESSED LORD said:

"I know the evil of Dhartaráshtra, great king, but we will make ourselves irreproachable to kings throughout the whole world. All kings together are no match to stand against me in battle when I am angry, like other animals against a lion. I have decided that if they behave improperly towards me in any way, I will scorch all the Kurus! My journey there will certainly not be in vain, Partha, even if all I achieve is that you are freed from blame." 72.85

YUDHI·SHTHIRA replied:

"If it pleases you, Krishna, then good luck! Go to the Káuravas and I will watch you return in good fortune, with
your aim achieved! Vishvak·sena, go to the Kurus and pla- 72.90
cate the Bháratas, my lord, so that we can all be well-minded towards each other and friendly. You are a brother and a friend, dear to Bibhátsu and to me. Your friendship is not in doubt, so good luck! Go to success! You know us, you know our enemies, you understand profit, and you know how to speak. Tell Suyódhana whatever is to our advantage, Krishna. Say whatever will help us, Késhava, even if peace needs to be made by deviating from what is right, or by some other means."

THE BLESSED LORD said:

"I HAVE HEARD what Sáñjaya had to say, and I have lis- 73.1
tened to you. I know their whole purpose as I do yours. Your mind relies upon moral law, but their thinking is intent on hostility. You would hold in high esteem whatever can be gained without resorting to war. Lord of earth, a life of sacrifice is not the task of a warrior. All hermits say that

āhur āśramiṇaḥ sarve, na bhaikṣaṃ kṣatriyaś caret.
jayo vadho vā saṃgrāme dhātr" ādiṣṭaḥ sanātanaḥ;
sva|dharmaḥ kṣatriyasy' âiṣa kārpaṇyaṃ na praśasyate.
73.5 na hi kārpaṇyam āsthāya śakyā vṛttir, Yudhiṣṭhira.
vikramasva, mahā|bāho, jahi śatrūn, paran|tapa!
atigṛddhāḥ, kṛta|snehā, dīrgha|kālaṃ, sah' ôṣitāḥ,
kṛta|mitrāḥ, kṛta|balā Dhārtarāṣṭrāḥ, paraṃ|tapa.
na paryāyo 'sti yat sāmyaṃ tvayi kuryur, viśāṃ pate,
balavattāṃ hi manyante Bhīṣma|Droṇa|Kṛp'|ādibhiḥ.
yāvac ca mārdaven' âitān, rājann, upacariṣyasi,
tāvad ete hariṣyanti tava rājyam, arin|dama.
n' ânukrośān, na kārpaṇyān, na ca dharm'|ârtha|kāraṇāt
alaṃ|kartuṃ Dhārtarāṣṭrās tava kāmam, arin|dama.
73.10 etad eva nimittaṃ te, Pāṇḍav', âstu: yathā tvayi
n' ânvatapyanta kaupīnaṃ tāvat kṛtv" âpi duṣ|karam.
pitā|mahasya Droṇasya, Vidurasya ca dhīmataḥ,
brāhmaṇānāṃ ca sādhūnāṃ, rājñaś ca, nagarasya ca
paśyatāṃ Kuru|mukhyānāṃ sarveṣām eva tattvataḥ
dāna|śīlaṃ, mṛduṃ, dāntaṃ, dharma|śīlam, anuvratam
yat tvām upadhiṇā, rājan, dyūte vañcitavāṃs tadā
na c' âpatrapate tena nṛśaṃsaḥ svena karmaṇā.
tathā|śīla|samācāre, rājan, mā praṇayaṃ kṛthāḥ;
vadhyās te sarva|lokasya, kiṃ punas tava, Bhārata?
73.15 vāgbhis tv a|pratirūpābhir atudat tvaṃ sah'|ânujam,
ślāghamānaḥ prahṛṣṭaḥ san bhrātṛbhiḥ saha bhāṣate:
‹etāvat Pāṇḍavānāṃ hi n' âsti kiñ cid iha svakam;

a warrior should not beg. Victory or slaughter in battle is what the creator has eternally ordained. This is the duty of
a warrior, and cowardice is not praised. For a living cannot 73.5
be sustained by resorting to cowardice, Yudhi·shthira. So advance, long-armed man, and kill your enemies, scorcher of the foe!

The excessively greedy sons of Dhrita·rashtra have become powerful, scorcher of the enemy, by making alliances and friendships through living with kings for a long time. There is no chance that they will treat you fairly, lord of earth, for they think they are stronger with Bhishma, Drona, Kripa, and so on. For as long as you behave towards them with leniency, king, they will steal your kingdom from you, enemy-tamer. The Dhartaráshtras will not grant your wish out of compassion or pity, nor by reason of virtue and profit, enemy-destroyer.

Let this be your evidence, Pándava: They did not even 73.10
regret their wicked deed of making you strip to your loincloth. When his grandfather, Drona, wise Vídura, the strict brahmins, the king, and the city, as well as the leading Kurus were all watching you, a mild, controlled, and faithful man of virtuous and generous conduct, that cruel man who tricked you deceitfully in the gambling match, king, was not ashamed of his wicked act.

King, don't feel any affection for a man who practices such conduct. They deserve death at the hands of the whole world, so how much more do they deserve death at your
hands, Bhárata? He struck at you and your brothers with 73.15
nasty words, delightedly boasting as he said to his own brothers: 'So now the Pándavas have nothing to their name

nāma|dheyaṃ ca gotraṃ ca tad apy eṣāṃ na śiṣyate!
kālena mahatā c' âiṣāṃ bhaviṣyati parābhavaḥ;
prakṛtiṃ te bhajiṣyanti naṣṭa|prakṛtayo mayi.›
Duḥśāsanena pāpena tadā dyūte pravartite
a|nāthavat tadā devī Draupadī su|dur|ātmanā
ākṛṣya keśe rudatī sabhāyāṃ rāja|saṃsadi
Bhīṣma|Droṇa|pramukhato ‹gaur, iti› vyāhṛtā muhuḥ!
73.20 bhavatā vāritāḥ sarve bhrātaro bhīma|vikramāḥ,
dharma|pāśa|nibaddhāś ca, na kiñ cit pratipedire,
etāś c' ânyāś ca paruṣā vācaḥ sa samudīrayan
ślāghate jñāti|madhye sma tvayi pravrajite vanam.
ye tatr' āsan samānītās, te dṛṣṭvā tvām an|āgasam
aśru|kaṇṭhā rudantaś ca sabhāyām āsate sadā.
na c' âinam abhyanandaṃs te rājāno brāhmaṇaiḥ saha;
sarve Duryodhanaṃ tatra nindanti sma sabhā|sadaḥ.
kulīnasya ca yā nindā, vadho vā, 'mitra|karśana,
mahā|guṇo vadho, rājan, na tu nindā ku|jīvikā.
73.25 tad" âiva nihato, rājan, yad" âiva nirapatrapaḥ,
ninditaś ca, mahā|rāja, pṛthivyāṃ sarva|rājabhiḥ.
īṣat|kāryo vadhas tasya yasya cāritram īdṛśam;
praskundena pratistabdhaś, chinna|mūla iva drumaḥ.
vadhyaḥ sarpa iv' ân|āryaḥ sarva|lokasya dur|matiḥ.
jahy enaṃ tvam, amitra|ghna, mā, rājan, vicikitsithāḥ!
sarvathā tvat|kṣamaṃ c' âitad rocate ca mam', ânagha,
yat tvaṃ pitari Bhīṣme ca praṇipātaṃ samācareḥ.

in this world! Not even their name and lineage will remain! In the great expanse of time they will meet their ruin, and since their natural position has been lost to me, they will die, becoming the five elements!'

While the gambling match was taking place, the wicked and terribly evil-souled Duhshásana dragged divine Dráupadi by the hair as she wept, for she had no one to protect her, and in the assembly where the kings had gathered, in front of Bhishma and Drona, he kept shouting 'Cow!' at
her incessantly! All your brothers of terrifying prowess, pre- 73.20
vented by you and bound by the chains of virtue, did not take any revenge. And saying these and other harsh words, Duryódhana boasted in the midst of his relatives when you had gone to the forest. Those who were gathered there and saw that you were innocent wept incessantly, tears choking their throats, as they sat in court.

The kings and brahmins did not praise him, and everyone sitting in court reproached Duryódhana. For a man with a family there is either censure or death, tormentor of your enemies, and the man of great virtue chooses death,
king, rather than a miserable life of blame. The impudent 73.25
man was killed right at that moment, king, when he was reproached by all the kings on earth, mighty sovereign.

It does not take much to kill someone of such behavior, for he is like a tree with its roots cut, resting on a single support. This ignoble and wicked-minded man deserves death at the hands of the whole world, just like a snake. Kill him, slayer of your enemies! Don't hesitate, king! However, it entirely befits you and also pleases me, sinless man, that you

aham tu sarva|lokasya gatvā chetsyāmi saṃśayam,
yeṣām asti dvidhā|bhāvo, rājan, Duryodhanaṃ prati.
73.30 madhye rājñām ahaṃ tatra prātipauruṣikān guṇān
tava saṃkīrtayiṣyāmi, ye ca tasya vyatikramāḥ.
bruvatas tatra me vākyaṃ dharm'|ârtha|sahitaṃ hitam
niśamya pārthivāḥ sarve nānā|janapad'|ēśvarāḥ
tvayi sampratipatsyante, dharm'|ātmā, satya|vāg, iti;
tasmiṃś c' âdhigamiṣyanti yathā lobhād avartata.
garhayiṣyāmi c' âiv' âinaṃ paura|jānapadeṣv api,
vṛddha|bālān upādāya cāturvarṇye samāgate.
śamaṃ vai yācamānas tvaṃ n' â|dharmaṃ tatra lapsyase;
Kurūn vigarhayiṣyanti, Dhṛtarāṣṭraṃ ca pārthivāḥ.
73.35 tasmin loka|parityakte kiṃ kāryam avaśiṣyate?
hate Duryodhane, rājan, yad anyat kriyatām iti?
yātvā c' âhaṃ Kurūn sarvān, yuṣmad artham a|hāpayan,
yatiṣye praśamaṃ kartuṃ, lakṣayiṣye ca ceṣṭitam,
Kauravāṇāṃ pravṛttiṃ ca gatvā yuddh'|âdhikārikām,
niśamya vinivartiṣye jayāya tava, Bhārata.
sarvathā yuddham ev' âham āśaṃsāmi paraiḥ saha;
nimittāni hi sarvāṇi tathā prādur bhavanti me.

practice reverence towards your father Dhrita·rashtra, and towards Bhishma.

I will go and cut out any doubt which remains within
those still in two minds about Duryódhana, king. In the 73.30
midst of the royalty I will describe your manly virtues and his sins. When they hear me speaking beneficial words which comply with moral duty and profit, all the kings and lords of various peoples will agree that you are a virtuous-souled speaker of the truth, and realize that he is a man who acts out of greed.

I will blame him among the townspeople and country people, bringing together the old and young at a meeting of the four castes. You will not attain any immorality in requesting peace, and the kings will blame the Kurus and
Dhrita·rashtra. What will there be left to do when the world 73.35
abandons him? When Duryódhana is dead, king, what else will need to be done?

So I will go to all the Kurus, and without damaging your cause I will strive to make peace. I will also observe their manner, and the Káuravas' progress and organization for war, and then I will leave and return for your victory, Bhárata. I expect no course but war with the enemy, for all the omens that have appeared are pointing to it.

mṛgāḥ śakuntāś ca vadanti ghoraṃ;
hasty|aśva|mukhyeṣu niśā|mukheṣu
ghorāṇi rūpāṇi; tath" âiva c' âgnir
varṇān bahūn puṣyati ghora|rūpān.
73.40 manuṣya|loka|kṣaya|kṛt su|ghoro
no ced anuprāpta ih' ântakaḥ syāt.
śastrāṇi, yantraṃ, kavacā, rathāṃś ca,
nāgān, hayāṃś ca pratipādayitvā
yodhāś ca sarve kṛta|niścayās te
bhavantu hasty|aśva|ratheṣu yattāḥ.
sāṅgrāmikaṃ te yad upārjanīyaṃ,
sarvaṃ samagraṃ kuru tan, nar'|êndra.
Duryodhano na hy alam adya dātuṃ
jīvaṃs tav' âitan, nṛpate, kathañ cit,
yat te purastād abhavat samṛddhaṃ
dyūte hṛtaṃ, Pāṇḍava|mukhya, rājyam.»

BHĪMA uvāca:

74.1 «YATHĀ YATH" âiva śāntiḥ syāt Kurūṇāṃ, Madhu|sūdana,
tathā tath" âiva bhāṣethā, mā sma yuddhena bhīṣayeḥ.
a|marṣī, jāta|saṃrambhaḥ, śreyo|dveṣī, mahā|manāḥ
n' ôgraṃ Duryodhano vācyaḥ; sāmn" âiv' âinaṃ samācareḥ.
prakṛtyā pāpa|sattvaś ca, tulya|cetās tu dasyubhiḥ,
aiśvarya|mada|mattaś ca, kṛta|vairaś ca Pāṇḍavaiḥ,
a|dīrgha|darśī, niṣṭhūrī, kṣeptā, krūra|parākramaḥ,
dīrgha|manyur, a|neyaś ca, pāp'|ātmā, nikṛti|priyaḥ,
74.5 mriyet' âpi na bhajyeta, n' âiva jahyāt svakaṃ matam;
tādṛśena śamaḥ, Kṛṣṇa, manye parama|duṣkaraḥ.

Animals and birds cry out horribly, as dusk falls elephants and horses take on horrific shapes, and so too the fire shows fearful forms of many colors. This would not be so unless 73.40
the time had come when ghastly death, the bringer of destruction to the world of men, had come. Let all your soldiers ready their weapons, machines, armor, chariots, elephants, and horses, become resolved, and attend to their elephants, horses, and chariots. Ensure that everything which is required for battle is completely ready, lord of men. While he lives now, Duryódhana is completely incapable of returning the flourishing kingdom—which was yours long ago, and which he stole in the gambling—back to you once again, sovereign leader of the Pándavas!"

BHIMA said:

"SPEAK TO THEM in whatever manner will bring about 74.1
peace with the Kurus, slayer of Madhu, but don't scare them with war. Duryódhana is impatient, full of fury, hateful of what is good, and great-spirited, so he should be not be spoken to roughly. Treat him placatingly. By nature he is truly evil, with a heart to match the *dasyus*; drunk with power and quarrelling with the Pándavas, he is short-sighted, cruel, insulting, pitiless in his prowess, deeply arrogant, ungovernable, evil-souled, and fond of deceit. He would die before 74.5
sharing, and will not let go of his own opinion. Peace with such a person, Krishna, will, I imagine, be extremely difficult.

suhṛdām apy avācīnas, tyakta|dharmā, priy'|ânṛtaḥ.
pratihanty eva suhṛdāṃ vācaś c' âiva manāṃsi ca.
sa manyu|vaśam āpannaḥ sva|bhāvaṃ duṣṭam āsthitaḥ
sva|bhāvāt pāpam abhyeti, tṛṇaiś channa iv' ôragaḥ.
Duryodhano hi yat|senaḥ, sarvathā viditas tava;
yac|chīlo, yat|sva|bhāvaś ca, yad|balo, yat|parākramaḥ.
purā prasannāḥ Kuravaḥ saha|putrās, tathā vayam
Indra|jyeṣṭhā iv' âbhūma modamānāḥ sa|bāndhavāḥ.
74.10 Duryodhanasya krodhena Bharatā, Madhu|sūdana,
dhakṣyante śiśir'|âpāye vanān' îva hut'|âśanaiḥ.
aṣṭā|daś' ême rājānaḥ prakhyātā, Madhu|sūdana,
ye samuccicchidur jñātīn, suhṛdaś ca sa|bāndhavān.
Asurāṇāṃ samṛddhānāṃ jvalatām iva tejasā
paryāya|kāle Dharmasya prāpte Kalir ajāyata.
Haihayānāṃ Mudāvarto, Nīpānāṃ Janamejayaḥ,
Bahulas Tālajaṅghānāṃ, Kṛmīṇām uddhato Vasuḥ,
Ajabinduḥ Suvīrāṇāṃ, Surāṣṭrāṇāṃ Ruṣaddhikaḥ,
Arkajaś ca Balīhānāṃ, Cīnānāṃ Dhautamūlakaḥ,
74.15 Hayagrīvo Videhānāṃ, Varayuś ca Mahaujasām,
Bāhuḥ Sundara|vaṃśānāṃ, Dīptākṣāṇāṃ Purūravāḥ,
Sahajaś Cedi|Matsyānāṃ, Pravīrāṇāṃ Vṛṣadhvajaḥ,
Dhāraṇaś Candravatsānāṃ, Mukuṭānāṃ Vigāhanaḥ,
Śamaś ca Nandivegānām. ity ete kula|pāṃsanāḥ
yug'|ânte, Kṛṣṇa, sambhūtāḥ kule ku|puruṣ'|âdhamāḥ.

He turns down his friends, has abandoned moral law, and is fond of lying. He crushes even his friends' advice and opinions. A slave to his anger, and set in his wicked nature, he follows evil out of his own inclination, like a snake concealed by grass. You know all about Duryódhana's armies, conduct, nature, strength, and prowess. Long ago the Kurus and their sons were peaceful, and we too were like Indra's
elders, enjoying ourselves with our relatives; but because of 74.10
Duryódhana's anger, the Bharatas will burn like the forests burn with fire at the end of winter, slayer of Madhu.

Eighteen kings are said, slayer of Madhu, to have destroyed their relatives, friends, and kin. At the time when Dharma's age had ended, Kali was born among the *ásura*s and flourished and blazed with splendor, Mudavárta was born among the Háihayas, Janam·éjaya among the Nipas, Báhula among the Tala·janghas, proud Vasu among the Krimis, Aja·bindu among the Suvíras, Rusháddhika among the Suráshtras, Árkaja among the Balíhas, Dhauta·múlaka
among the men of the lands to the north east, Haya·griva 74.15
among the Vidéhas, Várayu among the Maháujasas, Bahu among the lineage of the Súndaras, Puru·ravas among the Diptákshas, Sáhaja among the Chedi-Matsyas, Vrisha·dhvaja among the Pravíras, Dhárana among the Chandra·vatsas, Vigáhana among the Múkutas, and Shama among the Nandi·vegas. At the end of the age, Krishna, these lowest of the low were born into their respective families as the destroyers of their lineages.

apy ayaṃ naḥ Kurūṇāṃ syād yug'|ânte kāla|sambhṛtaḥ
Duryodhanaḥ kul'|âṅgāro jaghanyaḥ pāpa|pūruṣaḥ.
tasmān mṛdu śanair brūyā dharm'|ârtha|sahitaṃ hitam,
kām'|ânubaddhaṃ bahulaṃ; n' ôgram, ugra|parākrama.
74.20 api Duryodhanaṃ, Kṛṣṇa, sarve vayam adhaś|carāḥ
nīcair bhūtv" ânuyāsyāmo, mā sma no Bharatā naśan.
apy udāsīna|vṛttiḥ syād yathā naḥ Kurubhiḥ saha,
Vāsudeva, tathā kāryaṃ na Kurūn a|nayaḥ spṛśet.
vācyaḥ pitā|maho vṛddho, ye ca, Kṛṣṇa, sabhā|sadaḥ
bhrātṝṇām astu saubhrātraṃ, Dhārtarāṣṭraḥ praśāmyatām.
aham etad bravīmy evaṃ, rājā c' âiva praśaṃsati.
Arjuno n' âiva yuddh'|ârthī; bhūyasī hi day" Ârjune.»

VAIŚAMPĀYANA uvāca:

75.1 ETAC CHRUTVĀ mahā|bāhuḥ Keśavaḥ prahasann iva
a|bhūta|pūrvaṃ Bhīmasya mārdav'|ôpahitaṃ vacaḥ,
girer iva laghutvaṃ tac, chītatvam iva pāvake
matvā Rām'|ânujaḥ Śauriḥ Śārṅga|dhanvā Vṛkodaram
santejayaṃs tadā vāgbhir, mātariśv' êva pāvakam,
uvāca Bhīmam āsīnaṃ kṛpay" âbhipariplutam:

This wicked individual, Duryódhana, has also been prepared by time, born among us Kurus at the end of the age as the murdering firebrand who will consume his family. Therefore, speak slowly and gently to him in words which are beneficial and conform to virtue and profit, and which generally comply with his own wishes; but do not speak fiercely, hero of fierce prowess. We would all submit to Dur- 74.20
yódhana's superiority, Krishna, and serve him, sinking low, rather than destroy the Bharatas.

Vasudéva, neutrality should be forged between us and the Kurus, so that no misfortune touches upon the Kurus. Address elderly grandfather and those who sit in court, Krishna, in such a way that brotherliness may fill our brothers, and Dhartaráshtra may be appeased. This is what I have to say, and the king praises it. Árjuna is also against war, for Árjuna is filled with an abundance of compassion."

VAISHAMPÁYANA said:

WHEN LONG-ARMED Késhava had listened to Bhima's 75.1
words of gentleness, believing them to be as unprecedented as levity existing in a mountain or cold in a fire, Rama's younger brother Shauri, the wielder of the Sharnga bow, barely restrained himself from laughing, and as though he were inflaming Vrikódara with words just as the breeze inflames the fire, he spoke to Bhima as he sat there, brimming with pity:

ŚRĪ BHAGAVĀN uvāca:

«tvam anyadā Bhīmasena, yuddham eva praśaṃsasi
vadh'|âbhinandinaḥ krūrān Dhārtarāṣṭrān mimardiṣuḥ.
75.5 na ca svapiṣi, jāgarṣi, nyubjaḥ śeṣe, paraṃ|tapa,
ghorām a|śāntāṃ ruṣatīṃ sadā vācaṃ prabhāṣase.
niḥśvasann agnivat tena saṃtaptaḥ svena manyunā,
a|praśānta|manā, Bhīma, sa|dhūma iva pāvakaḥ.
ek'|ânte niḥśvasan śeṣe, bhār'|ārta iva dur|balaḥ;
api tvāṃ ke cid unmattaṃ manyante tad|vido janāḥ.
ārujya vṛkṣān nirmūlān gajaḥ parirujann iva,
nighnan padbhiḥ kṣitiṃ, Bhīma, niṣṭanan paridhāvasi.
n' âsmiñ jane 'bhiramase,* rahaḥ kṣipasi, Pāṇḍava,
n' ânyaṃ niśi divā c' âpi kadā cid abhinandasi!
75.10 a|kasmād smayamānaś ca rahasy āsse rudann iva,
jānvor mūrdhānam ādhāya ciram āsse pramīlitaḥ.
bhru|kuṭiṃ ca punaḥ kurvann, oṣṭhau ca vidaśann iva
abhīkṣṇaṃ dṛśyase, Bhīma; sarvaṃ tan manyu|kāritam.
‹yathā purastāt savitā dṛśyate śukram uccaran,
yathā ca paścān nirmukto dhruvaṃ paryeti raśmivān,
tathā, satyaṃ bravīmy etan, n' âsti tasya vyatikramaḥ,
hant" âhaṃ gaday" âbhyetya Duryodhanam a|marṣaṇam!›
iti sma madhye bhrātṝṇāṃ satyen' ālabhase gadām.
tasya te praśame buddhir dhriyate 'dya, paraṃ|tapa?

THE BLESSED LORD said:

"On all other occasions, Bhima·sena, you only approve of
war, desperate to crush the cruel Dhartaráshtras who take
pleasure in murder. You do not sleep but remain awake, 75.5
lying face down, scorcher of the enemy, and you always speak horrifying, violent, and irritable words. You sigh, scorched by your own fiery rage, Bhima, with an agitated mind like a smoky fire.

You lie on your own, groaning like a weak man pained by a burden. Some people even believe you are mad when they learn what's going on. You charge about, making the earth itself roar, just like an elephant tearing down uprooted trees, shattering and demolishing them with its feet, Bhima. You take no pleasure in the present company, but go off alone, son of Pandu, and are never pleased to see anyone else, night and day!

You sit alone and for no discernable reason laugh so hard 75.10
you're almost crying, and you sit for ages with your head between your knees and your eyes closed. Then again, you are frequently spotted furrowing your brows and nearly biting your lips open, Bhima. And all this is caused by your rage.

'Just as surely as the sun is seen first to rise brightly in the east, and just as surely as it later sets in the west, circling Meru with its ray, so I vow truly, and I will not break it, that I will kill intolerant Duryódhana with my mace!' This is what you promised in the midst of your brothers, swearing on the mace you held. Is your mind now resolved upon peace, scorcher of the foe?

75.15 aho yuddh'|âbhikāṅkṣāṇāṃ yuddha|kāla upasthite
cetāṃsi vipratīpāni, yat tvāṃ bhīr, Bhīma, vindati?
aho, Pārtha, nimittāni viparītāni paśyasi,
svapn'|ânte jāgār'|ânte ca tasmāt praśamam icchasi?
aho n' āśaṃsase kiñ cit puṃstvaṃ, klība iv', ātmani?
kaśmalen' âbhipanno 'si, tena te vikṛtaṃ manaḥ!

udvepate te hṛdayaṃ, manas te pratisīdati,
ūru|stambha|gṛhīto 'si, tasmāt praśamam icchasi!
a|nityaṃ kila martyasya, Pārtha, cittaṃ cal'|âcalam,
vāta|vega|pracalitā aṣṭhīlā śālmaler iva.
75.20 tav' âiṣā vikṛtā buddhir, gavāṃ vāg iva mānuṣī;
manāṃsi Pāṇḍu|putrāṇāṃ majjayaty a|plavān iva.
idaṃ me mahad āścaryaṃ, parvatasy' êva sarpaṇam,
yad īdṛśaṃ prabhāṣethā, Bhīmasen', â|samaṃ vacaḥ!

sa dṛṣṭvā svāni karmāṇi, kule janma ca, Bhārata,
uttiṣṭhasva; viṣādaṃ mā kṛthā, vīra, sthiro bhava!
na c' âitad anurūpaṃ te yat te glānir, arin|dama!
yad ojasā na labhate kṣatriyo, na tad aśnute!»

VAIŚAMPĀYANA UVĀCA:

76.1 TATH" ÔKTO Vāsudevena nitya|manyur a|marṣaṇaḥ
sad|aśvavat samādhāvad, babhāṣe tad|an|antaram:

Ah! Has fear found you, Bhima, now that the time for war has come and the minds of those who seek war start to waver? Ah! Do you see the signs going against you in your sleep or when you're awake, so that you now want peace, Partha? Ah! Perhaps you do not expect to see any manliness within yourself because you are emasculated like a eunuch? You are filled with weakness, so you've changed your mind! 75.15

Your heart is trembling, your mind is horrified, and your thighs have been caught out, paralysed! That is why you want peace! Indeed a mortal man's mind is as inconstant and fickle as *shálmali* pods moved by the force of the wind, Partha. This kind of thinking is as unbefitting for you as human speech among cattle, and it sinks the minds of Pandu's sons as though they were ship-wrecked men. You saying such odd things is as great a shock to me as it would be were a mountain to creep away, Bhima·sena! 75.20

Look at your own accomplishments, and your birth into such a lineage, Bhárata, and stand tall! Do not give in to dejection, hero, and be firm! This depression is not your style, enemy-tamer! A warrior gets nothing unless he takes it by force!"

VAISHAMPÁYANA said:

ADDRESSED BY Vasudéva in this manner, the intolerant and permanently enraged hero reared up like a fine horse and replied immediately: 76.1

BHĪMASENA uvāca:

«anyathā māṃ cikīrṣantam anyathā manyase, 'cyuta!
praṇīta|bhāvam atyarthaṃ, yudhi satya|parākramam
vetsi, Dāśārha, satyaṃ me, dīrgha|kālaṃ sah' ôṣitaḥ.
uta vā māṃ na jānāsi, plavan hrada iv' â|plavaḥ,
tasmād an|abhirūpābhir vāgbhir māṃ tvaṃ samarchasi.
kathaṃ hi Bhīmasenaṃ māṃ jānan kaś cana, Mādhava,
76.5 brūyād a|pratirūpāṇi yathā māṃ vaktum arhasi?
tasmād idaṃ pravakṣyāmi vacanaṃ, Vṛṣṇi|nandana,
ātmanaḥ pauruṣaṃ c' âiva, balaṃ ca na samaṃ paraiḥ!
sarvathā n' ārya|karm' âitat praśaṃsā svayam ātmanaḥ;
ativād'|âpaviddhas tu vakṣyāmi balam ātmanaḥ!
paśy' ême rodasī, Kṛṣṇa, yayor āsann imāḥ prajāḥ,
a|cale c', â|pratiṣṭhe c' âpy, an|ante, sarva|mātarau.
yad ime sahasā kruddhe sameyātāṃ śile iva,
aham ete nigṛhṇīyāṃ bāhubhyāṃ sa|car'|âcare.
paśy' âitad antaraṃ bāhvor mahā|parighayor iva!
76.10 ya etat prāpya mucyeta, na taṃ paśyāmi pūruṣam!
Himavāṃś ca, samudraś ca, vajrī vā Bala|bhit svayam
may" âbhipannaṃ trāyeran balam āsthāya, na trayaḥ!
yuddh'|ârhān kṣatriyān sarvān Pāṇḍaveṣv ātatāyinaḥ
adhaḥ pāda|talen' âitān adhiṣṭhāsyāmi bhū|tale.
na hi tvaṃ n' âbhijānāsi mama vikramam, Acyuta;
yathā mayā vinirjitya rājāno vaśa|gāḥ kṛtāḥ!
atha cen māṃ na jānāsi, sūryasy' êv' ôdyataḥ prabhām,

BHIMA·SENA replied:

"You assume the opposite of what I wanted to do, Áchyuta! You know the truth is that my very nature is brought
out in battle and that I am truly valiant, for you have lived
with me for long enough, Dashárha. Or perhaps you do not
know me, like a man swimming in a deep lake without a
boat, and that is the reason you attack me with inappropriate words. How could someone who knows me as Bhima·
sena say such ill-fitting things about me, Mádhava, as you 76.5
think you ought to say about me? So then, descendant of
the Vrishnis, I will tell you about my manliness and
strength, unmatched by others! It is anything but a noble
act to praise oneself, but, struck by your insults, I will indeed describe my strength to you!

Look at heaven and earth, Krishna, where the creatures
live, motionless and fluctuating, the infinite mothers of everything. If these should ever violently collide in anger like a
couple of rocks, then I would separate them with my arms,
along with all their moving and stationary parts. Look at
the space between these two arms like mighty iron bars! I 76.10
see no man who could escape once I have caught him! Even
Himálaya, the ocean, and the thunderbolt-wielding slayer
of Bala himself, the three together, could not defend the
man I have seized, when using my strength!

Killing all warriors who are worthy to fight against the Pándavas, I will pound them low into the surface of the ground with the sole of my foot. In reality you understand my prowess full well, Áchyuta; how I defeated the kings and made them subject to my will! And if you do not know my power, which is like the brilliance of the rising sun, then

vigāḍhe yudhi sambādhe vetsyase māṃ, Janārdana!
paruṣair ākṣipasi kiṃ, vraṇaṃ pūtim iv' ônnayan?
76.15 yathā|mati bravīmy etad, viddhi mām adhikaṃ tataḥ!
draṣṭ" âsi yudhi sambādhe pravṛtte vaiśase 'hani
mayā praṇunnān mātaṅgān, rathinaḥ, sādinas tathā!
tathā narān abhikruddhaṃ nighnantaṃ kṣatriya'|rṣabhān
draṣṭā māṃ tvaṃ ca lokaś ca vikarṣantaṃ varān varān!
na me sīdanti majjāno, na mam' ôdvepate manaḥ!
sarva|lokād abhikruddhān na bhayaṃ vidyate mama!
kiṃ tu sauhṛdam ev' âitat kṛpayā, Madhu|sūdana,
sarvāṃs titikṣe saṃkleśān, mā sma no Bharatā naśan.»

ŚRĪ BHAGAVĀN uvāca:

77.1 «BHĀVAṂ JIJÑĀSAMĀNO 'haṃ praṇayād idam abruvam,
na c' ākṣepān, na pāṇḍityān, na krodhān, na vivakṣayā.
ved' âhaṃ tava māhātmyam, uta te veda yad balam,
uta te veda karmāṇi; na tvāṃ paribhavāmy aham.
yathā c' ātmani kalyāṇaṃ sambhāvayasi, Pāṇḍava,
sahasra|guṇam apy etat tvayi sambhāvayāmy aham.
yādṛśe ca kule janma sarva|rāj'|âbhipūjite
bandhubhiś ca suhṛdbhiś ca, Bhīma, tvam asi tādṛśaḥ.
77.5 jijñāsanto hi dharmasya sandigdhasya, Vṛkodara,
paryāyaṃ n' âdhyavasyanti deva|mānuṣayor janāḥ.
sa eva hetur bhūtvā hi puruṣasy' ârtha|siddhiṣu,
vināśe 'pi sa ev' âsya sandigdhaṃ karma pauruṣam.

you will come to know me for what I am when I dive into the throng of battle, Janárdana!

Why do you strike out at me with harsh words as though draining the pus from a boil? I tell you what I think, but 76.15
be assured that I am greater even than that! You will see me bring down the elephants, chariots, and riders when the throng of battle gets underway on the day of butchery! You and the world will watch as I drag down the best of the best, killing men and bull-like warriors in my fury! My marrow is not sinking, and my mind is not dejected! I have no fear of the whole furious world! Whatever friendship I feel is from compassion, slayer of Madhu, for I will endure all troubles in order to prevent the destruction of the Bharatas."

THE BLESSED LORD replied:

"I MERELY SPOKE as I did out of friendship, wanting to 77.1
know your intentions, rather than from a desire to insult you, or show my learning, or from anger, or because I wanted to lecture. I know your magnanimity, I know your strength, I know your achievements, and I am not humiliating you. Just as you find good within yourself, Pándava, so I see a thousand virtues in you. You are exactly the sort of man you should be, Bhima, when born into a family respected by all kings, and so too are your relatives and friends.

People who want to know, Vrikódara, about the uncer- 77.5
tainty of moral law and about the divine and human, do not settle upon its true course. One and the same reason exists for a man's successes as well as his destruction, for human action is dubious. Things which are foreseen one

anyathā paridṛṣṭāni kavibhir doṣa|darśibhiḥ,
anyathā parivartante vegā iva nabhasvataḥ.

su|mantritaṃ, su|nītaṃ ca, nyāyataś c' ôpapāditam,
kṛtaṃ mānuṣyakaṃ karma daiven' âpi virudhyate.
daivam apy a|kṛtaṃ karma pauruṣeṇa vihanyate:
śītam, uṣṇaṃ, tathā varṣaṃ, kṣut|pipāse ca, Bhārata.
77.10 yad anyad diṣṭa|bhāvasya puruṣasya svayaṃ kṛtam
tasmād an|uparodhaś ca vidyate tatra lakṣaṇam.

lokasya n' ânyato vṛttiḥ, Pāṇḍav', ânyatra karmaṇaḥ
evaṃ buddhiḥ pravarteta, phalaṃ syād ubhay'|ânvaye.
ya evaṃ kṛta|buddhiḥ, sa karmasv eva pravartate;
n' â|siddhau vyathate tasya, na siddhau harṣam aśnute.
tatr' êyam anumātrā me, Bhīmasena, vivakṣitā;
n' âik'|ânta|siddhir vaktavyā śatrubhiḥ saha saṃyuge.
n' âtiprahīṇa|raśmiḥ syāt tathā bhāva|viparyaye;
viṣādam arched glāniṃ v" âpy, etam arthaṃ bravīmi te.

77.15 śvo|bhūte Dhṛtarāṣṭrasya samīpaṃ prāpya, Pāṇḍava,
yatiṣye praśamaṃ kartuṃ yuṣmad|artham a|hāpayan.
śamaṃ cet te kariṣyanti, tato 'n|antaṃ yaśo mama,
bhavatāṃ ca kṛtaḥ kāmas, teṣāṃ ca śreya uttamam.
te ced abhiniveksyante, n' âbhyupaiṣyanti me vacaḥ,
Kuravo yuddham ev' âtra ghoraṃ karma bhaviṣyati.

way by sages, who can see faults, turn out quite differently, like the onset of the wind.

Even human acts which are the product of well-advised, sensible policy and are properly accomplished, are obstructed by fate. But then again, an act of fate rather than a human creation, such as cold, heat, rain, hunger, and thirst, can be obstructed through human endeavor, Bhárata. On 77.10
the other hand, it is observed in the texts we inherit, that apart from the acts a man is fated to undertake, there are no obstacles to doing away with actions undertaken of one's own accord.

Action and nothing else is the way of the world, Pándava. So one should act, while being aware that the result will come into being through the natural order of both fate and personal effort. The man who understands this continues with his activities, and is neither upset by failure nor takes joy in success. This was the extent of what I wanted to say, Bhima·sena; success in war with the enemy is not the only option we should discuss. One should not let go of the reins too hastily when the tide turns, but should overcome despair or exhaustion. This is the crux of what I am saying.

When tomorrow dawns, I will go to Dhrita·rashtra's pres- 77.15
ence, Pándava, and I will try to make peace without damaging your cause. If they will make peace, then undying fame will be mine, your wishes will be granted, and they will gain the ultimate good. But if the Kurus are intent on their own position and do not approve of what I say, then there will be a terrible act of war.

asmin yuddhe, Bhīmasena, tvayi bhāraḥ samāhitaḥ,
dhūr Arjunena dhāryā syād, voḍhavya itaro janaḥ.
ahaṃ hi yantā Bībhatsor bhavitā saṃyuge sati;
Dhanañjayasy' âiṣa kāmo, na hi yuddhaṃ na kāmaye.
77.20 tasmād āśaṅkamāno 'haṃ, Vṛkodara, matiṃ tava
gadataḥ klībayā vācā tejas te samadīdipam.»

ARJUNA uvāca:

78.1 «UKTAM YUDHIṢṬHIREṆ' âiva yāvad vācyaṃ, Janārdana,
tava vākyaṃ tu me śrutva pratibhāti, param|tapa,
n' âiva praśamam atra tvaṃ manyase su|karaṃ, prabho,
lobhād vā Dhṛtarāṣṭrasya dainyād vā samupasthitāt.
a|phalaṃ manyase v" âpi puruṣasya parākramam,
na c' ântareṇa karmāṇi pauruṣeṇa bal'|ôdayaḥ.
tad idaṃ bhāṣitaṃ vākyaṃ tathā ca, na tath" âiva tat;
na c' âitad evaṃ draṣṭavyam a|sādhyam api kiñ cana.
78.5 kiṃ c' âitan manyase kṛcchram asmākam avasādakam,
kurvanti teṣāṃ karmāṇi yeṣāṃ n' âsti phal'|ôdayaḥ.
saṃpādyamānaṃ samyak ca syāt karma sa|phalaṃ, prabho,
sa tathā, Kṛṣṇa, vartasva, yathā śarma bhavet paraiḥ.
Pāṇḍavānāṃ Kurūṇāṃ ca bhavān naḥ prathamaḥ suhṛt,
surāṇām asurāṇāṃ ca yathā, vīra, Prajāpatiḥ.
Kurūṇāṃ Pāṇḍavānāṃ ca pratipatsva nirāmayam;
asmadd|hitam anuṣṭhānaṃ, manye, tava na duṣ|karam.
evaṃ ca kāryatām eti kāryaṃ tava, Janārdana;
gamanād evam eva tvaṃ kariṣyasi, Janārdana.

In this battle, Bhima·sena, the burden will be yours, the yoke will have to be borne by Árjuna, and other men will be carried along. I will be Bibhátsu's driver when the battle takes place, for that is Dhanañ·jaya's wish, and I do not desire to fight. It was because I was waiting for your opinion, 77.20
Vrikódara, that I said words like 'eunuch', thereby igniting your splendor."

ÁRJUNA said:

"YUDHI·SHTHIRA SAID what he needed to, Janárdana, and 78.1
having listened to what you have said, scorcher of the foe, it seems you do not think peace will be easy to achieve, lord, either because of Dhrita·rashtra's greed or because of our current wretched circumstances. You think that the mere prowess of man is fruitless, but also that one cannot achieve success without using strength.

What you have said may or may not be the case, but nothing should be viewed as unfeasible. You think that our 78.5
miserable situation puts an end to this plan of peace, but nevertheless, though they act, their actions against us have not yielded fruit. When an act is performed correctly, it bring results, lord, and so, Krishna, act so that we may have peace with our enemies.

Hero, you are the best friend of the Pándavas and the Kurus, just as Praja·pati is the principal friend of the gods and *ásuras*. Do what is in the best interest of the Kurus and Pándavas, for I believe that it is not difficult for you to act in our interest. If this is the case, then your task will be accomplished, Janárdana, and you will manage it merely by going there, Janárdana.

78.10 cikīrṣitam ath' ânyat te tasmin, vīra, dur|ātmani,
bhaviṣyati ca tat sarvaṃ, yathā tava cikīrṣitam.
śarma taiḥ saha vā no 'stu, tava vā yac cikīrṣitam,
vicāryamāṇo yaḥ kāmas tava, Kṛṣṇa, sa no guruḥ.
na sa n' ârhati duṣṭ'|ātmā vadhaṃ sa|suta|bāndhavaḥ;
yena Dharma|sute dṛṣṭā na sā śrīr upamarṣitā,
yac c' âpy a|paśyat" ôpāyaṃ dharmiṣṭhaṃ, Madhu|sūdana,
upâyena nṛśaṃsena hṛtā dur|dyūta|devinā?
katham hi puruṣo jātaḥ kṣatriyeṣu dhanur|dharaḥ
samāhūto nivarteta prāṇa|tyāge 'py upasthite?
a|dharmeṇa jitān dṛṣṭvā vane pravrajitāṃs tathā
78.15 vadhyatāṃ mama, Vārṣṇeya, nirgato 'sau Suyodhanaḥ!
na c' âitad adbhutaṃ, Kṛṣṇa, mitr'|ârthe yac cikīrṣasi.
kriyā kathaṃ ca mukhyā syān mṛdunā v", êtareṇa* vā?
atha vā manyase jyāyān vadhas teṣām an|antaram,
tad eva kriyatām āśu, na vicāryam atas tvayā.
jānāsi hi yath" âitena Draupadī pāpa|buddhinā
parikliṣṭā sabhā|madhye, tac ca tasy' ôpamarṣitam!
sa nāma samyag varteta Pāṇḍaveṣv, iti, Mādhava,
na me saṃjāyate buddhir bījam uptam iv' ōṣare.
tasmād yan manyase yuktaṃ, Pāṇḍavānāṃ hitaṃ ca yat,
tath" āśu kuru, Vārṣṇeya, yan naḥ kāryam an|antaram.»

Regardless of whether you want to deal with that wicked-souled man in another way, everything will turn out just as you intended it to. Let there be peace or war with those men if you wish, for any wish you ponder, Krishna, will have our respect. Doesn't that wicked-souled man, along with his sons and kin, deserve death? He couldn't stand the good fortune which he saw belonged to the son of Dharma, and unable to see a lawful way, slayer of Madhu, he stole it by the cruel method of using a fraudulent gambler! 78.10

How can a man born in the warrior caste as an archer refuse when challenged, even if it results in his giving up his life? When I saw that we were immorally defeated and going to the forest, then Suyódhana became mine to kill, 78.15
Varshnéya!

It is not surprising, Krishna, that you want to act to help your friends, but how will you perform this crucial task? Amicably or otherwise? Or perhaps you believe the best course would be their immediate murder, in which case let it be done quickly, and don't hesitate about it. You know how Dráupadi was molested by that evil-minded man in the middle of court, and how we tolerated it! The idea that Duryódhana would really act properly towards the Pándavas doesn't convince me, Mádhava. Wisdom in him is like seed sown on salty ground. So act quickly; do whatever you think appropriate and advantageous to the Pándavas, Varshnéya. Do what needs to be done for us immediately."

ŚRĪ BHAGAVĀN uvāca:

79.1 «EVAM ETAN, mahā|bāho, yathā vadasi, Pāṇḍava,
Pāṇḍavānāṃ Kurūṇāṃ ca pratipatsye nirāmayam.
sarvaṃ tv idaṃ mam' āyattaṃ, Bībhatso, karmaṇor dvayoḥ.
kṣetraṃ hi rasavac chuddhaṃ karmaṇ" âiv' ôpapāditam,
ṛte varṣān na, Kaunteya, jātu nirvartayet phalam.
tatra vai pauruṣaṃ brūyur āsekaṃ yatra kāritam;
tatra c' âpi dhruvaṃ paśyec choṣaṇaṃ daiva|kāritam.

tad idaṃ niścitam buddhyā pūrvair api mah"|ātmabhiḥ:
79.5 daive ca mānuṣe c' âiva saṃyuktaṃ loka|kāraṇam.
ahaṃ hi tat kariṣyāmi paraṃ puruṣa|kārataḥ;
daivaṃ tu na mayā śakyaṃ karma kartuṃ kathañ cana.

sa hi dharmaṃ ca lokaṃ ca tyaktvā carati dur|matiḥ.
na hi santapyate tena tathā|rūpeṇa karmaṇā.
tath" âpi buddhiṃ pāpiṣṭhāṃ vardhayanty asya mantriṇaḥ,
Śakuniḥ, sūta|putraś ca, bhrātā Duḥśāsanas tathā.
sa hi tyāgena rājyasya na śamaṃ samupaiṣyati
antareṇa vadhaṃ, Pārtha, s'|ânubandhaḥ Suyodhanaḥ;
na c' âpi praṇipātena tyaktum icchati dharma|rāṭ
yācyamānaś ca rājyaṃ sa na pradāsyati dur|matiḥ!

79.10 na tu manye sa tad vācyo, yad Yudhiṣṭhira|śāsanam;
uktaṃ prayojanaṃ yat tu dharma|rājena, Bhārata,
tathā pāpas tu tat sarvaṃ na kariṣyati Kauravaḥ.
tasmiṃś c' â|kriyamāṇe 'sau loke vadhyo bhaviṣyati,
mama c' âpi sa vadhyo hi, jagataś c' âpi, Bhārata,

THE BLESSED LORD replied:

"THE SITUATION does indeed stand just as you describe 79.1
it, long-armed Pándava, and I will do my best to bring about a state of affairs which benefits the Pándavas and Kurus. The whole matter of two outcomes—war or peace—rests on me, Bibhátsu. A field may be prepared through hard labour to be moist and weedless, but without rain, Kauntéya, it will produce no fruit. In this scenario one could argue that man-made irrigation could be organized, but even then one may find that fate causes the water to dry up.

Our high-spirited ancestors decided long ago, in their
wisdom, that it is a combination of fate and human exertion 79.5
which acts as the cause of things in the world. I will do my best as far as human agency goes, but I am not able to control fate to any extent.

That wicked-minded man acts having renounced moral law and the world, and is untroubled by behavior of this kind. His advisors, Shákuni, the *suta*'s son, and his brother Duhshásana, develop his most heinous plans. Suyódhana will not make peace by giving up the kingdom, Partha, before he and his kin are killed. The king of moral righteousness does not wish to renounce his kingdom through surrender, but that wicked-minded man will not return it when asked!

I do not believe that Yudhi·shthira's message should even 79.10
be given to him, for the evil Káurava will not do all that the king of righteousness's speech intends, Bhárata. In the event that the request is not acted upon, he will deserve death in this world. He will deserve death even at my hands and at the hands of the universe, Bhárata, since in boyhood he

yena kaumārake yūyaṃ sarve viprakṛtāḥ sadā,
vipraluptaṃ ca vo rājyaṃ nṛśaṃsena dur|ātmanā,
na c' ôpaśāmyate pāpaḥ śriyaṃ dṛṣṭvā Yudhiṣṭhire.
a|sakṛc c' âpy ahaṃ tena tvat|kṛte, Pārtha, bheditaḥ
na mayā tad gṛhītaṃ ca pāpaṃ tasya cikīrṣitam.
79.15 jānāsi hi, mahā|bāho, tvam apy asya paraṃ matam,
priyaṃ cikīrṣamāṇaṃ ca dharma|rājasya mām api.
sañjānaṃs tasya c' ātmānaṃ, mama c' âiva paraṃ matam,
a|jānann iva māṃ kasmād, Arjun', âdy' âbhiśaṅkase?
yac c' âpi paramaṃ divyaṃ, tac c' âpy anugataṃ tvayā
vidhānaṃ vihitaṃ, Pārtha. kathaṃ śarma bhavet paraiḥ?
yat tu vācā mayā śakyaṃ, karmaṇā v" âpi, Pāṇḍava,
kariṣye tad ahaṃ, Pārtha, na tv āśaṃse śamaṃ paraiḥ.
kathaṃ go|haraṇe hy ukto n' âitac charma tathā hitam,
yācyamāno hi Bhīṣmeṇa saṃvatsara|gate 'dhvani?
79.20 tad" âiva te parābhūtā, yadā saṃkalpitās tvayā!
lavaśaḥ kṣaṇaśaś c' âpi na ca tuṣṭaḥ Suyodhanaḥ!
sarvathā tu mayā kāryaṃ dharma|rājasya śāsanam;
vibhāvyaṃ tasya bhūyaś ca karma pāpaṃ dur|ātmanaḥ.»

NAKULA uvāca:

80.1 «UKTAṂ BAHU|VIDHAṂ vākyaṃ
dharma|rājena, Mādhava,
dharma|jñena, vadānyena,
śrutaṃ c' âiva hi tat tvayā.
matam ājñāya rājñaś ca Bhīmasenena, Mādhava,
saṃśamo bāhu|vīryaṃ ca khyāpitaṃ, Madhu|sūdana.
tath" âiva Phālgunen' âpi yad uktaṃ, tat tvayā śrutam;
ātmanaś ca mataṃ, vīra, kathitaṃ bhavitā sakṛt.

always bullied all of you, and that wicked-souled, cruel man even stole your kingdom because the evil creature could not bear to behold Yudhi·shthira's good fortune.

He tried to alienate me from you more than once, Partha,
but I did not accept his wicked plan. You know, long-armed 79.15
man, what his highest aim is, and you also know that I want to help the king of righteousness. Knowing his soul, and knowing my greatest goal, why do you now have doubts, Árjuna, as though unaware of the facts?

You also know and follow the highest divine statute, Partha, so how can there be peace with the enemy? I will do whatever I can, whether in word or deed, Pándava, but I do not hold out hope for peace with the enemy.

What of that time a year ago during the cattle-rustling? He did not mention the peace that is so beneficial then,
even when asked by Bhishma. You defeated them as soon 79.20
as you set your heart on it! But Suyódhana is not content to relinquish the slightest piece of land even for a moment! My task is always to follow the commands of the king of righteousness, so that wicked-souled man's evil deeds must be pondered once again."

NÁKULA said:

"YOU HAVE HEARD what the generous king of moral righ- 80.1
teousness, who understands duty, has had to say, Mádhava. Bhima·sena, who knows the king's opinion, Mádhava, spoke about refuge and also of his enormous strength, slayer of Madhu. You have also heard what Phálguna had to say, and you have repeatedly voiced my own opinion, hero.

sarvam etad atikramya, śrutvā para|mataṃ bhavān,
yat prāpta|kālaṃ manyethās, tat kuryāḥ, puruṣ'|ôttama.
80.5 tasmiṃs tasmin nimitte hi mataṃ bhavati, Keśava,
prāpta|kālaṃ manuṣyeṇa kṣamaṃ kāryam, arin|dama.
anyathā cintito hy arthaḥ, punar bhavati so 'nyathā;
a|nitya|matayo loke narāḥ, puruṣa|sattama.
anyathā buddhayā hy āsann asmāsu vana|vāsiṣu,
a|dṛśyeṣv anyathā, Kṛṣṇa, dṛśyeṣu punar anyathā.
asmākam api, Vārṣṇeya, vane vicaratāṃ tadā
na tathā praṇayo rājye, yathā samprati vartate.
nivṛtta|vana|vāsān naḥ śrutvā, vīra, samāgatāḥ
akṣauhiṇyo hi sapt' êmās tvat|prasādāj, Janārdana.
80.10 imān hi puruṣa|vyāghrān a|cintya|bala|pauruṣān
ātta|śastrān raṇe dṛṣṭvā na vyathed iha kaḥ pumān?
sa bhavān Kuru|madhye taṃ
sāntva|pūrvaṃ bhay'|ôttaram
brūyād vākyaṃ, yathā mando
na vyatheta Suyodhanaḥ?
Yudhiṣṭhiraṃ, Bhīmasenaṃ, Bībhatsuṃ c' â|parājitam,
Sahadevaṃ ca, māṃ c' âiva, tvāṃ ca, Rāmaṃ ca, Keśava,
Sātyakiṃ ca mahā|vīryaṃ,
Virāṭaṃ ca sah'|ātma|jam,
Drupadaṃ ca sah'|âmātyaṃ,
Dhṛṣṭadyumnaṃ ca, Mādhava,
Kāśi|rājaṃ ca vikrāntaṃ, Dhṛṣṭaketuṃ ca Cedi|pam
māṃsa|śoṇita|bhṛn martyaḥ pratiyudhyeta ko yudhi?

You have heard other people's thoughts on the matter, but ignore all this and do whatever you believe the occasion calls for, supreme person. There is an opinion for ev- 80.5
ery circumstance, Késhava, but a man must do whatever fits the situation at the time, enemy-tamer. A matter which was considered one way may well turn out quite differently, and so men in this world are inconstant in their beliefs, greatest of men.

Our outlook while we were living in the forest was quite different to our outlook when in disguise, Krishna, and when we were no longer under cover it changed again. When we were wandering in the forest, Varshnéya, our aim was not as intent upon our kingdom as it has now become. When word got out that we had returned from living in the forest, hero, these seven armed forces gathered through
your favor, Janárdana. What man on this earth would not 80.10
waver when he saw these tiger-like men whose strength and prowess defies comprehension, and that they have taken up their weapons for battle?

You should speak in the midst of the Kurus with words of conciliation before the fearsome threats, so that the fool Suyódhana does not tremble. Késhava, what mortal man of flesh and bone would fight in battle against Yudhi·shthira, Bhima·sena, undefeated Bibhátsu, Saha·deva, me, you, Rama, powerful Sátyaki, Viráta and his son, Drúpada and his advisors, Dhrishta·dyumna, the mighty king of Kashi, and Dhrishta·ketu the king of the Chedis, Mádhava?

80.15 sa bhavān gamanād eva sādhayiṣyaty a|saṃśayam
iṣṭam arthaṃ, mahā|bāho, dharma|rājasya kevalam.
Viduraś c' âiva, Bhīṣmaś ca, Droṇaś ca saha|Bāhlikaḥ,
śreyaḥ samarthā vijñātum ucyamānās tvay", ân|agha.
te c' âinam anuneṣyanti Dhṛtarāṣṭraṃ jan'|âdhipam,
taṃ ca pāpa|samācāraṃ sah'|âmātyaṃ Suyodhanam.
śrotā c' ârthasya Viduras, tvaṃ ca vaktā, Janārdana,
kam iv' ârthaṃ nivartantaṃ sthāpayetāṃ na vartmani?»

SAHADEVA uvāca:

81.1 «YAD ETAT kathitaṃ rājñā, dharma eṣa sanātanaḥ;
yathā ca yuddham eva syāt, tathā kāryam, arin|dama!
yadi praśamam iccheyuḥ Kuravaḥ Pāṇḍavaiḥ saha,
tath" âpi yuddhaṃ, Dāśārha, yojayethāḥ sah' âiva taiḥ!
kathaṃ nu dṛṣṭvā Pāñcālīṃ tathā, Kṛṣṇa, sabhā|gatām
a|vadhena praśāmyeta mama manyuḥ Suyodhane?
yadi Bhīm'|Ârjunau, Kṛṣṇa, dharma|rājaś ca dhārmikaḥ,
dharmam utsṛjya ten' âhaṃ yoddhum icchāmi saṃyuge!»

SĀTYAKIR uvāca:

81.5 «satyam āha, mahā|bāho, Sahadevo mahā|matiḥ;
Duryodhana|vadhe śāntis tasya kopasya me bhavet.
na jānāsi, yathā dṛṣṭvā cīr'|âjina|dharān vane
tav' âpi manyur udbhūto duḥkhitān prekṣya Pāṇḍavān?
tasmān Mādrī|sutaḥ śūro yad āha raṇa|karkaśaḥ,
vacanaṃ sarva|yodhānāṃ tan mataṃ, puruṣ'|ôttama.»

Doubtless the mere act of your going there means you will accomplish all that the king of righteousness desires as his goal, long-armed man. Vídura, Bhishma, Drona, and Báhlika are capable of understanding what is best when you tell them, sinless man. They will bring round Dhrita·rashtra, lord of his people, along with wicked-acting Suyódhana and his ministers. With Vídura listening, and you speaking, Janárdana, what matter can you not fix when it deviates from the path?" 80.15

SAHA·DEVA said:

"WHATEVER THE king says is eternal law; but arrange it so that we have a war, tamer of your enemies! Even if the Kurus want peace with the Pándavas, goad them into war, Dashárha! How could my fury at Suyódhana be calmed without murder, Krishna, when I saw the Pañchála princess mistreated when she entered the assembly? Even if Bhima, Árjuna, and the king of righteousness are law-abiding, then I will dispense with law—for I want to fight him in battle, Krishna!" 81.1

SÁTYAKI said:

"Long-armed man, intelligent Saha·deva speaks the truth. My anger will only be abated when Duryódhana is dead. Are you not aware of how your anger also flared up when you saw the wretched Pándavas wearing bark and antelope skins in the forest? For this reason, what the war-toughened hero son of Madri has said reflects the opinion of all warriors, greatest of people." 81.5

VAIŚAMPĀYANA uvāca:

evaṃ vadati vākyaṃ tu yuyudhāne mahā|matau,
su|bhīmaḥ siṃha|nādo 'bhūd yodhānāṃ tatra sarvaśaḥ.
sarve hi sarvaśo vīrās tad vacaḥ pratyapūjayan,
«sādhu! sādhv! iti» Śaineyaṃ harṣayanto yuyutsavaḥ.

VAIŚAMPĀYANA uvāca:

82.1 RĀJÑAS TU vacanaṃ śrutvā dharm'|ârtha|sahitaṃ, hitam,
Kṛṣṇā Dāśārham āsīnam abravīc choka|karśitā;
sutā Drupada|rājasya sv|asit'|âyata|mūrdhajā
saṃpūjya Sahadevaṃ ca, Sātyakiṃ ca mahā|ratham,
Bhīmasenaṃ ca saṃśāntaṃ dṛṣṭvā parama|durmanāḥ,
aśru|pūrṇ'|ēkṣaṇā vākyam uvāc' êdaṃ manasvinī.
«viditaṃ te, mahā|bāho dharma|jña Madhu|sūdana,
yathā nikṛtim āsthāya bhraṃśitāḥ Pāṇḍavāḥ sukhāt
82.5 Dhṛtarāṣṭrasya putreṇa s'|âmātyena, Janārdana,
yathā ca Sañjayo rājñā mantraṃ rahasi śrāvitaḥ.
Yudhiṣṭhirasya, Dāśārha, tac c' âpi viditaṃ tava
yath" ôktaḥ Sañjayaś c' âiva, tac ca sarvaṃ śrutaṃ tvayā.
‹pañca nas, tāta, dīyantāṃ grāmā, iti, mahā|dyute,
Avisthalaṃ, Vṛkasthalaṃ, Mākandīṃ, Vāraṇāvatam,
avasānaṃ, mahā|bāho, kañ cid ekaṃ ca pañcamam.›
iti Duryodhano vācyaḥ, suhṛdaś c' âsya, Keśava.
na c' âpi hy akarod vākyaṃ śrutvā, Kṛṣṇa, Suyodhanaḥ
Yudhiṣṭhirasya, Dāśārha, śrīmataḥ sandhim icchataḥ.

VAISHAMPÁYANA said:

While the wise Yuyudhána was speaking, a terrifying lion-like roar erupted from the warriors on all sides. All heroes on every side were paying their respect to his words, shouting "Bravo! Bravo!"—and they cheered the grandson of Shini with their clamor for war.

VAISHAMPÁYANA continued:

WHEN SHE HAD listened to the king's beneficial words, 82.1
conforming to both law and profit, Krishná, who was tormented with grief, spoke to Dashárha as he sat there. The woman with long, black hair, daughter of King Drúpada, honored Saha·deva and the warrior Sátyaki. Seeing even Bhima·sena being conciliatory made her extremely depressed, and, with her eyes full of tears, the spirited lady spoke.

"You know, long-armed, law-wise slayer of Madhu, how 82.5
the Pándavas were toppled from happiness, by Dhrita·rashtra's son and his ministers resorting to deception, Janárdana, and what counsels the king told Sáñjaya in secret. You also know how Yudhi·shthira spoke to Sáñjaya, Dashárha, for you have heard everything.

'Illustrious father, grant us five villages: Avísthala, Vrika·sthala, Makándi, Varanávata, and some other as the fifth and final one, long-armed man.' This is was supposed to be told to Duryódhana and his friends, Késhava. Suyódhana did nothing upon hearing the message from illustrious Yudhi·shthira who seeks peace, Krishna.

82.10 a|pradānena rājyasya yadi, Kṛṣṇa, Suyodhanaḥ
sandhim icchen, na kartavyaṃ tatra gatvā kathañ cana.
śakṣyanti hi, mahā|bāho, Pāṇḍavāḥ Sṛñjayaiḥ saha
Dhārtarāṣṭra|balaṃ ghoraṃ kruddhaṃ pratisamāsitum.
na hi sāmnā, na dānena śakyo 'rthas teṣu kaś cana;
tasmāt teṣu na kartavyā kṛpā te, Madhu|sūdana.

sāmnā dānena vā, Kṛṣṇa, ye na śāmyanti śatravaḥ
yoktavyas teṣu daṇḍaḥ syāj jīvitaṃ parirakṣatā.
tasmāt teṣu maha|daṇḍaḥ kṣeptavyaḥ kṣipram, Acyuta,
tvayā c' âiva, mahā|bāho, Pāṇḍavaiḥ saha Sṛñjayaiḥ.
82.15 etat samarthaṃ Pārthānāṃ tava c' âiva yaśas|karam
kriyamāṇaṃ bhavet, Kṛṣṇa, kṣatrasya ca sukh'|āvaham.
kṣatriyeṇa hi hantavyaḥ kṣatriyo lobham āsthitaḥ,
a|kṣatriyo vā, Dāśārha, sva|dharmam anutiṣṭhatā,
anyatra brāhmaṇāt, tāta, sarva|pāpeṣv avasthitāt;
gurur hi sarva|varṇānāṃ brāhmaṇaḥ prasṛt'|âgra|bhuk.

yath" â|vadhye vadhyamāne bhaved doṣo, Janārdana,
sa vadhyasy' â|vadhe dṛṣṭa, iti dharma|vido viduḥ.
yathā tvāṃ na spṛśed eṣa doṣaḥ, Kṛṣṇa, tathā kuru
Pāṇḍavaiḥ saha, Dāśārhaiḥ, Sṛñjayaiś ca sa|sainikaiḥ.
82.20 punar uktaṃ ca vakṣyāmi viśrambheṇa, Janārdana,
kā tu sīmantinī mādṛk pṛthivyām asti, Keśava?
sutā Drupada|rājasya vedi|madhyāt samutthitā,
Dhṛṣṭadyumnasya bhaginī tava, Kṛṣṇa, priyā sakhī,

If Suyódhana wants peace without returning the kingdom, Krishna, then you shouldn't go there and make peace at all. Long-armed man, the Pándavas and Sríñjayas are perfectly capable of handling Dhartaráshtra's furious and terrifying force. Since no matter can be resolved with those men through conciliation and generosity, they shouldn't be treated with compassion, slayer of Madhu. 82.10

We must use punishment with enemies who are not appeased through conciliation or generosity, Krishna, to protect our lives. Therefore, you, the Pándavas, and the Sríñjayas must quickly wreak enormous punishment upon them, long-armed Áchyuta.

This will bring power to the Parthas, bring you glory, and create future happiness for the warrior caste, Krishna. For a warrior who practices his own duty should kill another if he is set on greed, and even a non-warrior, Dashárha. The exception is a brahmin, my friend, even if he is intent on all evil, for the brahmin is the teacher of all castes and has first pick of food produced. 82.15

Men who understand their duty by the law know that it is a sin to kill a man who does not deserve it, Janárdana, but it is considered equally sinful not to kill a man who does deserve it. So take action with the Pándavas, Dashárhas, Sríñjayas, and their soldiers, to make sure this sin doesn't touch upon you, Krishna.

It has been said already, but I will say it again since we are close, Janárdana. What woman on earth is like me, Késhava? I am King Drúpada's daughter, born from the middle of an altar. I am Dhrishta·dyumna's sister and your dear friend, Krishna. As the wife of the Pándavas, who in splendor equal 82.20

Ājamīḍha|kulaṃ prāptā, snuṣā Pāṇḍor mah”|ātmanaḥ,
mahiṣī Pāṇḍu|putrāṇāṃ, pañc’|Êndra|sama|varcasām.
sutā me pañcabhir vīraiḥ pañca jātā mahā|rathāḥ,
Abhimanyur yathā, Kṛṣṇa, tathā te tava dharmataḥ.
s” âhaṃ keśa|grahaṃ prāptā parikliṣṭā sabhāṃ gatā,
paśyatāṃ Pāṇḍu|putrāṇāṃ tvayi jīvati, Keśava,
82.25 jīvatsu Pāṇḍu|putreṣu, Pañcāleṣv, atha Vṛṣṇiṣu,
dāsī|bhūt” âsmi pāpānāṃ sabhā|madhye vyavasthitā!
nirāmarṣeṣv a|ceṣṭeṣu prekṣamāṇeṣu Pāṇḍuṣu
‹pāhi mām! iti,› Govinda, manasā cintito ’si me.
yatra māṃ bhagavān rājā śvaśuro vākyam abravīt:
‹varaṃ vṛṇīṣva, Pāñcāli, var’|ârh” âsi matā mama.›
‹a|dāsāḥ Pāṇḍavāḥ santu sa|rathāḥ s’|āyudhā, iti›
may” ôkte yatra nirmuktā vana|vāsāya, Keśava!
evaṃ|vidhānāṃ duḥkhānām abhijño ’si, Janārdana.
trāyasva, puṇḍarīk’|âkṣa, sa|bhartṛ|jñāti|bāndhavān!
82.30 nanv ahaṃ, Kṛṣṇa, Bhīṣmasya Dhṛtarāṣṭrasya c’ ôbhayoḥ
snuṣā bhavāmi dharmeṇa, s” âhaṃ dāsī|kṛtā balāt.
dhik Pārthasya dhanuṣmattāṃ, Bhīmasenasya dhig balam,
yatra Duryodhanaḥ, Kṛṣṇa, muhūrtam api jīvati!
yadi te ’ham anugrāhyā, yadi te ’sti kṛpā mayi,
Dhārtarāṣṭreṣu vai kopaḥ sarvaḥ, Kṛṣṇa, vidhīyatām!»

five Indras, and the daughter-in-law of high-souled Pandu, I was adopted into the lineage of Aja·midha. I have had five warrior sons by five heroes, and they are lawfully as close to you as Abhimányu, Krishna.

I was grabbed by the hair and dragged along to court in the sight of the sons of Pandu while you lived, Késhava.
While the Pándavas, Pañchálas, and Vrishnis still lived, I 82.25
stood in the middle of court and was made a slave of evil men! Since the Pándavas watched and did nothing, refusing to give way to anger, I thought of you, Go·vinda, in my mind, calling out 'Protect me!' Then when the lord king, my father-in-law, said to me, 'Choose a favor, princess of Pañchála, for you deserve favors and honor from me,' I replied, 'Let the Pándavas be released from slavery with their chariots and weapons.' When I said this, they were indeed released, Késhava, but to live in the forest!

You are aware of the miseries I have suffered, lotus-eyed Janárdana, so protect me and my husbands, relatives, and
kin! Am I not both Bhishma's and Dhrita·rashtra's daughter- 82.30
in-law according to the law, Krishna? Yet I was forcibly made a slave! Shame on Partha's archery and shame on Bhima's strength if Duryódhana lives a moment longer, Krishna! If I deserve favor, and if you have any compassion for me, then direct all your anger at the Dhartaráshtras, Krishna!"

VAIŚAMPĀYANA uvāca:

ity uktvā mṛdu|saṃhāraṃ, vṛjin'|âgraṃ, su|darśanam,
su|nīlam, asit'|âpāṅgī sarva|gandh'|âdhivāsitam,
sarva|lakṣaṇa|sampannaṃ, mahā|bhujaga|varcasam
keśa|pakṣaṃ var'|ārohā gṛhya vāmena pāṇinā
82.35 padm'|âkṣī puṇḍarīk'|âkṣam upetya gaja|gāminī
aśru|pūrṇ'|ēkṣaṇā Kṛṣṇā Kṛṣṇaṃ vacanam abravīt:
«ayaṃ te, puṇḍarīk'|âkṣa, Duḥśāsana|kar'|ôddhṛtaḥ
smartavyaḥ sarva|kāryeṣu pareṣāṃ sandhim icchatā.
yadi Bhīm'|Ârjunau, Kṛṣṇa, kṛpaṇau sandhi|kāmukau
pitā me yotsyate vṛddhaḥ saha putrair mahā|rathaiḥ,
pañca c' âiva mahā|vīryāḥ putrā me, Madhu|sūdana,
Abhimanyuṃ puras|kṛtya yotsyante Kurubhiḥ saha!
Duḥśāsana|bhujaṃ śyāmaṃ
saṃchinnaṃ pāṃsu|guṇṭhitam
yady ahaṃ tu na paśyāmi,
kā śāntir hṛdayasya me?
82.40 trayo|daśa hi varṣāṇi pratīkṣantyā gatāni me
vidhāya hṛdaye manyuṃ pradīptam iva pāvakam.
vidīryate me hṛdayaṃ Bhīma|vāk|śalya|pīḍitam,
yo 'yam adya mahā|bāhur dharmam ev' ânupaśyati.»
ity uktvā bāṣpa|ruddhena kaṇṭhen' āyata|locanā
ruroda Kṛṣṇā s'|ôtkampaṃ, sa|svaraṃ, bāṣpa|gadgadam.
stanau pīn'|āyata|śroṇī sahitāv abhivarṣatī,
dravī|bhūtam iv' âtyuṣṇaṃ muñcatī vāri netra|jam.
tām uvāca mahā|bāhuḥ Keśavaḥ parisāntvayan:

VAISHAMPÁYANA said:

Having said this, the shapely hipped, black-eyed lady took hold of the side of her exceptionally beautiful, midnight-colored hair—soft to the touch, curled at the ends, scented with every perfume, endowed with all the approved attributes, and glistening like a huge snake—with
her left hand. The lotus-eyed lady with the gait of an ele- 82.35
phant approached the lotus-eyed man, and with eyes brimming with tears, Krishná said to Krishna:

"Lotus-eyed man, Duhshásana grabbed this hair in his hands; keep that in mind throughout the entire proceedings when you seek peace with the enemy. Even if Bhima and Árjuna have pity and wish for peace, my aged father will fight, with his warrior sons, Krishna! My five heroic sons will fight against the Kurus too, with Abhimányu at their head, slayer of Madhu!

If I do not see Duhshásana's dark-skinned arm severed and covered in dust, then what peace will my heart find?
Thirteen years have passed while I waited, concealing my 82.40
fury in my heart like a blazing fire. Bhima's words have torn my heart as though it were pierced by an arrow, for today that long-armed man only has eyes for the law."

When wide-eyed Krishná had said this she wept, her throat choked with tears, trembling and whimpering, stuttering with tears. That lady of full, round hips rained tears down onto her breasts and wept teardrops of liquid fire. Long-armed Késhava spoke to console her, saying:

«a|cirād drakṣyase, Kṛṣṇe, rudatīr Bharata|striyaḥ.
82.45 evaṃ tā, bhīru, rotsyanti nihata|jñāti|bāndhavāḥ,
hata|mitrā, hata|balā, yeṣāṃ kruddh" âsi, bhāmini.
ahaṃ ca tat kariṣyāmi Bhīm'|Ârjuna|yamaiḥ saha,
Yudhiṣṭhira|niyogena, daivāc ca vidhi|nirmitāt.

Dhārtarāṣṭrāḥ kāla|pakvā na cec chṛṇvanti me vacaḥ,
śeṣyante nihatā bhūmau śva|sṛgāl'|âdanī|kṛtāḥ.
caledd hi Himavān śailo, medinī śatadhā phalet,
dyauḥ patec ca sa|nakṣatrā, na me moghaṃ vaco bhavet!
satyaṃ te pratijānāmi, Kṛṣṇe, bāṣpo nigṛhyatām;
hat'|âmitrān śriyā yuktān a|cirād drakṣyase patīn.»

ARJUNA uvāca:

83.1 «KURŪṆĀM ADYA sarveṣāṃ bhavān suhṛd an|uttamaḥ,
sambandhī dayito nityam ubhayoḥ pakṣayor api.
Pāṇḍavair Dhārtarāṣṭrāṇāṃ pratipādyam an|āmayam;
samarthaḥ praśamaṃ c' âiva kartum arhasi, Keśava.
tvam itaḥ, puṇḍarīk'|âkṣa, Suyodhanam a|marṣaṇam
śānty|arthaṃ bhrātaraṃ brūyā yat tad vācyam, amitra|han.
tvayā dharm'|ârtha|yuktaṃ ced uktaṃ śivam an|āmayam,
hitaṃ n' ādāsyate bālo, diṣṭasya vaśam eṣyati.»

"It will not be long now till you see the Bharata women
weeping, Krishná. They too will cry, timid lady, when their 82.45
relatives and kin are dead. Those at whom you are furious, spirited lady that you are, have already lost their friends and armies. I, along with Bhima, Árjuna, and the twins, will act according to Yudhi·shthira's command and as the law of fate permits.

If the Dhartaráshtras, whose time is up, do not listen to what I have to say, then they will be left dead on the ground as food for dogs and jackals. Mount Himálaya may move, the earth may split into a hundred pieces, the sky and stars may fall, but my words will not prove fruitless! I promise you this truly, Krishná, so stop crying, for it will not be long now until you see your husbands meet with good fortune and your enemies dead."

ÁRJUNA said:

"AT THIS MOMENT you are the best friend of all Kurus, 83.1
for you have always been the cherished ally of both sides. You are capable of ensuring peace between the Pándavas and Dhartaráshtras and so you ought to do it, Késhava. Go to intolerant Suyódhana, lotus-eyed man, for the sake of peace, and tell our brother what he needs to hear, destroyer of your enemies. If you speak kindly and wholesome words which conform to virtue and profit and the foolish man will not accept your good advice, then he will become subject to the power of fate."

ŚRĪ BHAGAVĀN uvāca:

83.5 «dharmyam asmadd|hitaṃ c' âiva
Kurūṇāṃ yad an|āmayam,
eṣa yāsyāmi rājānaṃ
Dhṛtarāṣṭram abhīpsayā.»

VAIŚAMPĀYANA uvāca:

tato vyapeta|tamasi sūrye vimalavad gate,
Maitre muhūrte saṃprāpte, mṛdv|arciṣi divā|kare,
Kaumude māsi, Revatyāṃ śarad|ante him'|āgame,
sphīta|sasya|sukhe kāle kalpaḥ sattvavatāṃ varaḥ.
maṅgalyāḥ puṇya|nirghoṣā vācaḥ śṛṇvaṃś ca sūnṛtāḥ
brāhmaṇānāṃ pratītānām ṛṣīṇām iva Vāsavaḥ.
kṛtvā paurvāhṇikaṃ kṛtyaṃ, snātaḥ, śucir, alaṅkṛtaḥ
upatasthe vivasvantaṃ pāvakaṃ ca Janārdanaḥ,
83.10 ṛṣabhaṃ pṛṣṭha ālabhya, brāhmaṇān abhivādya ca,
agniṃ pradakṣiṇaṃ kṛtvā paśyan kalyāṇam agrataḥ.
tat pratijñāya vacanaṃ Pāṇḍavasya Janārdanaḥ
Śiner naptāram āsīnam abhyabhāṣata Sātyakim:
«ratha āropyatāṃ, śaṅkhaś, cakraṃ ca gadayā saha,
upāsaṅgāś ca, śaktyaś ca, sarva|praharaṇāni ca.
Duryodhanaś ca duṣṭ'|ātmā, Karṇaś ca saha|Saubalaḥ
na ca śatrur avajñeyo dur|balo 'pi balīyasā.»
tatas tan|matam ājñāya Keśavasya puraḥ|sarāḥ
prasasrur yojayiṣyanto rathaṃ cakra|gadā|bhṛtaḥ;
83.15 taṃ dīptam iva kāl'|âgnim ākāśa|gam iv' āśu|gam
sūrya|candra|prakāśābhyāṃ cakrābhyāṃ samalaṅkṛtam;
ardha|candraiś ca candraiś ca, matsyaiḥ sa|mṛga|pakṣibhiḥ,

THE BLESSED LORD replied:

"I will go to King Dhrita·rashtra, eager to obtain a settlement which is lawful and beneficial to us, as well as a healthy solution for the Kurus." 83.5

VAISHAMPÁYANA continued:

Then, when the darkness had vanished and a pure sun had risen, in the hour of Maitra, when the sun shines gently, in the month of Káumuda, under the Révati constellation, as the fall was waning and the winter arriving, when crops and happiness flourish, that greatest of living men was ready. He listened to the auspicious, holy prayers and the pleasant, truthful conversation of the firmly resolved brahmins, just as Vásava listens to the sages. Janárdana performed his morning rites, washed, purified, and adorned
himself, then worshipped the sun and fire. Touching a bull 83.10
on its back, he greeted the brahmins, circled the fire, and looked at the auspicious items in front of him.

Then Janárdana acknowledged what Pándava had to say and spoke to Shini's grandson, Sátyaki, as he was seated: "Pack the chariot with the conch, discus and mace, quivers, spears, and all missiles. Duryódhana, Karna, and Sáubala have wicked souls, and a stronger man should never disregard even a weak enemy."

Understanding Késhava's intention, his servants rushed to yoke the chariot of the wielder of the discus and mace.
The chariot blazed like the fire of armageddon and was 83.15
as swift as a bird, adorned with wheels which shone like the sun and moon. It was large and beautiful and gleamed

puṣpaiś ca vividhaiś citraṃ, maṇi|ratnaiś ca sarvaśaḥ,
taruṇ'|āditya|saṃkāśaṃ, bṛhantaṃ, cāru|darśanam,
maṇi|hema|vicitr'|âṅgaṃ, su|dhvajaṃ, su|patākinam;
s'|ûpaskaram, an|ādhṛṣyaṃ, vaiyāghra|parivāraṇam,
yaśo|ghnaṃ pratyamitrāṇāṃ, Yadūnāṃ nandi|vardhanam;
vājibhiḥ Śaibya|Sugrīva|Meghapuṣpa|Balāhakaiḥ
snātaiḥ saṃpādayām āsuḥ saṃpannaiḥ sarva|saṃpadā;
83.20 mahimānaṃ tu Kṛṣṇasya bhūya ev' âbhivardhayan
su|ghoṣaḥ patag'|êndreṇa dhvajena yuyuje rathaḥ.
tam Meru|śikhara|prakhyaṃ,
megha|dundubhi|niḥsvanam
āruruoha rathaṃ Śaurir,
vimānam iva kāma|gam.
tataḥ Sātyakim āropya prayayau puruṣ'|ôttamaḥ,
pṛthivīṃ c' ântarikṣaṃ ca ratha|ghoṣeṇa nādayan.
vyapoḍh'|âbhras tataḥ kālaḥ kṣaṇena samapadyata,
śivaś c' ânuvavau vāyuḥ, praśāntam abhavad rajaḥ.
pradakṣiṇ'|ânulomāś ca maṅgalyā mṛga|pakṣiṇaḥ
prayāṇe Vāsudevasya babhūvur anuyāyinaḥ.
83.25 maṅgaly'|ârtha|pradaiḥ śabdair anvavartanta sarvaśaḥ
sārasāḥ, śata|patrāś ca, haṃsāś ca Madhu|sūdanam.
mantr'|āhuti|mahā|homair hūyamānaś ca pāvakaḥ
pradakṣiṇa|mukho bhūtvā vidhūmaḥ samapadyata.
Vasiṣṭho, Vāmadevaś ca, Bhūridyumno, Gayaḥ, Krathaḥ,

like the freshly risen sun, decorated with half-moons, full-moons, fish, animals, birds, and with various flowers. Gems and jewels ensured it was generally colorful, and it had an excellent flag-pole and a banner decorated with various jewels and gold.

It was wonderfully embellished, unstoppable, and covered with tiger-skins. It destroyed the fame of enemies but augmented the joy of the Yadus. This was the chariot they yoked to the horses Shaibya, Sugríva, Megha·pushpa, and Baláhaka, all of whom were washed and furnished with the
full compliment of trappings. Further increasing Krishna's 83.20
majesty, the loud-booming chariot was topped with a banner depicting Gáruda, the lord of birds.

So it was that Shauri climbed onto the chariot that resembled the peak of Meru and thundered like clouds and drums; the chariot like the vehicle of the gods which goes where it pleases. Then the supreme person helped Sátyaki clamber up, and together they went off, making the earth and sky resound with the roar of the chariot. The clouds were instantly swept away, a gentle wind blew, and the dust was cleansed from the air.

Auspicious animals and birds followed Vasudéva, keeping to his right in natural order, as he set out on his journey. With cries prophesying luck, swans, woodpeckers, and 83.25
geese flew together around the slayer of Madhu. The fire, being fed with great offerings of oblations and mantras, became smokeless and rose with flames climbing to the right. Vasíshtha, Vama·deva, Bhuri·dyumna, Gaya, Kratha, Shukra, Nárada, Valmíka, Máruta, Kúshika, Bhrigu, and divine sages and brahmins together circumambulated

Śukra|Nārada|Vālmīkā, Marutaḥ, Kuśiko, Bhṛguḥ,
deva|brahma'|rṣayaś c' âiva Kṛṣṇaṃ Yadu|sukh'|āvaham
pradakṣiṇam avartanta sahitā Vāsav'|ânujam.
evam etair mahā|bhāgair maha"|rṣi|gaṇa|sādhubhiḥ
pūjitaḥ prayayau Kṛṣṇaḥ Kurūṇāṃ sadanaṃ prati.
83.30 taṃ prayāntam anuprāyāt Kuntī|putro Yudhiṣṭhiraḥ,
Bhīmasen'|Ârjunau c' ôbhau, Mādrī|putrau ca Pāṇḍavau,
Cekitānaś ca vikrānto, Dhṛṣṭaketuś ca Cedi|paḥ,
Drupadaḥ Kāśi|rājaś ca, Śikhaṇḍī ca mahā|rathaḥ,
Dhṛṣṭadyumnaḥ sa|putraś ca, Virāṭaḥ Kekayaiḥ saha,
saṃsādhan'|ârthaṃ prayayuḥ kṣatriyāḥ kṣatriya'|rṣabham.
tato 'nuvrajya Govindaṃ dharma|rājo Yudhiṣṭhiraḥ
rājñāṃ sakāśe dyutimān uvāc' êdaṃ vacas tadā.
yo vai na kāmān, na bhayān, na lobhān, n' ârtha|kāraṇāt
a|nyāyam anuvarteta, sthira|buddhir, a|lolupaḥ,
83.35 dharma|jño, dhṛtimān, prājñaḥ, sarva|bhūteṣu Keśavaḥ
īśvaraḥ sarva|bhūtānāṃ, deva|devaḥ sanātanaḥ,
taṃ sarva|guṇa|saṃpannaṃ, śrīvatsa|kṛta|lakṣanam
saṃpariṣvajya Kaunteyaḥ saṃdeṣṭum upacakrame.

YUDHIṢṬHIRA uvāca:

«yā sā bālyāt prabhṛty asmān paryavardhayat' âbalā,
upavāsa|tapaḥ|śīlā, sadā svasty|ayane ratā,
devat'|âtithi|pūjāsu guru|śuśrūṣaṇe ratā,
vatsalā, priya|putrā ca, priy" âsmākaṃ, Janārdana;
Suyodhana|bhayād yā no 'trāyat', âmitra|karśana,
mahato mṛtyu|saṃbādhād uddharan, naur iv' ârṇavāt,
83.40 asmat|kṛte ca satataṃ yayā duḥkhāni, Mādhava,

Krishna, the brother of Vásava, who brings happiness to the Yadus.

Once he had been honored by those illustrious throngs of great sages and holy men, Krishna set out to the Kurus' dwelling. Yudhi·shthira, son of Kunti, followed him as he 83.30
began his journey, as did Bhima·sena, Árjuna, both the sons of Madri and Pandu, powerful Chekitána, Dhrishta·ketu the king of the Chedis, Drúpada, the king of the Kashis, the warrior Shikhándin, Dhrishta·dyumna, Viráta and his sons, and the Kékayas. Warriors followed the bull-like warrior for the sake of his success.

As he followed him, glorious Yudhi·shthira, the king of righteousness, spoke to Go·vinda in the presence of the kings. Kauntéya embraced the man who never acted incor- 83.35
rectly out of love, fear, greed, or in the cause of profit—Késhava, the man of firm mind, without desire, who knows the law and is resolved and knowledgeable about all creatures; the lord of all creatures, eternal god of gods, endowed with every virtue and an auspicious curl of hair on his chest—and he began to instruct him:

YUDHI·SHTHIRA said:

"The woman who brought us up since our childhood, who always practices fasts and austerities, who delights in auspicious rituals, who takes pleasure in honoring the gods and guests as well as obeying gurus, who is affectionate to her offspring, dear to her sons, and dear to us, Janárdana; the lady who protected us from the danger of Suyódhana, enemy-plower, rescuing us at considerable personal risk of death, as a ship rescues men from drowning in the sea; the 83.40

anubhūtāny a|duḥkh'|ârhā, tāṃ sma pṛccher an|āmayam.
bhṛśam āśvāsayeś c' âināṃ putra|śoka|pariplutām,
abhivādya svajethās tvaṃ Pāṇḍavān parikīrtayan.
ūḍhāt prabhṛti duḥkhāni śvaśurāṇām, arin|dama,
nikārān a|tad|arhā ca paśyantī duḥkham aśnute.
api jātu sa kālaḥ syāt, Kṛṣna, duḥkha|viparyayaḥ,
yad ahaṃ mātaraṃ kliṣṭāṃ sukhaṃ dadyām, arin|dama?
pravrajanto 'nudhāvantīṃ kṛpanām putra|gṛddhinīm
rudatīm upahāy' âinām agacchāma vayaṃ vanam.
83.45 na nūnaṃ mriyate duḥkhaiḥ sā cej jīvati, Keśava,
tathā putr'|âdhibhir gāḍham ārtā hy Ānarta|satkṛta.
abhivādy" âtha sā, Kṛṣṇa, tvayā mad|vacanād, vibho,
Dhṛtarāṣṭraś ca Kauravyo, rājānaś ca vayo|'dhikāḥ.
Bhīṣmaṃ, Droṇaṃ, Kṛpaṃ c' âiva,
mahā|rājaṃ ca Bāhlikam,
Drauṇiṃ ca, Somadattaṃ ca,
sarvāṃś ca Bharatān prati,
Viduraṃ ca mahā|prājñaṃ Kurūṇāṃ mantra|dhāriṇam,
a|gādha|buddhiṃ, marma|jñaṃ svajethā, Madhu|sūdana.»
ity uktvā Keśavaṃ tatra rāja|madhye Yudhiṣṭhiraḥ
anujñāto nivavṛte Kṛṣṇaṃ kṛtvā pradakṣiṇam.
83.50 vrajann eva tu Bībhatsuḥ sakhāyaṃ puruṣa'|rṣabham
abravīt para|vīra|ghnaṃ Dāśārham a|parājitam:

lady who suffered constant miseries, though she deserved none, as the consequences of acting on our behalf—ask after her health, Mádhava.

Keep consoling her as she brims over with grief for her sons, and once you have greeted her, embrace her while celebrating the Pándavas. From the start of her marriage she has seen nothing but miseries and humiliation from her in-laws, tamer of your foes, though she does not deserve it, and she has gained only pain. Will there really be a time, Krishna, when we have a change of fortune and I will make my afflicted mother happy, enemy-tamer?

When we went to the forest we left her behind, and she ran after us as we went, crying, pitiably longing for her sons.
Surely one cannot die from one's miseries, Késhava, so she 83.45
may still live, well cared for by the Anártas, but greatly tormented over her sons. Please greet her on my behalf, lord Krishna, as well as Dhrita·rashtra Kaurávya and the kings who are our elders. Embrace Bhishma, Drona, Kripa, the great King Báhlika, Drona's son, Soma·datta, and all the Bharatas, as well as Vídura, advisor to the Kurus—a man of great learning, deep intelligence, and acute insight, O slayer of Madhu."

Once Yudhi·shthira had spoken in this way to Késhava in the midst of the kings, he bid him farewell, and after circling
Krishna, he turned back. Bibhátsu though went up to his 83.50
friend, the bull-like murderer of enemy heroes, undefeated Dashárha, and said to him:

«yad asmākaṃ, vibho, vṛttaṃ purā vai mantra|niścaye,
ardha|rājyasya, Govinda, viditaṃ sarva|rājasu.
tac ced dadyād a|saṅgena, sat|kṛty', ân|avamanya ca,
priyaṃ me syān, mahā|bāho, mucyeran mahato bhayāt.
ataś ced anyathā kartā Dhārtarāṣṭro 'n|upāyavit,
antaṃ nūnaṃ kariṣyāmi kṣatriyāṇāṃ, Janārdana!»

VAIŚAMPĀYANA uvāca:

evam ukte Pāṇḍavena samahṛṣyad Vṛkodaraḥ;
muhur muhuḥ krodha|vaśāt pravepata ca Pāṇḍavaḥ.
83.55 vepamānaś ca Kaunteyaḥ prākrośan mahato ravān
Dhanañjaya|vacaḥ śrutvā, harṣ'|ôtsikta|manā bhṛśam.
tasya taṃ ninadaṃ śrutvā saṃprāvepanta dhanvinaḥ,
vāhanāni ca sarvāṇi śakṛn|mūtre prasusruvuḥ.
ity uktvā Keśavaṃ tatra, tathā c' ôktvā viniścayam,
anujñāto nivavṛte pariṣvajya Janārdanam.
teṣu rājasu sarveṣu nivṛtteṣu Janārdanaḥ
tūrṇam abhyagamadd hṛṣṭaḥ Śaibya|Sugrīva|vāhanaḥ.
te hayā Vāsudevasya dārukeṇa pracoditāḥ
panthānam ācemur iva, grasamānā iv' âmbaram.
83.60 ath' âpaśyan mahā|bāhur ṛṣīn adhvani Keśavaḥ,
brāhmyā śriyā dīpyamānān sthitān ubayataḥ pathi.
so 'vatīrya rathāt tūrṇam, abhivādya Janārdanaḥ,
yathā|vṛttān ṛṣīn sarvān abhyabhāṣata pūjayan:
«kac cil lokeṣu kuśalaṃ? kaś cid dharmaḥ sv|anuṣṭhitaḥ?
brāhmaṇānāṃ trayo varṇāḥ kac cit tiṣṭhanti śāsane?»
tebhyaḥ prayujya tāṃ pūjāṃ provāca Madhu|sūdanaḥ:

"Long ago, lord Go·vinda, we decided on a resolution to ask for half the kingdom, and all the kings know it. If he returns it independently and behaves well without treating us contemptuously, then it would please me, long-armed man, and it would release them from great danger. But if Dhartaráshtra acts otherwise, unaware of the proper means, then I will surely put an end to the warriors, Janárdana!"

VAISHAMPÁYANA continued:

Vrikódara was excited by what the Pándava had said, and the son of Pandu repeatedly trembled under the power of
his rage. Shaking, Kauntéya bellowed, roaring at enormous 83.55
volume, for when he heard what Dhanañ·jaya had to say, he became extremely elevated with joy. Hearing his roaring, the archers trembled and all the horses passed dung and urine.

When he had spoken to Késhava in this way and told him of his decision, Árjuna bid him farewell, embraced Janárdana, and turned back. Then, as all the kings were returning, Janárdana set off quickly and happily, driving Shaibya and Sugríva, and the horses, urged on by Vasudéva's stick, seemed to sip the road and swallow the sky.

Long-armed Késhava saw sages blazing with brahmic 83.60
splendor standing on both sides on the road. So Janárdana swiftly got down from his chariot and greeted them, honoring all the sages as was customary, and said to them: "Is there health in the worlds? Is law well observed at all? Do the three other castes abide by the commands of the brahmins at all?" The slayer of Madhu paid his respects to them in this way, and then said to them: "Blessed sirs, where have

«bhagavantaḥ kva saṃsiddhāḥ? kā vīthī bhavatām iha?
kiṃ vā kāryaṃ bhagavatām? ahaṃ kiṃ karavāṇi vaḥ?
ken' ârthen' ôpasaṃprāptā bhagavanto mahī|talam?»
83.65 tam abravīj Jāmadagnya upetya Madhu|sūdanam,
pariṣvajya ca Govindaṃ sur'|âsura|pateḥ sakhā:
«deva'|rṣayaḥ puṇya|kṛto, brāhmaṇāś ca bahu|śrutāḥ,
rāja'|rṣayaś ca, Dāśārha, mānayantas tapasvinaḥ,
dev'|âsurasya draṣṭāraḥ purānasya, mahā|mate.
sametaṃ pārthivaṃ kṣatraṃ didṛkṣantaś ca sarvataḥ,
sabhā|sadaś ca rājānas, tvāṃ ca satyaṃ Janārdanam.
etan mahat prekṣaṇīyaṃ draṣṭuṃ gacchāma, Keśava,
dharm'|ârtha|sahitā vācaḥ śrotum icchāma, Mādhava,
tvay" ôcyamānāḥ Kuruṣu rāja|madhye, paraṃ|tapa.
Bhīṣma|Droṇ'|ādayaś c' âiva, Viduraś ca mahā|matiḥ,
83.70 tvaṃ ca, Yādava|śārdūla, sabhāyāṃ vai sameṣyatha.
tava vākyāni divyāni, tathā teṣāṃ ca, Mādhava,
śrotum icchāma, Govinda, satyāni ca hitāni ca.
āpṛṣṭo 'si, mahā|bāho; punar drakṣyāmahe vayam.
yāhy a|vighnena vai, vīra, drakṣyāmas tvāṃ sabhā|gatam,
āsīnam āsane divye, bala|tejaḥ|samāhitam.»

you found success? What path are you taking in this place? What do you need to do? What can I do for you? For what purpose have you come to the surface of the earth?"

Jamad·agni's son approached the slayer of Madhu, and 83.65
as an old friend of Brahma, the lord of gods and *ásura*s, he embraced Go·vinda and said to him:

"The celestial, pious-acting sages, the brahmins of advanced learning, the royal sages and respected ascetics, Dashárha, were once the spectators of the ancient battle between the gods and *ásura*s, great minded man. Now they want to watch the kings and warriors gathered at every turn, the kings sitting in court, and you, Janárdana, the essence of truth.

We are going to watch the great spectacle, Késhava, and we want to listen the words, full of law and profit, Mádhava, which you will address to the Kurus in the midst of the kings, scorcher of the enemy. Bhishma, Drona and so
on, wise Vídura, and you, tiger of the Yadus, will gather in 83.70
court. We want to hear you speak celestial words of both truth and advantage, Mádhava Go·vinda. Farewell, long-armed man. We will see you again. Go without obstruction, hero, and we will see you when you have arrived in court, endowed with strength and splendor, and are sitting on a celestial throne."

# NOTES

**Bold** *references are to the English text;* ***bold italic*** *references are to the Sanskrit text. An asterisk (*) in the body of the text marks the word or passage being annotated.*

2.5 ***sūta*** can mean "charioteer" or "herald" but is also used as a title of rank or position in court. For this reason, I leave the word untranslated. The phrase **suta's son** is commonly used as an epithet for Karna and Sáñjaya. See also BOWLES 2006: 548, notes to CSL VIII.1.5 and 2.9.

4.18 ***Kāmbojā, Ṛṣikā***: pre-sandhi forms, *metri causa*.

9.30 ***tariṣyati*** CE, *bhaviṣyati* K. The commentary glosses *bhaviṣyati* in the sense of the variant adopted from CE.

13.21 ***a/kampyam*** CE, *akampan* K. CE gives a clearer translation. Náhusha is unshakeable rather than merely unshaken.

16.4 **Sessions** translates ***sattra***, a great *soma* sacrifice lasting from thirteen to a hundred days. The word can also refer to any great sacrifice of equivalent pomp.

16.5 ***pratiṣṭhā*** is translated as **point of dissolution** in accordance with Nila·kantha's commentary.

16.17 ***Śakra*** CE, *śakta* K.

17.14 ***a/duṣṭaṃ*** CE, *adṛṣṭaṃ* K.

22.27 ***samīke*** CE, *samīkṣya* K.

22.36 ***samīke*** CE, *samīkṣya* K.

23.11 ***mahā/prajñāḥ . . . Drona/putraḥ?***: the order of the lines of these two verses follows that in CE; within each line the readings of K have been retained.

24.2 ***Dhārtarāṣṭrāḥ*** conj., *dhārtarāṣṭraḥ* K, *dhārtarāṣṭre* CE.

25.14 ***eva te*** CE, *evam evaṃ* K.

26.7 ***n' â/śreyān vā*** conj., *nāśreyān* K, *nāśreyasām* CE. K's reading would give a highly unusual ten-syllable *upajāti*, which my conjecture rectifies. Both here and in the next verse CE reads *n' â/śreyasām*, the basis for the present conjecture.

29.15 om. *tathā* CE, *tathā nakṣatrāṇi* K (hypermetrical).

29.25 ***yadṛcchayā*** CE, *yadicchayā* K.

29.28 ***vidyeta*** CE, *vidyati* K.

29.44 ***prauḍha*** CE, *prati* K.

29.46 ***Nakulaḥ*** CE, *nandanaḥ* K. CE has been adopted here to clarify which Pándava the text is referring to. Though *nandanaḥ* can mean "joy," in epic it more commonly means "son" or "descendant," neither of which would be appropriate here.

29.54 ***vyāghrān nīnaśo*** CE, *vyāghrānīnaśan* K.

30.17 ***praśāstā*** is here taken to be from *pra*√*śās*, though the form should more properly be *praśāsitā*. However, since CE also keeps this reading, it has been left as it is.

30.32 ***strībhir vṛddhābhir*** CE, *strībhiḥ savṛddhābhir* K.

31.16 ***sabhyāṃ*** conj., *kuntīṃ* K.

32.11 ***bhūyaś c' âto yac ca te 'gre mano 'bhūt*** CE, *bubhūṣate yac ca te 'gre "tmano 'bhūt* K.

32.21 ***tav' âp' îme*** CE, *tava hy amī* K.

32.21 ***nirayo vyapādi*** CE, *niyamen' ôdapādi* K.

33.16 Although verses 33.16–20 are rejected by CE and marked as dubious by K, they are nevertheless included here.

33.52 **The One without a second**: this phrase is used in the *Chāndogya Upaniṣad* at 6.2.1 and 6.2.2.

33.108 The story of **Prahráda's debate** begins at 35.5. A different version was told by Vídura years earlier during the dicing scene in 'The Great Hall,' CSL II.68.65ff.

33.113 ***yaḥ, sa*** CE, *yaś ca* K.

33.121 I have emended *moham* (K) to *śaucaṃ* (conj.) since "foolishness" is hardly fitting in a list of moral attributes.

35.6 **Svayam·vara**: a gathering of kings and nobles at which a princess acquires (often chooses) her husband.

35.26 ***c' âpy*** CE, *v" âpy* K.

35.45 This verse is almost identical to 33.73.

36.43 ***arthayed*** CE, *arcayed* K.

36.58 ***'/bhayam*** conj., *bhayam* K.

37.3 ***astu te*** CE, *aśnute* K. CE has been adopted here as the reading of K is most likely a corruption.

37.8 This verse is almost identical to 35.50.

37.14 ***n' ân/artha/kṛt, tyakta/kaliḥ*** CE, *n' ân/artha/kṛty" ākulitaḥ* K.

37.31–32 These two verses are almost identical to 35.52–53.

37.57 ***sv'/âdhyāye, prabhu/śatruṣu*** conj., *sv'/âdhyāya/prabhu/śatruṣu* K, *sv'/âdhyāye śatru/seviṣu* CE.

38.14–15 38.14cd and 15ab are almost identical to 37.62.

40.15 ***rudantaś*** CE, *rudanti* K.

41.2 Shánkara's commentary informs us that **Sanat·sujáta** is Sanat·kumára, the derivation of whose name means "born from Brahman."

42.1 Readers may find that the teachings of Sanat·sujáta which follow are not exact translations from the Sanskrit text. This is because explanations given in the Sanskrit commentary have been included to provide a fuller interpretation of the philosophical ideas. I have also included some interpretations from Shánkara's commentary. Shánkara (traditionally dated 788–820 CE) is considered to be one of India's greatest thinkers. His main theory was *advaita* or non-dualism.

42.16 ***sa krodha / lobhau mohavān antar' / ātmā*** K, *krodhāl lobhān moha/may'/ântar'/ātmā* CE. I have noted CE's reading on this verse since K is somewhat obscure, and both are unmetrical.

42.19 **Who commands ... wise one**: Sanat·sujáta has said that the individual's soul becomes Brahman by a process of renunciation, but Dhrita·rashtra here infers that it is the Supreme Soul that becomes an individual's soul according to the Nyaya logic that only similar things can become the same; but if this is the case, who impels Brahman to become an individual's soul? If Brahman is indeed the entire universe, due to its pervading and entering everything, then without the desire to act, how could it act? If the universe is Brahman's *līlā* or game, it would imply that Brahman was acting out of a motive of happiness. However, what can Brahman's happiness be when Brahman is apparently desireless?

42.20 This interpretation of ***nityāḥ*** as meaning "**eternal individual selves**" comes from Shánkara's commentary.

42.20 Sanat·sujáta answers Dhrita·rashtra's question by explaining that while the individual soul and Brahman, the supreme soul, are in some ways the same, they are not absolutely identical, for the individual soul is constrained by time, space, and other laws of the world in which we live, whereas Brahman is completely unconstrained. Brahman therefore retains its superiority over individual souls and it is not Brahman which becomes one with individual souls, but rather the other way around.

42.35 **To know**: while much of the present section is obscure, this verse is particularly odd. The use of ***hantum*** to mean "to know" is unprecedented. However, CE also retains this reading, and the commentary glosses it as translated.

43.55 This simile is known as *śākhā/candra/nyāya*, "the law of the moon upon the bough." By describing the moon (or **star** as in this example) in the distant sky as being on the branch of a nearby tree, one can point to the moon through the illusion of proximity. Such optical misperception is an epistemological device to guide someone to a notion which otherwise remains beyond their reach, as in **the highest aspect of the supreme soul** of this verse.

44.24 **No other ... exists**: this phrase is almost the exact equal of *Śvetāśvatara Upaniṣad* 3.8.

44.25 **White ... russet**: *Bṛhadāraṇyaka Upaniṣad* 4.4.9 also mentions the colors people suppose Brahman to be.

44.26 ***n' ābhāti*** conj., *ābhāti* K. A negative has been supplied here to make the sense clearer.

44.28 Here ***sāman*** is ***vimala***—"pure," but Manu calls it unholy.

45.4 This verse is almost identical to 43.19.

45.6 This verse is almost identical to 43.21.

45.8 ***te vai syur naraka/prasthā*** conj., *narakapratiṣṭhāste vai syur* K.

46.7 The **twelve parts** are presumably the five organs of action, the five senses of perception, mind, and understanding.

46.8 According to Shánkara, the **bee** represents one's individual self. The **honey** the bee drinks for half a month represents the karma one reaps in this life due to one's actions in a previous life.

46.9 Men without knowledge are like **birds without wings**, and men born as brahmins gain knowledge and fly to emancipation as winged birds.

46.26 **A man ... with water**: this simile is also found in the "Bhagavad Gita" 2.46.

46.28 Nila·kantha interprets that which exists as the present and that which does not exist as the past and future.

48.3 ***anvatrasto*** meaning "unhesitating" here is also attested in CE, but is not strictly grammatical. It is possibly ellipsis of *anavatrasta, metri causa*. Hypermetrical verses become metrical when *ava* is recited as *au*.

48.24 ***upāsaṅgād uddharan*** CE, *upāsaṅgānācarad* K.

48.24 ***paraḥśatān*** CE, *varāṅganānāṃ* (hypermetrical) K.

50.7 ***ā gopāl'/âvipālebhyo nandamānaṃ Yudhiṣṭhiram*** CE, *ā gopāl'/âvipālāś ca nandamānā Yudhiṣṭhiram* K.

55.8 ***na te*** CE, *tataḥ* K.

59.2 ***yathā dṛṣṭau mayā*** CE, *yathā dṛṣṭau yathā* K.

62.2 ***'/pratibhāsyat' îti*** CE, *pratibhāsyatīti* K.

63.3 ***yuktyā*** conj., *yugyā* K.

70.9 **the title of Hrishi·kesha ... divine attributes**: this is a theologically inspired popular etymology of the name. The actual etymology is more likely to be from the verbal root √*hṛṣ* and the noun *keśa*, referring to horripilation with joy.

72.3 ***Mādhava, saṃśritya*** CE, *mādhavamāśritya* K.

75.9 ***'bhiramase*** CE, *na ramase* K.

78.15 ***v", êtareṇa*** CE, *cetareṇa* K.

# GLOSSARY OF COMMON NAMES AND EPITHETS

Abhimányu Árjuna's son by Subhádra; husband of Uttará

Áchyuta Krishna

adítyas A collection of gods, descendants of Áditi

Agástya Sage; husband of Lopa·mudra

Agni The god of fire

Ahálya Wife of Gautama

Airávata Indra's elephant

Aja·bindu King of the Suvíras

Ajamídha Descendant of Aja·midha

Ambástha Name of a people

Ambikéya Descendant of Ámbika; Dhrita·rashtra

Anártas People who live in Anárta

Ándhaka Name of a tribe descended originally from Yadu

Anga Name of a people

Ángiras Sage; author of hymns and a code of laws; considered as a Praja·pati

Anúpaka Name of a people

Anuvínda Lord of Avánti

ápsaras Celestial nymphs; companions of the *gandhárvas*

Aríshta·nemi Gáruda's brother; used as a name of Krishna

Árjuna (1) Third of the Pándava brothers; also called Dhanañ·jaya, Partha, Phálguna, Savya·sachin, Jishnu, Bibhátsu, Kirítin, Víjaya, and Krishna. (2) See Kartavírya.

Árkaja King of the Balíhas

Ashvattháman Son of Drona and Kripi; great warrior and companion of the sons of Dhrita·rashtra

ASHVINS Divine twins; fathers of Nákula and Saha·deva

ÁSURA A class of demons

ATHÁRVAN Ángiras

ATHARVÁNGIRAS Ángiras

ATRÉYA Sage; descendant of Atri

BABHRU King of the Kashis

BÁHLIKA King of the Báhlikas; great-uncle of Dhrita·rashtra

BAHU King of the Súndaras

BÁHULA King of the Tala·janghas

BALA·DEVA Krishna's elder brother; also called Bala·rama and Sankárshana

BALÁHAKA One of Krishna's horses

BALI A Daitya

BALÍHA Name of a people

BANA An *ásura*; son of Bali

BHAGA·DATTA Prince of Prag·jyótisha

BHARAD·VAJA A sage; father of Drona

BHÁRATA Descendant of Bharata

BHARATA Legendary king, ancestor of Kuru; any of Bharata's descendants

BHÁRGAVA Descendant of Bhrigu

BHAUMA Demon Náraka

BHÁUMANA Vishva·karman

BHIMA Second of the Pándava brothers; also caleld Bhima·sena, Vrikódara, and Partha

BHISHMA Son of King Shántanu and Ganga, renowned for his wisdom and fidelity; also called Gangéya, Shántanava, and Deva·vrata

BHOJA Name of a people descended from Maha·bhoja

BHRIGU Sage, ancestor of a line of men

BHURI·DYUMNA Pious prince; son of Vira·dyumna

BHURI·SHRAVAS Ally of Duryódhana; son of Soma·datta

BIBHÁTSU Árjuna

BRAHMAN Ultimate creative power; the indescribable supreme soul

BRIHAS·PATI The deity in whom piety and religion are personified; the priest of the gods

CHANDRA·VATSA Name of a people

CHEDI·DHVAJA Warrior allied to the Káuravas

CHEKITÁNA Prince allied to the Pándavas

CHITRA·RATHA King of the *gandhárva*s

CHITRA·SENA A son of Dhrita·rashtra

CHITRA·VARMAN A son of Dhrita·rashtra

DAITYA A class of demons, descendants of Diti

DAMAYÁNTI Nala's wife

DÁNAVA A class of demons, descendants of Danu

DANTA·VAKTRA Name of a Karúsha prince

DÁRADA Name of a people who live above Peshawar

DASHÁRHA Krishna

DASYU Enemies of the gods

DEVA·DATTA Árjuna's conch

DEVA·VRATA Bhishma

DHÁRANA King of the Chandra·vatsas

DHARMA The personification of the law; a god; Yudhi·shthira's seminal father

DHAUMYA Family priest of the Pándavas

DHAUTA·MÚLAKA King of the northeastern lands in modern China

DHRISHTA·DYUMNA Son of Drúpada

DHRISHTA·KETU King of Chedi

DHRITA·RASHTRA The blind Kuru king; father of the hundred Káuravas, including Duryódhana

DITI An ancestress of demons

DRÁUPADI Wife of the five Pándava brothers; Drúpada's daughter; also called Krishná, Pañcháli, and Yajñaséni

DRONA Brahmin warrior; teacher of the Káuravas and Pándavas; father of Ashvatthâman

DRÚPADA King of the Pañchálas; father of Dhrishta·dyumna, Shikhándin, and Dráupadi

DÚHSAHA A son of Dhrita·rashtra

DUHSHÁSANA A son of Dhrita·rashtra

DÚRJAYA Hero warrior

DÚRMUKHA A son of Dhrita·rashtra

DURYÓDHANA Eldest son of Dhrita·rashtra; king of the Káuravas; also called Suyódhana

DVAITA FOREST The Pándavas spent some of their twelve-year exile here

DYUMAT·SENA Prince of Shalva; father of Sátyavat

EKA·LAVYA Son of Hiránya·dhanus

GADA Son of Vasu·deva

GANDHÁRA A people who live northeast of Peshawar, giving their name to Kandahar

GANDHÁRI Dhrita·rashtra's wife

GANDHÁRVA Celestial beings; companions of the *ápsarases*

GANDÍVA Árjuna's bow

GÁRUDA A bird deity; Vishnu's vehicle; son of Vínata; used as a name of Krishna

GÁUTAMA A sage; patronymic of Kripa

GO·VINDA Krishna

HÁIHAYA Name of a people

HÁNUMAN Monkey general; son of the wind god

HARDÍKYA Patronymic of Krita·varman

HARI Vishnu; also called Krishna

HAYA·GRIVA King of the Vidéhas

HIDÍMBA Giant *rákshasa* killed by Bhima·sena

HRISHI·KÉSHA Krishna

INDRA King of the gods; seminal father of Árjuna; also called Shakra, Vásava, and Mághavat

INDRÁNI Indra's wife

JALA·SANDHA King allied to the Káuravas

JAMAD·AGNI A sage, descendant of Bhrigu

JAMBHA Demon killed by Krishna

JANAM·ÉJAYA A king; direct descendant of the Pándavas, whose story is recited to him by Vaishampáyana

JANÁRDANA Krishna

JARA·SANDHA King of Mágadha and Chedi

JATÁSURA *Rákshasa* killed by Bhima·sena

JAYAD·RATHA Sindhu-Sauvíra king who fights for the Káuravas; Dhrita·rashtra's son-in-law

JAYAT·SENA King of Mágadha

KÁITAVYA Patronymic of Ulúka

KALA·KHAÑJA Race of *ásura*s

KALÍNGA Name of a people

KAMBÓJA Name of a people

KANSA Krishna's cousin and enemy

KARA·KARSHA Warrior allied to the Pándavas

KARNA Ally of Duryódhana; the Pándavas' older half-brother; son of Kunti and the Sun; foster-son of Ádhiratha and Radha; also called Radhéya, Vrisha, and Vasu·shena

KARSHNI Descendant of Krishna

KARTAVÍRYA A king, first name Árjuna, famous for a run-in with Jamad·agni and sons (see for example *Vanaparvan* CE III.116–17)

KARÚSHA Name of a people

KARÚSHAKA Chief of the Karúsha people

KASHI Name of a people

KAUNTÉYA Son of Kunti

KÁURAVA Descendant of Kuru

KÉKAYA Name of a warrior tribe

KÉSHAVA Krishna

KÍCHAKA General of King Viráta's army; brother of Queen Sudéshna of Matsya

KÍNNARA Celestial choristers

KIRÍTIN Árjuna

KRIMI Name of a people

KRIPA Son of the sage Sharádvat; raised by King Shántanu; teacher of the Pándavas and Káuravas; also called Sharádvata and Gáutama

KRISHNÁ Dráupadi

KRISHNA Avatar of the god Vishnu; allied to the Pándavas; also called Vasudéva, Madhu·súdana, Upéndra, Mádhava, Go·vinda, Hari, Pundarikáksha, Sátvata, Vrishabhékshana, Adhókshaja, Purushóttama, Anánta, Vishvak·shena, Dashárha, Hrishi·kesha, Késhava, and Áchyuta

KRITA·VARMAN Son of Hrídika

KRODHA·VASHA Evil spirits

KSHATRA·DEVA Warrior allied to the Pándavas

KSHEMA·DHURTI A warrior

KUBÉRA Lord of riches; leader of the *yakshas* and demons; also called Váishravana

KÚKURA Tribe descended from Ándhaka's son

KUNTI Wife of Pandu; mother of the three eldest Pándava brothers, and, by the Sun, of Karna

KURUS Descendants of Kuru; the Káuravas and Pándavas; sometimes just the sons of Dhrita·rashtra and their followers

KÚSHIKA Ancestor of Vishva·mitra

MÁDHAVA Usually denotes Krishna, but is also occasionally used for other Vrishnis

MADHU·SÚDANA Krishna

MADIRÁKSHA Brother of Shataníka and Viráta

MÁDRAVATI Madri

MADRI Pandu's second wife; mother of the Pándava twins Nákula and Saha·deva

MÁGHAVAT Indra

MAHÁUJASA Name of a people

MÁLAVA Name of a people who were allied to the Káuravas

MANU First man, and progenitor of the human race; archetypal sage

MATSYA Name of the people who live in Matsya

MEGHA·PUSHPA One of Krishna's horses

MUDAVÁRTA King of the Háihayas

MÚKUTA Name of a people

MURA A demon

NADI·JA 'River-born'; name of Bhishma

NÁGNAJIT A *gandhárva* prince

NÁHUSHA Human king of the gods who was deposed and turned into a snake

NÁKULA One of the Pándava twins (brother of Saha·deva); son of Madri and the Ashvins

NÁMUCHI A demon killed by Indra

NANDI·VEGA Name of a people

NARA The Primeval Man or eternal Spirit prevading the universe, always associated with Naráyana

NÁRADA A sage

NÁRAKA A demon; son of the earth

NARÁYANA Supreme deity; often refers to Vishnu; often associated with Nara

NIPA Name of a people

NISHÁDA King of a wild tribe

NIVÁTA·KÁVACHA A class of demons

PÁHLAVA Name for either the Parthians or Persians

PAKA A Daitya whom Indra killed

PÁNDAVA Son of Pandu

PANDU Younger brother of Dhrita·rashtra; legal father of the Pándavas; husband of Kunti and Madri

PÁRSHATA Patronymic of Drúpada and Dhrishta·dyumna

PASHU·PATI Epithet of Rudra-Shiva

PAULÓMA A class of demon

PÁURAVA Descendant of Puru

PHÁLGUNA Árjuna

PRABHÁDRAKA A class of handsome men

PRABHÁDRAKAS Warriors allied to the Pándavas

PRAHRÁDA Father of Viróchana

PRAJA·PATI The secondary creator or demiurge

PRATÍPA Father of Báhlika and Shántanu

PRAVÍRA Name of a people

PURU·MITRA A warrior allied the Káuravas

PURU·RAVAS King of the Diptákshas

RADHÉYA Karna

RÁKSHASA A class of demons

RAMA A shortened form for Bala·rama, elder brother of Krishna; or Jamad·agni's son Rama, a brahmin weapons-teacher and sometime slayer of kshatriyas

RAUHINÉYA Metronymic of Bala·rama

RÍSHIKA Name of a people

RUDRA Deity of storms

RUDRA Vedic storm god; later called Shiva

RUKMIN Eldest son of Bhíshmaka

RÚKMINI Sister of Rukmin; daughter of Bhíshmaka

RUSHÁDDHIKA King of the Suráshtras

SADHYA A class of celestial beings

SAHA·DEVA One of the Pándava twins (bother of Nákula); son of Madri and the Ashvins

SÁHAJA King of the Chedi-Matsyas

SAMBA Son of Krishna and Jámbavati

SANKÁRSHANA Bala·rama; also called Bala·deva

SANAT·SUJÁTA One of the seven mind-born sons of Brahma

SÁÑJAYA Son of Gaválgana; follower and envoy of Dhrita·rashtra

SARÁSVATA People from the Sarásvata area

SARÁSVATI Goddess of speech and learning

SATYA·BHAMA One of Krishna's eight wives

SÁTYAKA Sátyaki's father, or Sátyaki himself

SÁTYAKI A Vrishni warrior, grandson of Shini; also called Yuyudhána

SATYA·SANDHA A son of Dhrita·rashtra

SÁTYAVAT Son of Dyumat·sena; husband of Sávitri

SATYA·VRATA A warrior allied to the Pándavas

SAUBHA King of the Shalvas

SAUBHÁDRA Son of Subhádra; also called Abhimányu

SHACHI Indra's wife

SHAIBYA One of Krishna's horses

SHAKA Name of a tribe

SHAKRA Indra

SHÁKUNI Prince of Gandhára; son of Súbala; brother-in-law of Dhrita·rashtra; uncle of Duryódhana, for whom he wins the dicing match against Yudhi·shthira; also called Sáubala

SHALA A king; a son of Dhrita·rashtra

SHALVA King of the Shalvas

SHALVA Name of a people

SHÁLVAKA Ruler of the Shalvas

SHALYA King of Madra; brother of Madri

SHAMA King of the Nandi·vegas

SHÁMBARA Name of a demon

SHANKHA Viráta's eldest son

SHÁNTANU Father of Bhishma

SHÁRABHA Brother of the king of Chedi

SHARÁDVATA Patronymic of Kripa

SHAURI Patronymic of Vasudéva

SHIBI A people descended from Shibi

SHIKHÁNDIN Son (initially daughter) of Drúpada

SHINI Grandfather of Sátyaki

SHISHU·PALA Father of Dhrishta·ketu

SHIVA A name of Maha·deva, the great god associated with asceticism and destruction

SHRUTÁYUS A king of the Solar dynasty

SHUKRA Son of Bhrigu and preceptor of the Daityas

SHURA Ancestor of Krishna

SHURA·SENA Name of a people

SOMA The deified drink of victory

SOMA·DATTA A king allied to the sons of Dhrita·rashtra

SÚBALA King of Gandhára; father of Shákuni and of Dhrita·rashtra's wife Gandhári

SUBHÁDRA Sister of Krishna; wife of Árjuna; mother of Abhimányu

SUDÁKSHINA Uttará

SUDÉSHNA Queen of Matsya; wife of Viráta

SUGRÍVA One of Krishna's horses

SÚNDARA Name of a people

SURÁSHTRA Name of a people

SURYA·DATTA Matsyan royalty

SUSHÁRMAN King of the Trigártas

SUTA Charioteer; herald

TALA·JANGHA Name of a people

TRIGÁRTA Name of a people

TVASHTRI The heavenly builder

UGRA A son of Dhrita·rashtra

ULÚKA Son of Shákuni; king of the Ulúka people

UMA Shiva's wife; also called Párvati

UPÉNDRA Vishnu; also called Krishna

UTTAMÁUJAS A warrior from Pañchála

ÚTTARA Prince of Matsya; Viráta's son; brother of Uttará; = Bhumiñ·jaya

UTTARÁ Princess of Matsya; daughter of Viráta; sister of Uttara; wife of Abhimányu; also called Sudákshina

VAICHÍTRAVÍRYA Patronymic of Dhrita·rashtra

VAIKÁRTANA Karna

VAISHAMPÁYANA A brahmin, pupil of Vyasa; recites Vyasa's story of the Pándavas to King Janam·éjaya

VAIVÁSVATA Patronymic of Yama

VALA A demonic being defeated by Indra

VALMÍKA A sage; compare Valmíki, Vyasa's "Ramáyana" counterpart

VAMA·DEVA An ancient sage

VÁRAYU King of the Maháujasas

VARSHNÉYA Patronymic of Krishna and of any of the other Vrishnis

VÁRUNA Major god of the Vedic pantheon; later, god of the ocean

VÁSAVA Indra

VASHÁTI Name of a people

VASÍSHTHA A celebrated Vedic sage; owner of Nándani, the cow of plenty

VASUDÉVA Patronymic of Krishna

VICHÍTRA·VIRYA King of the Bháratas; son of Shántanu; half-brother of Bhishma; legal father of Dhrita·rashtra and Pandu

VIDÉHA Name of a people

VÍDURA Younger brother of Dhrita·rashtra and Pandu; son of Vyasa (on royal business) and Ámbika's maid

VIGÁHANA King of the Múkutas

VIKÁRNA A son of Dhrita·rashtra

VINDA Lord of Avánti

VIRÁTA King of Matsya

VIRÓCHANA An *ásura*; son of Prahráda

VISHNU Geat god, the preserver deity

VISHVA A class of gods

VISHVÁVASU A *gandhárva*

VIVÁSVAT Father of Yama

VIVÍMSHATI A son of Dhrita·rashtra

VRISHA·DHVAJA King of the Pravíras

VRISHNI Name of a tribe of people from whom Krishna is descended

VRITRA Vedic demon, the instigator of a universal drought; killed by Indra

VYASA DVAIPÁYANA Celebrated sage; seer and author of the story of the Pándavas; also known as Krishna; half-brother of Vichítra·virya; seminal father of Dhrita·rashtra, Pandu, and Vídura

YÁDAVAS Descendants of Yadu

YAJÑASÉNI Krishná

YAKSHA A spirit and lord of natural places, able to assume any shape

YAMA The god who rules over the spirits of the dead

YUDHI·SHTHIRA Eldest of the Pándavas; also called Bhárata, Partha, "best of the Kurus," and "king of righteousness."

YUYUDHÁNA Sátyaki

YUYÚTSU A half-caste son of Dhrita·rashtra

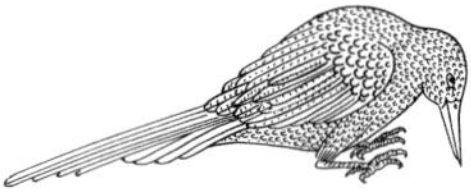

# INDEX

*Sanskrit words are given in the English alphabetical order, according to the accented CSL pronuncuation aid. They are followed by the conventional diacritics in brackets.*

# THE CLAY SANSKRIT LIBRARY

Current Volumes

For further details please consult the CSL website.

1. The Emperor of the Sorcerers (*Bṛhatkathāślokasaṃgraha*) (vol. 1 of 2) by *Budhasvāmin*. Sir James Mallinson
2. Heavenly Exploits (*Divyāvadāna*) Joel Tatelman
3. Maha·bhárata III: The Forest (*Vanaparvan*) (vol. 4 of 4) William J. Johnson
4. Much Ado about Religion (*Āgamaḍambara*) by *Bhaṭṭa Jayanta*. Csaba Dezső
5. The Birth of Kumára (*Kumārasaṃbhava*) by *Kālidāsa*. David Smith
6. Ramáyana I: Boyhood (*Bālakāṇḍa*) by *Vālmīki*. Robert P. Goldman
7. The Epitome of Queen Lilávati (*Līlāvatīsāra*) (vol. 1 of 2) by *Jinaratna*. R.C.C. Fynes
8. Ramáyana II: Ayódhya (*Ayodhyākāṇḍa*) by *Vālmīki*. Sheldon I. Pollock
9. Love Lyrics (*Amaruśataka, Śatakatraya & Caurapañcāśikā*) by *Amaru, Bhartṛhari & Bilhaṇa*. Greg Bailey & Richard Gombrich
10. What Ten Young Men Did (*Daśakumāracarita*) by *Daṇḍin*. Isabelle Onians
11. Three Satires (*Kalividambana, Kalāvilāsa & Bhallaṭaśataka*) by *Nīlakaṇṭha, Kṣemendra & Bhallaṭa* Somadeva Vasudeva
12. Ramáyana IV: Kishkíndha (*Kiṣkindhākāṇḍa*) by *Vālmīki*. Rosalind Lefeber

13. The Emperor of the Sorcerers (*Bṛhatkathāślokasaṃgraha*) (vol. 2 of 2) by *Budhasvāmin*. Sir James Mallinson
14. Maha·bhárata IX: Shalya (*Śalyaparvan*) (vol. 1 of 2) Justin Meiland
15. Rákshasa's Ring (*Mudrārākṣasa*) by *Viśākhadatta*. Michael Coulson
16. Messenger Poems (*Meghadūta, Pavanadūta & Haṃsadūta*) by *Kālidāsa, Dhoyī & Rūpa Gosvāmin*. Sir James Mallinson
17. Ramáyana III: The Forest (*Araṇyakāṇḍa*) by *Vālmīki*. Sheldon I. Pollock
18. The Epitome of Queen Lilávati (*Līlāvatīsāra*) (vol. 2 of 2) by *Jinaratna*. R.C.C. Fynes
19. Five Discourses on Worldly Wisdom (*Pañcatantra*) by *Viṣṇuśarman*. Patrick Olivelle
20. Ramáyana V: Súndara (*Sundarakāṇḍa*) by *Vālmīki*. Robert P. Goldman & Sally J. Sutherland Goldman
21. Maha·bhárata II: The Great Hall (*Sabhāparvan*) Paul Wilmot
22. The Recognition of Shakúntala (*Abhijñānaśākuntala*) (Kashmir Recension) by *Kālidāsa*. Somadeva Vasudeva
23. Maha·bhárata VII: Drona (*Droṇaparvan*) (vol. 1 of 4) Vaughan Pilikian
24. Rama Beyond Price (*Anargharāghava*) by *Murāri*. Judit Törzsök
25. Maha·bhárata IV: Viráta (*Virāṭaparvan*) Kathleen Garbutt
26. Maha·bhárata VIII: Karna (*Karṇaparvan*) (vol. 1 of 2) Adam Bowles
27. "The Lady of the Jewel Necklace" and "The Lady who Shows her Love" (*Ratnāvalī & Priyadarśikā*) by *Harṣa*. Wendy Doniger

28. The Ocean of the Rivers of Story (*Kathāsaritsāgara*) (vol. 1 of 7) by *Somadeva*. Sir James Mallinson
29. Handsome Nanda (*Saundarananda*) by *Aśvaghoṣa*. Linda Covill
30. Maha·bhárata IX: Shalya (*Śalyaparvan*) (vol. 2 of 2) Justin Meiland
31. Rama's Last Act (*Uttararāmacarita*) by *Bhavabhūti*. Sheldon Pollock. Foreword by Girish Karnad
32. "Friendly Advice" (*Hitopadeśa*) by *Nārāyaṇa* & "King Víkrama's Adventures" (*Vikramacarita*). Judit Törzsök
33. Life of the Buddha (*Buddhacarita*) by *Aśvaghoṣa*. Patrick Olivelle
34. Maha·bhárata V: Preparations for War (*Udyogaparvan*) (vol. 1 of 2) Kathleen Garbutt. Foreword by Gurcharan Das

## To Appear in 2008

"How the Nagas were Pleased" (*Nāgānanda*) by *Harṣa* &
"The Shattered Thighs" (*Ūrubhaṅga*) by *Bhāsa*
ANDREW SKILTON

Little Clay Cart (*Mṛcchakaṭikā*)
by *Śūdraka*. DIWAKAR ACHARYA

Maha·bhárata V: Preparations for War (*Udyogaparvan*) (vol. 2 of 2)
KATHLEEN GARBUTT

Maha·bhárata VI: Bhishma (*Bhīṣmaparvan*) (vol. 1 of 2)
ALEX CHERNIAK. Foreword by RANAJIT GUHA

Maha·bhárata VI: Bhishma (*Bhīṣmaparvan*) (vol. 2 of 2)
ALEX CHERNIAK

Maha·bhárata VIII: Karna (*Karṇaparvan*) (vol. 2 of 2)
ADAM BOWLES

The Ocean of the Rivers of Story (*Kathāsaritsāgara*) (vol. 2 of 7)
by *Somadeva*. SIR JAMES MALLINSON

The Ocean of the Rivers of Story (*Kathāsaritsāgara*) (vol. 3 of 7)
by *Somadeva*. SIR JAMES MALLINSON

Princess Kadámbari (*Kādambarī*) (vol. 1 of 3)
by *Bāṇa*. DAVID SMITH

The Quartet of Causeries (*Caturbhāṇī*)
by *Śūdraka, Śyāmilaka, Vararuci & Īśvaradatta*
CSABA DEZSŐ & SOMADEVA VASUDEVA

Seven Hundred Elegant Verses (*Āryāsaptaśatī*)
by *Govardhana*. FRIEDHELM HARDY